VICTORIAN TALES FOR GIRLS

VICTORIAN TALES FOR GIRLS

VICTORIAN TALES
FOR GIRLS

Edited with an Introduction by
MARGHANITA LASKI

LONDON
THE PILOT PRESS LTD
1947

First published in 1947 by
The Pilot Press Ltd., 45, Gt. Russell St., W.C.1.

Printed in Great Britain by
Charles Birchall & Sons, Ltd.,
London & Liverpool.

Contents

This Book *is* Dedicated *to*
Jennifer Lewis

INTRODUCTION   8

the family who can act as a Cinderella's godmother on suitable
occasions. But such an exciting occasion is likely to happen only
once in a book, and for the rest of the time our imaginary children
live a simple, close-knit and self-contained family life, playing
happily in the house and the countryside around
them, happy with pleasures so simple that to us they might
hardly seem pleasures at all, and moral to a degree

Introduction

Dear Jenny,

If you come to enjoy reading old-fashioned children's books as
much as I do, you will very soon find that you have made for yourself
a very clear and definite picture of Victorian family life. Whether
or not it is likely to be a true picture is a matter we can talk about
later; for the moment I want only to try to describe this picture
which will be, I think, the one in your mind as it is in mine.

The clearest picture I have is the one of the large family. I am
not quite sure how many children there are in it—probably seven or
eight—but some of them are girls and some are boys. The eldest
girl is almost grown-up (she is probably called Alice) and she has a
calm sweet face and is falling in love with the curate, though the
younger children won't find this out till the end of the book. There
is an almost grown-up brother and there are a few school-boy
brothers and there is a frail little youngest brother who may quite
well die young, particularly as he is so very imaginative and kind-
hearted; I always think that Chris in *Mary's Meadow*, who is just
this sort of boy, must be going to die before he grows up. Then,
somewhere in the middle of the family, comes the mad-cap tom-boy
daughter—though by our standards she is very sedate indeed—
who has untidy brown hair and wears a brown Holland overall,
and, if the book we are reading was written for girls, this particular
daughter will almost certainly be the heroine of it.

Our typical Victorian family live, of course, in a large, rambling,
old-fashioned country house with lots of attics and cellars and
out-buildings. On their nursery wall there hangs a cuckoo-clock
and in the corner by the door there stands a scrap-screen, just like
the one on the cover of this book. The nursery-maid carries the
children's meals up the long, long flights of stairs from the kitchen
where lives the red-faced harsh-voiced cook, unsympathetic to all
except the little ailing brother. Papa is probably a land-agent or a
vicar or a solicitor or something equally respectable in the professional
upper middle-class—for some reason, he is hardly ever an aristrocrat
and, for quite other reasons, he is never in trade. Papa himself is seldom very rich, though there is always a rich relation in

the family who can act as a Cinderella's godmother on suitable occasions. But such an exciting occasion is likely to happen only once in a book, and for the rest of the time our imaginary children live a simple, close-knit and self-contained family life, playing happily in the house and the garden and the countryside around them, happy with pleasures so simple that to us they might hardly seem pleasures at all, and moral to a degree quite startling to even quite moral children of to-day. Finally, and this above all, the whole family is certain, absolutely and completely certain, of present and future security in a country absolutely and certainly secure. I used to think that Victorian family life must have been the happiest family life that was ever lived.

But though the Victorian story-book that tells of the life of just such a family is far and away the most usual and typical one, it is certainly not the only one, and possibly *Mary's Meadow* represented an ideal for the Victorian child as it did for me. And I think that from these other less typical story-books we can find some other more realistic aspects of the lives of Victorian children, aspects that make their lives seem far less inviting than in the rosy picture I have just drawn.

I have already referred, for instance, to the good little boy who usually died. I haven't put in any such book because I wanted this omnibus to be happy rather than harrowing, but if you enjoy crying, you must try to read Florence Montgomery's *Misunderstood*. A horrifying number of Victorian children *did* die in childhood, and your imagination can play as miserably as mine on what these deaths must have meant in a loving compact family.

Then you must remember that the Victorian epoch was the great epoch of Empire-Building—and *someone* had to leave home and go overseas to build it. Who better than these Victorian Papas and Mamas, so upright in rectitude, so swift to discipline, exemplars that could not fail to mould the natives abroad as deftly as they moulded the children at home. The Army, the Indian Civil Service and suchlike were almost wholly stocked—in their upper grades, at least—by these upper-middle-class Victorian Papas, and it was rare indeed that Mama did not find that her duty lay in accompanying Papa wherever *his* duty called *him*. And it nearly always did call him to a climate quite unsuitable for children, and transport from these unsuitable climates back to Home was long and arduous and expensive, and so it happened that many Victorian children spent practically the whole of their childhoods without ever seeing their parents at all. What horrors this could mean for them, you can read in an unhappy story by Rudyard Kipling called *Baa Baa Black Sheep*. Even with the best will in the world, it might be impossible to find relations or good kind people who would take in children not their own, and the lonely miseries of the little girl in *The Carved Lions*, which you will find in this book, must have been far from uncommon.

I think, too, that there must have been other horrors in Victorian childhoods that we hear much less of in these books. Nowadays we know something of psychology and we think it wrong to frighten children with bogies and, if they frighten themselves, we comfort them and try to dispel the horrors. There were a lot of horrors going about in Victorian times. Many of the servants, for instance, were inevitably less well-educated and sensible than they would be to-day and would have frightened the children with the horrible stories with which they frightened themselves. The cheap 'shockers' of that period were often so shocking as to be quite revolting, and I cannot believe that somehow or other they didn't come into many children's hands. Even quite charming and harmless people like gipsies were frequently made terrifying as you can see in *The Runaways and the Gipsies* in this book; I can't imagine any modern child being frightened of gipsies. Remember, too, that Victorian children were not encouraged to talk of all the muddling fears that obsess nearly all children unless they are brought out into the open. Indeed, in some Victorian books, such untold fears can provide the whole theme of the story until at last, by some device, the bubble of terror is burst and the shivering child is at last comforted in friendly arms. Which is all very well, but look how miserable that poor child had been before anyone found out about it. It was not usual then to take much trouble to 'understand' children, and we find that the misunderstood child is an all too common theme in the Victorian story.

For, of course, not all families were large families, and death or accident could easily produce the unhappy only child. The sunny little Lord Fauntleroy is almost certainly an exception in fiction as in life, and we can read here from Mrs. Hodgson Burnett herself that the model for Little Lord Fauntleroy was not, in fact, an only child himself. Naturally, the Victorian only child had few of the opportunities for companionship that are available for only children to-day. There were no nursery-schools, and no opportunities for casual social intercourse in the days when no little girl could go out without a maid to accompany her and certainly could not play with any other little girl unless both sets of parents knew each other and came from the same social class. You will notice that in none of the books I have put in—except the *Gate of the Giant Scissors* where the heroine is an American girl—do any of the children casually meet and play with other children.

So I think that we now have the material for drawing another picture of Victorian family life that must have been quite as common as the one we first imagined; a picture of a little girl whose father and mother are away in India, whose brothers and sisters have died or have never been born, who lives in a town with elderly people who neither understand nor care for children, who has no friends and nothing to do, and neither the food nor the exercise nor the interests that make for healthy happy children. No, I don't think any longer that Victorian family lives were necessarily the happiest ever.

You will notice that in drawing this last miserable picture, the unhappy child I have put into it is a little girl. I had a good reason for this. Last year I was collecting stories for an omnibus volume for boys, and found that these, so long as they were good adventure stories, could have been written at any date and still be read by boys of to-day without any sense of incongruity. Adventures for boys seem to be timeless; a desert-island is a desert-island whether you reach it by schooner or seaplane, and a rogue elephant is just as roguish whether you attack him with an elephant-gun or a spear.

So when I first set about collecting material for this particular book, which is really meant for girls, I had hazily assumed that the same principle would apply and that a good girls' story, whenever written, would still remain ageless. I very quickly found out my mistake.

You see, it is not the surroundings in which a story takes place that sets the tone of the story; it is the way that people behave in them. Boys, apparently, have reacted to surrounding and circumstance in the same ways since time immemorial. Not so with girls.

Female emancipation has been so much a matter of course in my generation and, still more, in yours, that you and I take it for granted. But the lack of female emancipation is the great barrier that separates the girl of the Victorian stories from the girl of to-day and makes it impossible for you to enter into their feelings with the same ease and readiness that, say, your cousin Jonathan can enter into the feelings of Ralph and Jack and Peterkin in *Coral Island*. When you, turning the pages of this book, come upon *The Dove in the Eagle's Nest*, you will find Christina's maidenly shrinkings cowardly and rather silly. I doubt, myself, whether a real girl of that period would really have behaved in just this way. But Miss Yonge, who wrote the book, liked to think that she would, and more, knew that her girl readers would like to think so, too, for what Miss Yonge was really describing was *not* a fifteenth-century Germanic *mädchen* but an ideal Victorian maiden.

You, of course, cannot easily imagine a life where you cannot go out into the street by yourself; cannot read what books you choose; cannot swim and run and climb, do carpentry and wear shorts. You cannot easily imagine, instead, wearing at least two petticoats under your everyday frock, having your legs always covered with thick stockings, going to church at least once every Sunday and reading only improving books the rest of the day, and spending the whole of your childhood with never a thought of what you were going to be when you grew up, for, of course, when you did grow up, there was nothing for you to be but a married woman or a failure. I can hardly begin to imagine it myself, and you must find it more difficult than I. You are the longer emancipated.

And that is why, in collecting these old stories for you to read, I cannot ask you to approach them in quite the same way that you would approach a story actually written for your contemporaries. You have got to manage quite a feat of imagination first, unless, of course, you are only going to skim through them with a contemptuous smile for girls who certainly, by your standards, often behaved very oddly. I am asking you to remember that all the courage and self-reliance and initiative you will have the chance of showing throughout your life are in some measure accidents of circumstance. You have been born into an age when we expect these qualities from girls as from boys, and you will be glad, as I am, that this is so. But do not, please, despise these Victorian girls because they were seldom asked to display initiative or self-reliance or physical courage. I do think that they were very often being asked to show moral courage and often in circumstances far more adverse to its display than yours are.

It is rather the fashion to think that the Victorians were hypocritical, and you may well think these girls were only goody-goody and priggish. I earnestly believe that, if you think so, you will be wrong.

And I do hope, my dear Jenny, that you will enjoy these stories as much as I have enjoyed them all my life.

Your affectionate Aunt,

Marghanita.

Abbots Langley.   1947.

NOTE.—The original publication dates of the works included in this volume are as follows: Mary's Meadow, 1883-4;   The Runaways and the Gipsies, 1860; The Carved Lions, 1895;   The Dove in the Eagle's Nest, 1866;   The Gate of the Giant Scissors, 1898;   How Fauntleroy Occurred, 1894.

It remains to thank the owners of the relevant copyrights for permission to insert the following works: The Carved Lions (Mr. H. Molesworth), The Gate of the Giant Scissors (Jarrold & Sons), How Fauntleroy Occurred (Frederick Warne & Co. Ltd.).

Mary's Meadow

CHAPTER I

MOTHER IS ALWAYS trying to make us love our neighbours as ourselves.

She does so despise us for greediness, or grudging, or snatching, or not sharing what we have got, or taking the best and leaving the rest, or helping ourselves first, or pushing forward, or praising Number One, or being Dogs in the Manger, or anything selfish. And we cannot bear her to despise us!

We despise being selfish, too; but very often we forget. Besides, it is sometimes rather difficult to love your neighbour as yourself when you want a thing very much; and Arthur says he believes it is particularly difficult if it is your next-door neighbour, and that is why Father and the Old Squire quarrelled about the footpath through Mary's Meadow.

The Old Squire is not really his name, but that is what people call him. He is very rich. His place comes next to ours, and it is much bigger, and he has quantities of fields, and Father has only got a few; but there are two fields beyond Mary's Meadow which belong to Father, though the Old Squire wanted to buy them. Father would not sell them, and he says he has a right of way through Mary's Meadow to go to his fields, but the Old Squire says he has nothing of the kind, and that is what they quarrelled about.

Arthur says if you quarrel, and are too grown-up to punch each other's heads, you go to law; and if going to law doesn't make it up, you appeal. They went to law, I know, for Mother cried about it; and I suppose it did not make it up, for the Old Squire appealed.

After that he used to ride about all day on his grey horse, with Saxon, his yellow bull-dog, following him, to see that we did not trespass on Mary's Meadow. I think he thought that if we children were there, Saxon would frighten us, for I do not suppose he knew that we knew him. But Saxon used often to come with the Old Squire's Scotch Gardener to see our gardener, and when they were looking at the wall-fruit, Saxon used to come snuffing after us.

He is the nicest dog I know. He looks very savage, but he is only very funny. His lower jaw sticks out, which makes him grin, and some people think he is gnashing his teeth with rage. We think

15

it looks as if he were laughing—like Mother Hubbard's dog, when she brought home his coffin, and he wasn't dead—but it really is only the shape of his jaw. I loved Saxon the first day I saw him, and he likes me, and licks my face. But what he likes best of all are Bath Oliver Biscuits.

One day the Scotch Gardener saw me feeding him, and he pulled his red beard, and said, "Ye do weel to mak' hay while the sun shines, Saxon, my man. There's sma' sight o' young leddies and sweet cakes at hame for ye!" And Saxon grinned, and wagged his tail, and the Scotch Gardener touched his hat to me, and took him away.

The Old Squire's Weeding Woman is our nursery-maid's aunt. She is not very old, but she looks so, because she has lost her teeth, and is bent nearly double. She wears a large hood, and carries a big basket, which she puts down outside the nursery door when she comes to tea with Bessy. If it is a fine afternoon, and we are gardening, she lets us borrow the basket, and then we play at being weeding women in each other's gardens.

She tells Bessy about the Old Squire. She says—"He do be a real old skinflint, the Old Zquire a be!" But she thinks it "zim as if 'twas having ne'er a wife nor child for to keep the natur' in 'un, so his heart do zim to shrivel, like they walnuts Butler tells us of as a zets down for desart. The Old Zquire he mostly eats ne'er a one now's teeth be so bad. But a counts them every night when's desart's done. And a keeps 'em till the karnels be mowldy, and a keeps 'em till they be dry, and a keeps 'em till they be dust; and when the karnels is dust, a cracks aal the lot of 'em when desart's done, zo's no one mayn't have no good of they walnuts, since they be no good to he."

Arthur can imitate the Weeding Woman exactly, and he can imitate the Scotch Gardener too. Chris (that is Christopher, our youngest brother) is very fond of "The Zquire and the Walnuts." He gets nuts, or anything, like shells or bits of flower-pots, that will break, and something to hit with, and when Arthur comes to "*The karnels is dust*," Chris smashes everything before him, shouting "*A cracks aal the lot of 'em*," and then he throws the bits all over the place, with "*They be no good to he.*"

Father laughed very much when he heard Arthur do the Weeding Woman, and Mother could not help laughing too; but she did not like it, because she does not like us to repeat servants' gossip.

The Weeding Woman is a great gossip. She gossips all the time she is having her tea, and it is generally about the Old Squire. She used to tell Bessy that his flowers bloomed themselves to death, and the fruit rotted on the walls, because he would let nothing be picked, and gave nothing away, except now and then a grand present of fruit to Lady Catherine, for which the old lady returned no thanks, but only a rude message to say that his peaches were over-ripe, and he had better have sent the grapes to the Infirmary. Adela asked— "Why is the Old Squire so kind to Lady Catherine?" and Father said—"Because we are so fond of Lords and Ladies in this part of the country." I thought he meant the lords and ladies in the hedges, for we are very fond of them. But he didn't. He meant real lords and ladies.

There are splendid lords and ladies in the hedges of Mary's Meadow. I never can make up my mind when I like them best. In April and May, when they have smooth plum-coloured coats and pale green cowls, and push up out of last year's dry leaves, or in August and September, when their hoods have fallen away, and their red berries shine through the dusty grass and nettles that have been growing up round them all the summer out of the ditch.

Flowers were one reason for our wanting to go to Mary's Meadow. Another reason was the nightingale. There was one that used always to sing there, and Mother had made us a story about it.

We are very fond of fairy books, and one of our favourites is Bechstein's *As Pretty as Seven*. It has very nice pictures, and we particularly like "The Man in the Moon, and How He Came There;" but the story doesn't end well, for he came there by gathering sticks on Sunday, and then scoffing about it, and he has been there ever since. But Mother made us a new fairy tale about the nightingale in Mary's Meadow being the naughty woodcutter's only child, who was turned into a little brown bird that lives in the woods, and sits on a tree on summer nights, and sings to its father up in the moon.

But after our Father and the Old Squire went to law, Mother told us we must be content with hearing the nightingale from a distance. We did not really know about the lawsuit then, we only understood that the Old Squire was rather crosser than usual; and we rather resented being warned not to go into Mary's Meadow, especially as Father kept saying we had a perfect right so to do. I thought that Mother was probably afraid of Saxon being set at us, and, of course, I had no fears about him. Indeed, I used to wish that it could happen that the Old Squire, riding after me as full of fury as King Padella in the *Rose and the Ring*, might set Saxon on me, as the lions were let loose to eat the Princess Rosalba. "Instead of devouring her with their great teeth, it was with kisses they gobbled her up. They licked her pretty feet, they nuzzled their noses in her lap," and she put her arms "round their tawny necks and kissed them." Saxon gobbles us with kisses, and nuzzles his nose, and we put our arms round his tawny neck. What a surprise it would be to the Old Squire to see him! And then I wondered if my feet were as pretty as Rosalba's, and I thought they were, and I wondered if Saxon would lick them, supposing that by any possibility it could ever happen that I should be barefoot in Mary's Meadow at the mercy of the Old Squire and his bull-dog.

One does not, as a rule, begin to go to bed by letting down one's hair, and taking off one's shoes and stockings. But one night I was silly enough to do this, just to see if I looked (in the mirror) at all like the picture of Rosalba in the *Rose and the Ring*. I was trying to see my feet as well as my hair, when I heard Arthur jumping the three steps in the middle of the passage between his room and mine. I had only just time to spring into the window-seat, and tuck my feet under me, when he gave a hasty knock, and bounced in with his telescope in his hand.

"Oh, Mary," he cried, "I want you to see the Old Squire, with a great-coat over his evening clothes, and a squash hat, marching up and down Mary's Meadow."

And he pulled up my blind, and threw open the window, and arranged the telescope for me.

It was a glorious night. The moon was rising round and large out of the mist, and dark against its brightness I could see the figure of the Old Squire pacing the pathway over Mary's Meadow.

Saxon was not there; but on a slender branch of a tree in the hedgerow sat the nightingale, singing to comfort the poor, lonely old Man in the Moon.

LADY CATHERINE is Mother's aunt by marriage, and Mother is one of the few people she is not rude to.

She is very rude, and yet she is very kind, especially to the poor. But she does kind things so rudely that people now and then wish that she would mind her own business instead. Father says so, though Mother would say that is gossip. But I think sometimes that Mother is thinking of Aunt Catherine when she tells us that in kindness it is not enough to be good to others, one should also learn to be gracious.

Mother thought she was very rude to *her* once, when she said, quite out loud, that Father is very ill-tempered, and that, if Mother had not the temper of an angel, the house could never hold together. Mother was very angry, but Father did not mind. He says our house will hold together much longer than most houses, because he swore at the workman, and went to law with the builder for using dirt instead of mortar, so the builder had to pull down what was done wrong, and do it right; and Father says he knows he has a bad temper, but he does not mean to pull the house over our heads at present, unless he has to get bricks out to heave at Lady Catherine if she becomes quite unbearable.

We do not like dear Father to be called bad-tempered. He comes home cross sometimes, and then we have to be very quiet, and keep out of the way; and sometimes he goes out rather cross, but not always. It was what Chris said about that that pleased Lady Catherine so much.

It was one day when Father came home cross, and was very much vexed to find us playing about the house. Arthur had got a new Adventure Book, and he had been reading to us about the West Coast of Africa, and niggers, and tom-toms, and "going Fantee"; and James gave him a lot of old corks of the pantry, and let him burn them in a candle. It rained, and we could not go out, so we all blacked our faces with burnt cork, and played at the West Coast in one of the back passages, and at James being the captain of a slave ship, because he tried to catch us when we beat the tom-toms too near him when he was cleaning the plate, to make him give us rouge and whitening to tattoo with.

Dear Father came home rather earlier than we expected, and rather cross. Chris did not hear the front door, because his ears were pinched up with tying curtain rings on to them, and just at that minute he shouted, "I go Fantee!" and tore his pinafore right up the middle, and burst into the front hall with it hanging in two pieces by the armholes, his eyes shut, and a good grab of James's rouge-powder smudged on his nose, yelling and playing the tom-tom on what is left of Arthur's drum.

Father was very angry indeed, and Chris was sent to bed, and not allowed to go down to dessert; and Lady Catherine was dining at our house, so he missed her.

Next time she called, and saw Chris, she asked him why he had not been at dessert that night. Mother looked at Chris, and said, "Why was it, Chris? Tell Aunt Catherine." Mother thought he would say, "Because I tore my pinafore, and made a noise in the front hall." But he smiled, the grave way Chris does, and said, "Because Father came home cross." And Lady Catherine was pleased, but Mother was vexed.

I am quite sure Chris meant no harm, but he does say very funny things. Perhaps it is because his head is rather large for his body, with some water having got into his brain when he was very little, so that we have to take care of him. And though he does say very odd things, very slowly, I do not think any one of us tries harder to be good.

I remember once Mother had been trying to make us forgive each other's trespasses, and Arthur would say that you cannot *make* yourself feel kindly to them that trespass against you; and Mother said if you make yourself do right, then at last you get to feel right; and it was very soon after this that Harry and Christopher quarrelled, and would not forgive each other's trespasses in the least, in spite of all that I could do to try and make peace between them.

Chris went off in the sulks, but after a long time I came upon him in the toy-cupboard, looking rather pale and very large-headed, and winding up his new American top, and talking to himself.

When he talks to himself he mutters, so I could only just hear what he was saying, and he said it over and over again:

"*Dos first and feels afterwards.*"

"What are you doing, Chris?" I asked.

"I'm getting ready my new top to give to Harry. *Dos first feels afterwards.*"

"Well," I said, "Christopher, you *are* a good boy."

"I should like to punch his head," said Chris—and he said it in just the same sing-song tone—"but I'm getting the top ready. *Dos first and feels afterwards.*"

And he went on winding and muttering.

Afterwards he told me that the "feels" came sooner than he expected. Harry wouldn't take his top, and they made up their quarrel.

Christopher is very simple, but sometimes we think he is also a little sly. He can make very wily excuses about things he does not like.

He does not like Nurse to hold back his head and wash his face; and at last one day she let him go down-stairs with a dirty face, and then complained to Mother. So Mother asked Chris why he was so naughty about having his face washed, and he said, quite gravely, "I do think it would be *such pity* if the water got into my head again by accident." Mother did not know he had over heard about it, but she said, "Oh, Chris! Chris! that's one of your excuses." And he said, "It's not my *'scusis*. She lets a good deal get in—at my ears—and lather too."

But, with all his whimsical ways, Lady Catherine is devoted to Christopher. She likes him far better than any one of us, and he is very fond of her; and they say quite rude things to each other all along. And Father says it is very lucky, for if she had not been so fond of Chris, and so ready to take him too, Mother would never have been persuaded to leave us when Aunt Catherine took them to the South of France.

Mother had been very unwell for a long time. She has so many worries, and Dr. Solomon said she ought to avoid worry, and Aunt Catherine said worries were killing her, and Father said "Pshaw!" and Aunt Catherine said "Care killed the cat," and that a cat has nine lives, and a woman has only one; and then Mother got worse, and Aunt Catherine wanted to take her abroad, and she wouldn't go; and then Christopher was ill, and Aunt Catherine said she would take him too, if only Mother would go with her; and Dr. Solomon said it might be the turning-point of his health, and Father said "the turning-point which way?" but he thanked Lady Catherine and they didn't quarrel; and so Mother yielded, and it was settled that they should go.

Before they went, Mother spoke to me, and told me I must be a Little Mother to the others whilst she was away. She hoped we should all try to please Father, and to be unselfish with each other; but she expected me to try far harder than the others, and never to think of myself at all, so that I might fill her place whilst she was away. So I promised to try, and I did.

We missed Christopher sadly. And Saxon missed him. The first time Saxon came to see us after Mother and Chris went away, we told him all about it, and he looked very sorry. Then we said that he should be our brother in Christopher's stead, whilst Chris was away; and he looked very much pleased, and wagged his tail, and licked our faces all round. So we told him to come and see us very often.

He did not, but we do not think it was his fault. He is chained up so much.

One day Arthur and I were walking down the road outside the Old Squire's stables, and Saxon smelt us, and we could hear him run and rattle his chain, and he gave deep, soft barks.

Arthur laughed. He said, "Do you hear Saxon, Mary? Now I dare say the Old Squire thinks he smells tramps and wants to bite them. He doesn't know that Saxon smells his new sister and brother, and wishes he could go out walking with them in Mary's Meadow."

CHAPTER III

NOTHING comforted us so much whilst Mother and Chris were away as being allowed to play in the library.

We were not usually allowed to be there so often, but when we asked Father he gave us leave to amuse ourselves there at the time when Mother would have had us with her, provided that we did not bother him or hurt the books. We did not hurt the books, and in the end we were allowed to go there as much as we liked.

We have plenty of books of our own, and we have new ones very often: on birthdays and at Christmas. Sometimes they are interesting, and sometimes they are disappointing. Most of them have pretty pictures. It was because we had been rather unlucky for some time, and had had disappointing ones on our birthdays, that Arthur said to me, "Look here, Mary, I'm not going to read any books now but grown-up ones, unless it is an Adventure Book. I'm sick of books for young people, there's so much *stuff* in them."

We call it *stuff* when there seems to be going to be a story and it comes to nothing but talk; and we call it *stuff* when there is a very interesting picture, and you read to see what it is about, and the reading does not tell you, or tells you wrong.

Both Arthur and Christopher had had disappointments in their books on their birthdays.

Arthur jumped at his book at first, because there were Japanese pictures in it, and Uncle Charley had just been staying with us, and had brought beautiful Japanese pictures with him, and had told us Japanese fairy tales, and they were as good as Bechstein. So Arthur was full of Japan.

The most beautiful picture of all was of a stork, high up in a tall pine tree, and the branches of the pine tree, and the cones, and the pine needles were most beautifully drawn; and there was a nest with young storks in it, and behind the stork and the nest and the tall pine the sun was blazing with all his rays. And Uncle Charley told us the story to it, and it was called "The Nest of the Stork."

So when Arthur saw a stork standing among pine needles in his new book he shouted with delight, though the pine needles were rather badly done, with thick strokes. But presently he said, "It's not nearly so good a stork as Uncle Charley's. And where's the stem of the pine? It looks as if the stork were on the ground and on the top of the pine tree too, and there's no nest. And there's no sun. And, oh! Mary, what do you think is written under it? 'Crane and Water-reeds.' Well, I do call that a sell!"

Christopher's disappointment was quite as bad. Mother gave him a book with very nice pictures, particularly of beasts. The chief reason she got it for him was that there was such a very good picture of a toad, and Chris is so fond of toads. For months he made friends with one in the garden. It used to crawl away from him, and he used to creep after it, talking to it, and then it used to half begin to crawl up the garden wall, and stand on its hind legs, and let Chris rub its wrinkled back. The toad in the picture was exactly like Christopher's toad, and he ran about the house with the book in his arms begging us to read him the story about Dear Toady.

We were all busy but Arthur, and he said, "I want to go on with my water-wheel." But Mother said, "Don't be selfish, Arthur." And he said, "I forgot. All right, Chris; bring me the book." So they went and sat in the conservatory, not to disturb anyone. But very soon they came back, Chris crying, and saying, "It couldn't be the right one, Arthur"; and Arthur frowning, and saying, "It *is* the right story; but it's *stuff*. I'll tell you what that book's good for, Chris. To paint the pictures. And you've got a new paint-box." So Mother said, "What's the matter?" And Arthur said, "Chris thinks I haven't read him the right story to his Toad Picture. But I have, and what do you think it's about? It's about the silliest little girl you can imagine—a regular mawk of a girl—*and a frog*. Not a toad, but a F.R.O.G. frog! A regular hop, skip, jumping frog!"

Arthur hopped round the room, but Chris cried bitterly. So Arthur ran up to him and kissed him, and said, "Don't cry, old chap. I'll tell you what I'll do. You get Mary to cut out a lot of the leaves of your book that have no pictures, and that will make it like a real scrap-book; and then I'll give you a lot of my scraps and pictures to paste over what's left of the stories, and you'll have such a painting-book as you never had in all your life before."

So we did. And Arthur was very good, for he gave Chris pictures that I know he prized, because Chris liked them. But the very first picture he gave him was the "Crane and Water-reeds."

I thought it so good of Arthur to be so nice with Chris that I wished I could have helped him over his water-wheel. He had put Japan out of his head since the disappointment, and spent all his playtime in making mills and machinery. He did grind some corn into flour once, but it was not at all white. He said that was because the bran was left in. But it was not only bran in Arthur's flour. There was a good deal of sand too, from his millstones being made of sandstone, which he though would not matter. But it grinds off.

Down in the valley, below Mary's Meadow, runs the Ladybrook, which turns the old water-wheel of Mary's Mill. It is a very picturesque old mill, and Mother has made beautiful sketches of it. She caught the last cold she got before going abroad with sketching it—the day we had a most delightful picnic there, and went about in the punt. And from that afternoon Arthur made up his mind that his next mill should be a water-mill.

The reason I am no good at helping Arthur about his mills is that I am stupid about machinery; and I was so vexed not to help him, that when I saw a book in the library which I thought would do so, I did not stop to take it out, for it was in four very large volumes, but ran off at once, to tell Arthur.

He said, "What *is* the matter, Mary?"

I said, "Oh, Arthur! I've found a book that will tell you all about mills; and it is the nicest smelling book in the library."

"The nicest *smelling*? What's that got to do with mills?"

"Nothing, of course. But it's bound in russia, and I am so fond of the smell of russia. But that's nothing. It's a Miller's Dictionary, and it is in four huge volumes, 'with plates.' I should think you could look out all about every kind of mill there ever was a miller to."

"If the plates give sections and diagrams—" Arthur began, but I did not hear the rest, for he started off for the library at once, and I ran after him.

But when we got Miller's Dictionary on the floor, how he did tease me! For there was nothing about mills or millers in it. It was a Gardener's and Botanist's Dictionary, by Philip Miller; and the plates were plates of flowers, very truly drawn, like the pine tree in Uncle Charley's Jap. picture. There were some sections too, but they were sections of greenhouses, not of any kinds of mills or machinery.

The odd thing was that it turned out a kind of help to Arthur after all. For we got so much interested in it that it roused us up about our garden. We are all very fond of flowers, I most of all. And at last Arthur said he thought that miniature mills were really rather humbugging things, and it would be much easier and more useful to build a cold frame to keep choice auriculas and *half-hardies* in.

When we took up our gardens so hotly, Harry and Adela took up theirs, and we did a great deal, for the weather was fine.

We were surprised to find that the Old Squire's Scotch Gardener knew Miller's Gardener's Dictionary quite well. He said, "It's a gran' wurrk!" (Arthur can say it just like him.)

One day he wished he could see it, and smell the russia binding; he said he liked to feel a nice smell. Father was away, and we were by ourselves so we invited him into the library. Saxon wanted to come in too, but the gardener was very cross with him, and sent him out; and he sat on the mat outside and dribbled with longing to get in, and thudded his stiff tail whenever he saw anyone through the doorway.

The Scotch Gardener enjoyed himself very much, and he explained a lot of things to Arthur, and helped us to put away the Dictionary when we had done with it.

When he took up his hat to go, he gave one long look all round the library. Then he turned to Arthur (and Saxon took advantage of this to wag his way in and join the party), and said, "It's a rare privilege, the free entry of a book chamber like this. I'm hoping, young gentleman, that you're not insensible of it?"

Then he caught sight of Saxon, and beat him out of the room with his hat.

But he came back himself to say that it might just happen that he would be glad now and again to hear what was said about this or that plant (of which he would write down the botanical name) in these noble volumes.

So we told him that if he would bring Saxon to see us pretty often, we would look out anything he wanted to know about in Miller's Gardener's Dictionary.

CHAPTER IV

LOOKING round the library one day, to see if I could see any more books about gardening, I found the Book of Paradise.

It is a very old book, and very queer. It has a brown leather back—not russia—and stiff little gold flowers and ornaments all the way down, where Miller's Dictionary has gold swans in crowns, and ornaments.

There are a good many old books in the library, but they are not generally very interesting—at least not to us. So when I found that though this one had a Latin name on the title-page, it was written in English, and that though it seemed to be about Paradise, it was really about a garden, and quite common flowers, I was delighted, for I always have cared more for gardening and flowers than for any other amusement, long before we found Miller's Gardener's Dictionary. And the Book of Paradise is much smaller than the Dictionary, and easier to hold. And I like old, queer things, and it is very old and queer.

The Latin name is *Paradisi in sole Paradisus terrestris*, which we do not any of us understand, though we are all learning Latin;

so we call it the Book of Paradise. But the English name is—"Of a Garden of all sorts of pleasant flowers which our English ayre will permitt to be noursed up;" and on the top of every page is written "The Garden of Pleasant Flowers," and it says—"Collected by John Parkinson Apothecary of London, (and the King's Herbarist), 1629."

I had to think a minute to remember who was the king then, and it was King Charles I; so then I knew that it was Queen Henrietta to whom the book was dedicated. This was the dedication—

"To the Queen's Most Excellent Majesty.

"Madame,—Knowing your Majesty so much delighted with all the fair flowers of a Garden, and furnished with them as far beyond others, as you are eminent before them; this my work of a Garden, long before this intended to be published, and but now only finished, seemed as it were destined, to be first offered into your Highnesse hands, as of right challenging the propriety of Patronage from all others. Accept, I beseech your Majesty, this speaking Garden, that may inform you in all the particulars of your store, as well as wants, when you cannot see any of these fresh upon the ground: and it shall further encourage him to accomplish the remainder; who in praying that your Highnesse may enjoy the heavenly Paradise, after the many years' fruition of this earthly, submitteth to be your Majesties,

"in all humble devotion,

"John Parkinson."

We like queer old things like this, they are so funny! I liked the Dedication, and I wondered if the Queen's Garden really was an Earthly Paradise, and whether she did enjoy reading John Parkinson's book about flowers in the winter time, when her own flowers were no longer "fresh upon the ground." And then I wondered what flowers she had, and I looked out a great many of our chief favourites, and she had several kinds of them.

We are particularly fond of Daffodils, and she had several kinds of Daffodils, from the "Primrose Peerlesse,"[1] "of a sweet but stuffing scent," to "the least Daffodil of all,"[2] which the book says "was brought to us by a Frenchman called Francis le Vean, the honestest root-gatherer that ever came over to us."

The Queen had Cowslips too, though our Gardener despised

[1] *Narcissus medio lutens vulgaris.*
[2] *Narcissus minimus,* Parkinson. *N. minor,* Miller.

them when he saw them in my garden. I dug mine up in Mary's Meadow before Father and the Old Squire went to law; but they were only common Cowslips, with one Oxlip, by good luck. In the Earthly Paradise there were "double Cowslips, one within another." And they were called Hose-in-Hose. I wished I had Hose-in-Hose.

Arthur was quite as much delighted with the Book of Paradise as I. He said, "Isn't it funny to think of Queen Henrietta Maria gardening! I wonder if she went trailing up and down the walks looking like that picture of her we saw when you and I were in London with Mother about our teeth, and went to see the Loan Collection of Old Masters. I wonder if the Dwarf picked the flowers for her. I do wonder what Apothecary John Parkinson looked like when he offered his Speaking Garden into her Highness's hands. And what beautiful hands she had! Do your remember the picture, Mary? It was by Vandyck."

I remembered it quite well.

That afternoon the others could not amuse themselves, and wanted me to tell them a story. They do not like old stories too often, and it is rather difficult to invent new ones. Sometimes we do it by turns. We sit in a circle and one of us begins, and the next must add something, and so we go on. But that way does not make a good plot. My head was so full of the Book of Paradise that afternoon that I could not think of a story, but I said I would begin one. So I began—

"Once upon a time there was a Queen——"

"How was she dressed?" asked Adela, who thinks a good deal about dress.

"She had a beautiful dark-blue satin robe."

"*Princesse* shape?" inquired Adela.

"No; Queen's shape," said Arthur. "Drive on, Mary."

"And lace ruffles falling back from her Highness's hands——"

"Sweet!" murmured Adela.

"And a high hat, with plumes, on her head, and——"

"A very low dwarf at her heels," added Arthur.

"Was there really a dwarf, Mary?" asked Harry.

"There was," said I.

"Had he a hump, or was he only a plain dwarf?"

"He was a very plain dwarf," said Arthur.

"Does Arthur know the story, Mary?"

"No, Harry, he doesn't; and he oughtn't to interfere till I come to a stop."

"Beg pardon, Mary. Drive on."

"The Queen was very much delighted with all fair flowers, and she had a garden so full of them that it was called the Earthly Paradise."

There was a long-drawn and general "Oh!" of admiration.

"But though she was a Queen, she couldn't have flowers in the winter, not even in an Earthly Paradise."

"Don't you suppose she had a greenhouse, by the bye, Mary?" said Arthur.

"Oh, Arthur," cried Harry, "I do wish you'd be quiet: when you know it's a fairy story, and that Queens of that sort never had greenhouses or anything like we have now."

"And so the King's Apothecary and Herbarist, whose name was John Parkinson——"

"I shouldn't have thought he would have had a common name like that," said Harry.

"Bessy's name is Parkinson," said Adela.

"Well, I can't help it; his name *was* John Parkinson."

"Drive on, Mary!" said Arthur.

"And he made her a book, called the Book of Paradise, in which there were pictures and written accounts of her flowers, so that when she could not see any of them fresh upon the ground, she could read about them, and think about them, and count up how many she had."

"Ah, but she couldn't tell. Some of them might have died in the winter," said Adela.

"Ah, but some of the others might have got little ones at their roots," said Harry. "So that would make up."

I said nothing. I was glad of the diversion, for I could not think how to go on with the story. Before I quite gave in, Harry luckily asked, "Was there a Weeding Woman in the Earthly Paradise?"

"There was," said I.

"How was she dressed?" said Adela.

"She had a dress the colour of common earth."

"*Princesse* shape?" inquired Arthur.

"No; Weeding Woman shape. Arthur, I wish you wouldn't——"

"All right, Mary. Drive on."

"And a little shawl, that had partly the colour of grass, and partly the colour of hay."

"*Hay, dear!*" interpolated Arthur, exactly imitating a well-known sigh peculiar to Bessy's aunt.

"Was her bonnet like our Weeding Woman's bonnet?" asked Adela, in a disappointed tone.

"Much larger," said I, "and the colour of a Marigold."

Adela looked happier. "Strings the same?" she asked.

"No. One string canary-colour, and the other white."

"And a basket?" asked Harry.

"Yes, a basket, of course. Well, the Queen had all sorts of flowers in her garden. Some of them were natives of the country, and some of them were brought to her from countries far away, by men called Root-gatherers. There were very beautiful Daffodils in the Earthly Paradise, but the smallest of all the Daffodils——"

"A Dwarf, like the Hunchback?" said Harry.

"The Dwarf Daffodil of all was brought to her by a man called Francis le Vean."

"That was a *much* nicer name than John Parkinson," said Harry.

"And he was the honestest Root-gatherer that ever brought foreign flowers into the Earthly Paradise."

"Then I love him!" said Harry.

CHAPTER V

ONE sometimes thinks it is very easy to be good, and then there comes something which makes it very hard.

I liked being a Little Mother to the others, and almost enjoyed giving way to them. "Others first, Little Mothers afterwards," as we used to say—till the day I made up that story for them out of the Book of Paradise.

The idea of it took our fancy completely, the others as well as mine, and though the story was constantly interrupted, and never came to any real plot or end, there were no Queens, or dwarfs, or characters of any kind in all Bechstein's fairy tales, or even in Grimm, more popular than the Queen of the Blue Robe and her Dwarf, and the Honest Root-gatherer, and John Parkinson, King's Apothecary and Herbarist, and the Weeding Woman of the Earthly Paradise.

When I said, "Wouldn't it be a good new game to have an Earthly

Paradise in our gardens, and to have a King's Apothecary and Herbarist to gather things and make medicine of them, and an Honest Root-gatherer to divide the polyanthus plants and the bulbs when we take them up, and divide them fairly, and a Weeding Woman to work and make things tidy, and a Queen in a blue dress, and Saxon for the Dwarf"—the others set up such a shout of approbation that Father sent James to inquire if we imagined that he was going to allow his house to be turned into a bear-garden.

And Arthur said, "No. Tell him we're only turning it into a Speaking Garden, and we're going to turn our own gardens into an Earthly Paradise."

But I said, "Oh, James! please don't say anything of the kind. Say we're very sorry, and we will be quite quiet."

And James said, "Trust me, Miss. It would be a deal more than my place is worth to carry Master Arthur's messages to his Pa."

"I'll be the Honestest Root-gatherer," said Harry. "I'll take up Dandelion roots to the very bottom, and sell them to the King's Apothecary to make Dandelion tea of."

"That's a good idea of yours, Harry," said Arthur. "I shall be John Parkinson——"

"*My* name is Francis le Vean," said Harry.

"King's Apothecary and Herbarist," continued Arthur, disdaining the interruption. "And I'll bet you my Cloth of Gold Pansy to your Black Prince that Bessy's aunt takes three bottles of my dandelion and camomile mixture for 'the swimmings,' bathes her eyes every morning with my elder-flower lotion to strengthen the sight, and sleeps every night on my herb pillow (if Mary'll make me a flannel bag) before the week's out."

"I could make you a flannel bag," said Adela, "if Mary will make me a bonnet, so that I can be the Weeding Woman. You could make it of tissue-paper, with stiff paper inside, like all those caps you made for us last Christmas, Mary dear, couldn't you? And there is some lovely orange-coloured paper, I know, and pale yellow, and white. The bonnet was Marigold colour, was it not? And one string canary-coloured and one white. I couldn't tie them, of course, being paper; but Bessy's aunt doesn't tie her bonnet. She wears it like a helmet, to shade her eyes. I shall wear mine so too. It will be all Marigold, won't it, dear? Front *and* crown; and the white string going back over one shoulder and the canary string over the other. They might be pinned together behind, perhaps, if they were in my way. Don't you think so?"

I said "Yes," because if one does not say something, Adela never stops saying whatever it is she is saying, even if she has to say it two or three times over.

But I felt so cross and so selfish, that if Mother *could* have known she *would* have despised me!

For the truth was, I had set my heart upon being the Weeding Woman. I thought Adela would want to be the Queen, because of the blue dress, and the plumed hat, and the lace ruffles. Besides, she likes picking flowers, but she never liked grubbing. She would not really like the Weeding Woman's work; it was the bonnet that had caught her fancy, and I found it hard to smother the vexing thought that if I had gone on dressing the Weeding Woman of the Earthly Paradise like Bessy's aunt, instead of trying to make the story more interesting by inventing a marigold bonnet with yellow and white strings for her, I might have had the part I wished to play in our new game (which certainly was of my devising), and Adela would have been better pleased to be the Queen than to be anything else.

As it was, I knew that if I asked her she would give up the Weeding Woman. Adela is very good, and she is very good-natured. And I knew, too, that it would not have cost her much. She would have given a sigh about the bonnet, and then have turned her whole attention to a blue robe, and how to manage the ruffles.

But even whilst I was thinking about it, Arthur said: "Of course, Mary must be the Queen, unless we could think of something else— very good—for her. If we could have thought of something, Mary, I was thinking how jolly it would be, when Mother comes home, to have had *her* for the Queen, with Chris for her Dwarf, and to give her flowers out of our Earthly Paradise."

"She would look just like a Queen," said Harry.

"In her navy blue nun's cloth and Russian lace," said Adela.

That settled the question. Nothing could be so nice as to have Mother in the game, and the plan provided for Christopher also. I had no wish to be Queen, as far as that went. Dressing up, and walking about the garden would be no fun for me. I really had looked forward to clearing away big baskets full of weeds and rubbish, and keeping our five gardens and the paths between them so tidy as they had never been kept before. And I knew the weeds would have a fine time of it with Adela, as Weeding Woman, in a tissue-paper bonnet!

But one thing was more important than tidy gardens—not to be selfish.

I had been left as Little Mother to the others, and I had been lucky enough to think of a game that pleased them. If I turned selfish now, it would spoil everything.

So I said that Arthur's idea was excellent; that I had no wish to be Queen, that I thought I might, perhaps, devise another character for myself by and by; and that if the others would leave me alone, I would think about it whilst I was making Adela's bonnet.

The others were quite satisfied. Father says people always are satisfied with things in general when they've got what they want for themselves, and I think that is true.

I got the tissue-paper and the gum; resisted Adela's extreme desire to be with me and talk about the bonnet, and shut myself up in the library.

I got out the Book of Paradise too, and propped it up in an arm-chair, and sat on a footstool in front of it, so that I could read in between whiles of making the bonnet. There is an index, so that you can look out the flowers you want to read about. It was no use our looking out flowers, except common ones, such as Harry would be allowed to get bits of out of the big garden to plant in our little gardens, when he became our Honest Root-gatherer.

I looked at the Cowslips again. I am very fond of them, and so, they say, are nightingales; which is, perhaps, why that nightingale we know lives in Mary's Meadow, for it is full of cowslips.

The Queen had a great many kinds, and there are pictures of most of them. She had the Common Field Cowslip, the Primrose Cowslip, the Single Green Cowslip, Curled Cowslips, or Galli-gaskins, Double Cowslips, or Hose-in-Hose, and the Franticke or Foolish Cowslip, or Jackanapes on Horsebacke.

I did not know one of them except the Common Cowslip, but I remembered that Bessy's aunt once told me that she had a double cowslip. It was the day I was planting common ones in my garden, when our gardener despised them. Bessy's aunt despised them too, and she said the double ones were only fit for a cottage garden. I laughed so much that I tore the canary-coloured string as I was gumming it on to the bonnet, to think how I could tell her now that cowslips are Queen's flowers, the common ones as well as the Hose-in-Hose.

Then I looked out the Honeysuckle, it was page 404, and there were no pictures. I began at the beginning of the chapter; this was it, and it was as funnily spelt as the preface, but I could read it.

"Chap. cv. *Periclymemum*. Honeysuckles.

"The Honisucle that groweth wilde in euery hedge, although it be very sweete, yet doe I not bring it into my garden, but let it rest in his owne place, to serue their senses that trauell by it, or haue no garden."

I had got so far when James came in. He said—"Letters, Miss."

It was the second post, and there was a letter for me, and a book parcel; both from Mother.

Mother's letters are always delightful; and, like things she says, they often seem to come in answer to something you have been thinking about, and which you would never imagine she could know, unless she was a witch. This was *the knowing bit* in that letter:—

"*Your dear father's note this morning did me more good than bottles of tonic. It is due to you, my trustworthy little daughter, to tell you of the bit that pleased me most. He says—'The children seem to me to be behaving unusually well, and I must say, I believe the credit belongs to Mary. She seems to have a genius for keeping them amused, which luckily means keeping them out of mischief.' Now, good Little Mother, I wonder how you yourself are being entertained? I hope the others are not presuming on your unselfishness? Anyhow, I send you a book for your own amusement when they leave you a bit of peace and quiet. I have long been fond of it in French, and I have found an English translation with nice little pictures, and send it to you. I know you will enjoy it, because you are so fond of flowers.*"

Oh, how glad I was that I had let Adela be the Weeding Woman with a good grace, and could open my book parcel with a clear conscience!

I put the old book away and buried myself in the new one.

I never had a nicer. It was called *A Tour Round my Garden*, and some of the little stories in it—like the Tulip Rebecca, and the Discomfited Florists—were very amusing indeed; and some were sad and pretty, like the Yellow Roses; and there were delicious bits, like the Enriched Woodman and the Connoisseur Deceived; but there was no "stuff" in it at all.

Some chapters were duller than others, and at last I got into a very dull one, about the vine, and it had a good deal of Greek in it, and we have not begun Greek.

But after the Greek, and the part about Bacchus and Anacreon (I did not care about *them*; they were not in the least like the Discomfited Florists, or the Enriched Woodman!) there came this, and I liked it the best of all—

"At the extremity of my garden the vine extends in long porticoes, through the arcades of which may be seen trees of all sorts, and foliage of all colours. Here is an *azerolier* (a small medlar) which is covered in autumn with little scarlet apples, producing the richest effect. I have given away several grafts of this; far from deriving pleasure from the privation of others, I do my utmost to spread and render common and vulgar all the trees and plants that I prefer; it is as if I multiplied the pleasure and the chances of beholding them of all who, like me, really love flowers for their splendour, their grace, and their perfume. Those who, on the contrary, are jealous of their plants, and only esteem them in proportion with their conviction that no one else possesses them, do not love flowers; and be assured that it is either chance or poverty which has made them collectors of flowers, instead of being collectors of pictures, cameos, medals, or any other thing that might serve as an excuse for indulging in all the joys of possession, seasoned with the idea that others do not possess.

"I have even carried the vulgarization of beautiful flowers farther than this.

"I ramble about the country near my dwelling, and seek the wildest and least-frequented spots. In these, after clearing and preparing a few inches of ground, I scatter the seeds of my most favourite plants, which re-sow themselves, perpetuate themselves, and multiply themselves. At this moment, whilst the fields display nothing but the common red poppy, strollers find with surprise in certain wild nooks of our country, the most beautiful double poppies, with their white, red, pink, carnation, and variegated blossoms.

"At the foot of an isolated tree, instead of the little bindweed with its white flower, may sometimes be found the beautifully climbing convolvulus major, of all the lovely colours that can be imagined.

"Sweet peas fasten their tendrils to the bushes, and cover them with the deliciously-scented white, rose-coloured, or white and violet butterflies.

"It affords me immense pleasure to fix upon a wild-rose in a hedge, and graft upon it red and white cultivated roses, sometimes single roses of a magnificent golden yellow, then large Provence roses, or others variegated with red and white.

"The rivulets in our neighbourhood do not produce on their banks these forget-me-nots, with their blue flowers, with which the rivulet of my garden is adorned; I mean to save the seed, and scatter it in my walks.

"I have observed two young wild quince trees in the nearest wood; next spring I will graft upon them two of the best kinds of pears.

"And then, how I enjoy beforehand and in imagination, the pleasure and surprise which the solitary stroller will experience when he meets in his rambles with those beautiful flowers and these delicious fruits!

"This fancy of mine may, one day or another, cause some learned botanist who is herbarizing in these parts a hundred years hence, to print a stupid and startling system. All these beautiful flowers will have become common in the country, and will give it an aspect peculiar to itself; and, perhaps, chance or the wind will cast a few of the seeds or some of them amidst the grass which shall cover my forgotten grave!"

This was the end of the chapter, and then there was a vignette, a very pretty one, of a cross-marked, grass-bound grave.

Some books, generally grown-up ones, put things into your head with a sort of rush, and now it suddenly rushed into mine— "*That's what I'll be*! I can think of a name hereafter—but that's what I'll do. I'll take seeds and cuttings, and off-shoots from our garden, and set them in waste places, and hedges, and fields, and I'll make an Earthly Paradise of Mary's Meadow."

CHAPTER VI

The only difficulty about my part was to find a name for it. I might have taken the name of the man who wrote the book—it was Alphonse Karr,—just as Arthur was going to be called John Parkinson. But I am a girl, so it seemed silly to take a man's name. And I wanted some kind of title, too, like King's Apothecary and Herbarist, or Weeding Woman, and Alphonse Karr does not seem to have had any by-name of that sort.

I had put Adela's bonnet on my head to carry it safely, and was still sitting thinking, when the others burst into the library.

Arthur was first, waving a sheet of paper; but when Adela saw the bonnet, she caught hold of his arm and pushed forward.

"Oh, it's sweet! Mary, dear, you're an angel. You couldn't be better if you were a real milliner and lived in Paris. I'm sure you couldn't."

"Mary," said Arthur, "remove that bonnet, which by no means becomes you, and let Adela take it into a corner and gibber over it to herself. I want you to hear this."

"You generally do want the platform," I said, laughing. "Adela, I am very glad you like it. Tomorrow, if I can find a bit of pink tissue-paper, I think I could gum on little pleats round the edge of the strings as a finish."

I did not mind how gaudily I dressed the part of Weeding Woman now.

"You are good, Mary. It will make it simply perfect; and, kilts don't you think? Not box pleats?"

Arthur groaned.

"You shall have which you like, dear. Now, Arthur, what is it?"

Arthur shook out his paper, gave it a flap with the back of his hand, as you do with letters when you are acting, and said—"It's to Mother, and when she gets it, she'll be a good deal astonished, I fancy."

When I had heard the letter, I thought so too.

"To the Queen's Most Excellent Majestie—

"My Dear Mother,—This is to tell you that we have made you Queen of the Blue Robe, and that your son Christopher is a dwarf, and we think you'll both be very much pleased when you hear it. He can do as he likes about having a hump back. When you come home we shall give faire flowers into your Highnesse hands—that is, if you'll do what I'm going to ask you, for nobody can grow flowers out of nothing. I want you to write to John—write straight to him, don't put it in your letter to Father—and tell him that you have given us leave to have some of the seedlings out of the frames, and that he's to dig us up a good big clump of daffodils out of the shrubbery—and we'll divide them fairly, for Harry is the Honestest Root-gatherer that ever came over to us. We have turned the whole of our gardens into a *Paradisi in sole Paradisus terrestris*, if you can construe that; but we must have something to make a start. He's got no end of bedding things over—that are doing nothing in the Kitchen Garden and might just as well be in our Earthly Paradise. And please tell him to keep us a tiny pinch of seed at the bottom of every paper when he is sowing the annuals. A little goes a long way, particularly of poppies. And

you might give him a hint to let us have a flower-pot or two now
and then (I'm sure he takes ours if he finds any of our dead window-
plants lying about), and that he needn't be so mighty mean about
the good earth in the potting shed, or the labels either, they're dirt
cheap. Mind you write straight. If only you let John know that
the gardens don't entirely belong to him, you'll see that what's
spare from the big garden would more than set us going; and it
shall further encourage him to accomplish the remainder, who in
praying that your Highnesse may enjoy the heavenly Paradise
after the many years fruition of this earthly,

> "Submitteth to be, Your Maiestie's,
> "In all humble devotion,
> "JOHN PARKINSON,
> "King's Apothecary and Herbarist.

"P.S.—It was Mary's idea."

"My *dear* Arthur!" said I.

"Well, I know it's not very well mixed," said Arthur. "Not
half so well as I intended at first. I meant to write it all in the
Parkinson style. But then, I thought, if I put the part about John
in queer language and old spelling, she mightn't understand what
we want. But every word of the end comes out of the Dedication;
I copied it the other day, and I think she'll find it a puzzlewig
when she comes to it."

After which Arthur folded his paper and put it into an envelope
which he licked copiously, and closed the letter with a great deal
of display. But then his industry coming to an abrupt end, as it
often did, he tossed it to me, saying, "You can address it, Mary;"
so I enclosed it in my own letter to thank Mother for the book,
and I fancy she did write to our gardener, for he gave us a good
lot of things, and was much more good-natured than usual.

After Arthur had tossed his letter to me, he clasped his hands
over his head and walked up and down thinking. I thought he
was calculating what he should be able to get out of John, for when
you are planning about a garden, you seem to have to do so much
calculating. Suddenly he stopped in front of me and threw down
his arms. "Mary," he said, "if Mother were at home, she *would*
despise us for selfishness, wouldn't she just?"

"I don't think it's selfish to want spare things for our gardens,
if she gives us leave," said I.

"I'm not thinking of that," said Arthur; "and you're not selfish, you never are; but she would despise me, and Adela, and Harry, because we've taken your game, and got our parts, and you've made that preposterous bonnet for Adela to be the Weeding Woman in ——much she'll weed!——"

"I *shall* weed," said Adela.

"Oh, yes! You'll weed,—Groundsel!—and leave Mary to get up the docks and dandelions, and clear away the heap. But, never mind. Here we've taken Mary's game, and she hasn't even got a part."

"Yes," said I, "I have; I have got a capital part. I have only to think of a name."

"How shall you be dressed?" asked Adela.

"I don't know yet," said I. "I have only just thought of the part."

"Are you sure it's a good-enough one?" asked Harry, with a grave and remorseful air; "because, if not, you must take Francis le Vean. Girls are called Frances sometimes."

I explained, and I read aloud the bit that had struck my fancy.

Arthur got restless half-way through, and took out the Book of Paradise. His letter was on his mind. But Adela was truly delighted.

"Oh, Mary," she said. "It is lovely. And it just suits you. It suits you much better than being a Queen."

"Much better," said I.

"You'll be exactly the reverse of me," said Harry. "When I'm digging up, you'll be putting in."

"Mary," said Arthur, from the corner where he was sitting with the Book of Paradise in his lap, "what have you put a mark in the place about honeysuckle for?"

"Oh, only because I was just reading there when James brought the letters."

"John Parkinson can't have been quite so nice a man as Alphonse Karr," said Adela; "not so unselfish. He took care of the Queen's Gardens, but he didn't think of making the lanes and hedges nice for poor wayfarers."

I was in the rocking-chair, and I rocked harder to shake up something that was coming into my head. Then I remembered.

"Yes, Adela, he did—a little. He wouldn't root up the honeysuckle out of the hedges (and I suppose he wouldn't let his root-gatherers grub it up, either); he didn't put it in the Queen's Gardens, but left it wild outside——"

"To serve their senses that travel by it, or have no garden," interrupted Arthur, reading from the book, "and, oh, Mary! that reminds me—*travel—travellers*. I've got a name for your part just coming into my head. But it dodges out again like a wire-worm through a three-pronged fork. *Travel—traveller—travellers*—what's the common name for the—oh, dear! the what's his name that scrambles about in the hedges. A flower—you know?"

"Deadly Nightshade?" said Harry.

"Deadly fiddlestick!——"

"Bryony?" I suggested.

"Oh, no; it begins with C."

"Clematis?" said Adela.

"Clematis. Right you are, Adela. And the common name for Clematis is Traveller's Joy. And that's the name for you, Mary, because you're going to serve their senses that travel by hedges and ditches and perhaps have no garden."

"Traveller's Joy," said Harry. "Hooray!"

"Hooray!" said Adela, and she waved the Weeding Woman's bonnet.

It was a charming name, but it was too good for me, and I said so.

Arthur jumped on the rockers, and rocked me to stop my talking. When I was far back, he took the point of my chin in his two hands and lifted up my cheeks to be kissed, saying in his very kindest way, "It's not a bit too good for you—it's you all over."

Then he jumped off as suddenly as he had jumped on, and as I went back with a bounce he cried, "Oh, Mary! give me back that letter. I must put another postscript and another puzzlewig. 'P.P.S.—Excellent Majesty: Mary will still be our Little Mother on all common occasions, as you wished, but in the Earthly Paradise we call her Traveller's Joy.'"

CHAPTER VII

THERE ARE TWO or three reasons why the part of Traveller's Joy suited me very well. In the first place it required a good deal of trouble, and I like taking trouble. Then John was willing to let me do many things he would not have allowed the others to do, because he could trust me to be careful and to mind what he said.

On each side of the long walk in the kitchen garden there are flowers between you and the vegetables, herbaceous borders, with nice big clumps of things that have suckers, and off-shoots and seedlings at their feet.

"The Long Walk's the place to steal from if I wasn't an *honest* Root-gatherer," said Harry.

John had lovely poppies there that summer. When I read about the poppies Alphonse Karr sowed in the wild nooks of his native country, it made me think of John's French poppies, and paeony poppies, and ranunculus poppies, and carnation poppies, some very large, some quite small, some round and neat, some full and ragged like Japanese chrysanthemums, but all of such beautiful shades of red, rose, crimson, pink, pale blush, and white, that if they had but smelt like carnations instead of smelling like laudanum when you have the toothache, they would have been quite perfect.

In one way they are nicer than carnations. They have such a lots of seed, and it is so easy to get out. I asked John to let me have some of the heads. He could not possibly want them all, for each head has enough in it to sow two or three yards of border. He said I might have what seeds I liked, if I used scissors, and did not drag things out of the ground by pulling. But I was not to let the young gentlemen go seed-gathering. "Boys be so destructive." John said.

After a time, however, I persuaded him to let Harry transplant seedlings of the things that sow themselves and come up in the autumn, if they came up a certain distance from the parent plants. Harry got a lot of things for our Paradise in this way ; indeed, he would not have got much otherwise, except wild flowers ; and, as he said, "How can I be your Honest Root-gatherer if I mayn't gather anything up by the roots?"

I can't help laughing sometimes to think of the morning when he left off being our Honest Root-gatherer. He did look so funny and so like Chris.

A day or two before, the Scotch Gardener had brought Saxon to see us, and a new kind of mouldiness that had got into his grape vines to show to John.

He was very cross with Saxon for walking on my garden. (And I am sure I quite forgave him, for I am so fond of him, and he knew no better, poor dear!) But, though he kicked Saxon, the Scotch Gardener was kind to us. He told us that the reason our gardens do not do so well as the big garden, and that my *Jules Margottin* has not such big roses as John's *Jules Margottin* is because we have never renewed the soil.

Arthur and Harry got very much excited about this. They made the Scotch Gardener tell them what good soil ought to be made of, and all the rest of the day they talked of nothing but *compost*. Indeed, Arthur would come into my room and talk about compost after I had gone to bed.

Father's farming man was always much more good-natured to us than John ever was. He would give us anything we wanted. Warm milk when the cows were milked, or sweet-pea sticks, or bran to stuff the dolls' pillows. I've known him take his hedging-bill, in his dinner-hour, and cut fuel for our beacon fire, when we were playing at a French Invasion. Nothing could be kinder.

Perhaps we do not tease him so much as we tease John. But when I say that, Arthur says, "Now, Mary, that's just how you explain away things. The real difference between John and Michael is, that Michael is good-natured and John is not. Catch John showing me the duck's nest by the pond, or letting you into the cow-house to kiss the new calf between the eyes—if he were farm man instead of gardener!"

And the night Arthur sat in my room, talking about compost, he said, "I shall get some good stuff out of Michael, I know ; and Harry and I see our way to road-scrapings if we can't get sand ; and we mean to take precious good care John doesn't have all the old leaves to himself. It's the top-spit that puzzles us, and loam is the most important thing of all,"

"What is top-spit?" I asked.

"It's the earth you get when you dig up squares of grass out of a field like the paddock. The new earth that's just underneath. I expect John got a lot when he turfed that new piece by the pond, but I don't believe he'd spare us a flower-pot full to save his life."

"Don't quarrel with John, Arthur. It's no good."

"I won't quarrel with him if he behaves himself," said Arthur, "but we mean to have some top-spit somehow."

"If you aggravate him he'll only complain of us to Father."

"I know," said Arthur hotly, "and beastly mean of him, too, when he knows what Father is about this sort of thing."

"I know it's mean. But what's the good of fighting when you'll only get the worst of it?"

"Why, to show that you're in the right, and that you know you are," said Arthur. "Goodnight, Mary. We'll have a compost heap of our own this autumn, mark my words."

Next day, in spite of my remonstrances, Arthur and Harry came to open war with John, and loudly and long did they rehearse their grievances, when we were out of Father's hearing.

"Have we ever swept our own walks, except that once, long ago, when the German women came round with threepenny brooms?" asked Arthur, throwing out his right arm, as if he were making a speech. "And think of all the years John has been getting leaf mould for himself out of our copper beech leaves, and now refuses us a barrow-load of loam!"

The next morning but one Harry was late for breakfast, and then it seemed that he was not dressing; he had gone out—very early, one of the servants said. It frightened me, and I went out to look for him.

When I came upon him in our gardens, it was he who was frightened.

"Oh, dear," he exclaimed, "I thought you were John."

I have often seen Harry dirty—very dirty,—but from the mud on his boots to the marks on his face where he had pushed the hair out of his eyes with earthy fingers, I never saw him quite so grubby before. And if there had been a clean place left in any part of his clothes well away from the ground, that spot must have been soiled by a huge and very dirty sack, under the weight of which his poor little shoulders were bent nearly to his knees.

"What are you doing, Honest Root-gatherer?" I asked; "are you turning yourself into a hump-backed dwarf?"

"I'm not honest, and I'm not a Root-gatherer just now," said Harry, when he had got breath after setting down his load. He spoke shyly and a little surlily, like Chris when he is in mischief.

"Harry, what's that."?

"It's a sack I borrowed from Michael. It won't hurt it, it's had mangel-wurzels in already."

"What have you got in it now? It looks dreadfully heavy."

"It *is* heavy, I can tell you," said Harry, with one more rub of his dirty fingers over his face.

"You look half dead. What is it?"

"It's top-spit;" and Harry began to discharge his load on to the walk.

"Oh, Harry; where did you get it?"

"Out of the paddock. I've been digging up turfs and getting this out, and putting the turfs back, and stamping them down not to show, ever since six o'clock. It *was* hard work; and I was so afraid of John coming. Mary, you won't tell tales?

"No, Harry. But I don't think you ought to have taken it without Mother's leave."

"I don't think you can call it stealing," said Harry. "Fields are a kind of wild places anyhow, and the paddocks belong to Father, and it certainly doesn't belong to John."

"No," said I, doubtfully.

"I won't get any more; its dreadfully hard work," said Harry, but as he shook the sack out and folded it up, he added (in rather a satisfied tone), "I've got a good deal."

I helped him to wash himself for breakfast, and half-way through he suddenly smiled and said, "John Parkinson will be glad when he sees *you-know-what*, Mary, whatever the other John thinks of it."

But Harry did not cut any more turfs without leave, for he told me that he had a horrid dream that night of waking up in prison with a warder looking at him through a hole in the door of his cell, and finding out that he was in penal servitude for stealing top-spit from the bottom of the paddock, and Father would not take him out of prison, and that Mother did not know about it.

However, he and Arthur made a lot of compost. They said we couldn't possibly have a Paradise without it.

It made them very impatient. We always want the spring and summer and autumn and winter to get along faster than they do. But this year Arthur and Harry were very impatient with summer.

They were nearly caught one day by Father coming home just as they had got through the gates with Michael's old sack full of road-scrapings, instead of sand (we have not any sand growing near us, and silver sand is rather dear), but we did get leaves together and stacked them to rot into leaf mould.

Leaf mould is splendid stuff, but it takes a long time for the leaves to get mouldy, and it takes a great many, too. Arthur is rather impatient, and he used to say—"I never saw leaves stick on to branches in such a way. I mean to get into some of these old trees and give them a good shaking to remind them what time of the year it is. If I don't, we shan't have anything like enough leaves for our compost."

CHAPTER VIII

MOTHER WAS VERY much surprised by Arthur's letter, but not so much puzzled as he expected. She knew Parkinson's *Paradisus* quite well, and only wrote to me to ask, "What are the boys after with the old books? Does your Father know?"

But when I told her that he had given us leave to be in the library, and that we took great care of the books, and how much we enjoyed the ones about gardening, and all that we were going to do, she was very kind indeed, and promised to put on a blue dress and lace ruffles and be Queen of our Earthly Paradise as soon as she came home.

When she did come home she was much better, and so was Chris. He was delighted to be our Dwarf, but he wanted to have a hump, and he would have such a big one that it would not keep in its place, and kept slipping under his arm and into all sorts of queer positions.

Not one of us enjoyed our new game more than Chris did, and he was always teasing me to tell him the story I had told the others, and to read out the names of the flowers which "the real Queen" had in her "real paradise." He made Mother promise to try to get him a bulb of the real Dwarf Daffodil as his next birthday present, to put in his own garden.

"And I'll give you some compost," said Arthur. "It'll be ever so much better than a stupid book with 'stuff' in it."

Chris did seem much stronger. He had colour in his cheeks, and his head did not look so large. But he seemed to puzzle over things in it as much as ever, and he was just as odd and quaint.

One warm day I had taken the *Tour round my Garden* and was sitting near the bush in the little wood behind our house, when Chris came after me with a Japanese fan in his hand, and sat down cross-legged at my feet. As I was reading, and Mother has taught us not to interrupt people when they are reading, he said nothing, but there he sat.

"What is it, Chris?" said I.

"I am discontented," said Chris.

"I'm very sorry," said I.

"I don't think I'm selfish, particularly, but I'm discontented."

"What about?"

"Oh, Mary, I do wish I had not been away when you invented Paradise, then I should have had a name in the game."

"You've got a name, Chris. You're the Dwarf."

"Ah, but what was the Dwarf's name?"

"I don't know," I admitted.

"No; that's just it. I've only one name, and Arthur and Harry have two. Arthur is a Pothecary" (Chris could never be induced to accept Apothecary as one word), "and he's John Parkinson as well. Harry is Honest Root-gatherer, and he is Francis le Vean. If I'd not been away I should have had two names."

"You can easily have two names," said I. "We'll call the Dwarf Thomas Brown."

Chris shook his head.

"No, no. That wasn't his name; I know it wasn't. It's only stuff. I want another name out of the old book."

I dared not tell him that the Dwarf was not in the old book. I said:

"My dear Chris, you really are discontented; we can't all have double names. Adela has only one name, she is Weeding Woman and nothing else; and I have only one name, I'm Traveller's Joy, and that's all."

"But you and Adela are girls," said Chris, complacently. "The boys have two names."

I suppressed some resentment, for Christopher's eyes were beginning to look weary, and said:

"Shall I read to you for a bit?"

"No, don't read. Tell me things out of the old book. Tell me about the Queen's flowers. Don't tell me about daffodils, they make me think what a long way my off birthday is, and I'm quite discontented enough."

And Chris sighed, and lay down on the grass, with one arm under his head, and his fan in his hand; and, as well as I could remember, I told him all about the different varieties of Cowslips, down to the Frantincke, or Foolish Cowslip, and he became quite happy.

Dear Father is rather short-sighted, but he can hold a round glass in his eye without cutting himself. It was the other eye which was next to Chris at prayers the following morning; but he saw his legs, and the servants had hardly got out of the hall before he shouted, "Pull up your stockings, Chris!"—and then to Mother, "Why do you keep that sloven of a girl Bessy, if she can't dress the children decently? But I can't conceive what made you put that child into knickerbockers, he can't keep his stockings up."

"Yes, I can," said Christopher, calmly, looking at his legs.

"Then what have you got 'em down for?" shouted Father.

"They're not all down," said Chris, his head still bent over his knees, till I began to fear he would have a fit.

"One of 'em is, anyhow. I saw it at prayers. Pull it up."

"Two of them are," said Christopher, never lifting his admiring gaze from his stockings. "Two of them are down, and two of them are up, quite up, quite tidy."

Dear Father rubbed his glass and put it back into his eye.

"Why, how many stockings have you got on?"

"Four," said Chris, smiling serenely at his legs; "and it isn't Bessy's fault. I put 'em all on myself, every one of them."

At this minute James brought in the papers, and Father only laughed, and said, "I never saw such a chap," and began to read. He is very fond of Christopher, and Chris is never afraid of him.

I was going out of the room, and Chris followed me into the hall, and drew my attention to his legs, which were clothed in four stockings; one pair, as he said, being drawn tidily up over his knees, the other pair turned down with some neatness in folds a little above his ankles.

"Mary," he said, "I'm contented now."

"I'm very glad, Chris. But do leave off staring at your legs. All the blood will run into your head."

"I wish things wouldn't always get into *my* head, and nobody else's," said Chris, peevishly, as he raised it; but when he looked back at his stockings, they seemed to comfort him again.

"Mary, I've found another name for myself."

"Dear Chris! I'm so glad."

"It's a real one, out of the old book. I thought of it entirely by myself."

"Good Dwarf. What is your name?"

"*Hose-in-Hose*," said Christopher, still smiling down upon his legs.

CHAPTER IX

ALAS FOR the hose-in-hose!

I laughed over Christopher and his double stockings, and I danced for joy when Bessy's aunt told me that she had got me a fine lot of roots of double cowslips. I never guessed what misery I was about to suffer, because of the hose-in-hose.

I had almost forgotten that Bessy's aunt knew double cowslips. After I became Traveller's Joy I was so busy with wayside planting that I had thought less of my own garden than usual, and had allowed Arthur to do what he liked with it as part of the Earthly Paradise (and he was always changing his plans), but Bessy's aunt had not forgotten about it, which was very good of her.

The Squire's Weeding Woman is old enough to be Bessy's aunt, but she has an aunt of her own, who lives seven miles on the other side of the Moor, and the Weeding Woman does not get to see her very often. It is a very out-of-the-way village, and she has to wait for chances of a cart and team coming and going from one of the farms, and so get a lift.

It was the Weeding Woman's aunt who sent me the hose-in-hose.

The Weeding Woman told me—"Aunt be mortal fond of her flowers, but she've no notions of gardening, not in the ways of a gentleman's garden. But she be after 'em all along, so well as the roomatiz in her back do let her, with an old shovel and a bit of stuff to keep the frost out, one time, and the old shovel and a bit of stuff to keep 'em moistened from the drought, another time; cuddling of 'em like Christians. 'Ee zee, Miss, Aunt be advanced in years; her family be off her mind, zum married, zum buried; and it zim as if her flowers be like new childern for her, spoilt childern, too, as I zay, and most fuss about they that be least worth it, zickly uns and contrairy uns, as parents will. Many's time I do say to she—'Th' Old Zquire's garden, now, 'twould zim strange to thee, sartinly 'twould! How would 'ee feel to see Gardener zowing 's spring plants by the hunderd, and a-throwing of 'em away by the score when beds be vull, and turning of un out for bedding plants, and throwing they away when he 'eve made his cuttings?' And she 'low she couldn't abear it, no mote'n see Herod a mass-sakering of the Innocents. But if 'ee come to Bible, I do say Aunt put me in mind of the par'ble of the talents, she do, for what you give her she make ten of, while other folks be losing what they got. And 'tis well, too, for if 'twas not for givin' of un away, seeing's she lose nothin', and can't abear to destry nothin', and never takes un up but to set un again, six in place of one, as I say, with such a mossel of a garden, 'Aunt, where would you be?' And she 'low she can't tell, but the Lard would provide. 'Thank He,' I says, 'you be so out o' way, and 'ee back so bad, and past travelling, zo there be no chance of 'ee ever seein' Old Zquire's Gardener's houses and they stove plants;' for if Gardener give un a pot, sure's death her'd set it in the chimbly nook on frosty nights, and put bed-quilt over un, and any cold corner would do for she."

At this point the Weeding Woman became short of breath, and I managed to protest against taking so many plants of the hose-in-hose.

"Take un and welcome, my dear, take un and welcome," replied Bessy's aunt. "I did say to Aunt to keep two or dree, but 'One be aal I want,' her says, 'I'll have so many agin in a few years, dividin' of un in autumn,' her says. 'Thee've one foor in grave, Aunt,' says I, 'it don't altogether become 'ee to forecast autumns,' I says, 'when next may be your latter end, 's like as not.' 'Niece,' her says, 'I be no ways presuming. His will be done,' her says, 'but if I'm spared I'll rear un, and if I'm took, 'twill be where I sha'nt' want un. Zo let young lady have un,' her says. And there a be!"

When I first saw the nice little plants, I did think of my own garden, but not for long. My next and final thought was—"Mary's Meadow!"

Since I became Traveller's Joy, I had chiefly been busy in the hedge-rows by the high-roads, and in waste places, like the old quarry, and very bare and trampled bits, where there seemed to be no flowers at all.

You cannot say that of Mary's Meadow. Not to be a garden, it is one of the most flowery places I know. I did once begin a list of all that grows in it, but it was in one of Arthur's old exercise-books, which he had "thrown in," in a bargain we had, and there were very few blank pages left. I had thought a couple of pages would be more than enough, so I began with rather full accounts of the flowers, but I used up the book long before I had written out one half of what blossoms in Mary's Meadow.

Wild roses, and white bramble, and hawthorn, and dogwood, with its curious flowers; and nuts, and maple, and privet, and all sorts of bushes in the hedge, far more than one would think; and ferns, and the stinking iris, which has such splendid berries, in the ditch—the ditch on the lower side where it is damp, and where I meant to sow forget-me-nots, like Alphonse Karr, for there are none there as it happens. On the other side, at the top of the field, it is dry, and blue succory grows, and grows out on the road beyond. The most beautiful blue possible, but so hard to pick. And there are Lent lilies, and lords and ladies, and ground ivy, which smells herby when you find it, trailing about and turning the colour of Mother's "aurora" wool in green winters ; and sweet white violets, and blue dog violets, and primroses, of course, and two or three kinds of orchis, and all over the field cowslips, cowslips, cowslips—to please the nightingale.

And I wondered if the nightingale would find out the hose-in-hose, when I had planted six of them in the sunniest, cosiest corner of Mary's Meadow.

For this was what I resolved to do, though I kept my resolve to myself, for which I was afterwards very glad. I did not tell the others because I thought that Arthur might want some of the plants for our Earthly Paradise, and I wanted to put them all in Mary's Meadow. I said to myself, like Bessy's great-aunt, that "if I was spared" I would go next year and divide the roots of the six, and bring some off-sets to our gardens, but I would keep none back now. The nightingale should have them all.

We had been busy in our gardens, and in the roads and bye-lanes, and I had not been in Mary's Meadow for a long time before the afternoon when I put my little trowel, and a bottle of water, and the six hose-in-hose into a basket, and was glad to get off quietly and alone to plant them. The highways and hedges were very dusty, but there it was very green. The nightingale had long been silent, I do not know where he was, but the rooks were not at all silent; they had been holding a parliament at the upper end of the field this morning, and were now all talking at once, and flapping about the tops of the big elms which were turning bright yellow, whilst down below a flight of starlings had taken their place, and sat in the prettiest circles; and groups of hedge-sparrows flew and mimicked them. And in the fields round about the sheep baaed, and the air, which was very sweet, was so quiet that these country noises were the only sounds to be heard, and they could be heard from very far away.

I had found the exact spot I wanted, and had planted four of the hose-in-hose, and watered them from the bottle, and had the fifth in my hand, and the sixth still in the basket, when all these nice noises were drowned by a loud harsh shout which made me start, and sent the flight of starlings into the next field, and made the hedge-sparrows jump into the hedge.

And when I looked up I saw the Old Squire coming towards me, and storming and shaking his fist at me as he came. But with the other hand he held Saxon by the collar, who was struggling to get away from him and to go to me.

I had so entirely forgotten about Father's quarrel with the Squire, that when the sight of the old gentleman in a rage suddenly reminded me, I was greatly stupefied and confused, and really did not at first hear what he said. But when I understood that he was accusing me of digging cowslips out of his field, I said at once (and pretty loud, for he was deaf) that I was not digging up anything, but was planting double cowslips to grow up and spread amongst the common ones.

I suppose it did sound rather unlikely, as the Old Squire knew nothing about our game, but a thing being unlikely is no reason for calling truthful people liars, and that was what the Old Squire called me.

It choked me, and when he said I was shameless, and that he had caught me with the plants upon me, and yelled to me to empty my basket, I threw away the fifth and sixth hose-in-hose as if they had been adders, but I could not speak again. He must have been beside himself with rage, for he called me all sorts of names, and said I was my father's own child, a liar and a thief. Whilst he was talking about sending me to prison (and I thought of Harry's dream, and turned cold with fear), Saxon was tugging to get to me, and at last he got away and came rushing up.

Now I knew that the Old Squire was holding Saxon back because he thought Saxon wanted to worry me as a trespasser, but I don't know whether he let Saxon go at last because he thought I deserved to be worried, or whether Saxon got away of himself. When his paws were almost on me the Old Squire left off abusing me, and yelled to the dog, who at last, very unwillingly, went back to him,

but when he got to the Squire's feet he stopped, and pawed the
ground in the funny way he sometimes does, and looked up at his
master as much as to say, "You see, it's only play," and then turned
round and raced back to me as hard as he could lay legs to ground.
This time he reached me, and jumped to lick my face, and I threw
my arms round his neck and burst into tears.

When you are crying and kissing at the same time, you cannot
hear anything else, so what more the Old Squire said I do not
know.

I picked up my basket and trowel at once, and fled homewards
as fast as I could go, which was not very fast, so breathless was I
with tears and shame and fright.

When I was safe in our grounds I paused and looked back. The
Old Squire was still there, shouting and gesticulating, and Saxon
was at his heels, and over the hedge two cows were looking at him;
but the rooks and the starlings were far off in distant trees and fields.

And I sobbed afresh when I remembered that I had been called
a liar and a thief, and had lost every one of my hose-in-hose; and this
was all that had come of trying to make an Earthly Paradise of
Mary's Meadow, and of taking upon myself the name of Traveller's
Joy.

CHAPTER X

I TOLD no one. It was bad enough to think of by myself. I could
not have talked about it. But every day I expected that the Old
Squire would send a letter or a policeman, or come himself, and
rage and storm, and tell Father.

He never did; and no one seemed to suspect that anything had
gone wrong, except that Mother fidgeted because I looked ill, and
would show me to Dr. Solomon. It is a good thing doctors tell
you what they think is the matter, and don't ask you what you think,
for I could not have told him about the Squire. He said I was
below par, and that it was our abominable English climate, and he
sent me a bottle of tonic. And when I had taken half the bottle,
and had begun to leave off watching for the policeman, I looked
quite well again. So I took the rest, not to waste it, and thought
myself very lucky. My only fear now was that Bessy's aunt might
ask after the hose-in-hose. But she never did.

I had one more fright, where I least expected it. It had never occurred to me that Lady Catherine would take an interest in our game, and want to know what we had done, and what we were doing, and what we were going to do, or I should have been far more afraid of her than of Bessy's aunt. For the Weeding Woman has a good deal of delicacy, and often begs pardon for taking liberties; but if Aunt Catherine takes an interest, and wants to know, she asks one question after another, and does not think whether you like to answer or not.

She took an interest in our game after one of Christopher's luncheons with her.

She often asks Chris to go there to luncheon, all by himself. Father is not very fond of his going, chiefly, I fancy, because he is so fond of Chris, and misses him. Sometimes, in the middle of luncheon, he looks at Christopher's empty place, and says, "I wonder what those two are talking about over their pudding. They are the queerest pair of friends." If we ask Chris what they have talked about, he wags his head, and looks very well pleased with himself, and says, "Lots of things. I tell her things, and she tells me things." And that is all we can get out of him.

A few weeks afterwards, after I lost the hose-in-hose, Chris went to have luncheon with Aunt Catherine, and he came back rather later than usual.

"You must have been telling each other a good deal to-day, Chris," I said.

"I told her lots," said Chris, complacently. "She didn't tell me nothing, hardly. But I told her lots. My apple fritter got cold whilst I was telling it. She sent it away, and had two hot ones, new, on purpose for me."

"What *did* you tell her?"

"I told her your story; she liked it very much. And I told her Daffodils, and about my birthday; and I told her Cowslips—all of them. Oh, I told her lots. She didn't tell me nothing."

A few days later, Aunt Catherine asked us to tea, all of us—me, Arthur, Adela, Harry, and Chris. And she asked us all about our game. When Harry said, "I dig up, but Mary plants—not in our garden, but in wild places, and woods, and hedges, and fields," Lady Catherine blew her nose very loud, and said, "I should think you don't do much digging and planting in that field your Father went to law about?" and my teeth chattered so with fright that I think Lady Catherine would have heard them if she hadn't been blowing her nose. But, luckily for me, Arthur said, "Oh, we never go near Mary's Meadow now, we're so busy." And then Aunt Catherine asked what made us think of my name, and I repeated most of the bit from Alphonse Karr, for I knew it by heart now; and Arthur repeated what John Parkinson says about the "Honisucle that groweth wilde in euery hedge," and how he left it there, "to serue their senses that trauell by it, or haue no garden;" and then he said, " So Mary is called Traveller's Joy because she plants flowers in the hedges to serve their senses that travel by them."

"And who serves them that have no garden?" asked Aunt Catherine, sticking her gold glasses over her nose, and looking at us.

"None of us do," said Arthur, after thinking for a minute.

"Humph!" said Aunt Catherine.

Next time Chris was asked to luncheon, I was asked, too. Father laughed at me, and teased me, but I went.

I was very much amused by the airs which Chris gave himself at table. He was perfectly well-behaved, but, in his quiet old-fashioned way, he certainly gave himself airs. We have only one man indoors—James; but Aunt Catherine has three—a butler, a footman, and a second footman. The second footman kept near Christopher, who sat opposite Aunt Catherine (she made me sit on one side), and seemed to watch to attend upon him; but if Christopher did want anything, he always ignored this man, and asked the butler for it, and called him by his name.

After a bit, Aunt Catherine began to talk about the game again.

"Have you got anyone to serve them that have no garden, yet?" she asked.

Christopher shook his head, and said "No".

"Humph," said Aunt Catherine; "better take me into the game."

"Could you be of any use?" asked Christopher. "Toast and water, Chambers."

The butler nodded, as majestically as Chris himself, to the second footman, who flew to replenish the silver mug, which had been Lady Catherine's when she was a little girl. When Christopher had drained it (he is a very thirsty boy), he repeated the question: "Do you think you could be of any use?"

Mr. Chambers, the butler, never seems to hear anything that people say, except when they ask for something to eat or drink; and he does not often hear that, because he watches to see what you want, and gives it of himself, or sends it by the footman. He looks just as if he was having his photograph taken, staring at a point on the wall and thinking of nothing; but when Christopher repeated his question I saw Chambers frown. I believe he thinks Christopher presumes on Lady Catherine's kindness, and does not approve of it.

It is quite the other way with Aunt Catherine. Just when you would think she must turn angry, and scold Chris for being rude, she only begins to laugh, and shakes like a jelly (she is very stout), and encourages him. She said—

"Take care all that toast and water doesn't get into your head, Chris."

She said that to vex him, because, ever since he heard that he had water on the brain, Chris is very easily affronted about his head. He was affronted now, and began to eat his bread-and-butter pudding in silence, Lady Catherine still shaking and laughing. Then she wiped her eyes, and said—

"Never mind, old man, I'm going to tell you something. Put the sugar and cream on the table, Chambers, and you needn't wait."

The men went out very quietly, and Aunt Catherine went on—

"Where do you think I was yesterday? In the new barracks—a place I set my face against ever since they began to build it, and spoil one of my best peeps from the Rhododendron Walk. I went to see a young cousin of mine, who was fool enough to marry a poor officer, and have a lot of little boys and girls, no handsomer than you, Chris."

"Are they as handsome?" said Chris, who had recovered himself, and was selecting currants from his pudding, and laying them aside for a final *bonne bouche*.

"Humph! Perhaps not. But they eat so much pudding, and wear out so many boots, that they are too poor to live anywhere except in barracks."

Christopher laid down his spoon, and looked as he always looks when he is hearing a sad story.

"Is barracks like the workhouse, Aunt Catherine?" he asked.

"A good deal like the workhouse," said Aunt Catherine. Then she went on—"I told her Mother I could not begin calling at the barracks. There are some very low streets close by, and my coachman said he couldn't answer for his horses with bugles, and perhaps guns, going off when you least expect them. I told her I would ask them to dinner; and I did, but they were engaged. Well, yesterday I changed my mind, and I told Harness that I meant to go to the barracks, and the horses would have to take me. So we started.

When we were going along the upper road, between the high hedges, what do you think I saw?"

Chris had been going on with his pudding again, but he paused to make a guess.

"A large cannon, just going off?"

"No. If I'd seen that, you wouldn't have seen any more of me. I saw masses of wild clematis scrambling everywhere, so that the hedge looked as if somebody had been dressing it up in tufts of feathers."

As she said this, Lady Catherine held out her hand to me across the table very kindly. She has a fat hand, covered with rings, and I put my hand into it.

"And what do you think came into my head?" she asked.

"Toast and water," said Chris, maliciously.

"No, you monkey. I began to think of hedge-flowers, and travellers, and Traveller's Joy."

Aunt Catherine shook my hand here, and dropped it.

"And you thought how nice it was for the poor travellers to have such nice flowers," said Chris, smiling, and wagging his head up and down.

"Nothing of the kind," said Aunt Catherine, brusquely. "I thought what lots of flowers the travellers had already, without Mary planting any more; and I thought not one traveller in a dozen paid much attention to them—begging John Parkinson's pardon—and how much more in want of flowers people 'that have no garden' are; and then I thought of that poor girl in those bare barracks, whose old home was one of the prettiest places, with the lovliest garden, in all Berkshire."

"Was it an Earthly Paradise?" asked Chris.

"It was, indeed. Well, when I thought of her inside those brick walls, looking out on one of those yards they march about in, now they've cut down all the trees and planted sentry-boxes, I put my best bonnet out of the window, which always spoils the feather, and told Harness to turn his horses' heads, and drive home again."

"What for?" said Chris, as brusquely as Lady Catherine.

"I sent for Hobbs."

"Hobbs the Gardener?" said Chris.

"Hobbs the Gardener; and I told Chambers to give him the basket from the second peg, and then I sent him into the conservatory to fill it. Mary, my dear, I am very particular about my baskets. If ever I lend you my diamonds and you lose them I may forgive you—I shall know *that* was an accident; but if I lend you a basket, and you don't return it, don't look me in the face again. I always write my name on them, so there's no excuse. And I don't know a greater piece of impudence—and people are wonderfully impudent now-a-days—than to think that because a thing only cost fourpence you need not be at the trouble of keeping it clean and dry, and of sending it back."

"Some more toast and water, please," said Chris.

Aunt Catherine helped him, and continued—"Hobbs is a careful man—he had been with me ten years—he doesn't cut flowers recklessly as a rule, but when I saw that basket I said, 'Hobbs, you've been very extravagant.' He looked ashamed of himself, but he said, 'I understood they was for Miss Kitty, m'm. She's been used to nice gardens, m'm.' Hobbs lived with them in Berkshire before he came to me."

"It was very nice of Hobbs," said Chris, emphatically.

"Humph!" said Aunt Catherine, "the flowers were mine."

"Did you ever get to the barracks?" asked Chris, "and what was they like when you did?"

"They were as unlike Kitty's old home as anything could well be. She has made her rooms pretty enough, but it was easy to see she is hard up for flowers. She's got an old rose-coloured Sevres bowl that was my Grandmother's, and there it was, filled with bramble leaves and Traveller's Joy (which *she* calls Old Man's Beard; Kitty always would differ from her elders!), and a soup-plate full of forget-me-nots. She said two of the children had half-drowned themselves and lost a good straw hat in getting them for her. Just like their mother, as I told her."

"What did she say when you brought out the basket?" asked Chris, disposing of his reserve of currants at one mouthful, and laying down his spoon.

"She said, 'Oh! oh! oh!' till I told her to say something more amusing, and then she said, 'I could cry for joy!' and, 'Tell Hobbs he remembers all my favourites.'"

Christopher here bent his head over his empty plate, and said grace (Chris is very particular about his grace), and then got down from his chair and went up to Lady Catherine, and threw his arms round her as far as they would go, saying, "You are good. And I love you. I should think she thinked you was a fairy godmother."

After they had hugged each other, Aunt Catherine said, "Will you take me into the game, if I serve them that have no garden?"

Chris and I said "Yes" with one voice.

"Then come into the drawing-room," said Aunt Catherine, getting up and giving a hand to each of us. "And Chris shall give me a name."

Chris pondered a long time on this subject, and seemed a good deal disturbed in his mind. Presently he said, "I *won't* be selfish. You shall have it."

"Shall have what, you oddity?"

"I'm not a oddity, and I'm going to give you the name I invented for myself. But you'll have to wear stockings, two up and two down."

"Then you may keep *that* name to yourself," said Aunt Catherine. Christopher looked relieved.

"Perhaps you'd not like to be called Old Man's Beard?"

"Certainly not!" said Aunt Catherine.

"It *is* more of a boy's name," said Chris. "You might be the Franticke or Foolish Cowslip, but it is Jack an Apes on Horseback, too, and that's a boy's name. You shall be Daffodil, not a dwarf daffodil, but a big one, because you are big. Wait a minute—I know which you shall be. You shall be Nonsuch. It's a very big one, and it means none like it. So you shall be Nonsuch, for there's no one like you."

On which Christopher and Lady Catherine hugged each other afresh.

*   *   *   *   *   *

"Who told most to-day?" asked Father when we got home.

"Oh, Aunt Catherine. Much most," said Christopher.

CHAPTER XI

THE HEIGHT OF our game was in Autumn. It is such a good time for digging up, and planting, and dividing, and making cuttings, and gathering seeds, and sowing them, too. But it went by very quickly, and when the leaves began to fall they fell very quickly, and Arthur never had to go up the trees and shake them.

After the first hard frost we quite gave up playing at the Earthly Paradise; first, because there was nothing we could do, and, secondly, because a lot of snow fell, and Arthur had a grand idea of making snow statues all along the terrace, so that Mother could see them from the drawing-room windows. We worked very hard, and it was very difficult to manage legs without breaking; so we made most of them Romans in togas, and they looked very well from a distance, and lasted a long time, because the frost lasted.

And, by degrees, I almost forgot that terrible afternoon in Mary's Meadow. Only when Saxon came to see us I told him that I was very glad that no one understood his bark, so that he could not let out what had become of the hose-in-hose.

But when the winter was past, and the snowdrops came in the shrubbery, and there were catkins on the nut trees, and the missel-thrush we had been feeding in the frost sat out on mild days and sang to us, we all of us began to think of our gardens again, and to go poking about "with our noses in the borders," as Arthur said, "as if we were dogs snuffing after truffles." What we really were "snuffing after" were the plants we had planted in autumn, and which were poking and sprouting, and coming up in all directions.

Arthur and Harry did real gardening in the Easter holidays, and they captured Adela now and then, and made her weed. But Christopher's delight was to go with me to the waste places and hedges, where I had planted things as Traveller's Joy, and to get me to show them to him where they had begun to make a Spring start, and to help him to make up rambling stories, which he called "Supposings," of what the flowers would be like, and what this or that traveller would say when he saw them. One of his favourite *supposings* was—"Supposing a very poor man was coming along the road, with his dinner in a handkerchief; and supposing he sat down under the edge to eat it; and supposing it was cold beef, and he had no mustard; and supposing there was a seed on your nasturtium plants, and he knew it wouldn't poison him; and supposing he ate it with his beef, and it tasted nice and hot, like a pickle, wouldn't he wonder how it got there?"

But when the primroses had been out a long time and the cowslips were coming into bloom, to my horror Christopher began "supposing" that we should find hose-in-hose in some of the fields, and all my efforts to put this idea out of his head, and to divert him from the search, were utterly in vain.

Whether it had anything to do with his having had water on the brain I do not know, but when once an idea got into Christopher's head there was no dislodging it. He now talked of hose-in-hose constantly. One day he announced that he was "discontented" once more, and should remain so till he had "found a hose-in-hose."

I enticed him to a field where I knew it was possible to secure an occasional oxlip, but he only looked pale, shook his head distressingly, and said, "I don't think nothin' of oxlips." Coloured primroses would not comfort him. He professed to disbelieve in the time-honoured prescription, "Plant a primrose upside down, and it will come up a polyanthus." and refused to help me to make the experiment. At last the worst came. He suddenly spoke, with smiles—"I *know* where we'll find hose-in-hose! In Mary's Meadow. It's the fullest field of cowslips there is. Hurrah! Supposing we find hose-in-hose, and supposing we find green cowslips, and supposing we find curled cowslips or galligaskins, and supposing—"

But I could not bear it. I fairly ran away from him, and shut myself up in my room and cried. I knew it was silly, and yet I could not bear the thought of having to satisfy everybody's curiosity, and describe that scene in Mary's Meadow, which had wounded me so bitterly, and explain why I had not told of it before.

I cried, too, for another reason. Mary's Meadow had been dear to us all, ever since I could remember. It was always our favourite field. We had coaxed our nurses there, when we could induce them to leave the high-road, or when, luckily for us, on account of an epidemic, or for some reason or another, they were forbidden to go gossiping into the town. We had "pretended" fairies in the nooks of the delightfully neglected hedges, and we had found fairy-rings to prove our pretending true. We went there for flowers; we went there for mushrooms and puff-balls; we went there to hear the nightingale. What cowslip balls and what cowslip tea-parties it had afforded us! It is fair to the Old Squire to say that we were sad trespassers, before he and Father quarrelled and went to law. For Mary's Meadow was a field with every quality to recommend it to childish affections.

And now I was banished from it, not only by the quarrel, of which we had really not heard much, or realized it very fully, but by my own bitter memories. I cried afresh to think I should never go again to the corner where I always found the earliest violets; and then I cried to think that the nightingale would soon be back, and how that very morning, when I opened my window, I had heard the cuckoo, and could tell that he was calling from just about Mary's Meadow.

I cried my eyes into such a state that I was obliged to turn my attention to making them fit to be seen; and I had spent quite half-an-hour in bathing them and breathing on my handkerchief, and

dabbing them, which is more soothing, when I heard Mother
calling me. I winked hard, drew a few long breaths, rubbed my
cheeks, which were so white they showed up my red eyes, and ran
down-stairs. Mother was coming to meet me. She said—"Where
is Christopher?"

It startled me. I said, "He was with me in the garden, about—
oh, about an hour ago; have you lost him? I'll go and look for him."

And I snatched up a garden hat, which shaded my swollen eyelids,
and ran out. I could not find him anywhere, and becoming frightened, I ran down the drive, calling him as I went, and through the
gate, and out into the road.

A few yards farther on I met him.

That child is most extraordinary. One minute he looks like a
ghost; an hour later his face is beaming with a radiance that seems
absolutely to fatten him under your eyes. That was how he looked
just then as he came towards me, smiling in an effulgent sort of way,
as if he were the noonday sun—no less, and carrying a small nosegay
in his hand.

When he came within hearing he boasted, as if he had been
Caeser himself—

"I went; I found it. I've got them."

And as he held his hand up, and waved the nosegay—I knew all.
He had been to Mary's Meadow, and the flowers between his fingers
were hose-in-hose.

CHAPTER XII

"I WON'T BE selfish, Mary," Christopher said. "You invented the
game, and you told me about them. You shall have them in water
on your dressing-table; they might get lost in the nursery. Bessy
is always throwing things out. To-morrow I shall go and look for
galligaskins."

I was too glad to keep them from Bessy's observation, as well as
her unparalleled powers of destruction, which I knew well. I put
them into a slim glass on my table, and looked stupidly at them,
and then out of the window at Mary's Meadow.

So they had lived—and grown—and settled there—and were now
in bloom. *My* plants.

Next morning I was sitting, drawing, in the school-room window,

when I saw the Old Squire coming up the drive. There is no
mistaking him when you can see him at all. He is a big, handsome
old man, with white whiskers, and a white hat, and white gaiters,
and he generally wears a light coat, and a flower in his button-hole.
The flower he wore this morning looked like——, but I was angry
with myself for thinking of it, and went on drawing again, as well
as I could, for I could not help wondering why he was coming to
our house. Then it struck me he might have seen Chris trespassing,
and he might be coming at last to lay a formal complaint.

Twenty minutes later James came to tell me that Father wished
to see me in the library, and when I got there, Father was just
settling his eye-glass in his eye, and the Old Squire was standing on
the hearth-rug, with a big piece of paper in his hand. And then I
saw that I was right, and that the flowers in his button-hole were
hose-in-hose.

As I came in he laid down the paper, took the hose-in-hose out
of his button-hole in his left hand, and held out his right hand to
me, saying: "I'm more accustomed to public speaking than to
private speaking, Miss Mary. But—will you be friends with me?"

In Mary's Meadow my head had got all confused, because I was
frightened. I was not frightened to-day, and I saw the whole matter
in a moment. He had found the double cowslips, and he knew now
that I was neither a liar nor a thief. I was glad, but I could not feel
very friendly to him. I said, "You can speak when you are angry."

Though he was behind me, I could feel Father coming nearer, and
I knew somehow that he had taken out his glass again to rub it and
put it back, as he does when he is rather surprised or amused. I
was afraid he meant to laugh at me afterwards, and he can tease
terribly, but I could not have helped saying what came into my head
that morning if I had tried. When you have suffered a great deal
about anything, you cannot sham, not even politeness.

The Old Squire got rather red. Then he said, "I am afraid I am
very hasty, my dear, and say very unjustifiable things. But I am
very sorry, and I beg your pardon. Will you forgive me?"

I said, "Of course, if you're sorry, I forgive you, but you have
been a very long time in repenting."

Which was true. If I had been cross with one of the others, and
had borne malice for five months, I should have thought myself
very wicked. But when I had said it, I felt sorry, for the old gentleman made no answer. Father did not speak either, and I began to
feel very miserable. I touched the flowers, and the Old Squire

gave them to me in silence. I thanked him very much, and then I
said—

"I am very glad you know about it now . . . . I'm very glad they
lived. . . . I hope you like them ? . . . I hope, if you do like them,
that they'll grow and spread all over your field."

The Old Squire spoke at last. He said, "It is not my field any
longer."

I said, "Oh, why ?"

"I have given it away; I have been a long time in repenting, but
when I did repent I punished myself. I have given it away."

It overwhelmed me, and when he took up the big paper again, I
thought he was going, and I tried to stop him, for I was sorry I had
spoken unkindly to him, and I wanted to be friends.

"Please don't go," I said. "Please stop and be friends. And oh,
please, please don't give Mary's Meadow away. You mustn't
punish yourself. There's nothing to punish yourself for. I forgive
you with all my heart, and I'm sorry I spoke crossly. I have been
so very miserable, and I was so vexed at wasting the hose-in-hose,
because Bessy's great-aunt gave them to me, and I've none left.
Oh, the unkindest thing you could do to me now would be to give
away Mary's Meadow."

The Old Squire had taken both my hands in his and now he asked
very kindly—"Why, my dear, why don't you want me to give away
Mary's Meadow ?"

"Because we are so fond of it. And because I was beginning to
hope that now we're friends, and you know we don't want to steal
your things, or to hurt your field, perhaps you would let us play in it
sometimes, and perhaps have Saxon to play with us there. We are
so very fond of him, too."

"You are fond of Mary's Meadow ?" said the Old Squire.

"Yes, yes! We have been fond of it all our lives. We don't think
there is any field like it, and I don't believe there can be. Don't
give it away. You'll never get one with such flowers in it again.
And now there are hose-in-hose, and they are not at all common.
Bessy's aunt's aunt has only got one left, and she's taking care
of it with a shovel. And if you'll let us in we'll plant a lot of
things, and do no harm, we will indeed. And the nightingale will
be here directly. Oh, don't give it away!"

My head was whirling now with the difficulty of persuading him,
and I did not hear what he said across me to my father. But I
heard Father's reply—"Tell her yourself, sir."

On which the Old Squire stuffed the big paper into my arms, and put his hand on my head and patted it.

"I told you I was a bad hand at talking, my dear," he said, "but Mary's Meadow is given away, and that's the Deed of Gift which you've got in your arms, drawn up as tight as any rascal of a lawyer can do it, and that's not so tight, I believe, but what some other rascal of a lawyer could undo it. However, they may let you alone. For I've given it to you, my dear, and it is yours. So you can plant, and play, and do what you please there. 'You, and your heirs and assigns, for ever,' as the rascals say."

It was my turn now to be speechless. But as I stared blankly in front of me, I saw that Father had come round, and was looking at me through his eye-glass. He nodded to me, and said, "Yes, Mary, the Squire has given Mary's Meadow to you, and it is yours."

*   *   *   *   *   *

Nothing would induce the Old Squire to take it back, so I had to have it, for my very own. He said he had always been sorry he had spoken so roughly to me, but he could not say so, as he and Father were not on speaking terms. Just lately he was dining with Lady Catherine, to meet her cousins from the barracks, and she was telling people after dinner about our game (rather mean of her, I think, to let out our secrets at a dinner-party), and when he heard about my planting things in the hedges, he remembered what I had said. And next day he went to the place to look, and there were the hose-in-hose.

Oh, how delighted the others were when they heard that Mary's Meadow belonged to me.

"It's like having an Earthly Paradise given to you, straight off!" said Harry.

"And one that doesn't want weeding," said Adela.

"And oh, Mary, Mary!" cried Arthur. "Think of the yards and yards of top-spit. It does rejoice me to think I can go to you now when I'm making compost, and need not be beholden to that old sell-up-your-grandfather John for as much as would fill Adela's weeding basket, and that's about as small an article as anyone can make-believe with."

"It's very heavy when it's full," said Adela.

"Is everything hers?" asked Christopher. "Is the grass hers, and the trees hers, and the hedges hers, and the rooks hers, and the starlings hers, and will the nightingale be hers when he comes home, and if she could dig through to the other side of the world, would there be a field the same size in Australia that would be hers, and are the sheep hers, and——"

"For mercy's sake stop that catalogue, Chris," said Father. "Of course the sheep are not hers; they were moved yesterday. By the bye, Mary, I don't know what you propose to do with your property, but if you like to let it to me, I'll turn some sheep in to-morrow, and I'll pay so much a year, which I advise you to put into the Post Office Savings Bank."

I couldn't fancy Mary's Meadow always without sheep, so I was too thankful; though at first I could not see that it was fair that dear Father should let me have his sheep to look pretty in my field for nothing, and pay me, too. He is always teasing me about my field, and he teases me a good deal about the Squire, too. He says we have set up another queer friendship in the family, and that the Old Squire and I are as odd a pair as Aunt Catherine and Chris.

I am very fond of the Old Squire now, and he is very kind to me. He wants to give me Saxon, but I will not accept him. It would be selfish. But the Old Squire says I had better take him, for we have quite spoilt him for a yard dog by petting him, till he has not a bit of savageness left in him. We do not believe Saxon ever was savage; but I daren't say so to the Old Squire, for he does not like you to think you know better than he does about anything. There is one other subject on which he expects to be humoured, and I am careful not to offend him. He cannot tolerate the idea that he might be supposed to have yielded to Father the point about which they went to law, in giving Mary's Meadow to me. He is always lecturing me on encroachments, and the abuse of privileges, and warning me to be very strict about trespassers on the path through Mary's Meadow; and now that the field is mine, nothing will induce him to walk in it without asking my leave. That is his protest against the decision from which he meant to appeal.

Though I have not accepted Saxon, he spends most of his time with us. He likes to come for the night, because he sleeps on the floor of my room, instead of in a kennel, which must be horrid, I am sure. Yesterday, the Old Squire said, "One of these fine days, when Master Saxon does not come home till morning, he'll find a big mastiff in his kennel, and will have to seek a home for himself where he can."

Chris has been rather whimsical lately. Father says Lady Catherine spoils him. One day he came to me, looking very peevish, and said, "Mary, if a hedgehog should come and live in one of your hedges, Michael says he would be yours, he's sure.   If Michael finds him, will you give him to me?"

"Yes, Chris; but what do you want with a hedgehog?"

"I want him to sleep by my bed," said Chris.   "You have Saxon by your bed; I want something by mine. I want a hedgehog. I feel discontented without a hedgehog. I think I might have something the matter with my brain if I didn't get a hedgehog pretty soon. Can I go with Michael and look for him this afternoon?" and he put his hand to his forehead.

"Chris, Chris!" I said, "you should not be so sly. You're a real slyboots. Double-stockings and slyboots." And I took him on my lap.

Chris put his arms round my neck, and buried his cheek against mine.

"I won't be sly, Mary," he whispered; and then, hugging me as he hugs Lady Catherine, he added, "For I do love you; for you are a darling, and I do really think it always was yours."

"What, Chris?"

"If not," said Chris, "why was it always called MARY'S MEADOW?"

The Runaways and the Gipsies

The Runaways and the Gipsies

CHAPTER I

CLIMBING TREES

GRACE AND BERTRAM ASTLEY were twins, and, at the time my story begins, they were rather more than nine years old. They had several brothers and sisters younger than themselves, but none older; and in consequence of this they had been turned out of the nursery at an early age, as the younger ones multiplied, and had been left pretty much to amuse themselves, and to run wild about their father's park and grounds as they chose. They had thus acquired habits of independence beyond their years, which is often the case with the elder children of a large family.

Lord and Lady Astley had no very particular theories as to the bringing up of their children—his lordship contenting himself with requiring that they should always be dressed well and civilly behaved, and occasionally remarking that "Bertram ought to be at Eton by this time"; and her ladyship secretly resolving to keep him at home as long as she possibly could, and meantime doing her best to instil into the hearts of all her children the fear of God and a love of truth.

Bertram was a bold, fearless, handsome boy, always ready for any fun, provided Grace could share it with him; and hitherto there had been few difficulties in this proviso, for Grace was chiefly remarkable for her intense devotion to her twin brother—a devotion which appeared to swallow up all other feelings, all girlish fears, and childish tempers. Bertram was everything to her; and, under his able guidance and tuition, she could keep up with him in all his sports. Climbing trees and gates, scrambling through hedges, shooting with a little wooden cross-bow, exactly like Bertram's,—sliding in winter, cricketing in summer,—riding, walking, and, it might almost be said, dressing like her darling brother,—Grace Astley was but another Bertram. In one thing alone she surpassed him and differed from him. Grace was not only very quick at her books, but she delighted in them. She would have enjoyed the lesson-time, when she and Bertram had their mother's undivided attention; for, with the exception of Bertram's Latin, to which the clergyman of the parish devoted an hour daily, Lady Astley had hitherto managed to teach them herself; but the two hours after breakfast which she was able to devote to them were generally so irksome to poor Bertram that Grace found she could not look forward to them with any pleasure. Not that Bertram was a stupid boy: on the contrary he was quick and clever at everything except arithmetic, and could get through his work in a very short time if he chose to apply; but it was a choice that he did not often make, for somehow or another he generally fixed upon the lesson-hours as the best time for thinking, and he would sit with his books before him, gazing at them, and apparently busy with them, when his thoughts were wandering far away.

Sometimes Grace would forget herself for a short time in the absorbing interest of a compound long division sum, or even of a French exercise; but when, with burning cheeks and a bright face, she rose from her little corner to bring her slate or her book to her mother, her eye would fall on her poor Bertram as he lounged against the great school-room table, trying in vain to conquer the difficulties of the simple division, and helping himself thereto by drawing tiny ships filled with gigantic men,—or, what he excelled in much more, horses and dogs of all kinds and descriptions, round the unlucky sum; and then Grace's joy was over, and she wished she could give Bertram half her pleasure in her lessons, or that she did not care for them so much herself. It almost seemed to be unjust to him that she should like what gave him so much trouble. Her great consolation under this little trial arose from the fact of her being able to sympathize with him in his intense hatred of French verbs—for in this one branch of literature Grace took no pleasure whatever; and when they began to read history, she was quite happy, for his delight and interest were only to be equalled by her own, and were understood by no one but herself; for their gentle mother was surprised, in her own quiet way, at the interest Pinnock's Goldsmith's "Rome," and even "Mrs. Markham," excited in her children. She supposed children in these days were very different from what they were in her time, for she was quite certain that she and her sisters and brothers were equally indifferent to history and arithmetic; but, on the whole, she was rather proud of this new and striking feature of childhood, and she felt placidly convinced that there were no children like hers in the world.

The two hours over, Grace and Bertram were free to go where they chose, within the park. Dressed in their stout brown-holland gaberdines, happily they worked in their little gardens, or dug out caves in the sandy rocks behind the house. Lord Astley was much away from home, and so much engaged when he did come, that his children saw little of him. He was a clever man of the world, and many people asserted that he had never been anything else— that he had had no childhood, but was born a ready-made statesman. He had been an only child, and, having lost his parents in his baby- hood, had been brought up by a stern old aunt, who disapproved, on principle, of all childish amusements. Lord Astley, therefore, had grown up in utter ignorance of all such youthful vanities as delighted his own children; and, as for the said children, he looked upon them as a necessary part of his establishment—much as he regarded his servants, and his horses, and the handsome service of plate which had descended from father to son in the Astley family for many generations.

Lady Astley had lived much in the world before her marriage; but she did not now regret the world, although nothing could be much more retired than her life as it passed as Combe Astley. Among her children and her flowers she was happy, and she desired no more; she even occasionally wasted a sigh as the thought passed through her mind, that the time must come when her duty to her children would oblige her once more to quit her much-beloved solitude. During their father's short visits to his home, her chief care about Grace and Bertram hitherto had been to make them fit to be seen, and to keep them out of mischief. They had learnt, therefore, not to look forward to these visits with anything like pleasure, and were only too glad when their father's departure left them at liberty to return to their dear brown-holland dresses and wild habits.

Soon after these children had passed their ninth birthday, their happiness received a severe shock from a few words which they accidentally overheard between their father and mother. It was a bright warm spring day, and Lord Astley having arrived unex- pectedly from town, Bertram and Grace were running wild, as usual, after their morning lessons, instead of being caught up, like young horses, to be combed and dressed, as they always were when his lordship was expected.

On this particular morning there happened to be a wedding in the village, and the two children had climbed, by means of the huge old shrubbery trees, to the top of the very broad wall which comman- ded a good view of the church and village street, and here they were sitting side by side, perfectly indifferent to their great height from the ground, when their father and mother strolled slowly by in the avenue behind them.

Grace was just drawing her brother's attention to the bridal party, now issuing from the church, when Bertram, hearing his father's loud and important tones, exclaimed,—

"Hush, Gracey! There's mamma coming—and my father, too, I do believe. Keep quiet, and they will not see us here; the trees are nice and thick between us."

Gracey did hush directly; and Lord Astley was heard to say, in a voice of great decision, as if he was for ever setting at rest a disputed question,—

"My dear, the thing is settled; the children must have a governess. It will break the boy in for school; and as for Grace——"

The children were obliged to remain in ignorance as to the effect their father intended a governess to produce on Grace, for the end of his sentence was lost in the trees, and never reached their anxious little ears.

They looked at each other in dismay. A governess was an evil which they had never contemplated, and all their interest in the village wedding was gone for ever.

"Grace!" said Bertram, in a low tone, expressive of immense surprise and indignation at this unexpected insult, as he regarded it. "Grace! did you hear?—a *governess*—a real governess,—and for *me*—a big boy like me!—why, school would be better!" and he remained transfixed.

Grace felt as if she had never fully realized the horror of such an affliction before, now that she saw the terrible light in which Bertram regarded it; and when he went on to describe, in the most touching manner, how, on the arrival of the dreadful governess, they would never be allowed to stir beyond the house-door without her, never again visit the horses in the stables, nor the pigs in the pigsty, nor even to go to see the cows milked,—while climbing trees, ferreting and digging in their little gardens, would be regarded as equal to robbery and murder, and punished accordingly by this household tyrant,—Poor Grace could bear it no longer, but fairly burst into tears. As she seldom cried, Bertram was rather startled at this unexpected result of his words, and he began to console her with all the energy in his power.

"Never mind, Gracey, don't cry, and we'll manage her. I'll knock her down if she dares to follow us about. I ain't a boy for nothing. Look at this arm"—and he bared a sturdy little brown arm—"look, isn't this strong enough to beat any governess; I'll take care of you, never fear;" and he raised his voice in his excitement, till Grace begged him to stop.

"For," said she, "they are coming back; and, O Bertram! there is some one with them—perhaps it's the governess!"

"Nonsense," returned the boy; "governesses don't grow among the bluebells near the lodge, and that's where they've been. I wish they did grow there, the wretches!" added he, shaking his fist, "and I'd soon put a stop to them and their cruelty. Not that I care for myself though, Gracey, because I'm not a child now, you know; but what I think is, if they take it into their heads to send me to school, you'll be bullied into a scarecrow, and I sha'n't be able to help you; but, hush! here they come. Who *is* that with them?"

"Mr. De Verrie;" whispered Grace, "don't you see, now?"

"Hush!" repeated Bertram; and the two children sat like little mice on their high perch, while Lord and Lady Astley came slowly on, accompanied by their friend and neighbour Mr. De Verrie, whom they had met at the lodge-gate. Bertram and Grace hoped they should hear more about the governess now, as they fancied it must be a subject of great importance, and that everybody must be interested in it; and they were much disappointed at hearing, instead, only a few remarks about trees. The little party stopped just in front of a great tree which stood close to the children, so close that they were leaning against one of the branches which grew over the wall. Lord Astley was pointing out the beauties of this tree to his visitor, and they all looked up at it, and began to walk round to examine it. Bertram and Grace trembled on high, as Mr. De Verrie, advancing nearer than the others and peering up among the branches, caught sight of a little piece of brown-holland,— being neither more nor less than one of their gaberdines.

"Why, Lord Astley," he exclaimed, "you grow funny little brown flowers up in your trees."

"Eh? what?" said his lordship, who had dropped his cane, and was stooping to pick it up; "you must ask Lady Astley about the flowers,—she knows more about them than I do."

"I dare say she does; at least about these peculiar flowers," said Mr. De Verrie, smiling, and turning towards her, while she looked imploringly at him, and said, in a hurried voice,—

"I know nothing of flowers in trees; but come to my garden, and you shall see some worth looking at."

Mr. De Verrie did not remark her looks nor attend to her words, but he called again to Lord Astley to look up at the flowers, for he fancied that he would be amused at the situation of the children.

The poor man soon discovered his mistake. Lord Astley looked up, and saw, not only the brown-holland, but a little brown hand put gently out to gather it up out of sight.

"Holloa!" said he, in his loudest, most terrible voice, "who is there? Come down this instant, young vagabonds! This is always the way," he added, turning to Mr. De Verrie; "the ingratitude of these poor children is scandalous. In spite of all Lady Astley's schools, and charities, and rewards, there they are destroying my trees, as if there was no school in the parish. Come down, you young rascals!" he roared again.

Mr. De Verrie was very sorry for the children, still more sorry for having been the cause of getting them into the trouble he forsaw for them. He saw that they must be discovered—the sooner the better—and he said,—

"I don't think they are exactly rascals, Lord Astley, but more like your own children than anything else. Let me see;" and without another word, or waiting to be forbidden, he sprang on to one of the lowest branches, and, seizing a higher one, he swung himself up to where he could get a good view of the children, who still remained trembling on the wall. "Ah, Grace!" said he, as soon as he saw her little face peeping out, "how do you do? How did you get up there, and how do you intend to get down?—three questions for you in a breath, so don't answer one, but let me help you."

"No," said Grace, shrinking back.

"Come down!" roared father from below.

"Be careful, my dear, dear children, and make haste down," said their mother's gentle, tremulous voice; for she looked upon the tree as a burning house, and thought that every minute they remained in it increased their danger; while the children, regarding their father at this moment as something more to be dreaded than any burning house, were in no hurry to move. At another roar from Lord Astley, however, they began most cleverly to let themselves down from their height; but her mother's repeated exclamations of terror made poor little Grace so exceedingly nervous, that, although quite as good a climber as Bertram, and although she had been up and down that very tree hundreds of times before, she contrived, on this particular occasion, to lose her hold and slip,—not very far, however, for two huge friendly branches received her; and in another moment Mr. De Verrie was at her side, and with very little difficulty extricated her, and placed her in perfect safety by her mother's side.

Bertram now stood by her. Lord Astley's anger had been so much increased, and he felt it to be so entirely justified, by the sight of Grace's danger, that he could hardly thank Mr. De Verrie with becoming civility; but Mr. De Verrie was quite thanked enough by Lady Astley, whose tears, being in the habit of appearing at the shortest possible notice, were now, of course, flowing in the strongest consciousness of having every right to do so. Lord Astley scolded the children severely, and ordered them to their rooms for the rest of the day, and neither Lady Astley nor Mr. De Verrie said a word in their behalf, as they knew that it would be of no avail—for, although Lord Astley's naturally very violent temper was usually well under control, yet, when once it was aroused, he would bear no opposition, especially if the cause of his anger concerned in any way his household, in which he included, as before mentioned, his servants, his children, his horses, and his plate.

The children walked off, hand in hand, Grace crying quietly, but Bertram with his cheeks burning, and his head upright, taking very long steps, and longing to be tall and big, and almost to go back and answer his father.

When Lord Astley found that he was not opposed, his anger rapidly cooled down, and he consoled himself by talking most impressively to his wife and his guest on the subject of the impropriety of young ladies running wild about the country with their brothers; of his own extreme horror at the unfortunate brown-holland dresses; and he ended by pointing out how much better it would be for Grace to be dressed like a lady, and to spend her time in learning the harp or piano, declaring that he would that very day write to town for a governess,—which article of household furniture, apparently, his lordship expected to be able to order down from town from some repository or warehouse with as much ease as he would have obtained a pianoforte. Lady Astley mildly remarked, that "Grace was too young for the harp, and that she had done all her lessons before she went out, and really played very well on the piano for a child of her age; and as to dress, she was always well dressed when anybody was expected."

"And am I nobody?" inquired Lord Astley, in a tone of imposing dignity, and not the least as if he really wanted to know her opinion on the subject.

"Indeed, my dear," replied his gentle wife, "indeed, I always have them well dressed when you or any other company are expected, —only, you know, you never said you were coming to-day."

"And I am to be regarded as company in my own house, Lady Astley?" said he, in a tone which was intended to convey a depth of solemn sarcasm, but which really sounded so exactly like a simple question that her ladyship answered quietly,—

"Yes, my dear, if it is your wish. They only wear their old brown-hollands when they are alone with me here; and you know"—with a gentle sigh—"you know that is more than three-parts of the year."

Perhaps Lord Astley was tired of hearing of the brown-holland; at all events, he turned rather hastily to Mr. De Verrie as his wife spoke, and asked if he knew of a good governess,—though it was not very likely that a young man of one or two and twenty should know much about governesses—and no doubt Lord Astley would have thought of this if he had not been in a hurry to escape from brown-holland.

Now, strangely enough, it appeared that Mr. De Verrie did know of a governess, although he was a young man of one or two and twenty; and he hastened to tell Lord Astley that his youngest sister was just seventeen, and that his mother was very anxious to find a good situation and a happy home for Mrs. Abel, the lady who had filled the double situation of governess and friend to Laura De Verrie for the last seven years and a half. If either Lord or Lady Astley wonld like to talk to his mother about this lady, he would be delighted to drive her over any morning, or he would bring Mrs. Abel herself if they preferred.

Lord Astley was as pleased with this proposal as was consistent with his dignity, and as he generally was with any proposal that came from Mr. De Verrie, for he entertained a very high opinion of that young man's sense and abilities. Lady Astley, therefore, was obliged by her lord to write a very civil note to Mrs. De Verrie, for Reginald to take back, stating how very anxious she (Lady Astley) was to procure a governess for her children, and making many inquiries as to the likelihood of the situation suiting Mrs. Abel, and of Mrs. Abel's willingness to undertake the same. Reginald rode off with the note directly after luncheon; and Lady Astley, having watched his rapidly retreating figure till it was quite out of sight, went with her knitting and a heavy heart to hear from her husband a repetition of all his old lectures upon young lady proprieties and dress, embellished, on this occasion, with many additions and several pretty severe reprimands for her carelessness in having already allowed Grace to become such a tomboy; very little of which did her ladyship attend to, as her thoughts were completely taken up with wondering how the children had interpreted the order which sent them to their room,—whether they had retired to the solitude of their bed-rooms, or were quietly amusing themselves in the cheerful play-room, so soon and so sadly to be changed into the "school-room." At length, to her great delight, the superior claims of stewards, carpenters, and bailiffs, left her at liberty to creep out of the room.

"My love!" were the words that stopped her as she reached the door, "you are not going to pity and spoil those children; I will not have them down to-day Grace must learn to be ashamed of herself."

"Very well," said Lady Astley, leaving the room,

As she went along the passage to the play-room, it occurred to her to wonder what harm Bertram had done. It might be foolish for Grace to climb trees, but even Lord Astley had been heard to say that boys ought to be hardy; and one of his chief reasons for wishing to send the child early to school was, that he might grow up like other boys. "And what can be more like other boys than climbing trees?" thought Lady Astley, as she put her hand on the door of the play-room and pushed it open.

CHAPTER II

THE GOVERNESS

BERTRAM AND GRACE were sitting in the great window recess, looking very mournful and downcast, for so seldom did their father interfere with their pursuits, that a real scolding, as they called it, from him was quite an event, and a most disagreeable one, in their little lives. Even Bertram, his first anger and mortification over, was quite subdued; and they had been sitting for the last ten minutes just as their mother found them, in perfect silence, not daring to leave the room, longing for some one to break the monotony of their imprisonment, and yet dreading to receive a message from their father requiring their presence in the study—a room which they never entered without feelings of restraint at the very best of times.

Both the children came running up to Lady Astley as she entered the room. "Mamma, mamma!" said Grace, "Oh, mamma! is he very angry?—may'nt we go out?—Oh, mamma!" and they each seized a hand and clung to her.

"He is angry, Gracey," said their mother; "he thinks that little girls should not romp about and climb trees; and indeed, my dear child, it makes me quite tremble to think of the height you were from the ground, and you must promise me never to get up there again."

"But, mamma, *I* was there to take care of her," said Bertram, stoutly. "There wasn't the smallest atom of danger;—she never slipped before, only you flurried her by being frightened;—she climbs as well as I do."

"My dear boy, climbing is not a desirable accomplishment for a young lady, and I cannot allow your sister to do it any more. Gracey, my darling, you must promise me that you will never climb trees again."

Lady Astley put her arm round the little girl's waist, and drew her towards her in her own peculiarly gentle, engaging manner.

Promise never to climb trees again! Poor Grace! It was indeed a trial; for she knew perfectly well the value of a promise, and it never entered her head to give her word and then afterwards to break it,—and yet *how* to disobey her mother! Grace stood motionless, passively receiving her mother's caresses, but making no reply; while Bertram exclaimed, in a thorough passion—

"Grace! you must not promise—you *shall* not promise!"

"Bertram!" said Lady Astley.

It was but one word, but the sad tone in which it was uttered cut him to the heart far more than his father's many and angry words; and he turned away to the window, and stood with his back to his mother and sister, gazing out into the bright, lovely park, where the deer were grazing, in happy ignorance of the woes of their young master and mistress.

"Grace," continued Lady Astley, imploringly, "I must have your promise—I know I can trust you. My child, think of my misery if you were to fall from one of those dreadful trees, and perhaps be very much injured, or even killed. Grace, I shall not have a moment's peace when you are out of my sight. Indeed—indeed—"

Lady Astley was working herself up into a state of agony.

"Mamma, I promise!" burst from poor Grace; and she slid from her mother's arms, and, sinking on the floor, burst into a passion of tears.

Lady Astley was grieved to distress her little girl, but she was satisfied—she was more than satisfied—she was proud of her daughter's promise, and of her obedience—and she felt highly delighted at having so favourable a circumstance to report to her husband. She had no idea of what that promise cost Grace; and after telling the children that they must on no account leave that room without their father's permission, and advising them to keep as quiet as possible, she left them, to return to the study and watch for a favourable opportunity of obtaining a remission of their sentence by giving an account of Grace's promise.

The children, on being left to themselves, remained for some minutes, the one on the floor, the other at the window, without speaking. Grace was the first to move. She crept to Bertram and looked up in his face, half afraid to see how angry he was at the death-blow which she felt that she had given to many of their peculiar little plans and ways. He was still gazing out of the window, struggling to keep back the tears which for worlds he would not have been seen to shed.

"Bertram, I *could* not help it," said the little girl.

The boy turned to look at the little tearful face, and throwing his arm round his sister's neck, he kissed her, and answered, as if suddenly convinced of the truth of her words,—

"No, Gracey, you are right; but oh, Gracey!"— and his tone changed,—"think, only think, never, never, *never* to climb again; not the little beech, or the wall-tree, or even the great cedar, *never*— till you are quite grown up as much as mamma, and may do as you like. Oh, Gracey!" and as he named each favourite tree, he looked down into her face to see how she could bear it. The tears were still flowing, but the little face was firm.

"I know it, Bertram," she said; "I thought of it all when mamma was talking. It is giving up a great deal, but then it is for our own darling mamma, and I would do anything in the world for her. Don't you remember when we were wondering if we should have courage to leap down the gulf, like Marcus Curtius in Roman History, we said we would do it for mamma any day, and that would have been worse than giving up climbing?"

"I don't know that," said Bertram, doubtingly. "There would have been glory in that, at all events, and there is none in this."

Grace reminded him that the glory would have been of no good to them if they were dead; and they continued talking on the subject of glory and sacrifices till Bertram became so enchanted with the idea that he exclaimed,—

"I'll tell you what, Gracey, I'll give it up, too;—I'll go to mamma and promise to give up climbing."

"No, Bertram," said Grace, "that will never do. They won't like that; boys must climb. There are plenty of other great things for you to do."

"I don't know what," said Bertram, sadly; "and besides, if they like me to climb, why was my father so angry with me?"

"Oh, because it is spoiling the trees, that he does not like; besides, I don't think he was so angry with you, and perhaps if he had found you alone up there he would not have said much."

At this point in the discussion Lady Astley returned to tell the children that their father had forgiven them on hearing of Grace's promise, and that they had better go and make themselves fit to be seen.

To tell the truth, Lord Astley had very speedily forgotten all about the children in his multiplicity of business; and when their fault and punishment was recalled to his recollection by his wife, just as he had concluded a most satisfactory examination of his banker's book, he had remarked hastily, but with good humour,— "Oh, to be sure, let them out; but mind you, no more brown-holland suits; let them be dressed like gentlemen's children, and behave as such."

Lady Astley had tried to touch his heart by relating the promise Grace had made to climb no more, of which she thought so much herself; but he persisted in regarding it, most provokingly, as a thing of course that a child should promise to be good immediately after punishment, and would by no means be worked up to a pitch of admiration, or even to bestow another thought on the matter.

Mrs. De Verrie was a sensible, strong-minded woman, and her friendship might have been of great advantage to Lady Astley; but Lady Astley was slightly afraid of her, and disliked her rather blunt, plain-spoken manner, and as Mrs De Verrie was not a person to push her friendship when she saw it was not required, the two ladies met but seldom, although the son of the one was a great favourite at Combe Astley, and the children of the other were objects of much interest at Rangley Park, which was the name of the domain of the house of De Verrie.

Reginald De Verrie had taken a great fancy to Bertram Astley, and had often lamented to his mother and sister the strange, wild way in which, it was evident, these children would be allowed to grow up. "It does not signify," he would say, "now that they are so young, and it is well that they should be hardy; but Lady Astley has no idea of anything better for them as they get older. The boy sees no one but his sister and the servants, and some of these days, when he is suddenly taken from home and put to school, it will go hard with him. They are as wild as young colts, and as shy too. They run away and hide even when they see Laura and me riding up to the house, though we are friends enough if we do meet."

Mrs. De Verrie had sometimes asked the children to come to Rangley, but Lady Astley did not like them to go out alone, and "felt herself unequal to the exertion of accompanying them."

Reginald and his mother rejoiced in the prospect of introducing Mrs. Abel at Combe Astley, for they hoped that not only would she prove a real friend to the children, but that she might be the means of bringing them out of their solitude and making them associate with other children in the neighbourhood more than the pride of their father and the indolence of their mother had hitherto allowed them to do.

Lady Astley and Mrs. De Verrie interchanged a few notes on the subject, and it was finally settled that Mrs. Abel should go over to Combe Astley as soon as possible, to arrange preliminaries.

Unfortunately, Mrs. Abel was attacked by a severe cold, and was unable to go to Lady Astley's for some days, and before she was well enough to venture out, Lord Astley had returned to town; not, however, without extracting a promise from his wife that she would engage Mrs. Abel,—of whose fitness he entertained no doubts,— to undertake her new charge as soon as possible.

Now, to confess the truth, Lady Astley had quite as great a horror of a governess as her children had; for she, like her husband, was an only child, and had been entirely educated by her mother. She did not look forward with any pleasure to having a stranger domesticated in her home, and either constantly interfering between herself and her children, or entirely drawing away and monopolizing their affections. A spy upon her actions, and terribly in the way, she was convinced a governess would prove to be; nor did she incline to like her the better when she recollected that Mrs. Abel would come direct from Mrs. De Verrie, and had resided for so many years in that lady's family as to have established a right of friendship of which Lady Astley did not doubt she would avail herself as much as possible, as a consolation for the vexations and annoyances which she could not but find in a house where her presence was so little desired by any one member of the family; and by this means her ladyship feared to be drawn herself into that intimacy with Mrs. De

Verrie which it had been her almost unacknowledged object to avoid for so many years.

Both Lady Astley and her children, therefore, were at this time in a most uncomfortable state of suspense, with this difference in their sufferings: that whereas the mother knew from what quarter the blow might be expected, and that therefore her mind was comparatively at rest for the day on the subject after the arrival of the morning post, the children were living in perpetual dread, from morning till night, of the sudden arrival of their tyrant,—fearing every carriage, every gig, and even every cart, whether it came from the direction of Rangley or any other place,—and scarcely daring to venture forth to their more distant haunts for fear that the new governess should pounce upon them and at once marshal them into a state of terrible cleanliness and propriety.

At last, one bright morning, the expected letter arrived, announcing that Mrs. Abel was sufficiently recovered to wait on Lady Astley, and that Reginald De Verrie would drive her over that afternoon in his dog-cart; for his mother, having perceived that she herself was no favourite at Combe Astley, had decided that Mrs. Abel would be more likely to please if introduced in the first instance by another and more favoured individual.

On receiving this note, Lady Astley felt somewhat relieved, for she had been dreading the formal introduction—the long-winded praises of Mrs. Abel which she expected from Mrs. De Verrie, and she was sure that Reginald would do the thing much better, and set everybody at ease at once. It now occurred to her that the children ought to be told of what was hanging over them. Little thinking how much they already guessed, she went immediately to the playroom, where they were waiting for their usual lessons, and she told them, in a manner which she endeavoured to render as quiet and composed as usual—in which endeavour, however, she did not entirely succeed—that the little ones required so much of her attention, that she and their father thought it best to engage a lady to come to live in the house to assist with their lessons; "but," she continued with a sigh, as she wondered within her own mind how far the strong-minded and imperious governess she expected Mrs. Abel to prove would allow her to fulfil her own words,—"but I do not mean entirely to give up teaching you; I shall still come into the school-room every morning, at least at first, and till you get used to the new ways and greater strictness to which you must now accustom yourselves." And her eyes filled with tears as visions rose to her mind's eye of her little Grace in backboard and stocks for the improvement of her figure; and Bertram in perpetual disgrace and punishment for the sad long division sums which she really began to believe he could not master; and then, fearing she had said too much and given them but a sad idea of their governess, she added, in a voice which she strove to raise to cheerfulness but which only trembled the more in consequence, and thereby made her own dread of the new life more evident, and increased the terror which was stealing over the children's hearts,—"But I am sure you will like the lady who is coming; she is a very superior person, and will be very kind, and you will learn quite to love her."

To love a governess!—Bertram would have scorned the very idea at any other time; but there was something so strange in his mother's manner on this day, that he felt quite awestruck, and as Grace always followed in his lead, neither of the children spoke a word, but they hid their faces in Lady Astley's dress, while Grace gave free vent to her tears, and Bertram swallowed his with a choking feeling in his throat and a strong desire, in spite of his awe, to knock down every governess that had ever been invented, and especially this very superior one who made his mother cry. For although Bertram had seen her tears flow over and over again at an interesting book, or a tale of distress, or at the slight maladies and misfortunes of "the little ones," as, in the full consciousness of their nine years, he and Grace were in the habit of designating their younger brothers and sisters,—yet he did not, in his whole lifetime, remember ever to have seen such tears called forth for any matter concerning himself and Grace; so entirely apart, and in a little world of their own, had these two young ones passed their short lives. They loved their mother, and she loved them; but for comfort in all their little sorrows, for amusement, for sympathy, they had been all in all to each other. And now, when they saw her so strangely moved on a subject which concerned them alone, they felt that it must indeed be something very terrible which was hanging over them. Lady Astley gave them each a long, lingering kiss, highly suggestive of the idea that the new governess would never let her kiss them again, and telling them that they might have a whole holiday, and advising them to make the most of it, as it would probably be the last they would have for no one knew how long, she left the room, having, in perfect innocence, done all in her power to set the children against the governess, and to render that lady's task as difficult as it well could be.

Poor Mrs. Abel! Had you known what was passing at Combe Astley that morning, as you sat quietly in the pleasant drawing-room at Rangley Park, talking so cheerfully to Mrs. De Verrie of your new pupils,—of your kind hopes and plans for their good and amusement,—of the interest which you already felt in them and their gentle, amiable mother, and of the love which you were longing to bestow upon them; had you but seen all that was passing in their hearts about you, would you not have been ready to give them up for ever, and with them the pleasant prospect of remaining so near the pupil whom you must leave, and whom you love as a daughter and a friend—so near to her mother whom you esteem and look up to, and whom also you have learnt to love for her worth, in spite of her blunt manner?

Lady Astley need not have feared that because Mrs. De Verrie was blunt in her manner and strong in her mind, her daughter's governess must of necessity possess the same characteristics. No two women could be more different than Mrs. De Verrie and Mrs. Abel: the latter was an amiable, though eccentric, person, whom, when well known, it was impossible not to love, wherein she bore a much stronger resemblance to the lady whose house she was about to enter than to the lady whose house she was about to leave. For although Mrs. De Verrie's very good sense and real kindness of heart had gained her many true friends, yet it is right to remark that there still remained a considerable number among her acquaintances who found no difficulty whatever in not loving her at all:— for many are those who are influenced in their likes and dislikes far more by manner than by sterling worth.

Meantime, as Mrs. Abel had no idea of the feelings with which her new pupils and their mother were awaiting her arrival, she went upstairs with a light heart to put on her bonnet and shawl for her drive,—for she was one of those happy individuals who possess the enviable faculty of looking always on the sunny side,—and although she grieved much at the prospect of parting with the De Verries, she could not forget that she should be but seven miles from them; and besides, this was but a preliminary visit—the parting hour was not yet come.

And so Reginald and Mrs. Abel set off in the dog-cart, while Laura watched them drive away, and turned into the house, with tears in her eyes, as she thought how soon, how very soon, the day would come when her friend would drive away from that house for ever—only to return as an occasional visitor.

Laura was not hopeful and cheerful, like her governess; she "enjoyed bad health," as people say, though it would be difficult to imagine what enjoyment is to be found in that luxury. Weak nerves, too, were her sad portion; and the spirits of her mother and brother being often too much for her, she knew that she must sadly miss the more gentle and congenial spirit of Mrs. Abel, with whom alone did she venture to throw off the reserve which was natural to her. In everyday life she had been accustomed to seek for comfort and companionship in the cheerfulness of her governess;—but, had these two characters been tried in the battle of life, Laura's would have proved the stronger of the two; for she possessed what Mrs. Abel lacked—decision of character. But the one did not know her want, nor the other her power. With all her low spirits and her bad health, Laura would have made a better governess for the little Astleys than poor, happy, good Mrs. Abel, in spite of all her good-will and spirits. Mrs. Abel's eccentricities of dress and manner were highly calculated to excite the ridicule of two lively, clever children like Grace and Bertram, who would hardly be able to detect the real sterling worth concealed beneath much that was truly absurd.

But all things that be, are ordained for the best,—"even"—as a lady was once heard to remark—"even that rabbits should have long ears, though we know not why;" and therefore, no doubt, it was for some good end that Laura's decision and sense should be shut up in the drawing-room at Rangley Park, or should drive listlessly among the deep shady lanes of the country; while Mrs. Abel's indecision and weak judgment should be employed in the laborious task of curbing the youthful tempers of, and instilling all possible virtues and accomplishments into, Grace and Bertram Astley.

Laura De Verrie is sitting in her large pleasant window, watching the hay-makers pile up the huge cocks of hay in the field beyond her own peculiar garden, among the flower-beds of which her beautiful large St. Bernard dog is lazily reposing, watching for his young mistress to appear; and the sweet scent of the day is wafted to her by the gentle breeze, which ever and anon lifts and turns with a fluttering noise the leaves of the book which rests beside her; and Laura wonders whether she means to go out or to stay where she is, in dreamy listlessness, and then wonders again at the activity of her mother, who now appears below, decked in a huge sun-bonnet, and armed with a basket and a pair of scissors, passing through the smaller garden to reach her own, where she intends to spend the next hour in cutting roses; while Mrs. Abel and Reginald discourse cheerfully as the dog-cart bowls rapidly along the high road, and the splendid thoroughbred, which is Reginald's peculiar pride and favourite, arches his beautiful head and pricks up his small ears as his master whistles to him and he steps firmly along the smooth hard road. In the meantime, Bertram and Grace Astley are preparing for their first introduction to their new governess by hiding in the bushes near the gate at which they expect her to enter. Bertram had great ideas at first of jumping out and stabbing her; but they dwindled down to the less heroic and somewhat more feasible plan of frightening the horse, in hopes that they might run away, and that "she" might be thrown out, and perhaps sprain or break something, which happy accident would at least postpone her reign.

Lady Astley had told them her name, and that she was coming from Rangley, and they fancied that of course she would come in the Rangley barouche. When, therefore, they saw the dog-cart approaching, it never entered their heads that "she" might possibly be in it, until Bertram exclaimed,—"Why, it's Lofty!"

"Then it must be Mr. De Verrie," said Grace; "for he told mamma he would not trust anyone to drive Lofty but himself,—and, if it is Mr. De Verrie, perhaps she's with him."

"Nonsense, Gracey—governesses never come in dog-carts;—who ever heard of such a thing?" exclaimed Bertram, who evidently laid claim to great knowledge as to the natural history of governesses, although he had scarcely ever spoken to one in his life, while his reading on the all-important subject had been neither deep nor extensive.

"It is her, though, depend upon it," returned Grace, as the dog-cart approached.

"Then," said Bertram, solemnly,—being convinced in spite of himself,—"then, Gracey, I can't jump out—Lofty mustn't be frightened,—but you are my witness that I solemnly declare that I will make her a most dreadful face as she passes—a face that must frighten her into fits if she gets a good view of it; and you must make one, too."

"Oh, no, Bertram—not me."

"Grace, I command you!" said the boy, raising his finger with an imperative gesture,—"I command you, on your allegiance!

Remember, boys are made to command, and girls to obey. I heard my father say to mamma the other day."

Grace was always quelled by Bertram, especially when he used fine words which neither of them understood, a little practice in which he delighted. Therefore, she prepared to obey as the dog-cart approached the gate.

CHAPTER III.

THE GOVERNESS ON THE HAYSTACK

THE GROOM JUMPED down to open the gate, and the cart whisked past the children, who instantly pushed their little faces out of the bushes, and made two of the most hideous faces upon record at the retreating form of their governess; but it unfortunately happened that Reginald had caught sight of Gracey's bonnet in the bushes, and guessing that they would rather not be spoken to, he contented himself with laughingly telling Mrs. Abel, with a nod towards them *en passant*, that " there were her pupils watching for her;" in consequence of which, that lady turned her head just in time to get the view of Bertram's face, which he had foretold must send her into fits. It had not, however, the desired effect.

Mrs. Abel laughed heartily, and remarked that " they must be very funny children, and so different from dear Laura;—and therefore all the better for me, you know, though nothing could be more perfect than she is, dear girl; but then, you know, it is always an advantage to one to have fresh characters to study."

Reginald made no reply, the perfection of his sister being one of the points at which he was at variance with Mrs. Abel; for, whereas she would persist in seeing no faults in Laura, he could not but lament her extreme indolence and reserve, while he felt that she was capable of better things, and would have given worlds to induce her to make a friend and companion of himself, instead of being satisfied with the weak, friendly cheerfulness of her amiable governess.

Arrived at the house, they were ushered into the great drawing-room, where Lady Astley awaited their arrival. She was really glad to see Reginald, and as it was not in her nature to be ungracious to anyone, Mrs. Abel could not but be charmed with the reception she met with.

"I have brought you one, Lady Astley," said Mr. De Verrie, "who, I am sure, will prove as great an acquisition to your family as she will be a loss to ours."

Lady Astley secretly wished the loss was to be hers and the acquisition theirs, and yet she felt at once that she had nothing to fear from the overbearing conduct of the possessor of that bright, washed-out looking face, with the funny, twinkling eyes, and the thick, soft, old-fashioned flaxen curls, reposing in two huge masses on the forehead.

Reginald went on: "I can hardly believe that you have never seen Mrs. Abel before, so well and so long as I have had the pleasure of knowing you both; but my sister's long residence abroad must be the reason; and as I suppose you will have a great deal to say to Mrs. Abel, I will take a turn out and leave her with you."

Lady Astley begged him to stay, as all particulars had been arranged by letter, and she felt a slight tremor at the idea of being so soon deprived of the support which the presence of a third person afforded her.

"I think I have no secrets to discuss with Mrs. Abel as yet," said she, nervously, but with her sweetest smile; "and indeed I had rather you should stay, unless you wish to go to see after your beautiful horse, for I know that you do not think a groom fit to touch him;—but ours are quite used to our horses and to yours too, so often as you come. I am always glad to see you,—and the children love to see you ride Lofty,—you are so clever with horses; and indeed," and she turned to Mrs. Abel, "I do think it ought to form a part of every boy's education, and girl's as well. I hope you agree with me?"

Her ladyship waited for a reply, which Mrs. Abel gave in the form of the usual small laugh with which she was in the habit of beginning her sentences, and a "Certainly," while she wondered to herself, with slight trepidation, whether Lady Astley could possibly really mean that all boys and girls should be taught to be clever with horses, and if so whether she, Mrs. Abel, should be required to teach this accomplishment.

Lady Astley was quite satisfied with this her first little attempt at gaining for her children some promise of their accustomed liberty, and on the strength of it she said: "I should like you to see your little pupils, Mrs. Abel; I am sure you will soon learn to love them; and, as they are very shy, I am anxious that the first meeting should be over. I don't think you will have any very great difficulty with them, if once they can be got to look at you, for they are very clever children. They take after their father, and always know what they wish to do, which is a very good thing,—at least I always think decision is most desirable. They are far too clever for me, and I shall be quite glad to turn them over to you, though I shall wish to keep some of their lessons to myself at first. As for poor dear Bertram, I do not think he will ever conquer long division, although Grace thinks it pleasant; and I often think he has a great turn for mechanics, for when he was but two years old we could never get him away from the well in the yard. We can always tell a child's natural taste—do you not think so? I will ring for the children."

Mrs. Abel being rather at a loss for an answer to this complicated speech, contented herself with another laugh.

"I saw the children as we drove up," said Reginald; "so if you have no objection I will go and fetch them myself. It would be hard upon them to have to say, 'how do you do?' to two people at once;" and he left the room.

There was a silence for a moment, broken by Mrs. Abel, whose conscience had smitten her at the mention of Bertram's supposed taste for mechanics, knowing, as she well did, that her own tastes lay in a totally opposite direction.

Having sent forth her usual little laugh, as if to pave the way, she said: "Your ladyship mentioned mechanics. I feel it my duty to remark that I am quite ignorant on the subject. It was never required by Mrs. De Verrie; but though I think it right to mention this, I have no doubt I can easily get up enough of the science to be able to instruct your dear little boy for years to come. Mrs. De Verrie, I know, will be happy to render me any assistance in the matter."

Mrs. Abel seldom used fine words or formal expressions excepting on what she considered as matters of conscience; indeed, she was not often grave on any other subject, and it was unlucky that she was so on this occasion, for Lady Astley had been so entirely satisfied with the manner in which her long rambling speeches had been received, that she had really begun to like the "governess," when this unhappy sentence, and above all the double mention of her favourite aversion, Mrs. De Verrie, gave her a cold chill of disappointment.

"This is how it will be—I shall hear of nothing but the perfections of Mrs. De Verrie from morning till night," thought she, and she answered with her usual gentleness, but a slight flush on her cheeks:

"Oh, it will not be necessary to trouble Mrs. De Verrie at all—his lordship knows everything, and settles everything of that sort; and—"

"No trouble whatever, I assure you; Mrs. De Verrie will be too happy," interrupted Mrs. Abel.

"I do not think Bertram has the slightest turn that way now," replied Lady Astley; "it was quite a childish taste, and is quite gone,—ever since he tumbled in to the well from looking in too far."

Mrs. Abel was satisfied, and she made a movement which she thought was a bow, but which was not; and at this moment Reginald made his appearance with the children. He had had little trouble in finding them, but rather more in persuading them to come in with him.

"I am quite sure you will like Mrs. Abel," said he; "she is not the stiff, prim governess you expect. She is not like a governess at all, but is very funny, and says such odd, amusing things, that you will be obliged to laugh; and she laughs, too, a great deal more than I do, or you either."

"Will she go out with us?" anxiously inquired Bertram.

"That will be as your mamma likes," replied Reginald; "but I think you will soon ask her to go of your own accord. Why, I found my sister crying the other day because Mrs. Abel is going to leave her. She quite envies you having her."

"I'm sure she is very welcome to keep her!" was the ungracious rejoinder. "She's as deaf as a post, and a great deal uglier."

"Who? Laura, or Mrs. Abel?" asked Reginald, laughing.

"Oh, not Laura. I mean Mrs. Abel."

Reginald asked what made him think Mrs. Abel deaf.

"I heard you speak loud to her as you passed," said he, as they reached the house.

Mrs. Abel met them with a cheerful "How do you do, dears? I have been longing to make your acquaintance. I have *seen* you before, you know,—yes, I saw the funny faces you made at me out of the bushes,—very funny. Yes, I am sure we shall be friends— yes."

The children coloured up to the eyes, while Lady Astley looked rather shocked, and said,—

"Indeed, I hope they were not so rude; I trust you are mistaken."

"Oh! I dare say I am—quite so, no doubt—oh, yes," rejoined Mrs. Abel.

"No, you are not," said Bertram, in a hoarse, shy voice; "I did make a face at you, because I said I would, and I made Gracey do it, too."

"Funny children," laughed Mrs. Abel; "full of fun, but shy as yet! Yes,—oh, I feel sure we shall get on together. I am sure our tastes are just the same. I can see they are used to be a great deal out of doors; and so am I, you know, Mr. De Verrie, with dear Laura,—yes, always out."

Bertram longed to ask if Laura had a garden to dig in; but he did not dare to speak again, though he raised his eyes from the carpet, and took a good look at Mrs. Abel, while she rattled on to Lady Astley. Nobody was very sorry when Reginald said it was time to go, for Mrs. Abel never was sorry in her life; and Lady Astley had said all she had got to say, and did not want to be at the trouble of making more speeches.

Mrs. Abel was, as Reginald expected, in raptures during the whole drive, about "that sweet Lady Astley and those handsome children." And on the whole, Lady Astley was rather pleased than not with this first interview with Mrs. Abel; while Bertram confided to Grace that, "after all, she was not so bad as he expected, but certainly a good deal uglier than the old clerk," who had hitherto been to their young minds the *ne plus ultra* of all that is ugly. He added, moreover: "She laughs too much, and I think we can manage her, but mind, Gracey, we must not tell her any of our hiding-places, because we may want some place of retreat if she is very savage, and we can't tell yet. I believe they generally begin by being all right."

In a few days Mrs. Abel arrived to take up her abode at Coombe Astley, and very dreary to the children was their first school-room tea, presided over by a real governess, instead of their own favourite Emma, the second nurse, who now retired, *vice* Abel, promoted. They were rather cheered, however, by hearing Mrs. Abel declare that nothing should induce her to change the name of the room, unless their mamma insisted upon it.

"It has been called the play room till now," she said, "and why should we call it a schoolroom? I hope we shall play in it as much as ever. I suppose the school work has been always done here; and yet it has not been called a schoolroom yet."

Bertram afterwards pronounced that she had spoken like a sensible woman, and he shouldn't wonder if she were one after all. In a few days the children learnt to like her; and Lady Astley discovered that such a cheerful, happy spirit as Mrs. Abel's was so far from

being a check to her comfort that she sought her society as much
as possible after the daily lessons, which she very speedily gave up
to her entirely. Her manner of teaching was very good, and in
many things the children unconsciously preferred it to their mother's.
They felt that she took a more lively interest in their beloved history;
and as for the long division sum, it was in a fair way of being conquered.

When Mrs. Abel found how very welcome a visitor she was at
Lady Astley's work-table, and that, however well she got on with
the children during the school hours and at meals, they still preferred perfect liberty in their out of doors amusement, she very
willingly went with the tide, spending her spare time almost entirely
with Lady Astley, while the children ran wild as before. This happy
state of things lasted for about three weeks, with no drawback but
an occasional, momentary uncomfortableness on Lady Astley's part
at the very frequent mention of Mrs. De Verrie; but at the end of
the three weeks, a letter arrived from his lordship, announcing his
speedy advent at Coombe Astley. In consequence of which, as
usual, the children had to be caught up and dressed.

His lordship arrived, and was introduced to Mrs. Abel, with
whose old-fashioned appearance he was somewhat startled. He did
not, however, bestow a second thought on the matter, but concluded that the person who had educated so peculiarly ladylike a
girl as he had considered Miss De Verrie to be, the only time he
had ever seen her, must be perfectly competent to bring up his
own little girl.

The day after his arrival, on entering the drawing-room at half-
past twelve o'clock, he was surprised to find Mrs. Abel there,
reading aloud to his wife. He raised his eyebrows, but said nothing,
and merely passed through the room, supposing the children to be
in the school-room. In another hour, having occasion to return, he
was still more surprised at finding Mrs. Abel employed as before,
while at the same time he caught sight, through the open window,
of two little figures rushing across the lawn, one trundling a wheel-
barrow, and the other dragging a spade. Lady Astley looked up as
he shut the door, and said, in her usual calm voice,—

"I thought you were gone to Gatesford for the day, my love?
You said you should go at twelve."

"I did; but the man whom I wished to see came to me," said his
lordship shortly; and he turned to Mrs. Abel, and continued, "May I
ask where your pupils are at this moment?"

"Oh, certainly;" and Mrs. Abel gave her usual little laugh. "I don't in the least know where they are, or what they meant to do this morning; but I have no doubt I can find them directly. Shall I go?" And without waiting for a reply, the good woman began to trot out of the room with a gait peculiar to herself. Lord Astley stopped her.

"Oh, no trouble, I assure you," she began.

"A trouble which I could wish you spared," returned his lordship with an awful dignity, that struck even Mrs. Abel dumb for the moment. "Lady Astley, I fear, has been sadly wanting in her duty, both to you and to her children, for I cannot suppose that a lady so highly recommended by my friend Mrs. De Verrie would betray the trust reposed in her. I must beg you to be seated while I explain myself. Lady Astley was perfectly competent to the education of her children, as you must be well aware, but her health, and—and—numerous avocations,"—he glanced at the huge piece of work on which her ladyship was engaged, and cleared his throat,—"prevented her from—from—keeping them with her during the whole day. Under these circumstances, therefore, we thought it best to engage a person who—who—who—in short, could be constantly with them, and train them, especially my daughter, in those habits of elegance and good breeding which are so essential to them, and in which I have great reason to fear they are too deficient. I had hoped and expected that Lady Astley would have explained this herself, as I was unfortunately absent from home at the time of your arrival; but I see that she has left it for me to do. I trust we now understand one another." And his lordship rose to leave the room, while Mrs. Abel, who had ample time to recover herself during this long speech, hastened to say,—

"Oh, I assure your lordship I shall be delighted to be always with the dear children. I never left Laura De Verrie—sweet girl! and Mrs. De Verrie used often to say, 'Mrs. Abel, I mistook you for Laura's shadow!' and she has written to me twice to say how she misses her shadow—dear girl!—yes!"

Lord Astley bowed, and left the room, and soon after the house—having given a blow to the peace of his household, a blow which was destined to revert upon his own head in a manner of which he little dreamed.

From this day forward commenced a system of petty battles between the young Astleys and their governess, for while she was cheerfully striving to fulfil their father's commands, and never to lose sight of them, they, unable to comprehend this sudden change in her tactics, or to bear the constant surveillance over their movements, were again beginning to indulge in all their ancient and almost forgotten hatred for governesses, and to listen to all the foolish nonsense which servants are in general but too ready to talk to children on the subject.

Mrs. Abel was not judicious. She changed too suddenly, from leaving them quite to themselves to the opposite extreme; and, in spite of her great good nature, they were highly indignant, and rejoiced in what they considered as Bertram's wisdom in "not being taken in by her at first."

"Didn't I tell you, Gracey," said he, "that they all begin fairly, but they are sure to turn out villains at last. Now you see how wise it was not to tell her our hiding-places. To-morrow, when she goes to put on her bonnet to walk with us, we will slip out and hide."

Grace was quite willing; and, with her usual thought for Bertram's comfort, she slipped into her pocket one of his favourite story-books, well knowing that he would think it fun to sit in a hole for an hour or two in idleness. Bertram had been equally thoughtful for her comfort, and perhaps for his own, in another line; for he had secured a large basket of fruit, and concealed it not far from the stack which he intended should serve as their hiding-place that day. Accordingly, as soon as Mrs. Abel retired to put on her bonnet, the children flew down to the hall, and seizing their little hats, ran as fast as they could across the lawn, and through the shrubbery, to the rickyard beyond. Bertram set a ladder against a half-consumed haystack, and Gracey ran up it, followed speedily by her brother and his basket. Here, in a most delicious recess, they made themselves a very comfortable nest, and prepared to enjoy the book and fruit to their hearts' content.

They had not been there more than half an hour, however, before they heard a well-known and rather cracked, but eminently cheerful voice, inquiring of somebody if "Master Bertram and Miss Astley had passed that way." "Somebody" answered that he "didn't know not nuffin about 'em."

The children peeped out, and saw poor Mrs. Abel toiling along over the rough ground which surrounded the rickyard, holding her dress very high, and every now and then putting her hand up to shade her eyes while she looked anxiously around in search of them.

"Come back, Grace—she'll see us," said Bertram; and they retreated into their nest, and went on eating their fruit.

Presently a little rustling was heard below the stack, and somebody muttered, "They can't be up here—but I may as well see—yes;—they do get into such odd places—yes;"—and then a heavy step was put on the ladder, and began slowly to ascend.

"She'll never climb the ladder!" whispered Bertram.

"Impossible—a governess on a ladder!" responded his faithful copy; but, at the same time, the hard breathing, as of one using unwonted exertions, was heard to approach, and presently a huge straw bonnet with yellow bows appeared slowly arising above the top of the stack, and in another minute a pair of small laughing eyes met theirs; and with her well-known laugh, their governess exclaimed, "Ah, you little rogues, I have caught you! How pleasant! Why, you never told me where you were going to! Don't move; loves—don't move!" as they began to creep out of their den; "I should like to join you—yes—I've got my book too, and we'll make a merry little party—if I could but get over the ladder to you."

"There isn't room, I'm afraid," said Gracey, with a sinking heart, as the conviction forced itself upon her of the utter impossibility of escaping from such an enterprizing governess—one who was not even to be stopped by a ladder.

"Yes, there is room," said Bertram. "Hush, Gracey!—Lots of room, Mrs. Abel. Come on; I'll pull you up;" and he whispered to his sister, "Better to have her up here than to take a sober walk with her down there."

Besides, Bertram's heart was always touched by anything like courage, even in a woman; and so it was with a good will that he lent his small strength to assist Mrs. Abel over the top of the ladder and into their little nest. The three then busied themselves in arranging a place for the new arrival, and finally settled down very happily to their fruit and books, till they were roused by the sound of horses' feet on the soft turf in the distance.

Bertram stood up to reconnoitre, and perceived a lady and gentleman on horseback cantering up the park, while their pleasant ringing voices were borne to him by the breeze, which lightly lifted his own dark curls and the eccentric flaxen ones of his odd governess. A large dog ran before the riders; and as soon as Bertram percieved him, he waved his cap, and exclaimed, "It is Norna—here, Norna! here, here, he-re!" Norna being the name of Laura De Verrie's dog.

Mrs. Abel immediately essayed to spring upon her feet, to see what members of the Rangley family she might expect to greet; but, in the rapidity of her movement, she managed to entangle her feet in her dress in such a manner that she was forced to sink upon her knees, where she still remained, engaged in frantic and fruitless efforts to extricate her feet from her torn dress, and to regain her command of them, when Reginald and Laura De Verrie drew in their reins as they neared the stack. Laura's astonishment and Reginald's amusement at the position of their *ci-devant* governess was extreme. Mrs. Abel on her knees, plunging violently on the top of a haystack—an eminence which, to the best of their belief, she must have attained by means of a ladder—was a spectacle which they never could have imagined, even in the hours of their most juvenile romancing.

"Oh, my love—Laura! how delighted—how enchanted I am to see you! Wait a minute—I am coming down," said Mrs. Abel in an ecstasy of delight and perfect unconsciousness of the oddity of her situation. As she spoke, she succeeded in regaining her feet and, advancing to the side of the stack, she seized the top of the ladder, and prepared to descend,—first, by peeping down it, and then by putting one foot on the second step, very far in advance of the rest of her body,—talking rapidly the whole time. "So nice of you to come—I quite long to kiss you—how am I to get down?— so very nice—oh, backwards, perhaps,"—and here she turned suddenly round, and waved one leg out behind her in search of the ladder, by which means she managed to kick it completely down, and, losing her own balance, she fell forward on her face on the stack, and only saved herself from slipping quite off by catching hold of a thong which confined one of the trusses of hay.

"Stay," exclaimed Reginald, as he jumped from his horse, and flung the reign to his sister, "I'll take you down—though how or why you got up there surpasses the power of man to comprehend;" and with that he replaced the ladder against the stack, assisted Mrs. Abel to put her feet firmly on the steps, and soon placed her in safety on the ground. The children followed; and the little party set out for the house, Laura reining in her horse to keep back to Mrs. Abel's odd trot, and Reginald leading his in advance, with Bertram and Grace by his side.

CHAPTER IV

THE ROBBERS' DEN

REGINALD DE VERRIE had been curious to see how the children were getting on with their governess, but he had thought it best to keep aloof for some time. On this day, however, he had persuaded his sister to ride over with him to call on Lady Astley, and see what was going on, and he was not a little surprised at this first *coup d'oeil*. He managed, in the course of the visit, to get a few quiet words with Mrs. Abel, and he immediately inquired whether it was her usual custom at Combe Astley to pass the mornings on a haystack with her pupils. She laughed good-humouredly, and gave him an account of her interview with Lord Astley, which had obliged her to make so thorough a change in her first most successful management of the children, and so entirely overthrown the happy arrangement which enabled her to devote half her time to them and half to their mother, to the mutual satisfaction of all parties. Reginald advised her to try to win the little rebels by some of the long stories in which his sister used to delight, and for which Mrs. Abel was famous. She was enchanted at the idea, and, sanguine as usual, had not the smallest doubt of its success; and Reginald and Laura rode off, having actually obtained a promise from Lady Astley that "one of these days" Mrs. Abel and the two children should spend a long morning at Rangley Park.

The next day Mrs. Abel, with hearty good will, essayed the "story cure;" but homoepathy, or the water-cure, might have been tried with equal success. Her happy fairy tales, in which everything went right, and everybody had what everybody wished, exactly at the moment everybody wished for it, and the most marvellous feats were performed as if by magic, had no charms for children whose chief pleasure in that line was derived from sterner and far more noble accounts of Spartan fortitude and Roman heroism, and who delighted yet more in racing wild over hill and dale without any stories or books whatever.

They made several more attempts at escape, and various and strange were the hiding-places they selected; but in vain: Mrs. Abel was sure to find them out. This went on for some days; but at length Bertram hit upon a plan which, though slightly indefinite, was so full of delightful mystery and uncertainty that he felt sure it could not fail of success.

"Gracey," said he, "we have been foolish to waste our time in trying to hide so near home;—besides, now she knows pretty well where to look for us. We must go a long way off, and I have settled where. The Robbers' Den in Combe Wood will be the very place; and we will not go there only just to get away from her in play-time, we will regularly go and live there. Don't interrupt me,"—as Grace began eagerly with a "But." "Listen, and I will explain my plans. I have thought about it for an immense time—ever since her nasty long story about the magic cave."

"That was yesterday," put in Grace.

"Was it?—Well, never mind when;—but I didn't tell you before, because girls never can keep secrets, and I don't know what mightn't happen if she heard this. Now, what I mean to do is this. We must, by degrees, get everything that we can possibly want down to the den, and when it is quite ready we shall go and live there. Even if she knows where we are, I *know* she'll never dare to come, because she must cross the park, and she is a horrid coward at cows."

"But she might tell," suggested Grace.

"We'll find a way to stop her mouth," said Bertram, mysteriously; "besides, she never could find out. So now my commands to you are, collect together all the things we can possibly want for a very long time."

"What sort of things?" said Grace.

"Oh, I don't know—everything—anything you can get; we can't have too much; but that's your part. You know women must know best about keeping house and all that."

Grace felt quite grown up at this sentence, and said, "Perhaps I had better make a list for you to look over."

"Ah, yes, that might be better," said Bertram, with a consequential little nod: "meantime, I shall provide a basket of fruit, and the heavy things—railroad wrappers, I mean, and pillows, that would be too heavy for a woman to carry."

"But," said Grace, "when shall we be able to get them down—it is *such* a way?"

"Leave that to me," said Bertram, with another mysterious look.

"What shall we do to amuse ourselves in the den,—shan't we get tired of it?" was Grace's next idea.

"No," replied Bertram, deliberately; "no, I think not. Don't forget Pinnock's 'Rome,' and 'The Gipsies,' and 'Highwaymen and Robbers,' and that will do for us."

Grace ran off to make the list, which she slipped into her brother's hand next day as they went in to dinner. It was much as follows:—

Meat—a great deal.	Books and fruit. (B)
A paper of salt.	Our cross-bows.
Ditto of sugar.	A knife. String.
Loosifer matches and box.	Ralerode rappers.
Needles, and pins and thread.	Pilows.

Bertram graciously approved the list, adding of his own accord the item "arrows," and remarking that they need not be particular about "meat," for they could easily shoot rabbits with their bows; and besides, they might creep out at night and get a chicken from their own poultry-yard if they liked. "Remember to take knives and forks and spoons though," added he, as he left the room where this important conference had been held.

This new plan occupied the children for some days, and Mrs. Abel was perfectly satisfied that she had at last found the way to their hearts, through the delight they took, as she imagined, in her stories; for Bertram had pronounced it necessary to throw Mrs. Abel off her guard by being perfectly tractable till all their preparations for flight were complete. This conduct had another and most unhoped-for effect, extremely favourable to the children's plans. Mrs. Abel, finding them so quiet and so rapidly losing their wild ways and untidy habits, began gradually to leave them more alone, and even occasionally gave them a whole afternoon to themselves, while she devoted herself to Lady Astley, who was becoming quite fond of her.

These times were seized upon with avidity by the children to convey by slow degrees all their little goods and chattels, and many other things besides, to the "Robbers' Den," with which name they dignified a large cave which they imagined was known only to themselves. It was situated at the farthest end of a very ancient wood, which bounded the park on the side nearest Rangley. It had probably been the resort of smugglers in days gone by, as Combe Astley was but two miles distant from the sea, on the southern coast; and the surrounding country had been much pestered by the free-traders in the younger days of these children's father; and even now, although they were seldom heard of elsewhere, the peaceful inhabitants of Combe Astley, Rangley Park and the surrounding neighbourhood, were occasionally entertained rather than alarmed by the intelligence that a small schooner, supposed to be a smuggler, had been seen off Pester, the small fishing village nearest Lord Astley's park; and the coastguard was at times known to keep a sharp look-out in that quarter. The ground was very rocky about the cave, which was itself partly natural and partly artificial. The ruins of an old cottage stood some paces behind it, consisting merely of three shattered walls, and a space showing where a fireplace had been; while immediately below the ruin, from which the ground descended abruptly on each side, was a dark pond, the waters of which were almost black from the rich loamy earth of the place, and cold—to the children's fancy—with a supernatural coldness. This pond was completely shut in by trees, excepting on the side of the ruin. Sombre and heavy were the trees,—massive, and bending under the weight of their huge boughs; bending forward over the dark waters, as if they were trying to catch a glimpse of their own huge forms below. Lower and lower they bend, and lower still, the farther from the ruin, till one mighty monarch is laid low in the waters; and lighter brushwood and creeping moss have grown over his prostrate form in rich luxuriance, and have stolen among his dead, leafless branches, into the cold waters beneath. The park-wall was very low here, almost touching the ruin, and running by the side of the pond, although completely hid by the trees and brushwood. The lane leading to Rangley on the left, and Pester on the right, was on the other side of the wall; but it was a deep, rough lane, very little used excepting by visitors between Rangley Park and Combe Astley and the poor inhabitants of Pester, who brought fish to either place.

Most children would have been afraid to approach so gloomy a spot as the one just described; but Bertram's habits of independence and daring, and, above all, his familiarity with the place from his very babyhood, made him fearless regarding it, and Grace considered him protection enough under any circumstances and in any place.

In this cave, therefore, the children had already collected and concealed a great part of what they considered necessary, even to the knives and forks and spoons, when Reginald De Verrie rode over again, to persuade Lady Astley to fix a day for the visit to Rangley. Her ladyship was with very little trouble induced to consent that the expedition should take place on the following day; and, accordingly, at half-past eleven the next morning, the children, attired in their most worldly garments, plunged into the barouche after Mrs. Abel, and set out for Rangley Park, scarcely pleased with the unwonted indulgence, as they grudged the interruption to their important preparations, were afraid of Mrs. De Verrie, did not care for Laura, and hated their fine clothes. The holiday, however, was something, and the prospect of seeing Lofty, Norna, Laura's tame rabbits, and Reginald was still more.

They had to skirt Combe Wood for some way, and as they neared the spot where a glimpse of the ruin was visible, Bertram thought it prudent to direct Mrs. Abel's attention to some object in an opposite direction, and to talk very fast, as if he feared that the railroad wrappers and books would be discoursing in a loud voice, or the spoons, knives, and forks playing at hide-and-seek outside the wood.

Mrs. Abel, thinking no evil, was quite ready to look in any direction that anybody pleased, and Bertram was able to bestow a triumphant smile upon Grace, as, having quitted the park and turned up the lane in the Rangley direction, they again passed the ruin, but this time nearer yet, though separated by the park-wall, and he again repeated his little manoeuvre with equal success. Grace did not observe his glance, however, for, less wary, she was gazing with all her might and eyes into the wood. Bertram felt quite vexed at her want of caution, and touched her foot with his, under the seat, to recall her to her senses. The effect was instantaneous; but she took the first opportunity of whispering, when Mrs. Abel was looking the other way, "Secretus portentus," which were the words the children had agreed upon to be uttered as a sign whenever they had anything important to say to one another about their beloved secret. Bertram told Grace that it was Latin for "important secret", and she entirely believed it, and thought that she was very lucky in possessing a brother who could teach her Latin if she chose. Bertram nodded in answer to her whisper, for Grace's pride in the words often induced her to cry wolf when there was none.

The day passed happily with Mrs. Abel and Bertram. Grace would have enjoyed it too, but for her anxiety to speak to her brother alone, for she really had seen something that gave her some alarm as to the safety of their hiding-place, and still more of its now somewhat valuable contents. At Rangley it was impossible to get Bertram alone for one minute, and it was not till after their return home, when Mrs. Abel was gone to take off her bonnet, and the children were waiting for tea, that she was able to tell him what she had seen.

It will be remembered that the park-wall was low on the side of the Rangley lane, and there was a gap in the thick foliage exactly opposite the ruin. Through this gap Grace had distinctly seen two figures, both of men,—the one standing on the top of the hillock beneath which was their "Robbers' Den," and the other creeping among the brushwood in the direction of the pond. Grace finished this account, in a state of great excitement, by saying,—

"This shows that some people in the world do know the place as well as ourselves,—beggars or robbers, perhaps; and O, Bertram, the silver spoons! What *can* we do? I have been thinking of them all day. We must get them back to-night somehow, if they are not already gone, and never, never take them out again."

Bertram "pooh-poohed" it at first, and tried to quiet her with his usual "Nonsense, Gracey!" adding,—

"They might be there all day and never find out the cave, and they might be in the cave for a week and not find any of the things. Don't you know we hid them quite deep in the dark part, where few people would dare go."

But he could not help being rather alarmed himself; and at last he promised that he would go out directly after tea, and run down to bring back the spoons—if they were still to be found, which poor Gracey almost despaired of. He did so accordingly, and in a very short space of time re-appeared, singing as he entered the drawing-room, where his mother and Mrs. Abel and Grace were sitting,—

> "I've been roaming, I've been roaming,
>   Where the honeysuckle's sweet;
> And I'm coming, and I'm coming,
>   With *no* dust upon my feet."

The words "no dust" being pronounced with emphasis, for this was another of those secret signs in which these children delighted; the words being changed to "lots of dust," if any little plan in which they were engaged had failed; while by "no dust" Grace understood that all was right, and the spoons safe in the house again.

Lord Astley came home the next day, positively for one night only, and Mrs. Abel flew at him in the full assurance of his sharing her own exuberant joy at the success of her entire obedience to his orders, and was slightly shocked by the quiet unconcern with which he received her report. She could not help, however, giving him an account of the manner in which she and her pupils passed every half-hour in the day, and was rewarded for her pains by a few cold words expressive of his opinion that it was highly unnecessary to devote so much time to exercise and relaxation, and that, at all events, "a few hours in the afternoon might be reserved for study; two hours only in the morning were not, in his opinion, enough for the education of children, who were now, he believed, in their tenth year."

Accordingly, the next day, poor Mrs. Abel cheerfully, but reluctantly, informed Bertram and Grace that they must come to the play-room at four o'clock, for "just a few more lessons," as she expressed it.

Bertram was indignant. Such an infringement upon the rights of freeborn British children was not to be borne. Measures must be taken immediately, and a whispered "Secretus portentus" summoned Grace to a conference.

"Grace," he began, "I cannot stand this,—my mind is made up. We must run away to-night."

The short, stern sentences, and the "Grace," had their due effect upon her,—for Bertram never called her anything but "Gracey," excepting on occasions of great importance, or when he was angry with her. She made no opposition to his proposal therefore, and he went on,—

"I have been thinking seriously about the men you saw near the 'Robbers' Den;' and though they *might* have been only village boys, I do not think it would be safe for us to stay there long. I might bribe them not to tell, certainly (for I have five shillings in my purse), but it would be safer to go still farther off, and—do not be frightened —I mean to go to sea. We will creep out of the house to-night, and walk to Pester, where I will get on board a ship, and work my way out as cabin-boy, as many great men have done before me."

Grace's first thought was a pang of desolation at the idea of Bertram's leaving her; but, unselfish in her nature, she discussed his plans for some minutes before she even asked how she was to get back from Pester alone. Bertram's ideas on this point were highly indefinite.

"Perhaps, after all, Gracey, you had better stay behind," was his suggestion at length; but she scorned the idea of deserting him, and, at all events, would see him safe on the road, before she returned to have her tongue cut out, or endure any other of the tortures which Bertram assured her it was highly probable Mrs. Abel or his father would think fit to inflict upon her to extort from her the secret of his retreat.

At eight o'clock, as usual, the children went to bed.

Grace slept in a small room, opening into the one occupied by Mrs. Abel, and Bertram in just such another close by. Mrs. Abel's room and the play-room fronted the park, while the children's rooms formed the angle of the house, and their windows opened on to a balcony directly in front of the dark bushes which formed the boundary of the park and the beginning of the shrubbery. A flight of steps led from the balcony into a narrow walk below.

Bertram desired Grace to be ready for him at half-past ten, at which time the whole household would be in repose, as Lady Astley kept very early hours in the absence of her husband.

Grace lay awake as long as she could; in fact, till long after the time fixed, but at last, although she even tried holding her eyes open with her hands, she could not help falling asleep; and when she was roused, it was not by Bertram's tap at the window, or knock at the wall which separated their rooms, but by the usual "It's half-past seven, Miss Astley," from Emma.

Next morning Grace was rather afraid Bertram would be angry with her, but he was too thoroughly ashamed of having himself been overpowered by sleep when in the agonies of listening for the striking of each quarter of an hour, to dare even to meet her eye at the breakfast table, much less to be angry with her; and when Grace found an opportunity of begging his pardon in most humble terms, he was graciously pleased to pass over the offence. For this day, therefore, they were obliged to submit to the four-o'clock lessons, and before they went to bed Bertram told Grace that he had been thinking that it would be better for her to come to his room at the hour fixed, instead of the first plan of his going to her; "for," said he, "you are so much nearer Mrs. Abel, and, of course, the less noise made in your room the better; so as soon as you hear that all is quiet, come and whistle three times, with a turn in the last, close to my window; I shall come to it directly, and say 'Pax?' You must answer 'Proprius Gracius,' which is Latin for 'Your faithful Grace,' and then I shall know it is you, and shall come directly." "Very well," said Grace, delighted at the grandeur and mystery of the plan, " 'Proprius Gracius;' I shall remember," and she repeated the words to herself till everything seemed to say them. The servants walked to the sound, the younger children cried them, and the lively country dances which Mrs. Abel played to amuse them after tea said

"Proprius Gracius" so plainly that Grace was almost afraid Mrs. Abel herself must hear them, and, by some mysterious connection, through them discover the whole plot!

Grace possessed a peculiar talent often to be seen in grown persons but seldom in children—a talent which can be acquired with very little trouble by those who have any determination of strength or will, namely, the power of waking herself at any time that she chose. Accordingly, although she got into bed, and even dozed for some half-hours, she woke up thoroughly just as the large garden-clock struck ten; at the same time she heard the drawing-room bell ring, the door shut, and her mother's gentle step and rustling dress on the stairs, accompanied by Mrs. Abel's heavy trot, and the peculiar noise made by the knocking of the extinguishers against the hand candlesticks at each step taken by the bearers; she heard the subdued voices at the top of the stairs; Mrs. Abel's occasional breaking all bounds in an hysterical word, with her odd laugh, and Lady Astley's gentle "Hush!" Then came the good-nights and Mrs Abel's tip-toe entrance into her own room, and her attempt at gently closing the door, which, however, slipped from her hand and shut with a bang, causing the good lady to exclaim, in a very audible whisper, "Hush, my dear door, bless the thing."!

Grace waited for some time longer, hearing her good governess patter and trot about her room, and she was about to get up and commence her own operations when the door between the rooms opened just enough to admit a worthy, most benevolent, but anything but beautiful, night-capped face, decorated with two curl-papers of a size and form hitherto unknown to Grace. The face remained looking at her for one minute and then withdrew, with a muttered "Bless her, little lamb!" and a minute afterwards Grace heard the owner thereof flounder into her bed, which creaked and groaned as if it would rather not have received her. Then all was still. Grace's heart warmed towards the kind old lady, and she felt almost sorry to grieve her, as she was about to do, but Bertram must be obeyed: so as soon as the hard breathing in the next room assured her that all was safe, she slipped quietly out of bed and began dressing as noiselessly and as rapidly as possible, but with trembling hands and a beating heart. As she thrust her arms into her little warm bear-skin coat she heard the butler's creaking shoes as he ran upstairs to turn out the lamp and then ran down again. The steps died away in the distance, and then she knew that all was safe. That was the last legitimate noise to be heard in the house that night. She tied on her little hat, and was just approaching the window, when a thought struck her. Pursuit might be avoided for some hours if they could but put figures in their beds to represent themselves. The idea was followed by immediate action. Quick as thought she opened a large cupboard which took up one side of the room, and drew out, one after the other, two gigantic dolls. One of these she placed in her own bed, covering it with the bed-clothes, so as to look as like herself as possible, and with the other in her arms she again went to the window. Noiselessly she raised the loose old sash, and, stepping out, as noiselessly closed it. She trembled from head to foot at finding herself alone in the dark outer world; but she stole on tiptoe to Bertram's window, and gave the signal agreed on—the three whistles, with a turn in the last; and she waited breathlessly for the response, with the words "Proprius Gracius" trembling on her tongue. No answer—all was still. She repeated the signal; still no sound from within; while a slight breeze passing through the mass of dark foliage behind her, and gently moving the leaves with a mysterious sound, excited her already highly-wrought nerves to such a pitch of agony that, unable to bear the solitude a moment longer, she hastily put her hand to the window, and, lifting it quietly, entered the room and looked anxiously round.

CHAPTER V

THE GIPSIES

BERTRAM WAS SLEEPING peacefully in his little bed, with one sturdy little arm flung round his head, and the other clenching the bed-clothes with an energy highly characteristic of the child. The moon was shining through the trees upon his face, and their flickering shadows waved gently over it, giving, as Grace thought, a strange, unearthly, but beautiful expression to his countenance. His round and healthy cheek reposed calmly on the smooth, white pillow, while his luxuriant dark brown hair looked as glossy and unruffled as when he lay down to rest. Grace called him gently,—

"Bertram!"

He made no reply—no movement.

"Bertram!" said she, louder, and at the same time touching him. An impatient noise escaped his lips, while he turned heavily in his sleep; but his bed did not creak as Mrs. Abel's had done—perhaps it liked having him.

Grace now pulled him harder and called him louder, and after one or two more slight, impatient sounds, he roused himself, and sat up in bed, lazily opening his large, round eyes and gazing at her as if he thought she was part of his dream.

" 'Proprius Gracius,' Bertram!" said Grace, nervously; " 'Proprius Gracius!' and I am come, and it is time to go."

"Eh—what?" returned the sleepy boy, "Time—eh? Why do you bore me so—can't you let one sleep?"

"Hush!—not so loud! Don't you remember, Bertram, 'Proprius Gracius'—afternoon lessons? Come on—it is so cold to wait,"—for the poor little girl's very teeth were chattering with nervous cold and fear.

Bertram then rubbed his eyes, and looked at her again, as if perplexed; but the recollection of his wrongs and his plans at length reaching his torpid brain, he suddenly sprang up, exclaiming,—

"All right—I'll be with you directly—I forgot—I believe I was asleep."

Grace believed so too, and waited patiently till he was dressed and ready to set forth.

Bertram quite approved of the plan of putting the dolls in their beds, and helped Grace to arrange the one she had brought for his. He gave one look of regret round his little room as he prepared to step out of the window, saying with a sigh, "Ah, it will be many a long year before I sleep here again, I dare say. Grace, shall I take my cross-bow? I smuggled it up last night in case I should want it. It might be useful if we met any robbers."

Grace could not speak for a moment, for hot tears had risen to her eyes at Bertram's words, and she knew that he hated "women's tears" as he said, and he had even often told her that he had a very high opinion of her because she so seldom gave way to them. Could she forfeit that high opinion at such an hour! She was soon able however, to answer, "I wouldn't take it—it will only be in the way, I think."

"Think so?" said he. "Well, perhaps you are right; at all events, my arm is enough to defend *you*, I hope. Poor old Killdeer, though! I'm sorry to leave him. Take care of him, Gracey."

The bow was an old favourite, associated with many days of happiness in their young minds. They had named it after the rifle of the famous Leather-stocking.

Grace did not trust herself to answer, as she followed her brother through the window, which he carefully closed; and making her a sign to be quiet, he crept down the steps and into the bushes. Grace kept close at his heels, like a faithful dog. After a little pushing they came into one of the shrubbery walks. It was pitch-dark, for the trees met above their heads and concealed the light of the moon; but they knew the way well, and went on rapidly. Presently they came to a little low wicket-gate which opened on to the side of the hill on which their father's house stood. They passed through it, and paused for a moment to take breath, and to gaze around them. The moon was high in the heavens, and the vast plain before them was bathed in dew, which shone like a sheet of silver in her clear soft light; while the dark shadows of the trees, cast in motionless solemnity beneath them, looked, to the children's excited imaginations, like so many huge giants, caught and chained in strange shapes and attitudes by the magic power of the lady moon. The happy, peaceful home in which they had been born, and which had sheltered them all the years of their little lives, frowned upon them from the hill as if it would reproach them for leaving it. Its huge, mysterious-looking shadow stretched out towards them, as if to draw them back; while the great staircase window at the side—the only one which caught the moonlight—looked smilingly and benevolently down, as if it would ask them why they should flee from its large, comfortable recesses, and the luxuriant exotics which were blooming therein. There were neither deer nor cattle in the plain; they had all retired to rest in the woods or in the fern. No human life was abroad, but what was contained within those two strange little figures standing on the hill-side, and looking singularly out of place there at such an hour and far more creatures of sunshine than worshippers of the night.

"Come on," said Bertram, in a low voice, "we must not waste time,"—and he strode off, while Grace trotted by his side.

Now, could we have looked into the hearts of these two children at this time, we should have seen in that of Bertram Astley, although the originator and prime mover of this scheme, a very great doubt as to its success, while Grace's would have shown us nothing but the most entire faith in Bertram, his plans, and his words. Grace had no doubt but that the next sun would rise upon Bertram in a ship bound for some unknown country; and upon herself in her solitary play room, no longer gladdened by his presence; for she did not suppose he would allow her to accompany him very far on his way to Pester, and she only hoped she might be let to go at least to the park-gates.

Meantime, Bertram thought all the planning and the escape at night very good fun; but, although he did not confess it even to himself, sundry misgivings had been stealing into his mind, dating from the moment when he had sat up in his bed and seen Grace waiting for him. He did not like being roused from his nice sleep, and he had rather uncomfortable feelings about Combe Wood, through which they must pass; and as the time approached he began, too, to wonder what he should say to the captain of the ship, which he still believed he must find at Pester. However, he plodded on, rather ashamed of his fears, as Grace appeared by no means to share them.

"Gracey," said he, as they neared the wood, which certainly looked most terribly dark and ghost-like, "we won't go through the long drive by the lodge. We must avoid the lodge, or they'll hear us; so we'll go by the Robbers' Den, and over the wall at the ruin."

Accordingly, they turned off the great carriage-drive into a very narrow path at one side. Presently Grace asked Bertram if he was sure he was right.

"It seems to me as if we must have gone beyond the den. I am sure the brambles are not so thick that way—I can hardly drag through after you, and they make such a noise on my frock I'm afraid somebody will hear us."

"There's nobody near enough," answered Bertram, half wishing there had been, and carefully avoiding her questions, for he, too, began to find the brambles unusually thick and the way long.

They went on for some minutes in silence, carefully groping their way. At length Grace said, in a voice which heralded the approach of tears, "Bertram, I know we're wrong; and my legs do ache so, I *cannot* go on."

"Wait a bit Grace!" was the cheerful reply. "Cheer up heart a little longer; I see some light, and we'll soon be out of the wood."

"Then we *have* been going wrong all this time!" said Grace, in the same tone.

"Wrong!" returned Bertram. "Oh, no! Only, you see, I thought it better to go round just a *leetle* bit, to avoid the lodge. It's all right now. I know where we are; there's the ruin!"—and he stepped a little on one side to let her get a glimpse of it as the soft moonbeams fell upon it and lighted up every crevice and cranny in the old place.

"Why, we're coming to it from the Rangley side!" exclaimed Grace, in a whisper. "We must have gone all the way round by the great oak!"

Bertram's courage had been fast oozing out at his fingers' ends during his struggles in the brambles. His legs ached, too, and he was getting hotter and hotter as the form of each huge tree in succession appeared before him; and now, when he saw once again the clear calm moonlight and emerged from the thick brambles, he seemed to breathe more freely; but at the same time a strong sense of the comforts of rest and home, and an increasing unwillingness to plunge into the wide, wide world possessed him. He paused, considering how he should break to his credulous and faithful follower his sudden change of plan, and that he actually thought of getting home to bed as quickly and quietly as possible.

"Gracey, I am afraid you are *very* tired. We must rest a little," he began.

"Oh, no, no!" said Grace, earnestly. "Let us push on *now*, and rest later, nearer Pester!"

"Near Pester!—oh—ah! Well, but how will you get back alone?"

"I don't know," said Grace, trembling, though more with the fear that he meant to send her back that moment than anything else. "I don't care, Bertram. Never mind me, I shall manage. The chief thing now is to get you into the ship. You can send for me, you know, some day!"

"But I *must* mind you, Gracey. It is my place to protect you. It is too dark for you to go back alone. Robbers, or anything, might come. I shall take you back immediately!"

He doubled his little stick under his arm with an air of determination. Grace was miserable at the idea of his sacrificing his own interests for her, and was imploring him to go on, when he suddenly started and put his hand on hers, saying, in a whisper, "Hush, Gracey! didn't you see something! There, back among the bushes!"

"No!—where?—what?" said the frightened child, clinging to him.

"I declare!" said he, in a trembling whisper, "something light moved in those black trees!"

"Bertram! Bertram! I cannot go back through there—indeed, indeed I cannot!"

Bertram's dignity gave way completely at this new alarm, and his answer was a very meek, "No more can I, Gracey; what *shall* we do!"

"Let us get out of the wood and go home!" returned Grace; and she shook with fright.

"But it's all wood all round, except the wall," said the boy; "and my legs ache so. Let's creep into the cave and stay till morning."

"Oh, no, not the cave! not the cave!" said Grace in an agony. We'll get into the ruin—it's light there, and we can hide in the fireplace."

Bertram agreed, and they went on as fast as their trembling limbs would allow, and were soon snugly curled up in what had once been the fireplace. Here they nestled together very cold and very tired—frightened at every leaf that moved near them—not daring to look round, and thinking that daytime would never, never come again. Before they had been there ten minutes they were both fast asleep.

At the same moment that Grace and Bertram Astley emerged from their father's shrubbery and stood alone on the hill-side, a gipsy cart might have been seen wending its way along the high road between Rangley Park and Henley,—a large seaport town situated about three miles from Pester. Some of the gipsies were in the cart, while others walked by the side, and some few lagged behind. One young girl, with long black hair and eyes of an almost unnatural brilliancy, walked by the side of the horse, which was a better-looking animal than those usually seen among the gipsies.

As the cart came up to and almost passed the turning off to Combe Astley and Pester, a shrill voice from the cart exclaimed sharply—"The deuce is in you, Nora, girl! Whatever are ye dreaming on? Take the turn, girl and mind what yer arter—do!"

Nora did not speak a word, but she turned the horse's head, and the heavy lumbering cart creaked wearily down into the deep ruts of the unfrequented lane with a jolt that elicited many an oath from those within the rickety yellow walls of the vehicle.

Nora walked slowly on, for she was sadly tired, and had been on foot many hours that day; but still she kept her post by Drudo's head, for she loved the horse, and well she knew that from none but herself would he receive kindness.

"We'll be having a fine sail to-night, Nat," said she, looking up into the heavens, now spangled by myriads of stars.

"Yes," replied a gruff voice, whose owner had moved forward

to her side, "if the wind ba'ant a rising ag'in; it's sagged jolly sin'
the morning."

"I hope Black Sam won't keep us waiting," said the girl; "I
hate that place."

"Ai!" returned her companion; "there's no doubt but what it's
terrible ellinge and drearsome; but Black Sam's up to snuff."

They walked on in silence for some time. Presently Nora
shivered, and drawing her rag of a cloak round her slight form,
remarked,—"I've a bad feeling about this lane. I wish I hadn't
forgot the money, and we wouldn't ha' come this way."

"You're full o' bad feelings, to-night," returned the man, shortly.

"I wonder why it's called the Headless Lane?" said Nora,
musingly, and without noticing his remark.

" 'Cause o' the wife o' one o' them 'ere lords up at the Combe.
They say she walks up and down the lane o' summer nights with her
head in her hands, a-groaning," replied the man.

"I hope we shan't meet her—d'ye think we shall?" said a tall
sprightly gipsy, who had joined them at the beginning of Nat's
speech.

"Belike," said he in answer; "there ain't no odds, nor no sinifica-
tion, as I sees."

The tall gipsy drew nearer, and seemed to dislike the idea, but
Nora dragged dreamily on in silence.

They now approached the wall of Lord Astley's park, and, after
skirting it for some little way, the broad square shadow of the ruin
appeared before them, thrown straight across the lane. The moon
sailed on in the heavens, and now she was behind the ruin, and
Bertram and Grace lay in darkness, still fast asleep.

"Halt!" said the shrill voice from the gipsy cart.

"Wo-o, Dru!" said Nora's gentle tones; and a shrivelled and
ragged old gipsy, of most forbidding aspect, began to clamber out
of the cart, muttering and mumbling as she knocked against the
shafts.

"Nora, girl, you'll go with me and get the money," said she,
sharply; "Nat'll stay wi' the horse."

Nora obeyed, and together they approached the wall. Nora
sprung lightly to the top, and pulled the old woman over with less
trouble than might have been imagined, though not without eliciting
groans and curses in abundance. The two women then crept to the
back of the ruin, passing close to the unconscious children, but
without perceiving them. The brushwood was very thick here;

but the old woman, lifting a huge mass of it aside, disclosed a trap-door in the rock. Nora opened it with ease, and old Gran began to grope her way down. Nora dropped lightly after her. They stood in a passage scooped out of the hill. It was very narrow, and not long, and they soon entered a cave exactly behind, and, in fact, joining on to the "Robbers' Den." At present there was no communication between the two, although originally the inner cave had been but a continuation of the outer one. The gipsies were in utter darkness; but Gran proceeded to strike a light and secure the money—cleverly concealed in the ground—which was so covered with dead leaves that had drifted through a crevice in the top of the cave that no eye but the most practised could have guessed at the treasures it contained. This was one of the great hoarding-places of the gipsies, and many and various were the stores herein concealed.

Grace and Bertram would, indeed, have started with fright could they have seen what was passing so near them. The old woman on her knees on the ground,—her shrivelled claw-like hands busily employed among the bright coins, but covered with the wet clammy earth in which she had been muddling to reach them,—her nails standing out long and black, and giving a finish scarcely human to the withered form. Her coarse grey hair escaped in bunches from the dirty blue handkerchief which served as her head-dress, and every line in her hard puckered face was seamed with dirt, rendered distinct by the faint light of the lantern which her companion held towards her.

That lantern cast its light upon but one other being. Nora stood beside her, with one hand resting on her side, her whole form slightly drooping in an attitude of extreme languor, like a parched flower pining for the summer rain. Her long black hair fell around her like a veil, and the red handkerchief which had confined it had been thrown back from her head. Her eyes were large and deep, and so heavy that it seemed to be an effort to her to lift them to your face, and when you met their gaze there was no escaping from its mournful earnestness. They were shaded now by the large heavy eyelids, with their long black fringes resting on the pale thin cheeks. But for the black hair and eyes you would not have taken Nora for a gipsy, so white were her hands and so white her face. And now the task was done, and the gipsies left the cave, Nora first, still holding the lantern. It was harder work for the old woman to get out of the trap-door than it had been for her to drop down, and her words on the occasion were not at all like angels' visits in any way. All having been put as before, they again crept round the ruin, Nora still being first with the lantern. She rounded the corner; the light fell upon the little sleepers. Nora glanced round the ruins and started. She had seen them. Her next impulse was to pass on as if she had not seen them, that her mother's attention might not be drawn to them likewise. It was too late. Her start had been observed, and its cause was perceived.

"Ah!" said the old gipsy, "ah! what will this be?" and she hobbled up to the children and bent down over them, peering with her half-blind eyes into their faces.

Grace turned and half opened her eyes, and sharp and shrill was the shriek she gave at that haggard old face so close to hers. She might have thought she was in her own little bed and dreaming, but still she screamed. Quick as thought the gipsy's hard, bony hand was on her mouth, tight, tight, keeping back the screams, and poor little Grace was caught up in her arms and held firmly beneath her cloak.

Bertram awoke at Grace's scream; but his dream was more pleasant than hers,—Nora's thin arm was round him, and her mournful eyes were looking in his face. He did not scream but only looked again, thinking he was dreaming still—wondering, and hoping his pleasant vision would not pass.

Two of the gipsies had jumped over the wall before Grace's scream was well finished, and now they snatched Bertram from Nora, and before he had time to recover from his astonishment his mouth was stopped, and he was in the cart, jolting along the lane as fast as poor Dru could gallop. Gran sat beside him, with Grace in her arms, and her hard hand was still on the poor child's mouth. Grace still struggled and tried to scream, and the old woman shook her roughly, and told her "if she didn't leave off and lie like a lamb she'd soon find a way to quiet her for ever." Grace was quiet enough then, and Nora begged to be allowed to take her—for Nora was in the cart too. But the old gipsy would not give her up, so Nora sat down by Bertram, and bent over him, trying to save him from the rough jolting, which shook everything and everybody in the cart. Presently, by Gran's directions, she poured a few drops from a dirty glass bottle into a still more dirty blue mug. The poor children were, by threats, induced to swallow this, and they obeyed in deadly fear. They went on at a rapid pace for about a mile, and then Nat, who had now taken the reins and was sitting in front of the cart, suddenly pulled up, saying, " 'Tain't no good pegging along this ere way; if we are afore Black Sam we'll only be having to wait, and the others won't be up this hour." Old Gran answered only by an oath, to which Nat paid no attention but went on, angrily, "How ever did them 'ere children get in there this time o' night, and what was you a thinking on, a-snapping on 'em up, you old fool! I'd like to know what good they'll do us, 'cept 'tis a bringing you to the gallows, where you'd ought to a bin by rights these forty years."

"When you is chief, or chief's widdy, speak so, and not afore, my chick," returned the old woman, with a horrible grin, whereby she displayed a long row of gum, toothless but for two long front incisors, which, when her mouth again closed, resumed their usual place over the lower lip, and considerably below the upper, from which they protruded.

The man made no reply, for the elder gipsy possessed considerable authority over the gang; and the cart jolted wearily on for the remaining two miles; and, in spite of their fright, Bertram and Grace were both fast asleep by the time they reached Pester, or rather the small creek in which the gipsies expected to meet their friends the smugglers, which creek was somewhat to the right of the village, from which it was concealed by a rise in the beachy ground. There was but little beach here, and the lane, which for some time had little deserved the name, being no more than an open cart-track, crossed by many others on the half marsh, half beach common, reached nearly to the sea. As the gipsies approached, they perceived another party and another cart coming up from the left, and signs of recognition passed between the two caravans. A boat, with two rough-looking men, was waiting for them in the cove, and another now appeared rowing rapidly from a ship, which lay with flapping sails at a short distance from the shore. A few words of explanation passed between the two gipsy parties, while the old gipsy, Gran, seemed to be giving a somewhat sulky account of the capture of the children to a tall, commanding-looking man of the party. He was evidently much annoyed and perplexed at first, but finally appeared to yield to her persuasions, and accordingly gave some directions to several of the gipsies; in consequence of which, Nora and the still sleeping children, with old Gran, were put into the first boat, with almost all the goods and chattels from the cart, and rowed off to the ship. The contents of the blue mug, though not given in kindness, were of the greatest service to the poor little wanderers, for they slept on in the boat; and still they slept when they were lifted up the side of the ship, and received by savage-looking men, with rough beards and rougher ways.

The boats plied backwards and forwards several times between the ship and the shore, until all the gipsies and, last of all, their horses, were on board. The carts had been taken to the village as soon as they were emptied, and left there, as usual, under care of some friends—for all the inhabitants of that dirty little fishing-town were on the very best terms with the gipsies and smugglers who frequented the place.

When all was ready, the ship sailed slowly away from the coast, leaving far behind the dirty little village, Headless Lane, and Combe Astley, the good-natured governess, the lesson-books, and the kind mother, whom Grace and Bertram had only left, as it turned out, to join a set of wild, lawless wanderers.

CHAPTER VI

THE GYPSY VOYAGE AND CAMP.

AND NOW THE drug which Gran had given the children began to lose its power, and the rolling of the vessel—for the wind was rising—helped to rouse them from their death-like sleep. Grace was the first to wake, and she opened her eyes and gazed around her, wondering where she could be, and how she got into such a strange place. Her head ached dreadfully, and was so heavy that she could hardly lift it from the bundle of rags on which she had been thrown. She had little time to wonder, for soon everything seemed to be going round and round, and she became dreadfully sick. Between the paroxysms the poor child cried very much, and longed—ah, how she longed!—for her own dear mamma's cool, soft hand to hold her poor little throbbing head! She was dreadfully frightened, too, at being alone; but she was too weak and too sick to move or to call out, and she ached and trembled all over from the unusual exposure to the night air to which she had been subjected. She and Bertram had been put away in the cabin, and there was only one dim tallow candle, stuck all on one side in a hole in the rickety wooden table in the middle. Grace did not see that Bertram was just behind her till he too awoke, and began to look round and move about.

"Oh! Gracey, Gracey!" said he, "where are we? Why does everything move so?"

Grace could only groan, and Bertram, a far better sailor, crept to her side, and put his little hot hand to her head. He didn't mind the rolling of the vessel, or the noises and smells with which they were surrounded, but his head throbbed, and he could not remember what had happened to them, for he had hardly shaken off the effects of the drug. The poor children were left alone for some hours, till they became faint from exhaustion.

The gipsies were bound for the north of England; and, instead of travelling by land, as they usually did, they engaged one of the gang, the Black Sam of whom Nora and Nat spoke, and who was a smuggler as well as a gipsy, and owned one or two small vessels, to take them by sea, as they greatly dreaded the cholera which was at that time raging in the southern and midland counties.

A small party of the gipsies had been sent round by Headless Lane to secure some money, which Nora had forgotten when sent there some time before, but they were all to meet—as, in fact, they did—at Pester Creek, to be conveyed on board Black Sam's ship. They were a rough, bad lot; but it had never been part of their trade, nor would it have answered to them, to steal children. Hubert, their head, or chief as they called him, was both puzzled and vexed at the strange chance which had almost obliged them to take off the young Astleys. He had wished at first to send them straight home, but old Gran had disuaded him from this by holding out hopes that a reward would be offered for them, and also by representations of the danger of letting them go without discovering how much of the secret of the cave and passage they knew,—for she persisted in declaring that they were awake when she found them, and that they must have heard her talking with Nora about the treasure and the trap-door.

The discussion, or rather quarrel, was resumed as soon as the sailing of the ship left the gipsies at liberty, and so excited did they become on the subject that the sun was high in the heavens before anyone thought of going to see after the little ones.

Nora, overcome with fatigue and sea-sickness, was lying on deck, on a sort of couch made for her by the kindness of one of the gang,—for poor Nora was loved by them all. By the time she was able to creep up again, many hours had gone by, and still the chief and old

Gran were at issue about the children, and still the poor little half-fainting victims were alone below. Nora approached Gran, and asked what had become of "them?"

"Down below," was the short reply; and Nora crept down the stairs, or rather ladder, to the cabin. The light was still flickering, and looked strange and dreary in the broad sunshine. Grace had sunk quite back upon her rags, with her white parched lips open as she gasped for breath. Bertram was curled up at her side, supporting his aching head with both his hands. Nora was touched at the sight of their helpless misery, and with all her little strength she raised poor Grace's head.

Bertram turned at the sound, and said, in a hoarse voice, "Water— O, please, give us water!"

She fetched some, which he drank with avidity; and she then made Grace as comfortable as she could, wetting her lips with brandy, and, after a little, succeeding in pouring some down her throat. The poor child revived greatly after this, and soon was able to sit up, leaning her head against Nora's shoulder, though she was too much exhausted to speak. Bertram sat up, too, and looked better.

"What's your name?" he began. "Where are we, and why are we here?"

"I am Nora," said the girl, in a low, musical voice as she slowly lifted her eyes from his sister's face to his own.

"Nora? What Nora?" he repeated; and then changing his tone—"Oh, if you could give me something to eat!"

Nat came in at that moment, and Nora begged him to fetch her some food. He was "a man of Kent," and had joined the gipsies a year or two before. A rough, bad specimen was he; but every one did as Nora wished. He obeyed, therefore, and soon returned with a portion of a most savoury mess, to which no one had more right than Bertram and Grace Astley, seeing that it was chiefly composed of rabbits from their father's woods. Grace could not eat; but Nora and Bertram did justice to the repast; and then the poor boy began to recall the past. They ate in silence; but, when he had finished, he turned to Nora, and said,—

"'Where are we now? and where are we going to? Are we going to mamma? Oh! why did you take us!" and the sobs began to burst forth.

Nora's eyes filled with tears.

"We are going to the north," she said; "we shall live there a long time, but I will beg them to let you stay with me. I may not go out as they do, I am weak; and if they will let you stay, I will make you happy."

"But who are they?" persisted Bertram; and Grace opened her eyes and listened, too.

"We are gipsies," said Nora, slowly, as if each word was dragged from her.

Both the children began to cry.

"Hush! oh pray, pray, hush!" said Nora, imploringly, as the door burst open, and old Gran hobbled in.

"What are ye kicking up this confounded noise for!" she exclaimed, as she hit Bertram a blow that sent him against the sharp corner of the table, the blood streaming from his face.

Grace screamed, and Nora sprung up to catch him as he fell. The old witch gave Grace a ringing box on the ear, and called to Nora to "leave palavering the brat and tend to her."

Hubert appeared at the door before Nora could obey, and just as old Gran was about to bestow a blow upon her, he arrested her arm from behind, exclaiming, "Strike Nora! No one shall dare to strike Nora, not even her mother!"

Nora looked her thanks as she supported the prostrate boy, and Gran hobbled off, cursing as she went.

"Nora!" said the chief, "I give these children to your charge, till we leave the ship."

Another grateful look from Nora, and he left the cabin. Nora did her best to comfort her young charge, but with poor success; that day was a sad and a long one for the trio. At night Nora told them that they must go to sleep, if they could, where they were, for there were no better beds to be had.

"But I haven't said my prayers," said Grace; and she tried to raise herself on her knees; but then came the recollection of the last time she had knelt in prayer, at her own little low chair, in her own little room at home; and the visions of that home and of her own gentle mamma rose before her, and the poor child cried bitterly. After a time, however, she roused herself sufficiently to go through her usual prayer, although the old familiar words " Bless papa and mamma, and all my dear brothers and sisters," called forth her tears afresh. Bertram was nearly as bad, and Nora watched them both with heartfelt pity, not, however, unmingled with envy, for she, too, longed to pray; but she knew not how, and she resolved that, at a fitter time, she would find out from the children all about that great God to whom she saw them raise their tearful faces and baby voices in such simple confidence. For Grace and Bertram prayed this night as they had never really prayed before. The words came from their hearts, and when they had done, they received their reward. They were calmer far, and they lay down to rest with a composure which astonished Nora.

The gipsies soon came pouring down into the cabin, for several of them slept there, although, as the nights were fine, most of them preferred the deck, both for meals and sleep. Few of them took any notice of the children, who, roused by the noise, were terribly frightened at the strange, wild forms and faces with which they were surrounded, and clung to Nora. They slept, however; but awaking very early the next morning before any of the gipsies were astir, their eyes met as they were staring round the room in fresh alarm and wonder at finding themselves in so strange a place.

"Bertram," said Grace, in a whisper, "is it a bad dream, and shall we awake and find ourselves at home?"

"No, Gracey darling," said the boy; "it is true. These are bad gipsies, and they have stolen us, and I don't know what will become of us. This is a ship we are in. I heard them talk last night."

"So did I, Bertram,—and oh, such bad words! Bertram, that tall, black woman said 'devil' so often, I hid my face not to hear. O mamma! mamma!"

"Don't cry, Gracey darling!" said Bertram, crying himself; "we'll run away!"

Next day Nora whispered to them, as the other gipsies were leaving the cabin, that they had better pretend to be ill still.

"For then," said she, " I can keep you here; if you are well, Gran'll get ye. Gran's my mother."

Bertram shrank from her at this news; but her mournful looks and sweet, low voice soon overcame his horror. It was no great stretch for them to pretend to be ill, for Grace was dreadfully weak, and Bertram suffering a good deal from his contact with the table the day before.

A long, long day was this again. Nora's head was giving her such violent pain that she could hardly stir, and the other gipsies were tired of waiting upon her, or, more likely, forgot her altogether. The poor children were again nearly famished; but Bertram was kneeling by Nora's side, stroking her head gently, and Grace was clasping one of the gipsy's thin hands in both hers, when a great noise and stir on deck caused them all three to start. Voices were now heard approaching the cabin.

"Mamma!" said Grace, joyfully, as she raised her head and prepared to spring up.

"Nora! Nora!" said a voice outside.

Poor Nora's face flushed, and her beautiful eyes were lifted from the ground as the door was pushed open, and a tall young gipsy came eagerly forward. His happy countenance fell as he caught sight of her face.

"My poor Nora!—darling Nora! you are worse! Curse them, there is none to take care of you when I am away; and they make me leave you; but by——I will not again!"

"Hush! Charlie," said Nora, faintly; but she gladly rested her weary head on his firm, broad shoulder, and then her eyes closed again, and for some minutes no one spoke. At last Bertram said,—

"She has had no food to-day,—no one has brought us anything."

Charlie, who had been gazing gloomily on Nora's face, turned sharply at these words, and laying her head gently down, he left the cabin, but soon returned with a cup of tea. He held it to her lips, and the beautiful eyes slowly opened and turned up to his.

"Tea!" said Nora, in a tone of surprise.

"I brought it for you, Nora. I was waiting at D—— for Black Sam's Nancy, and I came off in a boat as soon as I saw her," said he softly.

The tea revived her, and Charlie was at liberty to attend to the children.

The rest of the voyage was performed with more comfort to them, as Charlie, who belonged to the tribe, remained, and devoted himself to them and Nora, and was able to procure for them many things which the poor young Astleys were now obliged to consider as luxuries, although hitherto they had looked upon them as the merest necessaries of life.

"We land in another hour, Nora darling," said Charlie at length; and the two children started up. Any change, they fancied, must be for the better; for, in spite of Charlie's and Nora's kindness, they had done little but cry for home and mamma, and beg Nora to take them back. And Nora would cry, too, and soothe them, and ask them questions about home.

"Gran says," continued Charlie, "that there must be a change here;" and he signed significantly towards the children.

"A change!—what change? Oh, don't kill us— *please* don't

kill us—we will do anything in the world!" screamed the children.

"No one's a goin' to hurt ye as long as ye don't hurt Nora," replied Charlie, pulling them away as they clung to her. "Gran's a coming," he added; and Gran hobbled into the cabin, followed by another gipsy carrying some rags and wigs of different sorts. She proceeded to seize Grace.

The terror which the poor little girl had entertained for the old woman ever since that dreadful whisper in the cart kept her pale and mute, while her once beautiful but now tangled and matted curls were cut quite close to her head. The gipsy then divested her of all her nice clothes, and clad her completely in rags,—first rubbing her face, and neck, and chest, and hands, and arms all over with walnut-juice,—finally fixing, with consummate art, a flaxen wig upon her head.

Charlie had carried off Bertram, and now appeared leading a little brown-skinned, red-headed boy, clothed likewise in rags and tatters, whom Grace could by no means recognize as her own darling brother.

Regardless of the children's tears, Gran and the other gipsy laughed heartily at the metamorphoses, and Charlie joined in the merriment, until he saw Nora's tearful face lifted imploringly towards him.

The landing soon commenced with great activity. The children were left with Nora to the last by Charlie's management, and were then conveyed straight to the cart. It was late in the evening when they arrived at the vast common which was to terminate their travels for some time. A drizzling rain was falling, and the three friends remained in the cart while the gipsy-women made their preparations for supper—Nora in a half-dozing state, Bertram, with his already pale and dirty little face pressed against one of the tiny windows at the side, gazing wearily out into the increasing darkness, and poor Grace crying quietly but bitterly. The child had done little else since she left her home, for she pined dreadfully for the kindness and comforts to which she had been accustomed, and her little tender face was quite blistered with her tears.

There were many other gipsy encampments on this common,—for it was a wild spot, and was, in fact, a kind of headquarters of the tribe,—and for some days the party to which Bertram and Grace belonged were busy coming and going, settling themselves and hunting up their friends.

Meantime, poor Nora did not seem to recover from the fatigue

of her sea-voyage, but spent almost all her time on her couch of
rags. When the sun was not too powerful, she would creep out
and rest under one of the grassy banks between which the tents
were pitched, and the carts—for several had met them at landing—
were drawn up. Bertram and Grace followed her like her shadow,
all three instinctively avoiding the rest of the tribe excepting Charlie,
who joined them whenever he could, which, however, was not often,
for Hubert always seemed to know, by magic, the instant he came
to them, and was sure to send for him on some pretext or another.
The children, and Nora, and old Gran, her mother, had a tent to
themselves; but the old woman was out all day, and the greater
part of the night, too, sometimes. She generally came back very
tipsy, and always in a bad temper, so Nora and the little ones pretended to be asleep when they heard her. She was the widow of
the last chief—a weak man, whom she had completely ruled, and
through him the tribe, who still, from long habit, paid some deference
to her; but her temper was fast destroying her influence over them.

One evening, she suddenly entered the tent at an unusually early
hour, and in a worse humour than ever. Nora and the children
had just returned from the bank, and were standing near the
entrance watching Charlie, who had been with them and was now
going to join a noisy supper-party assembled at some distance
round a low smouldering fire.

Gran exclaimed, angrily, giving Bertram a push as she came up,
"Idling, as usual, you young varlet. Nora, girl, you spile 'em for
any good. I'll take 'em out wi' me to-morrow, and find 'em work.
Them as eats must work. and them as doesn't work ma'n't eat!"

This speech was interspersed with many an oath, and Bertram's
pale face flushed, while Grace clung trembling to Nora, whispering,
"Don't let me go! Oh, keep me! save me!"

"They ain't fit for work, mother!" said Nora, feebly; "they ain't
been brought up to it like us."

"Like us, you fool!" said the old beldame. "Like me, you mean:
d—l a stroke o' work you've been good for; bad enough in your
father's time, and wussur a great deal sin' Hubert keeps you up
to yeer nonsense."

Nora made no reply, and the old woman mumbled on in the
same strain till sleep overpowered her. Grace was suddenly awoke
at early dawn next day to the consciousness that the scarcely human
face and two hideous fangs of the old gipsy were within an inch
of her pillow; and before she could recover her breath enough to

scream, the thin, skinny finger was held up, and a voice, that excited every nerve in her brain to agony, whispered, "Don't scream; Nora sleeps!"

The right chord had been touched. Grace glanced towards the poor girl as she moved uneasily on her wretched bed, with one cheek flushed like fire, and the other deadly pale, while the mournful expression of her sad face was sad to behold; and frightened as she was, Grace could not find it in her heart to disturb Nora, nor even to call Bertram, for fear of waking her. Trembling, she arose at the gipsy's whispered commands, and put on her few miserable rags.

"Step lightly, and follow me," was the next order; and Grace obeyed.

Her heart sank as she crept from under the tent after the old tyrant, and she even hesitated and looked back, and was on the point of screaming, when a hard hand gripped her throat, and the old gipsy, in another moment, lifted her some paces from the spot, and then, putting her down with a shake, bade her "be quiet, or that scream should be her last."

"Let me pray! oh, let me pray!" said the poor child, in a whisper, firmly believing that her last hour was come.

The only answer Gran vouchsafed was seizing her again and running off with her till they were some paces beyond the most scattered tents of the encampment. She then set her down again, and, roughly snatching off the flaxen wig, she proceeded to rub all over the child's head and short-cropped hair some stuff out of a dirty bottle, which she took from her pocket. In a few minutes Grace's hair was as decidedly golden as it had been before a decided and very dark brown.

"Now," said the old hag, "you are my grandchild, remember; and if you say one word—remember, one word—I'll wuss than wallop ye, and Nora, too. D'ye ken—ye're *dumb—dumb*!" she repeated, with horrible emphasis.

Poor Grace trotted many weary miles that day after old Gran. They went through towns and villages, and Gran begged of some people and told others their fortunes; and admirably did she change her tone to suit the different individuals whom she met; for she was a clever woman, though a bad one. She had travelled much, and could assume at pleasure any dialect that pleased her, Irish, or Scotch, or provincial. Some people passed them by without paying any attention to Gran's whine, or her saucy "Will I tell yer fortune, my pretty lady! Ah, it's a good one, I see, by the bright een!"

Some were moved by her apparent misery, or by the little girl's piteous looks, and gave them pence; and one well-dressed little boy, who was driving his hoop in a street, stopped and gave her a large piece of bread that he was munching. Grace looked after him as he ran happily off, and longed to make him know how different she was to what she appeared to be. She felt dreadfully ashamed of her rags the first time they met a carriage full of ladies, and yet she would have given anything to have been in that carriage, safe from the old woman who watched her so narrowly.

As they passed through a field, between two villages, a respectable old lady, walking just in front of them, dropped something. Gran hurried on to pick it up. It was a purse! Bright coins glittered and peeped through the network.

"Shall I run on and give it her?" asked Grace, listlessly, though hardly able to walk, at the same time offering to take it.

A slap on the cheek, and a "D—l take ye!" was the only reply; and Grace perceived, to her horror, that Gran meant to keep the booty; and not only that, but the old woman had the audacity to hobble after the owner, and beg "a few halfpence—for she hadn't a farthing in the world, and neither she nor the child, dear lamb! had tasted a bit that blessed day."

The old lady stumped on, asserting that she "never gave to tramps," and little suspecting that in the present case the "tramp" would have been far more able to give to her.

After this, Gran found many opportunities of pilfering in a small way, and Grace's misery increased. That night she slept under a hedge, with no companion but the old gipsy. The poor child cried herself to sleep. Her feet were blistered and her head ached with so much walking, but the next day she had to be off again betimes. And thus she passed many days—although at last her little, delicate feet became so sore that Gran was forced to carry her, which greatly increased the old woman's ill-humour.

Nora and Bertram, on waking the morning that Gran had for the second time stolen Grace, at first supposed that she had crept out alone—but her prolonged absence alarmed them greatly; nor was their alarm diminished at hearing from Charlie that some others of the tribe had seen Gran and the child at break of day making for the Stantley road; and that the old woman had been extremely violent the night before, at the gathering of the elders, when a quarrel had arisen regarding the stolen children—some of the tribe being anxious that the reward offered for them should be claimed; while others, of whom Gran was one, were of opinion that there would be more danger than profit in giving them up;—that hot words had ensued, during which she had been reproached with wanting to rule all, when she contributed nothing to the common hoard. At this her passion had become ungovernable, and she had flung away from the fire—muttering, with fearful oaths, that she would find a way of making money by the children; adding something to the effect that they belonged to her, and her only, which words had not been thought worthy of attention at the time, but were now recalled, with many gloomy forebodings, when it was discovered that she had actually made off with Grace. There was nothing to be done. To follow her would only make matters worse—for by the rules of the tribe, she, having taken the child in the first instance, was alone answerable for its safety; besides which, Hubert was loth to enrage one who possessed secrets of the last consequence to many of their number.

Poor Bertram heard all that Charlie was telling Nora, and he saw that they both thought very seriously of Grace's danger, and the idea possessed his mind that the wicked old woman had taken his poor little sister to sell as a slave, nor could all their representations and assurances persuade him to the contrary. How or where he imagined this desirable object was to be accomplished is not known,—whether Grace was to be led through towns and villages, while Gran hallooed loudly, "Girl to sell—who'll buy a girl?" or whether she was to be hung up in a shop window, with other articles of commerce, marked in large letters, "For sale, price £5," he had not paused to determine,—but that for sale she was, to all intents and purposes, he felt certain, and he mourned accordingly.

CHAPTER VII

THE OLD MAN

ALL THIS TIME, although Nora and her little companions had had many long talks about the happy home which, but a few weeks back, the latter had been so willing to leave, and to return to which they would now have been too glad, still Nora had never yet summoned courage to question them upon that subject, which, more than others (excepting perhaps *one*) interested her now—I mean religion. Nora knew that there was a God above, and that good people prayed to him; and she had heard that if she was good in this world, he would reward her in the world to come; and that if she were wicked here, she would be punished there. She had heard, too, of our Saviour, and she knew that he had come down among us; and this was all the poor girl's religion. Her delicate health, sweet temper, and sensitive nature, had preserved her from much harm; but that very sensitiveness was also the source of much misery to her, for it had, from long indulgence, grown into a morbid dread of doing the least thing which she imagined might be displeasing to the Almighty, and draw down his wrath upon her; for Nora had never learnt to look upon God as a father, nor did she know that "perfect love casteth out fear." These wretched feelings increased as her failing health strengthened her tendency to low spirits; and her natural reserve of character would have prevented her from uttering a word on the subject even had there been a single person in all her world with whom such confidence had been possible. But though all the tribe loved Nora in their own rough way, there was no one to whom she could have related her doubts and fears with the slightest hope of their being understood, even had she been so inclined. Charlie had loved her from their childhood, but even he could not understand her, although he was more to her than all the world besides. Charlie's love—the thought of Charlie, was the one bright calm spot in her dark and troubled mind, and even this at times was not unclouded; for although she never tried to look on into the dim future, yet she could not wholly banish a vague and almost unacknowledged, but sadly increasing, foreboding which crept into her heart at times—a foreboding that whispered to her that she must die—die alone and in her earliest youth—long, long before Charlie could take her from her wretched mother's tent, and from the wandering life so unsuited to her, and which he, too, for her sake, was beginning to long to leave. Poor Nora! Her heart was indeed a sad and lonely one, in spite of all Charlie's efforts to cheer her. He, poor fellow, wilfully closed his eyes to what was but too plain to all the others,—that Nora might be among them yet a very little while; and if a doubt—a pang— did cross his heart as he gazed into her mournful, speaking eyes, or at her almost transparent cheek, he resolutely drove it back, determined to read nothing that was therein written save the refined beauty so rare among that wild race.

The young Astleys had been sources of the greatest comfort to Nora, although she bitterly reproached herself with having been the cause of their misfortunes. She had listened with avidity to their talk of home and happy days gone by. She was their only friend in their wretched banishment. Not to love her would have been impossible, had they known her even in their days of happiness; but now they were rapidly learning to forget that she was but a gipsy girl, and to talk to her with more openness than they had ever shown to any one else in the world. They would run on for hours with a host of reminiscences, while Nora would lie perfectly still, encouraging their confidence with her sad, beautiful eyes, and now and then asking some question which drew forth long descriptions of "Mamma's beautiful, gentle ways," or Mrs. Abel's funny ones, and of all the little brothers and sisters, and every room and corner of the "dear, darling house at home," as Gracey called it,—till Nora felt as if she knew it all quite as well as the children did; and she thought that it must be a very fairyland, and the people who lived there must be happier than she had fancied it possible for anyone to be in this world. Lady Astley especially she longed to see. She could not tell her doubts to the children, from a strange feeling that they were too far above her,—that if they heard all that was in her heart, they must despise her; and yet, with an inconsistency not unusual in her state of health, she fancied that to this sweet, gentle mother of whom they talked she could open her mind without any fear,—and to this fancy she clung with a strange tenacity, pining for its realization as for something which would for ever set her mind at ease, and even perhaps make her strong as others; for she felt, truly, that could she be at peace, it would go far to improve her health. But now Grace had gone, and Bertram was too restless and miserable about her to talk of anything else. It was a very bad day with Nora, and though the sun was shining brightly and the birds were singing merrily, the poor girl could not leave the tent, nor even her wretched bed, till very late in the afternoon when, with the help of Bertram's shoulder, she crept out to the mossy bank, intending to remain there till the cold evening air warned her to return. Bertram stayed with her for some time, but at last begged to be allowed to go round the encampment and to climb the opposite mound, with a restless hope that by so doing he might by chance see something of Grace and the old woman.

"The gipsies are all out, and I shan't meet anybody, Nora," said he, "and I'll promise to come back;" for he had heard Gran's threats, "that Nora should suffer for it if the children escaped," too often not to be well aware how great must be her dread in losing sight of them.

She could not wish to deny him this slight gratification, and he was soon out of sight

Before he had been gone many minutes, old Drudo, who had been grazing at some distance, but gradually getting nearer, now came quite close to her, hoping to receive, as usual, something from her hands.

Grace and Bertram had become great friends with the old horse, and he was in the habit of coming to them to be fed and patted whenever they were sitting with Nora out of doors; and now the poor horse pushed its worthy old nose into Nora's lap, and bent its ears forward, asking for its accustomed portion. Nora was half lying, half sitting on the ground, and, though not generally nervous about horses, she felt too weak and ill on this day to bear the great head so close to her, and she wished Bertram would come back. She tried to raise herself to look round for him, at the same time pushing old Drudo away with all her little strength. The movement brought on a violent fit of coughing, with a feeling of intense oppression on her chest. It was followed by a sensation of relief; but, at the same moment, the green mossy bank, upon which she leaned forward, was dyed with the blood which flowed from her mouth. Few can tell the pang of hopeless, bitter agony that shot through the poor girl at that moment. Then, for the first time, did she realize the awful truth that she must die, and in an instant the words seemed as if seared into her heart—"I must die—die!" There they were, burning with an intensity that imparted an untold anguish to every breath she drew. A terror seized her, too, that her last hour was at hand—that she must die alone; and even at that dreadful hour the thought of Charlie was with her. She could not speak, but her lips formed the words, "Save me—oh, save me, Charlie!" Most of the other gipsies were gone to a fair, and those that were left were too far off to hear her, even had she been able to call. The common having a bad name, few people frequented it; but happily for our poor Nora on this sad day, one solitary individual was jogging along on his old grey pony, and just at this moment was preparing to cross the ravine in which the dying girl was lying. It was an old man, and one who had travelled much and seen and

E

felt much, both of sickness and sorrow, and yet his heart had not become callous to suffering. He had paused for a moment before descending the bank from which he just caught sight of the gipsy tents, for he had been warned to avoid them in these their own retreats, as they were reported to be suspicious and revengeful in the extreme towards anyone whom they imagined to be a spy upon them; and he hesitated between running the risk of provoking their anger and the disagreeable alternative of going a long way round. A moment's scrutiny convinced him, however, that the encampment was all but deserted. A few dirty children alone were playing by a heap of stones at the farther end of the ravine, and two or three miserable-looking horses jumped spasmodically near them, their wretched legs confined by shackles; but there were no fierce-looking men or wild dirty women, and the old man leisurely got off his horse, and began to descend the steep bank on which he stood. At this moment his eye fell on a horse, of a somewhat better description than the others, standing in a far more free and unshackled attitude, with its head drooping over the figure of a girl—a figure bending almost to the ground. The strange couple were but a few paces from the old man, and he lost no time in approaching them. The horse started as he came up, throwing back his head and snorting as if to forbid a stranger to touch the body of his young mistress, and *but* a body the old man at first feared it was, so motionless was the girl. Another moment, and a faint groan re-assured him. He gently raised her from the ground; her face was deadly pale, and her eyes half-closed; but she was not fainting—one thought now en-grossed her mind, with a force that excluded all outer objects. Could she—might she—but live to see Charlie once more, but once, and she would be "content to die."

The old man looked round for some fitting place for her; to leave her where she was, was impossible. Her mother's tent was the nearest, and there was a longer space between it and any other. Gently he lifted her in his arms and carried her towards it, while poor Drudo followed, with drooping head, apparently well aware of the hopeless state of his only friend; and the old man's own patient pony stood in dogged unconcern at the trouble its old master was having. The old man laid her on the bed from which she had but lately risen, and then returned to his own well-filled saddle-bags to seek for some simple remedy that might be of service to her. As he returned to her side, she slowly opened her eyes and gazed at him; but it was a stony, stolid gaze at first, and when it brightened into her own peculiar, imploring expression, there was mingled with it no surprise at the unusual figure bending over her, and one word only escaped from her lips.

"Charlie!" she whispered; but the single word, or rather the tone in which that word was uttered, spoke volumes of love and fear, fear that "Charlie" would not be in time.

"You must not talk, my poor child," said the old man, kindly; "I will fetch Charlie when I have done all I can for you!"—and he proceeded to apply the means which his not slight knowledge of medicine dictated.

"Now," said he, "I would willingly stay with you if I could, but it must not be. I will try to find someone in the tents who can take care of you, and who will understand my directions; and now, my poor child, may God bless you, and spare you, and in His own good time take you to Himself!"

"I must die?" interrupted Nora, in a startling whisper. The words were uttered in the form of a question, but of one the answer to which none could doubt.

"We must all die!" said the old man, with solemnity.

"But now?—soon?" persisted Nora, in the same tone; for the words "and spare you" had given her one ray of hope, and she fixed her eyes upon him as if she would pierce through and through any attempt at deceit.

"My poor, poor child," said the old man, "and is it so hard to die? Oh, if it but pleased the Almighty to take me in your stead, and to spare you, if only for the few short months that might be my lot on earth, that you may have time to prepare for death! It is a weary, dreary world, without the love of God; but no wonder that you have not found it so yet."

He paused a moment, and then resumed: "If God wills it, you may yet live. It may be but a few short years, or even months; in all human probability it can be but months; but, O my child, do not neglect this warning,—prepare to meet thy God!"

Nora's tears were flowing freely at this solemn appeal, and her thin hands were clasped together, but she could not speak.

At this moment a noise outside the tent attracted the old man's attention, and he went out just in time to rescue the saddle-bags from the claws of the gipsy children, who, having caught sight of the sober figure of the old pony, had lost no time in attacking him. The old man tried to make them understand the cause of his lingering in their domain, but the little rebels pretended not to understand his words, and only answered by shouts and shrieks, and, in some cases, by running away. Leading his pony, he then sought the farther tents, in hopes of finding someone to whose care he might confide his patient. One very old and hopelessly deaf woman was, however, the only living being he could discover. After a few fruitless efforts at making her comprehend his errand, he gave it up in despair and, returning to Nora's tent, he tore two leaves out of his memorandum-book and wrote in a legible hand a few simple directions for her treatment, adding at the end these words, "If these directions are followed, I see no reason why, with the blessing of God, this poor girl should not live some weeks, or it may be months."

He then read it to Nora, telling her that he did so in case it should happen that none of her tribe could read; but as this was most unlikely, he should leave it pinned to the tent. Having done this, he once more blessed her and left the tent, without observing two merry little black eyes that were watching him from behind the entrance the whole time. It was getting dark as he mounted his pony and jogged slowly out of the valley. No sooner was he fairly out of sight than the little black eyes peeped farther out of their hiding-place, and the small owner thereof followed cautiously and quietly. Nora was lying quite still, with her eyes closed. The child crept in on her hands and knees, then slowly raised herself upon her feet and looked round. Her eyes were first directed to the spot where she had seen the strange man pin the paper. Its bright, smooth surface and shining edges excited her cupidity, and she hastened to snatch it down. Turning round, she first perceived Nora's deathlike form, rendered the more terrible by the fast-fading light. She flew from the tent as if she had seen a ghost—and was soon in the midst of her young companions, declaring to the wondering little ones how the old man who had driven them from his pony had first written down some words, and then read them out over poor Nora; that the words said she should not live many weeks, and, accordingly, that she was already lying dead in her tent, while the old man had escaped.

With one accord all the children set off for Nora's tent, outside of which they spent the next ten minutes,—the boldest among them cautiously approaching to peep in, in hopes of seeing a real dead body that they had known in life. But the increasing darkness jealously guarded the features, and the dim, still outline of a form was all that the bravest could descry.

Just at this moment Bertram, who had wandered on and on, fancying he saw his sister in every distant form of sheep or cow on the common, and had for some time lost his way, now returned to the bank where he had left Nora. He was rather surprised not to find her there; but he supposed Charlie had come back and taken her in. He went on towards Gran's tent, and wondered to see the ragged little party which surrounded it. Why should they peep in and crowd round that tent usually so neglected? Why should they seem to fear to enter it? Some of the children now caught sight of him, and in a moment he was surrounded. Some seized his ragged little coat—some his arms and hands—some mischievous ones took the opportunity of the confusion to give him sly kicks and pinches, and one sturdy little rebel sprung up and clung to his neck, nearly strangling the poor child,—for all were delighted to get Nora's boy, as they had learnt to call him, into their power at last, and all screamed and shouted around him. Poor Bertram did not at all understand or like this strange greeting. The words "Don't go in—don't go in!" were the first he could distinguish in the confusion. "Why?"—he struggled out the word between the dirty fingers which one of his tormenters placed over his mouth, evidently in the belief that although their own noise was of no consequence, one word from "Nora's boy" would wake the dead girl,—a most undesirable object, of course. "She's dead—she's dead!" screamed many small voices,—"you must not disturb her." Bertram sprang forward, dragging with him several future thieves, robbers and housebreakers. "Let him go, he'll be tarned," shouted one of the biggest; and, in another instant, Bertram was where none dared follow—at Nora's side. Could it be true? Was his last, his only friend, gone from him for ever? Must he henceforth make one of the unruly tribe outside? All childish fear of death was lost in this appalling dread. "Nora, Nora," said the poor boy, in a voice of agony; "Nora! you are not dead—you shall not die!" and he took one of her attenuated hands in both his little chubby ones. Nora slowly turned her head towards him and smiled. His voice was the first thing that roused her from the dreamy state in which she had remained ever since the old man left her. Bertram burst into tears. He did not see—he did not notice the sad change that had come over during his short absence. It was enough now that she was not dead, as they had so cruelly told him, and his poor little troubled spirit was soothed and relieved by his tears. The dark hours of night came on, and slowly passed away, and the

young heir to wealth and rank still lay curled up on the ground by
the side of the dying gipsy girl. He neither moved nor spoke—
perhaps he slept—and yet, if she but moved her hand, his little head
was raised from his hands and his eyes fixed upon her, and not one
whispered request for "water" was unheard. He did not ask what
had brought her to this state: he was satisfied that at least she was
with him still, and there he sat, scarcely daring to breathe, for fear
of disturbing Nora, watching the soft moonlight gradually descending
the opposite bank, and creeping and stealing in succession over
each dark tent in the valley.

The girl had relapsed into a dreamy, half-dozing state, and thus
she remained till morning brought several of the other gipsies to
see after her. Great kindness was shown to both her and Bertram,
but several attempts were made to draw him from her side, and to
persuade him to join the wild games of the other children. He
clung in such fear to Nora's hand, however,—and, above all, she
seemed so unwilling to part from him, that they were at last allowed
to have their own way, which was to be left as much as possible to
themselves.

In the course of that day almost all the gipsies returned to the
valley, and many and various were the news, and strange the tales
and adventures, that were told round the fires that night; but Nora
and Bertram heard none of it; their little tent was as a convent in
the midst of a populous city, and they knew nothing of what was
going on.

CHAPTER VIII

NORA AND CHARLIE

THAT DAY and the next passed, and still no news of Grace, and
still was Bertram carefully and tenderly nursing poor Nora. And
she was better, though but very, very little. There was great weakness, and great disinclination for speaking; but she was, as it were,
more alive than she had been. In proportion as she rallied, she
grew restless, and poor Bertram's task became more difficult to him,
and more than ever he longed for Grace, or, at least, Charlie; but

Charlie had been sent out on a long expedition, and the poor boy felt that he had no hope of ever seeing his darling sister again.

Nora now liked him to sit by her and talk. The sound of his pleasant child-voice seemed to soothe her during the long, weary hours of the day; but she could make him little answer, and he was often somewhat puzzled to know how to amuse her. She liked best to hear about Combe Astley and his mamma; but these were just the subjects most painful to the poor little fugitive. He could not now speak of them without crying, so forcibly did they bring "Gracey" to his mind, and so bitterly did he miss this last little bit of home. At last, one day, when Nora was particularly restless, it occurred to him that she might like to hear him repeat something pretty and soothing.

"I wish I knew as much poetry as Gracey does," said he. "She could say lots and lots of pieces to you. She knows—'Around the Fire one Wintry Night,' out of the little green book; and 'My Name is Norval,' and Mrs. Somebody's 'Lament over her Dead Bird;' and oh, a lot more, besides Gray's 'Elegy,'—at least most of it, because I know mamma was giving her a penny for every verse that she learnt; but I can't say anything except a bit of —'Friends! Romans! countrymen!' and that isn't poetry—besides, you wouldn't care for that. I know some verses out of the Bible though, if you would like that; would you?"

"Yes—O yes!" was the whispered reply; and the gipsy girl turned her large sad eyes full upon him, and waited eagerly.

Bertram repeated the fifty-third chapter of Isaiah, which he had learnt during the last Passion Week; and Nora, attracted by the beauty and poetry of the language, though unable to understand the meaning, rewarded him with a whispered,—

"More—say more."

Bertram pondered, and then said,—

"I don't think I know any more whole chapters; but I can say verses." And he began accordingly:—"Whom the Lord loveth He chasteneth, and scourgeth every son whom he receiveth." He stopped for a moment, and then added, as if he had just thought of something: "Nora, do you know, I think God must love you very much. You see he has let you be ill, and it says he chasteneth people that he loves."

Nora shook her head, but whispered, "Go on."

He thought she meant with the verses, and he proceeded: "'Come unto me all ye that labour and are heavy laden, and I will give you rest. Take my yoke upon you, and learn of me, for I am meek and lowly in heart, and ye shall find rest unto your souls; for my yoke is easy and my burden light.' "

A low sob interrupted the child.

"Nora, I have tired you," said he; "I am so sorry."

"No," sobbed poor Nora; "say it again."

He repeated the verse; and there was a silence in that lowly tent, in which words like these had never before been heard.

Nora's faint sobs subsided. Bertram's head had fallen on her hand, and his thoughts had wandered far away. He was thinking of the last time he had repeated that verse, when he stood by his sister's side, before his own beautiful mamma, who was sitting with Mrs. Abel on the great bench on the lawn in front of his happy home. He had gabbled it over then, longing to have done, that he might be free to run where he liked. Sorrow had touched his young heart, and far differently did he utter those blessed words now, as, far, far from his friends and his home, he crouched in poverty and loneliness by the dying gipsy's bed.

"Say it again," repeated Nora; and he obeyed.

She interrupted him at the first words.

"You can go to Him; you are good. I can't," was her whisper.

Nora was forced to pause for breath between every few words.

"O Nora!" replied Bertram, "don't you know you mustn't say that, because there was a Man in the Bible called our Saviour good,— even our Saviour himself,—and He stopped him, and said, 'There is none good but one, and that is God.' "

"But you pray," replied Nora, in the same short whisper—" "you pray; I can't."

"Not now, because you are so ill," replied the boy; "but when you are better, you will say your prayers again."

"I never prayed," was the reply.

"Ah, Nora! you are ill now, and cannot, perhaps; but all grown-up people pray, though children forget sometimes. I often forgot before I was——"

"Stolen" he was going to say—but, with instinctive delicacy, he changed his sentence——

"Before I came away. I didn't think so much about goodness till I came here, and was unhappy—at least, I mean, till Gracey said it wouldn't do to run away from here, but that we must pray to God to let us get back to mamma, and so we do. She said because of that verse, 'Whatsoever ye shall ask in my name, that will I do.' "

"Teach me!" whispered the gipsy.

"Teach you what, Nora?" was the simple reply.

"To pray," said Nora.

"O Nora! anyone can pray—at least anyone whom God teaches, mamma says; and she told me to begin by asking Him to teach me how, and then to say, at the end, 'For Jesus Christ's sake' "—and the child bowed his head with reverence.

"Pray for me," said Nora.

"We do every night, Nora—Gracey and I both. We settled it that night we got into the tent, and you kept us from Gran. We say, 'Pray God to bless Nora for being kind to us, and make her well.' "

"Pray now—here," persisted Nora.

Bertram paused; for, although his heart had been opened by his own sorrows, and by pity for the sick girl, he shrank from taking the great, and, as it appeared to him, the "grown-up" office of praying for and with another person. But Nora's imploring eyes were fixed upon him, and he could not refuse. He knelt up by her side, therefore, and clasped his little hands together, as he had been taught to do at home, and said, in his peculiarly musical and childish voice,—

"O Lord God! I beseech Thee to teach me to pray for poor Nora. If it please Thee, make her well and strong like me, and able to pray to Thee again. Give her strength and patience to bear to be ill as long as it is Thy will. Teach her to love Thee and to obey Thee. Hear my prayer, for Jesus Christ's sake. Amen."

Could Lady Astley have seen her boy at this moment, would she have found it in her heart still to grieve for his loss—for his sufferings and privations?

As Bertram concluded his little prayer, Nora's head was turned from him, and burning tears were raining down her face, and dropping through her thin fingers; but she was happier now. For the first time, in what had seemed to the poor girl a long, long life— although it numbered but seventeen years—for the first time, the message of peace had visited her weary, aching heart, and she was comforted. There was much to be done yet—much to be heard— much to be explained and understood; and to help her—to do the work of a minister of God—there was but one little child, but this was enough; for "with God all things are possible."

Unconsciously, our little Bertram was, by God's blessing, ful- filling a mission to which many of the noblest and best among us have aspired—for which they have prayed in vain. His few simple words and childlike remarks and explanations were suited both to the capacity of his hearer and to the grandeur and importance of a subject often rendered intricate and—alas! that it should be so—wearisome, by long, wordy, so-called explanations.

The days passed more quickly now, and Bertram had little trouble in amusing Nora.

One evening they had been talking for some time, and Nora was quite tired. She had been sitting up too, for some hours that day; but, in spite of her fatigue, she felt better than she had done since the beginning of her illness, and very, very happy. She knew that she must die, but she did not feel afraid, except, perhaps, now and then for a minute at the idea of the actual dying. She had lost the far worse thoughts that had haunted her for so long. Her very ignorance was of service to her. There were no rooted prejudices and opinions to be overcome. Her mind was open to receive the simple teaching of a child—and as a little child did she hear His holy Word.

Her only earthly care was now for Charlie,—to see him once more and to tell him—to *make* him feel what she felt about the love of God and our Saviour; and she fancied, poor child, that her great love for Charlie must have power to turn him to repentance and faith. To persuade him to this—to induce him to leave the wild gipsy life, and to take Bertram home to his parents—was the task which Nora had resolved should be hers to accomplish before she might close her eyes on this sad toiling world. On this evening she lay pondering over it all, when a sound fell on her ear which raised a flush on her pale face—a sound which was so distant that none but herself would have heard it. Bertram had just left her to borrow something from one of the other tents, and she was alone. The sound was repeated. It was nearer this time, and still nearer it came, and the bitter tears sprang for one moment to Nora's eyes as she remembered that she could no longer answer Charlie's well-known call, or go forth to meet him, as she used to do; and then, for the first time, she remembered the shock her altered appearance must give him, and she would have given worlds to recall Bertram, to send him to meet Charlie, and prepare him to see her. But she could do nothing but lie still and wait, having at least the comfort of knowing that he would not pass her by; that hers would be the first tent he entered. But Nora did not recognize this as a comfort, but as a matter of course; for she had never for one moment had reason to doubt his entire love for her, and she would sooner have expected to find herself queen of England than to find Charlie care for anyone but herself.

The faithful and careful little Bertram met Charlie some paces from the tent, just as the latter was beginning to feel rather alarmed at receiving no answer to his repeated signals, for he well knew that Nora would not be risking the night air at this time. She must be in her tent. Why, then, did she not answer?

"Charlie," said the gentle voice of Bertram Astley, "I'm glad to see you back; so will Nora be—very glad; she's not been so well since you went, and has been in bed a long time, but she has been up to-day and is better. Come on."

The last words were, to say the least, unnecessary, as the gipsy was some paces in advance of Bertram at the moment, having stridden forward rapidly at the first mention of Nora's illness.

He entered the tent, but the darkness prevented him from seeing anything.

"Nora," said he—"Nora, where are you?"

He listened breathlessly.

"Here, lying down," said a whisper from one corner. "Charlie— my own Charlie!"

He groped his way towards her, more frightened than he chose to confess at the change, or rather loss of voice.

"My darling Nora; what have they done to you? Was it Gran?"

He always had an indefinite idea that any mischief, especially any evil to Nora, must by some mysterious means have been caused by that old woman, of whom he had the greatest horror, and of whom he had often been heard to remark that he could not imagine how she ever managed to have such a daughter as Nora. Bertram had run back to the great fire to light a candle, which, as a great privilege, was allowed to Nora; the sun and moonlight, or when these were not to be had, the blaze of fires, serving for the gipsies in most cases.

When the boy returned to the tent he found Nora looking so happy, and with such a lovely little colour in the cheek which was turned towards him, that he felt quite sure she must get well soon now.

Nora had longed for the light, that she might once more see the face she loved so well, the only one in all this vast wilderness of faces that she ever cared to look upon.

Charlie had dreaded it. He pretended it dazzled his eyes—that " it was so jolly to sit in the dark ;" but in truth he feared to see what that light might show him, though still he dared not own his fears even to himself, but pushed them back, and tried to escape from them. Yet, when the light came, he turned eagerly to Nora. Their eyes met. It was a long, lingering gaze. It seemed that neither of them could turn away, and yet each was reading what they would wish never to know. Charlie read that she must die, and she saw that he must be miserable. Poor girl! Her misery would have been increased fourfold had she been old enough to know that the more wretched he was at this moment the greater the probability of his finding consolation after she was gone. Her love for him had been her life; the love of him the one thing—the one object of her life; and it was but too unlikely that his love for her had been but one of many objects of passing interest—passing, though strong, and to be succeeded perhaps by many another as strong and as fleeting. But Nora knew none of this, and would not have believed it had she been told, nor would Charlie.

Charlie's eye fell beneath the feverish brilliancy of hers.

"My darling Nora, you have been ill indeed; but I know you must soon be well," said he. "I ain't to go again, and I've brought you a great many nice things—tea and candles, and, above all, some stuff that always cures people that are like you. I went to a doctor, and told him all about you, and he gave me one bottle, and is going to send more to Cross-stone at ten tomorrow, and I'll go and fetch it. I've paid him, Nora, so you needn't dread to take it. It'll make you fat and strong, he says, and like other people—not that I want you to be like the others though," added the young man fondly. "You are much better, to my mind. You never were like them, Nora darling. How came you so very, very different?"

Nora's heart beat very fast, and her courage almost failed her. She saw that he must be told. She had hoped that the sight of her would have done something towards preparing him to hear the sad truth; but when he went on to say, "Nora darling, you'll never be strong till you leave this wild tent life and live in a quiet cottage of your own," she felt that she must delay it no longer.

"Charlie!" she began, in a faint whisper, and then stopped from utter inability to proceed, so fast and so painfully was her heart throbbing.

But he bent his head forward and listened.

She went on confusedly and quickly, "Charlie, darling. It may never come—most likely never! I am ill, Charlie; but I am not—I am not afraid to die!"

The last words seemed as if spoken in spite of herself. There was a silence. His head was hid. This was not what Nora had expected. Bursts of grief and much agitation she had looked for, but not for this. She was frightened.

"Speak to me, Charlie, speak!" she whispered.

He neither moved nor spoke, but his head bowed lower and lower, and his whole frame was bent in agony.

"I have so much to say and so little time," were the next words that broke the silence, and she touched his hard, rough hand with her feeble dying one.

The touch or the words roused him. There was a deep sob which shook him from head to foot. The spell was broken and his tears flowed. Nora knew that this was bad for her. She felt each sob in every fibre of her frame; but it was better to bear than the awful sustained pause had been. Perhaps, however, she had hardly realized how painful it would be to see her own noble, manly Charlie melted to tears like an infant; and there is indeed something very terrible in the violent grief of a young man. Old men may weep, because they know that they have been men, and that nobody can deny the fact; middle-aged men may weep, because they know that they are men, and that everybody can see it; but a young man will not willingly be seen to weep until long after his claim to manhood is established, as the boyish fear of weakness and "girlism" and the dread of ridicule cling to the species most pertinaciously.

"Nora! it *is* not true. You shall not, must not, cannot——" He could not even say the word "die."

Poor Nora! Was it to be done all over again? But at least the idea had entered his mind. She looked around for Bertram to speak for her, but, with a tact rare even among his elders, the child had retired to his little couch in another corner of the tent and was fast asleep.

"Charlie, listen! I was very ill and alone. A kind old man came; he saved me, and said good words—beautiful words! I asked, and he said I must—die. He"—and she glanced at Bertram—"he prayed, and taught me; and, Charlie, I am ready. But, oh! be safe, be happy too!—believe in Jesus!"

She could say no more; but Charlie was alarmed at her gasping for breath, and the exhausted expression that came over her face.

"Nora! you shall not speak another word. I will hear anything to-morrow, when you are better, so that you rest now. I shall go."

"One minute—wait!" gasped the poor girl. "He—the old man—left a paper to tell; it is pinned on the tent!"

He rose to look, feeling as if nothing he read or saw could make any difference to his wretchedness; but anything to please Nora. He searched in vain of course, and soon left the tent, to wander in misery during the whole night over the common, longing, wishing to die, and firmly believing that he would do so immediately if he could. Nora was thoroughly worn out, and much disappointed at this unsatisfactory interview. She slept little that night, and when she did doze, her dreams were so fearful and her waking so painful, that she could not help wishing she might never sleep again. As morning dawned, Charlie wandered towards the encampment, pining and yet dreading to see Nora again, and half tempted to hope that the last night's interview had been but a horrible dream, of which the long night's wandering was but a continuation. His hope, such as it was, was soon crushed. Bertram was on the look out for him, and ran up the valley to meet him.

"Good morning, Charlie," began the boy; "Nora told me to watch for you, and I've been twice to your tent. She wants me to tell you everything, to prepare you, she said, because she can't talk much, and then, if you know most, she can finish, you know, and you'll understand. She has had a bad night, but I think she is dozing now."

"What does she want me to know?" said Charlie gloomily, standing stock-still.

"I can't tell, if you look so, Charlie," said the boy, "because it is very beautiful,—it is about her being so happy to die and go to Jesus Christ, who died for her—only she has two things on her mind," and Bertram forgot all about Charlie's looks and went on, warming with his subject: "one is about you; she does so want you to love God and our Saviour like her, and to pray with her. She said it would make her quite happy. I do believe, Charlie," continued the child, lifting his little woe-worn face up to the gipsy's,— "I do believe that you are the only person in the world she cares for."

Charlie's lip quivered, and he turned away, seating himself on a fallen tree close at hand, and hiding his face in his hands, while Bertram's musical tones ran on—

"You know," said he, mysteriously, drawing closer to Charlie and looking round, as if he feared Gran might hear,—"you know, though Gran is her mother, she can't be very fond of her, because she is so very bad. Charlie! do you know, I didn't know anybody could be so bad, and say such things, before I came here, and yet Nora has heard it always."

Charlie groaned, and interrupted the boy to ask what was the other thing on Nora's mind.

"I do not know," said he; "she said she must tell you that herself. Perhaps it is to see the old man again. I must tell you all that;" and he related all the particulars which Nora had been unable to give the night before, and ended by dwelling at length on Nora's great anxiety that Charlie should "learn to be good."

Charlie listened without speaking, and when Bertram had quite done, he only asked, "When may I see her?"

"As soon as she wakes. She said she would like you to feed her this morning," said Bertram, disregarding the apparent inattention to his own long story, as few older people could have done.

"To feed her!" These words opened a new and terrible view of her extreme debility to poor Charlie, and he impatiently sprang up, and walked towards the tent. Bertram ran in before him, to see if Nora was awake; and, as Charlie waited outside, he listlessly stooped to pick up a piece of paper which was partly concealed by the canvas. There was writing on the paper, but half erased; and, without knowing what he was about, he read the only distinguishable words:—" . . . this poor girl should not live many weeks, or it may be months." Had the anguish of the past night been as nothing? Was it all to come over again. The paper dropped from his hand, and he turned away with a fresh burst of agony .

It was the old man's paper, and Charlie knew it too well.

CHAPTER IX

AGNES VERNON

NOT FAR FROM the common on which our gipsies had pitched their tents was situated a small watering-place,—small at present, but rapidly increasing both in size and fashion. It consisted of a nucleus of houses, dignified with the name of "The Town" by its inhabitants, and of a few villas stretching out on each side, all professing to be more or less "elegant" or "desirable" till they were let, and then ceasing to make any professions at all. The very last and most detached of these "elegant family residences" was a long, low house, consisting of but two stories, the lowest of which was jealously guarded by a fierce-looking green verandah, while the windows in the one above were so close together that the heavy, projecting, tent-like blinds which protected them gave to the house the appearance of a chest-of-drawers with the top drawer left half pulled out. There was a little bit of green in front of the house, which thought itself a garden, but was decidedly mistaken. Shrubs bounded it on each side, and a little green fence and gate stood in front of it, to proclaim to the world that the bit of green was not public property, but was sacred to the inhabitants of the long, low house, whosoever they might chance to be at the time. At present, a Mrs. Vernon and her daughter Agnes were the enviable possessors of the house, garden, fence, and gate; and, as Agnes is at this moment sitting at the open window of her room finishing a letter, we will take the liberty of peeping over her shoulder. The window is a French one, and opens on to the veranda. Agnes has just come in from her ride, and has not taken off her habit. Her hat and gloves and whip are on the table by her side. She writes,—

"I have this moment come in from riding, and found your letter waiting for me on the drawing-room table. I left this unfinished in the morning in case there should be anything dreadful, important, or destructive to impart. But there is nothing. Mamma will 'be delighted to see you,' and all that; and, as for me, I don't dare to say whether I am glad or not, after your terrible sentence about 'romantic young ladies,' for fear you should set me down as one. By the by, I'm afraid I *must* be getting very romantic, now I come to think of it, which I assure you I never did before, and my reason is, that to-day, as I was riding along, I met the most horrible, supernatural—no, I mean unearthly-looking gipsy woman that ever was invented. Her (I must say it, so rub it out or look the other way) diabolical expression haunts me, but, happily, yet more so does the strangely mournful, pitiful look of the child she was carrying on her back. It was a girl, old enough to have been walking, but her tender little feet were bleeding, and she looked quite faint and exhausted. She fixed her eyes upon me as I passed, with a look that I shall never forget to my dying day.

"There!—don't you think my symptoms are very bad? That

'strangely mournful look,' and the 'tender little feet,' have a most dangerous appearance about them. But the last sentence I consider fatal. I mean the one beginning 'She fixed,' and ending with 'my dying day.' The fact is, that romance is the fashionable epidemic of this rural retreat, and I must have caught it of some of the young ladies whom I see daily strewed on the beach, attired in red petticoats and cocked hats. Under these appalling circumstances, perhaps you had better bring all your sober common sense here as soon as possible, and if you will add to it, as you pass through London, some French chocolate, you will greatly oblige me. It may be some consolation to you to hear that one great reason why I really do long to see you is, that I don't think I remember you quite as well as I did; I don't think of you quite as much as I did at first; and worse still, I can't *exactly* recall the peculiar wave—I should say air—of your nose. I discovered this sad truth yesterday, when, having drawn a caricature of you engaged in dancing a hornpipe with your sister's old governess, and having shown it to mamma, she exclaimed vehemently against your nose, and declared I had not done justice to it. Oh dear! when people begin to talk of the rights of women, and to call for justice for a nose, I really must go and dress; so you see, as I can think and talk of *you* with such unbecoming levity, I can't be romanticated past cure.

"Adieu, your most affectionate

"AGNES VERNON."

And Agnes sealed up her letter, and directed it to

"Reginald De Verrie, Esq.,
"Rangley Park,
"Henley."

And then she began to dress for a *tete-a-tete* dinner with her mother, talking to herself the while in a half-loud voice.

"It's all very well laughing it off," were her first words; "but the truth is, I cannot get that child's eyes out of my head. I believe I have thought of nothing but tortured children ever since he told me about those poor little Astleys. I cannot help now having a feeling that this child might be one of them, though I did not dare to suggest it even to him, for he said it was *impossible* that they should have been stolen; but yet one never knows."

She was silent for a few minutes, and then sat down to wait for her maid, slowly unweaving the thick, smooth plaits of her dark hair the while. Presently she added,—

"Yes; he certainly is as decided and unimaginative as I am the contrary of both; and when I am with him, I often think of that detestable Mrs. Elton's speech to Jane Fairfax in Miss Austen's 'Emma,'—'What a perfect character you and I should make if we could be shaken together.' But I suppose it is dreadfully presumptuous to think I could improve upon him in any way. It is not at all *en regle*. O dear! I am afraid I make a very bad lovess. I *cannot* look upon him as a model lover, so I shall not wait any longer for Macnade, but dress myself."

Agnes Vernon had been engaged to Reginald De Verrie for about half a year, and they were only waiting the return of her youngest brother from the Cape to be married. They believed that they were very fond of one another. Reginald, indeed, was quite sure of his own affection for her; but in the distance, in Agnes's mind there lurked sundry faint and unconfessed doubts, which must have gained in strength and importance, if she would have paused in the happy whirl of her life—paused to think and to enquire. But Agnes never thought. She was a very butterfly, and her happiness was a very surface happiness. There was no store set aside for a rainy day. What she believed to be thinking was no more than musing—jumping from subject to subject by an unconnected train of thought, without ever arriving at any conclusion.

Exactly at the moment when Agnes Vernon was signing her name at the conclusion of the letter to Mr. De Verrie, old Gran, with many a bright and ill-gotten coin in her dirty old pocket, and the anything but bright, but equally ill-gotten, Grace on her back, was once more approaching the encampment in which her poor daughter still continued to die, and Charlie and Bertram to mourn with perseverence that would have been most praiseworthy had it not been involuntary.

Charlie's grief fitted him better now than when last we saw him, though bad was that better, and very hard to bear. He had had many long talks with Nora, sometimes alone, sometimes with Bertram, and he thoroughly understood her wishes, and was resolved that, at least as far as regarded Bertram, they should be fulfilled to the very letter. He would take the boy home and deliver him up to his parents with his own hands, be the risk what it might;

and he told her that he only waited till Hubert and the greater part
of the gang were out together before he started with the child,
but in truth he could not bear to tear himself from her.

Nora had had a long talk with Hubert one day, when, at her
request, Charlie had taken Bertram for a walk on the common.
Hubert had long loved Nora himself, and he felt that he had a
right in her which none other could have, for it had been a custom
among this tribe, from time immemorial, for the chief to marry one
of the daughters of his predecessor. Hubert had been elected at
the death of Nora's father, and she was an only child. She sent
for him, therefore, to tell him—what he had feared for some time
past—that she must die; and she entreated him, in a few forcible
words, to take measures to find out what her mother had done with
Grace; to protect her and Bertram as long as they were with the
tribe ; and, finally, at least to connive in Charlie's plan for returning
them to their parents.

Hubert was deeply touched by the earnestness of her words. He
promised all that she required, and he did yet more; for instead of
almost invariably sending for Charlie if anyone was required, he
now left him entirely with her.

The "stuff" which the doctor had given to Charlie for her was
neither more nor less than cod-liver oil; and certainly its effects
were most wonderful at first. It seemed to stand in the stead of
all eating and drinking to the poor girl, and finally it brought back
her appetite. She was now able to creep out in the sunshine with
the help of Charlie's strong arm; and he was tremblingly daring to
think that he might hope; but he never got any further than that,
though Bertram openly and joyously declared his conviction that
she would soon be quite strong, and able to go with him and Charlie
"back to mamma,"—for Nora had told him that he was to be taken
home.

Poor Nora herself had no doubts. There was a feeling within
her that told her she must die; and although the new medicine was
of more benefit to her than it would have been to a person who had
been accustomed to good living, yet she was right.

As Gran and Grace approached the tent of the former, the child
lifted up her little feeble head and strained her eyes towards it, full
of hopes, and longings and fears, about her darling brother; but no
one was stirring. Gran hobbled on, grumbling as usual, and when
she reached the tent, she flung Grace down, as if she had been but
a bundle, swearing at her for giving so much trouble, and for daring

to have arms and legs enough to be about as heavy as a moderate sized terrier.

Nora and Charlie and Bertram were together, as usual; the latter was repeating aloud all the verses he could remember out of the Bible, now and then adding some simple remark of his own, while the others listened in silence.

At Gran's sudden entrance Charlie and Bertram started up, and in a moment the boy was at his sister's side, half out of his mind with mingled joy at seeing her again, and grief at the miserable appearance she presented. Her little, round, fat face had grown quite thin and pale; it was very dirty, too, and one or two red marks showed but too plainly the traces of old Gran's nails, while the flaxen hair was tangled and untidy.

Unconciously Bertram had forgotten the changes that had been effected in them both before they had left the ship. He had been thinking of Grace as the pretty little dark-haired home sister, and he could scarcely recognize her in this disguise.

Gran received the news of her daughter's illness with a fresh burst of bad language, chiefly directed against the unfortunate girl herself for having presumed to be ill without her amiable mother's permission, and for being so different from all the other gipsies.

Nora and her two companions felt that all peace and quiet had fled from that tent the moment old Gran put her foot in it, and they busied themselves, as far as they dared, in comforting and pitying poor little Grace, who was too thoroughly worn out and ill to do anything but lie quite still and cry quietly, still keeping her eyes fixed on Bertram, as if she could hardly yet believe that she really saw him again.

Although Gran was, as a matter of course, ill-tempered and violent on the night of her return to her so-called home, she was in reality highly pleased with the success of her expedition. The sickly appearance and mournful looks of poor little Grace had gained for her tormentor many an extra penny; and so elated was the old woman by her good fortune, that at a grand council held by the gipsies a few days after her return, she openly pronounced that there was "luck about those children," and strongly recommended, and graciously permitted, that Bertram should be made use of in the affair which they were now discussing, declaring that she would be satisfied to go equal shares with them in the spoil, and would not ask more, even if—through the loan of her boy—they got more than was calculated upon. This offer was listened to with avidity.

The plot was neither more nor less than to rob Agnes Vernon of the beautiful present that Reginald De Verrie had brought her from town, and of the contents of that present. It was not the French chocolate,—although he had brought her a large supply of that,—but it was a most costly and handsome dressing-case; and in the soft velvet of the deep drawer at the bottom sparkled many a gem, both "rich and rare,"—almost all wedding presents from the numerous circle of friends and relations whose high-sounding names will doubtless be dragged ere long into the notice of her marriage in the newspapers. The gipsies, in league with another numerous circle of friends and relations, namely, the smugglers, entertained not the remotest intention of allowing Agnes, either Vernon or De Verrie, to indulge in the worldly vanity of wearing these vain baubles any more. One of the gang had, in the garb of indigent poverty, watched her as she displayed them to a friend one day; and another had ascertained that she was in the habit of sleeping with her window open. Nothing, therefore, could be easier than to slip into her room and quietly march off with the dressing-case and its valuable contents. The smugglers' boat would be close at hand ready to receive the booty, and two or three of the gipsies, and convey them to a distant land, where the jewels might be disposed of without exciting suspicion. This was a plan which could scarcely fail of success; but there existed one great difficulty. Agnes slept with an open window, it is true, but not wide enough open to admit a man's body, and the difficulty was in finding a child small enough, strong enough, sharp enough, and sufficiently tractable for the job; and until Gran proposed Bertram it had seemed that the whole thing would, in all probability, fall to the ground for want of this model child-thief; for this kind of robbery was not usual to the gipsies, consequently the children of the tribe were by no means well educated in the line of villainy now required.

This great prize, however, promised to be so easily obtained that Hubert could not but feel it hard that it should be slipping from his grasp only for the want of one small-sized, first-class villain, when he had so many of all other sorts and sizes at his command. He doubted greatly, however, at first, as to Bertram's tractability—of his strength, size, and quickness, he was sure, but could he be made to do his part?

Gran grinned a hideous grin, and shook her skinny finger at him, while she declared that "she would answer for the brat; *she* would manage him." As no one doubted her capabilities of managing

this or any other brat, it was immediately decided that Bertram
should be at once the victim and the chief actor in the next scene
in which these amiable and praiseworthy people intended to act.

The next night was fixed upon as the latest term that Agnes
could be permitted to enjoy her jewels. The only difficulty was,
how to get the boy from his constant companions,—Grace, Nora,
and Charlie; and this Gran willingly undertook to accomplish.

Hubert felt sadly guilty of violating his promise to Nora; but the
oath which he had taken on being elected chief left him, in fact,
no will of his own in the matter, and all he could do to ease his
conscience was, to take care to be out of the way all day, that there
might be no possibility of an appeal from Nora, which could only
make him more unhappy, and could be of no use whatever to the
poor child.

Gran's diplomacy in this case was of a bold and straightforward
nature, that really did her credit. Instead of stealing off Bertram
as she had stolen his sister, and as she might very well have done,
she told Nora outright that the boy was to go out with her that
night, and she said it before Charlie, Grace, and Bertram himself.
She had her reward, and a rich reward it was. She had the delight
of seeing tears in abundance from Nora and Grace, horror on the
faces of both the children, of being entreated and implored by all,
and, finally, of seeing Nora quite overcome with her agitation, and
obliged to go to bed with a violent headache; while she could not
but feel that Charlie was only restrained by consideration for Nora
from abusing her mother. Hubert had acted wisely in keeping
aloof, for a whisper from Nora sent Charlie to summon the chief,
who, of course, was not to be found.

At the appointed time, therefore, poor Bertram was led forth,
looking "like a little martin," as one of his tiny sisters was heard
to say in after years, when telling the story of "Bertram and Grace
and the gipsies" to a new nursery-maid. The poor boy kissed
Nora, who felt as if she was about to lose her mainstay; for Charlie's
state of mind was so unsettled that she could not now look up to
him for comfort.

Gran sneered at this parting, and said, "He'll be back in two or
three hours, you fool!" at which words the children brightened up;
but Nora shook her head, and she felt a foreboding that in this
world she should never again set eyes on the child whom she had
learnt to love as she never thought to love any one but Charlie.
Bertram's dignity had been left behind at Combe Astley, every

particle of it, and he evinced no disdain at the "woman's tears" which rained down Gracey's cheek. He even sobbed himself, but was at last obliged to turn from the tent and follow the wretched old woman to where two of the gang were waiting for her with a cart, into which she scrambled. The men got up by her, Bertram was lifted in behind, and off they jolted. The poor child had a most uncomfortable time of it; every step taken by the horse threw him roughly against one side of the cart, only to be thrown back again to the other immediately, and he soon became all over bruises. They drove on for a long time without stopping. It was a dark night, but the men knew the way well, and as for the horse, he could have taken it blindfold. Occasionally, but at long intervals, they passed some gipsy settlement. The fire—or perhaps there might be two—cast a red and flickering light over the wild, dark faces and figures around them, and as sticks, or other fuel, were thrown on the flames, glanced up brightly, lighting up the low brown tents and rickety old carts, and a portion of the common beyond. Bertram was too miserable to admire fine effects of light and shade, his companions were equally indifferent, and on they drove till the camps and the common were left behind, and they came out into a narrow lane. Here they got out of the cart, which they backed behind a great tree. One of the men was left with the horse and cart, while the other, with Gran and Bertram, set out once more on foot. They soon left the lane, and turned across some fields by a footpath which took them by a gentle descent to the back of the house which contained Agnes Vernon, her mother, her jewels, and several servants—not to mention Reginald De Verrie himself, being one more than the gipsies had calculated upon; for although they never for a moment contemplated the possibility of any of the peaceful inhabitants of this desirable family residence being awakened by the entrance of one small villain into Miss Vernon's room, yet they did very well know that the said entrance would be attended with great risk as long as there was a young gentleman about the place; forasmuch as nobody could ever foresee at what hour of day or night such an individual might not choose to be smoking, either indoors or out—specimens having been known to retire to bed at seven o'clock in the morning, rising to breakfast at three o'clock in the afternoon of one and the same day. That Reginald De Verrie had returned to town or to Rangley Park, the gipsies were pretty sure, and it was with the utmost confidence of success that they approached the small gate which led from the fields into a very narrow slip of grass behind the house. This slip contained a well, covered by some thin planks; and a miniature walk led from it through the bushes to the front of the house, coming out close under the window of the room in which Agnes slept. At this gate Gran stopped with Bertram, while their companion unclosed it, and went through to reconnoitre, and to see that the window was open.

CHAPTER X.

THE RESCUE

THE MOMENT HAD now arrived which Gran had fixed upon to inform Bertram of the part he had to perform.

"Ye're to goo alang arter Bill," said she, "an' he'll show ye the winder—thin ye mus' crep in, and ye'll see a grat box wi' a leather cover an' letters on it; it's mine; and ye'll bring it me and take no heed o' the gal sleeping in the room."

Bertram felt the box was not hers, and in a moment his horrible position presented itself to his mind. Either to commit a great sin, or, as he doubted not, to die a violent death by the hands of an old gipsy woman, and never, never again to hear the sweet voices of his home—never, never more to see the beautiful face of his darling mother, or his own twin sister. The poor boy's teeth chattered and his knees trembled with fright. He put up his little hands to entreat the hard-hearted old gipsy to have pity on him; but his tongue clung to the roof of his mouth, and the words that seemed bursting from his heart would go no farther than his throat.

The gipsy stooped and whispered in his ear, and that whisper he never forgot to his dying day.

"If you scream, you die;" and the hissing sound of the last word rung in his ear and sank deep into his heart, as Bill reappeared.

"All right," was his whispered assurance: "winder open—gal asleep—box on a table near her. Boy all right?"

Gran nodded an affirmative, and pushed the poor child towards him.

Bertram heard his own heart throbbing against his side as he tottered, rather than walked, after the man through the dark shrubs.

They rounded the corner of the house. Bill pointed to the half-open window, and a hard gripe from behind on the boy's little delicate arm warned him that the old gipsy was not far off, and nearly elicited the shriek which it was intended to prevent. Bertram would have given worlds at that moment if the earth would have opened and swallowed him up. The earth was by no means so obliging, however, and, nearly sick with fear, he prepared to creep into the room on his hands and knees—one of the gipsies lifting aside the slight muslin blind which hung before the window. Another moment and his head and shoulders were in the room—the window creaked—Agnes Vernon turned in her sleep, and a deep sigh and half a word escaped her. A rough detaining hand was laid upon Bertram's leg, and he paused—his head drooping from the faintness of extreme fear. In after life he often and often recalled the agony of that moment. No sound broke the deathlike silence save the gentle rippling of the waves on the beach, and the hard breathing of the old gipsy grandmother behind him.

There was a lamp in the room, and its faint, sickly light fell straight across a small table, upon which stood the unconscious cause of so much sin and misery—the dressing-case. Yet fainter and more sickly was the light as it faded away upon the calm face of Agnes Vernon, as she slept peacefully, little dreaming of the strange things that were passing so close to her. How sad it is to feel how careless and unconcerned we are but too often obliged to be, of the anguish and misery that is going on so near to us,—so near that it is not unfrequently woven in with the story of our lives ; and yet we do not heed it—we do not know it. It is too near us, and we look beyond it, and give out pity and our help to distant objects. And when we hear of sorrow bravely borne, we wonder and admire, little dreaming of the richness of strength, the wealth of endurance, that in silence and in sorrow has been living among us—bearing and enduring, it may be, for our own sakes. Yes, there are ghosts among us—black, shadowy objects, unseen by the many, but casting a solemn, ever-chilling, ever-weighing gloom over those to whom they are visible.

Poor Bertram! But he cannot long to get out of his uncomfortable position more than I long to help him out.

A whispered "Go on!" soon sent him, creeping and trembling, into the room. Slowly and noiselessly he raised himself to his feet, and looked round. The gipsies anxiously watched him. On tip-toe he passed the light—he approached the box.

"All right—he'll do it!" whispered Gran, with an oath.

Not so fast, amiable and most fascinating specimen of age and hilarity. In another moment, as if touched by an electric machine, impelled by an uncontrollable terror, Bertram sprang forward, dropped on his knees by the side of the yet sleeping girl, and, burying his head in the bed-clothes,—clinging to them with the strength of despair,—he exclaimed in a piercing scream,—

"Save me—oh, save me!"

Agnes awoke; and not being at all romantic, her first idea—and it was instantly acted upon—was to scream loudly. Almost before she was awake, however, the window was thrown open with a jerk— a man bounded into the room, and, seizing up the child as if he had been a small-sized dog, rushed out again, dealing the poor boy a violent blow on the head as he did so.

Agnes heard him leap over the palings, and run away down the road. Her own screams were stopped from utter fright. She could not raise her voice above a whisper; but she could, and she did, ring the bell till it broke.

Scarcely had she commenced this praiseworthy employment, however, when a shout from the road broke upon her ear—another, and yet another!

And that voice!—she knew that voice if she knew any voice on earth. It was Reginald's, and the sound of it brought back her own.

She sprang to the door of her room, and screamed, "Help—help! They are killing him—he is dead! Help—help!"

And now another and more terrible sound fell on her ear, and put a stop to her own lively exclamations, while she paused in horror. A crash—it seemed to Agnes of falling chimneys—a crash, a splash, and a shriek—and *such* a shriek—so unearthly and fearful, that as it died away, and at the same moment the servants came rushing up and down, poor Agnes, in very terror, sprang with one bound into bed, and buried herself deep, deep under the bed-clothes, trying in vain to stifle the sounds yet ringing in her ears.

But where was Reginald? Why was he out at such an hour?

Reginald De Verrie had, as the gipsies were well aware, made his adieux to Agnes and her mother that very morning, and set out for town; but, as they did *not* know, he had, whether purposely or not, missed the train, and had accordingly returned to spend another four-and-twenty hours at the long, low two-storied house. When Agnes and her mother retired to bed, Reginald, with a cigar-case and a railroad wrapper, repaired to the beach to enjoy the contents of the former, and to ponder upon the vicissitudes of human life in general, and of his own in particular.

So interested had he become in the one or the other of these occupations, that he had disregarded alike the decreasing time and the increasing darkness. Rousing himself at length, however, he began slowly to tramp up the beach, and was about half-way from the road, when shriek number one—being Bertram's—broke the solemn silence of the night. Almost at the same moment the window of the room in which Agnes slept was flung open, and he saw a man spring in, and as rapidly out again, bearing something in his arms.

Let anybody who wishes to form an idea of Reginald's situation and difficulties put himself into as violent a passion as possible, and then begin to run, or rather to try to run, up a steep stony beach. The great round loose stones and the myriads of tiny ones will combine together in one vast league to sink beneath his feet—to roll back, to pull him back, to play him false in every and the most aggravating way. At length he gained the road in spite of their villany; and then rage lent him the wings which she is supposed to keep for such occasions. Even passions have their etiquette and customs, like men and women. Thus Rage and Fear lend out wings when required;—Love beams, generally in the eye, but occasionally, though rarely, in every feature;—Envy and Jealousy each have a weakness for gnawing at the heart;—Pity lends out sorrowing tears,—and so on. Therefore, when Reginald De Verrie wanted to catch the robbers whom he imagined to be running away with his beloved Agnes—with whom, of course, everybody in the world must want to run away—Rage very obligingly and properly lent him a couple of wings, with which he so speedily gained ground on the loaded villain, that that villain, with an oath, dropped the load on the ground, and redoubled his speed. Then Rage went away with the wings, and Reginald pounced upon the load, and, alas! raised from the ground—not his own Agnes—but a little ragged, red-headed, gipsy boy—dirty, insensible, and covered with blood from a great and recent cut on his head! Although Reginald De Verrie could not but be disappointed at finding that his lady-love had not been thrown down on a hard high road in the middle of the night, by a housebreaker, and therefore that he could not enjoy the extreme pleasure and felicity of saving her, yet he was not hard hearted enough to vent his disappointment upon the poor beggar-child who had undergone the experience in her stead. He raised the boy from the ground, therefore, and turned back to the house. He was met by some of the servants, armed in various manners, pokers and tongs forming a large feature in the accoutrements, which in one case consisted of a small fender in one hand and a glass water-bottle in the other.

Thus escorted, and still bearing his ragged trophy, he returned in a sort of triumphant procession to that house which he had quitted but a few hours before in a solitude which was ignominious by comparison.

Agnes had meantime emerged from her retreat, and attired herself in a dressing-gown which contrasted pleasantly with the one in which her lady mother had seen fit to envelop her tall, stooping form. They stood side by side in the doorway, while a bevy of maids formed a somewhat striking background.

"It is the child that screamed and woke me!" exclaimed Agnes, as Reginald approached, and a clearer idea of the confusing, startling events of the last few minutes began to dawn upon her at the sight of that little red head. "Oh, he is dead—he is hurt! In here—bring him here!" she continued, opening the door of her own room, where the faint light still burnt boldly on, in no wise daunted by the stronger beams of the many candles that now flitted about in cold and trembling hands.

Macnade, Mrs. Vernon's maid, had taken Bertram from the panting Reginald, and she followed Agnes into the room and laid him, still insensible, upon the bed to which he had clung so imploringly but a few minutes before in life and in strength. Now he rested on it, motionless, to all appearance dead. Reginald despatched someone immediately for a doctor, and then set off himself to rouse the proper officials to take measures for the apprehension of the villains who had, he doubted not, attempted to break into the house, for a few words from Agnes had given him a pretty true idea of the state of the case. Till the doctor arrived nothing could be done for the poor boy except shutting down and securely fastening that fatal window to prevent the re-appearance of the enemy ; of which catastrophe Mrs. Vernon and several of the maids seemed to be in momentary expectation. This dangerous service having been heroically executed without loss of life or limb—the blind having been drawn down and the shutters closed, "for fear they should see the lights and shoot us, the wretches!" as Mrs. Vernon remarked—that lady, sleepy, nervous, and slipshod, crept up to bed again. Most of the maids followed her example, and Agnes, Macnade, and one housemaid were left to keep watch over the boy, whom one of them feared, and the other two hoped, was dead. Not that either Macnade or the housemaid were unfeeling or hard-hearted; very much the contrary;—neither of them could bear the sight of a dead mouse, and Jane had been known to shed tears at the death of a favourite old cat which had inhabited the Vernon kitchen for many years, and it is highly probable that they will pay the same compliment to Bertram if I kill him; but the love of excitement, of the marvellous, the terrible, of anything, in fact, to break the monotony of life, was so strong both in Macnade and in Jane that although they firmly believed that they hoped the child would live, they could not help gazing on that little mute form with an intensity of interest arising from the unconfessed feeling that if he were to draw one breath, everything must go on sadly as usual; but that every moment that he delayed that breath rendered the stirring possibility of a funeral and a sight more likely.   Just as the doctor's ring was heard at the door, Bertram did draw a breath—another, and yet another—and as the good but withal sleepy man entered the room, the child began slowly to open his eyes.

"He will live!" exclaimed Agnes.

And it soon became evident that he had every intention of doing so. He had received a severe blow on the head from the hard, cruel hand of the man Bill, and was covered with bruises from having been thrown violently on the road. Of these latter, however, the doctor thought nothing. The head was the only thing for which he feared. The prolonged insensibility and the seeming deepness of the cut at first made him fear a concussion of the brain, although he allowed that the former might have been merely a fainting-fit; of the latter he could not judge in its present state. Some of the hair surrounding the cut must be immediately removed. He called for a pair of scissors, and began to carry his words into effect, while Macnade held the light towards him, and Agnes stood by, watching attentively. Snip, snip went the scissors.

"Hallo!" exclaimed the doctor, "hallo! what's this?"

"My goodness gracious me!" ejaculated Macnade, as the red wig came half off in the left hand of the good doctor, while his right grasped the scissors. "A disguise, by all that's sacred," said the astonished man, while Jane screamed in the distance.

But it was a poor, weak scream, the last of a long and powerful line, and it was treated with the contempt and ignominy which usually fall to the lot of poor descendants.

Doctor Halling now carefully disengaged the rest of the wig from under the boy's head, and disclosed to view his own dark hair— short now, but still considerably grown since the sad day on which it had been so closely cropped.

"A disguise," repeated the doctor; "a stolen child, no doubt! poor boy, poor boy!"

"Stolen!" exclaimed Agnes, in an eager whisper; "then it is Bertram Astley;" and with her usual impetuosity she rushed out of the room, bounded upstairs three steps at a time, and burst into her mother's room to communicate the startling idea; for Agnes had been much interested in Reginald's sad story of the disappearance of the young Astleys, and Mrs. Vernon had fancied herself much interested also at the time, although she had only heard the beginning of the story, having lost the end, and forgotten to inquire whether the children were ever found again, in the delights of ordering dinner, to which duty she had been summoned at the moment Reginald had chosen to tell his tale.

As soon as she fully comprehended the drift of the somewhat incoherent expressions with which Agnes almost overwhelmed her, and as soon as she could recall to mind who Grace and Bertram Astley were, and that she had felt and suffered so deeply for them and for their dear parents, she insisted upon getting up to look at the child, with a sort of vague idea that she must find his name written on his face, although everyone else had failed to discover it.

Agnes was raving to rush off somewhere, anywhere, to tell some-body, anybody, the great news, and to work off the excitement that incited her to perform a series of inimitable gymnastics round her mother's dressing-table, by way of helping out her explanation.

Mrs. Vernon, however, would keep her to help her on once more with the antiquated dressing-gown, and to answer her innumerable questions.

Just as they reached the bottom of the stairs, the house-door opened to admit Reginald, and two policemen come to inspect the premises.

Agnes sprang towards him, dancing in a manner somewhat unexpected and novel to the eyes of those tall officials. "It is Bertram Astley; we have found them—it is them, and Grace was the girl; oh, come!" she exclaimed.

"Bertram Astley — Grace — Agnes! — who is — what?" said Reginald, rapidly and confusedly.

"Come and look," repeated Agnes, springing to the door of her own room, where Bertram was; but at this moment Jane came out with her finger on her lip, and a request from the doctor that Miss Vernon would be kind enough to keep the house quieter, if possible. He was still busy about the child's head, but would come to her in the dining-room as soon as it was dressed; meantime he wished to be left alone with his patient and the maids.

Reginald could hardly be restrained from at least looking in, but was finally conquered, and dragged off to the dining-room, to hear the tale of the wig from Agnes, and an elaborate account of her own feelings from Mrs. Vernon.

At last Doctor Halling made his appearance and his report. He repeated his conviction that the wound in the head was the only thing of the least consequence, adding that he could hardly tell yet the extent of the injury, but was of opinion that the wig had softened the severity of the blow. He opened his eyes when he heard of the suspicions to which the discovery of the wig had given rise, and delivered it as his decided opinion that they were right; upon which Agnes commenced another gymnastic, and Mrs. Vernon cast up her eyes and took a look at the dirty chandelier hanging from the ceiling. But the doctor would not hear of any attempt at recognition for the present. Perfect quiet was essential, he said. The child had evidently been much reduced, and any shock in his weak state might be of serious consequence. The most he would allow was that, if the boy fell asleep, Reginald might go in to look at, and, if possible, identify him; but even then he must keep out of sight.

The doctor now took his leave, promising to return the next day; and Reginald joined the policemen, to consult them as to what steps could be taken for the recovery of Grace, if the sick boy should prove to be Bertram.

Jane entered in a short time to say that the boy was asleep, and Reginald, who returned at the same moment, went to look at him. His heart beat fast as he gently opened the door.

Macnade sat by the bed in which reposed the slight form of our poor Bertram. His face was wan and thin, and as pale as the brown dye of the walnut-juice would allow; but in spite of that—in spite of the bandages on his head and the short-cropped hair—Reginald had no doubt it was Bertram Astley whom he saw stretched before him, ragged, wounded, helpless, dying perhaps. How different from the sleeping Bertram whom Grace had looked upon in his own little room at home some months before; and how different from the

Bertram whom Reginald had last seen in health and strength, jumping gaily into his father's carriage with his merry little sister and his governess. Where was that sister now? Reginald was almost tempted to disobey the doctor, and to wake Bertram at once to ask for Grace; but instead of committing this act of insanity, he returned to the dining-room to assure Agnes of the truth of her suspicions, and to receive as many blessings and thanks from Mrs. Vernon as if Agnes had been the lost child and he had just found her and restored her to a disconsolate mother.

After so much hard blessing, Mrs. Vernon began to experience fatigue. She would not be persuaded that Reginald was not tired to death also, and she insisted upon his retiring to bed at once. Therefore the good lady once more crept upstairs, followed and lighted by her son-in-law elect, while Agnes stole softly into her own room, to spend the few remaining hours of the night in an arm-chair, first taking a good look at the little sleeping hero, as she considered him to be.

No sooner was Mrs. Vernon safe in her own apartment, than Reginald stole noiselessly down the stairs again, and in a few minutes was on his way to the town to obtain more assistance to scour the common, no doubt now existing in his mind that the children had been stolen, and that Grace would be found among the gipsies.

Breakfast was late the next morning at the long, low house, for everybody was tired, and it was nearly eleven o'clock before Mrs. Vernon and Agnes met in the dining-room. Reginald was not there, and a messenger was despatched to his room to inquire if he would have his breakfast sent up to him. It then appeared that he not only was not in the house, but that his bed had not been occupied that night. Poor Mrs. Vernon had hardly time to imagine every possible misfortune for him, before she was destined to receive another shock.

Macnade opened the door, pale and trembling, with a "Could I speak to you, ma'am?" which called forth a volley of questions from both ladies.

"Is he hurt, Macnade? What is it? More robbers? anything stolen?" etc.

Macnade came in, and faltered out the words,—

"Please, ma'am, yes; they've found one in the well."

"One!—one what?" exclaimed both ladies at once.

And it appeared that on "the boy"—an article pertaining to every household—going to draw water at the well, he found the planks disturbed, dashed aside in fact, and the body of an old woman sunk deep into the water. At first he had been unable to imagine what prevented the buckets from rising as usual; but, obtaining help, the terrible object had soon been brought to light. The face was indeed dreadful to behold, so distorted were the features, so inhuman the expression.

Whatever may be the fate of Grace Astley, she need no longer fear the harsh treatment nor dread the fearful language of old Gran the gipsy. The old woman had missed her path in the flurry of her flight, and, instead of turning to the left for the little gate, she had turned to the right—over—and, alas! into the well!

And now Agnes recalled to mind the unearthly shriek which put the finishing stroke to her alarm, and had sent her flying into bed the night before,—that never-to-be-forgotten night!

The moment that it had been suggested to Reginald that the beggar boy whom he had picked up might be no other than Bertram Astley, his chief object had been to obtain a sufficient force to search the common—so well known as a resort of gipsies; and he had hurried off the policemen for that purpose before they had time for a strict examination of the premises, or they must have discovered the body of old Gran, and Mrs. Vernon might have been spared this last shock, from which she did not recover for some days, and which implanted in her mind so deep a horror of all wells that she never again hired a house which boasted in its back-yard so dangerous and useless a disfigurement. During the remainder of the stay by the sea-side she steadfastly refused to pass through the little walk leading to the unlucky well, and to the little white gate, as she entertained a most reasonable fear that more dead gipsies might be strewn about among the bushes.

Reginald returned ere long, worn out and dispirited. The common was vast, the gipsies' encampments many and scattered, and his search had been in vain, and not without danger. No trace of Grace could be found.

CHAPTER XI

ANOTHER MOVE

AND BILL and Grace and Nora!—what of them? As soon as Bill became aware that he was no longer pursued, he slackened his pace, but only to take breath, and he was not long in gaining the spot where his comrade with the horse and cart awaited him. A few hurried words explained the failure of the plot and the capture of the boy, and then followed a consultation respecting Gran. Was it worth while to wait for her, or could she shift for herself? It was a choice of evils. If they waited, it would give time for pursuit; but by leaving the place of meeting they might be the cause of her capture, and of ill-effects to the whole tribe. The smugglers, too, must be warned, and not left to linger in expectation of the booty. It was decided that Bill should return immediately to the tents, with horse and cart, to inform Hubert of the catastrophe, and that the other man should first repair to the top of the cliffs to the right, to make the signal of danger to the smugglers, and then endeavour to see after Gran; if possible to bring her back to the encampment, or at least to discover whether she had likewise succeeded in effecting her escape, or had fallen into the hands of the enemy.

Bill drove off, venting his rage and disappointment on the poor, innocent old horse, and before long was reporting himself and relating his tale to Hubert and a few expectant elders. Great was the consternation when it was known that one had been taken who had so much power, and but too likely so good a will, to injure them, as Bertram Astley. Instant flight was unanimously decided upon, and even a total separation and dispersion of the tribe for a short period, till the affair and the search should be blown over, which, as Hubert remarked, might be hoped for in a very short time, but for the girl, seeing that no real harm had been done and no goods taken; but then there *was* the girl, and as long as she remained in the tribe they must expect pursuit and persecution. By this able manoeuvre Hubert hoped to induce the elders to propose that Grace should return to her parents; but he hoped in vain. Grace was the property of Gran, and only Gran could dispose of her. Hubert, unsupported, could not alter the laws and regulations of the tribe, and with a sigh and a thought for Nora, he relinquished the attempt.

The news of danger and removal spread like wildfire through the tents. Every human being was up and stirring, and Charlie felt a pang at his heart as he thought that, well or ill, Nora must be moved now. He ran to prepare her and Grace for the sudden change, and to tell them what had happened. They were both greatly excited. Nora was at first full of hope and thankfulness that Bertram was in safe hands, and that her prayers for him were in a fair way of being answered; but soon the poor girl was completely taken up with what was to her, in her sad state, the terrible idea of the journey. She who had hardly left her tent for so long a time, now to undertake a sea-voyage and a jolting, rambling journey of hundreds of miles! Of her mother and her danger Nora naturally thought but little, being so perfectly accustomed to the long absences and hair-breadth escapes in which the old lady had indulged during a long and eventful life.

Grace meantime hardly knew whether to be glad or sorry—Bertram had escaped, that was joy; but then he might have been hurt, even killed, and her sobs came quickly at the thought. If he were safe, he would tell people where to find her, and they would come and take her to her own mamma; but then this moving! How could Bertram or anybody else tell where she might be taken to next; and now, wherever it was, she must be alone, without him, and alone she must bear not only the sad changes in her way of life, but the uncertainty as to his fate. On the whole, sorrow predominated, and Grace cried bitterly as she helped Charlie in his thoughtful preparations for their comfort during the journey.

A messenger had been despatched in all speed to alter the signal of warning to the smugglers into one summoning them to be ready to take off the tribe, for Hubert had resolved that those among them with whom the children were best acquainted must leave that coast together, and shape their future course according to circumstances. If they were discovered and pursued, as he could hardly hope they would not be, it might be necessary to remain on board for a long time, and possibly even to sail to some far-off land—to leave old England, it might be, for years. If, however, the embarkation could be effected without exciting remark or suspicion, his plan was that they should be landed by degrees and at different places, to meet again at a given time and place, possibly even in a few weeks if all went well.

The remainder of the tribe dispersed immediately in different directions; many, of whom Bertram was supposed to have seen so little that he could not recognize them even if her were to meet them or to be confronted with them, were left behind among the other gipsies on the common, to keep a sharp look-out for what was going on, and to inform Gran of their plans, should she make her appearance, as no one doubted but that she would, sooner or later.

All prospered under the able management of Hubert. The removal and embarkation were effected with marvellous rapidity and perfect secrecy, in the usual retired, almost desert spot, and with little trouble to anyone but poor Nora and her two attendants, who both felt for her, and Grace a good deal for her poor little self too. They looked back on the valley as they left it in the last of the lumbering old carts, and though they had all suffered much during the short time they had spent between those huge grassy banks, they could not leave it without a strange feeling of regret ; Nora especially, for she felt that she was taking her last look upon a place that had been, from time to time, her home for many long and dreary months, and one, moreover, in which she had first known the only real and true happiness. It is strange that one should feel regret at leaving even a spot in which one has suffered and sorrowed; but so it is.

Bertram's whole system had received a severe shock from the privations and trials he had endured since he left his happy home, and especially from the *finale* of his gipsy life; the last scene in which he had been so cruelly treated. It was some days, therefore, before Reginald was allowed to make himself known, and then— who can describe that meeting? Bertram was duly prepared by good Doctor Halling, who had become much interested in "the case," as he persisted in calling the little boy. And when Reginald entered the room, Bertram perfectly beamed all over from head to foot with joy, and clung round Mr. De Verrie's neck, kissing him as heartily as if he had never been dignified, or talked of "woman's tears and foolery" in his life. But this is looking on too fast, for there were many long days in which the poor child remained perfectly still and helpless, not positively unconscious, but without seeming to notice anything or anybody about him, taking everything that was given to him, however disagreeable, with a sort of hasty, frightened obedience, that was more painful to witness than violence would have been; for it was so unnatural, and suggested the idea of his having been worried and persecuted into a perpetual state of

fear. The first symptom of improvement was in the large dark
eyes, which began to wander inquiringly round the room, settling
finally upon Agnes, who was sitting writing by his side. When
she moved, the large eyes followed her unceasingly wherever she
went.

As soon as she saw them fixed upon her, she came up to the bed.
"You are better now, are you not, Bertram?" said she kindly,
smiling at him.

"Yes," said he, still gazing at her, as if it was a comfort to have
something pretty for those tired eyes to rest upon.   "Who are you?"

"I am Agnes—Agnes Vernon—and I am going to take care of
you till you are well," said she. "Won't that be nice?—and you
shall not go back to the bad people any more, and we will get Grace
very soon."

Agnes thought this a most clever and composing speech, but she
found that, on the contrary, she could hardly have done worse than
to mention Grace, or any subject likely to excite him. He looked
for a moment as if he did not understand what she was saying; but
the familiar name of Grace found its way at length to his weak brain,
and he looked anxiously round, and asked repeatedly, "Is she here?
Bring her; where is she? Nora!" gradually working himself into
such a state of excitement that Agnes became quite alarmed. After
this, all allusions to the past were strictly forbidden by the doctor
until "the case" became much stronger, and it was not until a day or
two after the first interview with Reginald De Verrie that the poor
little "case" could bear any questioning on the subject.

The gipsies thus obtained a great advantage. Not the slightest
clue could be obtained that might lead to the discovery of the where-
abouts of poor Grace. When by degrees the whole story came out,
the valley, in fact the whole common, was again examined with yet
more care—but, of course, the former was utterly deserted; in fact
no one could be quite sure of the identity of the place from Bertram's
not very lucid description. The other gipsies on the common
were questioned and examined, and the body of the old woman,
it was hoped, might be the means of bringing to light some of the
gang, but all was in vain. Nobody claimed the body, and it was
quietly interred in the little churchyard behind the town, through
which the old woman had passed in health and strength but a very
short time before.

Reginald had despatched a telegraphic message to Lord Astley
as soon as possible, to inform him of the event, and he was much

surprised when two days passed without bringing any signs of his lordship. He now wrote both to Combe Astley and to London, in spite of the dissuasions of Mrs. Vernon, who urged that as long as Bertram remained in so critical a state, it would be far better to leave his parents in utter ignorance respecting him. Judging by what her own feelings would be in a similar case, she said that she felt quite certain Lady Astley would much rather not hear anything "till it was decided one way or the other." Agnes, though rather shocked at hearing that her mother would rather not be sent for if she were ill at a distance, for fear of finding her alive, but would prefer waiting till she was dead, strongly advocated the opposite opinion, and Reginald, either trusting to his own good sense and knowledge of Lord and Lady Astley, or feeling it a duty to yield to the wishes of the girl to whom he was engaged, from a vague idea of how often he should expect the same compliment from the girl he married, decided upon writing to Lord Astley.

His letter was just what might have been expected from one English gentleman to another, short, and to the point—too short, and too much to the point, Agnes thought; and she could not but feel injured and hurt that such an opportunity of cleverly breaking by a letter a startling event, which might cause an irremediable shock to the person destined to hear it, should have been wasted upon a gentleman, instead of falling to the lot or pen of a lady. Lady Astley had felt the loss of her children more than a casual observer would have supposed possible in one so passive. True, she was passive, she was cold, but not to her children; for them she lived; her love of them had become her very life; and when two of them were rudely and suddenly torn from her, without preparation and without hope, she drooped and pined. In the few months of her children's absence, Lady Astley lived more years than the six-and-thirty which she counted up to that time. Her dark hair was deeply tinged with grey, and the comfortable languor, hitherto expressed by her *tout ensemble*, had given place to a settled, woe-worn look of hopeless, helpless misery, which seemed to be weighing her down rapidly to the grave.

As to Lord Astley, nothing could at first exceed his indignation at the disappearance of his children. It was everybody's fault. Mrs. Abel and his wife first of all were to blame, and then, in due order, everybody that ventured to approach his infuriated lordship. The whole corps of servants,—housemaids grooms, gamekeepers, nursery-maids, cooks, and foot-men; the De Verries, for recommending the governess, who had not watched by the children night and day; the clergyman of the parish, for not inculcating better maxims in his sermons—maxims that might teach the world to keep children within bounds; everybody—every one was to blame, excepting and saving only himself. He had done his duty; he had left his children to the care of an incompetent mother and an all but superannuated governess. He had taught them to fear him by his harsh, stern manners; he had let them see that their mother feared him. This was bringing them up betimes to bear the privations and harshness of the world. What more could be expected from a model father?

This fine frenzy could not last long, however, and when it subsided, Lord Astley arrived at that real love for his children which no one imagined him to possess less than he did himself. And when one by one every means which he took for discovering what had become of them proved vain, he became most properly and truly miserable. Self-reproach also attacked him, and Combe Astley became more than ever distasteful to him, as recalling to his mind too forcibly those two hitherto neglected but not much loved little ones, whom he might never hope to see again. With his own grief, his pity and affection for his wife increased; and, as she more than shared his horror of their home, and evidently pined to leave it, with a strange, sickly fancy that elsewhere she might hear of the lost ones—*there*, never,—he resolved to shut up or let the place. Reginald's letter, with a telegraphic message forwarded from Coombe Astley, found Lord and Lady Astley in London, still engaged in fruitless inquiries and researches, talking of going abroad, but still lingering on from week to week, to follow up some "last hope" or "positive clue." The general idea at first had seemed to be that the children had wandered out of sight, why or wherefore no tongue could tell, and had fallen into the lake, or some of the ponds in the park. But every place containing as much as a foot of water, was dragged and drained to no purpose. The contents of the Robbers' Den were, of course, discovered in the search, and threw just so much light on the subject as to suggest to some who remembered their own youthful days, the idea that the little ones had meditated a running away for some time past. The discovery of the dolls in the little beds was proof that their departure had been voluntary, but further than this nothing could be imagined. Gipsies were suggested; but the unanswered advertisements and unclaimed rewards lessened week by week, day by day, the likelihood of this view of the subject; for what object could gipsies have in stealing children, but to gain a reward for having found them astray, and bringing them back.   Besides, gipsies do not travel so quickly but that they must have been found in the miles and miles of country scoured and minutely examined the very next and for many succeeding days.   The only evidence in favour of this solution of the problem was, that there had been a gang of gipsies at the outskirts of Lord Astley's property, about ten miles off, and that they could not be traced after that eventful night.

The gamekeepers considered it as certain that "Master Bertram and Miss Astley had been stolen by gipsies, because there had been a deal o' poaching lately," especially out in the direction where the gipsies had been seen.

Besides all this, the wife of one of the keepers, who lived in the lodge nearest to Headless Lane and Coombe Wood, declared that she was awoke in the middle of that very night by a scream; that she had listened, expecting it to be repeated; but, hearing no more, she had supposed that it must have been fancy, and had gone to sleep again, though it was so vivid to her mind that she could not help feeling that it was real.

It is said that there is honour among thieves, and it is certain that, whatever the worthies of Pester might suspect with regard to their allies, the gipsies and smugglers, and the young runaways, no hints reached the despairing parents from that quarter—not a word which might have led to a suspicion of the truth, in spite of all the rewards offered.

Lady Astley was seldom able to leave her room before the middle of the day, and her husband was at his solitary breakfast, when Reginald's letter was, with several others, put into his hands.   It chanced to be the first he opened, and it is but proper to remark that his feelings may be better imagined than described; and, therefore, although I had much rather describe them, I will not. I must mention, however, that ever since his grief had become more subdued, his lordship had found a slight, a very slight, consolation in considering himself "an altered man."   He felt " altered."   He knew he was " altered,"—" broken-hearted and altered."

That was the proper thing to say of him now, just as people used to call him "dignified, and a man of great weight and influence," before his loss.   And he knew that people did say it as he walked gravely and sadly along the streets, where he used to walk gravely and grandly. The words "altered and broken-hearted" seemed to him to be graven in large letters above the doorway of his heart. And in his heart was nothing but one great sorrow, swallowing up all else excepting a little consciouness of self which lurked in a corner. When Reginald's letter told him, therefore, that Bertram was actually found, his first thought was one of thankfulness, but his second was a sudden recollection that he need no longer be an altered man; and such a mass of contradictions is man, that Lord Astley really experienced a tinge of regret at being thus speedily called upon to resign his new character. It was but a tinge, however, and his next thought was for his wife. How, in her weak state, would she bear this news, as sudden as unhoped for?

Mrs. Abel was still with them, for Lady Astley could not bear to part with one who seemed to her weak mind the last lingering link connected with her lost darlings; so, together with the brown holland dresses, a few worn books and broken toys, which once delighted the hearts of Bertram and Grace, Mrs. Abel was preserved; and Lord Astley now thought of her as the fittest person to undertake the task from which he shrunk in his manly cowardice.

Mrs. Abel was sent for, and Mrs. Abel came, unchanged since we saw her last, with the same lumps of flaxen hair on each side of her odd cap; attired in the same wondrous garment of peculiar fashion, and of a pattern that raises in one's mind a longing to know the bold genius that originated it. There was the same odd trot, too, and the same, but perhaps a little less of the insane little laugh. She had been sitting with Lady Astley, as usual, attempting to console her, and when she came into the dining-room and found his lordship waiting for her, she fancied that she had been sent for to give her report of the poor invalid, and accordingly began immediately,— "Oh! Lord Astley, I'm sure she's better—more cheerful—talks more—yes—sent for me half an hour earlier than usual, by the clock on the stairs—and I have been talking to her since—yes—and read a letter—yes—one I had this morning from a dear friend—poor dear soul—she's lost eight near relations since January—yes—since January—and I thought Lady Astley would like to hear it, because, poor dear soul, she is so cheerful and doesn't mind a bit—eight new, I mean near, relations, and she only writes a little deady here and there."

Lord Astley had made several efforts at breaking in with his great news; but finding all his smaller attempts in vain, and roused by the eight dead relations into a state of frenzy, highly unbecoming in an altered man, he now burst forth with a stentorian "Madam!" which completely quelled Mrs. Abel for one minute, during which time he uttered the magic words, "Bertram is found."

There was no mistaking these words. They fell straight upon her brain and were received at once. Mrs. Abel gave a wild stare, an hysterical yell, and burst into tears; she sobbed and she laughed, and putting a gigantic handkerchief up to her face, she plunged off into the very middle of the room in a series of ecstatic but indescribable prances. She believed she was going to a sofa, to cry among its cushions, and Lord Astley believed so too, only there was no sofa in the room, and she had pranced past all the chairs and still was running on, in an inflated exaggeration of her usual trot.

"Oh! I knew it, I knew it," exclaimed she between her sobs and little yells of joy. "I always knew it—they are not lost—oh, dear—oh, dear—oh!"

Lord Astley saw that he might as soon expect a witty remark from a black cow as help from Mrs. Abel, and his first object now was to prevent her from bursting into his wife's room and killing her upon the spot with the news. Having succeeded in shutting the poor kind-hearted old lady up in her own room, there to take the remainder of the violent exercise to which she appeared inclined, he went himself to Lady Astley, and, as gradually as was consistent with words, he told her that one of her darlings was safe.

Lady Astley started, and Lady Astley cried very much, as might have been expected; but she also did what Lord Astley had not expected of her. Knowing her indolent, inert disposition, he had not imagined that she would insist upon setting off immediately to Bertram. *Insist*—yes, actually to rouse herself to such a pitch of determination that he felt that he could not advise even a short delay, for that rest which appears to form so essential a part of the lives of most ladies of the present day, who rest before dinner and after dinner, before driving and after driving; in fact, before and after every event, whether great or small.

Lord Astley yielded for once in his life to the wishes of his wife. It was the last dying action of his altered manhood.

At this time Bertram had not even been allowed to see Reginald, and as soon as Dr. Halling heard that "the case" possessed a father and mother who were on the road to see it, he begged that they would delay their journey at least for a few days; there was, however, no time to communicate his desires; Lady Astley, still retaining the command, insisted on pushing rapidly on, even to the door of the long, low house. If she could but see her child, sleeping or waking, even if he were not to be allowed to see her, she felt she should be happier: she could not rest until she had seen him.

Lodgings were therefore taken as near as possible to the Vernon's, and day after day, for hours and hours, poor Lady Astley would linger about that house; sitting either on the beach or in the tiny would-be garden, to watch and wait till she was told that Bertram slept; and then stealing on tip-toe up to the window, to gaze at the little, thin, but almost idolized features.

She was most reluctant to allow Mr. De Verrie to be the first to make himself known to the child, but here her husband interfered in his old way, and she found that all the authority which she was ever to hope to exercise over him had been spent entirely in the effort of bringing him as far as the long, low house.

But the day did really come at last, though Lady Astley began to fear that it never would, when she might go into the very room where her child was living, and see those little arms, no longer sturdy, stretched out towards herself; and, in another minute, her own beautiful boy, her darling one, was safe in his mother's arms.

Who can hope to tell in words the happiness of that meeting? Every fibre of the boy's weak frame was vibrating with an intensity of happiness. He could not look enough. He could not leave her hand for one moment. It was "mamma" again: his own darling mamma, with a voice that nobody else ever had, to his mind. Every movement, every look was "mamma,"—a coming back to his old home ways. He could not realize it; he could not believe it. It must be a dream, and somebody would take her away; and from that minute Bertram could not bear her out of his sight without uneasiness.

It was long, indeed, since his weary eyes had looked on anything so comforting as his mother's face; and for Lady Astley, she not only felt that her treasure was her own again, but that it was such a treasure as nobody else in the world ever had or could have.

After the first joy, however, the thought of poor little Grace was a sad drawback. Every means failed to discover her or the gipsies, and the repeated and prolonged disappointments were very bad both for Lady Astley and Bertram, the sufferings of the former being greatly heightened by the accounts of gipsy life which she received from the latter.

In the mean time the cause of all this anxiety, poor Grace, the innocent victim to a brother's dislike of four-o'clock lessons and governesses, was suffering most acutely from the consequences of a sea-voyage, made under every possible disadvantage. The crowded cabin, the noise, dirt and confusion, were quite too much for the delicate child. Nora, too, felt the change, the journey, and all the disagreeables as much as her little charge; and Charlie, thoroughly alarmed for her, had as much on his hands as he could well manage, with nursing them both, which he did as tenderly as any number of mothers or grandmothers could have done. The smugglers were coasting slowly along, gradually getting rid of the gipsies, and here and there stopping for hours at a time "on business," mysterious to Nora and Grace, and even to Charlie, though he had perhaps a better idea of the signification of the word in this instance than had the other two. After many days of this life, Nora became so palpably worse that Charlie could bear it no longer, and he begged and entreated that he and Nora might be put on shore the very next time they touched anywhere, although the original plan had been for them to remain in the ship to the very last.

"It was as much as her life was worth," the poor boy declared, "to keep her another hour on board ship;" and though Hubert felt but too surely that her hours were already numbered, he had not the heart to refuse the request, especially when he found that the poor dying girl herself was pining for "green fields and trees" as she said; and when, further, Nora entreated that Grace might be let go with her, Hubert assented, without a word as to her future fate. Not a syllable about what Charlie was to do with her when he had no longer Nora to care for. Perhaps Hubert may have felt, as he wrung the hand of the young gipsy, his subject, who had robbed him of the love that was his right,—perhaps he may have felt at that moment that this too was a last farewell; that never again should he see that strong handsome boy, or the pretty ladylike child, any more than he might dare to hope ever again to rest his eyes upon the drooping girl, whose transparent hand he could not have kissed with greater reverence had she been the first lady of the land.

Poor Hubert! It was a love that would have softened him and drawn him from the wild bad ways of his people. But it was taken from him. The one bright light that had hitherto been the charm of his rough life—the star that had travelled on before him—his guardian angel, the thought of whom had kept him from much that was wrong, and filled his heart with good soothing thoughts—this was gone from him for ever—a long and endless for ever. On, on will he go in the great, the dreary ocean of life, in which we are all wandering; but for him henceforth all will be darkness. And for her? She too must travel here a little, little while. Her light will brighten and increase; through one cloud it must pass—but one: and that one will not dim the glory, as she comes out purified and glorified among the angels of God.

CHAPTER XII

HOME AGAIN

CHARLIE'S ONLY IDEA, his one thought was but for Nora. He had money, and his first wish was to take a lodging for her in the quietest part of the little seaport at which they had been landed. But Nora too had one wish, one hope, and it was to see Grace restored to her own home, once more in her mother's arms; and she implored with such wild eagerness that Charlie would take her straight to Combe Astley, that he could not refuse her, although his heart was torn with the conviction that her strength must sink under the fatigue of a long and slow journey. But Nora had evidently set her heart on this one thing with an energy so new in her, that Charlie was more than startled. Her repugnance to the place they were in amounted to a positive horror. She entreated him that she might not die there, although the discussion took place on the beach where she was resting after the fatigue of landing and she had therefore seen nothing of the town. It was to no purpose that Charlie represented this to her. She could only repeat her entreaties that he would take her from the sight of the terrible sea, on which she had suffered so much. She knew she could not walk, she could not stand the jolting of a cart, even supposing any one could be found to trust them with the hire of one, which was most unlikely; but there was the railroad, and she pointed to the hissing, panting engine, the smoke of which was visible from where they sat. Surely that would take them to Combe Astley. She could not die till she had seen "the lady," as she called the child's mother. She must give her back her child.

It was more painful to Charlie to see Nora unhappy and in a state of excitement than anything else, and he carried, more than helped, her to the station, which, fortunately, was not far distant, although he could not overcome his astonishment at her strange determination, for he well knew that Nora had never travelled by rail in her life, and that her alarm at the idea had been considerable in days gone by. Her horror of the little seaport was not assumed; but all fears, all and every other feeling, were lost and forgotten in her one great desire to get Grace to her mother. Every moment that they were apart was a burden to Nora. It was a small station, and but few trains stopped at it. Our little party had to wait some hours, but the kindness of a porter afforded them the accommodation of the tiny waiting-room, which chanced to be empty. At last a train did stop. It was very full, and as several people had come up to go on by it, Charlie had some difficulty in finding a seat for Nora, and in guarding her from the crowd and crush. His anger was rising at each fresh push from the busy throng, and he was beginning to fear that the train would go off without them, when he was suddenly addressed by an eccentric and benevolent old gentleman, who was at that moment passing: a sort of worthy of whom so many are inserted between the leaves of books, that it appears but few are left for real life. This specimen was attracted by the strange little group on the platform,—the reckless, angry anxiety of the dark gipsy boy, and the death-like face of the drooping girl at his side.

It was evening; and as one of the porters ran past with a lantern, its light was cast for one moment upon our wanderers, and Nora lifted her eyes to the old man's face, as, looking at her, but speaking rather to her companion, he hastily asked if they were going on by this train, and if so, advising them to be quick, he offered his assistance, which was gladly accepted; and in another moment Charlie was guiding Nora's feeble steps towards a first-class carriage; and, with the help of the kind old man, the exhausted girl was lifted in. Grace, hitherto unnoticed, was put in after her, and Charlie, with the old gentleman, followed. The bell rang—close to the carriage, of course—nearly deafening the invalid, and making Charlie long to kill the ringer. There was a shriek, and they were off; slowly at first, but soon rushing away at full speed, and the old man, bent forward to draw up the window to keep the cool evening air from the white, white face, shaded now by a yet whiter hand. Charlie sat by her side, holding her other hand in both his, and watching her with an anxiety which was painful to witness, for death was written in every line of her form and face. The little girl cowered in the farthest corner, and the old man looked at each in turn, and looked again and again. He felt that they had a history, and he longed to know it; but poor and wretched as they were, there was something sacred in their deep sorrow, which kept him from asking more. They did not seem to belong to this busy, rapid world; and not only did they not demand sympathy, but he felt that it would but disturb and increase the silent, unobtrusive grief.

It was a long journey even by rail, and to Nora and one of her companions it seemed endless. After the first half-hour she could scarcely be easy a moment in any position, and although she bore it bravely, yet her repeated moaning, "Move me, move me!" was agony to poor Charlie, and drew tears from the kind old man. Grace slept a great deal; and at last, long, long after morning had dawned, poor Nora sank into an uneasy slumber, which lasted till the train stopped at the station at which they were to alight. Here she awoke, but she seemed hardly sensible, and quite unable to move or exert herself in the least.

"What will you do, my poor boy?" asked the old man compassionately, after they had carried Nora to the waiting-room, and placed her in one of the hard, shiny horsehair chairs.

Charlie was standing hopelessly by her, and he turned and looked up in the face of the speaker, as if he could not take in his words.

"Can I help you? Where do you wish to take her?" continued his new friend.

Charlie could only shake his head; and there was a silence, during which time nothing was heard but the hard, catching breath of the dying girl,—for it was a small station, and the noises consequent on the arrival of a train had soon subsided. Nora herself broke that silence. She raised her eyes, as if suddenly awake to what was passing. The dark eyes had lost their unnatural brightness,—a dimness was stealing over them; they wandered painfully from Charlie to the old man, and then rested on Grace, and Charlie bent to catch the faint whisper, "Take her," were the only words he could hear; but he understood.

"Nora, I *cannot* leave you; don't make me go!"

She shook her head, and asked,—

"How far?"

"To Combe Astley?—half a mile," was his reply.

Another whisper—"Go—come again."

Charlie hesitated. He could not—he would not leave her so.

"What is it?" asked the old man, who lingered still,—for the whisper had been lost to all but Charlie.

The gipsy explained,—

"She won't be easy till I take this child home; it's half a mile. How can I leave her?"

Grace had been too much awed to speak; but now her little voice was heard,—

"She could go alone—she knew all the way; and mamma would come back and bring something to take Nora home."

No one listened to this proposal, and the old man at the same moment offered to take the child to her home, never doubting but that it would be to some cottage in Astley Park, for he had heard Charlie mention the place as being but half a mile distant. Charlie was too thankful, and Grace, seeing that it was all arranged, turned to Nora to give her one last, almost fearful kiss, for the little girl was awed at the sudden change which had come over her who had been for so long her chief companion. Nora feebly returned the kiss, and then her head sank again on her breast, and she relapsed into her former half-conscious state; but as the sobbing child and her companion left the room, Nora roused up once more to look after them, and her eyes fell on Charlie, who was crouched at her feet, his head buried in his hands.

"Go!" she whispered; "her mother—go!"

He started. It was a loud, thrilling whisper.

"Nora—don't send me from you—not now!" he implored—and the head fell forward again, and her eyes closed.

Charlie crept yet nearer to her chair, and took the hand that hung down with such an expression of feebleness and death in every line. He bent his head on that hand, and he fixed his eyes on the face before him as if his earnest gaze could keep back the fast fleeting breath. It came with greater and increasing difficulty now every moment—and the moments flew, and yet it seemed that the end would never come. There was a chance at last. The parched lips parted. There was one long breath, and the eyes half-opened. Was she trying to speak? He sprang up and bent his head to her lips.

"Charlie!"

He just caught the lingering, halting word. The breath stopped. There was one more long, long sigh. Nora was dead.

And the porters and railway-clerks sauntered up and down, laughing and joking carelessly outside that window with the stiff blind; and a country boy passed whistling merrily by the other window, which looked out on the beautiful country and the smooth grass fields; and the train that had just stopped at the station rushed on with its cargo of human life—of hopes and fears, happiness and misery. What did they care that one who, but a few minutes before had been a fellow-traveller, was now lying dead, and that another had been struck by a far worse death—the death of all happiness in this life—the blow that strikes all that has made our life, and yet that leaves us living and breathing still.

Nora had sent happiness to many that morning. She was gone to far greater happiness herself. But Charlie stood alone in his great sorrow. There was no joy for him.

The evening before had seen a very different arrival at that station. Lord and Lady Astley and Bertram, who was now, if not strong, at least well enough to be moved, had left the long, low house, the Vernons and Reginald, a day or two before, and by easy stages had reached Combe Astley on the very evening that had witnessed the landing of our poor gipsies and Grace.

The news of the safe return of the son and heir of the house of Astley, had spread far and wide, and at an early hour the next morning the house was surrounded by the poorer tenantry of the estate and by numbers of people who had experienced Lady Astley's kindness. The higher class of tenants, too, assembled together, and appeared on horseback in a long array, to congratulate " his lordship and the family."

His lordship had not been quite unprepared for this ebullition of feeling, and huge barrels of ale were broached, and long tables spread out under the old trees, which in the good old times had witnessed many a rejoicing of landlord and tenant—the good old feudal times, which are so comfortable to talk of, and which it is so convenient to wish back again; but which, if they were to come by any mistake or accident, would disgust and shock us so dreadfully.

There was "open house" at Combe Astley this day, and Lord Astley, with his wife and Bertram at his side, was just coming out of the house to thank his friends for coming to sympathize with him and to drink his ale. The appearance of the family was greeted with loud cheers.

"Long live my lord—my lady!" but, above all, "Long life to the

young lord!" as they persisted in calling Bertram, were the words
that burst with one accord from that multitude as Bertram thought
it.

Lady Astley bowed in answer to the many hats and handkerchiefs
that waved around, and tears ran down her cheeks, while her husband
stood uncovered, and little Bertram, still pale from the effects of
his illness, took off his straw hat in imitation of his father, and
struggled not to imitate his mother too, by crying.

When the shouting had somewhat subsided, the oldest tenant
on the estate advanced in front of the crowd, and addressed the little
party standing on the steps.

He was a very old man, nearly ninety, but hale and hearty *yet*,
though feeble. His hair was as white as snow, and very long, and
it floated over his blue coat as the wind played with it, raising it
gently and letting it fall daintily as he spoke.

"He was a plain-spoken man," he said, "and there was many a
better, and a richer, and a more knowing in books and such-like,
on the estate, but they'd asked him to speak, and he wouldn't say no
to 'em, because there wasn't one as had known his lordship and the
family as long, or loved 'em better than he did—he could say that.
He'd had been born on the estate, and he'd died on it—at least his
father had, and he hoped he should, and he must say this one thing,
that there never was anything like the family, nor ever would be—
he believed that. He'd lived in the reign of four lords—ay! that he
had—and they'd always been good landlords and kind friends to
him and his, and he'd pray for 'em or drink their health any day;"
and the good old patriarch wandered on in this strain for some
time, thoroughly melting the hearts of Lady Astley and Mrs. Abel
at least.

After some time he arrived at his chief subject, which was, as
Mrs. Abel afterwards expressed it to Mrs. De Verrie, "to thank
Lord and Lady Astley and everybody for Bertram's being safe again,
and to say how glad they all were, and what a nice boy he was,
and that he must be as good as his father and the other lords. Lor'
bless me, I hope he won't be so solemn as dear Lord Astley, or I
shall never be able to teach him his lessons! And then he went on
to say what a pity it was Grace wasn't found too, and where could
she be, and then Lady Astley cried more than ever."

When the old man's speech was over, and he ended it by proposing
the health of "Lord and Lady Astley, and may they live long, and

when they die may they go down to the grave with golden honours like the rising sun!"

Then Lord Astley returned thanks in a short speech of real feeling, and the tears stood in his eyes, as, with a softened heart, he felt that he must yet be an altered and a better man, but, thanks be to God, not a broken-hearted one.

With his still weeping wife, who mourned the more for Grace in the midst of the general rejoicing, and with Bertram, he then walked round the different tables, and by his kindness and his softened manner, he won more hearts in that hour than in all the preceding ones of his "reign" at the home of his fathers.

Suddenly a worthy old farmer, rising in a sort of paroxysm of affection for the family, proposed the health of "Bertram" alone. It was drunk with enthusiasm—three times three; and Bertram coloured with pleasure and excitement, as he stood by his father's side, with his hat in his hand, bowing round to every one with a mixture of shyness and boldness that enchanted Mrs. Abel beyond measure.

"Why, my boy," said his father; "you ought to thank them yourself. I can't stand up for a man like you as I should for mamma."

"May I, mamma?" said the boy, half-longing, half-frightened, looking up to his mother.

"May you?—of course you may, my brave boy," said Lord Astley, delighted and surprised at such a question. "Up with you. There you are! Steady— now then!" and in less than a moment Bertram was mounted on the table.

Oh, how his heart beat, and how the colour mounted to his very temples, with a rushing sound in his ears, and a momentary dizziness, when he found that every one waited for *him*—a little boy—to speak! For one moment his tongue clung to the roof of his mouth, and he could not, oh, he could not, say the words that were so ready just now!

But the moment his little figure was seen on that table one unanimous shout burst from the people; one deep hearty long "hurrah" coming from their very hearts, and rending, as such a shout ought to rend, the very air. It gave him his courage again; and, as it died away, his clear, childish voice rose in the deep silence that followed. Every word was heard, so still, so breathless, were all around.

"My friends," he said, "I wanted to thank you myself, and mamma said I might. I çan't speak like papa or Mr. Alton" (the old man with the white hair), "but I can say how much I thank you all for being so glad to see me, and for—and for drinking my health. There is only one thing I want now to be quite hap——"

He stops suddenly. His colour rushes to his face again. Is he frightened? No. His voice changes. "Oh, take me down! somebody take me down, please! Gracey!—there she is—oh!"

Before the words were well uttered, and before his father had time to turn, a strong faithful arm had lifted him from the table, and he was rushing, tearing at headlong speed through the crowd, which parted on each side as he advanced towards one of the large old trees which reared its huge form at some little distance. It was one that he and Gracey had gazed at on the miserable night in which they had left their home. And who stood beneath it now?

"Gracey, my darling!"

"Bertram!"

The crowd waved and opened again as Lord Astley rapidly pushed through, and he stood to see his children locked in each other's arms, sobbing for very joy. There was another and *such* a shout! And Lord Astley was crying too; he could not help it. As for Mrs. Abel, she seized an unfortunate schoolboy, who had the ill luck to be standing near her at the moment, and began kissing and embracing him with such energy that he never got over it, but remained an idiot for life.

But nobody cared for that, and nobody cared that Charlie had lost his Nora—the only, the one thing he cared for in all this vast, dreary world—for Grace and Bertram are together again *at home*. One is dressed in rags and one in purple and fine linen; and great is the contrast as they cling together under that ancient tree. And the wind rises and clasps together the huge arms of the old tree above them, and all is joy.

Bertram could hardly give her up to her father, and Lord Astley raised her in his arms and took her to her mother; and as he put her in her mother's arms, he uncovered his head once more, and he thanked God aloud for this blessing also.

The multitude is easily led and swayed, and many were the heads uplifted to God on that autumn morning in fervent thankfulness—though some scarcely knew for what they thanked. It was the feeling—the spontaneous sympathy that filled all hearts to overflowing.

Lady Astley ought to have fainted, and although it is of no consequence to any one else, it is extremely inconvenient to me that she did not. I shall have no other opportunity of describing a fainting fit.

Mrs. Abel, having discovered that her idiot was not Bertram, let him go, and pranced round the real Bertram, ready to seize him or his sister at every opportunity.

After the first joy was over, Grace began to tell her little story, or rather only the part which concerned poor Nora.

"She is very, very ill at the station,—Charlie is there; but we must go—I promised to bring mamma."

Certainly the running away had not been in vain, for at least the smallest word from either Grace or Bertram was now law to the inhabitants of Combe Astley—Lord and Lady Astley included. The carriage was ordered, and after Lord Astley had once more thanked his people for their kind sympathy, and begged them to enjoy themselves and make the most of this happy day, the family retired to the house. Grace was quickly dressed in her own attire, and the Astley carriage was shortly conveying them all to the station.

The old man had disappeared. Grace had looked for him as soon as she could think of anything besides "Mamma and Bertram," but he was gone. He had not found out whose child he had undertaken to convey to her parents until they had reached the park-gates. He was feeling too much for the sorrow he had just left to wish to talk, and Grace was crying too much to speak; but when she got nearer home, and every old, familiar object rose one after another before her, childlike, her grief was over and her tears dried; and when she expressed her astonishment at the crowd which was round the house, and "wondered whether papa was at home, or only mamma," he began to rouse himself to ask questions. They pushed through the crowd, nobody recognizing Grace in her rags; and they had just reached the tree as Bertram mounted the table.

Grace's cry of "Bertram, Bertram! mamma!" was lost in the shout that followed, and a "Hush!" from her companion kept her silent till Bertram's eye, in wandering over the crowd of faces, fell upon that one so well-known, and lately so longed for, so missed. The old man only waited to see the meeting between the brother and sister before he set out on his return to the station, which he, being on foot, reached only just as Lady Astley's carriage drove up. He had desired the porters not to disturb the sick girl or the boy in the waiting-room till his return, and he had supported this order by a gratuity and the promise of more. He now inquired anxiously of this man, "How are those poor people?"

"Quiet enough," was the reply. "I looked in just now, and they're all right."

The old man's hand was on the door, and he pushed it open just as Lord and Lady Astley and the children got out of the carriage. Charlie had sunk back to his old position at Nora's feet. He was literally crouched up all of a heap. Her hand was tightly clasped between both of his, his head thrown slightly back, and his eyes, staring wide open, were fixed upon her face. Was he learning by heart every feature, every line, of that face which would so soon be taken from his sight for ever. ? He neither moved nor spoke as the old man, followed by the Astleys, advanced into that strange chamber of death. Many a traveller, many a passenger, had that comfortless room received and sent forth again, but never before had a long, long journey, been thus brought to a close within its walls. It had afforded rest to many—discomfort to many; but such rest as this of Nora's, such wretchedness as that of the gipsy boy,—never.

One glance told the elder of the party that all was over. The gipsy was far beyond the thanks which Lady Astley longed to pour forth to her.

But Bertram and Grace, Bertram especially, eager to see the friend of his wanderings, pushed forward from behind the others, and were rushing towards the motionless couple. A something—a feeling of awe—stopped them half-way: they felt that it was death, but they did not know it.

There was an awful silence. No one moved or spoke.

The old man could bear it no longer. The children's looks of bewilderment, the sudden change from their late joy, was too painful to him. It was too like real life to be natural in children. He stepped lightly forward, and whispered to Bertram, "My child, she is dead."

Then Bertram sprang forward: "Charlie, poor Charlie!" he exclaimed.

How strange the clear ringing voice sounded to the ears of those within that silent room—the voice lifted so lately in such different tones.

He burst into tears and flung himself by the side of Charlie, while Grace clung tremblingly to her newly found mother, as if she feared death would snatch her too from all she loved.

Charlie just turned his head for one moment and then resumed his earnest gaze at the senseless face.

Lord Astley came up and gently led away his boy. He put the children into the carriage with his wife and returned himself to the poor gipsies.

Charlie paid no attention to anything that was said to him, but he fiercely resisted every attempt that was made to touch Nora.

After every means had failed to rouse him, the old man suggested that the children should be brought back.

Lord Astley was unwilling to subject them again to such scenes of sorrow, but he yielded to the entreaties of the stranger, and fetched the children.

They advanced timidly now and clung to their father.

"Speak to him," said the old man.

"What shall I say?" whispered the trembling Grace.

"Tell him that *she* would wish him to go with you could she speak. Say he must not leave her here, but must take her with him—with you."

"Charlie!" said the low voices of both children at once, and two small hands were laid on his rough ones, which still held the hand of death—"Charlie!" Grace went on, "Nora wouldn't like to stay here. People will come soon, Charlie. She would like you to come with us, and she will come too;" and Grace looked up at her father, half fearing that she had said something wrong. But he made her a sign to go on, for Charlie moved and listened as she spoke.

"It would be so horrid when people come, Charlie," said the little girl.

She had touched the right chord. The boy sprung up, and now his chief anxiety was to move "her" before the station was again full. It was done.

In death the poor gipsy reposed on such a soft downy bed as she had never seen in life. She was taken to Combe Astley.

Her death sadly marred the joy of the children at their return home; they had so longed for her to see and know the much-talked of mamma, and all the home ways and places. Their chief pleasure for long was in talking of her to one another or to their mother.

Charlie remained in the same stunned, tearless state for days. It was not till he stood by Nora's grave, and heard the earth rattle on her coffin, that he gave way. Then he flung himself on the ground with a groan that went to the hearts of the few poor villagers who stood round the grave. But tears came and he was better. He never left the Astleys again. It did not seem to enter his head that the world could have any place for him but by Nora's grave; and he would spend hours and hours there in perfect idleness. The children alone could draw him away, and he became after a time their constant companion. Mrs. Abel was quite content that it should be so, for she declared herself to be quite in love with "the poor, dear, darling, broken-hearted gipsy;" which announcement was the cause of a grand consultation between two of the younger children as to whether, if Mrs. Abel did marry Charlie, they would both go away, and "be gipsies;" or whether Charlie would remain at Combe Astley, and be "another governess for Bertram and Gracey." The said Bertram and Grace thought no more of running away, but submitted very quietly to afternoon lessons and the restraints of a school-room life, which seemed light to them after all they had gone through during their gipsy days.

It is believed that Bertram entered the army when he grew up, and that he took Charlie with him as his servant. I have heard, too, that he found the gipsy experience of a camp-life very useful during the terrible winter of 1854-5 amid the horrors of a Crimean campaign.

The   Carved   Lions

CHAPTER I

OLD DAYS

IT IS ALREADY a long time since I was a little girl. Sometimes, when I look out upon the world and see how many changes have come about, how different many things are from what I can remember them, I could believe that a still longer time had passed since my childhood than is really the case. Sometimes, on the contrary, the remembrance of things that then happened comes over me so very vividly, so very *real*-ly, that I can scarcely believe myself to be as old as I am.

I can remember things in my little girlhood more clearly than many in later years. This makes me hope that the story of some part of it may interest children of to-day, for I know I have not forgotten the feelings I had as a child. And after all, I believe that in a great many ways children are very like each other in their hearts and minds, even though their lives may seem very different and very far apart.

The first years of my childhood were very happy, though there were some things in my life which many children would not like at all. My parents were not rich, and the place where we lived was not pretty or pleasant. It was a rather large town in an ugly part of the country, where great tall chimneys giving out black smoke, and streams—once clear sparkling brooks, no doubt—whose water was nearly as black as the smoke, made it often difficult to believe in bright blue sky or green grass, or any of the sweet pure country scenes that children love, though perhaps children that have them do not love them as much as those who have not got them do.

I think that was the way with me. The country was almost the same as fairyland to me—the peeps I had of it now and then were a delight I could not find words to express.

But what matters most to children is not *where* their home is, but *what* it is. And our home was a very sweet and loving one, though it was only a rather small and dull house in a dull street. Our father and mother did everything they possibly could to make us happy, and the trial of living at Great Mexington must have been far worse for them than for us. For they had both been accustomed to rich homes when they were young, and father had never expected that he would have to work so hard or in the sort of way he had to do, after he lost nearly all his money.

When I say "us," I mean my brother Haddie and I. Haddie—whose real name was Haddon—was two years older than I, and we two were the whole family.   My name—*was* I was going to say, for now there are so few people to call me by my Christian name that it seems hardly mine—my name is Geraldine.   Somehow I never had a "short" for it, though it is a long name, and Haddie was always Haddie, and "Haddon" scarcely needs shortening.   I think it was because he nearly always called me Sister or "Sis."

Haddie was between ten and eleven years old and I was nine when the great change that I am going to tell you about came over our lives.   But I must go back a little farther than that, otherwise you would not understand all about us, nor the meaning of the odd title I have chosen for my story.

I had no governess and I did not go to school.   My mother taught me herself, partly, I think, to save expense, and partly because she did not like the idea of sending me to even a day-school at Great Mexington.   For though many of the families there were very rich, and had large houses and carriages and horses and beautiful gardens, they were not always very refined.   There were good and kind and unselfish people there as there are everywhere, but there were some who thought more of being rich than of anything else—the sort of people that are called "purse proud."   And as children very often take after their parents, my father and mother did not like the idea of my having such children as my companions—children who would look down upon me for being poor, and perhaps treat me unkindly on that account.

"When Geraldine is older she must go to school," my father used to say, "unless by that time our ship comes in and we can afford a governess.   But when she is older it will not matter so much, as she will have learnt to value things at their just worth."

I did not then understand what he meant, but I have never forgotten the words.

I was a very simple child.   It never entered my head that there was anything to be ashamed of in living in a small house and having only two servants.   I thought it would be *nice* to have more money, so that mamma would not need to be so busy and could have more pretty dresses, and above all that we could then live in the country, but I never minded being poor in any sore or ashamed way.   And I thought it would be nice to have lots of other little girls to play with. I remember once saying so to mamma, but she shook her head.

"I don't think you would like it as much as you fancy you would," she said. "Not at present at least. When you are a few years older I hope to send you for some classes to Miss Ledbury's school, and by that time you will enjoy the good teaching. But except for the lessons, I am quite sure it is better and happier for you to be at home, even though you find it rather lonely sometimes."

And in his way Haddie said much the same. School was all very well for boys, he told me. If a fellow tried to bully you, you could bully him back. But girls weren't like that—they couldn't fight it out. And when I said to him I didn't want to fight, he still shook his head, and repeated that I wouldn't like school at all—some of his friends' sisters were at school and they hated it.

Still, though I did not often speak of it, the wish to go to school, and the belief that I should find school-life very happy and interesting, remained in my mind. I often made up fancies about it, and pictured myself doing lessons with other little girls and reading the same story-books and playing duets together. I could not believe that I should not like it. The truth was, I suppose, that I was longing for companions of my own age.

It was since Haddie went to school that I had felt lonely. I was a great deal with mamma, but of course there were hours in the day when she was taken up with other things and could not attend to me. I used to long then for the holidays to come so that I should have Haddie again to play with.

My happiest days were Wednesdays and Saturdays, for then he did not go to school in the afternoon. And mamma very often planned some little treat for us on those days, such as staying up to have late tea with her and papa when he came in from his office, or reading aloud some new story-book, or going a walk with her in the afternoon and buying whatever we liked for our own tea at the confectioner's.

Very simple treats—but then we were very simple children, as I have said already.

Our house, though in a street quite filled with houses, was some little way from the centre of the town, where the best shops were—some years before, our street had, I suppose, been considered quite in the country. We were very fond of going to the shops with mamma. We thought them very grand and beautiful, though they were not nearly as pretty as shops are nowadays, for they were much smaller and darker, so that the things could not be spread out in the attractive way they are now, nor were the things themselves nearly as varied and tempting.

There was one shop which interested us very much. It belonged to the principal furniture-maker of Mexington. It scarcely looked like a shop, but was more like a rather gloomy private house very full of heavy dark cabinets and tables and wardrobes and chairs, mostly of mahogany, and all extremely good and well made. Yes, furniture, though ugly, really was very good in those days—I have one or two relics of my old home still, in the shape of a leather-covered armchair and a beautifully-made chest of drawers. For mamma's godmother had helped to furnish our house when we came to Mexington, and she was the sort of old lady who when she *did* give a present gave it really good of its kind. She had had furniture herself made by Cranston—that was the cabinetmaker's name—for her home was in the country only about three hours' journey from Mexington—and it had been first-rate, so she ordered what she gave mamma from him also.

But it was not because the furniture was so good that we liked going to Cranston's. It was for quite another reason. A little way in from the front entrance to the shop, where there were glass doors to swing open, stood a pair of huge lions carved in very dark, almost black, wood. They were nearly, if not quite, as large as life, and the first time I saw them, when I was only four or five, I was really frightened of them. They guarded the entrance to the inner part of the shop, which was dark and gloomy and mysterious-looking, and I remember clutching fast hold of mamma's hand as we passed them, not feeling at all sure that they would not suddenly spring forward and catch us. But when mamma saw that I was frightened, she stopped and made me feel the lions and stroke them to show me that they were only wooden and could not possibly hurt me. And after that I grew very fond of them, and was always asking her to take me to the "lion shop."

Haddie liked them too—his great wish was to climb on one of their backs and play at going a ride.

I don't think I thought of that. What I liked was to stroke their heavy manes and fancy to myself what I would do if, all of a sudden, one of them "came alive," as I called it, and turned his head round and looked at me. And as I grew older, almost without knowing it, I made up all sorts of fairy fancies about the lions—I sometimes thought they were enchanted princes, sometimes that they were real lions who were only carved in the wood in the day-time, and at night walked about wherever they liked.

So, for one reason or another, both Haddie and I were always very pleased when mamma had to look in at Cranston's.

This happened oftener than might have been expected, considering that our house was small, and that my father and mother were not rich enough often to buy new furniture. For mamma's god-mother seemed to be always ordering something or other at the cabinet-maker's, and as she knew mamma was very sensible and careful, she used to write to her to explain to Cranston about the things she wanted, or to look at them before he sent them home, to see that they were all right. And Cranston was always very polite indeed to mamma.

He himself was a stout, red-faced, little, elderly man, with grey whiskers, which he brushed up in a fierce kind of way that made him look like a rather angry cat, though he really was a very gentle and kind old man. I thought him much nicer than his partner, whose name was Berridge, a tall, thin man, who talked very fast, and made a great show of scolding any of the clerks or workmen who happened to be about.

Mr. Cranston was very proud of the lions. They had belonged to his grandfather and then to his father, who had both been in the same sort of business as he was, and he told mamma they had been carved in "the East." I didn't know what he meant by the East, and I don't now know what country he was alluding to—India or China or Japan. And I am not sure that he knew himself. But 'the East" sounded far away and mysterious—it might do for fairyland or brownieland, and I was quite satisfied. No doubt, wherever they came from, the lions were very beautifully carved.

Now I will go on to tell about the changes that came into our lives, closing the doors of these first happy childish years, when there scarcely seemed to be ever a cloud on our sky.

One day, when I was a month or two past nine years old, mamma said to me just as I was finishing my practising—I used to practise half an hour every other day, and have a music lesson from mamma the between days—that she was going out to do some shopping that afternoon, and that, if I liked, I might go with her.

"I hope it will not rain," she added, "though it does look rather threatening. But perhaps it will hold off till evening."

"And I can take my umbrella in case it rains," I said. I was very proud of my umbrella. It had been one of my last birthday presents. "Yes, mamma, I should like to come very much. Will Haddie come too?"

For it was Wednesday—one of his half-holidays.

"To tell the truth," said mamma, "I forgot to ask him this morning if he would like to come, but he will be home soon—it is nearly luncheon time. I daresay he will like to come, especially as I have to go to Cranston's."

She smiled a little as she said this. Our love for the carved lions amused her.

"Oh yes, I am sure he will like to come," I said. "And may we buy something for tea at Miss Fryer's on our way home?"

Mamma smiled again.

"That will be two treats instead of one," she said, "but I daresay I can afford two or three pence."

Miss Fryer's was our own pet confectioner, or pastry-cook, as we used to say more frequently then. She was a Quakeress, and her shop was very near our house, so near that mamma let me go there alone with Haddie. Miss Fryer was very grave and quiet, but we were not at all afraid of her, for we knew that she was really very kind. She was always dressed in pale grey or fawn colour, with a white muslin shawl crossed over her shoulders, and a white net cap beautifully quilled and fitting tightly round her face, so that only a very little of her soft grey hair showed. She always spoke to us as "thou" and "thee," and she was very particular to give us exactly what we asked for, and also to take the exact money in payment. But now and then, after the business part had been all correctly settled, she would choose out a nice bun, or sponge-cake, or two or three biscuits, and would say "I give thee this as a present." And she did not like us to say "Thank you, Miss Fryer," but "Thank you, friend Susan." I daresay she would have liked us to say "Thank thee," but neither Haddie nor I had the courage for that!

I ran upstairs in high spirits, and five minutes after when Haddie came in from school he was nearly as pleased as I to hear our plans.

"If only it does not rain," said mamma at luncheon.

Luncheon was, of course, our dinner, and it was often mamma's dinner really too. Our father was sometimes so late of getting home that he liked better to have tea than a regular dinner. But mamma always called it luncheon because it seemed natural to her.

"I don't mind if it does rain," said Haddie, "because of my new mackintosh."

Haddie was very proud of his mackintosh, which father had got him for going to and coming from school in rainy weather. Mackintoshes were then a new invention, and very expensive compared with what they are now. But Haddie was rather given to catching cold, and at Great Mexington it did rain very often— much oftener than anywhere else, I am quite sure.

"And Geraldine doesn't mind because of her new umbrella," said mamma. "So we are proof against the weather, whatever happens."

It may seem strange that I can remember so much of a time now so very long ago. But I really do—of that day and of those that followed it especially, because, as I have already said, they were almost the close of the first part of our childish life.

That afternoon was such a happy one. We set off with mamma, one on each side of her, hanging on her arms, Haddie trying to keep step with her, and I skipping along on my tiptoes. When we got to the more crowded streets we had to separate—that is to say, Haddie had let go of mamma's arm, so that he could fall behind when we met more than one person. For the pavements at Mexington were in some parts narrow and old-fashioned.

Mamma had several messages to do, and at some of the shops Haddie and I waited outside because we did not think they were very interesting. But at some we were only too ready to go in. One I remember very well. It was a large grocer's. We thought it a most beautiful shop, though nowadays it would be considered quite dull and gloomy, compared with the brilliant places of the kind you see filled with biscuits and dried fruits of all kinds of groceries tied up with ribbons, or displayed in boxes of every colour of the rainbow. I must say I think the groceries themselves were quite as good as they are now, and in some cases better, but that may be partly my fancy, as I daresay I have a partiality for old-fashioned things.

Mamma did not buy all our groceries at this grand shop, for it was considered dear. But certain things, such as tea—which cost five shillings a pound then—she always ordered there. And the grocer, like Cranston, was a very polite man. I think he understood that though she was not rich, and never bought a great deal, mamma was different in herself from the grandly-dressed Mexington ladies who drove up to his shop in their carriages, with a long list of all the things they wanted. And when mamma had finished giving her order, he used always to offer Haddie and me a gingerbread biscuit of a very particular and delicious kind. They were large round biscuits, of a nice bright brown colour, and underneath they had thin

white wafer, which we called " eating paper." They were crisp
without being hard. I never see gingerbreads like them now.

"This is a lucky day, mamma," I said, when we came out of the
grocer's. "Mr. Simeon never forgets to give us gingerbreads when
he is there himself."

"No," said mamma, "he is a very kind man. Perhaps he has got
Haddies and Geraldines of his own, and knows what they like."

"And now are we going to Cranston's?" asked my brother.

Mamma looked at the paper in her hand. She was very careful
and methodical in all her ways, and always wrote down what she had
to do before she came out.

"Yes," she said, "I think I have done everything else. But I
shall be some little time at Cranston's. Mrs. Selwood has asked me
to settle ever so many things with him—she is going abroad for the
winter, and wants him to do a good deal of work at Fernley while she
is away."

CHAPTER II

A HAPPY EVENING

HADDIE AND I were not at all sorry to hear that mamma's call at
Cranston's was not to be a hurried one.

"We don't mind if you are ever so long," I said; "do we, Haddie?"

"No, of course we don't," Haddie agreed. "I should like to spend
a whole day in those big showrooms of his. Couldn't we have jolly
games of hide-and-seek, Sis? And then riding the lions! I wish
you were rich enough to buy one of the lions, mamma, and have it
for an ornament in the hall, or in the drawing-room."

"We should need to build a hall or a drawing-room to hold it,"
said mamma, laughing. "I'm afraid your lion would turn into a
white elephant, Haddie, if it became ours."

I remember wondering what she meant. How could a lion turn
into an elephant? But I was rather a slow child in some ways.
Very often I thought a thing over a long time in my mind if I did
not underatnd it before asking any one to explain it. And so before
I said anything it went out of my head, for here we were at Cranston's
door.

There was only a young shopman to be seen, but when mamma told him she particularly wanted to see Mr. Cranston himself, he asked us to step in and take a seat while he went to fetch him.

We passed between the lions. It seemed quite a long time since we had seen them, and I thought they looked at us very kindly. I was just nudging Haddie to whisper this to him when mamma stopped to say to us that we might stay in the outer room if we liked; she knew it was our favourite place, and in a few minutes we heard her talking to old Mr. Cranston, who had come to her in the inner showroom through another door.

Haddie's head was full of climbing up on to one of the lions to go a ride. But luckily he could not find anything to climb up with, which was a very good thing, as he would have been pretty sure to topple over, and Mr. Cranston would not have been at all pleased if he had scratched the lion.

To keep him quiet I began talking to him about my fancies. I made him look close into the lions' faces—it was getting late in the afternoon, and we had noticed before we came in that the sun was setting stormily. A ray of bright orange-coloured light found its way in through one of the high-up windows which were at the back of the show-room, and fell right across the mane of one of the lions and almost into the eyes of the other. The effect on the dark, almost black, wood of which they were made was very curious.

"Look, Haddie," I said suddenly, catching his arm, "doesn't it really look as if they were smiling at us—the one with the light on its face especially? I really do think there's something funny about them—I wonder if they are enchanted."

Haddie did not laugh at me. I think in his heart he was fond of fancies too, though he might not have liked the boys at school to know it. He sat staring at our queer friends nearly as earnestly as I did myself. And as the ray of light slowly faded, he turned to me.

"Yes," he said, "their faces do seem to change. But I think they always look kind."

"They do to us," I said confidently, "but sometimes they are quite fierce. I don't think they looked at us the way they do now the first time they saw us. And one day one of the men in the shop shoved something against one of them and his face frowned—I'm sure it did."

"I wonder if he'd frown if I got up on his back," said Haddie.

"Oh do leave off about climbing on their backs," I said. "It wouldn't be at all comfortable—they're so broad, you couldn't sit cross-legs, and they'd be as slippery as anything. It's much nicer to make up stories about them coming alive in the night, or turning into black princes and saying magic words to make the doors open like in the Arabian Nights."

"Well, tell me stories of all they do then," said Haddie condescendingly.

"I will if you'll let me think for a minute," I said. "I wish Aunty Etta was here—she does know such lovely stories."

"I like your's quite as well," said Haddie encouragingly, "I don't remember Aunty Etta's; it's such a long time since I saw her. You saw her last year, you know, but I didn't."

"She told me one about a china parrot, a most beautiful green and gold parrot, that was really a fairy," I said. "I think I could turn it into a lion story, if I thought about it."

"No," said Haddie, "you can tell the parrot one another time. I'd rather hear one of your own stories, new, about the lions. I know you've got some in your head. Begin, do—I'll help you if you can't get on."

But my story that afternoon was not to be heard. Just as I was beginning with, "Well, then, there was once an old witch who lived in a very lonely hut in the middle of a great forest," there came voices behind us, and in another moment we heard mamma saying,

"Haddie, my boy, Geraldine, I am quite ready."

I was not very sorry. I liked to have more time to make up my stories, and Haddie sometimes hurried me so. It was Aunty Etta, I think, who had first put it into my head to make them. She was *so* clever about it herself, both in making stories and in remembering those she had read. And she *had* read a lot. But she was away in India at the time I am now writing about; her going so far off was a great sorrow to mamma.

Haddie and I started up at once. We had to be very obedient, what father called "quickly obedient," and though he was so kind he was very strict too.

"My children are great admirers of your lions, Mr. Cranston,' mamma said; and the old man smiled.

"They are not singular in their taste, madam," he said. "I own that I am very proud of them myself, and when my poor daughter was a child there was nothing pleased her so much as when her mother or I lifted her on to one of them, and made believe she was going a ride."

Haddie looked triumphant.

"There now you see, Sis," he whispered, nudging me.

But I did not answer him, for I was listening to what mamma was saying.

"Oh, by the bye, Mr. Cranston," she went on, "I was forgetting to ask how your little grandchild is. Have you seen her lately?"

Old Cranston's face brightened.

"She is very well, madam, I thank you," he replied. "And I am pleased to say that she is coming to stay with us shortly. We hope to keep her through the winter. Her stepmother is very kind, but with little children of her own, it is not always easy for her to give as much attention as she would like to Myra, and she and Mr. Raby have responded cordially to our invitation."

"I am very glad to hear it—very glad indeed," said mamma. "I know what a pleasure it will be to you and Mrs. Cranston. Let me see—how old is the little girl now—seven, eight?"

"*Nine*, madam, getting on for ten indeed," said Mr. Cranston with pride.

"Dear me," said mamma, "how time passes! I remember seeing her when she was a baby—before we came to live here, of course, once when I was staying at Fernley, just after——"

Mamma stopped and hesitated.

"Just after her poor mother died—yes, madam," said the old man quietly.

And then we left, Mr. Cranston respectfully holding the door open.

It was growing quite dark; the street lamps were lighted and their gleam was reflected on the pavement, for it had been raining and was still quite wet underfoot. Mamma looked round her.

"You had better put on your mackintosh, Haddie," she said. "It may rain again. No, Geraldine dear, there is no use opening your umbrella till it does rain."

My feelings were divided between pride in my umbrella and some reluctance to have it wet! I took hold of mamma's arm again, while Haddie walked at her other side. It was not a very cheerful prospect before us—the gloomy dirty streets of Mexington were now muddy and sloppy as well—though on the whole I don't know but what they looked rather more cheerful by gaslight than in the day. It was chilly too, for the season was now very late autumn, if not winter. But little did we care—I don't think there could have been found anywhere two happier children than my brother and I that dull rainy evening as we trotted along beside our mother. There was the feeling of *her* to take care of us, of our cheerful home waiting

for us, with a bright fire and the tea-table all spread. If I had not
been a little tired—for we had walked a good way—in my heart I
was just as ready to skip along on the tips of my toes as when we
first came out.

"We may stop at Miss Fryer's, mayn't we, mamma?" said Haddie.

"Well, yes, I suppose I promised you something for tea," mamma
replied.

"How much may we spend?" he asked. "Sixpence—do say
sixpence, and then we can get enough for you to have tea with us too."

"Haddie," I said reproachfully, "as if we wouldn't give mamma
something however little we had!"

"We'd offer it her of course, but you know she wouldn't take
it," he replied. "So it's much better to have really enough for all."

His way of speaking made mamma laugh again.

"Then I suppose it must be sixpence," she said, "and here we are
at Miss Fryer's. Shall we walk on, my little girl, I think you must
be tired, and let Haddie invest in cakes and run after us?"

"Oh no, please mamma, dear," I said, "I like so to choose too."

Half the pleasure of the sixpence would have been gone if Haddie
and I had not spent it together.

"Then I will go on," said mamma, "and you two can come after
me together."

She took out her purse and gave my brother the promised money,
and then with a smile on her dear face—I can see her now as she
stood in the light of the street-lamp just at the old Quakeress's
door—she nodded to us and turned to go.

I remember exactly what we bought, partly, perhaps, because it
was our usual choice. We used to think it over a good deal first
and each would suggest something different, but in the end we
nearly always came back to the old plan for the outlay of our sixpence,
namely, half-penny crumpets for threepence—that meant *seven*, not
six; it was the received custom to give seven for threepence—and
half-penny Bath buns for the other threepence—seven of them too,
of course. And *Bath* buns, not plain ones. You cannot get these
now—not at least in any place where I have lived of late years. And
I am not sure but that even at Mexington they were a *specialité* of
dear old Miss Fryer's. They were so good; indeed, everything she
sold was thoroughly good of its kind. She was so honest, using the
best materials for all she made.

That evening she stood with her usual gentle gravity while we
discussed what we should have, and when after discarding sponge-

cakes and finger-biscuits, which we had thought of "for a change," and partly because finger-biscuits weighed light and made a good show, we came round at last to the seven crumpets and seven buns, she listened as seriously and put them up in their little paper bags with as much interest as though the ceremony had never been gone through before. And than just as we were turning to leave, she lifted up a glass shade and drew out two cheese-cakes, which she proceeded to put into another paper bag.

Haddie and I looked at each other. This was a lovely present. What a tea we should have!

"I think thee will find these good," she said with a smile, "and I hope thy dear mother will not think them too rich for thee and thy brother."

She put them into my hand, and of course we thanked her heartily. I have often wondered why she never said "thou wilt," but always "thee will," for she was not an uneducated woman by any means.

Laden with our treasures Haddie and I hurried home. There was mamma watching for us with the door open. How sweet it was to have her always to welcome us!

"Tea is quite ready, dears," she said. "Run upstairs quickly, Geraldine, and take off your things, they must be damp. I am going to have my real tea with you, for I have just had a note from your father to say he won't be in till late and I am not to wait for him."

Mamma sighed a little as she spoke. I felt sorry for her disappointment, but, selfishly speaking, we sometimes rather enjoyed the evenings father was late, for then mamma gave us her whole attention, as she was not able to do when he was at home. And though we were very fond of our father, we were—I especially, I think—much more afraid of him than of our mother.

And that was such a happy evening! I have never forgotten it. Mamma was so good and thoughtful for us, she did not let us find out in the least that she was feeling anxious on account of something father had said in his note to her. She was just perfectly sweet.

We were very proud of our spoils from Miss Fryer's. We wanted mamma to have one cheese-cake and Haddie and I to divide the other between us. But mamma would not agree to that. She would only take a half, so that we had three-quarters each.

"Wasn't it kind of Miss Fryer, mamma?" I said.

"Very kind," said mamma. "I think she is really fond of children though she is so grave. She has not forgotten what it was to be a child herself."

Somehow her words brought back to my mind what old Mr.
Cranston had said about his little grand-daughter.

"I suppose children *are* all rather like each other," I said. "Like
about Haddie and that little girl riding on the lions."

Haddie was not very pleased at my speaking of it; he was beginning
to be afraid of seeming babyish.

"That was *quite* different," he said. "She was a baby and had to
be held on. It was the fun of climbing up *I* cared for."

"She wasn't a baby," I said. "She's nine years old, he said she
was—didn't he, mamma?"

"You are mixing two things together," said mamma. "Mr.
Cranston was speaking first of his daughter long ago when she was a
child, and then he was speaking of *her* daughter, little Myra Raby,
who is now nine years old."

"Why did he say my "poor" daughter?" I asked.

"Did you not hear the allusion to her death? Mrs. Raby died
soon after little Myra was born. Mr. Raby married again—he is a
clergyman not very far from Fernley——"

"A clergyman," exclaimed Haddie. He was more worldly-wise
than I, thanks to being at school. "A clergyman, and he married
a shopkeeper's daughter."

"There are very different kinds of shopkeepers, Haddie," said
mamma. "Mr. Cranston is very rich, and his daughter was very
well educated and very nice. Still, no doubt Mr. Raby was in a
higher position than she, and both Mr. Cranston and his wife are
very right-minded people, and never pretend to be more than they
are. That is why I was so glad to hear that little Myra is coming to
stay with them. I was afraid the second Mrs. Raby might have
looked down upon them perhaps."

Haddie said no more about it. And though I listened to what
mamma said, I don't think I quite took in the sense of it till a good
while afterwards. It has often been like that with me in life. I
have a curiously "retentive" memory, as it is called. Words and
speeches remain in my mind like unread letters, till some day, quite
unexpectedly, something reminds me of them, and I take them out,
as it were, and find what they really meant.

But just now my only interest in little Myra Raby's history was
a present one.

"Mamma," I said suddenly, "if she is a nice little girl like what
her mamma was, mightn't I have her to come and see me and play
with me? I have never had a little girl to play with, and it is so dull

sometimes—the days that Haddie is late at school, and when you are busy. Do say I may have her—I'm sure old Mr. Cranston would let her come, and then I might go and play with her sometimes perhaps. Do you think she will play among the furniture—where the lions are?"

Mamma shook her head.

"No, dear," she answered. "I am quite sure her grandmother would not like that. For, you see, anybody might come in to the shop or show-rooms, and it would not seem nice for a little girl to be playing there—not nice for a carefully brought-up little girl, I mean."

"Then I don't think I should care to go to her house," I said, "but I would like her to come here. Please let her, mamma dear."

But mamma only said,

"We shall see."

After tea she told us stories—some of them we had heard often before, but we never tired of hearing them again—about when she and Aunty Etta were little girls. They were lovely stories—real ones of course. Mamma was not as clever as Aunty Etta about making up fairy ones.

We were quite sorry when it was time to go to bed.

After I had been asleep for a little that night I woke up again—I had not been very sound asleep. Just then I saw a light, and mamma came into the room with a candle.

"I'm not asleep, dear mamma," I said. "Do kiss me, again."

"That is what I have come for," she answered.

And she came up to the bedside and kissed me, oh so sweetly—more than once. She seemed as if she did not want to let go of me.

"Dear mamma," I whispered sleepily, "I *am* so happy—I'm always happy, but to-night I feel so *extra* happy somehow."

"Darling," said mamma.

And she kissed me again.

CHAPTER III

COMING EVENTS

THE SHADOW of coming changes began to fall over us very soon after that.

Indeed, the very next morning at breakfast I noticed that mamma looked pale and almost as if she had been crying, and father was, so to say, "extra" kind to her and to me. He talked and laughed more than usual, partly perhaps to prevent our noticing how silent dear mamma was, but mostly I think because that is the way men do when they are really anxious or troubled.

I don't fancy Haddie thought there was anything wrong—he was in a hurry to get off to school.

After breakfast mamma told me to go and practice for half an hour, and if she did not come to me then, I had better go on doing some of my lessons alone. She would look them over afterwards. And as I was going out of the room she called me back and kissed me again —almost as she had done the night before.

That gave me courage to say something. For children were not, in my childish days, on such free and easy terms with their elders as they are now. And kind and gentle as mamma was, we knew very distinctly the sort of things she would think forward or presuming on our part.

"Mamma," I said, still hesitating a little.

"Well, dear," she replied. She was buttoning, or pretending to button, the band of the little brown holland apron I wore, so that I could not see her face, but something in the tone of her voice told me that my instinct was not mistaken.

"Mamma," I repeated, "may I say something? I have a feeling that—that you are—that there is something the matter."

Mamma did not answer at once. Then she said very gently, but quite kindly,

"Geraldine, my dear, you know that I tell you as much as I think it right to tell any one as young as you—I tell you more, of our plans and private matters and such things, than most mothers tell their little daughters. This has come about partly through your being so

202

much alone with me. But when I *don't* tell you anything, even though you may suspect there is something to tell, you should trust me that there is good reason for my not doing so."

"Yes," I said, but I could not stifle a little sigh. "Would you just tell me one thing, mamma," I went on; "it isn't anything that you're really unhappy about, is it?"

Again mamma hesitated.

"Dear child," she said, "try to put it out of your mind. I can only say this much to you, I am *anxious* more than troubled. There is nothing the matter that should really be called a trouble. But your father and I have a question of great importance to decide just now, and we are very—I may say really *terribly*—anxious to decide for the best. That is all I can tell you. Kiss me, my darling, and try to be your own bright little self. That will be a comfort and help to me."

I kissed her and I promised I would try to do as she wished. But it was with rather a heavy heart that I went to my practising. What *could* it be? I did try not to think of it, but it would keep coming back into my mind. And I was only a child. I had no experience of trouble or anxiety. After a time my spirits began to rise again—there was a sort of exitement in the wondering what this great matter could be. I am afraid I did not succeed in putting it out of my mind as mamma wished me to do.

But the days went on without anything particular happening. I did not speak of what mamma had said to me to my brother. I knew she did not wish me to do so. And by degrees other things began to make me forget about it a little. It was just at that time, I remember, that some friend—an aunt on father's side, I think—sent me a present of *The Wide, Wide World,* and while I was reading it I seemed actually to live in the story. It was curious that I should have got it just then. If mamma had read it herself I am not sure that she would have given it to me. But after all, perhaps it served the purpose of preparing me a *little*—a very little—for what was before me in my own life.

It was nearly three weeks after the time I have described rather minutely that the blow fell, that Haddie and I were told the whole. I think, however, I will not go on telling *how* we were told, for I am afraid of making my story too long.

And of course, however good my memory is, I cannot pretend that the conversations I relate took place *exactly* as I give them. I think I give the *spirit* of them correctly, but now that I have come to the telling of distant facts, perhaps it will be better simply to narrate them.

You will remember my saying that my father had lost money very unexpectedly, and that this was what had obliged him to come to live at Mexington and work so hard. He had got the post he held there —it was in a bank—greatly through the influence of Mrs. Selwood, mamma's godmother, who lived in the country at some hour's distance from the town, and whose name was well-known there, as she owned a great many houses and other property in the immediate neighbourhood.

Father was very glad to get this post, and very grateful to Mrs. Selwood. She took great interest in us all—that is to say, she was interested in Haddie and me because we were mamma's children, though she did not care for or understand children as a rule. But she was a faithful friend, and anxious to help father still more.

Just about the time I have got to in my story, the manager of a bank in South America, in some way connected with the one at Great Mexington, became ill, and was told by the doctors that he must return to England and have a complete rest for two years. Mrs. Selwood had money connection with this bank too, and got to hear of what had happened. Knowing that father could speak both French and Spanish well, for he had been in the diplomatic service as a younger man, she at once applied for the appointment for him, and after some little delay she was told that he should have the offer of it for the two years.

Two years are not a very long time. even though the pay was high, but the great advantage of the offer was that the heads of the bank at Mexington promised, if all went well for that time, that some permanent post should be given to father in England on his return. This was what made him more anxious to accept the proposal than even the high pay. For Mrs. Selwood found out that he would not be able to save much of his salary, as he would have a large house to keep up, and would be expected to receive many visitors. On this account the post was never given to an unmarried man.

"If he accepts it," Mrs. Selwood wrote to mamma, "you, my dear Blanche, must go with him, and some arrangement would have to be made about the children for the time. I would advise your sending them to school."

Now I think my readers will not be at a loss to understand why our dear mother had looked so troubled, even though on one side this event promised to be for our good in the end.

Father was allowed two or three weeks in which to make up his mind. The heads of the Mexington bank liked and respected him very much, and they quite saw that there were two sides to the question of his accepting the offer. The climate of the place was not very good—at least it was injurious to English people if they stayed there for long—and it was perfectly certain that it would be madness to take growing children like Haddie and me there.

This was the dark spot in it all to mamma, and indeed to father too. They were not afraid for themselves. They were both strong and still young, but they could not for a moment entertain the idea of taking *us*. And the thought of the separation was terrible.

You see, being a small family, and living in a place like Great Mexington, where my parents had not many congenial friends, and being poor were obliged to live carefully, *home* was everything to us all. We four were the whole world to each other, and knew no happiness apart.

I do not mean to say that I felt or saw all this at once, but looking back upon it from the outside, as it were, I see all that made it a peculiarly hard case, especially—at the beginning, that is to say—for mamma.

It seems strange that I did *not* take it all in—all the misery of it, I mean—at first, nor indeed for some time, not till I had actual experience of it. Even Haddie realised it more in anticipation than I did. He was two years older, and though he had never been at boarding-school, still he knew something of school life. There were boarders at his school, and he had often seen and heard how, till they got accustomed to it at any rate, they suffered from home-sickness, and counted the days to the holidays.

And for us there were not to be any holidays! No certain prospect of them at best, though Mrs. Selwood said something vaguely about perhaps having us at Fernley for a visit in the summer. But it was very vague. And we had no near relations on mamma's side except Aunty Etta, who was in India, and on father's no one who could possibly have us regularly for our holidays.

All this mamma grasped at once, and her grief was sometimes so extreme that, but for Mrs. Selwood, I doubt if father would have had the resolution to accept. But Mrs. Selwood was what is called "very sensible," perhaps just a little hard, and certainly not *sensitive*. And she put things before our parents in such a way that mamma felt it her duty to urge father to accept the offer, and father felt it *his* duty to put feelings aside and do so.

They went to stay at Fernley from a Saturday to a Monday to talk it well over, and it was when they came back on the Monday that we were told.

Before then I think we had both come to have a strong feeling that something was going to happen. I, of course, had some reason for this in what mamma had said to me, though I had forgotten about it a good deal, till this visit to Fernley brought back the idea of something unusual. For it was *very* seldom that we were left by ourselves.

We did not mind it much. After all, it was only two nights and one *whole* day, and that a Sunday, when my brother was at home, so we stood at the door cheerfully enough, looking at our father and mother driving off in the clumsy, dingy old four-wheeler—though that is a modern word—which was the best kind of cab known at Mexington.

But when they were fairly off Haddie turned to me, and I saw that he was very grave. I was rather surprised.

"Why, Haddie," I said, "do you mind so much? They'll be back on Monday."

"No, of course I don't mind *that*," he said. "But I wonder why mamma looks so—so awfully trying-not-to-cry, you know."

"Oh," I said, "I don't think she's quite well. And she hates leaving us."

"No," said my brother, "there's something more."

And when he said that, I remembered the feeling I had had myself. I felt rather cross with Haddie; I wanted to forget it quite.

"You needn't try to frighten me like that," I said. "I meant to be quite happy while they were away—to please mamma, you know, by telling her so when she comes back."

Then Haddie, who really was a very good-natured, kind boy, looked sorry.

"I didn't mean to frighten you," he said; "perhaps it was my fancy. I don't want to be unhappy while they're away, I'm sure. I'm only too glad that to-day's Saturday and to-morrow Sunday."

And he did his very best to amuse me. We went out a walk that afternoon with the housemaid—quite a long walk, though it was winter. We went as far out of the town as we could get, to where there were fields, which in spring and summer still looked green, and through the remains of a little wood, pleasant even in the dullest season. It was our favourite walk, and the only pretty one near the town. There was a brook at the edge of the wood, which still did its best to sing merrily, and to forget how dingy and grimy its clear waters became a mile or two further on; there were still a few treasures in the shape of ivy sprays and autumn-tinted leaves to gather and take home with us to deck our nursery.

I remember the look of it all so well. It was the favourite walk of many besides ourselves, especially on a Saturday, when the hard-worked Mexington folk were for once free to ramble about—boys and girls not much older than ourselves among them, for in those days children were allowed to work in factories much younger than they do now. We did not mind meeting some of our townsfellows. On the contrary, we felt a good deal of interest in them and liked to hear their queer way of talking, though we could scarcely understand anything they said. And we were very much interested indeed in some of the stories Lydia, who belonged to this part of the country, told us of her own life, in a village a few miles away, where there were two or three great factories, at which all the people about worked—men, women, and children too, so that sometimes, except for babies and very old people, the houses seemed quite deserted.

"And long ago before that," said Lydia, "when mother was a little lass, it was such a pretty village—cottages all over with creepers and honeysuckle—not ugly rows of houses as like each other as peas. The people worked at home on their own hand-looms then."

Lydia had a sense of the beautiful!

On our way home, of course, we called at Miss Fryer's—this time we had a whole shilling to spend, for there was Sunday's tea to think of as well as to-day's. We had never had so much at a time, and our consultation took a good while. We decided at last on seven crumpets and seven Bath buns as usual, and in addition to these, three large currant tea-cakes, which our friend Susan told us would be all the better for toasting if not too fresh. And the remaining threepence we invested in a slice of sweet sandwich, which she told us would be perfectly good if kept in a tin tightly closed. The old Quakeress for once, I have always suspected, departed on this occasion from her rule of exact payment for all purchases, for it certainly seemed a very large slice of sweet sandwich for threepence.

We were rather tired with our walk that evening and went to bed early. Nothing more was said by Haddie about his misgivings. I think he hoped I had forgotten what had passed, but I had not. It had all come back again, the strange feeling of change and trouble in the air which had made me question mamma that morning two or three weeks ago.

But I did not as yet really believe it. I had never known what sorrow and trouble actually are. It is not many children who reach even the age I was then with so sunny and peaceful an experience of life. That anything could happen to us—to *me*—like what happened to "Ellen" in *The Wide, Wide World*, I simply could not believe; even though if any one had talked to me about it and said that troubles must come and *do* come to all, and to some much more than to others, and that they might be coming to us, I should have agreed at once and said yes, of course I knew that was true.

The next day, Sunday, was very rainy. It made us feel dull, I think, though we did not really mind a wet Sunday as much as another day, for we never went a walk on a Sunday. It was not thought right, and as we had no garden the day would have been a very dreary one to us, except for mamma.

She managed to make it pleasant. We went to church in the morning, and in the evening too sometimes. I think all children like going to church in the evening; there is something grown-up about it. And the rest of the day mamma managed to find interesting things for us to do. She generally had some book which she kept for reading aloud on Sunday—Dr. Adams's *Allegories*, "The Dark River" and others, were great favourites, and so were Bishop Wilberforce's *Agathos*. Some of them frightened me a little, but it was a rather pleasant sort of fright, there was something grand and solemn about it.

Then we sang hymns sometimes, and we always had a very nice tea, and mamma, and father too now and them, told us stories about when they were children and what they did no Sundays. It was much stricter for them than for us, though even for us many things were forbidden on Sundays which are now thought not only harmless but right.

Still, I never look back to the quiet Sundays in the dingy Mexington street with anything but a feeling of peace and gentle pleasure.

CHAPTER IV

ALL SETTLED

THAT SUNDAY—that last Sunday I somehow feel inclined to call it—stands out in my memory quite differently from its fellows. Both Haddie and I felt dull and depressed, partly owing no doubt to the weather, but still more, I think, from that vague fear of something being wrong which we were both suffering from, though we would not speak of it to each other.

It cleared up a little in the evening, and though it was cold and chilly we went to church. Mamma had said to us we might if we liked, and Lydia was going.

When we came in, cook sent us a little supper which we were very glad of; it cheered us up.

"Aren't you thankful they're coming home tomorrow?" I said to Haddie. "I've never minded their being away so much before."

They had been away two or three times that we could remember, though never for longer than a day or two.

"Yes," said Haddie, "I'm very glad."

But that was all he said.

They did come back the next day, pretty early in the morning, as father had to be at the bank. He went straight there from the railway station, and mamma drove home with the luggage. She was very particular when she went to stay with her godmother to take nice dresses, for Mrs. Selwood would not have been pleased to see her looking shabby, and it would not have made her any more sympathising or anxious to help, but rather the other way. Long afterwards—at least some years afterwards, when I was old enough to understand—I remember Mrs. Selwood saying to me that it was mamma's courage and good management which made everybody respect her.

I was watching at the dining-room window, which looked out to the street, when the cab drove up. After the heavy rain the day before, it was for once a fine day, with some sunshine. And sunshine was rare at Great Mexington, especially in late November.

Mamma was looking out to catch the first glimpse of me; of course she knew that my brother would be at school. There was a sort of sunshine on her face, at least I thought so at first, for she was smiling. But when I looked more closely there was something in the smile which gave me a queer feeling, startling me almost more than if I had seen that she was crying.

I think for my age I had a good deal of self-control of a certain kind. I waited till she had come in and kissed me and sent away the cab and we were alone. Then I shut the door and drew her to father's special arm-chair beside the fire.

"Mamma, dear," I half said, half whispered, "what is it?"

Mamma gave a sort of gasp or choke before she answered. Then she said,

"Why, dear, why should you think—oh, I don't know what I am saying," and she tried to laugh.

But I wouldn't let her.

"It's something in your face, mamma," I persisted.

She was silent for a moment.

"We had meant to tell you and Haddie this evening," she said, "father and I together; but perhaps it is better. Yes, my Geraldine, there is something. Till now it was not quite certain, though it has been hanging over us for some weeks, ever since——"

"Since that day I asked you—the morning after father came home so late and you had been crying?"

"Yes, since then," said mamma.

She put her arm round me, and then she told me all that I have told already, or at least as much of it as she thought I could under-stand. She told it quietly, but she did not try not to cry—the tears just came trickling down her face, and she wiped them away now and then. I think the letting them come made her able to speak more calmly.

And I listened. I was very sorry for her, very *very* sorry. But you may think it strange—I have often looked back upon it with wonder myself, though I now feel as if I understood the causes of it better—when I tell you that I was *not* fearfully upset or distressed myself. I did not feel inclined to cry, *except* out of pity for mamma. And I listened with the most intense interest, and even curiosity. I was all wound up by excitement, for this was the first great event I had ever known, the first change in my quiet child-life.

And my excitement grew even greater when mamma came to the subject of what was decided about us children.

"Haddie of course must go to school," she said; "to a larger and better school—Mrs. Selwood speaks of Rugby, if it can be managed.

He will be happy there, every one says. But about you, my Geraldine."

"Oh, mamma," I interrupted, "do let me go to school too. I have always wanted to go, you know, and except for being away from you, I would far rather be a boarder. It's really being at school then. I know they rather look down upon day-scholars—Haddie says so."

Mamma looked at me gravely. Perhaps she was just a little disappointed, even though on the other hand she may have felt relieved too, at my taking the idea of this separation, which to her over-rode *everything*, which made the next two years a black cloud to her, so very philosophically. But she sighed. I fancy a suspicion of the truth came to her almost at once and added to her anxiety—the truth that I did not the least realise what was before me.

"We *are* thinking of sending you to school, my child," she said quietly, "and of course it must be as a boarder. Mrs. Selwood advises Miss Ledbury's school here. She has known the old lady long and has a very high opinion of her, and it is not very far from Fernley in case Miss Ledbury wished to consult Mrs. Selwood about you in any way, or in case you were ill."

"I am very glad," I said. "I should like to go to Miss Ledbury's." My fancy had been tickled by seeing the girls at her school walking out two and two in orthodox fashion. I thought it must be delightful to march along in a row like that, and to have a partner of your own size to talk to as much as you liked.

Mamma said no more just then. I think she felt at a loss what to say. She was afraid of making me unnecessarily unhappy, and on the other hand she dreaded my finding the reality all the worse when I came to contrast it with my rose-coloured visions.

She consulted father, and he decided that it was best to leave me to myself and my own thoughts.

"She is a very young child still," he said to mamma. (All this of course I was told afterwards.) "It is quite possible that she will *not* suffer from the separation as we have feared. It may be much easier for her than if she had been two or three years older."

Haddie had no illusions. From the very first he took it all in, and that very bitterly. But he was, as I have said, a very good boy, and a boy with a great deal of resolution and firmness. He said nothing to discourage me. Mamma told him how surprised she was at my way of taking it, and he agreed with father that perhaps I would not be really unhappy.

And I do think that my chief unhappiness during the next few weeks came from the sight of dear mamma's pale, worn face, which she could not hide, try as she might to be bright and cheerful.

There was of course a great deal of bustle and preparation, and all children enjoy that, I fancy. Even Haddie was interested about his school outfit. He was to go to a preparatory school at Rugby till he could get into the big school. And as far as school went, he told me he was sure he would like it very well, it was only the—but there he stopped.

"The what?" I asked.

"Oh, the being all separated," he said gruffly.

"But you'd have had to go away to a big school some day," I reminded him. "You didn't want always to go to a day-school."

"No," he allowed, "but it's the holidays."

The holidays! I had not thought about that part of it.

"Oh, I daresay something nice will be settled for the holidays," I said lightly.

In one way Haddie was very lucky. Mrs. Selwood had undertaken the whole charge of his education for the two years our parents were to be away. And after that "we shall see," she said.

She had great ideas about the necessity of giving a boy the very best schooling possible, but she had not at all the same opinion about *girls'* education. She was a clever woman in some ways, but very old-fashioned. Her own upbringing had been at a time when *very* little learning was considered needful or even advisable for our sex. And as she had good practical capacities, and had managed her own affairs sensibly, she always held herself up both in her own mind and to others as a specimen of an *un*learned lady who had got on far better than if she had had all the "'ologies," as she called them, at her fingers' ends.

This, I think, was one reason why she approved of Miss Ledbury's school, which, as you will hear, was certainly not conducted in accordance with the modern ideas which even then were beginning to make wise parents ask themselves if it was right to spend ten times as much on their son's education as on their daughters'.

"Teach a girl to write a good hand, to read aloud so that you can understand what she says, to make a shirt and make pudding and to add up the butcher's book correctly, and she'll do," Mrs. Selwood used to say.

"And what about accomplishments?" some one might ask.

"She should be able to play a tune on the piano, and to sing a nice English song or two if she has a voice, and maybe to paint a wreath of flowers if her taste lies that way. That sort of thing would do no harm if she doesn't waste time over it," the old lady would allow, with great liberality, thinking over her own youthful acquirements no doubt.

I daresay there was a foundation of solid sense in the first part of her advice. I don't see but that girls nowadays might profit by some of it. And in many cases they *do*. It is quite in accordance with modern thought to be able to make a good many "puddings," though home-made shirts are not called for. But as far as the "accomplishments" go, I should prefer none to such a smattering of them as our old friend considered more than enough.

So far less thought on Mrs. Selwood's part was bestowed on Geraldine—that is myself, of course—than on Haddon, as regarded the school question. And mamma *had* to be guided by Mrs. Selwood's advice to a great extent just then. She had much so to do and so little time to do it in, that it would have been impossible for her to go hunting about for a school for me more in accordance with her own ideas. And she knew that personally Miss Ledbury was well worthy of all respect.

She went to see her once or twice to talk about me, and make the best arrangements possible. The first of these visits left a pleasanter impression on her mind than the second. For the first time she saw Miss Ledbury alone, and found her gentle and sympathising, and full of conscientious interest in her pupils, so that it seemed childish to take objection to some of the rules mentioned by the schoolmistress which in her heart mamma did not approve of.

One of these was that all the pupils' letters were to be read by one of the teachers, and as to this Miss Ledbury said she could make no exception. Then, again, no story-books were permitted, except such as were read aloud on the sewing afternoons. But if I spent my holidays there, as was only too probable, this rule should be relaxed.

The plan for Sundays, too, struck my mother disagreeably. "My poor Geraldine," she said to father, when she was telling him all about it, "I don't know how she will stand such a dreary day."

Father suggested that I should be allowed to write my weekly letter to them on Sunday, and mamma said she would see if that could be.

And then father begged her not to look at the dark side of things.

"After all," he said, "Geraldine is very young, and will accommodate herself better than you think to her new circumstances. She will enjoy companions of her own age too. And we know that Miss Ledbury is a good and kind woman—the disadvantages seem trifling, though I should not like to think the child was to be there for longer than these two years."

Mamma gave in to this. Indeed, there seemed nothing else to do. But the second time she went to see Miss Ledbury, the schoolmistress introduced her niece—her "right hand," as she called her— a woman of about forty, named Miss Aspinall, who, though only supposed to be second in command, was really the principal authority in the establishment, much more than poor old Miss Ledbury, whose health was failing, realised herself.

Mamma did not take to Miss Aspinall. But it was now far too late to make any change, and she tried to persuade herself that she was nervously fanciful.

And here, perhaps, I had better say distinctly, that Miss Aspinall was not a bad or cruel woman. She was, on the contrary, truly conscientious and perfectly sincere. But she was wanting in all finer feelings and instincts. She had had a hard and unloving childhood, and had almost lost the power of caring much for anyone. She loved her aunt after a fashion, but she thought her weak. She was just, or wished to be so, and with some of the older pupils she got on fairly well. But she did not understand children, and took small interest in the younger scholars, beyond seeing that they kept the rules and were not complained of by the under teachers who took charge of them. And as the younger pupils were very seldom boarders it did not very much matter, as they had their own homes and mothers to make them happy once school hours were over.

Mamma did not know that there were scarcely any boarders as young as I, for when she first asked about the other pupils, Miss Ledbury, thinking principally of lessons, said, "oh yes," there was a nice little class just about my age where I should feel quite at home.

A few days before *the* day—the day of separation for us all— mamma took me to see Miss Ledbury. She thought I would feel rather less strange if I had been there once, and had seen the lady who was to be my schoolmistress.

I knew the house—Green Bank, it was called—by sight. It was a little further out of the town than ours, and had a melancholy bit of garden in front, and a sort of playground at the back. It was not a large house—indeed, it was not really large enough for the number of people living in it—twenty to thirty boarders, and a number of day-scholars, who of course helped to fill the school-rooms and to make them hot and airless, four resident teachers, and four or five servants. But in those days people did not think nearly as much as now about ventilation and lots of fresh air, and perfectly pure water, and all such things, which we now know to be quite as important to our health as food and clothes.

Mamma rang the bell. Everything about Green Bank was neat and orderly, prim, if not grim. So was the maid-servant who opened the door, and in answer to mamma's inquiry for Miss Ledbury, showed us into the drawing-room, a square moderate-sized room, at the right hand of the passage.

I can remember the look of that room even now, perfectly. It was painfully neat, not exactly ugly, for most of the furniture was of the spindle-legged quaint kind, to which everybody now gives the general name of "Queen Anne." There were a few books set out on the round table, there was a cottage piano at one side, there were some faint water-colours on the wall, and a rather nice clock on the white marble mantelpiece, the effect of which was spoilt by a pair of huge "lustres," as they were called, at each side of it. The carpet was very ugly, large and sprawly in pattern, and so was the hearth-rug. They were the newest things in the room, and greatly admired by Miss Ledbury and her niece, who were full of the bad taste of the day in furniture, and would gladly have turned out all the delicate spidery-looking tables and chairs to make way for heavy and cumbersome sofas and ottomans, but for the question of expense, and perhaps for the sake of old association on the elder lady's part.

There was no fire, though it was November, and mamma shivered a little as she sat down, possibly, however, not altogether from cold. It was between twelve and one in the morning—that was the hour at which Miss Ledbury asked parents to call.

Afterwards, when I got to know the rules of the house, I found that the drawing-room fire was never lighted except on Wednesday and Saturday afternoons, or on some very special occasion.

I stood beside mamma. Somehow I did not feel inclined to sit down. I was full of a strange kind of excitement, half pleasant, half frightening. I think the second half prevailed as the moments went on. Mamma did not speak, but I felt her hand clasping my shoulder.

Then at last the door opened.

CHAPTER V

AN UNPROMISING BEGINNING

MY FIRST SIGHT of Miss Ledbury was a sort of agreeable disappointment. She was not in the least like what I had imagined, though
till I did see her I do not think I knew that I had imagined anything!
She had been much less in my thoughts than her pupils; it was the
idea of companions, the charm of being one of a party of other girls,
with a place of my own among them, that my fancy had been full of.
I don't think I cared very much what the teachers were like.

What I did see was a very small, fragile-looking old lady, with
quite white hair, a black or purple—I am not sure which, anyway it
was dark—silk dress, and a soft fawn-coloured cashmere shawl. She
had a white lace cap, tied with ribbons under her chin, and black lace
mittens. Looking back now, I cannot picture her in any other dress.
I cannot remember ever seeing her with a bonnet on, and yet she
must have worn one, as she went to church regularly. Her face
was small and still pretty, and the eyes were naturally sweet, sometimes they had a twinkle of humour in them, sometimes they looked
almost hard. The truth was that she was a gentle, kind-hearted
person by nature, but a narrow life and education had stunted her
power of sympathy, and she thought it wrong to give way to feeling.
She was conscious of what she believed to be weakness in herself,
and was always trying to be firm and determined. And since her
niece had come to live with her, this put-on sternness had increased.

Yet I was never really afraid of Miss Ledbury, though I never—
well perhaps that is rather too strong—almost never, I should say,
felt at ease with her.

I was, I suppose, a very shy child, but still now the circumstances
of my life had not brought this out.

This first time of seeing my future schoolmistress I liked her very
much. There was indeed something very attractive about her—
something almost "fairy-godmother-like" which took my fancy.

We did not stay long. Miss Ledbury was not without tact, and
she saw that the mention of the approaching parting, the settling the
day and hour at which I was to come to Green Bank to stay, were
very, very trying to mamma. And I almost think her misunderstanding of me began from that first interview. In her heart I fancy

she was shocked at my coolness, for she did not know, or if she ever had known, she had forgotten, much about children—their queer contradictory ways of taking things, how completely they are sometimes the victims of their imagination, how little they realise anything they have had no experience of.

All that the old lady did not understand in me, she put down to my being spoilt and selfish. She even, I believe, thought me forward.

Still, she spoke kindly—said she hoped I should soon feel at home at Green Bank, and try to get on well with my lessons, so that when my dear mamma returned she would be astonished at the progress I had made.

I did not quite understand what she said—the word "progress" puzzled me. I wondered if it had anything to do with the Pilgrim's Progress, and I was half inclined to ask if it had, and to tell her that I had read the history of Christian and his family quite through, two or three times. But mamma had already got up to go, so I only said "Yes" rather vaguely, and Miss Ledbury kissed me somewhat coldly.

As soon as we found ourselves outside in the street again, mamma made some little remark. She wanted to find out what kind of impression had been left on me, though she would not have considered it right to ask me straight out what I thought of the lady who was going to be my superior—in a sense to fill a parent's place to me.

And I remember replying that I thought Miss Ledbury must be very, very old—nearly a hundred, I should think.

"Oh dear no, not nearly as old as that," mamma said quickly. "You must not say anything like that, Geraldine. It would offend her. She cannot be more than sixty."

I opened my eyes. I thought it would be very nice to be a hundred.

But before I had time to say more, my attention was distracted. For just at that moment, turning a corner, we almost ran into the procession I was so eager to join—Miss Ledbury's girls, returning two and two from their morning constitutional.

I felt my cheeks grow red with exitement. I stared at them, and some of them, I think, looked at me. Mamma looked at them too, but instead of getting red, her face grew pale.

They passed so quickly, that I was only able to glance at two or three of the twenty or thirty faces. I looked at the smallest of the train with the most interest, though one older face at the very end caught my attention almost without my knowing it.

When they had passed I turned to mamma.

"Did you see that little girl with the rosy cheeks, mamma? The one with a red feather in her hat. *Doesn't* she look nice?"

"She looked a good-humoured little person," said mamma. In her heart she thought the rosy-faced child rather common-looking and far too showily dressed, but that was not unusual among the rich Mexington people, and she would not have said anything like that to me. "I did notice one *very* sweet face," she went on, "I mean the young lady at the end—one of the governesses no doubt."

I had, as I said, noticed her too, and mamma's words impressed it upon me. Mamma seemed quite cheered by this passing glimpse, and she went on speaking.

"She must be one of the younger teachers, I should think. I hope you may be in her class. You must tell me if you are when you write to me, and tell me her name."

I promised I would.

The next two or three days I have no clear remembrance of at all. They seemed all bustle and confusion—though through everything I recollect mamma's pale drawn face, and the set look of Haddie's mouth. He was so determined not to break down. Of father we saw very little—he was terribly busy. But when he was at home, he seemed to be always whistling, or humming a tune, or making jokes.

"How pleased father seems to be about going so far away," I said once to Haddie. But he did not answer.

He—Haddie—was to go a part of the way in the same train as father and mamma. They were to start on the Thursday, and I was taken to Green Bank on Wednesday morning. Father took me—and Lydia. I was such a little girl that mamma thought Lydia should go with me to unpack and arrange my things, and she never thought that anyone could object to this. For she had never been at school herself, and did not know much about school ways. I think the first beginning of my troubles and disappointments was about Lydia.

Father and I were shown into the drawing-room. But when the door opened this time, it was not to admit gentle old Miss Ledbury. Instead of her in came a tall thin woman, dressed in grey—she had black hair done rather tightly, and a black lace bow on the top of her head.

Father was standing looking out of the window, and I beside him holding his hand. I was not crying. I had had one sudden convulsive fit of sobs early that morning when mamma came for a moment into my room, and for the first time it *really* came over me that I was leaving her. But she almost prayed me to try not to cry, and the feeling that I was helping her, joined to the excitement I was in, made it not so very difficult to keep quiet. I do not even think my eyes were red.

Father turned at the sound of the door opening.

"Miss Ledbury," he began.

"Not Miss Ledbury. I am Miss Aspinall, her *niece*," said the lady; she was not pleased at the mistake.

"Oh, I beg your pardon," said poor father. "I understood——"

"Miss Ledbury is not very well this morning," said Miss Aspinall. "She deputed me to express her regrets."

"Oh certainly," said father. "This is my little daughter—you have seen her before, I suppose?"

"No," said the lady, holding out her hand. "How do you do, my dear?"

I did not speak. I stared up at her, I felt so confused and strange. I scarcely heard what father went on to say—some simple messages from mamma about my writing to them, and so on, and the dates of the mails, the exact address, etc., etc., to all of which Miss Aspinall listened with a slight bend of her head or a stiff "indeed," or "just so."

This was not encouraging. I am afraid even father's bouyant spirits went down: I think he had some idea that if he came himself he would be able to make friends with my schoolmistress and be able to ensure her special friendliness. But it was clear that nothing of this kind was to be done with the niece.

So he said at last,

"Well, I think that is all. Good-bye, my little woman, then. Good-bye, my darling. She will be a good girl, I am sure, Miss Aspinall; she has been a dear good child at home."

His voice was on the point of breaking, but the governess stood there stonily. His praise of me was not the way to win her favour. I do believe she would have liked me better if he had said I had been so naughty and troublesome at home that he trusted the discipline of school would do me good. And when I glanced up at Miss Aspinall's face, something seemed to choke down the sob which was beginning again to rise in my throat.

"Good-bye, my own little girl," said father. One more kiss and he was gone.

My luggage was in the hall—which was really a passage scarcely deserving the more important name—and beside it stood Lydia. Miss Aspinall looked at her coldly.

"Who——" she began, when I interrupted her.

"It's Lydia," I said. "She's come to unpack my things. Mamma
sent her."

"Come to unpack your things," repeated the governess. "There
must be some mistake—that is quite unecessary. There is no
occasion for you to wait," she said to poor Lydia, with a slight gesture
towards the door.

Lydia grew very red.

"Miss Geraldine won't know about them all, I'm afraid," she
began. "She has not been used to taking the charge of her things
yet."

"Then the sooner she learns the better," said Miss Aspinall, and
Lydia dared not persist. She turned to me, looking ready to burst
out crying again, though, as she had been doing little else for three
days, one might have thought her tears were exhausted.

"Good-bye, dear Miss Geraldine," she said, half holding out her
arms. I flew into them. I was beginning to feel very strange.

"Good-bye, dear Lydia," I said.

"You will write to me, Miss Geraldine?"

"Of course I will; I know your address," I said. Lydia was going
to her own home to work with a dressmaker sister in hopes of coming
back to us at the end of the two years.

"Miss Le Marchant" (I think I have never said that our family
name was Le Marchant), said a cold voice, "I really cannot wait any
longer; you must come upstairs at once to take off your things."

Lydia glanced at me.

"I beg pardon," she said; and then she too was gone.

Long afterwards the poor girl told me that her heart was nearly
bursting when she left me, but she had the good sense to say nothing
to add to mamma's distress, as she knew that my living at Green
Bank was all settled about. She could only hope the other governesses might be kinder than the one she had seen.

Miss Aspinall walked upstairs, telling me to follow her. It was
not a very large house, but it was a high one and the stairs were
steep. It seemed to me that I had climbed up a long way when at
last she opened a door half-way down a dark passage.

"This is your room," she said, as she went in.

I followed her eagerly. I don't quite know what I expected. I
had not been told if I was to have a room to myself or not. But at
first I think I was rather startled to see three beds in a room not
much larger than my own one at home—three beds and two wash-
hand stands, a large and a small, two chests of drawers, a large and a

small also, which were evidently considered to be toilet-tables as well, as each had a looking-glass, and three chairs.

My eyes wandered round. It was all quite neat, though dull. For the one window looked on to the side-wall of the next-door house, and much light could not have got in at the best of times, added to which, the day was a very grey one. But the impression it made upon me was more that of a tidy and clean servants' room than of one for ladies, even though only little grls.

I stood still and silent.

"This is your bed," said Miss Aspinall next, touching a small white counterpaned iron bedstead in one corner—I was glad it was in a corner. "The Miss Smiths are your companions. They share the large chest of drawers, and your things will go into the smaller one."

"There won't be nearly room enough," I said quickly. I had yet to learn the habit of not saying out whatever came into my head.

"Nonsense, child," said the governess. "There must be room enough for you if there is room enough for much older and——" she stopped. "At your age many clothes are not requisite. I think, on the whole, it will be better for you not to unpack or arrange your own things. One of the governesses shall do so, and all that you do not actually require must stay in your trunk and be put in the box-room."

I did not pay very much attention to what she said. I don't think I clearly understood it, for, as I have said, in some ways I was rather a slow child. And my thoughts were running more on the Miss Smiths and the rest of my future companions than on my wardrobe. If I had taken in that it was not only my clothes that were in question, but that my little household gods, my special pet possessions, were not to be left in my own keeping, I would have minded much more.

"Now take off your things at once," said Miss Aspinall. "You must keep on your boots till your shoes are got out, but take care not to stump along the passages. Do your hands want washing? No, you have your gloves on. As soon as you are ready, go down two flights of stairs till you come to the passage under this on the next floor. The door at the end is the second class schoolroom, where you will be shown your place."

Then she went away, leaving me to my own reflections. Not a word of sympathy or encouragement, not a pat on my shoulder as she passed me, nor a kindly glance out of her hard eyes. But at the time I scarcely noticed this. My mind was still full of not unpleasant excitement, though I was beginning to feel tired and certainly very confused and bewildered.

I sat down for a moment on the edge of my little bed when Miss Aspinall left me, without hastening to take off my coat and bonnet. We wore bonnets mostly in those days, though hats were beginning to come into fashion for young girls.

"I wish there were only two beds, not three," I said to myself. "And I would like the little girl with the rosy face to sleep in my room. I wonder if she's Miss Smith perhaps. I wonder if there's several little girls as little as me. I'd like to know all their names, so as to write and tell them to mamma and Haddie."

The inclination to cry had left me—fortunately in some ways, though perhaps if I had made my *debut* in the schoolroom looking very woe-begone and tearful I should have made a better impression. My future companions would have felt sorry for me. As it was, when I had taken off my things I had made my way downstairs as I had been directed, and opening the schoolroom door—I remember wondering to myself what second class schoolroom could mean: would it have long seats all round, something like a second-class railway carriage?—walked in coolly enough.

The room felt airless and close, though it was a cold day. And at the first glance it seemed to me perfectly full of people—girls— women indeed in my eyes many of them were, they were so much bigger and older than I—in every direction, more than I could count. And the hum of voices was very confusing, the *hums* I should say, for there were two or three different sets of reading aloud, or lessons repeating, going on at once.

I stood just inside the door. Two or three heads were turned in my direction at the sound I made in opening it, but quickly bent over their books again, and for some moments no one paid any attention to me. Then suddenly a governess happened to catch sight of me. It was the same sweet-faced girl whom mamma had noticed at the end of the long file in the street.

She looked at me once, then seemed at a loss, then she looked at me again, and at last said something to the girl beside her, and getting up from her seat went to the end of the room, and spoke to a small elderly woman in a brown stuff dress, who was evidently another governess.

This person—I suppose I should say lady—turned round and stared at me. Then she said something to the younger governess, nothing very pleasant, I fancy, for the sweet-looking one—I had better call her by her name, which was Miss Fenmore—went back to her place with a heightened colour.

You may ask how I can remember all these little particulars so exactly. Perhaps I do not quite do so, but still, all that happened just then made a very strong impression on me, and I have thought it over so much and so often, especially since I have had children of my own, that it is difficult to tell quite precisely how much is real memory, how much the after knowledge of how things must have been, to influence myself and others as they did. And later, too, I talked them over with those who were older than I at the time, and could understand more.

So there I stood, a very perplexed little person, though still more perplexed than disappointed, by the door. Now and then some head was turned to look at me with a sort of stealthy curiosity, but there was no kindness in any of the glances, and the young governess kept her eyes turned away. I was not a pretty child. My hair was straight and not noticeable in any way, and it was tightly plaited, as was the fashion, *unless* a child's hair was thick enough to make pretty ringlets. My face was rather thin and pale, and there was nothing of dimpling childish loveliness about me. I was rather near-sighted too, and I daresay that often gave me a worried, perhaps a fretful expression.

After all, I did not have to wait very long. The elderly governess finished the page she was reading aloud—she may have been dictating to her pupils, I cannot say—and came towards me.

"Did Miss Aspinall send you here?" she said abruptly.

I looked up at her. She seemed to me no better than our cook, and not half so good-natured.

"Yes," I said.

"Yes," she repeated, as if she was very shocked. "Yes *who*, if you please? Yes, Miss ——?"

"Yes, Miss," I said in a matter-of-fact way.

"What manners! Fie!" said Miss ——; afterwards I found her name was Broom. "I think indeed it was quite time for you to come to school. If you cannot say my name, you can at least say ma'am."

I stared up at her. I think my trick of staring must have been rather provoking, and perhaps even must have seemed rude, though it arose entirely from my not understanding.

"I don't know your name, Miss—ma'am," I said.

I spoke clearly. I was not frightened. And a titter went round the forms. Miss Broom was angry at being put in the wrong.

"Miss Aspinall sent you to my class, *Miss Broom's* class," she said.

"No, ma'am—Miss Broom—she didn't."

The governess thought I meant to be impertinent—impertinent, poor me!

And with no very gentle hand, she half led, half pushed me towards her end of the room, where there was a vacant place on one of the forms.

"Silence, young ladies," she said, for some whispering was taking place. "Go on with your copying out."

And then she turned to me with a book.

"Let me hear how you can read," she said.

CHAPTER VI

A NEW WORLD

I COULD READ aloud well, unusually well, I think, for mamma had taken great pains with my pronunciation. She was especially anxious that both Haddie and I should speak well, and not catch the Great Mexington accent, which was both peculiar and ugly.

But the book which Miss Broom had put before me was hardly a fair test. I don't remeber what it was—some very dry history, I think, bristling with long words, and in very small print. I did not take in the sense of what I was reading in the very least, and so, of course, I read badly, tumbling over the long words, and putting no intelligence into my tone. I think, too, my teacher was annoyed at the purity of my accent, for no one could possible have mistaken *her* for anything but what she was—a native of Middleshire. She corrected me once or twice, then shut the book impatiently.

"Very bad," she said, "very bad indeed for eleven years old."

" I am not eleven, Miss Broom," I said. " I am only nine past."

"Little girls must not contradict, and they must not be rude," was the reply.

What had I said that could be called rude? I tried to think, thereby bringing on myself a reprimand for inattention, which did not have the effect of brightening my wits, I fear.

I think I was put through a sort of examination as to all my acquirements. I know I came out of it very badly, for Miss Broom pronounced me so backward that there was no class, not even the youngest in the school, which I was really fit for. There was nothing for it, however, but to put me in the lowest class, and she said I must do extra work in play hours to make up to my companions.

Even my French, which I now *know* must have been good, was found fault with by Miss Broom, who said my accent was extraordinary. And certainly, if her's was Parisian, mine must have been worse than that of Stratford-le-Bow!

Still I was not unhappy. I thought it must be always like that at school, and I said to myself I really would work hard to make up to the others, who were so much, much cleverer than I. And I sat contentedly enough in my place, doing my best to learn a page of English grammar by heart, from time to time peeping round the table, till, to my great satisfaction and delight, I caught sight of the rosy-cheeked damsel at the farther end of the table.

I was so pleased that I wonder I did not jump up from my place and run round to speak to her, forgetful that though I had thought so much of her, she had probably never noticed me at all the only other time of our meeting, or rather passing each other.

But I felt Miss Broom's eye upon me, and sat still. I acquitted myself pretty fairly of my page of grammar, leading to the dry remark from the governess that it was plain I "could learn if I chose." As this was the first thing I had been given to learn, the implied reproach was not exactly called for. But none of Miss Broom's speeches were remarkable for being appropriate. They depended much more on the mood she happened to be in herself than upon anything else.

I can clearly remember most of that day. I have a vision of a long dining-table, long at least it seemed to me, and a plateful of roast mutton and potatoes which I could not manage to finish, followed by rice pudding with which I succeeded better, though I was not in the least hungry. Miss Aspinall was at one end of the table, Miss Broom at the other, and Miss Fenmore, who seemed always to be jumping up to ring the bell or hand the governesses something or other that had been forgotten by the servant, sat somewhere in the middle.

No one spoke unless spoken to by one of the teachers. Miss

H

Aspinall shot out little remarks from time to time about the weather, and replied graciously enough to one or two of the older girls who ventured to ask if Miss Ledbury's cold, or headache, was better.

Then came the grace, followed by a shoving back of forms, and a march in order of age, or place in class rather, to the door, and thence down the passage to what was called the big schoolroom—a room on the ground floor, placed where by rights the kitchen should have been, I fancy. It was the only large room in the house, and I think it must have been built out beyond the original walls on purpose.

And then—there re-echo on my ears even now the sudden bursting out of noise, the loosening of a score and a half of tongues, girls' tongues too, forcibly restrained since the morning. For this was the recreation hour, and on a wet day, to make up for not going a walk, the "young ladies" were allowed from two to three to chatter as much as they liked—in English instead of in the fearful and wonderful jargon yclept "French."

I stood in a corner by myself, staring, no doubt. I felt profoundly interested. This was a *little* more like what I had pictured to myself, though I had not imagined it would be quite so noisy and bewildering. But some of the girls seemed very merry, and their laughter and chatter fascinated me—if only I were one of them, able to laugh and chatter too! Should I ever be admitted to share their fun?

The elder girls did not interest me. They seemed to me quite grown-up. Yet it was from their ranks that came the first token of interest in me—of notice that I was there at all.

"What's your name?" said a tall thin girl with fair curls, which one could see she was very proud of. She was considered a beauty in the school. She was silly, but very good-natured. She spoke with a sort of lisp, and very slowly, so her question did not strike me as rude. Nor was it meant to be so. It was a mixture of curiosity and amiability.

"My name," I repeated, rather stupidly. I was startled by being spoken to.

"Yes, your name. Didn't Miss Lardner say what's your name? Dear me—don't stand gaping there like a monkey on a barrel-organ," said another girl.

By this time a little group had gathered round me. The girls composing it all laughed, and though it does not sound very witty— to begin with, I never heard of a monkey "gaping"—I have often thought since that there was some excuse for the laughter. I was small and thin, and I had a trick of screwing up my eyes which made them look smaller than they really were. And my frock was crimson merino with several rows of black velvet above the hem of the skirt.

I was not offended. But I did not laugh. The girl who had spoken last was something of a tomboy, and looked upon also as a wit. Her name was Josephine Mellor, and her intimate friends called her Joe. She had very fuzzy red hair, and rather good brown eyes.

"I say," she went on again, "what *is* your name? And are you going to stay for dinner every day, or only when it rains, like Lizzie Burt?"

Who was Lizzie Burt? That question nearly set my ideas adrift again. But the consciousness of my superior position fortunately kept me to the point.

"I am going to be at dinner always," I said proudly. "I am a boarder."

The girls drew a little nearer, with evidently increased interest.

"A boarder," repeated Josephine. "Then Harriet Smith'll have to give up being baby. You're ever so much younger than her, I'm sure."

"What are you saying about me?" said Harriet, who had caught the sound of her own name, as one often does.

"Only that that pretty snub nose of yours is going to be put out of joint," said Miss Mellor mischievously.

Harriet came rushing forward. She was my rosy-cheeked girl! Her face was redder than usual. I felt very vexed with Miss Mellor, even though I did not quite understand her.

"What are you saying?" the child called out. "I'm not going to have any of your teasing, Joe."

"It's not teasing—it's truth," said the elder girl. "You're not the baby any more. *She*," and she pointed to me, "she's younger than you."

"How old are you?" said Harriet roughly.

"Nine past," I said. "Nine and a half."

"Hurrah! Hurrah!" shouted Harriet. "I'm only nine and a month. I'm still the baby, Miss Joe."

She was half a head at least taller than I, and broad in proportion.

"What a mite you are, to be sure," said Miss Mellor, "nine and a half and no bigger than that."

I felt myself getting red. I think one or two of the girls must have had perception enough to feel a little sorry for me, for one of them—I fancy it was Miss Lardner—said in a good-natured patronising way,

"You haven't told us your name yet, after all."

"It's Geraldine," I said. "That's my first name, and I'm always called it."

"Geraldine what?" said the red-haired girl.

"Geraldine Theresa Le Marchant—that's all my names."

"My goodness," said Miss Mellor, "how grand we are! Great Mexington's growing quite aristocratic. I didn't know monkeys had such fine names."

Some of the girls laughed, some, I think, thought her as silly as she was.

"Where do you come from?" was the next question.

"Come from?" I repeated. "I don't know."

At this they all did laugh, and I suppose it was only natural. Suddenly Harriet Smith made a sort of dash at me.

"Oh, I say," she exclaimed. "I know. She's going to sleep in our room. I saw them putting sheets on the bed in the corner, but Jane wouldn't tell me who they were for. Emma," she called out loudly to a girl of fourteen or fifteen, "Emma, I say, she's going to sleep in our room I'm sure."

Emma Smith was taller and thinner and paler than her sister, but still they were rather like. Perhaps it was for that very reason that they got on so badly—they might have been better friends if they had been more unlike. As it was, they quarrelled constantly, and I must say it was generally Harriet's fault. She was very spoilt, but she had something hearty and merry about her, and so had Emma. They were the daughters of a rich Great Mexington manufacturer, and they had no mother. They were favourites in the school, partly I suspect because they had lots of pocket money, and used to invite their companions to parties in the holidays. But they were not mean or insincere, though rough and noisy—more like boys than girls.

Emma came bouncing forward.

"I say," she began to me, "if it's true you're to sleep in our room I hope you understand you must do what I tell you. I'm the eldest. You're not to back up Harriet to disobey me."

"No," I said. "I don't want to do anything like that."

"Well, then," said Harriet, "you'll be Emma's friend, not mine."

My face fell, and I suppose Harriet saw it. She came closer to me and looked at me well, as if expecting me to answer. But for the first time since I had been in my new surroundings I felt more than bewildered—I felt frightened and lonely, terribly lonely.

"Oh, mamma," I thought to myself, "I wish I could see you to tell you about it. It isn't a bit like what I thought it would be."

But I said nothing aloud. I think now that if I had burst out crying it would have been better for me, but I had very little power of expressing myself, and Haddie had instilled into me a great horror of being a cry-baby at school.

In their rough way, however, several of the girls were kind-hearted, the two Smiths perhaps as much so as any. Harriet came close up to me.

"I'm only in fun," she said; "of course we'll be friends. I'll tell you how we'll do," and she put her fat little arm around me in a protecting way which I much appreciated. "Come over here," she went on in a lower voice, "where none of the big ones can hear what we say," and she drew me, nothing loth, to the opposite corner of the room.

As we passed through the group of older girls standing about, one or two fragments of their talk reached my ears.

"Yes—I'm sure it's the same. He's a bank clerk, I think. I've heard papa speak of them. They're awfully poor—come-down-in-the-world sort of people."

"Oh, then, I expect when she's old enough she'll be a governess—perhaps she'll be a sort of teacher here to begin with."

Then followed some remark about looking far ahead, and a laugh at the idea of "the monkey" ever developing into a governess.

But after my usual fashion it was not till I thought it over afterwards that I understood that it was I and my father they had been discussing. In the meantime I was enjoying a confidential talk with Harriet Smith—that is to say, I was listening to all she said to me; she did not seem to expect me to say much in reply.

I felt flattered by her condescension, but I did not in my heart feel much interest in her communications. They were mostly about Emma—how she tried to bully her, Harriet, because she was five years older, and how the younger girl did not intend to stand it much longer. Emma was as bad as a boy.

"As bad as a boy," I repeated. "I don't know what you mean."

"That's because you've not got a brother, I suppose," said Harriet. "Our brother's a perfect nuisance. He's so spoilt—papa lets him do just as he likes. Emma and I hate the holidays because of him

being at home. But it's the worst for me, you see. Emma hates
Fred bullying her, so she might know I hate her bullying me."

This was all very astonishing to me.

"I have a brother," I said after a moment or two's reflection.

"Then you know what it is. Why didn't you say so?" asked
Harriet.

"Because I don't know what it is. Haddie never teases me. I
love being with him."

"My goodness! Then you're not like most," said Harriet elegantly,
opening her eyes.

She asked me some questions after this—as to where we lived, how
many servants we had, and so on. Some I answered—some I
could not, as I was by no means as worldly-wise as this precocious
young person.

She gave me a great deal of information about school—she hated
the governesses, except the old lady, and she didn't care about her
much. Miss Broom was her special dislike. But she liked school
very well, she'd been there a year now, and before that she had a
daily governess at home, and it was very dull indeed. What had I
done till now—had I had a governess?

"Oh no," I said. "I had mamma."

"Was she good to you," asked my new friend, "or was she very
strict?"

I stared at Harriet. Mamma was strict, but she was very, very
good to me. I said so.

"Then why are you a boarder?" she asked. "We've not got a
mamma, but even if we had I'm sure she wouldn't teach us herself.
I suppose your mamma isn't rich enough to pay for a governess
for you."

"I don't know," I said simply. I had never thought in this way
of mamma's teaching me, but I was not at all offended. "I don't
think any governess would be as nice as mamma."

"Then why have you come to school?" inquired Harriet.

"Because"—"because father and mamma have to go away," I
was going to say, when suddenly the full meaning of the words
seemed to rush over me. A strange giddy feeling made me shut my
eyes and I caught hold of Harriet's arm.

"What's the matter?" she said wonderingly, as I opened my eyes
and looked at her again.

"I'd rather not talk about mamma just now," I said. "I'll tell
you afterwards."

"Up in our room," said Harriet, "oh yes, that'll be jolly. We've got all sorts of dodges."

But before she had time to explain more, or I to ask her why "dodges"—I knew the meaning of the word from Haddie—were required, a bell rang loudly.

Instantly the hubbub ceased, and there began a sort of silent scramble—the elder girls collecting books and papers and hurrying to their places; the younger ones rushing upstairs to the other schoolroom, I following.

In a few minutes we were all seated round the long tables. It was sewing afternoon, and to my great delight I saw that Miss Fenmore, the pretty governess whom I had taken such a fancy to, though I had not yet spoken to her, was now in Miss Broom's place.

Mamma had provided me with both plain work and a little simple fancy work, but as my things were not yet unpacked, I had neither with me, and I sat feeling awkward and ashamed, seeing all the other busily preparing for business.

"Have you no work, my dear?" said Miss Fenmore gently. It was the first kind speech I had had from a governess.

"It isn't unpacked," I said, feeling my cheeks grow red, I did not know why.

Miss Fenmore hesitated for a moment. Then she took out a stocking—or rather the beginning of one on knitting-needles.

"Can you knit?" she asked.

"I can knit plain—plain and purl—just straight on," I said. "But I've never done it round like that."

"Never mind, you will learn easily, as you know how to knit. Come and sit beside me, so that I can watch you."

She made the girls sit a little more closely, making a place for me beside her, and I would have been quite happy had I not seen a cross expression on several faces, and heard murmurs of "favouring," "spoilt pet," and so on.

Miss Fenmore, if she heard, took no notice. And in a few moments all was in order. We read aloud in turns—the book was supposed to be a story-book, but it seemed to me very dull, though the fault may have lain in the uninteresting way the girls read, and the constant change of voices, as no one read more than two pages at a time. I left off trying to listen and gave my whole attention to my knitting, encouraged by Miss Fenmore's whispered "very nice— a little looser," or "won't it be nice to knit socks for your father or brother, if you have a brother?"

I nodded with a smile. I was burning to tell her everything. Already I felt that I loved her dearly—her voice was as sweet as her face. Yet there were tones in the former and lines in the latter telling of much sorrow and suffering, young as she was. I was far too much of a child to understand this. I only felt vaguely that there was something about her which reminded me of mamma as she had looked these last few weeks.

And my heart was won.

CHAPTER VII

GATHERING CLOUDS

AFTER THAT FIRST day at Green Bank, the remembrance of things in detail is not so clear to me.

To begin with, the life was very monotonous. Except for the different lessons, one day passed much like another, the principal variety being the coming of Sunday and the two weekly half-holidays—Wednesday and Saturday. But to me the half-holidays brought no pleasure. I think I disliked them more than lesson days, and most certainly I disliked Sundays most of all.

Looking back now, I think my whole nature and character must have gone through some curious changes in these first weeks at school. I grew older very rapidly.

There first came by degrees the great *disappointment* of it all—for though I am anxious not to exaggerate anything, it was a bewildering "disillusionment" to me. Nobody and nothing were what I had imagined they would be. Straight out of my sheltered home, where every thought and tone and word were full of love, I was tossed into this world of school, where, though no doubt there were kind hearts and nice natures as there are everywhere, the whole feeling was different. Even the good-nature was rough and unrefined—the tones of voice, the ways of moving about, the readiness to squabble, though very likely it was more a kind of bluster than anything worse, all startled and astounded me, as I gradually awoke from my dream of the delights of being at school surrounded by companions.

And there was really a prejudice against me, both among teachers and pupils. A story had got about that my family was very, very poor, that father had had to go abroad on this account, and that my schooling was to be paid for out of charity. So even my gentleness, my soft way of speaking, the surprise I was too innocent to conceal at much that I saw, were all put down to my "giving myself airs." And I daresay the very efforts I made to please those about me and to gain their affection did more harm than good. Because I clung more or less to Harriet Smith, my room-mate, and the nearest to me in age, I was called a little sneak, trying to get all I could "out of her," as she was such a rich little girl.

I overheard these remarks once or twice, but it was not for some time that I in the least knew what they meant, and so I daresay the coarse-minded girls who made them thought all the worse of me because I did not resent them and just went quietly on my own way.

What I did want from Harriet was sympathy; and when she was in the humour to pay attention to me, she did give me as much as it was in her to give.

I shall never forget the real kindness she and Emma too showed me that first night at Green Bank, when a great blow fell on me after we went upstairs to go to bed.

Some one had unpacked my things. My nightdress was lying on the bed, my brushes and sponges were in their places, and when I opened the very small chest of drawers I saw familiar things neatly arranged in them. But there seemed so few—and in the bottom drawer only one frock, and that my oldest one, not the pretty new one mamma had got me for Sundays or any special occasion.

"Where can all my other things be?" I said to Harriet, who was greatly interested in my possessions.

"What more have you?" she said, peering over my shoulder.

I named several.

"And all my other things," I went on, "not clothes, I don't mean, but my workbox and my new writing-desk, and the picture of father and mamma and Haddie"—it was before the days of "carte-de-visite" or "cabinet" photographs; this picture was what was called a "daguerreotype" on glass, and had been taken on purpose for me at some expense—"and my china dog and the rabbits, and my scraps of silk, and all my puzzles, and, and——" I stopped short, out of breath with bewilderment. "Can they be all together for me to unpack myself?" I said.

Emma, the most experienced of the three, shook her head.

"I'm afraid," she was beginning, when the door opened, and Miss Broom's face appeared.

"Young ladies," she said, "I cannot have this. No talking after the last bell has rung. My dear Miss Smith, you are not usually so forgetful. If it is *you*, Miss Marchant, it is a very bad beginning, disobedience the very first evening."

"She didn't know," said both the girls. "It isn't her fault." "And if she had known," Harriet went on, "she couldn't have helped it. Miss Broom, somebody's took such a lot of her things. Tell her, Gerry."

Under her protection I repeated the list of missing articles, but before I had got to the end the governess interrupted me.

"You are a most impertinent child," she said, "to say such a thing. There are no thieves at Green Bank—what a mind you must have! Your things are safely packed away. Such as you really need you shall have from time to time as I or Miss Aspinall think fit. The frock you have on must be kept as your best one, and you must wear the brown check every day. You have far too many clothes— absurd extravagance—no wonder——" but here she had the sense to stop short.

I did not care so much about my clothes.

"It's the other things I mind," I began, but Miss Broom, who was already at the door, again interrupted.

"Nonsense," she said. "We cannot have the rooms littered with rubbish. Miss Aspinall left it to me. You may have your Biblical dissected maps on Sundays, and perhaps some of the other puzzles during the Christmas holidays, but young ladies do not come to school to amuse themselves, but to work hard at their lessons."

I dared not say anything more. There may have been some reason in putting away a certain number of my treasures, for dear mamma, in her wish to do all she possibly could for my happiness, had very probably sent more things with me then was advisable. But I was not a silly spoilt child; I had always been taught to be reasonable, and I would have given in quite cheerfully if Miss Broom had put it before me in any kindly way.

I was not quite without defence, however.

"I don't see but what you might let her have some things out," said Emma. "Harry and I have. Look at the mantlepiece—the china figures and the Swiss chalets are our ornaments, and there's quite room for some more."

But Miss Broom was by this time at the door, which shut after her sharply without her saying another word.

"Horrid old cat," said both the Smiths.

I said nothing, for if I had I knew I should have burst into tears. But after I was ready for bed and had said my prayers, I could not help the one bitter complaint.

"I wouldn't mind anything else if only she'd let me have papa and mamma's picture," I said.

"Of *course* you should have that," said Emma. "I'm sure Miss Ledbury would let you have it. I think even Miss Aspinall would. Don't be unhappy, Gerry, I'll see if I can't do something for you tomorrow."

And with this consolation I fell asleep. Nor did Emma forget her promise. The next day I found my daguerreotype installed on the mantelpiece, where it stayed all the time I was at school.

My happiest days were those of our French lessons, for then Miss Fenmore was the teacher. She spoke French very well, and she was most kind and patient. Yet for some reason or other she was not much liked in the school. There was a prejudice against her as there was against me: partly, because she did not belong to that part of the country, she was said to "give herself airs;" partly, I think, because she was quiet and rather reserved; partly, I am afraid, because some of the elder girls were jealous of her extreme loveliness. She was as kind to me as she dared to be, but I had no lessons from her except French, and she has since told me that she did not venture to show me anything like partiality, as it would only have made my life still harder and lonelier.

The remembrances which stand out the most clearly in my mind will give a fair idea of my time at Green Bank. The next great trouble I had came on my first Sunday there.

It had been settled that I was to write to mamma once a week— by every mail, that is to say. The usual day for writing home was Wednesday, the half-holiday, but as the South American mail left England that very day, mamma had arranged with Miss Ledbury that I should be allowed to add a little on Sundays to my letter, as otherwise my news would be a whole week late before it left.

So on the first Sunday afternoon I got out my writing things with great satisfaction, and when Miss Broom asked me what I was going to do, I was pleased to be able to reply that Miss Ledbury had given leave for a Sunday letter. Miss Broom said something to

Miss Aspinall, but though they both looked very disapproving, they said no more.

I wrote a long letter. This time, of course, it had to be a complete one, as I had only come to Green Bank on the Thursday. I poured out my heart to mamma, but yet, looking back now and recalling, as I know I can, pretty correctly, all I said, I do not think it was exaggerated or wrong. I tried to write cheerfully, for childish as I was in many ways, I did understand that it would make mamma miserable to think I was unhappy.

I was just closing the envelope when Miss Broom entered the room.

"What are you doing?" she said. "Dear, dear you don't mean to say you have been all this afternoon writing that letter? What a waste of time! No, no, you must not do that. Miss Ledbury will seal it."

"It doesn't need sealing," I replied. "It is a gumming-down envelope."

But she had come close to me, and drew it out of my hand.

"No letters leave this house without being first read by Miss Ledbury or Miss Aspinall," she said. "Why do you stare so? It is the rule at every school," and so in those days I suppose it was. "If you have written nothing you should not, you have no reason to dread its being seen."

"Yes, I have," I replied indignantly. Even the three or four days I had been at school had made me months older. "I have," I repeated. "Nobody would say to strangers all they'd say to their own mamma."

I felt my face growing very red; I pulled the letter out of the envelope and began to tear it across. But Miss Broom's strong hands caught hold of mine.

"You are a very naughty girl," she said, "a very naughty girl indeed. I saw at once how spoilt and self-willed you were, but I never could have believed you would dare to give way to such violent temper."

She dragged the letter out of my fingers—indeed, I was too proud to struggle with her—and left the room. I sat there in a sort of stupefied indifference. That day had been the worst I had had. There was not the interest of lessons, nor the daily bustle which had always something enlivening about it. It was so dull, and oh so different from home! The home-sickness which I was too ignorant to give a name to began to come over me with strides;

but for my letter to mamma I felt as if I could not have lived through
that afternoon. For even the Smiths were away. They were what
was called "weekly boarders," going home every Saturday at noon
and staying till Monday morning.

The indifference did not last long. Gradually both it and the
indignation broke down. I laid my head on the table before me
and burst into convulsive crying.

I do not think I cried loudly. I only remember the terrible
sort of shaking that went through me—I had never felt anything
like it in my life—and I remember trying to choke down my sobs for
fear of Miss Broom hearing me and coming back.

Some one opened the door and looked in. I tried to be perfectly
quiet. But the some one, whoever it was, had seen and perhaps
heard me, for she came forward, and in another moment I felt an
arm steal gently round me, while a voice said softly, very softly,

"My poor little girl, what *is* the matter?" and looking up, I saw
that the new-comer was Miss Fenmore.

"Oh," I said through my tears, "it's my letter, and she's taken it
away—that horrid, *horrid* Miss Broom."

And I told her the whole story.

Miss Fenmore was very wise as well as kind. I have often
wondered how she had learnt so much self-control in her short life,
for though then she seemed quite "old" to me, I now know she
cannot have been more than eighteen or nineteen. But she had had a
sad life—that of an orphan since childhood. I suppose sorrow had
done the work of years in her case—work that is indeed often not
done at all! For she had a character which was good soil for all
discipline. She was naturally so sweet and joyous—she seemed born
with rose-coloured spectacles.

"Dear child," she said, "try not to take this so much to heart. I
daresay your letter will be sent just as it is. Miss Broom is sure to
apply to Miss Aspinall, perhaps to Miss Ledbury. And Miss
Ledbury is really kind, and she must have had great experience in
such things."

But the last words were spoken with more hesitation. Miss
Fenmore knew that the class of children composing Miss Ledbury's
school had not had a home like mine.

Suddenly she started up—steps were coming along the passage.

"I must not talk to you any more just now," she said, "I came to
fetch a book."

After all, the steps did not come to the schoolroom. So after sitting there a little longer, somewhat comforted by the young governess's words, I went up to my own room, where I bathed my eyes and smoothed my hair, mindful of Haddie's warning—not to get the name of a cry-baby!

Late that evening, after tea, I was sent for to Miss Ledbury in the drawing-room. It was a very rainy night, so only a few of the elder girls had gone to church. Miss Ledbury herself suffered sadly from asthma, and could never go out in bad weather. This was the first time I had seen her to speak to since I came.

I was still too unhappy to feel very frightened, and I was not naturally shy, though I seemed so, owing to my difficulty in expressing myself. And there was something about the old lady's manner, gentle though she was, which added to my constraint. I have no doubt she found me very dull and stupid, and it must have been disappointing, for she did mean to be kind.

She spoke to me about my letter which she had read, according to her rule, to which she said she could make no exceptions. I did not clearly understand what she meant, so I just replied "No, ma'am," and "Yes, ma'am." She said the letter should be sent as it was, but she gave me advice for the future which in some ways was very good. Could I not content myself with writing about my own affairs—my lessons, the books I was reading, and so on? What was the use of telling mamma that I did not like Miss Aspinall, and that I could not bear Miss Broom? Would it please mamma, or would it make school-life any happier for me to take up such prejudices? These ladies were my teachers and I must respect them. How could I tell at the end of three days if I should like them or not?

I felt I *could* tell, but I did not dare to say so. All I longed for was to get away. So when the old lady went on putting words into my mouth, as it were, about being wiser for the future, and not touchy and fanciful, and so on, I agreed with her and said "No, ma'am" and "Yes, ma'am" a few more times, meekly enough. Then she kissed me, and again I felt that she meant to be kind and that it was wrong of me to disappoint her, but somehow I could not help it. And I went upstairs to bed feeling more lonely than ever, now that I quite understood that my letters to mamma must never be anything more than I would write to a stranger—a mere mockery, in short.

There was but one person I felt that I could confide in. That was Miss Fenmore. But the days went on and she seemed to take less instead of more notice of me. I did not understand that her position, poor girl, was much more difficult than mine. If she had

seemed to pet me or make much of me it would only have made
Miss Broom still more severe to me, and angry with her. For, as
was scarcely to be wondered at, Miss Broom was very indignant
indeed at the way I had spoken of her in my letter to mamma. And
Miss Fenmore was entirely at that time dependent upon her position
at Green Bank. She had no home, and if she brought displeasure
upon herself at Miss Ledbury's her future would look very dark
indeed.

Yet she was far from selfish. Her caution was quite as much for
my sake as for her own.

CHAPTER VIII

'NOBODY—*NOBODY*'

THE HISTORY of that first week might stand for the history of
several months at Green Bank. That is why I have related it
as clearly as possible. In one sense I suppose people would say
my life grew easier to me, that is to say I got more accustomed to
it, but with the "growing accustomed," increased the loss of hope
and spring, so I doubt if time did bring any real improvement.

I became very dull and silent. I seemed to be losing the power
of complaining, or even of wishing for sympathy. I took some
interest in my lessons, and almost the only pleasure I had was when
I got praise for them. But that did not often happen, not as often
as it should have done, I really believe. For the prejudice against
me on the part of the upper teachers did not wear off. And I can
see now that I must have been a disagreeable child.

Nor did I win more liking among my companions. They
gradually came to treat me with a sort of indifferent contempt.

"It's only that stupid child," I would hear said when I came
into the room.

The Christmas holidays came and went, without much improving
matters. I spent them at school with one or two other pupils,
much older than I. Miss Broom went away, and we were under
Miss Aspinall's charge, for Miss Ledbury had caught a bad cold

and her niece would not leave her. I preferred Miss Aspinall to Miss Broom certainly, but I had half hoped that Miss Fenmore would have stayed. She too went away, however, having got a "holiday engagement,"which she was very glad of she told me when she bade me goodbye. I did not understand what she meant, beyond hearing that she was glad to go, so I said nothing about being sorry.

"She doesn't care for me," I thought.

I saw nothing of Haddie, though he wrote that he was very happy spending the holidays at the house of one of his schoolfellows, and I was glad of this, even while feeling so utterly deserted myself.

It was very, very dull, but I felt as if I did not mind. Even mamma's letters once a fortnight gave me only a kind of tantalising pleasure, for I knew I dared not *really* answer them. The only thing I felt glad of was that she did not know how lonely and un-happy I was, and that she never would do so till the day—the day which I could scarcely believe would ever, *ever* come—when I should see her again, and feel her arms round me, and know that all the misery and loneliness were over!

Some new pupils came after the Christmas holidays, and one or two of the elder girls did not return. But the new boarders were older than I and took no notice of me, so their coming made no difference. One event, however, did interest me—that was the appearance at certain classes two or three times a week of a very sweet-looking little girl about my own age. She was pretty and very nicely dressed, though by no means showily, and her tone of voice and way of speaking were different from those of most of my companions. I wished she had come altogether, and then I might have made friends with her. "Only," I said to myself unselfishly, "she would most likely be as unhappy as I am, so I shouldn't wish for it."

One of the classes she came to was the French one—the class which, as I have said, Miss Fenmore taught. And Miss Fenmore seemed to know her, for she called her by her Christian name—"Myra." The first time I heard it I felt quite puzzled. I knew I had heard it before, though I could not remember where or when, except that it was not very long ago. And when I heard her last name, "Raby"—"Miss Raby" one of the other teachers called her—and put the two together—"Myra Raby"—I felt more and more certain I had heard them spoken of before, though I was equally certain I had never seen the little girl herself.

I might have asked Miss Fenmore about her, but it did not enter my head to do so: that was one of my odd childish ways. And it was partly, too, that I was growing more and more reserved and silent. Even to Harriet Smith I did not talk half as much as at first, and she used to tell me I was growing sulky.

I took great interest in watching for Myra's appearance. I daresay if I could make a picture of her now she would seem a quaint old-fashioned little figure to you, but to me she seemed perfectly lovely. She had pretty brown hair, falling in ringlets round her delicate little face; her eyes were grey, very soft and gentle, and she had a dear little rosebud of a mouth. She was generally dressed in pale grey merino or cashmere, with white lace frilled round the neck and short sleeves—all little girls wore short sleeves then, even in winter; and once when I caught a glimpse of her getting into a carriage which was waiting for her at the door, I was lost in admiration of her dark green cloth pelisse trimmed with chinchilla fur.

"She must be somebody very rich and grand," I thought. But I had no opportunity of getting to know more of her, than a nice little smile or a word or two of thanks if I passed her a book at the class or happened to sit next to her. For she always left immediately after the lesson was over.

Up to Easter she came regularly. Then we had three weeks' holidays, and as before, Miss Fenmore went away. She was pleased to go, but when she said goodbye to me I thought she looked sad, and she called me "my poor little girl."

"Why do you say that?" I asked her. She smiled and answered that she did not quite know; she thought I looked dull, and she wished I were going too.

"Are you less unhappy than when you first came to school?" she said, looking at me rather earnestly. It was very seldom she had an opportunity of speaking to me alone.

"No," I replied, "I'm much unhappier when I think about it. But I'm getting not to think, so I don't care."

She looked still graver at this. I fancy she saw that what I said was true. I was growing dulled and stupefied, as it were, for want of any one to sympathise with me or draw me out, though I did not know quite how to put this into words. As I have said before, I was not a child with much power of expression.

Miss Fenmore kissed me, but she sighed as she did so.

"I wish——" she began, but then she stopped. "When I come

back after Easter," she said more cheerfully, "I hope I may somehow manage to see more of you, dear Geraldine."

"Thank you," I answered. I daresay my voice did not sound as if I did thank her or as if I cared, though in my heart I was pleased, and often thought of what she had said during the holidays, which I found even duller than the Christmas ones had been.

They came to an end at last, however, but among the returning governesses and pupils there was no Miss Fenmore. Nor did Myra Raby come again to the classes she used to attend. I wondered to myself why it was so, but for some time I knew nothing about Miss Fenmore, and in the queer silent way which was becoming my habit I did not ask. At last one day a new governess made her appearance, and then I overheard some of the girls saying she was to take Miss Fenmore's place. A sort of choke came into my throat, and for the first time I realised that I *had* been looking forward to the pretty young governess's return.

I do not remember anything special happening for some time after that. I suppose Easter must have been early that year, for when the events occurred which I am now going to relate, it was still cold and wintry weather—very rainy at least, and Mexington was always terribly gloomy in rainy weather. It seems a long stretch to look back upon—those weeks of the greatest loneliness I had yet known—but in reality I do not think it could have been more than three or four.

I continued to work steadily—even hard—at my lessons. I knew that it would please mamma, and I had a vague feeling that somehow my getting on fast might shorten the time of our separation, though I could not have said why. I was really interested in some of my lessons, and anxious to do well even in those I did not like. But I was not quick or clever, and often, very often, my hesitation in in expressing myself made me seem far less intelligent than I actually was. Still I generally got good marks, especially for *written* tasks, for the teachers, though hard and strict, were not unprincipled. They did not like me, but they were fair on the whole, I think.

Unluckily, however, about this time I got a bad cold. I was not seriously ill, but it hung about me for some time and made me feel very dull and stupid. I think, too, it must have made me a little deaf, though I did not know it at the time. I began to get on less well at lessons, very often making mistakes and replying at random, for which I was scolded as if I did it out of carelessness.

And though I tried more and more to prepare my lessons perfectly, things grew worse and worse.

At last one day they came to a point. I forget what the lesson was, and it does not matter, but every time a question came to me I answered wrongly. Once or twice I did not hear, and when I said so, Miss Broom, whose class it was, was angry, and said I was talking nonsense. It ended in my bursting into tears, which I had never done before in public since I had been at Green Bank.

Miss Broom was very annoyed. She said a great deal to me which between my tears and my deafness I did not hear, and at last she must have ordered me to go up to my room, for her tone grew more and more angry.

"Do you mean to defy me?" she said, so loud that I heard her plainly.

I stared, and I do not know what would have happened if Harriet Smith, who was near me, had not started up in her good-natured way.

"She doesn't hear; she's crying so," she said. "Gerry, dear, Miss Broom says you're to go up to your room."

I was nothing loth. I got up from my seat and made my way more by feeling than seeing—so blinded was I by crying—to the door, and upstairs.

Arrived there, I flung myself on the end of my bed. It was cold, and outside it was raining, raining—it seems to me now that it never left off raining at Mexington that spring; the sky, I if had looked out of the window, was one dull grey sheet. But I seemed to care for nothing—just at first the comfort of being able to cry with no one to look at me was all I wanted. So I lay there sobbing, though not loudly.

After some little time had passed the downstairs bell rang—it was afternoon, and the bell meant, I knew, preparation for tea. So I was not very surprised when the door opened and Emma and Harriet came in—they were both kind, Harriet especially, though her kindness was chiefly shown by loud abuse of Miss Broom.

"You'd better take care, Harry," said her sister at last, "or you'll be getting into disgrace yourself, which certainly won't do Gerry any good. Do be quick and make yourself tidy, the tea-bell will be ringing in a moment. Hadn't you better wash your face and brush your hair, Gerry—you do look such a figure."

"I can't go down unless Miss Broom says I may," I replied, "and I don't want any tea," though in my heart I knew I was feeling hungry. Much crying often makes children hungry; they are not like grown-up people.

"Oh, nonsense," said Emma. "You'd feel ever so much better if you had some tea. What *I* think you're so silly for is *minding*—why need you care what that old Broom says? She daren't beat you or starve you, and once you're at home again you can snap your fingers at school and governesses and—"

Here Harriet said something to her sister in a low voice which I did not hear. It made Emma stop.

"Oh, well, I can't help it," she said, or something of that kind. "It doesn't do any good to cry like that, whatever troubles you have," she went on.

I got up slowly and tried to wash away some of the traces of my tears by plunging my face in cold water. Then Harriet helped me to smooth my hair and make myself look neat. Emma's words had had the effect of making me resolve to cry no more if I could help it. And a moment or two later I was glad I had followed her advice, for one of the elder girls came to our room with a message to say that I was to go down to tea, and after tea I was to stay behind in the dining-room as Miss Aspinall wished to speak to me.

"Very well," I said. But the moment the other girl had gone both Emma and Harriet began again.

"That horrid old Broom," said Harriet, "just fancy her complaining to Miss Aspinall."

And "Promise me, Gerry," said Emma, "not to mind what she says, and whatever you do, don't cry. There's nothing vexes old Broom so much as seeing we don't care—mean old cat."

I could scarcely help laughing, my spirits had got up a little—that is to say, I felt more angry than sad now. I felt as if I really did *not* much care what was said to me.

And I drank my tea and ate my thick slices of bread and butter with a good appetite, though I saw Miss Broom watching me from her end of the table; and when I had finished I felt, as Emma had said I should, "ever so much better"—that is to say, no longer in the least inclined to cry.

Nor did I feel nervous or frightened when Miss Aspinall—all the others having gone—seated herself in front of me and began her talk. It began quite differently from what I had expected. She was a good woman, and not nearly so bad-tempered as Miss Broom, though hard and cold, and I am sure she meant to do me good. She talked about how changed I had been of late, my lessons so much less well done, and how careless and inattentive I seemed. There was some truth in it. I knew my lessons had not been so well done, but I also knew I had not been careless or inattentive.

"And worst of all," continued the governess, "you have got into such a habit of making excuses that it really amounts to telling untruths. Several times, Miss Broom tells me, you have done a wrong lesson or not done one at all, and you have maintained to her that you had not been told what you *had* been told—there was something about your French poetry yesterday, which you *must* have known you were to learn. Miss Broom says you positively denied it."

I was getting very angry now—I had wanted to say I was sorry about my lessons, but now that I was accused of not speaking the truth I felt nothing but anger.

"I never tell stories," I said very loudly; "and if Miss Broom says I do, I'll write to mamma and tell her. I *won't* stay here if you say such things to me."

Miss Aspinall was quite startled; she had never seen me in a passion before, for I was usually considered in the school as sulky rather than violent-tempered. For a moment or two she stared, too astonished to speak. Then

"Go back to your room," she said. "I am sorry to say I must lay this before Miss Ledbury."

I got up from my seat—Miss Aspinall had not kept me standing— and went upstairs again to my room, where I stayed for the rest of the evening, my supper—a cup of milk and a piece of dry bread— being brought me by a servant, and with it a message that I was to undress and go to bed, which I was not sorry to do.

I lay there, not asleep, and still burning with indignation, when Harriet came up to bed. She had not been told not to speak to me, very likely the teachers thought I would be asleep, and she was very curious to know what had passed. I told her all. She was very sympathising, but at the same time she thought it a pity I had lost my temper with Miss Aspinall.

"I don't know how you'll get on now," she said, "with both her and Miss Broom so against you. You should just not have minded— like Emma said."

"Not mind her saying I told stories," I burst out. Harriet did not seem to think there was anything specially annoying in that. "Well," I went on, "*I* mind it, whether you do or not. And I'm *going* to mind it. I shall write to mamma and tell her I can't stay here any more, and I'm sure when she hears it she'll do *something*. She won't let me stay here. Or—or—perhaps father will fix to come home again and not stay as long as two years there."

"I don't think he'll do that," said Harriet mysteriously.

"What do you mean? What do you know about it?" I asked, for something in her voice struck me.

"Oh, nothing—I shouldn't have said it—it was only something I heard," she replied, looking rather confused.

"Something you heard," I repeated, starting up in bed and catching hold of her. "Then you *must* tell me. Do you mean there's been letters or news about father and mamma that I don't know about?"

"No, no," said Harriet. "Of course not."

"Then what do you mean? You shall tell me—if you don't," I went on, more and more excitedly, "I'll—" I hesitated—"I'll tell you what I'll do, I'll go straight downstairs, just as I am, in my nightgown, to Miss Ledbury herself, and tell her what you've said. I don't care if she beats me, I don't care what she does, but I *will* know."

Harriet tried to pull herself away.

"What a horrid temper you're getting, Gerry," she said complainingly. "Just when I hurried up to bed as quick as I could to talk to you. It's nothing, I tell you—only something I heard at home, and Emma said I wasn't ever to tell it you."

I clutched her more firmly.

"You shall tell me, or I'll do what I said."

Harriet looked really frightened.

"You'll not tell Emma, then? You promise?"

I nodded. "I promise."

"Well, then, it was only one day—papa was talking about somebody going to South America, and I said that was where your papa and mamma had gone, and papa asked your name, and then he said he had seen your papa at the bank, and it was a pity he hadn't been content to stay there. It was such a bad climate where he'd gone—lots of people got ill and died there, unless they were rich enough to live out of the town, and he didn't suppose any one who'd only been a clerk in the bank here would be that. And Emma said, couldn't your papa and mamma come back if they got ill, and he said if they waited till then it would be rather too late. There's some fever people get there, that comes all of a sudden. And besides that, your papa must have promised he'd stay two years—they always do."

As she went on, my heart fell lower and lower—for a moment or two I could not speak. All sorts of dreadful fears and imaginings began to fill my mind; perhaps my parents had already got that terrible illness Harriet spoke of, perhaps one or both of them had already died. I could have screamed aloud. I felt I could not bear it—I must write to mamma a letter that nobody should read. I must see somebody who would tell me the truth—Haddie, perhaps, knew more than I did. If I could go to him! But I had no money and no idea of the way, and Miss Aspinall would never, *never* let me even write to ask him. Besides, I was in disgrace, very likely they would not believe me if I told them why I was so miserable; they had already said I told stories, and then I must not get Harriet into trouble.

What *should* I do? If only Miss Fenmore had still been there, I felt she would have been sorry for me, but there was nobody—*nobody*.

I turned my face away from my little companion, and buried it in the pillow. Harriet grew frightened.

"What are you doing, Gerry?" she said. "Why don't you speak? Are you doing to sleep or are you crying? Very likely your papa and mamma won't get that illness. I wish I hadn't told you."

"Never mind," I said. "I'm going to sleep."

"And you won't tell Emma?" Harriet repeated.

"Of course not—don't you believe my word? Do you too think that I tell stories?"

I tried to get rid of my misery by letting myself grow angry.

"You're very cross," said Harriet; but all the same I think she understood me better than she could express, for she kissed me and said, "Do go to sleep—don't be so unhappy."

CHAPTER IX

OUT IN THE RAIN

IT WOULD BE an exaggeration to say that I did not sleep that night. Children often sleep very heavily when they are specially unhappy, and I was unhappy enough, even before Harriet's telling me what she had heard. But though I did sleep, I shall never forget that night. My dreams were so miserable, and when I awoke—very early in the morning—I could scarcely separate them from real things. It was actually not so bad when I was quite awake, for then I set myself thoroughly to think it all over.

I could not bear it—I could not go on without knowing if it was true about father and mamma. I could not bear my life at school, if the looking forward to being with them again, before *very* long, was to be taken from me. I must write a letter to mamma that no one would see; but first—yes, first I must know how much was true. Whom could I ask? Haddie? Perhaps he knew no more than I did, and it was just as difficult to write to him as to mamma. Then suddenly another thought struck me—Mrs Selwood, old Mrs. Selwood, if I could but see her. Perhaps if I wrote to her she would come to see me; mamma always said she was very kind, though I know she did not care much for children, especially little girls. Still I thought I would try, though it would be difficult, for I should not like Miss Ledbury to know I had written to Mrs. Selwood secretly. She would be so angry, and I did not want to make Miss Ledbury angry. She was much nicer than the others. Once or twice the idea came to me of going straight to her and telling her how miserable I was, but that would bring in Harriet, and oh, how furious the other governesses would be! No, I would try to write to Mrs. Selwood—only, I did not know her address. I only knew the name of her house—Fernley—that would not be enough, at least I feared not. I would try to find out; perhaps Harriet could ask some one when she went home.

My spirits rose a little with all this planning. I am afraid that the life I led was beginning to make me unchildlike and concealed in my ways. I enjoyed the feeling of having a secret and, so to say, outwitting my teachers, particularly Miss Broom. So, though I was looking pale and my eyes were still very swollen, I think Harriet

248

was surprised, and certainly very glad, to find that I was not very miserable or upset.

A message was sent up to say I was to go down to breakfast with the others. And after prayers and breakfast were over I went into the schoolroom as usual.

That morning did not pass badly; it happened to be a day for lessons I got on well with—written ones principally, and reading aloud. So I got into no fresh disgrace. It was a very rainy day, there was no question of going out, and I was sent to practise at twelve o'clock till the dressing-bell rang for the early dinner. That was to keep me away from the other girls.

As soon as dinner was over Miss Broom came to me with a French poetry book in her hand.

"This is the poem you should have learnt yesterday," she said, "though you denied having been told so. Miss Aspinall desires you to take it upstairs to your room and learn it, as you can do perfectly, if you choose, by three o'clock. Then you are to come downstairs to the drawing-room, where you will find her."

"Very well," I said, as I took the book, "I will learn it."

They were going to let me off rather easily, I thought, and possibly, just *possibly*, if Miss Ledbury was in the drawing-room too and seemed kind, I might ask her to give me leave to write to Mrs. Selwood just to say how very much I would like to see her, and then if I *did* see her I could tell her what Harriet had said, without risking getting Harriet into trouble.

So I set to work at my French poetry with good will, and long before three o'clock I had learnt it perfectly. There was a clock on the landing half-way down the staircase which struck the quarters and half-hours. I heard the quarter to three strike and then I read the poem right through six times, and after that, closing the book, I said it aloud to myself without one mistake, and then just as the clock began "*burr*-ing" before striking the hour I made my way quietly down to the drawing-room.

I tapped at the door.

"Come in," said Miss Aspinall.

She was standing beside Miss Ledbury, who was sitting in an arm-chair near the fire. She looked very pale, her face nearly as white as her hair, and it made me feel sorry, so that I stared at her and forgot to curtsey as we always were expected to do on entering a room where any of the governesses were.

"Do you not see Miss Ledbury?" said Miss Aspinall sharply.

I felt my cheeks get red, and I turned back towards the door to make my curtsey.

"I—I forgot," I said, and before Miss Aspinall had time to speak again, the old lady held out her hand.

"You must try to be more thoughtful," she said, but her voice was gentle. "Now give me your book," she went on, "I want to hear your French verses myself."

I handed her the book, which was open at the place. I felt very glad I had learnt the poetry so well, as I wished to please Miss Ledbury.

"Begin, my dear," she said.

I did so, repeating the six or eight verses without any mistake or hesitation.

Miss Ledbury seemed pleased and relieved.

"Very well said—now, my dear child, that shows that you can learn well when you try."

"Of course she can," said Miss Aspinall.

"But more important than learning your lessons well," continued Miss Ledbury, "is to be perfectly truthful and honest. What has distressed me, Geraldine, has been to hear that when—as may happen to any child—you have forgotten a lesson, or learnt it imperfectly, instead of at once owning your fault, you have tried to screen yourself behind insincere excuses. That was the case about these very verses, was it not, Miss Aspinall?" (Miss Ledbury always called her niece "Miss Aspinall" before any of us.)

"It was," replied Miss Aspinall. "Miss Broom will tell you all the particulars," and as she spoke Miss Broom came in.

Miss Ledbury turned to her.

"I wish you to state exactly what you have had to complain of in Geraldine Le Marchant," she said. And Miss Broom, with a far from amiable expression, repeated the whole—my carelessness and ill-prepared lessons for some time past, the frequent excuses I made, saying that she had not told me what she certainly had told me, my forgetting my French poetry altogether, and persisting in denying that it had been given out.

I did not hear clearly all she said, but she raised her voice at the end, and I caught her last words. I felt again a sort of fury at her, and I gave up all idea of confiding in Miss Ledbury, or of trying to please any one.

Miss Ledbury seemed nervous.

"Geraldine has said her French poetry perfectly," she said. "I think she has taken pains to learn it well."

"It is some time since she has said any lesson perfectly to *me*, I am sorry to say," snapped Miss Broom.

Miss Ledbury handed her the book.

"You can judge for yourself," she said. "Repeat the verses to Miss Broom, Geraldine."

Then a strange thing happened. I really wanted to say the poetry well, partly out of pride, partly because again something in Miss Ledbury's manner made me feel gentler, but as I opened my mouth to begin, the words entirely left my memory. I looked up—possibly a little help, a syllable just to start me, would have set me right, but instead of that I saw Miss Broom's half-mocking, half-angry face, and Miss Aspinall's cold hard eyes. Miss Ledbury I did not look at. In reality I think both she and Miss Aspinall were afraid of Miss Broom. I do not think Miss Aspinall was as hard as she seemed.

I drew a long breath—no, it was no use. I could not recall one word.

"I've forgotten it," I said.

Miss Aspinall gave an exclamation—Miss Ledbury looked at me with reproach. Both believed that I was not speaking the truth, and that I had determined not to say the verses to Miss Broom.

"Impossible," said Miss Aspinall.

"Geraldine," said Miss Ledbury sadly but sternly. "do not make me distrust you."

I grew stony. Now I did not care. Even Miss Ledbury doubted my word. I almost think if the verses had come back to me then, I would not have said them. I stood there, dull and stupid and obstinate, though a perfect fire was raging inside me.

"Geraldine," said Miss Ledbury again, still more sadly and sternly.

I was only a child, and I was almost exhausted by all I had gone through. Even my pride gave way. I forgot all that Emma and Harriet had said about not crying, and, half turning away from the three before me, I burst into a loud fit of tears and sobbing.

Miss Ledbury glanced at her niece. I think the old lady had hard work to keep herself from some impulsive kind action, but I suppose she would have thought it wrong. But Miss Aspinall came towards me, and placed her arm on my shoulders.

"Geraldine," she said, and her voice was not unkind, "I beg you to try to master this naughty obstinate spirit. Say the verses again, and all may be well."

"No, no," I cried. "I can't, I can't. It is true that I've forgotten them, and if I could say them I wouldn't now, because you all think me a story-teller."

She turned away really grieved and shocked.

"Take her upstairs to her room again," said Miss Ledbury. "Geraldine, your tears are only those of anger and temper."

I did not care now. I suffered myself to be led back to my room, and I left off crying almost as suddenly as I had begun, and when Miss Aspinall shut the door, and left me there without speaking to me again, I sat down on the foot of my bed as if I did not care at all, for again there came over me that strange stolid feeling that nothing mattered, that nothing would ever make me cry again.

It did not last long, however. I got up in a few minutes and looked out of the window. It was the dullest afternoon I had ever seen, raining, raining steadily, the sky all gloomy no-colour, duller even than grey. It might have been any season, late autumn, mid-winter; there was not a leaf, or the tiniest beginning of one, on the black branches of the two or three trees in what was called "the garden"—for my window looked to the back of the house— not the very least feeling of spring, even though we were some way on in April. I gave a little shiver, and then a sudden thought struck me. It would be a very good time for getting out without any one seeing me—no one would fancy it possible that I would venture out in the rain, and all my schoolfellows and the governesses were still at lessons. What was the use of waiting here? They might keep me shut up in my room for—for ever, perhaps—and I should never know about father and mamma, or get Mrs. Selwood's address or be allowed to write to her, or—or any one. I would go.

It took but a few minutes to put on my things. As I have said, there was a queer mixture of childishness and "old-fashioned-ness", as it is called, about me. I dressed myself as sensibly as if I had been a grown-up person, choosing my thickest boots and warm jacket, and arming myself with my waterproof cape and umbrella. I also put my purse in my pocket—it contained a few shillings.

Then I opened the door and listened, going out a little way into the passage to do so. All was quite quiet—not even a piano was to be heard, only the clock on the landing sounded to me much louder than usual. If I had waited long, it would have made me nervous. I should have begun to fancy it was talking to me like Dick Whittington's bells, though, I am sure, it would not have said anything half so cheering!

But I did not wait to hear. I crept downstairs, past one school-room with its closed door, and a muffled sound of voices as I drew quite close to it, then on again, past the downstairs class-room, and along the hall to the front door. For that was what I had made up my mind was the best, bold as it seemed. I would go right out by the front door. I knew it opened easily, for we went out that way on Sundays to church, and once or twice I had opened it. And nobody would ever dream of my passing out that way.

It was all managed quite easily, and almost before I had time to take in what I had done, I found myself our in the road some little distance from Green Bank, for as soon as the gate closed behind me I had set off running from a half-nervous fear that some one might be coming in pursuit of me. I ran on a little further, in the same direction, that of the town, for Miss Ledbury's house was in the outskirts—then, out of breath, I stood still to think what I should do.

I had not made any distinct plan. The only idea clearly in my mind was to get Mrs. Selwood's address, so that I could write to her. But as I stood there, another thought struck me. I would go home—to the house in the dull street which had never seemed dull to me! For there, I suddenly remembered, I might find one of our own servants. I recollected Lydia's telling me that cook was probably going to "engage" with the people who had taken the house. And cook would be sure to know Mrs. Selwood's address, and—perhaps—cook would be able to tell me something about father and mamma. She was a kind woman—I would not mind telling her how dreadfully frightened I was about them since Harriet Smith had repeated what she had heard.

I knew the way to our house, at least I thought I did, though afterwards I found I had taken two or three wrong turnings, which had made my journey longer. It was scarcely raining by this time, but the streets were dreadfully wet and muddy, and the sky still dark and gloomy.

At last I found myself at the well-known corner of our steet—how often I had run round it with Haddie, when we had been allowed to go on some little errand by ourselves! I had not passed this way since mamma went, and the feeling that came over me was very strange. I went along till I came to our house, number 39;

then, in a sort of dream, I mounted the two or three steps to the door, and rang the bell. How well I knew its sound! It seemed impossible to believe that Lydia would not open to me, and that if I hurried upstairs I should not find mamma sitting in her usual place in the drawing-room!

But of course it was not so. A strange face met me as the door drew back, and for a moment or two I felt too confused to speak, though I saw the servant was looking at me in surprise.

"Is—can I see cook?" I got out at last.

"Cook," the maid repeated. "I'm sure I can't say. Can't you give me your message—Miss?" adding the last word after a little hesitation.

"I'd rather see her, please. I want to ask her for Mrs. Selwood's address. Mrs. Selwood's a friend of mamma's, and I'm sure cook would know. We used to live here, and Lydia said cook was going to stay."

The servant's face cleared, but her reply was not encouraging. "Oh," she said, "I see. But it's no use your seeing our cook, Miss. She's a stranger. The other one—Sarah Wells was her name——"

"Yes, yes," I exclaimed, "that's her."

"She's gone—weeks ago. Her father was ill, and she had to go home. I'm sorry, Miss"—she was a good-natured girl—"but it can't be helped. And I think you'd better go home quick. It's coming on to rain again, and it'll soon be dark, and you're such a little young lady to be out alone."

"Thank you," I said, and I turned away, my heart swelling with disappointment.

I walked on quickly for a little way, for I felt sure the servant was looking after me. Then I stopped short and asked myself again "what should I do?" The girl had advised me to "go home"— "home" to Green Bank, to be shut up in my room again, and be treated as a story-teller, and never have a chance of writing to Mrs. Selwood or any one! No, that I would not do. The very thought of it made me hasten my steps as if to put a greater distance between myself and Mrs. Ledbury's house. And I walked on some way without knowing where I was going except that it was in an opposite direction from school.

It must have been nearly six o'clock by this time, and the gloomy day made it already dusk. The shops were lighting up, and the glare of the gas on the wet pavement made me look about me.

I was in one of the larger streets now, a very long one, that led right out from the centre of the town to the outskirts. I was full of a strange kind of excitement; I did not mind the rain, and indeed it was not very heavy; I did not feel lonely or frightened, and my brain seemed unusually active and awake.

"I know what I'll do," I said to myself; "I'll go to the big grocer's where they give Haddie and me those nice gingerbreads, and I'll ask *them* for Mrs. Selwood's address. I remember mamma said Mrs. Selwood always bought things there. And—and—I won't write to her. I'll go to the railway and see if I've money enough to get a ticket, and I'll go to Mrs. Selwood and tell her how I can't bear it any longer. I've got four shillings, and if that isn't enough I daresay the railway people wouldn't mind if I promised I'd send it them."

I marched on, feeling once more very determined and valiant. I thought I knew the way to the big grocer's quite well, but when I turned down a street which looked like the one where it was, I began to feel a little confused. There were so many shops, and the lights in the windows dazzled me, and the worst of all, I could not remember the name of the grocer's. It was something like Simpson, but not Simpson. I went on, turning again more than once, always in hopes of seeing it before me, but always disappointed. And I was beginning to feel very tired; I must, I suppose, have been really tired all the time, but my excitement had kept me up.

At last I found myself in a much darker street than the others. For there were few shops in it, and most of the houses were offices of some kind. It was a wide street and rather hilly. As I stood at the top I saw it sloping down before me; the light of the tall lamps glimmered brokenly in the puddles, for it was raining again more heavily now. Suddenly, as if in a dream, some words came back to me, so clearly that I could almost have believed some one was speaking. It was mamma's voice.

"You had better put on your mackintosh, Haddie," I seemed to hear her say, and then I remembered it all—it came before me like a picture—that rainy evening not many months ago when mamma and Haddie and I walked home so happily, we two tugging at her arms, one on each side, heedless of the rain or the darkness, or anything except that we were all together.

I stood still. Never, I think, was a child's heart more nearly breaking.

CHAPTER X

TAKING REFUGE

For a minute or two I seemed to feel nothing; then there came over me a sort of shiver, partly of cold, for it *was* very cold, partly of misery. I roused myself, however. With the remembrance of that other evening had come to me also the knowledge of where I was. Only a few yards down the sloping street on the left-hand side came a wide stretch of pavement, and there, in a kind of angle, stood a double door, open on both sides, leading into a small outer hall, from which again another door, glazed at the top, was the entrance to Cranston's show-rooms.

I remembered it all perfectly. Just beyond the inner entrance stood the two carved lions that Haddie and I admired so much. I wished I could see them again, and—yes—a flash of joy went through me at the thought—I could get Mrs. Selwood's address quite as well from old Mr. Cranston as from the big grocer!

As soon as the idea struck me I hurried on, seeming to gain fresh strength and energy. It was almost dark, but a gas-lamp was burning dimly above the lintel, and inside, on the glass of the inner door, were the large gilt letters "Cranston and Co."

I ran up the two or three broad shallow steps and pushed open the door, which was a swing one. It was nearly time for closing, but that I did not know. There was no one to be seen inside, not, at least, in the first room, and the door made no noise. But there stood the dear lions—I could not see them very clearly, for the place was not brightly lighted, but I crept up to them, and stroked softly the one nearest me. They seemed like real friends.

I had not courage to go into the other show-room, and all was so perfectly still that I could scarcely think any one was there. I thought I would wait a few minutes in hopes of some one coming out, of whom I could enquire if I could see Mr. Cranston. And I was now beginning to feel so tired—so very tired, and so cold.

In here, though I did not see any fire, it felt ever so much warmer than outside. There was no chair or stool, but I found a seat for myself on the stand of the farther-in lion—each of them had a heavy wooden stand. It seemed very comfortable, and I soon found that by moving on a little I could get a nice rest for my head against the lion's body. A strange pleasant sense of protection and comfort came over me.

"How glad I am I came in here," I said to myself. "I don't mind if I have to wait a good while. It is so cosy and warm." I no longer made any plans. I knew I wanted to ask for Mrs. Selwood's address, but that was all I thought of. What I should do when I had got it I did not know; where I should go for the night, for it was now quite dark, I did not trouble about in the least. I think I must have been very much in the condition I have heard described, of travellers lost in the snow—the overpowering wish to stay where I was and rest, was all I was conscious of. I did not think of going to sleep. I did not know I was sleepy.

And for some time I knew nothing.

The first thing that caught my attention was a very low murmur— so low that it might have been merely a breath of air playing in the keyhole; I seemed to have been hearing it for some time before it took shape, as it were, and grew into a softly-whispering voice, gradually gathering into words.

"Poor little girl; so she has come at last. Well, as you say, brother, we have been expecting her for a good while, have we not?"

"Yes, indeed, but speak softly. It would be a pity to awake her. And what we have to do can be done just as well while she sleeps."

"I don't agree with you," said the first speaker. "I should much prefer her being awake. She would enjoy the ride, and she is an intelligent child and would profit by our conversation."

"As you like," replied number two. "I must be off to fetch the boy. She will perhaps be awake by the time I return."

And then—just as I was on the point of starting up and telling them I *was* awake—came a sound of stamping and rustling, and a sort of whirr and a breath of cold air, which told me the swing door had been opened. And when I sat straight up and looked about me, lo and behold, there was only one lion to be seen—the stand of his brother was empty!

"I—please I *am* awake," I said rather timidly. "It was me you were talking about, wasn't it?"

"I—'it was I'—the verb to be takes the same case after it as before it," was the reply, much to my surprise and rather to my disgust. Who would have thought that the carved lions bothered about grammar!

I

"It was I, then," I repeated meekly. I did not want to give any offence to my new friend. "Please—I heard you saying something—something about going a ride. And where has the—the other Mr. Lion gone? I heard about—a boy."

"You heard correctly," my lion replied, and I knew somehow that he was smiling, or whatever lions do that matches smiling. "My brother has gone to fetch *your* brother—we planned it all some time ago—we shall meet on the sea-shore and travel together. But we should be starting. Can you climb up on to my back?"

"Oh yes," I said quite calmly, as if there was nothing the least out of the common in all this, "I'm sure I can."

"Catch hold of my mane," said the lion; "don't mind tugging, it won't hurt," and—not to my surprise, for nothing surprised me— I felt my hands full of soft silky hair, as the lion shook down his long wavy mane to help my ascent.

Nothing was easier. In another moment I was cosily settled on his back, which felt deliciously comfortable, and the mane seemed to tuck itself round me like a fleecy rug.

"Shut your eyes," said my conductor or steed, I don't know which to call him; "go to sleep if you like. I'll wake you when we meet the others."

"Thank you," I said, feeling too content and comfortable to disagree with anything he said.

Then came a feeling of being raised up, a breath of colder air, which seemed to grow warm again almost immediately, and I knew nothing more till I heard the words, "Here they are."

I opened my eyes and looked about me. It was night—overhead in the deep blue sky innumerable stars were sparkling, and down below at our feet I heard the lap-lap of rippling waves. A dark, half-shadowy figure stood at my right hand, and as I saw it more clearly I distinguished the form of the other lion, with—yes, there was some one sitting on his back.

"Haddie," I exclaimed.

"Yes, yes, Geraldine, it's me," my brother's own dear voice replied. "We're going right over the sea—did you know?—isn't it splendid? We're going to see father and mamma. Hold out your hand so that you can feel mine."

I did so, and my fingers clasped his, and at that moment the brother lions rose into the air, and down below, ever fainter and fainter, came the murmur of the sea, while up above, the twinkling stars looked down on what surely was one of the strangest sights they had ever seen in all their long, long experience!

Then again I seemed to know nothing, though somehow, all through, I felt the clasp of Haddie's hand and knew we were close together.

A beautiful light streaming down upon us, of which I was conscious even through my closed eyelids, was the next thing I remember. It seemed warm as well as bright, and I felt as if basking in it.

"Wake up, Geraldine," said Haddie's voice.

I opened my eyes. But now I have come to a part of my story which I have never been able, and never shall be able, to put into fitting words. The scene before me was too beautiful, too magically exquisite for me even to succeed in giving the faintest idea of it. Still I must try, though knowing that I cannot but fail.

Can you picture to yourselves the loveliest day of all the perfect summer days you have ever known—no, more than that, a day like summer and spring in one—the richness of colour, the balmy fragrance of the prime of the year joined to the freshness, the indescribable hopefulness and expectation which is the charm of the spring? The beauty and delight seemed made up of everything lovely mingled together—sights, sounds, scents, feelings. There was the murmur of running streams, the singing of birds, the most delicious scent from the flowers growing in profusion and of every shade of colour.

Haddie and I looked at each other—we still held each other by the hand, but now, somehow, we were standing together on the grass, though I could not remember having got down from my perch on the lion's back.

"Where are the lions, Haddie?" I said.

Haddie seemed to understand everything better than I did.

"They're all right," he replied, "resting a little. You see we've come a long way, Geraldine, and so quick."

"And where are we?" I asked. "What is this place, Haddie? Is it fairyland or—or—heaven?"

Haddie smiled.

"It's not either," he said. "You'll find out the name yourself. But come, we must be quick, for we can't stay very long. Hold my hand tight and then we can run faster."

I seemed to know that something more beautiful than anything we had seen yet was coming. I did not ask Haddie any more questions, even though I had a feeling that he knew more than I did.

He seemed quite at home in this wonderful place, quite able to guide me. And his face was shining with happiness.

We ran a good way, and very fast. But I did not feel at all tired or breathless. My feet seemed to have wings, and all the time the garden around us grew lovelier and lovelier. If Haddie had not been holding my hand so fast I should scarcely have been able to resist stopping to gather some of the lovely flowers everywhere in such profusion, or to stand still to listen to the dear little birds singing so exquisitely overhead.

"It must be fairyland," I repeated to myself more than once, in spite of what Haddie had said.

But suddenly all thoughts of fairyland or flowers, birds and garden, went out of my head, as Haddie stopped in his running.

"Geraldine," he half whispered, "look there."

"There" was a little arbour a few yards from where we stood, and there, seated on a rustic bench, her dear face all sunshine, was mamma!

She started up as soon as she saw us and hastened forward, her arms outstretched.

"My darlings, my darlings," she said, as Haddie and I threw ourselves upon her.

She did look so pretty; she was all in white, and she had a rose—one of the lovely roses I had been admiring as we ran—fastened to the front of her dress.

"Mamma, mamma," I exclaimed, as I hugged her, "oh, mamma, I am so happy to be with you. Is this your garden, mamma, and may we stay with you always now? Wasn't it good of the lions to bring us? I have been so unhappy, mamma—somebody said you would get ill far away. But nobody could get ill here. Oh, mamma, you will let us stay always."

She did not speak, but looking at Haddie I saw a change in his face.

"Geraldine," he said, "I told you we couldn't stay long. The lions would be scolded if we did, and you know you must say your French poetry."

And then there came over me the most agonising feeling of disappointment and misery. All the pent-up wretchedness of the last weeks at school woke up and overwhelmed me like waves of dark water. It is as impossible for me to put this into words as it was for me to describe my exquisite happiness, for no words ever succeed in expressing the intense and extraordinary sensations of some dreams. And of course, as you will have found out by this time, the strange adventures I have been relating were those of a dream, though I still, after all the years that have passed since then, remember them so vividly.

It was the fatal words "French poetry" that seemed to awake me—to bring back my terrible unhappiness, exaggerated by the fact of my dreaming.

"French poetry," I gasped, "oh Haddie, how can you remind me of it?"

Haddie suddenly turned away, and I saw the face of one of the lions looking over his shoulder, with, strange to say, a white frilled cap surrounding it.

"You must try to drink this, my dear," said the lion, if the lion it was, for as I stared at him the brown face changed into a rather ruddy one—a round good-humoured face, with pleasant eyes and smile, reminding me of mamma's old nurse who had once come to see us.

I stared still more, and sat up a little, for, wonderful to relate, I was no longer in the lovely garden, no longer even in the show-room leaning against the lion: I was in bed in a strange room which I had never seen before. And leaning over me was the owner of the frilled cap, holding a glass in her hand.

"Try to drink this, my dearie," she said again, and then I knew it was not the lion but this stranger who had already spoken to me.

I felt very tired, and I sank back again upon the pillow. What did it all mean? Where was I? Where had I been? I asked myself this in a vague sleepy sort of way, but I was too tired to say it aloud, and before I could make up my mind to try I fell asleep again.

The room seemed lighter the next time I opened my eyes. It was in fact nearly the middle of the day, and a fine day—as clear as it ever was in Great Mexington. I felt much better and less tired now, almost quite well, except for a slight pain in my throat which told me I must have caught cold, as my colds generally began in my throat.

"I wonder if it was with riding so far in the night," I first said to myself, with a confused remembrance of my wonderful dream. "I didn't feel at all cold on the lion's back, and in the garden it was lovelily warm."

Then, as my waking senses quite returned, I started. It had been only a dream—oh dear, oh dear! But still, *something* had happened—I was certainly not in my little bed in the corner of the room I shared with Emma and Harriet Smith at Green Bank. When had my dream begun, or was I still dreaming?

I raised myself a little, very softly, for now I began to remember the good-humoured face in the frilled cap, and I thought to myself that unless its owner were a dream too, perhaps she was still in the room, and I wanted to look about me first on my own account.

What there was to see was very pleasant and very real. I felt quite sure I was not dreaming now, wherever I was. It was a large old-fashioned room, with red curtains at the two windows and handsome dark wood furniture. There was a fire burning cheerfully in the grate and the windows looked very clean, even though there was a prospect of chimney-tops to be seen out of the one nearest to me, which told me I was still in a town. And then I began to distinguish sounds outside, though here in this room it was so still. There were lots of wheels passing, some going quickly, some lumbering along with heavy slowness—it was much noisier than at Miss Ledbury's or at my own old home. Here I seemed to be in the very heart of a town. I began to recall the events of the day before more clearly. Yes, up to the time I remembered leaning against the carved lion in Mr. Cranston's show-room all had been real, I felt certain. I recollected with a little shiver the scene in the drawing-room at Green Bank, and how they had all refused to believe I was speaking the truth when I declared that the French poetry had entirely gone out of my head. And then there was the making up my mind that I could bear school no longer, and the secretly leaving the house, and at last losing my way in the streets.

I had meant to go to Mrs. Selwood's, or at least to get her address and write to her—but where was I now?—what should I do?

My head grew dizzy again with trying to think, and a faint miserable feeling came over me and I burst into tears.

I did not cry loudly. But there was some one watching in the room who would have heard even a fainter sound than that of my sobs—some one sitting behind my bed-curtains whom I had not seen, who came forward now and leant over me, saying, in words and voice which seemed curiously familiar to me,

"Geraldine, my poor little girl."

CHAPTER XI

KIND FRIENDS

It was Miss Fenmore. I knew her again at once. And she called me "my poor little girl"—the very words she had used when she said goodbye to me and looked so sorry before she went away for the Easter holidays, never to come back, though she did not then know it, to Green Bank.

"You remember me, dear?" she said, in the sweet tones I had loved to hear. "Don't speak if you feel too ill or if it tires you. But don't feel frightened or unhappy, though you are in a strange place—everything will be right."

I felt soothed almost at once, but my curiosity grew greater.

"When did you come?" I said. "You weren't here when I woke before. It was—somebody with a cap—first I thought it was one of the lions."

The sound of my own voice surprised me, it was so feeble and husky, and though my throat did not hurt me much I felt that it was thick and swollen.

Miss Fenmore thought I was still only half awake or light-headed, but she was too sensible to show that she thought so.

"One of the lions?" she said, smiling. "You mean the carved lions that Myra is so fond of. No—that was a very funny fancy of yours—a lion with a cap on! It was old Hannah that you saw, the old nurse. She has been watching beside you all night. When you awoke before, I was out. I went out very early."

She spoke in a very matter-of-fact way, but rather slowly, as if she wanted to be sure of my understanding what she said. And as my mind cleared and I followed her words I grew more and more anxious to know all there was to hear.

"I don't understand," I said, "and it hurts me to speak. Is this your house, Miss Fenmore, and how do you know about the lions? And who brought me in here, and why didn't I know when I was put in this bed?"

Miss Fenmore looked at me rather anxiously when I said it hurt me to speak.   But she seemed pleased, too, at my asking the questions so distinctly.

"Don't speak, dear," she said quietly, "and I will explain it all. The doctor said you were not to speak if it hurt you."

"The doctor," I repeated.   Another puzzle!

"Yes," said Miss Fenmore, "the doctor who lives in this street— Dr. Fallis.   He knows you quite well, and you know him, don't you ? Just nod your head a little, instead of speaking."

But the doctor's name brought back too many thoughts for me to be content with only nodding my head.

"Dr. Fallis," I said.   "Oh, I would so like to see him. He could tell me——" but I stopped.   "Mrs. Selwood's address" I was going to say, as all the memories of the day before began to rush over me. "Why didn't I know when he came ?"

"You were asleep, dear, but he is coming again," said Miss Fenmore quietly.   "He was afraid you had got a sore throat by the way you breathed.   You must have caught cold in the evening down in the show-room by the lions, before they found you."

And then she went on to explain it all to me.   I was in Mr. Cranston's house!—up above the big show-rooms, where he and old Mrs. Cranston lived.   They had found me fast asleep, leaning against one of the lions—the old porter and the boy who went round late in the evening to see that all was right for the night, though when the rooms were shut up earlier no one had noticed me.   I was so fast asleep, so utterly exhausted, that I had not awakened when the old man carried me up to the kitchen, just as the servants were about going to bed, to ask what in the world was to be done with me; nor even later, when, on Miss Fenmore's recognising me, they had undressed and settled me for the night in the comfortable old-fashioned "best bedroom," had I opened my eyes or spoken.

Old Hannah watched beside me all night, and quite early in the morning Dr. Fallis, who fortunately was the Cranston's doctor too, had been sent for.

"He said we were to let you have your sleep out," said Miss Fenmore, "though by your breathing he was afraid you had caught cold.   How is your throat now, dear ?"

"It doesn't hurt very much." I said, "only it feels very shut up."

"I expect you will have to stay in bed all to-day," she replied. "Dr. Fallis will be coming soon and then we shall know."

"But—but," I began; then as the thought of it all came over me still more distinctly I hid my face in the pillow and burst into tears.

"Must I go back to school?" I said. "Oh, Miss Fenmore, they will be so angry—I came away without leave, because—because I couldn't bear it, and they said I told what wasn't true—that was almost the worst of all. Fancy if they wrote and told mamma that I told lies."

"She would not believe it," said Miss Fenmore quietly; "and besides, I don't think Miss Ledbury would do such a thing, and she always writes to the parents herself, I know. And she *is* kind and good, Geraldine."

"P'raps she means to be," I said among my tears, "but it's Miss Aspinall and—and—Miss Broom. I think I hate her, Miss Fenmore. Oh, I shouldn't say that—I never used to hate anybody. I'm getting all wrong and naughty, I know," and I burst into fresh sobs.

Poor Miss Fenmore looked much distressed. No doubt she had been told to keep me quiet and not let me excite myself.

"Geraldine, dear," she said, "do try to be calm. If you could tell me all about it quietly, the speaking would do you less harm than crying so. Try, dear. You need not speak loud."

I swallowed down my tears and began the story of my troubles. Once started I could not have helped telling her all, even if it had hurt my throat much more than it did. And she knew a good deal already. She was a girl of great natural quickness and full of sympathy. She seemed to understand what I had been going through far better than I could put it in words, and when at last, tired out, I left off speaking, she said all she could to comfort me. There was no need for me to trouble about going back to Green Bank just now. Dr. Fallis had said I must stay where I was for the present, and when I saw him I might tell him anything I liked.

"He will understand," she said, "and he will explain to Miss Ledbury. I have seen Miss Ledbury this morning already, and—"

"Was she dreadfully angry?" I interrupted.

"No, dear," Miss Fenmore replied. "She had been terribly frightened about you, and Miss Aspinall and some of the servants had been rushing about everywhere. But Miss Ledbury is very good, as I keep telling you, Geraldine. She is very sorry to hear how unhappy you have been, and if she had known how anxious you were about your father and mother she would have tried to comfort you. I wish you had told her."

"I wanted to tell her, but Miss Broom was there, and they thought I told stories," I repeated.

"Well, never mind about that now. You shall ask Dr. Fallis, and I am sure he will tell you you need not be so unhappy."

It was not till long afterwards that I knew how very distressed poor old Miss Ledbury had been, and how she had blamed herself for not having tried harder to gain my confidence. Nor did I fully understand at the time how very sensibly Miss Fenmore had behaved when Mr. and Mrs. Cranston sent her off to Green Bank to tell of my having, without intending it, taken refuge with them; she had explained things so that Miss Ledbury, and indeed Miss Aspinall, felt far more sorry for me than angry with me.

Just as Miss Fenmore mentioned his name there came a tap at the door, and in another moment I saw the kind well-known face of our old doctor looking in.

"Well, well," he began, looking at me with a rather odd smile, "and how is the little runaway? My dear child, why did you not come to me, instead of wandering all about Great Mexington streets in the dark and the rain? Not that you could have found anywhere better for yourself than this kind house, but you might have been all night downstairs in the cold! Tell me, what made you run away like that—no, don't tell me just yet. It is all right now, but I think you have talked enough. Has she had anything to eat?" and he turned to Miss Fenmore. Then he looked at my throat and listened to my breathing, and tapped me and felt my pulse and looked at my tongue before I could speak at all.

"She must stay in bed all to-day," he said at last. "I will see her again this evening," and he went on to give Miss Fenmore a few directions about me, I fidgeting all the time to ask him about father and mamma, though feeling too shy to do so.

"Geraldine is very anxious to tell you one of the chief causes of her coming away from Green Bank as she did," said Miss Fenmore. And then she spoke of the gossip that had reached me through Harriet Smith about the terribly unhealthy climate my parents were in.

Dr. Fallis listened attentively.

"I wanted to write to Mrs. Selwood, and I thought Mr. Cranston would tell me her address," I said, though I almost started when I heard how hoarse and husky my voice sounded. "Can you tell it me? I do so want to write to her."

"Mrs. Selwood is abroad, my dear, and not returning till next month," said Dr. Fallis; but when he saw how my face fell, he added quickly, "but I think I can tell you perhaps better than she about your parents. I know the place—Mr. Le Marchant consulted me about it before he decided on going, as he knew I had been there

myself in my young days. Unhealthy? No, not if people take
proper care. Your father and mother live in the best part—on high
ground out of the town—there is never any fever there. And I
had a most cheerful letter from your father quite lately. Put all
these fears out of your head, my poor child. Please God you will
have papa and mamma safe home again before long. But they
must not find such a poor little white shrimp of a daughter when
they come. You must get strong and well and do all that this kind
young lady tells you to do. Goodbye—goodbye," and he hurried off.

I was crying again by this time, but quietly now, and my tears
were not altogether because I was weak and ill. They were in great
measure tears of relief—I was so thankful to hear what he said about
father and mamma.

"Miss Fenmore," I whispered, "I wonder why they didn't take
me with them, if it's a nice place. And then there wouldn't have
been all these dreadful things."

"It is quite a different matter to take a child to a hot climate,"
she said. "Grown-up people can stand much that would be very
bad for girls and boys. When I was little my father was in India,
and my sister and I had to be brought up by an aunt in England."

"Did you mind?" I said eagerly. "And did your papa soon
come home? And where was your mamma?"

Miss Fenmore smiled, but there was something a little sad in her
smile.

"I was very happy with my aunt," she said; "she was like a mother
to me. For my mother died when I was a little baby. Yes, my
father has been home several times, but he is in India again now,
and he won't be able to come back for good till he is quite old.
So you have much happier things to look forward to, you see,
Geraldine."

That was true. I felt very sorry for Miss Fenmore as I lay
thinking over what she had been telling me. Then another idea
struck me.

"Is Mrs. Cranston your aunt?" I said. "Is that why you are
living here?"

Miss Fenmore looked up quickly.

"No," she replied; "I thought somehow that you understood.
I am here because I am Myra Raby's governess—Myra Raby, who
used to come for some lessons to Green Bank."

"Oh!" I exclaimed. This explained several things. "Oh yes,"
I went on, "I remember her, and I know she's Mr. Cranston's

granddaughter—he was speaking of her to mamma one day. I should like to see her, Miss Fenmore. May I?"

Miss Fenmore was just going to reply when again there came a tap at the door, and in answer to her "Come in" it opened and two figures appeared.

I could see them from where I lay, and I shall never forget the pretty picture they made. Myra I knew by sight, and as I think I have said before, she was an unusually lovely child. And with her was a quite old lady, a small old lady—Myra was nearly as tall as she—with a face that even I (though children seldom notice beauty in elderly people) saw was quite charming. This was Mrs. Cranston.

I felt quite surprised. Mr. Cranston was a rather stout old man, with spectacles and a big nose. I had not thought him at all "pretty," and sonehow I had fancied Mrs. Cranston must be something like him and I gave a sigh of pleasure as the old lady came up to the side of the bed with a gentle smile on her face.

"Dr. Fallis gave us leave to come in to see you, my dear," she said. "Myra has been longing to do so all the morning."

"I've been wanting to see her too," I said, half shyly. "And—please—it's very kind of you to let me stay here in this nice room. I didn't mean to fall asleep downstairs. I only wanted to speak to Mr. Cranston."

"I'm sure Mr. Cranston would be very pleased to tell you anything he can that you want to know, my dear. But I think you mustn't trouble just now about anything except getting quite well," said the old lady. "Myra has been wanting to come to see you all the morning, but we were afraid of tiring you."

Myra came forward gently, her sweet face looking rather grave. I put out my hand, and she smiled.

"May she stay with me a little?" I asked Mrs. Cranston.

"Of course she may—that's what she came for," said the grandmother heartily. "But I don't think you should talk much. Missie's voice sounds as if it hurt her to speak," she went on, turning to Miss Fenmore.

"It doesn't hurt me much," I said. "I daresay I shall be quite well to-morrow. I am so glad I'm here—I wouldn't have liked to be ill at school," and I gave a little shudder. "I'm quite happy now that Dr. Fallis says it's not true about father and mamma getting ill at that place, and I don't want to ask Mr. Cranston anything now, thank you. It was about Mrs. Selwood, but I don't mind now."

I had been sitting up a little—now I laid my head down on the pillows again with a little sigh, half of weariness, half of relief.

Mrs. Cranston looked at me rather anxiously.

"Are you very tired, my dear?" she said. "Perhaps it would be better for Myra not to stay just now."

"Oh, please let her stay," I said; "I like to see her."

So Myra sat down beside my bed and took hold of my hand, and though we did not speak to each other, I liked the feeling of her being there.

Mrs. Cranston left the room then, and Miss Fenmore followed her. I think the old lady had made her a little sign to do so, though I did not see it. Afterwards I found out that Mrs. Cranston had thought me looking very ill, worse than she had expected, and she wanted to hear from Miss Fenmore if it was natural to me to look so pale.

I myself, though feeling tired and disinclined to talk, was really happier than I had been for a very long time. There was a delightful sensation of being safe and at home, even though the kind people who had taken me in, like a poor little stray bird, were strangers. The very look of the old-fashioned room and the comfortable great big four-post bed made me hug myself when I thought how different it all was from the bare cold room at Green Bank, where there had never once been a fire all the weeks I was there. It reminded me of something—what was it? Oh yes, in a minute or two I remembered. It was the room I had once slept in with mamma at grand-mamma's house in London, several years before, when I was quite a little girl. For dear grandmamma had died soon after we came to live at Great Mexington. But there was the same comfortable old-fashioned feeling: red curtains to the window and the bed, and a big fire and the shiny dark mahogany furniture. Oh yes, how well I remembered it, and how enormous the bed seemed, and how mamma tucked me in at night and left the door a little open in case I should feel lonely before she came to bed. It all came back to me so that I forgot where I was for the moment, till I felt a little tug given to the hand that Myra was still holding, and heard her voice say very softly,

"Are you going to sleep, Geraldine?"

This brought me back to the present.

"Oh no," I said, "I'm not sleepy. I was only thinking," and I told her what had come into my mind.

She listened with great interest.

"How unhappy you must have been when your mamma went away," she said. 'I can't remember my own mamma, but mother " —she meant her step-mother—"is so kind, and granny is so sweet. I've never been lonely."

"You can't fancy what it's like," I said. "It wasn't only mamma's going away; I know Haddie—that's my brother—loves her as much as I do, but he's not very unhappy, because he likes his school. Oh, Myra, what *shall* I do when I have to go back to school? I'd rather be ill always. Do you think I'll have to go back to-morrow?"

Myra looked most sympathising and concerned.

"I don't think you'll be quite well to-morrow," was the best comfort she could give me. "When I have bad colds and sore throats they always last longer than one day."

"I'd like to talk a great lot to keep my throat from getting quite well," I said, "but I suppose that would be very naughty."

"Yes," said Myra with conviction, "I'm sure it would be. You really mustn't talk, Geraldine; granny said so. Mayn't I read aloud to you? I've brought a book with me—it's an old story-book of mamma's that she had when she was a little girl. Granny keeps them here all together. This one is called *Ornaments Discovered.*"

"Thank you," I said. "Yes, I should like it very much."

And in her gentle little voice Myra read the quaint old story aloud to me. It was old-fashioned even then, for the book had belonged to her mother, if not in the first place to her grandmother. How very old-world it would seem to the children of to-day—I wonder if any of you know it? For I am growing quite an old woman myself, and the little history of my childhood that I am telling you will, before long, be half a century in age, though its events seem as clear and distinct to me as if they had only happened quite recently! I came across the little red gilt-leaved book not long ago in the house of one of Myra's daughters, and with the sight of it a whole flood of memories rushed over me.

It was not a very exciting story, but I found it very interesting, and now and then my little friend stopped to talk about it, which I found very interesting too. I was quite sorry when Miss Fenmore, who had come back to the room and was sitting quietly sewing, told Myra that she thought she had read enough, and that it must be near dinner-time.

"I will come again after dinner," said Myra, and then I whispered something to her. She nodded; she quite understood me. What I said was this:

"I wish you would go downstairs and tell the carved lions that they made me very happy last night, and I *am* so glad they brought me back here to you, instead of taking me to Green Bank."

"Where did they take you to in the night?" said Myra with great interest, though not at all as if she thought I was talking nonsense.

"I'll tell you all about it afterwards," I said. "It was beautiful. But it would take a long time to tell, and I'm rather tired."

"You are looking tired, dear," said Miss Fenmore, who heard my last words, as she gave me a cupful of beef-tea. "Try and go to sleep for a little, and then Myra can come to sit with you again."

I did go to sleep, but Myra was not allowed to see me again that day, nor the next—nor for several days after, except for a very few minutes at a time. For I did not improve as the kind people about me had hoped I would, and Dr. Fallis looked graver when he came that evening than he had done in the morning. Miss Fenmore was afraid she had let me talk too much, but after all I do not think anything would have made any great difference. I had really been falling out of health for months past, and I should probably have got ill in some other way if I had not caught cold in my wanderings. I do not very clearly remember thos days of serious illness. I knew whenever I was awake that I was being tenderly cared for, and in the half-dozing, half-dreaming state in which many hours must have been passed, I fancied more than once that mamma was beside me, which made me very happy. And though never actually delirious, I had very strange though not unpleasant dreams, especially about the carved lions; none of them, however, so clear and real as the one I related at full in the last chapter.

On the whole, that illness left more peaceful and sweet memories than memories of pain. Through it all I had the delightful feeling of being cared for and protected, and somehow it all seemed to have to do with the pair of lions downstairs in Mr. Cranston's show-room.

CHAPTER XII

GOOD NEWS

I don't suppose there was anything really infectious about my illness, though nowadays whenever there is any sort of sore throat people are very much on their guard. Perhaps they were not so cautious long ago. However that may have been, Myra was not banished from my room for very long. I rather think, indeed, that she used to creep in and sit like a little mouse behind the curtains before I was well enough to notice her.

But everything for a time seemed dreamy to me. The first event I can quite clearly recall was my being allowed to sit up for an hour or two, or, more correctly speaking, to *lie* up, for I was lifted on to the sofa and tucked in almost as if I were still in bed.

That was a very happy afternoon. It was happy for several reasons, for that morning had brought me the first letter I had had from dear mamma since she had heard of my bold step in running away from school! Lying still and silent for so many hours as I had done, things had grown to look differently to me. I began to see where and how I had been wrong, and to think that if I had been more open about my troubles, more courageous—that is to say, if I had gone to Miss Ledbury and told her everything that was on my mind—I need not have been so terribly unhappy or caused trouble and distress to others.

A little of this mamma pointed out to me in her letter, which was, however, so very kind and loving, so full of sorrow that I had been so unhappy, that I felt more grateful than I knew how to express. Afterwards, when we talked it all over, years afterwards even, for we often talked of that time after I was grown up and married, and had children of my own, mamma said to me that she *could* not blame me though she knew I had not done right, for she felt so broken-hearted at the thought of what I had suffered.

It had been a mistake, no doubt, to send me to Green Bank, but mistakes are often overruled for good. I am glad to have had the experience of it, as I think it made me more sympathising with others. And it made me determine never to send any child of mine, or any child I had the care of, to a school where there was so little feeling of *home*, so little affection and gentleness—above all, that dreadful old-world rule of letters being read, and the want of trust and confidence in the pupils, which showed in so many ways.

A few days after I received mamma's letter I was allowed to write to her. It was slow and tiring work, for I was only able to write a few lines at a time, and that in pencil. But it was delightful to be free to say just what I wanted to say, without the terrible feeling of Miss Aspinall, or worse still Miss Broom, judging and criticising every line. I thanked mamma with my whole heart for not being angry with me, and to show her how truly I meant what I said, I promised her that when I was well again and able to go back to school I would try my very, very best to get on more happily.

But I gave a deep sigh as I wrote this, and Myra, who was sitting beside me, looked up anxiously, and asked what was the matter.

"Oh, Myra," I said, "it is just that I can't bear to think of going back to school. I'd rather never get well if only I could stay here till mamma comes home."

"Dear little Geraldine," said Myra—she often called me "little" though she was *scarcely* any taller than I—"dear little Geraldine, you mustn't say that. I don't think it's right. And, you know, when you are quite well again things won't seem so bad to you. I remember once when I was ill—I was quite a little girl then"— Myra spoke as if she was now a very big girl indeed!—"I think it was when I had had the measles, the least thing vexed me dreadfully. I cried because somebody had given me a present of a set of wooden tea-things in a box, and the tea ran out of the cups when I filled them! Fancy crying for that!"

"I know," I said, "I've felt like that too. But this is a *real* trouble, Myra—a real, very bad, dreadful trouble, though I've promised mamma to try to be good. Do you think, Myra, that when I'm back at school your grandmamma will sometimes ask me to come to see you?"

"I'm sure——" my little friend began eagerly. But she was interrupted. For curiously enough, just at that moment Mrs. Cranston opened the door and came in. She came to see me every day, and though at first I was just a tiny bit afraid of her—she seemed to me such a very old lady—I soon got to love her dearly, and to talk to her quite as readily as to kind Miss Fenmore.

"What is my little girl sure about?" she said. "And how is my other little girl to-day? Not too tired," and she glanced at my letter. "You have not been writing too much, dearie, I hope?"

"No, thank you," I replied, "I'm not tired."

"She's only rather unhappy, granny," said Myra.

"I think that's a very big 'only,'" said Mrs. Cranston. "Can't you tell me, my dear, what you are unhappy about?"

I glanced at Myra, as if asking her to speak for me. She understood.

"Granny," she said. "Poor little Geraldine is unhappy to think of going away and going back to school."

Mrs. Cranston looked at me very kindly.

"Poor dear," she said, "you have not had much pleasure with us, as you have been ill all the time."

"I don't mind," I said. "I was telling Myra, only she thought it was naughty, that I'd rather be ill always if I was with kind people, than—than—be at school where nobody cares for me."

"Well, well, my dear, the troubles we dread are often those that don't come to pass. Try to keep up your spirits and get quite well and strong, so that you may be able to enjoy yourself a little before both you and Myra leave us."

"Oh, is Myra going away?" I said. "I thought she was going to live here always," and somehow I felt as if I did not mind *quite* so much to think of going away myself in that case.

"Oh no," said the old lady, "Myra has her own home where she must spend part of her time, though grandfather and I hope to have her here a good deal too. It is easy to manage now Miss Fenmore is with her always."

In my heart I thought Myra a most fortunate child—*two* homes were really hers; and I—I had none. This thought made me sigh again. I don't know if Myra guessed what I was thinking of, but she came close up to me and put her arms round my neck and kissed me.

"Geraldine," she whispered, by way of giving me something pleasant to think of, perhaps, "as soon as you are able to walk about a little I want you to come downstairs with me to see the lions."

"Yes," I said in the same tone, "but you did give them my message, Myra?"

"Of course I did, and they sent you back their love, and they are very glad you're better, and they want you very much indeed to come to see them."

Myra and I understood each other quite well about the lions, you see.

I went on getting well steadily after that, and not many days later

I went downstairs with Myra to the big show-room to see the lions. It gave me such a curious feeling to remember the last time I had been there, that rainy evening when I crept in, as nearly broken-hearted and in despair as a little girl could be. And as I stroked the lions and looked up in their dark mysterious faces, I could not get rid of the idea that they knew all about it, that somehow or other they had helped and protected me, and when I tried to express this to Myra she seemed to think the same.

After this there were not many days on which we did not come downstairs to visit our strange play-fellows, and not a few interesting games or "actings," as Myra called them, did we invent, in which the lions took their part.

We were only allowed to be in the show-rooms at certain hours of the day, when there were not likely to be any customers there. Dear old Mrs. Cranston was as particular as she possibly could be not to let me do anything or be seen in any way which mamma could possibly have disliked.

And before long I began to join a little in Myra's lessons with Miss Fenmore—lessons which our teacher's kind and "understand-ing" ways made delightful. So that life was really very happy for me at this time, except of course for the longing for mamma and father and Haddie, which still came over me in fits, as it were, every now and then, and except—a still bigger "except"—for the dreaded thought of the return to school which must be coming nearer day by day.

Myra and I never spoke of it. I tried to forget about it, and she seemed to enter into my feeling without saying anything.

I had had a letter from mamma in answer to the one I wrote to her just after my illness In it she said she was pleased with all I said, and my promise to try to get on better at Green Bank, but "in the meantime," she wrote, "what we want you to do is to get *quite* strong and well, so put all troubling thoughts out of your head and be happy with your kind friends."

That letter had come a month ago, and the last mail had only brought me a tiny little note enclosed in a letter from mamma to Mrs. Cranston, with the promise of a longer one "next time." And "next time" was about due, for the mail came every fortnight, one afternoon when Myra and I were sitting together in our favourite nook in the show-room.

"I have a fancy, Myra," I said, "that something is going to happen.

My lion has been so queer to-day—I see a look on his face as if he knew something."

For we had each chosen one lion as more particularly our own.

"I think they always look rather like that," said Myra dreamily. "But I suppose something must happen soon.   I shall be going home next week."

"Next week." I repeated.   "Oh, Myra!"

I could not speak for a moment.   Then I remembered how I had made up my mind to be brave.

"Do you mind going home?" I asked.   "I mean, are you sorry to go?"

"I'm always sorry to leave grandpapa and grandmamma," she said, "and the lions, and this funny old house.   But I'm very happy at home, and I shall like it still better with Miss Fenmore.   No, I wouldn't be unhappy—I'd be very glad to think of seeing father and mother and my little brothers again—I wouldn't be unhappy, except for—you know, Geraldine—for leaving you," and my little friend's voice shook.

"Dear Myra," I said.   "But you mustn't mind about me.   I'm going to try——" but here I had to stop to choke down something in my throat.   "After all," I went on, after a moment or two, "more than a quarter of the time that father and mamma have to be away is gone.   And perhaps in the summer holidays I shall see Haddie."

"I wish——" Myra was beginning, but a voice interrupted her. It was Miss Fenmore's.

"I have brought you down a letter that has just come by the second post, Geraldine, dear," she said; "a letter from South America."

"Oh, thank you," I said, eagerly seizing it.

Miss Fenmore strolled to the other side of the room, and Myra followed her, to leave me alone to read my letter.   It was a pretty long one, but I read it quickly, so quickly that when I had finished it, I felt breathless—and then I turned over the pages and glanced at it again.   I felt as if I could not believe what I read.   It was too good, too beautifully good to be true.

"Myra," I gasped, and Myra ran back to me, looking quite startled.   I think I must have grown very pale.

"No, no," I went on, "it's nothing wrong.   Read it, or ask Miss Fenmore—she reads writing quicker.   Oh, Myra, isn't it beautiful?"

They soon read it, and then we all three kissed and hugged each other, and Myra began dancing about as if she had gone out of her mind.

"Geraldine, Geraldine, I can't believe it," she kept saying, and Miss Fenmore's pretty eyes were full of tears.

I wonder if any of my readers can guess what this delightful news was? It was not that mamma was coming home—no, that could not be yet. But next best to that it certainly was.

It was to tell me this—that *till* dear father and she returned, my home was to be with Myra, and I was to be Miss Fenmore's pupil too. Wherever Myra was, there I was to be—principally at her father's vicarage in the country, but some part of the year with her kind grandparents at Great Mexington. It was all settled and arranged—of course I did not trouble my head about the money part of it, though afterwards mamma told me that both Mr. and Mrs. Raby and the Cranstons had been most exceedingly kind, making out that the advantage of a companion for their little girl would be so great that all the thanking should be on their side, though, of course, they respected father too much not to let him pay a proper share of all the expense. And it really cost less than my life at Green Bank, though father was now a good deal richer, and would not have minded paying a good deal more to ensure my happiness.

There is never so much story to tell when people are happy, and things go rightly; and the next year or two of my life, except of course for the separation from my dear parents, were *very* happy. Even though father's appointment in South America kept him and mamma out there for nearly three years instead of two, I was able to bear the disappointment in a very different way, with such kind and sympathising friends at hand to cheer me, so that there is nothing bitter or sad to look back to in that part of my childhood. Haddie spent the summer holidays with me, either at Crowley Vicarage, or sometimes at the sea-side, where Miss Fenmore took care of us three. Once or twice he and I paid a visit to Mrs. Selwood, which we enjoyed pretty well, as we were together, though otherwise it was rather dull.

And oh, how happy it was when father and mamma at last came home! no words can describe it. It was not *quite* unmixed pleasure— nothing ever is, the wise folk say—for there was the separation from Myra and her family. But after all, that turned out less than we feared. Miss Fenmore married soon after, and as father had now a good post in London, and we lived there, it was settled that Myra should be with us, and join in my lessons for a good part of the year, while I very often went back to Crowley with her for the summer holidays. And never without staying a few days at Great Mexington, to see Mr. and Mrs. Cranston and the lions!

Many years have passed since I went there for the last time. Myra's grandparents have long been dead—my own dear father and mother are dead too, for I am growing quite old. My grandchildren are older now than I was when I ran away from the school at Green Bank. But once, while mamma was still alive and well, she and I together strolled through the streets of the grim town, which had for a time been our home, and lived over the old days again in fancy. I remember how tightly I clasped her hand when we passed the corner where once was the old Quakeress's shop—all changed now— and walked down the street, still not very different from what it had been, where we used to live.

There was no use in going to Mr. Cranston's show-rooms—they had long been done away with. But the lions are still to be seen. They stand in the hall of Myra's pretty house in the country, where she and Haddon, her husband, have lived for many years, ever since my brother left the army and they came home for good from India.

I spend a part of every year with them, for I am alone now. They want me to live with them altogether, but I cling to a little home of my own. Our grandchildren know the lions well, and stroke their smooth sides, and gaze up into their dark faces just as Myra and I used to do. So I promised them that some time I would write out the simple story that I have now brought to a close.

The Dove in the Eagle's Nest

CHAPTER I

THE UPPER LATTICES of a tall, narrow window were open, and admitted the view, of first some richly-tinted vine leaves and purpling grapes, then, in dazzling freshness of new white stone, the lacework fabric of a half-built minster spire, with a mason's crane on the summit ; and beyond, peeping through every crevice of the exquisite open fretwork, was the intensely blue sky of early autumn.

The interior of the room was wainscoted, the floor paved with bright red and cream-coloured tiles, and the tall stove in one corner decorated with the same. The eastern end of the apartment was adorned with an exquisite small group carved in oak, representing the carpenter's shop at Nazareth, with the Holy Child instructed by Joseph in the use of tools, and the Mother sitting with her book, "pondering these things in her heart." All around were blocks of wood and carvings in varying states of progress—some scarcely shaped out, and others in perfect completion. On the work-table itself, growing under the master's hand, was a long wreath, entirely composed of leaves and seed-vessels in their quaint and beauteous forms—the heart-shaped shepherd's purse, the mask-like skull-cap, and the crowned urn of the henbane. The starred cap of the poppy was actually being shaped under the tool, copied from a green capsule, surmounted with purple velvety rays, which, together with its rough and wavy leaf, was held in the hand of a young maiden who knelt by the table, watching the work with eager interest.

She was not a beautiful girl. She was too small, too slight, too retiring for such a description. If there was something lily-like in her drooping grace, it was not the queen-lily of the garden, that she resembled, but the retiring lily of the valley—so purely, transparently white was her skin, scarcely tinted by a roseate blush on the cheek, so tender and modest the whole effect of her slender figure, and the soft, downcast, pensive brown eyes, utterly dissimilar in hue from those of all her friends and kindred, except perhaps the bright, quick ones of her uncle, the master-carver. Otherwise, his portly form, open visage, and good-natured stateliness, as well as his furred cap and gold chain, were thoroughly those of the German burgo-master[1] of the fifteenth century; but those glittering black eyes had not ceased to betray their French, or rather Walloon, origin, though for several generations back the family had been settled at Ulm. Perhaps, too, it was Walloon quickness and readiness of wit that had made them, so soon as they became affiliated, so prominent in all the councils of the good free city, and so noted for excellence in art and learning.

Master Gottfried Sorel had had a scapegrace younger brother named Hugh, who had scorned both books and tools, had been the plague of the workshop, and, instead of coming back from his wandering-year of improvement, had joined a band of roving lanzknechts.[2] No more had been heard of him for a dozen or fifteen years, when he suddenly arrived at the paternal mansion at Ulm, half dead with intermittent fever, and with a young, broken-hearted, and nearly expiring wife, his spoil in his Italian campaigns. His rude affection had utterly failed to console her for her desolated home and slaughtered kindred, and it had so soon turned to brutality that, when brought to comparative peace and rest in his brother's home, there was nothing left for the poor Italian but to lie down and die, commending her babe in broken German to Hausfrau[3] Johanna, and blessing Master Gottfried for his flowing Latin assurances that the child should be to them even as the little maiden who was lying in the God's acre upon the hillside.

And verily the little Christina had been a precious gift to the bereaved couple. Her father had no sooner recovered than he re-turned to his roving life, and, except for a report that he had been seen among the retainers of one of the robber-barons of the Swabian Alps, nothing had been heard of him. Meantime, both the burgo-master and his wife did their utmost to forget that the gentle little girl was not their own ; they set all their hopes and joys on her, and, making her supply the place at once of son and daughter, they bred her up in all the refinements and accomplishments in which the free citizens of Germany took the lead in the middle and latter part of the fifteenth century. To aid her aunt in all housewifely arts, to prepare dainty food and varied liquors, and to spin, weave, and broider, was only a part of Christina's training; her uncle likewise set great store by her sweet Italian voice, and caused her to be carefully taught to sing and play on the lute, and he likewise de-

---

[1] Chief magistrate of a town, like our mayor.
[2] Horsemen armed with lances.   [3] Literally "house-woman" = mistress.

lighted in hearing her read aloud to him from the hereditary store of MSS. and from the dark volumes that began to proceed from the press. Nay, Master Gottfried had made experiments in printing and wood-engraving on his own account, and had found no head so intelligent, no hand so desirous to aid him, as his little Christina's. Some fine bold woodcuts had been produced by their joint efforts; but these less important occupations had of late been set aside by the engrossing interest of the interior fittings of the great "Dome Kirk," which for nearly a century had been rising by the united exertions of the burghers, without any assistance from without. The foundation had been laid in 1377; and at length, in the year of grace 1472, the crown of the apse had been closed in, and matters were so forward that Master Gottfried's stall work was already in requisition for the choir.

"Three cubits more," he reckoned. "Child, hast thou found me fruits enough for the completing of this border?"

"Oh, yes, mine uncle. I have the wild rosehip, and the flat shield of the moonwort, and a pea-pod, and more whose names I know not. But should they all be seed and fruit?"

"Yea, truly, my Stina, for this wreath shall speak of the goodly fruits of a completed life."

"I have scarce seed-pods enough in store, uncle; might we not seek some rarer shapes in the herb-garden of Master Gerhard, the physician? He, too, might tell me the names of some of these."

"True, child; or we might ride into the country beyond the walls, and seek them. What, little one, wouldst thou not?"

"So we go not far," faltered Christina, colouring.

"Ha, thou hast not forgotten the fright thy companions had from the Schlangenwald reitern[1] when gathering May-dew? Fear not, little coward; if we go beyond the suburbs we will take Hans and Peter with their halberts. But I believe thy silly little heart can scarce be free for enjoyment if it can fancy a reiter within a dozen leagues of thee."

"At your side I would not fear. That is, I would not vex thee by my folly, and I might forget it," replied Christina, looking down.

" My gentle child!" the old man said approvingly. "Moreover, if our good Kaiser has his way, we shall soon be free of the reitern of Schlangenwald, and Adlerstein, and all the rest of the mouse-trap barons. He is hoping to form a league of us free imperial cities with all the more reasonable and honest nobles, to preserve the

---

[1] Riders, *i.e.* armed horsemen.

peace of the country, and, when all are united against them, my lords-mousers must needs become pledged to the league, or go down before it."

"Ah! that will be well," cried Christina. "Then will our wagons be no longer set upon at the Debateable Ford by Schlangenwald or Adlerstein; and our wares will come safely, and there will be wealth enough to raise our spire! Oh, uncle, what a day of joy will that be when Our Lady's great statue will be set on the summit!"

"A day that I shall scarce see, and it will be well if thou dost," returned her uncle, "unless the hearts of the burghers of Ulm return to the liberality of their fathers, who devised that spire! But what trampling do I hear?"

There was indeed a sudden confusion in the house, and, before the uncle and niece could rise, the door was opened by a prosperous apple-faced dame, exclaiming in a hasty whisper, "Housefather, oh, housefather, there are a troop of reitern at the door, dismounting already"; and, as the master came forward, brushing from his furred vest the shavings and dust of his work, she added in a more furtive, startled accent, "and, if I mistake not, one is thy brother!"

"He is welcome," replied Master Gottfried, in his cheery, fearless voice; " he brought us a choice gift last time he came; and it may be he is ready to seek peace among us after his wanderings. Come hither, Christina, my little one; it is well to be abashed, but thou art not a child who need fear to meet a father."

Down the stair the three proceeded, and reached the stone hall that lay beyond it, just as there entered a thin wiry man, in a worn and greasy buff suit, guarded on the breast and arms with rusty steel, and a battered helmet with the vizor up, disclosing a weather-beaten bronzed face, with somewhat wild dark eyes, and a huge grizzled moustache forming a straight line over his lips. The poor child's heart died within her as she perceived the mutual recognition between her uncle and the newcomer; and, while Master Gottfried held out his hands, with a cordial greeting of "Welcome home, brother Hugh," she trembled from head to foot, as she sank on her knees, and murmured, "Your blessing, honoured father."

"Ha, What, this is my girl? What says she? My blessing, eh? There then, thou hast it, child, such as I have to give, though they'll tell thee at Adlerstein that I am more wont to give the other sort of blessing! Now, give me a kiss, girl, and let me see thee! How now!" as he folded her in his rough arms, "thou art a mere feather, as slight as our sick Jungfrau[1] herself." And then, regarding her, as she stood drooping, "Thou art not half the woman thy mother was!"

"True!" replied Hausfrau Johanna, in a marked tone; "but both she and her poor babe had been so harassed and wasted with long journeys and hardships, that with all our care of our Christina, she has never been strong or well-grown. The marvel is that she lived at all."

"Well, well," returned the lanzknecht, "she will answer the purpose well enough, or better than if she were fair enough to set all our fellows together by the ears for her. Camilla, I say—no, what's her name, Christina?—put up thy gear and be ready to start with me to-morrow morning for Adlerstein."

"For Adlerstein?" re-echoed the housemother, in a tone of horrified dismay; and Christina would have dropped on the floor but for her uncle's sustaining hand, and the cheering glance with which he met her imploring look.

"Let us come up to the gallery, and understand what you desire, brother," said Master Gottfried gravely. "Fill the cup of greeting, Hans. Your followers shall be entertained in the hall," he added.

"Ay, ay," quoth Hugh, "I will show you reason over a goblet of the old Rosenburg."[2]

So saying, the trooper crossed the lower room, and clanked up the oaken stairs to the gallery, the reception-room of the house. It had tapestry hangings to the wall, and cushions both to the carved chairs and deep windows, which looked out into the street.

"Just as it was in the old man's time," said the soldier, throwing himself into the housefather's chair. "Here, Camilla, girl, unlace my helmet! What, know'st not how? What is a woman made for but to let a soldier free of his trappings? Thou hast done it! There!"

"What would you with Christina, brother?" gravely asked Master Gottfried, seating himself on the opposite side of the stove, while out of sight the frightened girl herself knelt on the floor, her head on her aunt's knees, trying to derive comfort from Dame Johanna's clasping hands, and vehement murmurs that they would not let their child be taken from them. Alas! these assurances were little in accordance with Hugh's rough reply, "And what is it to you what I do with mine own?"

"Only this, that, having bred her up as my child and intended heiress, I might have some voice."

"Oh! in choosing her mate! Some mincing artificer, I trow! Hast got him here? If I like him, and she likes him, I'll bring her back when her work is done."

"There is no such person as yet in the case," said Gottfried. "Christina is not yet seventeen, and I would take my time to find an honest, pious burgher, who will value this precious jewel of mine."

"And let her polish his flagons to the end of her days," laughed Hugh grimly, but manifestly somewhat influenced by the notion of his brother's wealth. "And who told thee, Goetz, that I would do aught with the girl that should hinder her from being the very same fat, sourkrout-cooking,[1] pewter-scrubbing housewife of thy mind's eye?"

"I have heard nothing of thy designs as yet, brother Hugh, save that thou wouldst take her to Adlerstein, which men greatly belie if it be not a nest of robbers."

"Aha! thou hast heard of Adlerstein! We have made the backs of your jolly merchants tingle as well as they could through their well-lined doublets! Ulm knows of Adlerstein, and the Debateable Ford!"

"It knows little to its credit," said Gottfried gravely; "and it knows also that the Emperor is about to make a combination against all the Swabian robber-holds, and that such as join not in it will fare the worse."

"Let Kaiser Fritz catch his bear ere he sells its hide! He has never tried to mount the Eagle's Ladder! Why, man, Adlerstein might be held against five hundred men by sister Johanna with her rock and spindle! 'Tis a free barony, Master Gottfried, I tell thee —has never sworn allegiance to Kaiser or Duke of Swabia either! Freiherr[2] Eberhard is as much a king on his own rock as Kaiser Fritz ever was of the Romans, and more too, for I never could find out that they thought much of our king at Rome; and, as to gainsaying our old Freiherr, one might as well leap over the abyss at once."

"Yes, those old free barons are pitiless tyrants," said Gottfried, "and I scarce think I can understand thee aright when I hear thee say thou wouldst carry they daughter to such an abode."

"It is the Freiherr's command," returned Hugh. "Look you, they have had wondrous ill-luck with their children; the Freiherrinn Kunigunde has had a dozen at least, and only two are alive, my young Freiherr and my young Lady Ermentrude; and no wonder, you

---

[1] A favourite German dish made of pickled cabbage, etc.
[2] "Baron" is the nearest English equivalent.

would say, if you could see the gracious Freiherrinn. She is Adlerstein herself by birth, married her cousin, and is prouder and more
dour than our old Freiherr himself—fitter far to handle shield than
swaddled babe. And now our Jungfrau has fallen into a pining
waste, that 'tis a pity to see how her cheeks have fallen away, and
how she mopes and fades. Now, the old Freiherr and her brother,
they both dote on her, and would do anything for her. They
thought she was bewitched, so we took old Mother Ilsebill and tried
her with the ordeal of water; but, look you, she sank as innocent as
a puppy dog, and Ursel was at fault to fix on any one else. Then one
day, when I looked into the chamber, I saw the poor maiden sitting
with her head hanging down, as if 'twas too heavy for her, on a
high-backed chair, no rest for her feet, and the wind blowing keen
all round her, and nothing to taste but scorched beef, or black bread
and sour wine, and her mother rating her for foolish fancies that gave
trouble. And, when my young Freiherr was bemoaning himself
that we could not hear of a Jew physician passing our way to catch
and bring up to cure her, I said to him at last that no doctor could
do for her what gentle tendence and nursing would, for what the
poor maiden needed was to be cosseted and laid down softly, and fed
with broths and possets, and all that women know how to do with
one another. A proper scowl and hard words I got from my lady,
for wanting to put burgher softness into an Adlerstein; but my old
lord and his son opened on the scent at once. 'Thou hast a
daughter?' quoth the Freiherr. 'So please your gracious lordship,'
quoth I; 'that is, if she still lives, for I left her a puny infant.' "Well,'
said my lord, 'if thou wilt bring her here, and her care restores my
daughter, then will I make thee my body squire, with a right to a
fourth part of all the spoil, and feed for two horses in my stable.'
And young Freiherr Eberhard gave his word upon it."

Gottfried suggested that a sick nurse was the person required
rather than a child like Christina; but, as Hugh truly observed, no
nurse would voluntarily go to Adlerstein, and it was no use to wait
for the hopes of capturing one by raid or foray. His daughter was
at his own disposal, and her services would be repaid by personal
advantages to himself which he was not disposed to forgo; in effect
these were the only means that the baron had of requiting any
attendance upon his daughter.

The plentiful supper, full cup of wine, the confections, the soft
chair, together perhaps with his brother's grave speech, soon had
the effect of sending Reiter Hugh into a doze, whence he started to

accept civilly the proposal of being installed in the stranger's room, where he was speedily snoring between two feather-beds.

Then there could be freedom of speech in the gallery, where the uncle and aunt held anxious counsel over the poor little dark-tressed head that sill lay upon good Johanna's knees. The dame was indignant and resolute: Take the child back with him into a very nest of robbers!—her own innocent dove, whom they had shielded from all evil like a very nun in a cloister! She should as soon think of yielding her up to be borne off by the great Satan himself with his horns and hoofs.

"Hugh is her father, housewife," said the master-carver. "Heaven knows how I love her, but Heaven also knows that I see no means of withholding her from one whose claim is closer than my own."

In the meantime, Christina was rising from the floor, and stood before them with loose hair, tearful eyes, and wet, flushed cheeks. " It must be thus," she said, in a low, but not unsteady voice. "I can bear it better since I have heard of the poor young lady, sick and with none to care for her. I will go with my father; it is my duty. I will do my best; but oh! uncle, so work with him that he may bring me back again."

"Duty, indeed!" exclaimed Johanna. "As if any duty could lead a silly, helpless child among that herd of evil men and women, with a good-for-nothing father!"

"I will take care that he knows it is worth his while to restore her safe to us. Nor do I think so ill of Hugh as thou dost, mother. And, for the rest, Heaven and the saints must be her guard till she shall return to us."

There was always the hope that, whether the young lady died or recovered, the conclusion of her illness would be the term of Christina's stay at Adlerstein, and with this trust Johanna must content herself. Half the night was spent by the aunt and niece in preparing Christina's wardrobe for her sudden journey.

Many a tear was shed over the tokens of the little services she was wont to render, her half-done works, and pleasant studies so suddenly broken off; and all the time Hausfrau Johanna was running on with a lecture on the diligent preservation of her discretion, with plentiful warnings against swaggering men-at-arms, drunken lanzknechts, and young barons. Christina had best never stir a yard from her lady's chair, when forced to meet them. All this was interspersed with motherly advice how to treat the sick lady, and receipts for cordials and possets; for Johanna began to regard the case as a sort of second-hand one of her own. Nay, she even turned it over in her mind whether she should not offer herself as the Lady Ermentrude's sick-nurse, as being a less dangerous commodity than her little niece; but fears for the well-being of the master-carver, and his Wirthschaft,[1] and still more the notion of gossip Gertrude Grundt hearing that she had ridden off with a wild lanzknecht, made her at once reject the plan, without even mentioning it to her husband or his niece.

By the time Hugh Sorel rolled out from between his feather-beds, and was about to don his greasy buff, a handsome new suit, finished point device, and a pair of huge boots to correspond, had been laid by his bedside.

"Ho, ho! Master Goetz," said he, as he stumbled into the Stube,[2] "I see thy game. Thou wouldst make it worth my while to visit the father-house at Ulm. ?"

"It shall be worth thy while, indeed, if thou bringest me back my white dove," was Gottfried's answer.

"And how if I bring her back with a strapping reiter son-on-law?" laughed Hugh. "What welcome should the fellow receive?"

"That would depend on what he might be," replied Gottfried; and Hugh, his love of tormenting a little allayed by satisfaction in his buff suit, and by an eye to a heavy purse that lay by his brother's hand on the table, added, "Little fear of that. Our fellows would look for lustier brides than yon little pale face. 'Tis whiter than ever this morning,—but no tears. That is my brave girl."

"Yes, father, I am ready to do thy bidding," replied Christina meekly.

"That is well, child. Mark me, no tears. So long as thou art good daughter to me, thou shaft find me good father to thee"; and for a moment there was a kindliness in his eye which made it sufficiently like that of his brother to give some consolation to the shrinking heart that he was rending from all it loved ; and she steadied her voice for another gentle profession of obedience.

"Well said, child. Now canst sit on old Nibelung's croup? His back-bone is somewhat sharper than if he had battened in a citizen's stall; but, if thine aunt can find thee some sort of pillion, I'll promise thee the best ride thou hast had since we came from Innspruck, ere thou canst remember."

"Christina has her own mule," replied her uncle, "without troubling Nibelung to carry double."

[1] Household management.   [2] Sitting-room.

J

"Ho! her own! An overfed burgomaster sort of a beast, that will turn restive at the first sight of the Eagle's Ladder! However, he may carry her so far, and, if we cannot get him up the mountain, I shall know what to do with him," he muttered to himself.

But Hugh, like many a gentleman after him, was recusant at the sight of his daughter's luggage; and yet it only loaded one sumpter mule, besides forming a few bundles which could be easily bestowed upon the saddles of his two knappen,[1] while her lute hung by a silken string on her arm. Both she and her aunt thought she had been extremely moderate; but his cry was, What could she want with so much? Her mother had never been allowed more than would go into a pair of saddle-bags; and his own Jungfrau—she had never seen so much gear together in her life; he would be laughed to scorn for his presumption in bringing such a fine lady into the castle; it would be well if Freiherr Eberhard's bride brought half as much.

Still he had a certain pride in it—he was, after all, by birth and breeding a burgher—and there had been evidently a softening and civilising influence in the night spent beneath his paternal roof, amid old habits, and perhaps likewise in the submission he had met with from his daughter; and, though he growled and muttered a little, he at length was won over to consent, chiefly, as it seemed, by Christina's obliging readiness to leave behind the bundle that contained her holiday kirtle.

He had been spared all needless irritation. Before his waking, Christina had been at the priest's cell, and had received his last blessings and counsels, and she had, on the way back, exchanged her farewells and tears with her two dearest friends, Barbara Schmidt and Regina Grundt, confiding to the former her cage of doves, and to the latter the myrtle, which, like every German maiden, she cherished in her window, to supply her future bridal wreath. Now pale as death, but so resolutely composed as to be almost disappointing to her demonstrative aunt, she quietly went through her home partings; while Hausfrau Johanna adjured her father by all that was sacred to be a true guardian and protector of the child, and he could not forbear from a few tormenting auguries about the lanzknecht son-in-law.

Master Gottfried was going to ride as far as the confines of the free city's territory, and his round, sleek, cream-coloured palfrey, used to ambling in civic processions, was as great a contrast to raw-

---

[1] Attendants.

boned, wild-eyed Nibelung, all dappled with misty grey, as was the stately, substantial burgher to his lean, hungry-looking brother.

As beneath the trellised porches that came down from the projecting gables of the burghers' houses many a well-known face gazed and nodded, as they took their way through the crooked streets, many a begger or poor widow waved her a blessing. Out into the market-place, with its clear fountain adorned with arches and statues, past the rising Dome Kirk, where the swarms of workmen unbonneted to the marter-carver, and the reiter paused with an irreverent sneer at the small progress made since he could first remember the building. The tears had wellnigh blinded Christina in a gush of feeling that came on her unawares, and her mule had his own way as he carried her under the arch of the tall and beautifully-sculptured bridge tower, and over the noble bridge across the Danube.

Her uncle spoke much, low and earnestly, to his brother. She knew it was in commendation of her to his care, and an endeavour to impress him with a sense of the kind of protection she would require, and she kept out of ear-shot. It was enough for her to see her uncle still, and feel that his tenderness was with her, and around her. But at last he drew his rein. "And now, my little one, the daughter of my heart, I must bid thee farewell," he said.

Christina could not be restrained from springing from her mule, and kneeling on the grass to receive his blessing, her face hidden in her hands, that her father might not see her tears.

"The good God bless thee, my child," said Gottfried, who seldom invoked the saints; "bless thee, and bring thee back in His own good time. Thou hast been a good child to us; be so to thine own father. Do thy work, and come back to us again."

The tears rained down his cheeks, as Christina's head lay on his bosom, and then with a last kiss he lifted her again on her mule, mounted his horse, and turned back to the city, with his servant.

Hugh was merciful enough to let his daughter gaze long after the retreating figure ere he summoned her on. All day they rode, at first through meadow lands and then through more broken, open ground, where at midday they halted.

The evening began to advance, and Christina was very weary, as the purple mountains that she had long watched with a mixture of fear and hope began to look more distinct, and the ground was often in abrupt ascents. Her father, without giving space for complaints, hurried her on. He must reach the Debateable Ford ere dark. It was, however, twilight when they came to an open space, where, at the foot of thickly forest-clad rising ground, lay an expanse of turf and rich grass, through which a stream made its way, standing in a wide tranquil pool as if to rest after its rough course from the mountains. Above rose, like a dark wall, crag upon crag, peak on peak, in purple masses, blending with the sky; and Hugh, pointing upwards to a turreted point, apparently close above their heads, where a star of light was burning, told her that there was Adlerstein, and this was the Debateable Ford.

In fact, as he explained, while splashing through the shallow expanse, the stream had changed its course. It was the boundary between the lands of Schlangenwald and Adlerstein, but it had within the last sixty years burst forth in a flood, and had then declined to return to its own bed, but had flowed in a fresh channel to the right of the former one. The Lords of Adlerstein claimed the ground to the old channel, the Counts of Schlangenwald held that the river was the landmark; and the dispute had a greater importance than seemed explained from the worth of the rushy space of ground, for this was the passage of the Italian merchants on their way from Constance, and every load that was overthrown in the river was regarded as the lawful prey of the noble on whose banks the catastrophe befell.

Any freight of goods was anxiously watched by both nobles, and it was not their fault if no disaster befell the travellers. Hugh talked of the Schlangenwald marauders with bitterness, but manifestly did not breathe freely till his whole convoy were safe across both the wet and the dry channel. He led the way up through the trees, and finally arrived at a miserable little hut, which served the purpose of an inn.

He was received with much obsequiousness, and was plainly a great authority there. Christina, weary and frightened, descended from her mule, and was put under the protection of a wild, rough-looking peasant woman, who stared at her like something from another world, but at length showed her a nook behind a mud partition, where she could spread her mantle, and at least lie down, and tell her beads unseen, if she could not sleep in the stifling, smoky atmosphere, amid the sounds of carousal among her father and his fellows.

A great hound came up and smelt to her. His outline was so wolfish, that she had nearly screamed; but, more in terror at the men who might have helped her than even at the beast, she tried to smoothe him, and found him licking her hand, and wagging his long rough tail. And he finally lay down at her feet, as though to protect her.

"Is it a sign that good angels will not let me be hurt ?" she thought, and, wearied out, she slept.

Christina awoke to a scene most unlike that which had been wont to meet her eyes in her own little wainscoted chamber high in the gabled front of her uncle's house. It was a time when the imperial free towns of Germany had advanced nearly as far as those of Italy in civilisation, and had reached a point whence they retrograded grievously during the Thirty Years' War. The country immediately around them shared the benefits of their civilisation, and the free peasant proprietors lived in great ease and prosperity, in beautiful and picturesque farmsteads, enjoying a careless abundance, and keeping numerous rural or religious feasts, where old Teutonic mythological observances had received a Christian colouring and adaptation.

In the mountains, or around the castles, it was usually very different. The elective constitution of the empire, the frequent change of dynasty, the many disputed successions, had combined to render the soverign authority uncertain and feeble, and it was seldom really felt save in the hereditary dominions of the Kaiser for the time being. Thus, while the cities advanced in the power of self-government, and the education it conveyed, the nobles, especially those whose abodes were not easily accessible, were often practically under no government at all, and felt themselves accountable to no man. The old wild freedom of the Suevi, and other Teutonic tribes, still technically, and in many cases practically existed. The Heretogen, Heerzogen, or, as we call them, Dukes, had indeed accepted employment from the Kaiser as his generals, and had received rewards from him; the Gerefen, or Graffen, of all kinds were his judges, the titles of both being proofs of their holding commissions from, and being thus dependent on, the court. But the Freiherren, a word very inadequately represented by our French term of baron, were absolutely free, "never in bondage to any man," holding their own, and owing no duty, no office; poorer, because unendowed by the royal authority, but holding themselves infinitely higher, than the pensioners of the Court. Left behind, however, by their neighbours, who did their part by society, and advanced with it, the Freiherren had been for the most part obliged to give up their independence and fall into the system, but so far in the rear, that they ranked, like the barons of France and England, as the last order of nobility.

Still, however, in the wilder and more mountainous parts of the country, some of the old families of unreduced, truly free Freiherren lingered, their hand against every man, every man's hand against them, and ever becoming more savage, both positively and still more proportionately, as their isolation and the general progress around them became greater. The House of Austria, by gradually absorbing hereditary states into its own possessions, was, however, in the fifteenth century, acquiring a preponderance that rendered its possession of the imperial throne almost a matter of inheritance, and, moreover, rendered the supreme power far more effective than it had ever previously been. Friedrich III., a man still in full vigor, and with an able and enterprising son already elected to the succession, was making his rule felt, and it was fast becoming apparent that the days of the independent baronies were numbered, and that the only choice that would soon be left them would be between making terms and being forcibly reduced. Von Adlerstein was one of the oldest of these free families.

And the wilderness of their territory was what might be expected from their hostility to all outward influences. The hostel, if it deserved the name, was little more than a charcoal-burner's hut, hidden in the woods at the foot of the mountain, serving as a halting-place for the Freiherren's retainers ere they attempted the ascent. The inhabitants were allowed to ply their trade of charring wood in the forest on condition of supplying the castle with charcoal, and of affording a lodging to the followers on occasions like the present.

Grimy, half clad, and brawny, with the whites of his eyes gleaming out of his black face, Jobst the Kohler startled Christina terribly when she came into the outer room, and met him returning from his night's work, with his long stoking-pole in his hand. Her father shouted with laughter at her alarm.

"Thou thinkest thyself in the land of the kobolds and dwarfs, my girl! Never mind, thou wilt see worse than honest Jobst before thou hast done. Now, eat a morsel and be ready—mountain air will make thee hungry ere thou art at the castle. And, hark thee, Jobst, thou must give stable-room to yon sumpter-mule for the present, and let some of my daughter's gear lie in the shed."

"Oh, father!" exclaimed Christina in dismay.

"We'll bring it up, child, by piecemeal," he said in a low voice, "as we can; but if such a freight came to the castle at once, my lady would have her claws on it, and little more wouldst thou ever see thereof. Moreover, I shall have enough to do to look after thee up the ascent, without another of these city-bred beasts."

"I hope the poor mule will be cared for. I can pay for——" began Christina; but her father squeezed her arm, and drowned her soft voice in his loud tones.

"Jobst will take care of the beast, as belonging to me. Woe betide him, if I find it the worse!"

"Look you, Christina," said Hugh Sorel, as soon as he had placed her on her mule, and led her out of hearing, "if thou hast any gold about thee, let it be the last thing thou ownest to any living creature up there." Then, as she was about to speak—"Do not even tell me. I *will* not know." The caution did not add much to Christina's comfort; but she presently asked, "Where is thy steed, father?"

"I sent him up to the castle with the Schneiderlein and Yellow Lorentz," answered the father. "I shall have ado enough on foot with thee before we are up the Ladder."

The father and daughter were meantime proceeding along a dark path through oak and birch woods, constantly ascending, until the oak grew stunted and disappeared, and the opening glades showed steep, stony, torrent-furrowed ramparts of hillside above them, looking to Christina's eyes as if she were set to climb up the cathedral side like a snail or a fly. She quite gasped for breath at the very sight, and was told in return to wait and see what she would yet say to the Adlerstreppe, or Eagle's Ladder. Yet, alarmed as she was, there was something in the exhilaration and elasticity of the mountain air that gave her an entirely new sensation of enjoyment and life, and seemed to brace her limbs and spirits for whatever might be before her.

Having passed beyond the region of wood, they had come forth upon the mountain-side. A not immoderately steep slope of boggy, mossy-looking ground, with bare rocks here and there rising, went away above; but the path turned round the shoulder of the mountain, and to the left, on a ledge of rock cut off apparently on their side by a deep ravine, and with a sheer precipice above and below it, stood a red stone pile, with one turret far above the rest.

"And this is Schloss[1] Adlerstein?" she exclaimed.

"That is Schloss Adlerstein; and there shalt thou be in two hours' time, unless the devil be more than usually busy, or thou mak'st a fool of thyself. If so, not Satan himself could save thee."

---

[1] Castle.

It was well that Christina had resolution to prevent her making
a fool of herself, for she could only shut her eyes, trusting that her
father did not see her terror. Soon the turn round to the side of
the mountain was made, and the road became a mere track worn
out on the turf on the hillside, with an abyss beneath, close to the
edge of which the mule, of course, walked.

When she ventured to look again, she perceived that the ravine
was like an enormous crack open on the mountain-side, and that
the stream that formed the Debateable Ford flowed down the
bottom of it. The ravine itself went probably all the way up the
mountain, growing shallower as it ascended higher; but here, where
Christina beheld it, it was extremely deep, and savagely desolate
and bare. She now saw that the Eagle's Ladder was a succession
of bare gigantic terraces of rock, of which the opposite side of the
ravine was composed, and on one of which stood the castle.

The fearful steepness of the ground absorbed all Christina's
attention. The road, or rather stairs, came down to the stream at
the bottom of the fissure, and then went again on the other side
up still more tremendous steeps, which Hugh climbed with a staff,
sometimes with his hand on the bridle, but more often only keeping
a watchful eye on the sure-footed mule, and an arm to steady his
daughter in the saddle when she grew absolutely faint with giddiness
at the abyss around her.

Presently a voice was heard above—"What, Sorel, hast brought
her! Trudchen is wearying for her."

The words were in the most boorish dialect and pronunciation,
the stranger to Christina's ears, because intercourse with foreign
merchants, and a growing affectation of Latinism, had much refined
the city language to which she was accustomed; and she was surprised to perceive by her father's gesture and address that the
speaker must be one of the lords of the castle. She looked up, and
saw on the pathway above her a tall, large-framed young man, his
skin dyed red with sun and wind, in odd contrast with his pale
shaggy hair, moustache, and beard, as though the weather had
tanned the one and bleached the other. His dress was a still
shabbier buff suit than her father had worn, but with a richly
embroidered belt sustaining a hunting-horn with finely chased
ornaments of tarnished silver, and an eagle's plume was fastened
into his cap with a large gold Italian coin. He stared hard at the
maiden, but vouchsafed her no token of greeting—only distressed
her considerably by distracting her father's attention from her mule

by his questions about the journey, all in the same rude, coarse tone and phraseology. Some amount of illusion was dispelled. Christina was quite prepared to find the mountain lords dangerous ruffians, but she had expected the graces of courtesy and high birth; but, though there was certainly an air of command and freedom of bearing about the present specimen, his manners and speech were more uncouth than those of any newly-caught apprentice of her uncle.

By this time a last effort of the mule had climbed to the level of the castle. As her father had shown her, there was precipice on two sides of the building; on the third, a sheer wall of rock going up to a huge height before it reached another of the Eagle's Steps; and on the fourth, where the gateway was, the little beck had been made to flow in a deep channel that had been hollowed out to serve as a moat, before it bounded down to swell the larger water-course in the ravine. A temporary bridge had been laid across; the drawbridge was out of order. Christina was told to dismount and cross on foot. The unrailed board, so close to the abyss, and with the wild water foaming above and below, was dreadful to her; and she hung back with an involuntary shudder, as her father, occupied with the mule, did not think of giving her a hand. The young baron burst out into an unrestrained laugh, but at the same time he roughly took her hand, and almost dragged her across, saying, "City bred—ho, ho!" "Thanks, sir," she strove to say, but she was very near weeping with the terror and strangeness of all around.

The low-browed gateway, barely high enough to admit a man on horseback, opened before her, almost to her feelings like the gate of the grave, and she could not help crossing herself, with a silent prayer for protection, as she stepped under it, and came into the castle court—not such a court as gave its name to fair courtesy, but, if truth must be told, far more resembling an ill-kept, ill-savoured stable-yard, with the piggeries opening into it. The Sorel family had brought cleanliness from Flanders, and Hausfrau Johanna was scrupulously dainty in all her appointments. Christina scarcely knew how she conveyed herself and her blue kirtle across the bemired stones to the next and still darker portal, under which a wide but rough ill-hewn stair ascended. These stairs led into the castle hall. There was a long table, with rough men-at-arms lounging about, and staring rudely at her; and at the upper end, by a great open chimney, sat, half dozing, an elderly man, more rugged in feature than his son; and yet, when he roused himself and spoke to Hugh, there was a shade more of breeding, and less of clownishness, in his voice and deportment, as if he had been less entirely devoid of training. A tall darkly-robed woman stood beside him, whose huge towering cap made her look gigantic in the dim light of the smoky hall. Her features had been handsome, but had become hardened into a grim wooden aspect; and with sinking spirits Christina paused at the step of the dais, and made her reverence, wishing she could sink beneath the stones of the pavement out of sight of these terrible personages.

"So that's the wench," was Freiherrinn Kunigunde's greeting. "She looks like another sick baby to nurse; but I'll have no trouble about her; that is all. Take her up to Ermentrude; and thou, girl, have a care thou dost her will, and puttest none of thy city fancies into her head."

"And hark thee, girl," added the old Freiherr, sitting up. " So thou canst nurse her well, thou shalt have a new gown and a stout husband."

"That way," pointed the lady towards one of the four corner towers; and Christina moved towards it. The younger Freiherr stepped before her, went striding two or three steps at a time up the turret stair, and, before Christina had wound her way up, she heard a thin, impatient voice say, "Thou saidst she was come, Ebbo."

"Yes, even so," she heard Freiherr Eberhard return; "but she is slow and town-bred. She was afraid of crossing the moat." And then both laughed, so that Christina's cheeks tingled as she emerged from the turret into another vaulted room. "Here she is," quoth the brother; "now will she make thee well."

It was a very bare and desolate room, with no hangings, and scarcely any furniture, except a great carved bedstead, one wooden chair, a table, and some stools. On the bare floor, in front of the fire, her arm under her head, and a profusion of long hair falling round her like flax from a distaff, lay wearily a little figure, beside whom Sir Eberhard was kneeling on one knee.

"Here is my sisterling," said he, looking up to the newcomer. " They say you burgherwomen have ways of healing the sick. Look at her. Think you can heal her?"

In an access of dumb shyness Ermentrude half rose, and effectually hindered any observations on her looks by hiding her face away upon her brother's knee. It was the gesture of a child of five years old, but Ermentrude's length of limb forbade Christina to suppose her less than fourteen or fifteen. "What, wilt not look at her?" he said, trying to raise her head; and then, holding out one of her wasted, feverish hands to Christina, he again asked, with a wistfulness that had a strange effect from the large, tall man, almost ten years her elder, "Canst thou cure her, maiden?"

"I am no doctor, sir," replied Christina; "but I could, at least, make her more comfortable. The stone is too hard for her."

"I will not go away; I want the fire," murmured the sick girl, shivering.

Christina quickly took off her own thick cloth mantle, well lined with dressed lambskins, laid it on the floor, rolled the collar of it over a small log of wood—the only substitute she could see for a pillow—and showed an inviting couch in an instant. Ermentrude let her brother lay her down, and then was covered with the ample fold. She smiled as she turned up her thin, wasted face, faded into the same whitey-brown tint as her hair. "That is good," she said, but without thanks; and, feeling the soft lamb's-wool: "Is that what you burgherwomen wear? Father is to give me a furred mantle, if only some court dame would pass the Debateable Ford. But the robbers got the last before ever we could get down. Jobst was so stupid. He did not give us warning in time; but he is to be hung next time if he does not."

"Never mind, Trudchen," answered the brother kindly; "meantime I have kept all the wild catskins for thee, and maybe this— this—*she* could sew them up into a mantle for thee."

"Oh, let me see!" cried the young lady eagerly; and Sir Eberhard, walking off, presently returned with an armful of the beautiful brindled furs of the mountain cat. Ermentrude sat up, and regarded the placing out of them with great interest; and thus her brother left her employed, and so much delighted that she had not flagged, when a great bell proclaimed that it was the time for the noontide meal, for which Christina, in spite of all her fears of the company below stairs, had been constrained by mountain air to look forward with satisfaction.

Ermentrude, she found, meant to go down, but with no notion of the personal arrangements that Christina had been wont to think a needful preliminary. With all her hair streaming, down she went, and was so gladly welcomed by her father that it was plain that her presence was regarded as an unusual advance towards recovery, and Christina feared lest he might already be looking out for the stout husband. She had much to tell him about the catskin cloak, and then she was seized with eager curiosity at the sight of Christina's bundles, and especially at her lute, which she must hear at once.

"Not now," said her mother, "there will be jangling and jingling enough by and by—meat now."

The whole establishment were taking their places—or rather tumbling into them. A battered, shapeless metal vessel seemed to represent the salt-cellar, and next to it Hugh Sorel seated himself, and kept a place for her beside him. Otherwise she would hardly have had seat or food. She was now able to survey the imnates of the castle. Besides the family themselves, there were about a dozen men, all ruffianly-looking, and of much lower grade than her father, and three women. One, old Ursel, the wife of Hatto the forester, was a bent, worn, but not ill-looking woman, with a motherly face; the younger ones were hard, bold creatures, from whom Christina felt a shrinking recoil. The meal was dressed by Ursel and her kitchen boy. From a great cauldron, goat's flesh and broth together were ladled out into wooden bowls. That every one provided their own spoon and knife—no fork—was only what Christina was used to in the most refined society, and she had the implements in a pouch hanging to her girdle; but she was not prepared for the unwashed condition of the bowls, nor for being obliged to share that of her father. Hungry as she was, she did not find it easy to take food under these circumstances, and she was relieved when Ermentrude was overcome by the turmoil, grew giddy, and was carried upstairs by her father, who laid her down upon her great bed, and left her to the attendance of Christina. Ursel had followed, but was petulantly repulsed by her young lady in favour of the newcomer and went away grumbling.

Nestled on her bed, Ermentrude insisted on hearing the lute, and Christina had to creep down to fetch it, with some other of her goods, in trembling haste.

Low and softly, with a voice whence she could scarcely banish tears, and in dread of attracting attention, Christina sung to the sick girl, who listened with a sort of rude wonder, and finally was lulled to sleep. Christina ventured to lay down her instrument and move towards the window, heavily mullioned with stone, barred with iron, and glazed with thick glass; being in fact the only glazed window in the castle. To her great satisfaction it did not look out over the loathsome court, but over the opening of the ravine. A stone thrown from the window would have gone straight down, she knew not where. Close to her ears rushed the descending waterfall in its leap over the rock side, and her eyes could rest themselves on the green meadow land below, and the smooth water of the Debateable Ford; nay—far, far away beyond retreating ridges of wood and field—she thought she could track a silver line, and guided by it, a something that might be a city. Her heart lept towards it, but she was recalled by Ermentrude's fretfully imperious voice.

"I was only looking forth from the window, lady," she said, returning.

"Ah! thou saw'st no travellers at the Ford?" cried Ermentrude, starting up with lively interest.

"No, lady; I was gazing at the far distance. Know you if it be indeed Ulm that we see from these windows?"

"I do not know. Let me see," said Ermentrude, rising; but at the window her pale blue eyes gazed vacantly as if she did not know what she was looking at or for.

"Ah! if the steeple of the Dome Kirk were but finished, I could not mistake it," said Christina. "How beauteous the white spire will look from hence!"

"Dome Kirk?" repeated Ermentrude; " what is that?"

Such an entire blank as the poor child's mind seemed to be was inconceivable to the maiden, who had been bred up in the busy hum of men, where the daily interests of a self-governing municipality were an unconscious education.

Ermentrude von Adlerstein had, on the contrary, not only never gone beyond the Kohler's hut on the one side, and the mountain village on the other, but she had never seen more of life than the festival at the wake at the hermitage chapel there on Midsummer Day. The only strangers who ever came to the castle were disbanded lanzknechts who took service with her father, or now and then a captive whom he put to ransom. She knew absolutely nothing of the world, except for a general belief that Freiherren lived there to do what they chose with other people, and that the House of Adlerstein was the freest and noblest in existence. Also there was a very positive hatred to the House of Schlangenwald, and no less to that of Adlerstein Wildschloss, for no reason that Christina could discover save that, being a younger branch of the family, they had submitted to the Emperor. To destroy either the Graf von Schlangenwald, or her Wildschloss cousin, was evidently the highest gratification Ermentrude could conceive; and, for the rest, that her father and brother should make successful captures at the Debateable Ford was the more abiding, because more practicable hope. She had no further ideas, except perhaps to elude her mother's severity, and to desire her brother's success in chamois-hunting. The only mental culture she had ever received was that old Ursel had taught her the Credo, Pater Noster, and Ave, as correctly as might be expected from a long course of traditionary repetitions of an incomprehensible language. And she knew besides a few German rhymes and jingles, half Christian, half heathen, with a legend or two which, if the names were Christian, ran grossly wild from all Christian meaning or morality. As to the amenities, nay, almost the proprieties, of life, they were less known in that baronial castle than in any artisan's house at Ulm.

And this was Christina's charge, whom she must look upon as the least alien spirit in this dreadful castle of banishment! The young and old lords seemed to her savage bandits, who frightened her only less than did the proud sinister expression of the old lady.

Long, long did the maiden weep and pray that night after Ermentrude had sunk to sleep. She strained her eyes with homesick longings to detect lights where she thought Ulm might be; and, as she thought of her uncle and aunt, the poodle and the cat round the stove, the maids spinning and the prentices knitting as her uncle read aloud some grave good book, most probably the legend of the saint of the day, and contrasted it with the rude, gruff sounds of revelry that found their way up the turret stairs, she could hardly restrain her sobs from awakening the young lady whose bed she was to share.

CHAPTER II

LIFE IN SCHLOSS ADLERSTEIN was little less intolerable than Christina's imagination had depicted it. It was entirely devoid of all the graces of chivalry, and its squalor and coarseness, magnified into absurdity by haughtiness and violence, were almost inconceivable. Fortunately for her, the inmates of the castle resided almost wholly below stairs in the hall and kitchen, and in some dismal dens in the thickness of their walls.

Freiherrinn Kunigunde hardly ever mounted to her daughter's chamber. All her affection was centred on the strong and manly son, of whom she was proud, while the sickly pining girl, who would hardly find a mate of her own rank, and who had not even dowry enough for a convent, was such a shame and burthen to her as to be almost a distasteful object. But perversely, as it seemed to her, the only daughter was the darling of both father and brother, who were ready to do anything to gratify the girl's sick fancies, and hailed with delight her pleasure in her new attendant. Old Ursel was at first rather envious and contemptuous of the childish, fragile stranger, but her gentleness disarmed the old woman; and, when it was plain that the young lady's sufferings were greatly lessened by tender care, dislike gave way to attachment, and there was little more murmuring at the menial services that were needed by the two maidens, even when Ermentrude's feeble fancies, or Christina's views of dainty propriety, rendered them more onerous than before. She was even heard to rejoice that some Christian care and tenderness had at last reached her poor neglected child.

It was well for Christina that she had such an ally. The poor child never crept downstairs to the dinner or supper, to fetch food for Ermentrude, or water for herself, without a trembling and shrinking of heart and nerves.

Her father, whom she looked on as a cultivated person in comparison with the rest of the world, did his best for her after his own views, and gradually brought her all the properties she had left at

303

Kohler's hut.   Therewith she made a great difference in the aspect
of the chamber, under the full sanction of the lords of the castle.
Wolf, deer, and sheep skins abounded; and with these, assisted by
her father and old Hatto, she tapestried the lower part of the bare
grim walls, a great bear's hide covered the neighbourhood of the
hearth, and cushions were made of these skins, and stuffed from
Ursel's stores of feathers.   All these embelishments were watched
with great delight by Ermentrude, who had never been made of so
much importance, and was as much surprised as relieved by such
attentions.   She was too young and too delicate to reject civilisation,
and she let Christina braid her hair, bathe her, and arrange her
dress, with sensations of comfort that were almost like health.   To
train her into occupying herself was, however, as Christina soon
found, in her present state, impossible.   She could spin and sew
a little, but hated both; and her clumsy, listless fingers only soiled
and wasted Christina's needles, silk, and lute strings, and such
damage was not so easily remedied as in the streets of Ulm.   She
was best provided for when looking on at her attendant's busy
hands, and asking to be sung to, or to hear tales of the active, busy
scenes of the city life.

The gentle nursing and the new interests made her improve in
health, so that her father was delighted, and Christina began to
hope for a return home.   Sometimes the two girls would take the
air, either, on still days, upon the battlements; or they would find
their way to a grassy nook on the mountain-side, where Christina
gathered gentians and saxifrage, trying to teach her young lady that
they were worth looking at.   Once the quiet mule was brought into
requisition; and, with her brother walking by her, and Sorel and
his daughter in attendance, Ermentrude rode towards the village of
Adlerstein.   It was a collection of miserable huts, on a sheltered
slope towards the south, where there was earth enough to grow
some wretched rye and buckwheat, subject to severe toll from
the lord of the soil.   Perched on a hollow rock above the
slope was a rude little church, over a cave where a hermit had once
lived and died in such odour of sanctity that, his day happening to
coincide with that of St. John the Baptist, the Blessed Friedmund
had acquired the credit of the lion's share both of the saint's honours
and of the old solstitial feast of Midsummer.   This wake was the
one gaiety of the year, and attracted a fair which was the sole occasion
of coming honestly by anything from the outer world; nor had his
cell ever lacked a professional anchorite.

This was Christina's first sight of a church since her arrival, except that in the chapel, which was a dismal neglected vault, where a ruinous altar and mouldering cruifix testified to its sacred purpose. The old baron had been excommunicated for twenty years, ever since he had harried the wains of the Bishop of Augsburg on his way to the Diet; and, though his household and family were not under the same sentence, "Sunday didna come abune the pass." Christina's entreaty obtained permission to enter the little building, but she had knelt there only a few moments before her father came to hurry her away, and her supplications that he would some day take her to mass there were whistled down in the wind; and indeed ther hermit was a layman, and the church was only served on great festivals by a monk from the convent of St. Ruprecht, on the distant side of the mountain, which was further supposed to be in the Schlangenwald interest. Her best chance lay in infusing the desire into Ermentrude, who, by watching her prayers and asking a few questions, had begun to acquire a few clearer ideas. And what Ermentrude wished had always hitherto been acquiesced in by the two lords.

The elder baron came little into Christina's way. He meant to be kind to her, but she was dreadfully afraid of him, and, when he came to visit his daughter, shrank out of his notice as much as possible, shuddering most of all at his attempts at civilities. His son she viewed as one of the thick-witted giants meant to be food for the heroism of good knights of romance. Except that he was fairly conversant with the use of weapons, and had occasionally ridden beyond the shadow of his own mountain, his range was quite as limited as his sister's; and he had an equal scorn for all beyond it. His unfailing kindness to his sister was, however, in his favour, and he always eagerly followed up any suggestion Christina made for her pleasure. He certainly did not admire the little, slight, pale bower-maiden, but he seemed to look upon her like some strange, almost uncanny, wise spirit out of some other sphere, and his manner towards her had none of the offensive freedom apparent in even the old man's patronage. It was, as Ermentrude once said, laughing, almost as if he feared that she might do something to him.

Christina had expected to see a ruffian, and had found a boor; but she was to be convinced that the ruffian existed in him. Notice came up to the castle of a convoy of wagons, and all was excitement. Men-at-arms were mustered, horses led down the Eagle's Ladder, and an ambush prepared in the woods. The autumn rains were already swelling the floods, and the passage of the ford would be difficult enough to afford the assailants an easy prey.

The Freiherrinn Kunigunde herself, and all the women of the castle, hurried into Ermentrude's room to enjoy the view from her window. The young lady herself was full of eager expectation, but she knew enough of her maiden to expect no sympathy from her, and loved her well enough not to bring down on her her mother's attention; so Christina crept into her turret, unable to withdraw her eyes from the sight, trembling, weeping, praying, longing for power to give a warning signal. Could they be her own townsmen stopped on the way to dear Ulm?

She could see the wagons in mid-stream, the warriors on the bank; she heard the triumphant outcries of the mother and daughter in the outer room. She saw the overthrow, the struggle, the flight of a few scattered dark figures on the farther side, the drawing out of the goods on the nearer.

She was glad that Ermentrude went down with her mother to watch the return of the victors. She crouched on the floor, sobbing, shuddering with grief and indignation, and telling her beads alike for murdered and murderers, till, after the sounds of welcome and exultation, she heard Sir Eberhard's heavy tread, as he carried his sister upstairs. Ermentrude went up at once to Christina.

"After all, there was little for us!" she said. "It was only a wain of wine barrels; and now will the drunkards downstairs made good cheer. But Ebbo could only win for me this chain and medal, which was round the old merchant's neck."

"Was he slain?" Christina asked, with pale lips.

"I only know I did not kill him," returned the baron; "I had him down and got the prize, and that was enough for me. What the rest of the fellows may have done, I cannot say."

"But he has brought thee something, Stina," continued Ermentrude. "Show it to her, brother."

"My father sends you this for your care of my sister," said Eberhard, holding out a brooch that had doubtless fastened the band of the unfortunate wine-merchant's bonnet.

"Thanks, sir; but, indeed, I may not take it," said Christina, turning crimson, and drawing back.

"So!" he exclaimed in amaze; then bethinking himself—"They are no townsfolk of yours, but Constance cowards."

"Take it, take it Stina, or you will anger my father," added Ermentrude.

"No, lady, I thank the barons both, but it were sin in me," said Christina, with trembling voice.

"Look you," said Eberhard: "we have the full right—'tis a seignorial right—to all the goods of every wayfarer that may be overthrown in our river—as I am a true knight!" he added earnestly.

"A true knight!" repeated Christina, pushed hard, and very indignant in all her terror. "The true knight's part is to aid, not rob, the weak." And the dark eyes flashed a vivid light.

"Christina!" exclaimed Ermentrude, in the extremity of her amazement, "know you what you have said?—that Eberhard is no true knight!"

He meanwhile stood silent, utterly taken by surprise, and letting his little sister fight his battles.

"I cannot help it, Lady Ermentrude," said Christina, with trembling lips, and eyes filling with tears. "You may drive me from the castle—I only long to be away from it—but I cannot stain my soul by saying that spoil and rapine are the deeds of a true knight."

"My mother will beat you," cried Ermentrude passionately, ready to fly to the head of the stairs; but her brother laid his hand upon her.

"Tush, Trudchen; keep thy tongue still, child! What does it hurt me?" And he turned on his heel and went downstairs.

Christina crept into her turret, weeping bitterly and with many a wild thought. Would they visit her offence on her father? Would they turn them both out together? If so, would not her father hurl her down the rocks rather than return her to Ulm? Could she escape? And as she felt her helplessness, the selfish thoughts passed into a gush of tears for the murdered man, lying suffering there, and for his possible wife and children watching for him. Presently Ermentrude peeped in.

"Stina, Stina, don't cry; I will not tell my mother! Come out, and finish my kerchief! Come out! No one shall beat you."

"That is not what I wept for, lady," said Christina. "I do not think you would bring harm on me. But I grieve for the bloodshed that I must see, and for that poor merchant."

"Oh," said Ermentrude, "you need not fear for him! I saw his own folk return and lift him up. But what is he to thee or to us?"

"I am a burgher maid, lady," said Christina, recovering herself, aware that it was of little use to bear testimony to such an auditor as poor little Ermentrude against the deeds of her own father and brother, which had in reality the sort of sanction Sir Eberhard had mentioned.

Still she could not but tremble at the thought of her speech, and went down to supper in greater trepidation than usual, dreading that she should be expected to thank the Freiherr for his gift. But, fortunately, manners were too rare at Adlerstein for any such omission to be remarkable, and the whole establishment was in a state of noisy triumph and merriment over the excellence of the French wine they had captured, so that she slipped into her seat unobserved.

Ermentrude was eagerly presented with draughts by both father and brother, and presently Sir Eberhard exclaimed, turning towards the shrinking Christina with a rough laugh, "Maiden, I trow thou wilt not taste?"

Christina shook her head.

"What's this?" asked her father, close to whom she sat. "Is't a fast-day?"

There was a pause. Many were present who regarded a fast-day much more than the lives or goods of their neighbours. Christina again shook her head.

"No matter," said good-natured Sir Eberhard, evidently wishing to avert any ill consequences from her. "'Tis only her loss."

The mirth went on rough and loud, and Christina felt this the worst of all the miserable meals she had partaken of in fear and trembling at this place of her captivity. Ermentrude, too, was soon in such a state of excitement, that not only was Christina's woman-hood bitterly ashamed and grieved for her, but there was a serious danger that she might at any moment break out with some allusion to her maiden's recusancy in her reply to Sir Eberhard.

Presently, however, Ermentrude laid down her head and began to cry—violent headache had come on—and her brother took her in his arms to carry her up the stairs; but his potations had begun before hers, and his step was far from steady; he stumbled more than once on the steps, shook and frightened his sister, and set her down weeping petulantly. And then came a more terrible moment; his awe of Christina had passed away; he swore that she was a lovely maiden, with only too free a tongue, and that a kiss must be the seal of her pardon. She spoke resolutely—

"Sir Eberhard, your sister is ill—you are in no state to be here. Go down at once, nor insult a maiden."

Probably the low-toned softness of the voice, so utterly different from the shrill wrangling notes of all the other women he had known, took him by surprise. He was still sober enough to be subdued, almost cowed, by resistance of a description unlike all he had ever seen; his alarm at Christina's superior power returned in full force, he staggered to the stairs.

Ermentrude had so much fever all that night and the next day that no going down could be thought of. Nobody came near the maidens but Ursel, and she described one continued orgy that made Christina shudder again with fear and disgust. Yet there might have been worse even than this; for old Ursel whispered that at the bottom of the stairs there was a trap-door. Did the maiden know what it covered? It was an oubliette.[1] There was once a Strasburg armourer who had refused ransom, and talked of appealing to the Kaiser. He trod on that door and—— Ursel pointed downwards. "But since that time," she said, "my young lord has never brought home a prisoner."

No wonder that all this time Christina cowered at the discordant sounds below, trembled, and prayed while she waited on her poor young charge, who tossed and moaned in fever and suffering. She was still far from recovered when the materials of the debauch failed, and the household began to return to its usual state. She was soon restlessly pining for her brother; and when her father came up to see her, received him with scant welcome, and entreaties for Ebbo. The old Freiherr went down, promising that her brother should come.

With a fluttering heart Christina awaited the noble whom she had perhaps insulted, and whose advances had more certainly insulted her. Would he visit her with his anger, or return to that more offensive familiarity? She longed to flee out of sight when his heavy tread was heard; but she could not even take refuge in her turret, for Ermentrude was leaning against her. Somehow, the step was less assured than usual; he absolutely knocked at the door; and, when he came in, he acknowledged her by a slight inclination of the head. If she only had known it, this was the first time that head had ever been bent to any being, human or Divine; but all she did perceive was that Sir Eberhard was in neither of the moods she dreaded, only desperately shy and sheepish, and extremely ashamed, not indeed of his excess, which would have been, even to a much tamer German baron, only a happy accident, but of what had passed between himself and her.

[1] A secret dungeon with no other entrance than a trapdoor.

He was much grieved to perceive how much ground Ermentrude had lost, and gave himself up to comforting her; and in a few days more, in their common cares for the sister, Christina lost her newly-acquired horror of the brother, and could not but be grateful for his forbearance; while she was almost entertained by the increased awe of herself shown by this huge robber baron.

Ermentrude had by no means recovered the ground she had lost, before the winter set in; and blinding snow came drifting down day and night, rendering the whole view, above and below, one expanse of white, only broken by the peaks of rock which were too steep to sustain the snow.

In spite of all endeavours to guard the windows and keep up the fire, the cold withered the poor child like a fading leaf, and she needed more and more of tenderness and amusement to distract her attention from her ailments. Christina's resources were unfailing. Out of the softer pine and birch woods provided for the fire, she carved a set of draughtsmen, and made a board by ruling squares on the end of a settle, and painting the alternate ones with a compound of oil and charcoal. Even the old baron was delighted with this contrivance, and the pleasure it gave his daughter. He remembered playing at draughts in that portion of his youth which had been a shade more polished, and he felt as if the game were making Ermentrude more like a lady. Christina was encouraged to proceed with a set of chessmen, and the shaping of their characteristic heads under her dexterous fingers was watched by Ermentrude like something magical.

Christina had brought her own books—a library of extraordinary extent for a maiden of the fifteenth century, but which she owed to her uncle's connection with the arts of wood-cutting and printing. A Vulgate[1] from Dr. Faustus's own press, a mass book and breviary, Thomas à Kempis's *Imitation*, and the *Nuremburg Chronicle*, all in Latin, and the poetry of the gentle Minnesinger and bird-lover, Walther von Vogelweide, in the vernacular; these were her stock, which Hausfrau Johanna had viewed as a foolish encumbrance, and Hugh Sorel would never have transported to the castle unless they had been so well concealed in Christina's kirtles that he had taken them for parts of her wardrobe.

Most precious were they now, when, out of the reach of all teaching save her own, she had to infuse into the sinking girl's mind the great mysteries of life and death, so that she might not leave the

[1] Latin Bible.

world without more hope or faith than her heathen forefathers. For that Ermentrude would live Christina had never hoped, since that fleeting improvement had been cut short by the fever of the wine-cup. She knew she could not cure, but she felt she could comfort, cheer, and soften, and she no longer repined at her enforced sojourn at Adlerstein. She heartily loved her charge, and could not bear to think how desolate Ermentrude would be without her. And now the poor girl had become responsive to her care. She was infinitely softened in manner, and treated her parents with forms of respect new to them; she had learnt even to thank old Ursel, dropped her imperious tone, and struggled with her petulance; and, towards her brother, the domineering, uncouth adherence was becoming real, tender affection; while the dependent, reverent love she bestowed upon Christina was touching and endearing in the extreme.

Freiherr von Adlerstein saw the change, and congratulated himself on the effect of having a town-bred bower-woman; nay, spoke of the advantage it would be to his daughter, if he could persuade himself to make the submission to the Kaiser which the late improvements decided on at the Diet were rendering more and more inevitable. *Now* how happy would be the winner of his gentle Ermentrude!

Freiherr Eberhard was more strongly convinced than was his father of the untenableness of their present position. Hugh Sorel's reports of what he heard at Ulm had shown that the league that had been discussed at Regensburg was far more formidable than anything that had ever previously threatened Schloss Adlerstein, and that if the Graf von Schlangenwald joined in the coalition, there would be private malice to direct its efforts against the Adlerstein family. Feud-letters or challenges had been made unlawful for ten years, and was not Adlerstein at feud with the world?

Nor did Eberhard look on the submission with the sullen rage and grief that his father felt in bringing himself to such a declension from the pride of his ancestors. What the young baron heard upstairs was awakening in him a sense of the poorness and narrowness of his present life. Ermentrude never spared him what interested her; and, partly from her lips, partly through her appeals to her attendant, he had learnt that life had better things to offer than independence on these bare rocks, and that homage might open the way to higher and worthier exploits than preying upon overturned wagons.

He believed nothing of his sister's slow declension in strength, ascribing all the change he saw to the bitter cold, and seeing but little even of that alteration, though he spent many hours in her room, holding her in his arms, amusing her, or talking to her and to Christina. All Christina's fear of him was gone. As long as there was no liquor in the house, and he was his true self, she felt him to be a kind friend, bound to her by strong sympathy in the love and care for his sister. She could talk almost as freely before him as when alone with her young lady; and as Ermentrude's religious feelings grew stronger, and were freely expressed to him, surely his attention was not merely kindness and patience with the sufferer.

"Like an army defeated,
The snow had retreated"

out of the valley, whose rich green shone smiling round the pool into which the Debateable Ford spread. The waterfall had burst its icy bonds, and dashed down with redoubled voice, roaring rather than babbling. The dark peaks of rock came out all glistening with moisture, and the snow only retained possession of the deep hollows and crevices, into which, however, its retreat was far more graceful than when, in the city, it was trodden by horse and man, and soiled with smoke.

Ermentrude had a love for the white sheet that lay covering a gorge running up from the ravine. She watched its diminution day by day with a fancy that she was melting away with it ; and, indeed, it was on the very day that a succession of drifting showers had left the sheet alone, and separated if from the masses of white above, that it first fully dawned upon the rest of the family that, for the little daughter of the house, spring was only bringing languor and sinking instead of recovery.

Then it was that Sir Eberhard listened to her entreaty that she might not die without a priest, and comforted her by passing his word to her that, if—he would not say *when*—the time drew near, he would bring her one of the priests who had only come from St. Ruprecht's cloister on great days, by a sort of sufferance, to say mass at the Blessed Friedmund's hermitage chapel.

The time was slow in coming. Easter had passed—the sheet of snow had dwindled to a mere wreath—the ford looked blue in the sunshine—the cascade tinkled merrily down its rock—mountain primroses peeped out, when, as Father Norbert came forth from saying his ill-attended Pentecostal mass, and was parting with the infirm peasant hermit, a tall figure strode up the pass, and, as the

villagers fell back to make way, stood before the startled priest, and
said, in a voice checked with grief, " Come with me."

" Wherefore dost thou seek me?" demanded Father Norbert.

"For my sister," replied Eberhard, his voice thickening again.
"My little sister lies at the point of death, and I have sworn to her
that a priest she shall have. Wilt thou come, or shall I drag thee
down the pass?"

"I come, I come with all my heart, sir knight," was the ready
response. "A few moments and I am at your bidding."

As Norbert appeared with the pyx and other appliances that he
had gone to fetch, the Freiherr held out his hand with an offer to
"carry his gear for him"; and, when the monk refused, with an
inward shudder at entrusting a sacred charge to such unhallowed
hands, replied, "You will have work enow for both hands ere the
castle is reached."

But Father Norbert was by birth a sturdy Switzer, and thought
little of these Swabian Alps; and he climbed after his guide through
the most rugged passages of Eberhard's shortest and most per-
pendicular cut without a moment's hesitation, and with agility
worthy of a chamois. The young baron turned for a moment, when
the level of the castle had been gained, perhaps to see whether he
were following, but at the same time came to a sudden speechless
pause.

On the white masses of vapour that floated on the opposite side
of the mountain was traced a gigantic shadowy outline of a hermit,
with head bent eagerly forward, and arm outstretched.

The monk crossed himself. Eberhard stood still for a moment,
and then said hoarsely, "The Blessed Friedmund! He is come
for her"; then strode on towards the postern gate, followed by
Father Norbert.

Sir Eberhard led the way up the turret stairs to the open door,
and the monk entered the death-chamber. The baron sat near
the fire in the large wooden chair, half turned towards his daughter,
as one who must needs be present, but with his face buried in his
hands, unable to endure the spectacle. Nearer was the tall form
of his wife, standing near the foot of the bed, her harsh features
somewhat softened by the feelings of the moment. Ursel waited
at hand, with tears running down her furrowed cheeks.

For such of these Father Norbert was prepared; but he little
expected to meet so pure and sweet a gaze of reverential welcome
as beamed on him from the soft dark eyes of the little white-cheeked

maiden who sat on the bed, holding the sufferer in her arms. Still less had he anticipated the serene blessedness that sat on the wasted features of the dying girl, amid all the anguish of labouring breath.

She smiled, held up her hand, and thanked her brother. Her father scarcely lifted his head, her mother made a rigid curtsey, and with a grim look of sorrow coming over her features, laid her hand over the old baron's shoulder. "Come away, Herr Vater,"[1] she said; "he is going to hear her confession, and make her too holy for the like of us to touch."

The old man rose up, and stepped towards his child. Ermentrude held out her arms to him, and murmured:

"Father, father, pardon me; I would have been a better daughter if I had only known——" He gathered her in his arms—he was quite past speaking—and only gave her repeated kisses, laid her down on her pillows, then rushed to the door, and the passionate sobs of the strong man's uncontrolled nature might be heard upon the stair. Kunigunde leant down to kiss her; and, in return to her repetition of her entreaty for pardon, replied, "Thou hast it, child, if it will ease thy mind; but it is all along of these new fancies that ever an Adlerstein thought of pardon. There, there, I blame thee not, poor maid; if thou wert to die, it may be even best as it is. Now must I to thy father; he is troubled enough about this gear."

But when Eberhard moved towards his sister, she turned to the priest, and said imploringly, "Not far, not far! Oh, let them," pointing to Eberhard and Christina, "let them not be quite out of sight!"

"Out of hearing is all that is needed, daughter," replied the priest; and Ermentrude looked content as Christina moved towards the empty north turret, where with the door, open she was in full view, and Eberhard followed her thither. Gravely and sadly both stood there. Christina looked up the hillside for the snow-wreath. The May sunshine had dissolved it; the green pass lay sparkling without a vestige of its white coating. Her eyes full of tears, she pointed the spot out to Eberhard. He understood; but, leaning towards her, told, under his breath, of the phantom he had seen. Her eyes expanded with awe of the supernatural. "It was the Blessed Friedmund," said Eberdard. "Never hath he so greeted one of our race since the pious Freiherrinn Hildegarde. Maiden, hast thou brought us back a blessing?"

"Ah! well may she be blessed—well may the saints stoop to greet her," murmured Christina, with strangled voice, scarcely able to control her sobs.

Father Norbert came towards them. The simple confession had been heard, and he sought the aid of Christina in performing the last rites of the Church.

Eberhard was not excluded during the final services by which the soul was to be dismissed from its earthly dwelling-place. True, he comprehended little of their import, and nothing of the words, but he gazed meekly, with uncovered head, and a bewildered look of sadness, while Christina made her responses and took her part with full intelligence and deep fervour. Ermentrude lay calm, and, as it were, already rapt into a higher world.

She was all but gone when the rite of extreme unction was completed, and they could only stand round her, Eberhard, Christina, Ursel, and the old baroness, who had returned again, watching the last flutterings of the breath, the window thrown wide open that nothing might impede the passage of the soul to the blue vault above.

The priest spoke the beautiful commendation, "Depart, O Christian soul." There was a faint gesture in the midst for Christina to lift her in her arms, but her last look was for her brother, her last murmur, "Come after me, Ebbo."

CHAPTER III

ERMENTRUDE VON ADLERSTEIN slept with her forefathers in the vaults of the hermitage chapel, and Christina Sorel's work was done.

Surely it was time for her to return home, though she should be more sorry to leave the mountain castle than she could ever have believed possible. She entreated her father to take her home, but she received a sharp answer that she did not know what she was talking of: the Schlangenwald reitern were besetting the roads; and, moreover, the Ulm burghers had taken the capture of the Constance wine in such dudgeon that for a retainer of Adlerstein to show himself in the streets would be asking for the wheel.[1]

[1] An instrument of torture which revolved with the victim bound on it.

But was there any hope for her? Could he not take her to some nunnery midway, and let her write to her uncle to fetch her from thence?

He swore at woman's pertinacity, but allowed at last that if the plan, talked of by the barons, of going to make their submission to the Emperor at Linz, with a view to which all violence at the ford had ceased, should hold good, it might be possible thus to drop her on their way.

With this Christina must needs content herself. Ermentrude's death had deprived her of the sole object of her residence at Schloss Adlerstein, and it had infinitely increased the difficulties of her position. No one interfered with her possession of the upper room and its turrets; and it was only at meal-times that she was obliged to mingle with the other inhabitants, who, for the most part, absolutely overlooked the little shrinking pale maiden: but with one exception, and that the most perplexing of all. She had been on terms with Freiherr Eberhard that were not easily broken off. All through his sister's decline she had been his comforter, assistant, director, living in intercourse and sympathy that ought surely to cease when she was no longer his sister's attendant, yet which must be more than ever missed in the full freshness of the stroke.

The next time she heard the well-known tread on the stair, she fled into her own turret chamber, and shut the door. Her heart beat fast. She could hear Sir Eberhard moving about the room, and listened to his heavy sigh as he threw himself into the large chair. Presently he called her by name, and she felt it needful to open her door and answer respectfully:

"What would you, my lord?"

"What would I? A little peace, and heed to her who is gone. To see my father and mother one would think that a partridge had but flown away. I have seen my father more sorrowful when his dog had fallen over the abyss. Sit down, Christina," he said, dragging a chair nearer the hearth. "My heart is sore, and I cannot bear the din below."

"Ah! sir; pardon me. I must to the kitchen," said Christina, crossing her hands over her breast, to still her trembling heart, for she was very sorry for his grief, but moving resolutely.

"Must? And wherefore? Thou hast nought to do there; speak truth! Why not stay with me?" as his great light eyes opened wide.

"A burgher maid may not sit down with a noble baron."

"The devil! Has my mother been plaguing thee, child?"

"No, my lord," said Christina, "she recks not of me; but"—steadying her voice with great difficulty—"it behoves me the more to be discreet."

"And you would not have me come here?" he said, with a wistful tone of reproach.

"I have no power to forbid you; but if you do, I must betake me to Ursel in the kitchen," said Christina, very low, trembling and half choked.

"Among the rude wenches there!" he cried, starting up. "Nay, nay, that shall not be! Rather will I go. But this is very cruel of thee, maiden," he added, lingering.

"Oh, my lord," returned Christina, "you are kind and generous, make it not hard for me to do what other maidens less lonely have friends to do for them!"

"Kind and generous!" said Eberhard, leaning over the back of the chair as if trying to begin a fresh score. "This from you, who told me once I was no true knight!"

"I shall call you a true knight with all my heart," cried Christina, the tears rushing into her eyes, "if you will respect my loneliness," and retreating at once through the door of the staircase, whence she made her way to the kitchen, and with great difficulty found an excuse for her presence there.

It had been a hard struggle with her compassion and gratitude, and, poor little Christina felt with dismay, with something more than these. Else was it that, even while principle and better sense summoned her back to Ulm, she experienced a deadly weariness of the city-pent air, of the grave, heavy roll of the river, nay, even of the quiet, well-regulated household? Why did such a marriage as she had thought her natural destiny, with some worthy kind-hearted brother of the guild, become so hateful to her that she could only aspire to a convent life? And why was the interchange of greetings, the few words at meals, worth all the rest of the day beside to her? Her own heart was the traitor. She wept apart, and resolved, and prayed, cruelly ashamed of every start of joy or pain that the sight of Eberhard cost her. From almost the first he had sat next her at the single table that accommodated the whole household at meals, and the custom continued, though on some days he treated her with sullen silence, which she blamed herself for not rejoicing in; sometimes he spoke a few friendly words; but he observed, better than she could have dared to expect, her test of his true knighthood, and never again forced himself into her apartment, though now and then he came to the door with flowers, with mountain strawberries, and once with two young doves. "Take them, Christina," he said, "they are very like yourself"; and he always delayed so long that she was forced to be resolute, and shut the door on him at last.

Once, when there was to be a mass at the chapel, Hugh Sorel, between a smile and a growl, informed his daughter that he would take her thereto. To her amazement and pleasure, the young baron was at church, and when, on the way home, he walked beside her mule, she could see no need of sending him away.

He had been in no school of the conventionalities of life, and, when he saw that Hugh Sorel's presence had obtained him this favour, he wistfully asked, "Christina, if I bring your father with me, will you not let me in?"

"Entreat me not, my lord," she answered, with fluttering breath.

She felt the more that she was right in this decision, when she encountered her father's broad grin of surprise and diversion, at seeing the young baron help her to dismount.

The effect was a new entreaty, that he would find means of sending her home. It brought upon her the hearing put into words what her own feelings had long shrunk from confessiong to herself.

"Father, let me go home! My mind is—is to return to my uncle and aunt," said Christina, with clasped hands. "And oh, father, as you were the son of a true and faithful mother, be a father to me now! Jeer not your motherless child, but help her."

Hugh Sorel was touched by this appeal, and at length bethought him that, among the merchants who frequented the Midsummer fair at the Blessed Friedmund's Wake, a safe escort might be found to convey her back to Ulm.

Midsummer-day arrived, and the village of Adlerstein presented a most unusual spectacle. The wake was the occasion of a grand fair for all the mountain-side, and it was an understood thing that the barons, instead of molesting the pedlars, merchants, and others who attended it, contented themselves with demanding a toll from every one who passed the Kohler's hut on the one side, or the Gemsbock's Pass on the other; and this toll, being the only coin by which they came honestly in the course of the year, was regarded as a certainty and highly valued. Moreover, it was the only time that any purchases could be made, and the flotsam of the ford did not always include all even of the few requirements of the inmates of the castle; it was the only holiday, sacred or secular, that ever gladdened the Eagle's Rock.

So all the inmates of the castle prepared to enjoy themselves, except the heads of the house. The Freiherr had never been at one of these wakes since the first after he was excommunicated, when he had stalked round to show his indifference to the sentence; and the Freiherrinn snarled out such sentences of disdain towards the concourse, that it might be supposed that she hated the sight of her kind; but Ursel had all the household purchases to make, and the kitchen underlings were to take turns to go and come, as indeed were the men-at-arms, who were set to watch the toll-bars.

Christina had packed up a small bundle, for the chance of being unable to return to the castle without missing her escort, though she hoped that the fair might last two days, and that she should thus be enabled to return and bring away the rest of her property. She was more and more resolved on going, but her heart was less and less inclined to departure. And bitter had been her weeping through all the early light hours of the long morning—weeping that she tried to think was all for Ermentrude.

So tear-stained was her face, that, ashamed that it should be seen, she wrapped it closely in her hood and veil when she came down and joined her father. The whole scene swam in tears before her eyes when she saw the green slope from the chapel covered with tents and booths, and swarming with pedlars and mountaineers in their picturesque dresses. Women and girls were exchanging the yarn of their winter's spinning for bright handkerchiefs; men drove sheep, goats, or pigs to barter for knives, spades, or weapons; others were gazing at simple shows—a dancing bear or ape—or clustering round a Minnesinger; many even then congregating in booths for the sale of beer. Farther up, on the flat space of sward above the chapel, were some lay-brothers, arranging for the representation of a mystery—a kind of entertainment which Germany owed to the English who came to the Council of Constance, and which the monks of St. Ruprecht's hoped might infuse some religious notions into the wild ignorant mountaineers.

First, however, Christina gladly entered the church. Crowded though it was, it was calmer than the busy scene without.

Hugh Sorel decided on going into the fair in quest of an escort for his daughter, but as she saw Father Norbert and another monk ascending from the stairs leading to the hermit's cell, Christina begged to be allowed to remain in the church, where she was sure to be safe, instead of wandering about with him in the fair.

He was glad to be unencumbered, though he thought her taste unnatural; and, promising to return for her when he had found an escort, he left her.

Father Norbert had come for the very purpose of hearing confessions, and Christina's next hour was the most comfortable she had spent since Ermentrude's death.

After this, however, the priests were called away, and long, long did Christina first kneel and then sit in the little lonely church, hearing the various sounds without, and imagining that her father had forgotten her, and that he and all the rest were drinking.

Hours of waiting and nameless alarm must have passed, for the sun was waxing low, when she heard steps coming up the hermit's cell, and a head arose above the pavement which she recognised with a wild throb of joy, but, repressing her sense of gladness, she only exclaimed, "Oh, where is my father?"

"I have sent him to the toll at the Gemsbock's Pass," replied Sir Eberhard, who had by this time come up the stairs, followed by Brother Peter and the two lay assistants Then, as Christina turned on him her startled eyes in reproach for such thoughtlessness, he came towards her, and, bending his head and opening his hand, he showed on his palm two gold rings. "There, little one," he said; "now shalt thou never again shut me out."

Her senses grew dizzy. "Sir," she faintly said, "this is no place to delude a poor maiden."

"I delude thee not. The brother here waits to wed us."

"Impossible! a burgher maid is not for such as you."

"None but a burgher maid will I wed," returned Sir Eberhard, with all the settled resolution of habits of command. "See, Christina, thou art sweeter and better than any lady in the land. I love thee as never knight loved lady. I love thee so that I have not spoken a word to offend thee when my heart was bursting; and"— as he saw her irrepressible tears—"I think thou lovest me a little."

"Ah!" she gasped with a sob, "let me go."

"Thou canst not go home; there is none here fit to take charge of thee. Or if there were, I would slay him rather than let thee go. No, not so," he said, as he saw how little those words served his cause; "but without thee I were a mad and desperate man. Christina, I will not answer for myself if thou dost not leave this place my wedded wife."

"Oh!" implored Christina, "if you would only betroth me, and woo me like an honourable maiden from my home at Ulm!"

"Betroth thee, ay, and wed thee at once," replied Eberhard, who, all along, even while his words were most pleading, had worn a look and manner of determined authority and strength, good-natured indeed, but resolved. "I am not going to miss my opportunity, or balk the friar."

The friar, who had meantime been making a few arrangements for the ceremony, advanced towards them. He was an easy-going man, who came prepared to do any office that came in his way on such festival days; and peasant marriages at such times were not uncommon. But something now staggered him, and he said, anxiously:

"This maiden looks convent-bred! Herr Reiter, pardon me; but if this be the breaking of a cloister, I can have none of it."

"No such thing," said Eberhad; "she is town-bred, that is all."

"You would swear it, on the holy mass yonder, both of you?" said the friar, still suspiciously.

"Yea," replied Eberhard, "and so dost thou, Christina."

This was the time if ever to struggle against her destiny. The friar would probably have listened to her if she had made any vehement opposition, and if not, a few shrieks would have brought perhaps Father Norbert, and certainly the whole population; but the horror and shame of being found in such a situation, even more than the probability that she might meet with vengeance rather than protection, withheld her. Had she hated and loathed Sir Eberhard, perhaps she had striven harder, but his whole demeanour constrained and quelled her. and the chief effort she made against yielding was the reply, "I am no cloister maid, father, but——"

The "but" was lost in the friar's jovial speech. "Oh, then, all is well! Hast confessed of late?"

"This morning, but——" said Christina, and "This morning," to her great joy, said Eberhard, and, in her satisfaction thereat, her second "but——" was not followed up.

The friar asked their names, and both gave the Christian name alone; then the simple rite was solemnised in its shortest form. Christina had, by very force of surprise and dismay, gone through all without signs of agitation, except the quivering of her whole frame, and the icy coldness of the hand, where Eberhard had to place the ring on each finger in turn.

But each mutual vow was a strange relief to her long-tossed and

K

divided mind, and it was rest indeed to let her affection have its will, and own him indeed as a protector to be loved instead of shunned. When all was over, and he gathered the two little cold hands into his large one, his arm supporting her trembling form, she felt for the moment, poor little thing, as if she could never be frightened again.

Parish registers were not, even had this been a parish church, but Brother Peter asked, when he had concluded, "Well, my son, which of his flock an I to report to your Pfarrer[1] as linked together?"

"The less your tongue wags on that matter till I call on you, the better," was the stern reply. "Look you, no ill shall befall you if you are wise, but remember, against the day I call you to bear witness, that you have this day wedded Baron Eberhard von Adlerstein the younger, to Christina, the daughter of Hugh Sorel, the Esquire of Ulm."

"Thou hast played me a trick, Sir Baron!" said the friar, somewhat dismayed, bit more amused, looking up at Eberhard, who, as Christina now saw, had divested himself of his gilt spurs, gold chain, silvered belt and horn, and eagle's plume, so as to have passed for a simple lanzknecht. "I would have had no such gear as this!"

"So I supposed," said Eberhard cooly.

"Young folks! young folks!" laughed the friar. "Well, so thou hast a pretty, timid lambkin there, Sir Baron. Take care you use her mildly."

Eberhard looked into Christina's face with a smile, that to her, at least, was answer enough; and he held out half a dozen links of his gold chain to the friar, and tossed a coin to each of the lay-brethren.

"Not for the poor friar himself," explained Brother Peter, on receiving this marriage-fee; "it all goes to the weal of the brotherhood."

"As you please," siad Eberhard. "Silence, that is all! And thy friary——?"

"The poor house of St. Francis at Offingen for the present, noble sir," said the priest. "There will you hear of me, if you find me not. And now, fare thee well, my gracious lady. I hope one day thou wilt have more words to thank the poor brother who has made thee a noble baroness."

At that moment a sudden glow and glare of light broke out on the eastern rock, illuminating the fast darkening little church with a flickering glare, that made her start in terror as if the fires of heaven

1 Parson.

were threatening this stolen marriage; but the friar and Eberhard both exclaimed, "The Needfire alight already!" And she recollected how often she had seen these bonfires on Midsummer night shining red on every hill around Ulm. Loud shouts were greeting the uprising flame, and the people gathering thicker and thicker on the slope. The friar undid the door to hasten out into the throng, and Eberhard said he had left his spurs and belt in the hermit's cell, and must return thither, after which he would walk home with his bride.

Eberhard, after his first few words, was silent, and seemed solely absorbed in leading her safely along the rocky path, sometimes lifting her when he thought her in danger of stumbling. It was one of the lightest, shortest nights of the year, and a young moon added to the brightness in open places, while in others it made the rocks and stones cast strange elvish shadows. The distance was not entirely lost; other fires could be seen, like beacons, on every hill, and the few lights in the castle shone out like red fiery eyes in its heavy dark pile of building.

Before entering, Eberhard paused, pulled off his own wedding-ring, and put it into his bosom, and taking his bride's hand in his, did the same for her, and bade her keep the ring till they could wear them openly.

"Alas! then," said Christina, "you would have this secret?"

"Unless I would have to seek thee down the oubliette, my little one," said Eberhard; "or, what might even be worse, see thee burnt on the hillside for bewitching me with thine arts! No, indeed, my darling. Were it only my father, I could make him love thee; but my mother—I could not trust her where she thought the honour of our house concerned. It shall not be for long. Thou knowest we are to make peace with the Kaiser, and then will I get me employment among Kurfurst[1] Albrecht's companies of troops, and then shalt thou prank it as my Lady Freiherrinn, and teach me the ways of cities·"

"Alas! I fear me it has been a great sin!" sighed the poor little wife.

"For thee—thou couldst not help it," said Eberhard; "for me—who knows how many deadly ones it may hinder? Cheer up, little one; no one can harm thee while the secret is kept."

Christina had no choice but submission; but it was a sorry bridal evening, to enter her husband's home in shrinking terror; with the

1 Elector: one of the princes who elected the Emperor.

threat of the oubliette before her, and with a sense of shame and deception hanging upon her, making the wonted scowl of the old baroness cut her with remorse and dread.

She did indeed sit beside her bridegroom at the supper but how little like a bride! even though he pushed the salt-cellar, as if by accident, below her place.

Poor child! After she had crept away to her own room, glad that her father was not yet returned, she wept bitterly over the wrong that she felt she had done to the kind uncle and aunt, who must now look in vain for their little Christina, and would think her lost to them. At least she had had the Church's blessing— but that, strange to say, was regarded, in burgher life before the Reformation, as rather the ornament of a noble marriage than as essential to the civil contract; and a marriage by a priest was regarded by the citizens rather as means of eluding the need of obtaining the parents' consent, than as a more regular and devout manner of wedding. However, Christina felt this the one drop of peace. The blessings and prayers were warm at her heart, and gave her hope. And as to drops of joy, of them there was no lack, for had not she now a right to love Eberhard with all her heart and conscience, and was not it a wonderful love on his part that had made him stoop to the little white-faced burgher maid, despised even by her own father? Oh, better far to wear the maiden's uncovered head for him than the myrtle wreath for any one else!

CHAPTER IV

THE POOR LITTLE unowned bride tried to extort Eberhard's permission to let her father know how it was; but Eberhard laughed, saying he believed the old fox knew just as much as he chose; and, in effect, Sorel, though now and then gratifying his daughter's scruples, by serving as a shield to her meetings with the young baron, never allowed himself to hear a hint of the true state of affairs. This state of things lasted much longer than there had been reason to expect at the time of the marriage. The two Freiherren then intended to set out in a very short time to make their long-talked-of submission to the Emperor at Ratisbon; but, partly from their German tardiness of movement, partly from the obstinate delays interposed by the proud old Freiherrinn, who was averse to the measure, partly from reports that the Court was not yet arrived at Ratisbon, the expedition was again and again deferred, and did not actually take place till September was far advanced.

Poor Christina would have given worlds to go with them, and even entreated to be sent to Ulm with an avowal of her marriage to her uncle and aunt, but of this Eberhard would not hear. He said the Ulmers would thus gain a hostage, and hamper his movements. Eberhard was fully determined to enroll himself in some troop, either Imperial, or, if not, among the Free Companies, among whom men of rank were often found, and he would then fetch or send for his wife and avow her openly, so soon as she should be out of his mother's reach. He longed to leave her father at home, to be some protection to her, but Hugh Sorel was so much the most intelligent and skilful of the retainers as to be absolutely indispensable to the party. The troop numbered about ten men-at-arms, only three being left at home to garrison the castle—namely, Hatto, Hans and Squinting Mätz. If needful, the villagers could always be called in to defend the castle: but of this there was little or no danger—the Eagle's Steps were defence enough in themselves, and the party were not likely to be absent more than a week or ten days—a grievous length of time, poor Christina thought, as she stood straining her eyes on the top of the watch-tower, to watch them as far as possible along the plain.

Reluctantly had she gone down to the noontide meal, feeling, though her husband and father were far less of guardians than they should have been, yet that there was absolute rest, peace, and protection in their presence compared with what it was to be alone with Freiherrinn Kunigunde and her rude women without them. A few sneers on her daintiness and uselessness had led her to make an offer of assisting in the grand chopping of sausage-meat and preparation of winter stores, when one of the maids who had been sent to fetch beer from the cellar came back with startled looks, and the exclamation, "There is the Schneiderlein riding up the Eagle's Ladder upon Freiherr Ebbo's white mare!"

All the women sprang up together, and rushed to the window, whence they could indeed recognise both man and horse; and presently it became plain that both were stained with blood, weary

and spent; indeed, nothing but extreme exhaustion would have
induced the man-at-arms to trust the tired, stumbling horse up such
a perilous path.

Loud were the exclamations. "This shameful expedition! Only
harm could befall. This is thy doing, thou mincing city-girl."

The angry and dismayed cries all blended themselves in confusion
in the ears of the only silent woman present, as, holding herself a
little in the rear of the struggling, jostling little mob of women, who
hardly made way even for their acknowledged lady, she followed
with failing limbs the universal rush to the entrance as soon as man
and horse had mounted the slope and were lost sight of.

A few moments more, and the throng of expectants was at the
foot of the hall steps, just as the lanzknecht reached the arched
entrance. His comrade Hans took his bridle, and almost lifted him
from his horse; he reeled and stumbled as, pale, battered, and bleeding, he tried to advance to Freiherrinn Kunigunde, and, in answer
to her hasty interrogation, faltered out, "Ill news, gracious lady.
We have been set upon by the accursed Schlangenwaldern, and I am
the only living man left."

Christina scarce heard even these last words; senses and powers
alike failed her, and she sank back on the stone steps in a death-like
swoon.

When she came to herself she was lying on her bed, Ursel and
Else, another of the women, busy over her, and Ursel's voice was
saying, "Ah, she is coming round. Look up, sweet lady, and fear
not. You are our gracious Lady Baroness."

"Is he here? Oh, has he said so? Oh, let me see him—Sir
Eberhard," faintly cried Christina with sobbing breath.

"Ah, no, no," said the old woman; "but see here," and she lifted
up Christina's powerless, bloodless hand, and showed her the ring
on the finger. Her bosom had been evidently searched when her
dress was loosened in her swoon, and her ring found and put in its
place. "My dear young Freiherr, the boy that I nursed," and the
old woman's burst of tears brought back the truth to Christina's
reviving senses.

"Oh, tell me," she said, trying to raise herself, "was it indeed so?
Oh, say it was not as he said!"

"Ah, woe's me, woe's me, that it was even so," lamented Ursel;
"but oh, be still; look not so wild, dear lady. The dear, true-hearted
young lord, he spent his last breath in owning you for his true lady,
and in bidding us cherish you and our young baron that is to be.

And the gracious lady below—she owns you; there is no fear of her now; so vex not yourself, dearest, most gracious lady."

Christina did not break out into the wailing and weeping that the old nurse expected; she was still far too much overwhelmed, and she entreated to be told all, lying still, but gazing at Ursel with piteous, bewildered eyes. Ursel and Else helping one another out, tried to tell her, but all they knew was that the party had been surprised at night in a village hostel by the Schlangenwaldern, and all slain, though the young baron had lived long enough to charge the Schneiderlein with his commendation of his wife to his mother; but all particulars had been lost in the general confusion.

"Oh, let me see the Schneiderlein," implored Christina, by this time able to rise and cross the room to the large carved chair; and Ursel turned to her underling, saying, "Tell the Schneiderlein that the gracious Lady Baroness desires his presence."

Else's wooden shoes clattered downstairs, but the next moment she returned. "He cannot come; he is quite spent, and he will let no one touch his arm till Ursel can come, not even to get off his doublet."

"I will go to him," said Christina, and, revived by the sense of being wanted, she moved at once to the turret, where she kept some rag and some ointment. Ursel made no objection further than to look for something that could be at once converted into a widow's veil—being in the midst of her grief quite alive to the need that no matronly badge should be omitted—but nothing came to hand in time, and Christina was descending the stairs, on her way to the kitchen, where she found the fugitive man-at-arms seated on a rough settle, his head and wounded arm resting on the table, while groans of pain, weariness, and impatience were interspersed with imprecations on the stupid, awkward girls who surrounded him.

Pity and the instinct of affording relief must needs take the precedence even of the desire to hear of her husband's fate; and, as the girls hastily whispered, "Here she is!" and the lanzknecht hastily tried to gather himself up, and rise with tokens of respect, she bade him remain still, and let her see what she could do for him. She bade at once that some water should be heated, and some of the broth of the dinner set on the fire; then with the shears at her girdle, and her soft, light fingers, she removed the torn strip of cloth that had been wound round the arm, and cut away the sleeve, showing the arm not broken, but gashed at the shoulder, and thence the whole length grazed and wounded by the descent of the sword down to the wrist. So tender was her touch, that he scarcely winced or moaned under her hand; and, when she proceeded, with Ursel's help, to bathe the wound with the warm water, the relief was such that the wearied man absolutely slumbered during the process, which Christina protracted on that very account. She then dressed and bandaged the arm, and proceeded to skim—as no one else in the castle would do—the basin of soup, with which she then fed her patient as he leant back in the corner of the settle, at first in the same somnolent, half-conscious state in which he had been ever since the relief from the severe pain; but after a few spoonfuls the light and life came back to his eye, and he broke out, "Thanks, thanks, gracious lady! This is the Lady Baroness for me! My young lord was the only wise man! Thanks, lady; now am I my own man again. I am your man, lady, for life or death!" And, before she knew what he was about, the gigantic Schneiderlein had slid down on his knees, seized her hand, and kissed it—the first act of homage to her rank, but most startling and distressing to her. "Nay," she faltered, "prithee do not; thou must rest. Only if—if thou canst only tell me if he, my own dear lord, sent me any greeting, I would wait to hear the rest till thou hast slept."

"Ah! the dog of Schlangenwald!" was the first answer; then, as he continued, "You see, lady, we had ridden merrily as far as Jacob Müller's hostel, the traitor,"—it became plain that he meant to begin at the beginning. There, the Schneiderlein proceeded to say, they put up for the night, entirely unsuspicious of evil; Jacob Müller, who was known to himself, as well as to Sorel and to the others, assuring them that the way was clear to Ratisbon, and that he heard the Emperor was most favourably disposed to any noble who would tender his allegiance. Jacob's liquors were brought out, and were still in course of being enjoyed, when the house was suddenly surrounded by an overpowering number of the retainers of Schlangenwald, with their count himself at their head. He had been evidently resolved to prevent the timely submission of the enemies of his race, and suddenly presenting himself before the elder baron, had challenged him to instantaneous battle, claiming credit to himself for not having surprised them when asleep. The disadvantage had been scarcely less than if this had been the case, for the Adlersteinern were all half intoxicated, and far inferior in numbers—at least, on the showing of the Schneiderlein—and a desperate fight had ended by his being flung aside in a corner, bound fast by the ankles and wrists, the only living prisoner, except his young lord, who, having several terrible wounds, the worst in his chest, was left unbound.

Both lay helpless, untended, and silent, while the revel that had been so fatal to them was renewed by their captors, who finally all sunk into a heavy sleep. The torches were not all spent, and the moonlight shone into the room, when the Schneiderlein, desperate from the agony caused by the ligature round his wounded arm, sat up and looked about him. A knife thrown aside by one of the drunkards lay near enough to be grasped by his bound hands, and he had just reached it when Sir Eberhard made a sign to him to put it into his hand, and therewith contrived to cut the rope round both hands and feet—then pointed to the door.

There was nothing to hinder an escape; the men slept the sleep of the drunken; but the Schneiderlein would have lingered with a hope of saving his master. But Everhard shook his head, and signed again to escape; then, making him bend down close to him, he used all his remaining power to whisper, as he pressed his sword into the retainer's hand:

"Go home; tell my mother—all the world—that Christina Sorel is my wife, wedded on the Friedmund Wake by Friar Peter of Offingen, and if she should bear a child, he is my true and lawful heir. My sword for him—my love to her. And if my mother would not be haunted by me, let her take care of her."

These words were spoken with extreme difficulty, for the nature of the wound made utterance nearly impossible, and each broken sentence cost a terrible effusion of blood. The final words brought on so choking and fatal a gush that, said the Schneiderlein, "he fell back as I tried to hold him up, and I saw that it was all at an end, and a kind and friendly master and lord gone from me. I laid him down, and put his cross on his breast that I had seen him kissing many a time that evening; and I crossed his hands, and wiped the blood from them and his face. And lady, he had put on his ring; I trust the robber caitiffs may have left it to him in his grave. And so I came forth, walking soft, and opening the door in no small dread, not of the snoring swine, but of the dogs without. But happily they were still, and even by the door I saw all our poor fellows stark and stiff."

"My father?" asked Christina.

"Ay, with his head cleft open by the Graf himself. He died like a true soldier, lady, and we have lost the best head among us in him. Well, the knave that should have watched the horses was as drunken as the rest of them, and I made a shift to put the bridle on the white mare and ride off."

Such was the narrative of the Schneiderlein, and all that was left to Christina was the picture of her husband's dying effort to guard her, and the haunting fancy of those long hours of speechless agony on the floor of the hostel, and how direful must have been his fears for her. Sad and overcome, yet not sinking entirely while any work of comfort remained, her heart yearned over her companion in misfortune, the mother who had lost both husband and son; and all her fears of the dread Freiherrinn could not prevent her from bending her steps, termbling and palpitating as she was, towards the hall, to try whether the daughter-in-law's right might be vouchsafed to her, of weeping with the elder sufferer.

The Freiherrinn sat by the chimney, rocking herself to and fro, and holding consultation with Hatto. She started as she saw Christina approaching, and made a gesture of repulsion; but, with the feeling of being past all terror in this desolate moment, Christina stepped nearer, knelt, and, clasping her hands, said, "Your pardon, lady."

"Pardon!" returned the harsh voice, even harsher for very grief, "thou hast naught to fear, girl. As things stand, thou canst not have thy deserts. Dost hear?"

"Ah, lady, it was not such pardon that I meant. If you would let me be a daughter to you."

"A daughter! A wood-carver's girl to be a daughter of Adlerstein!" half laughed the grim baroness. "Hark ye all, this is the Frau Freiherrinn, Freiherr Eberhard's widow, to be honoured as such," she added, raising her voice. "There, girl, thou hast what thou didst strive for. Is not that enough?"

"Alas! lady," said Christina, her eyes swimming in tears, "I would fain have striven to be a comforter, or to weep together."

"What! to bewitch me as thou didst my poor son and daughter, and wellnigh my lord himself! Girl! Girl! Thou knowst I cannot burn thee now; but away with thee; try not my patience too far."

And, more desolate than ever, the crushed and broken-hearted Christina, a widow before she had been owned a wife, returned to the room that was now so full of memories as to be even more home than Master Gottfried's gallery at Ulm.

CHAPTER V

WHO CAN DESCRIBE the dreariness of being snowed-up all the winter with such a mother-in-law as Freiherrinn Kunigunde?

Yet it was well that the snow came early, for it was the best defence of the lonely castle from any attack on the part of the Schlangenwaldern, the Swabian Legaue, or the next heir, Freiherr Kasimir von Adlerstein Wildschloss. The elder baroness had, at least, the merit of a stout heart, and, even with her sadly reduced garrison, feared none of them. Probably the Schlangewald count knew how tough a morsel the castle was like to prove, and Wildschloss was serving at a distance, for nothing was heard of either during the short interval while the roads were still open. During this time an attempt had been made through Father Norbert to ascertain what had become of the corpses of the two barons and their followers, and it had appeared that the count had carried them all off from the inn, no doubt to adorn his castle with their limbs, or to present them to the Emperor in evidence of his zeal for order.

Christina had some consoling intercourse with the priest while all this was pending; but throughout the winter she was entirely cut off from every creature save the inmates of the castle, where, as far as the old lady was concerned, she only existed on sufferance, and all her meekness and gentleness could not win for her more than the barest toleration.

That Eberhard had for a few hours survived his father, and that thus the Freiherrin Christina was as much the dowager baroness as Kunigunde herself, was often insisted on in the kitchen by Ursel, Hatto, and the Schneiderlein, whom Christina had unconsciously rendered her most devoted servant, not only by her daily care of his wound, but by her kind, courteous words, and by her giving him his proper name of Heinz, dropping the absurd *nom de guerre* of the Schneiderlein, or little tailor, which had been originally conferred on him in allusion to the valiant Tailorling who boasted of having killed seven flies at a blow, and had been carried on chiefly because of the contradiction between such a title and his huge,

brawny strength and fierce courage. He would have died to serve
her, and she might have headed an opposition party in the castle,
had she not been quite indifferent to all save her grief; and, except
by sitting above the salt at the empty table, she laid no claim to any
honours or authority, and was more seldom than ever seen beyond
what was now called her own room.

At last, when for the second time she was seeing the snow wreaths
dwindle, and the drops shine forth in moisture again, while the
mountain paths were set free by the might of the springtide sun,
she spoke almost for the first time with authority, as she desired
Heinz to saddle her mule, and escort her to join in the Easter mass
at the Blessed Friedmund's Chapel. It was a glorious, sparkling
Easter Day, lovely blue sky above, herbage and flowers glistening
below, snow dazzling in the hollows, peasants assembling in holiday
garb, and all rejoicing. Even the lonely widow, in her heavy veil
and black mufflings, took hope back to her heart, and smiled when
at the church door a little child came timidly up to her with a madder-
tinted Easter egg—a gift once again like the happy home customs of
Ulm. She gave the child a kiss—she had nothing else to give, but
the sweet face sent it away strangely glad.

The festival mass in all its exultation was not fully over, when
anxious faces began to be seen at the door, and whisperings went
round, and many passed out. Nobody at Adlerstein was particular
about silence in church, and, when the service was not in progress,
voices were not even lowered, and, after many attempts on the part
of the Schneiderlein to attract the attention of his mistress, his
voice immediately succeeded the *Ite missa est*.[1] "Gracious lady, we
must be gone. Your mule is ready. There is a party at the Debateable Ford, whether Schlangewald or Wildschloss we know not yet,
but either way you must be the first thing placed in safety."

Christina turned deadly pale. Sheltered as her girlhood had
been in the quiet city, she had never been brought in contact with
warfare, and her nervous, timid temperament made the thought
most appalling and frightful to her, certain as she was that the old
baroness would resist to the uttermost; and a shudder passed over
her whenever the serfs, hastily summond to augment the garrison,
came hurrying down the path, or turning aside into the more rugged
and shorter descents.

Even when she crept up the castle stairs, she was met with an
angry rebuke for having taken away the Schneiderlein, by far the

[1] The last words of the Service: "Go, mass is over."

most availing among the scanty remnant of the retainers of Adler-stein. Attempting no answer, and not even daring to ask from what quarter came the alarm, Christina made her way out of the turmoil to that chamber of her own, the scene of so much fear and sorrow, and yet of some share of peace and happiness. But from the window, near the fast subsiding waters of the Debateable Ford, could plainly be seen the small troop of warriors, of whom Jobst the Kohler had brought immediate intelligence. The sun glistened on their armour, and a banner floated gaily on the wind; but they were a fearful sight to the inmates of the lonely castle.

A stout heart was, however, Kunigunde's best endowment; and she arranged and armed her garrison, perfectly resolved against any submission, and confident in the strength of her castle; nay, not without a hope of revenge either against Schlangenwald or Wild-schloss, whom, as a degenerate Adlerstein, she hated only less than the slayer of her husband and son.

The afternoon of Easter Day passed away without any movement on the part of the enemy, and it was not till the following day that they could be seen struggling through the ford, and preparing to ascend the mountain.

The new-comers could hardly have had any hostile intentions, for, though well armed and accoutred, their numbers did not exceed twenty-five. The banner borne at their head was an azure one, with a white eagle, and their leader could be observed looking with amazement at the top of the watch-tower, where the same eagle had that morning been hoisted for the first time since the fall of the two Freiherren.

So soon as the ascent had been made, the leader wound his horn, and, before the echoes had died away among the hills, Hatto, acting as seneschal, was demanding his purpose.

"I am Kasimir von Adlerstein Wildschloss," was the reply. "I have hitherto been hindered by stress of weather from coming to take possession of my inheritance. Admit me, that I may arrange with the widowed Frau Freiherrin as to her dower and residence."

"The widowed Frau Freiherrinn, born of Adlerstein," returned Hatto, "thanks the Freiherr von Adlerstein Wildschloss; but she holds the castle as guardian to the present head of the family, the Freiherr von Adlerstein.

"It is false, old man," exclaimed Wildschloss; "the Freiherr had no other son."

"No," said Hatto, "but Freiherr Eberhard hath left us twin heirs, our young lords, for whom we hold this castle."

"This trifling will not serve!" sternly spoke the knight. "Eberhard von Adlerstein died unmarried."

"Not so," returned Hatto, "our gracious Frau Freiherrinn, the younger, was wedded to him at the last Friedmund Wake, by the special blessing of our good patron, who would not see our house extinct."

"I must see thy lady, old man," said Sir Kasimir impatiently, not in the least crediting the story. She consented to an interview with the claimant of the inheritance, and descended to the gateway for the purpose. The court was at its cleanest, the thawing snow having newly washed away its impurities, and her proud figure, under her black hood and veil, made an imposing appearance as she stood tall and defiant in the archway.

Sir Kasimir was a handsome man of about thirty, of partly Polish descent, and endowed with Slavonic grace and courtesy, and he had likewise been employed in negotiations with Burgundy, and had acquired much polish and knowledge of the world.

"Lady," he said, "I regret to disturb and intrude on a mourning family, but I am amazed at the tidings I have heard; and I must pray of you to confirm them."

"I thought they would confound you," composedly replied Kunigunde.

"And pardon me, lady, but the Diet is very nice in requiring full proofs. I would be glad to learn what lady was chosen by my deceased cousin Eberhard."

"The lady is Christina, daughter of his esquire, Hugh Sorel, of an honourable family at Ulm."

"Ha! I know who and what Sorel was!" exclaimed Wildschloss. "Lady cousin, thou wouldst not stain the shield of Adlerstein with owning aught that cannot bear the examination of the Diet!"

"Sir Kasimir," said Kunigunde proudly, "had I known the truth ere my son's death, I had strangled the girl with mine own hands! But I learnt it only by his dying confession; and, had she been a beggar's child, she was his wife, and her babies are his heirs."

"I must see the Frau herself," said Wildschloss.

For one moment Kunigunde hesitated, but suddenly a look of malignant satisfaction crossed her face. She spoke a few words to Squinting Mätz, and then replied that Sir Kasimir should be allowed to satisfy himself, but that she could admit no one else into the castle;

hers was a widow's household, the twins were only a few hours old, and she could not open her gates to admit any person besides himself.

So resolved on judging for himself was Adlerstein Wildschloss that all this did not stagger him; for, even if he had believed the old lady's story, there would have been no sense of intrusion in such a visit to the mother.

But when Baron Kasimir had clanked up the turret stairs, and had been led to the bedside, he was completely taken by surprise. Instead of the great, flat-faced, coarse comeliness of a German wench, he saw a delicate, lily-like face, white as ivory, and the soft, sweet brown eyes under their drooping lashes, so full of innocence and sad though thankfully content, with her arm encircling the two little swaddled babes, whose red faces and bald heads alone were allowed to appear above their mummy-like wrappings; and he could only make an obeisance lower and infinitely more respectful than that with which he had favoured the Baroness née von Adlerstein, with a few words of inquiry and apology.

"Which of them is the head of our family?" he added, looking at the two undistinguishable little chrysalises, so exactly alike that Christina herself was obliged to look for the black ribbon, on which a medal had been hung, round the neck of the elder. Sir Kasimir put one knee to the ground as he kissed the red cheek of the infant and the white hand of the mother.

"Lady cousin," he said to Kunigunde, who had stood by all this time with an anxious, uneasy, scowling expression on her face, "I am satisfied. I own this babe as the true Freiherr von Adlerstein, and far be it from me to trouble his heritage. Rather point out the way in which I may serve you and him. Shall I represent all to the Emperor, and obtain his wardship, so as to be able to protect you from any attacks by the enemies of the house?

"Thanks, sir," returned the elder lady severely, seeing Christina's gratified, imploring face. "The right line of Adlerstein can take care of itself without greedy guardians appointed by usurpers. Our submission has never been made, and the Emperor cannot dispose of our wardship."

And Kunigunde looked defiant, regarding herself and her grandson as quite as good as the Emperor, and ready to blast her daughter-in-law with her eyes for murmuring gratefully and wistfully, "Thanks, noble sir, thanks!"

"Let me at least win a friendly right in my young cousins," said Sir Kasimir. "They are not baptized? Let me become their godfather."

Christina's face was all joy and gratitude, and even the grand-mother made no objection; in fact, it was the babes' only chance of a noble sponsor; and Father Norbert, who had already been making ready for the baptism, was sent for from the hall. Kunigunde, meantime, moved about restlessly, went half-way down the stairs, and held counsel with some one there; Ursel, likewise, bustled about, and Sir Kasimir remained seated on the chair that had been placed for him near Christina's bed.

She was again to thank him, and add, "It may be that you will have more cause than the lady grandmother thinks to remember your offer of protection to my poor orphans. Their father and grandfather were, in very deed, on their way to make submission."

"That is well known to me," said Sir Kasimir. "Lady, I will do all in my power for you. The Emperor shall hear the state of things; and, while no violence is offered to travellers," he added, lowering his tone, "I doubt not he will wait for full submission till this young baron be of age to tender it."

"We are scarce in force to offer violence," said Christina, sighing. "I have no power to withstand the Lady Baroness. I am like a stranger here; but oh, sir, if the Emperor and Diet will be patient with this desolate house, my babes shall strive to requite their mercy by loyalty. And the blessing of the widow and fatherless will fall on you, most generous knight," she added fervently, holding out her hand.

"I would I could do more for you," said the knight. "Ask, and all I can do is at your service."

"Ah, sir," cried Christina, her eyes brightening, "there is one most inestimable service you could render me—to let my uncle, Master Gottfried, the wood-carver of Ulm, know where I am, and of my state, and of my children. It is eighteen months since they had any tidings from her who was as a daughter to them."

"I will see them myself," said Kasimir; "I know the name. Carved not Master Gottfried the stall-work at Augsburg?"

"Yes, indeed!" exclaimed Christina. "Oh, sir, thanks indeed! Bear to the dear, dear uncle and aunt their child's duteous greetings, and tell them she loves them with all her heart, and prays them to forgive her, and to pray for her and her little ones! And," she added, "my uncle may not have learnt how his brother, my father, died by his lord's side. Oh, pray him to have masses sung for my father and my own dear lord."

As she promised, Ursel came to make the babes ready for their baptism, and Sir Kasimir moved away towards the window. Ursel was looking uneasy and dismayed, and, as she bent over her mistress, she whispered, "Lady, the Schneiderlein sends you word that Mätz has called him to help in removing the props of the door you wot of when *he* yonder steps across it. He would know if it be your will?"

The oubliette! This was Frau Kunigunde's usage of the relative who was doing his best for the welfare of her grandson's! Christina's whole countenance looked so frozen with horror, that Ursel felt as if she had killed her on the spot; but the next moment a flash of relief came over the pale features, and the trembling lip commanded itself to say, "My best thanks to good Heinz! Say to him that I forbid it. If he loves the life of his master's children, he will abstain! Tell him so. My blessings on him if this knight leave the castle safe, Ursel." And her terrified, earnest eyes impelled Ursel to hasten to do her bidding; but whether it had been executed, there was no knowing, for almost immediately the Freiherrinn and Father Norbert entered, and Ursel returned with them. Nay, the message given, who could tell if Heinz would be able to act upon it?

Seldom could such a christening have taken place as that of which Christina's bedroom was the scene—the mother scarcely able even to think of the holy sacrament for the horror of knowing that the one sponsor was already exulting in the speedy destruction of the other; and, poor little feeble thing, rallying the last remnants of her severely-tried powers to prevent the crime at the most terrible of risks.

The elder babe received from his grandmother the hereditary name of Eberhard, but Sir Kasimir looked at the mother inquiringly, ere he gave the other to the priest. Christina had wellnigh said, "Oubliette," but recalling herself in time, she feebly uttered the name she had longed after from the moment she had known that two sons had been her Easter gift, "Gottfried," after her beloved uncle. But Kunigunde caught the sound, and exclaimed, "No son of Adlerstein shall bear a base craftsman's name. Call him Racher (the avenger)"; and in the word there already rang a note of victory and revenge that made Christina's blood run cold. Sir Kasimir marked her trouble. "The lady mother loves not the sound," he said kindly. "Lady, have you any other wish? Then will I call him Friedmund."

Christina had almost smiled. To her the omen was of the best. Baron Friedmund had been the last common ancestor of the two branches of the family, the patron saint was so called, his wake was her wedding-day; the sound of the word imported peace. And so the second little baron received the name of Friedmund, and then the Knight of Wildschloss, perceiving, with consideration rare in a warrior, that the mother looked worn out and feverish, at once prepared to kiss her hand and take leave.

"One more favour, Sir Knight," she said, lifting up her head, while a burning spot rose on either cheek, "I beg of you to take my two babes down, in your own arms, and show them to your men, owning them as your kinsmen and godsons."

Sir Kasimir looked exceedingly amazed, as if he thought the lady's senses taking leave of her, and Dame Kunigunde broke out into declarations that it was absurd, and she did not know what she was talking of; but she repeated almost with passion, "Take them, take them; you know not how much depends on it." Ursel, with unusual readiness of wit, signed and whispered that the young mother must be humoured; till the knight, in a good-natured, confused way, submitted to receive the two little bundles in his arms, while he gave place to Kunigunde, who hastily stepped before him in a manner that made Christina trust that her precaution would be effectual.

The room was reeling round with her. The agony of those few minutes was beyond all things unspeakable. What had seemed just before like a certain way of saving the guest, without real danger to her children, now appeared instead the most certain destruction to all, and herself the unnatural mother who had doomed her new-born babes for a stranger's sake. She could not even pray; she would have shrieked to have them brought back, but her voice was dead within her, her tongue clave to the roof of her mouth, ringings in her ears hindered her even from listening to the descending steps. She lay as one dead, when ten minutes afterwards the cry of one of her babes struck on her ear, and the next moment Ursel stood beside her, laying them down close to her, and saying exultingly, "Safe! safe out at the gate, and down the hillside, and my old lady ready to gnaw off her hands for spite!"

CHAPTER VI

THE GRANDMOTHER HAD softened for a few moments at the birth of the children, with satisfaction at obtaining twice as much as she had hoped; but the frustration of her vengeance upon Kasimir of Adlerstein Wildschloss had renewed all her hatred, and she had no scruple in abusing "the burgher-woman" to the whole household for her artful desire to captivate another nobleman. It was the favourite reproach whenever she chose to vent her fury on the mute, blushing weeping young widow, whose glance at her babies was her only appeal against the cruel accusation.

On Midsummer eve, Heinz the Schneiderlein, who had all day been taking toll from the various attendants at the Friedmund Wake, came up and knocked at the door. He had a bundle over his shoulder and a bag in his hand, which last he offered to her.

"The toll! It is for the Lady Baroness."

"You are my Lady Baroness. I levy toll for this my young lord."

"Take it to her, good Heinz, she must have the charge, and needless strife I will not breed."

The angry notes of Dame Kunigunde came up: "How now, knave Schneiderlein! Cone down with the toll instantly. It shall not be tampered with! Down, I say, thou thief of a tailor."

"Go; prithee go, vex her not," entreated Christina.

"Coming, lady!" shouted Heinz, and, disregarding all further objurgations from beneath, he proceeded to deposit his bundle, and explain that it had been entrusted to him by a pedlar from Ulm, who would likewise take charge of anything she might have to send in return; and he then ran down just in time to prevent a domiciliary visit from the old lady.

From Ulm! The very sound was joy; and Christina with trembling hands unfastened the cords and stitches that secured the canvas covering, within which lay folds on folds of linen, and in the midst a rich silver goblet, long ago brought by her father from Italy, a few of her own possessions, and a letter from her uncle secured with black floss silk, with a black seal.

339

She kissed it with transport, but the contents were somewhat chilling by their grave formality. The opening address to the "honour-worthy Lady Baroness and love-worthy niece," conveyed to her a doubt on good Master Gottfried's part whether she were still truly worthy of love. The slaughter at Jacob Muller's had been already known to him, and he expressed himself as relieved, but greatly amazed, at the information he had received from the Baron of Adlerstein Wildschloss, who had visited him at Ulm.

Freiherr von Adlerstein Wildschloss had further requested him to make known that, feud-briefs having regularly passed between Schlangenwald and Adlerstein, and the two barons not having been within the peace of the empire, no justice could be exacted for their deaths; yet, in consideration of the tender age of the present heirs, the question of forfeiture or submission should be waived till they could act for themselves, and Schlangenwald should be withheld from injuring them so long as no molestation was offered to travellers. It was plain that Sir Kasimir had well and generously done his best to protect the helpless twins, and he sent respectful but cordial greetings to their mother. These, however, were far less heeded by her than the coldness of her uncle's letter. She had drifted beyond the reckoning of her kindred, and they were sending her her property and bridal linen, as if they had done with her, and had lost their child in the robber-baron's wife. Yet at the end there was a touch of old times in offering a blessing, should she still value it, and the hopes that heaven and the saints would comfort her; "for surely, thou poor child, thou must have suffered much, and, if thou willest still to write to thy city kin, thine aunt would rejoice to hear that thou and thy babes were in good health."

Whenever her little ones left her any leisure, she spent this, her first wedding-day, in writing so earnest and loving a letter as must assure the good burgomaster that, except in having suffered much and loved much, his little Christina was not changed since she had left him.

No answer could be looked for till another wake-day; but, when it came, it was full and loving, and therewith were sent a few more of her favourite books, a girdle, and a richly-scented pair of gloves, together with two ivory boxes of comfits, and two little purple silk, gold-edged, straight narrow garments, and tight round brimless lace caps, for the two little barons. Nor did henceforth a wake-day pass by without bringing some such token, not only delightful as gratifying Christina's affection by the kindness that suggested them, but supplying absolute wants in the dire stress of poverty at Schloss Adlerstein. Christina durst not tell her mother-in-law of the terms on which they were unmolested. Indeed, while the Count of Schlangenwald was in the neighbourhood, his followers took care to secure all that could be captured at the Debateable Ford, and the broken forces of Adlerstein would have been insane had they attempted to contend with such superior numbers. That the castle remained unattacked was attributed by the elder baroness to it own merits; nor did Christina undeceive her. They had no intercourse with the outer world, except that once a pursuivant arrived with a formal intimation from their kinsman, the Baron of Adlerstein Wildschloss, of his marriage with the noble Fraulein, Countess Valeska von Trautbach, and a present of a gay dagger for each of his godsons.

The last silver cup the castle had possessed had to be given as a reward to the pursuivant. The cup could indeed be ill spared. The cattle and swine, the dues of the serfs, and the yearly toll at the wake were the sole resources of the household; and though there was no lack of meat, milk, and black bread, sufficient garments could scarce be come by, with all the spinning of the household, woven by the village webster, of whose time the baronial household, by prescriptive right, owned the lion's share.

These matters little troubled the two beings in whom Christina's heart was wrapped up. Though running about barefooted and bareheaded, they were healthy, handsome, straight-limbed, noble-looking creatures, so exactly alike, and so inseparable, that no one except herself could tell one from the other save by the medal of Our Lady worn by the elder, and the little cross carved by the mother for the younger. They were tall for their age, but with the slender make of their foreign ancestry; and, though their fair rosy complexions were brightened by mountain mists and winds, their rapidly darkening hair, and large liquid brown eyes, told of their Italian blood.

They were never quarrelsome. Either from the influence of her gentleness, or from their absolute union, they could do and enjoy nothing apart, and would as soon have though of their right and left hands falling out as of Ebbo and Friedel disputing. Ebbo, however, was always the right hand. *The* Freiherr, as he had been called from the first, had, from the time he could sit at the table at all, been put into the baronial chair with the eagle carved at the back; every member of the household from his grandmother downwards, placed him foremost, and Friedel followed their example, at the less loss to himself, as his hand was always in Ebbo's, and all their doings were in common. Sometimes, however, the mother doubted whether there would have been this perfect absence of all contest had the medal of the firstborn chanced to hang round Friedmund's neck instead of Eberhard's.

> " It fell about the Lammas tide,
> When moor men win their hay,"

that all the serfs of Adlerstein were collected to collect their lady's hay to be stored for the winter's fodder of the goats, and of poor Sir Eberhard's old white mare, the only steed as yet ridden by the young barons.

The boys were fourteen years old. So monotonous was their mother's life that it was chiefly their growth that marked the length of her residence in the castle. Otherwise there had been no change, except that the elder baroness was more feeble in her limbs, and still more irritable and excitable in temper. There were no events, save a few hunting adventures of the boys, or the yearly correspondence with Ulm; and the same life continued, of shrinking in dread from the old lady's tyrannous dislike.

The boys' love was entirely given to their mother. Far from diminishing with their dependence on her, it increased with the sense of protection; and, now that they were taller than herself, she seemed to be cherished by them more than ever. Moreover, she was their oracle. Quick-witted and active-minded, loving books the more because their grandmother thought signing a feud-letter the utmost literary effort becoming to a noble, they never rested till they had acquired all that their mother could teach them; or rather, they then became more restless than ever. Long ago had her whole store of tales and ballads become so familiar, by repetition, that the boys could correct her in the smallest variation; reading and writing were mastered as for pleasure; and the *Nuremberg Chronicle*, with its wonderful woodcuts, excited such a passion of curiosity that they must needs conquer its Latin and read it for themselves.

The soft dreamy eye was becoming Friedel's characteristic, as fire and keenness distinguished his brother's glance. When at rest, the twins could be known apart by their expression, though in all other respects they were as alike as ever; and let Ebbo look thoughtful or Friedel eager, and they were again undistinguishable; and, indeed, they were constantly changing looks. They shared all occupations; and it was by the merest shade that Ebbo excelled with the weapon, and Friedel with the book or tool. For the artist nature was in them, not intentionally excited by their mother, but far too strong to be easily discouraged. They had long daily gazed at Ulm in the distance, hoping to behold the spire completed; and the illustrations in their mother's books excited a strong desire to imitate them. The floor had often been covered with charcoal outlines even before Christina was persuaded to impart the rules she had learnt from her uncle; and her carving-tools were soon seized upon.

One regret their mother had, almost amounting to shame. Every virtuous person believed in the efficacy of the rod; but her sons had never felt the weight of a blow, except once when their grandmother caught them carving a border of eagles and doves round the hall table, and then Ebbo had returned the blow with all his might. As to herself, if she ever worked herself up to attempt chastisement, the baroness was sure to fall upon her for insulting the noble birth of her sons, and thus gave them a triumph far worse for them than impunity. In truth, the boys had their own way, or rather the baron had his way, and his way was Baron Friedmund's. Poor, bare, and scanty as were all the surroundings of their life, everything was done to feed their arrogance, with only one influence to counteract their education in pride and violence—a mother's influence, indeed, but her authority was studiously taken from her, and her position set at naught, with no power save what she might derive from their love and involuntary honour, and the sight of the pain caused her by their wrongdoings.

And so the summer's hay-harvest was come.

The full muster of serfs appeared, for Frau Kunigunde admitted of no excuses, and the sole absentee was a widow who lived on the ledge of the mountain next above that on which the castle stood. Her son reported her to be very ill, and with tears in his eyes entreated Baron Friedel to obtain leave for him to return to her, since she was quite alone in her solitary hut, with no one even to give her a drink of water. Friedel rushed with the entreaty to his grandmother, but she laughed it to scorn. Lazy Koppel only wanted an excuse, or, if not, the woman was old and useless, and men could not be spared.

Grieved and discomfited, Friedel betook himself to his mother and brother.

"Foolish lad not to have come to me!" said the young baron. "Where is he? I'll send him at once."

But Christina interposed an offer to go and take Koppel's place beside his mother, and her skill was so much prized over all the mountain-side, that the alternative was gratefully accepted, and she was escorted up the steep path by her two boys to the hovel, where she spent the day in attendance on the sick woman.

Evening came on, the patient was better, but Koppel did not return, nor did the young barons come to fetch their mother home, and, beginning to suspect something amiss, she at length set off, and half-way down met Koppel, who replied to her question, "Ah, then, the gracious lady has not heard of our luck. Excellent booty, and two prisoners! The young baron has been a hero indeed, and has won himself a knightly steed." And, on her further interrogation, he added, that an unusually rich but small company had been reported by Jobst the Kohler to be on the way to the ford, where he had skilfully prepared a stumbling-block. The gracious baroness had caused Hatto to call all the haymakers together, and they had fallen on the travellers by the straight path down the crag. "Ach! did not the young baron spring like a young antelope? And in midstream down came their pack-horses and their wares? Some of them took to flight, but, *pfui*, there were enough for my young lord to show his mettle upon. Such a prize the saints have not sent since the old baron's time."

Christina pursued her walk in dismay at this new beginning of freebooting in its worst form, overthrowing all her hopes. The best thing that could happen would be the immediate interference of the Swabian League, while her sons were too young to be personally held guilty. Yet this might involve ruin and confiscation; and, apart from all consequences, she bitterly grieved that the stain of robbery should have fallen on her hitherto innocent sons.

Every peasant she met greeted her with praises of their young lord, and, when she mounted the hall steps, she found the floor strewn with bales of goods.

"Mother," cried Ebbo, flying up to her, "have you heard? I have a horse! and Friedel is to ride him by turns with me. Where is Friedel? And, mother, Heinz said I struck as good a stroke as any of them; and I have a sword for Friedel now. Why does he not come? And, motherling, this is for you, a gown of velvet, a real black velvet, that will make you fairer than Our Lady at the convent. Come to the window and see it, mother dear."

The boy was so joyously excited that she could hardly withstand his delight, but she did not move.

"Don't you like the velvet?" he continued. "We always said that the first prize we won, the motherling should wear velvet. Do but look at it."

"Woe is me, my Ebbo!" she sighed, bending to kiss his brow.

He understood her at once, coloured, and spoke hastily and in defiance. "It was in the river, mother, the horses fell; it is our right."

"Fairly, Ebbo?" she asked in a low voice.

"Nay, mother, if Jobst *did* hide a branch in mid-stream, it was no doing of mine; and the horses fell. The Schlangenwaldern don't even wait to let them fall. We cannot live, if we are to be so nice and dainty."

"Ah! my son, I thought not to hear you call mercy and honesty mere niceness."

"What do I hear?" exclaimed Frau Kunigunde, entering. "Are you chiding and daunting this boy, as you have done with the other?"

"My mother may speak to me!" cried Ebbo hotly.

"And quench thy spirit with whining fooleries! Take the baron's bounty, woman, and vex him not after his first knightly exploit."

"Heaven knows, and Ebbo knows," said the trembling Christina, "that, were it a knightly exploit, I were the first to exult."

"Thou! thou craftsman's girl! dost presume to call in question the knightly deeds of a noble house! There!" cried the furious baroness, striking her face. "Now! dare to be insolent again." Her hand was uplifted for another blow, when it was grasped by Everhard, and, the next moment, he likewise held the other hand, with youthful strength far exceeding hers. She had often struck his mother before, but not in his presence, and the greatness of the shock seemed to make him cool and absolutely dignified.

"Be still, grandame," he said. "No mother, I am not hurting her," and indeed the surprise seemed to have taken away her rage and volubility, and unresistingly she allowed him to seat her in a chair. Still holding her arm, he made his clear voice resound through the hall, saying, "Retainers all, know that, as I am your lord, so is my honoured mother lady of the castle, and she is never to be gainsaid, let her say or do what she will."

"You are right, Herr Freiherr," said Heinz. "The Frau Christina is our gracious and beloved dame. Long live the Freiherrin Christina!" And the voices of almost all the serfs present mingled in the cry.

"And hear you all," continued Eberhard, "she shall rule all, and never be trampled on more. Grandame, you understand?"

The old woman seemed confounded, and cowered in her chair without speaking. Christina, almost dismayed by this silence, would have suggested to Ebbo to say something kind or consoling; but at that moment she was struck with alarm by his renewed inquiry for his brother.

"Friedel! Was not he with thee?"

"No; I never saw him!"

Ebbo flew up the stairs, and shouted for his brother; then, coming down, gave orders for the men to go out on the mountain-side, and search and call. He was hurrying with them, but his mother caught his arm. "Oh, Ebbo, how can I let you go? It is dark, and the crags are so perilous!"

"Mother, I cannot stay!" and the boy flung his arms round her neck, and whispered in her ear, "Friedel said it would be a treacherous attack, and I called him a craven. Oh, mother, we never parted thus before! Oh, where is he?"

Infected by the boy's despairing voice, yet relieved that Friedel at least had withstood the temptation, Christina still held Ebbo's hand, and descended the steps with him. The clear blue sky was fast showing the stars, and into the evening stillness echoed the long, loud calls, cast back from the other side of the ravine. Ebbo tried to raise his voice, but broke down in the shout, and, choked with agitation, said, "Let me go, mother. None know his haunts as I do!"

"Hark!" she said, only grasping him tighter.

Thinner, shriller, clearer came a far-away cry from the heights, and Ebbo thrilled from head to foot, then sent up another pealing mountain shout, responded to by a call so pitched as to be plainly not an echo. "Towards the Red Eyrie," said Hans.

"He will have been to the Ptarmigan's Pool," said Ebbo, sending up his voice again, in hopes that the answer would sound less distant; but, instead of this, its intonations conveyed, to these adepts in mountain language, that Friedel stood in need of help.

"Up after him!" said Ebbo, emitting a variety of shouts intimating speedy aid, and receiving a halloo in reply. Equipped with a rope and sundry torches of pinewood, Heinz and two of the serfs were speedily ready, and Christina implored her son to let her come so far as where she should not impede the others. He gave her his arm, and Heinz held his torch so as to guide her up a winding path, not in itself very steep, but which she could never have climbed had daylight shown her what it overhung. Guided by the constant exchange of calls, they reached a height where the wind blew cold and wild, and Ebbo pointed to an intensely black shadow overhung by a peak rising like the gable of a house into the sky. "Yonder lies the tarn, he said. "Don't stir. This way lies the cliff. Fried—mund!"

"Here!—this way! Under the Red Eyrie," called back the wanderer; and steering their course round the rocks above the pool, the rescuers made their way towards the base of the peak, which was the summit of the mountain, the top of the Eagle's Ladder, the highest step of which they had attained. The peak towered over them, and beneath, the castle lights seemed as if it would be easy to let a stone fall straight down on them.

Friedel's cry seemed to come from under their feet. "I am here! I am safe; only it grew so dark that I durst not climb up or down."

The Schneiderlein explained that he would lower down a rope, which, when fastened round Friedel's waist, would enable him to climb safely up; and, after a breathless space, the torchlight shone upon the longed-for face, and Friedel springing on the path cried, "The mother!—and here!"

"Oh, Friedel, where have you been? What is this in your arms?"

He showed them a little white kid.

"Whence is it, Friedel?"..

He pointed to the peak, saying "I was lying on my back by the tarn, when my lady eagle came sailing overhead, so low that I could see this poor little thing, and hear it bleat."

"Thou has been to the Eyrie—the inaccessible Eyrie!" exclaimed Ebbo, in amazement.

"That's a mistake. It is not hard after the first," said Friedel. "I only waited to watch the old birds out again."

"Robbed the eagles! And the young ones?"

"Well," said Friedmund, as if half ashamed, "they were twin eaglets, and their mother had left them, and I felt as though I could not harm them; so I only bore off their provisions, and stuck some feathers in my cap. But by that time the sun was down, and soon I could not see my footing; and, when I found that I had missed the path, I thought I had best nestle in the nook where I was, and wait for day."

Not a single word passed between them upon Ebbo's exploits. Whether Friedel had seen all from the heights, or whether he intuitively perceived that his brother preferred silence, he held his peace, and both were solely occupied in assisting their mother down the pass, the difficulties of which were far more felt now than in the excitement of the ascent.

Ursel reported that Dame Kunigunde had scarcely spoken again, but had retired, like one stunned, into her bed. Friedel was half asleep after the exertions of the day; Ebbo did not speak, and both soon betook themselves to their little turret chamber within their mother's.

CHAPTER VII

"FRIEDEL, WAKE!"

"Is it day?" said Friedel, slowly wakening, and crossing himself as he opened his eyes. "Surely the sun is not up?"

"We must be before the sun!" said Ebbo, who was on his feet, beginning to dress himself. "Hush, and come! Do not wake the mother."

Carrying their shoes, they crossed their mother's chamber, and crept downstairs. Ebbo muttered to his brother, "Stand thou still there, and pray the saints to keep her asleep"; and then, with bare feet, moved noiselessly behind the wooden partition that shut off his grandmother's box-bedstead from the rest of the hall. She lay asleep, with open mouth, snoring loudly, and on her pillow lay the bunch of castle keys, that was always carried to her at night. It was a moment of peril when Ebbo touched it; but he had nerved himself to be both steady and dexterous, and he secured it without a jingle, and then, without entering the hall, descended into a passage lit by a rough opening cut in the rock. Friedel, who began to comprehend, followed him close, and at the first door he fitted in, and with some difficulty, turned a key, and pushed open the door of a vault, where morning light, streaming through the grated window, showed two captives, who had started to their feet, and now stood regarding the pair in the doorway as if they thought their dreams were multiplying the young baron who had led the attack.

"Signori——" began the principal of the two; but Ebbo spoke.

"Sir, you have been brought here by mistake in the absence of my mother, the lady of the castle. If you will follow me, I will restore all that is within my reach, and put you on your way."

The merchant's knowledge of German was small, but the purport of the words was plain, and he gladly left the damp, chilly vault. Ebbo pointed to the bales that strewed the hall. "Take all that can be carried," he said. "Here is your sword and your purse," he said. "I will bring out your horse and lead you to the pass."

"Give him food," whispered Friedel; but the merchant was too anxious to have any appetite. Only he faltered in broken German a proposal to pay his respects to the Signora Castellana,[1] to whom he owed so much.

"No! *Dormit in lecto*,"[2] said Ebbo, with a sudden inspiration caught from the Latinised sound of some of the Italian words, but colouring desperately as he spoke.

The Latin proved most serviceable, and the merchant understood that his property was restored, and made all speed to gather it together and transport it to the stable. One or two of his beasts of burden had been lost in the fray, and there were more packages than could well be carried by the merchant, his servant, and his horse. Ebbo gave the aid of the old white mare—now very white indeed—and in truth the boys pitied the merchant's fine young bay for being put to base trading uses.

They patted the creature's neck with such fervent admiration that the merchant longed to present it to them, when he saw that the old white mare was the sole steed they possessed, and watched their tender guidance both of her and of the bay up the rocky path so familiar to them.

"But, ah, *signorini miei*,[3] I am an *infelice*,[4] *infelicissimo*, ever persecuted by *le Fate*."

"By whom? A count like Schlangenwald?" asked Ebbo.

"*Das Schicksal*,"[5] whispered Friedel.

"Three long, miserable years did I spend as a captive among the Moors, having lost all, my ships and all I had, and being forced to row their galleys."

"Galleys!" exclaimed Ebbo; "there are some pictured in our *World History before Carthage*. Would that I could see one."

"The signorino would soon have seen his fill, were he between the decks, chained to the bench for weeks together, without ceasing to row for twenty-four hours together, with a renegade standing

[1] Lady of the Castle.   [2] " She is asleep in bed."
[3] My young sirs.   [4] Unlucky, most unlucky.

over to lash us, or to put a morsel into our mouths if we were faint-ing."

"The dogs! Do they thus use Christian men?" cried Friedel.

"*Si, si—ja wohl.*[1] There were a good fourscore of us, and among them a Tedesco,[2] a good man and true, from whom I learnt your tongue."

"Our tongue!—from whom?" asked one twin of the other.

"A Tedesco, a fellow-countryman of *sue eccellenze.*"

"*Deutscher!*"[3] cried both boys, turning in horror, "our Germans so treated by the pagan villains?"

"Yea, truly, *signorini miei.* This fellow-captive of mine was a *cavaliere* in his own land, but he had been betrayed and sold by his enemies, and he mourned piteously for *la sposa sua*—his bride, as they say here. A goodly man and a tall, piteously cramped in the narrow deck, I grieved to leave him there when the good *confraternita* at Genoa paid my ransom. Having learnt to speak *il Tedesco*, and being no longer able to fit out a vessel, I made my venture beyond the Alps; but, alas! till this moment fortune had still been adverse. My mules died of the toil of crossing the mountains; and, when with reduced baggage I came to the river beneath there—when my horses fell and my servants fled, and the peasants came down with their hayforks—I thought myself in hands no better than those of the Moors themselves."

"It was wrongly done," said Ebbo, in an honest, open tone, though blushing. "I have indeed a right to what may be stranded on the bank, but never more shall foul means be employed for the overthrow."

The boys had by this time led the traveller through the Gems-bock's Pass, within sight of the convent. "There," said Ebbo, "will they give you harbourage, food, a guide, and a beast to carry the rest of your goods. We are now upon convent land, and none will dare to touch your bales; so I will unload old Schimmel."

"Ah, signorino, if I might offer any token of gratitude——"

"Nay," said Ebbo, with boyish lordliness, "make me not a spoiler."

"If the signorini should ever come to Genoa," continued the trader, "and would honour Gian Battista dei Battiste with a call, his whole house would be at their feet."

"Thanks; I would that we could see strange lands!" said Ebbo. "But come, Friedel, the sun is high, and I locked them all into the castle to make matters safe."

[1] Yes, yes: yes, indeed.   [2] German.   [3] German.

"May the liberated captive know the name of his deliverers, that he may commend it to the saints?" asked the merchant.

"I am Eberhard, Freiherr von Adlerstein, and this is Freiherr Friedmund, my brother. Farewell, sir."

"Strange," muttered the merchant, as he watched the two boys turn down the pass, "strange how like one barbarous name is to another. Eberardo! That was what we called *il Tedesco*, and, when he once told me his family name, it ended in *stino*; but all these foreign names sound alike. Let us speed on, lest these accursed peasants should wake, and be beyond the control of the signorino."

"Ah!" sighed Ebbo, as soon as he had hurried out of reach of the temptation, "small use in being a baron if one is to be no better mounted!"

"Thou art glad to have let that fair creature go free, though," said Friedel.

"Nay, my mother's eyes would let me have no rest in keeping him. Otherwise—— Talk not to me of gladness, Friedel! Thou shouldst know better. How is one to be a knight with nothing but a beast old enough to be his grandmother?"

"Knighthood of the heart may be content to go afoot." said Friedel.

"Pfui, Friedel; what boots heart without spur? I am sick of being mewed up here within these walls of rock! No sport, not even with falling on a traveller. I am worse off than ever were my forefathers! I know all about freebooting being a deadly sin, and, moreover, that it will bring the League about our ears; and it was a cowardly trick of Jobst to put those branches in the stream. Did I not go over it last night till my brain was dizzy? But still, it is but living and dying like our fathers, and I hate tameness or dulness, and it is like a fool to go back from what one has once begun."

"No; it is like a brave man, when one has begun wrong," said Friedel.

"But then I thought of the grandame triumphing over the gentle mother—and I know the mother wept over her beads half the night. She *shall* find she had had her own way for once this morning. But, hark! there's an outcry at the castle! They have found out that they are locked in! Ha! ho! hilloa, Hatto, how like you playing prisoner?"

Ebbo would have amused himself with the dismay of his garrison a little longer, had not Friedel reminded him that their mother might be suffering for their delay, and this suggestion made him march in hastily. He found her standing drooping under the pitiless storm which Frau Kunigunde was pouring out at the highest pitch of her cracked, trembling voice, one hand uplifted and clenched, the other grasping the back of a chair, while her whole frame shook with rage too mighty for her strength.

"Grandame," said Ebbo, striding up to the scene of action, "cease. Remember my words yestereve."

"She has stolen the keys! She has tampered with the servants! She has released the prisoner—thy prisoner, Ebbo! She has cheated us as she did with Wildschloss! False burgherinn! I trow she wanted another suitor! Bane—pest of Adlerstein!"

Friedmund threw a supporting arm round his mother, but Ebbo confronted the old lady. "Grandmother," he said, "I freed the captive. I stole the keys—I and Friedel! No one else knew my purpose. He was my captive, and I released him because he was foully taken. I have chosen my lot in life," he added; and, standing in the middle of the hall, he took off his cap, and spoke gravely: "I will not be a treacherous robber-outlaw, but, so help me God, a faithful, loyal, godly nobleman. And thou, grandame, peace! Such reverence shalt thou have as befits my father's mother; but henceforth mine own lady mother is the mistress of this castle, and whoever speaks a rude word to her offends the Freiherr von Alderstein."

That last day's work had made a great step in Ebbo's life, and there he stood, grave and firm, ready for the assault; for, in effect, he and all besides expected that the old lady would fly at him or at his mother like a wild cat; but she took them all by surprise by collapsing into her chair and sobbing piteously. Ebbo, much distressed, tried to make her understand that she was to have all care and honour; but she muttered something about ingratitude, and continued to exhaust herself with weeping, spurning away all who approached her; and thenceforth she lived in a gloomy, sullen acquiescence in her deposition.

Christina inclined to the opinion that she must have had some slight stroke in the night, for she was never the same woman again; her vigour had passed away, and she would sit spinning, or rocking herself in her chair, scarcely alive to what passed, or scolding and fretting like a shadow of her old violence. Nothing pleased her but the attentions of her grandsons, and happily she soon ceased to know them apart, and gave Ebbo credit for all that was done for her by Friedel, whose separate existence she seemed to have forgotten; and though the reins of government fast dropped from the aged hands, they were but gradually and cautiously assumed by the younger baroness.

In time there was a shade of greater civilisation about the castle, though impeded both by dire poverty and the doggedness of the old retainers. At least the court was cleared of the swine, and, within doors, the table was spread with dainty linen out of the parcels from Ulm, and the meals served with orderliness that annoyed the boys at first, but soon became a subject of pride and pleasure.

Frau Kunigunde lingered long, with increasing infirmities. After the winter day, when, running down at a sudden noise, Friedel picked her up from the hearthstone, scorched, bruised, almost senseless, she accepted Christina's care with nothing worse than a snarl, and gradually seemed to forget the identity of her nurse with the interloping burgher girl.

The old lady's first failure had been in the summer of 1488; it was the Advent season of 1489, when the snow was at the deepest, and the frost at the hardest, that the two hardy mountaineer grandsons fetched over the pass Father Norbert, and a still sturdier, stronger monk, to the dying woman.

"Are we in time, mother?" asked Ebbo, from the door of the upper chamber, where the Adlersteins began and ended life, shaking the snow from his mufflings. Ruddy with exertion in the sharp wind, what a contrast he was to all within the room!

"Who is that?" said a thin, feeble voice.

"It is Ebbo. It is the baron," said Christina. "Come in, Ebbo She is somewhat revived."

"Will she be able to speak to the priest?" asked Ebbo.

"Priest!" feebly screamed the old woman. "No priest for me! My lord died unshriven, unassoilzied. Where he is, there will I be. Let a priest approach me at his peril!"

Stony insensibility ensued; nor did she speak again, though life lasted many hours longer. The priests did their office ; for, impenitent as the life and frantic as the words had been, the opinions of the time deemed that their rites might yet give the departing soul a chance, though the body was unconscious.

When all was over, snow was again falling, shifting and drifting. The corpse of Kunigunde, preserved—we must say the word— salted, was placed in a coffin, and laid in that chapel to await the melting of the snows, when the vault at the Hermitage could be opened. And this could not be effected till Easter had nearly come round again, and it was within a week of their sixteenth birthday

L

that the two young barons stood together at the coffin's head, serious indeed, but more with the thought of life than of death.

For the first time in her residence at Adlerstein, now full half her life, the Freiherrinn Christina ventured to send a messenger to Ulm, who undertook to convey to Master Gottfried Sorel her letter, informing him of the death of her mother-in-law, and requesting him to send the same tidings to the Freiherr von Adlerstein Wildschloss, the kinsman and godfather of her sons.

She was used to wait fifty-two weeks for answers to her letters, and was amazed when, at the end of three, two stout serving-men were guided by Jobst up the pass. They bore a letter of invitation to her and her sons to come at once to her uncle's house. The King of the Romans, and perhaps the Emperor, were to come to the city early in the summer, and there could be no better opportunity of presenting the young barons to their sovereign. Sir Kasimer of Adlerstein Wildschloss would meet them there for the purpose, and would obtain their admission to the League, in which all Swabian nobles had bound themselves to put down robbery and oppression, and outside which there was nothing but outlawry and danger.

"So must it be?" said Ebbo, between his teeth, as he leant moodily against the wall, while his mother was gone to attend to the fare to be set before the messengers.

"What! art not glad to take wing at last?" exclaimed Friedel, cut short in an exclamation of delight.

"Take wing, forsooth! To be the guest of a greasy burgher, and call cousin with him! Fear not, Friedel; I'll not vex the motherling. Heaven knows she has had pain, grief, and subjection enough in her lifetime, and I would not hinder her visit to her home; but I would she could go alone, nor make us show our poverty to the swollen city folk, and listen to their endearments. I charge thee, Friedel, do as I do; be not too familiar with them. I shall not lightly yield my freedom to king or kaiser. Maybe there is no help for it; but it irks me to think that I should be the last Lord of Adlerstein to whom the title of Freiherr is not a mockery."

"Methinks there will be freedom in rushing at last into the great far-off!" said Friedel—the boy's eye expanded and glistened with eagerness. "Here we are prisoners—to ourselves, if you like—but prisoners still, pent up in the rocks, seeing no one, hearing scarce an echo from the knightly or the poet world, not from all the wonders that pass. Oh, Ebbo, think of being in the midst of life, with lance and sword, and seeing the Kaiser—the Kaiser of the holy Roman Empire!"

"With lance and sword, well and good; but would it were not at the cost of liberty!"

However, Ebbo forbore to damp his mother's joy, save by the one warning—"Understand, mother, that I will not be pledged to anything. I will not bend to the yoke ere I have seen and judged for myself."

The manly sound of the words gave a sweet sense of exultation to the mother, even while she dreaded the proud spirit, and whispered "God direct thee, my son."

The journey was to be at once, so as to profit by the escort of Master Sorel's men. Means of transport were scanty, but Ebbo did not choose that the messengers should report the need, and bring back a bevy of animals at the burgher's expense; so the mother was mounted on the old white mare, and her sons and Heinz trusted to their feet. By setting out early ,on a May morning the journey could be performed ere night, and the twilight would find them in the domains of the free city, where their small numbers would be of no importance. As to their appearance, the mother wore a black woollen gown and mantle, and a black silk hood tied under her chin, and sitting loosely round the stiff frame of her white cap—a nun-like garb, save for the soft brown hair, parted over her brow, and more visible than she sometimes thought correct, but her sons would not let her wear it out of sight.

The brothers had piece by piece surveyed the solitary suit of armour remaining in the castle; but, though it might serve for defence it could not be made to fit for display, and they must needs be contented with blue cloth, spun, woven, dyed, fashioned, and sewn at home, chiefly by their mother, and by her embriodered on the breast with the white eagle of Adlerstein. Short blue cloaks and caps of the same, with an eagle plume in each, and leggings neatly fashioned of deerskin, completed their equipments. Ebbo wore his father's sword, Friedel had merely a dagger and crossbow. There was not a gold chain, not a brooch, not an approach to an ornament among the three, except the medal that had always distinguished Ebbo, and the coral rosary at Christina's girdle. Her own trinkets had gone in masses for the souls of her father and husband; and though a few costly jewels had been found in Frau Kunigunde's hoards, the mode of their acquisition was so doubtful, that it had seemed fittest to bestow them in alms and masses for the good of her soul.

The sun had lately set, and the moon was silvering the Danube, when the travellers came full in view of the imperial free city.

The gates were closed, and the serving-men had to parley at the barbican ere the heavy door was opened to admit the party to the bridge, between deep battlemented stone walls.

A hearty voice proceeded from the lighted guardroom in the thickness of the gateway. "Freiherrinn von Adlerstein! Is it she? Then must I greet my old playmate!" And the captain of the watch appeared among upraised lanterns and torches that showed a broad, smooth, plump face beneath a plain steel helmet.

"Welcome, gracious lady, welcome to your old city. What! do you not remember Lippus Grundt, your poor Valentine?"

"Master Philip Grundt!" exclaimed Christina, amazed at the breadth of visage and person; "and how fares it with my good Regina?"

"Excellent well, good lady. She manages her trade and house as well as the good man Bartolaus Fleischer himself. Blithe will she be to show you her goodly ten, as I shall my eight," he continued.

Then signing with her hand, Christina said, "I have my sons likewise to show."

"Ah, on foot!" muttered Grundt, as a not well-conceived apology for not having saluted the young gentlemen. "I greet you well, sirs," with a bow, most haughtily returned by Ebbo, who was heartily wishing himself on his mountain. "Two lusty, well-grown young men indeed, to whom my Martin will be proud to show the humours of Ulm. A fair good-night, lady!"

Well did Christina know the turn down the street, darkened by the overhanging brows of the tall houses. The familiar porch was reached, the familiar knock resounded on the iron-studded door. Friedel lifted his mother from her horse, and felt that she was quivering from head to foot, and at the same moment the light streamed from the open door on the white horse, and the two young faces, one eager, the other with knit brows and uneasy eyes. A kind of echo pervaded the house, "She is come! she is come!" and as one in a dream Christina entered, crossed the well-known hall, looked up to her uncle and aunt on the stairs, perceived little change on their countenances, and sank upon her knees, with bowed head and clasped hands.

"My child! my dear child!" exclaimed her uncle, raising her with one hand, and crossing her brow in benediction with the other. "Art thou indeed returned?" and he embraced her tenderly.

"Welcome, fair niece!" said Hausfrau Johanna, more formally. "I am right glad to greet you here."

"Dear, dear mother!" cried Christina, courting her fond embrace by gestures of the most eager affection, "how have I longed for this moment, and, above all, to show you my boys! Herr Uncle, let me present my sons—my Eberhard, my Friedmund." And she stood with a hand on each, proud that their heads were so far above her own, and looking still so slight and girlish in figure that she might better have been their sister than their mother. The cloud that the sudden light had revealed on Ebbo's brow had cleared away, and he made an inclination neither awkward nor ungracious in its free mountain dignity and grace, but not devoid of mountain rusticity and shy pride, and far less cordial than was Friedel's manner. Both were infinitely relieved to detect nothing of the greasy burgher, and were greatly struck with the fine venerable head before them; indeed, Friedel would, like his mother, have knelt to ask a blessing, had he not been under command not to outrun his brother's advances towards her kindred.

"Welcome, fair young sirs!" said Master Gottfried; "welcome both for your mother's sake and your own! Come to the gallery, and let me see thee better."

And, ceremoniously giving his hand, he proceeded to lead his niece up the stairs, while Ebbo, labouring under ignorance of city forms and uncertainty of what befitted his dignity, presented his hand to his aunt with an air that half amused, half offended the shrewd dame.

"All is as if I had left you but yesterday!" exclaimed Christina. "Uncle, have you pardoned me? You bade me return when my work was done."

"I should have known better, child. Such return is not to be sought on this side the grave. Thy work has been more than I then thought of."

"Ah! and now will you deem it begun—not done!" softly said Christina, though with too much heartfelt exultation greatly to doubt that all the world must be satisfied with two such boys, if only Ebbo would be his true self.

The luxury of the house was a great contrast to the bare walls and scant necessaries of Schloss Adlerstein; but Ebbo was resolved not to expose himself by admiration, and did his best to stifle Friedel's exclamations of surprise and delight. Were not these citizens to suppose that everything was tenfold more costly at the baronial castle? And truly the boy deserved credit for the consideration for his mother, which made him merely reserved, while he felt like a wild eagle in a poultry yard. It was no small proof of his affection to forbear more interference with his mother's happiness than was the inevitable effect of that intuition which made her aware that he was chafing and ill at ease. For his sake, she allowed herself to be placed in the seat of honour, though she longed, as of old, to nestle at her uncle's feet, and be again his child; but, even while she felt each acceptance of a token of respect as almost an injury to them, every look and tone was showing how much the same Christina she had returned.

"Ah, little one!" said her uncle, after duly contemplating her; "the change is all for the better! Thou art grown a wondrously fair dame. There will scarce be a lovelier in the Kaiserly train."

Ebbo almost pardoned his great-uncle for being his great-uncle.

"When she is arrayed as becomed the Frau Freiherrinn," said the housewife aunt, looking with concern at the coarse texture of her black sleeve. "I long to see our own lady ruffle it in her new gear. I am glad that the lofty pointed cap has passed out; the coif becomes my child far better, and I see our tastes still accord as to fashion."

"Fashion scarce came above the Debateable Ford," said Christina, smiling. "I fear my boys look as if they came out of the *Weltgeschichte*,[1] for I could only shape their garments after my remembrance of the gallants of eighteen years ago."

"Their garments are your own shaping?" exclaimed the aunt, now in an accent of real, not conventional respect.

"Spinning and weaving, shaping and sewing," said Friedel, coming near to let the housewife examine the texture.

"Close woven, even threaded, smooth tinted! Ah, Stina, thou didst learn something! Thou wert not quite spoilt by the house-father's books and carvings."

"I cannot tell whose teachings have served me best, or been the most precious to me," said Christina, looking from one to another with earnest love.

"Thou art a good child. Ah! little one, forgive me; you look so

---

[1] *History of the World.*

like our child that I cannot bear in mind that you are the Frau
Freiherrinn."

"Nay, I should deem myself in disgrace with you, did you keep
me at a distance, and not *thou* me, as your little Stina." she fondly
answered, half regretting her fond, eager movement, as Ebbo seemed
to shrink together with a gesture perceived by his uncle.

"It is my young lord there who would not forgive the freedom,"
he said good-humouredly, though gravely.

"Not so," Ebbo forced himself to say; "not so, if it makes my
mother happy."

He held up his head rather as if he thought it a fool's paradise,
but Master Gottfried answered, "The noble Freiherr is, from all I
have heard, too good a son to grudge his mother's duteous love
even to burgher kindred."

There was something in the old man's frank dignified tone of
grave reproof that at once impressed Ebbo with a sense of the true
superiority of that wise and venerable old age to his own petulant
baronial self-assertion. He had both head and heart to feel the
burgher's victory, and with a deep blush, though not without
dignity, he answered, "Truly, sir, my mother has ever taught us
to look up to you as her kindest and best——"

He was going to say "friend," but a look into the grand benignity
of the countenance completed the conquest, and he turned it into
"father." Friedel at the same instant bent his knee, exclaiming,
"It is true what Ebbo says! We have both longed for the day.
Bless us, honoured uncle, as you have blessed my mother."

"Truly and heartily, my fair youths," said Master Gottfried, with
the same kind dignity, "do I pray the good God to bless you, and
render you faithful and loving sons, not only to your mother, but to
your fatherland."

Their mother was ready to weep for joy. There was now no
drawback to her bliss, since her son and her uncle had accepted
one another; and she repaired to her own beloved old chamber a
happier being than she had been since she had left its wainscoted
walls.

CHAPTER VIII

AFTER HAVING ONCE accepted Master Gottfried, Ebbo froze towards him and Dame Johanna no more, save that a naturally imperious temper now and then led to fitful stiffness and momentary haughtiness, which were easily excused in one so new to the world and afraid of compromising his rank. In general he could afford to enjoy himself with a zest as hearty as that of the simpler-minded Friedel.

They were early afoot, but not before the heads of the household were coming forth for the morning devotions at the cathedral; and the streets were stirring into activity, and becoming so peopled that the boys supposed that it was a great fair day. They had never seen so many people together even at the Friedmund Wake, and it was several days before they ceased to exclaim at every passenger as a new curiosity.

They were delighted to receive instruction from a travelling student then attending the schools of Ulm; also lessons in music and singing were gladly accepted, and from their uncle's carving they could not keep their hands. Ebbo had begun by enjoining Friedel to remember that the work that had been sport in the mountains would be basely mechanical in the city, and Friedel as usual yielded his private tastes; but on the second day Ebbo himself was discovered in the workshop, watching the magic touch of the deft workman, and he was soon so enticed by the perfect appliances as to take tool in hand and prove himself not unadroit in the craft. Friedel, however, excelled in delicacy of touch and grace and originality of conception, and produced such workmanship that Master Gottfried could not help stroking his hair and telling him it was a pity he was not born to belong to the guild.

"I cannot spare him, sir," cried Ebbo; "priest, scholar, minstrel, artist—all want him."

"What, Hans of all streets, Ebbo?" interrupted Friedel.

"And guildmaster of none," said Ebbo, "save as a warrior; the rest only enough for a gentleman! For what I am thou must be."

But Ebbo did not find fault with the skill Friedel was bestowing on his work—a carving in wood of a dove brooding over two young eagles—the device that both were resolved to assume. When their mother asked what their lady-loves would say to this, Ebbo looked up, and with the fullest conviction in his lustrous eyes declared that no love should ever rival his motherling in his heart.

The youths held aloof from the burghers, for Master Gottfried wisely desired to give them time to be tamed before running risk of offence, either to, or by, their wild shy, pride; and their mother contrived to time her meetings with her old companions when her sons were otherwise occupied. Master Gottfried made it known that the marriage portion he had designed for his niece had been entrusted to a merchant trading in peltry to Moscovy, and the sum thus realised was larger than any bride had yet brought to Adlerstein. Master Gottfried would have liked to continue the same profitable speculations with it; but this would have been beyond the young baron's endurance, and his eyes sparkled when his mother spoke of repairing the castle, refitting the chapel, having a resident chaplain, cultivating more land, increasing the scanty stock of cattle, and attempting the improvements hitherto prevented by lack of means, and the first pleasant sense of wealth came in the acquisition of horses, weapons, and braveries. In his original mood, Ebbo would rather have stood before the Diet in his homespun blue than have figured in cloth of gold at the burghers expense; but he had learned to love his uncle, he regarded the marriage portion as family property, and, moreover, he sorely longed to feel himself and his brother well mounted, and scarcely less to see his mother in a velvet gown.

Here was his chief point of sympathy with the housemother, who, herself precluded from wearing miniver, velvet, or pearls, longed to deck her niece therewith, in time to receive Sir Kasimir of Adlerstein Wildschloss, as he had promised to meet his godsons at Ulm. The knight's marriage had lasted only a few years, and had left him no surviving children except one little daughter, whom he had placed in a nunnery at Ulm, under the care of her mother's sister. His lands lay higher up the Danube, and he was expected at Ulm shortly before the Emperor's arrival. He had been chiefly in Flanders with the King of the Romans, and had only returned to Germany when the Netherlanders had refused the regency of Maximilian, and driven him out of their country, depriving him of the custody of his children.

Pfingsttag, or Pentecost Day, was the occasion of Christina's first full toilette, and never was bride more solicitously or exultingly arrayed than she, while one boy held the mirror and the other criticised and admired as the aunt adjusted the pearl-bordered coif, and long white veil floating over the long-desired black velvet dress. How the two lads admired and gazed, caring far less for their own new and noble attire! Friedel was indeed somewhat concerned that the sword by his side was so much handsomer than that which Ebbo wore, and which, for all its dinted scabbard and battered hilt, he was resolved never to discard.

It was a festival of brilliant joy. Wreaths of flowers hung from the windows; rich tapestries decked the Dome Kirk, and the relics were displayed in shrines of wonderful costliness of material and beauty of workmanship; little birds, with thin cakes fastened to their feet, were let loose to fly about the church, in strange allusion to the event of the day, and the clergy wore their most gorgeous robes. The Lady of Adlerstein came out, leaning on Ebbo's arm, with Friedel on her other side, but her steps were checked by a call from Master Gottfried just behind. "Frau Freiherrinn, Junkern, not so fast. Here is your noble kinsman."

A tall, fine-looking person, in the long rich robe worn on peaceful occasions, stood forth, doffing his eagle-plumed bonnet, and, as the lady turned and curtsied low, he put his knee to the ground and kissed her hand, saying, "Well met, noble dame; I felt certain that I knew you when I beheld you in the Dome."

"He was gazing at her all the time," whispered Ebbo to his brother; while their mother, blushing, replied, "You do me too much honour, Herr Freiherr."

"Once seen, never to be forgotten," was the courteous answer; "and truly, but for the stately height of these my godsons, I would not believe how long since our meeting was."

Thereupon, in true German fashion, Sir Kasimir embraced each youth in the open street, and then, removing his long embroidered Spanish glove, he offered his hand, or rather the tips of his fingers, to lead the Frau Christina home.

Master Sorel had invited him to become his guest at a festival meal in honour of the great holiday, at which were to be present several wealthy citizens with their wives and families. Ebbo had resolved upon treating them with courteous reserve and distance; but he was surprised to find his cousin of Wildschloss comporting himself among the burgomasters and their dames as freely as though they had been his equals, and to see that they took such demeanour as perfectly natural. Quick to perceive, the boy gathered that the gulf between noble and burgher was so great that no intimacy could bridge it over, no reserve widen it, and that his own bashful hauteur was almost a sign that he knew that the gulf had been passed by his own parents; but shame and consciousness did not enable him to alter his manner, but rather added to its stiffness.

"The Junker is like an Englishman," said Sir Kasimir, who had met many English exiles at the court of Burgundy.

After the lengthy meal, the tables were removed, the long gallery was occupied by musicians, and Master Gottfried crossed the hall to tell his eldest grandnephew that to him he should depute the opening of the dance with the bride of the Rathsherr, Ulrich Burger. Ebbo blushed up to the eyes, and muttered that he prayed his uncle to excuse him.

"So!" said the old citizen, really displeased; "thy kinsman might have proved to thee that it is no derogation of thy lordly dignity. I have been patient with thee, but thy pride passes——"

"Sir," interposed Friedel hastily, with a look between shame and merriment, "it is not that; but you forget what poor mountaineers we are. Never did we tread a measure save now and then with our mother on a winter evening, and we know no more than a chamois of your intricate measures."

Master Gottfried looked perplexed, for these dances were matters of great punctilio. It was but seven years since the Lord of Praunstein had defied the whole city of Frankfort because a damsel of that place had refused to dance with one of his cousins; and, though "fist-right" and letters of challenge had been made illegal, yet the whole city of Ulm would have resented the affront put on it by the young Lord of Adlerstein. Happily the Freiherr of Adlerstein Wildschloss was at hand. "Herr Burgomaster," he said, "let me commence the dance with your fair lady neice. By your testimony," he added, smiling to the youths, "she can tread a measure. And, after marking us, you may try your success with the Rathsherrin."

Christina would gladly have transferred her noble partner to the Rathsherrin, but she feared to mortify her good uncle and aunt further, and consented to figure alone with Sir Kasimir in one of the majestic, graceful dances performed by a single couple before a gazing assembly. So she let him lead her to her place, and they bowed and bent, swept past one another, and moved in interlacing lines and curves, with a grand slow movement that displayed her quiet grace and his stately port and courtly air.

"See," said Friedel, who had been watching the steps, "it will be easy to dance it now. It is a figure my mother once tried to teach us. I remember it now."

"Then go and do it, since better may not be."

"Nay, but it should be thou."

"Who will know which of us it is?"

Friedel came forward, and the substitution was undetected by all save their mother and uncle; by the latter only because, addressing Ebbo, he received a reply in a tone such as Friedel never used.

Natural grace, quickness of ear and eye, and a skilful partner, rendered Friedel's so fair a performance that he ventured on sending his brother to attend the councilloress with wine and comfits; while he in his own person performed another dance with the city dame next in pretension, and their mother was amused by Sir Kasimir's remark, that the second son danced better than the elder, but both must learn.

Sir Kasimir lodged at a neighbouring hostel; but he spent much time with his cousins, and tried to make them friends with his squire, Count Rudiger. A great offence to Ebbo was, however, the criticisms of both knight and squire on the bearing of the young barons in military exercises. Truly, with no instructor but the rough lanzknecht Heinz, they must, as Friedel said, have been born paladins to have equalled youths whose life had been spent in chivalrous training.

The crossbow was the only weapon with which they excelled; and, as shooting was a favourite exercise with the burghers, their proficiency was not as exclusive as had seemed to Ebbo a baronial privilege. Harquebuses were novelties to them, and they despised them as burgher weapons, in spite of Sir Kasimir's assurance that firearms were a great subject of study and interest to the King of the Romans. The name of this personage was, it may be feared, highly distasteful to the Freiherr von Adlerstein, both as Wildschloss's model of knightly perfection, and as one who claimed submission from his haughty spirit. When Sir Kasimir spoke to him on the subject of giving his allegiance, he stiffly replied, "Sir, that is a question for ripe consideration."

"It is the question, "said Wildschloss, rather more lightly than agreed with the baron's dignity, "whether you like to have your castle pulled down about your ears."

"That has never happened yet to Adlerstein!" said Ebbo proudly.

"No, because since the days of the Hohenstaufen there has been neither rule nor union in the empire.   But times are changing fast, my Junker, and within the last ten years forty castles such as yours have been consumed by the Swabian League, as though they were so many walnuts."

"The shell of Adlerstein was too hard for them, though.   They never tried."

"And wherefore, friend Eberhard?   It was because I represented to the Kaiser and the Graf von Wurtemberg that little profit and no glory would accrue from attacking a crag full of women and babes, and that I, having the honour to be your next heir, should prefer having the castle untouched and under the peace of the empire, so so long as that peace was kept.   When you should come to years of discretion, then it would be for you to carry out the intention wherewith your father and grandfather left home."

"Then we have been protected by the peace of the empire all this time?" said Friedel, while Ebbo looked as if the notion were hard of digestion.

"Even so; and, had you not freely and nobly released your Genoese merchant, it had gone hard with Adlerstein."

"Could Adlerstein be taken?" demanded Ebbo triumphantly.

"Your grandmother thought not," said Sir Kasimir, with a shade of irony in his tone.   "It would be a troublesome siege; but the league numbers 1500 horse, and 9000 foot, and, with Schlangenwald's concurrence, you would be assuredly starved out."

Ebbo was so much the more stimulated to take his chance; but Friedel put in the question to what the oaths would bind him.

"Only to aid the Emperor with sword and counsel in field or Diet, and thereby win fame and honour such as can scarce be gained by carrying prey to yon eagle roost."

"One may preserve one's independance without robbery," said Ebbo coldly.

"Nay, lad; did you ever hear of a wolf that could live without marauding? or if he tried, would he get credit for so doing?"

"After all," said Friedel, "does not the present agreement hold till we are of age?   I suppose the Swabian League would attempt nothing against minors unless we break the peace?"

"Probably not; I will do my utmost to give the Freiherr there time to grow beyond his grandmother's maxims," said Wildschloss. "If Schlangenwald do not meddle in the matter, he may have the next five years to decide whether Adlerstein can hold out against all Germany."

"Freiherr Kasimir von Adlerstein Wildschloss," said Eberhard, turning solemnly on him, "I do you to wit once for all that threats will not serve me. If I submit, it will be because I am convinced it is right. Otherwise we had rather both be buried in the ruins of our castle, as its last free lords."

"So!" said the provoking kinsman; "such burials look grim when the time comes, but happily it is not coming yet!"

Meantime, as Ebbo said to Friedel, how much might happen— a disruption of the empire, a crusade against the Turks, a war in Italy, some grand means of making the Diet value the sword of a free baron without chaining him down to gratify the greed of hungry Austria. If only Wildschloss could be shaken off! But he only became constantly more friendly and intrusive, almost paternal.

He even asked leave to bring his little daughter Thekla from her convent to see the Lady of Adlerstein. She was a pretty, flaxen-haired maiden of five years old. in a round cap, and long narrow frock, with a little cross at the neck. She had never seen any one beyond the walls of the nunnery; and, when her father took her from the lay-sister's arms, and carried her to the gallery, where sat Haus-frau Johanna, in dark green slashed with cherry colour, Master Gottfried, in sober crimson, with gold medal and chain, Freiherrinn Christina, in silver-broidered black, and the two Junkern stood near in the shining mail in which they were going to the tilt-yard, she turned her head in terror, struggled with her scarce known father, and shrieked for Sister Grethel.

"It is all to sheen," she sobbed, in the lay-sister's arms; "I do not want to be in Paradise yet, among the saints! Oh! take me back! The two bright, holy Michaels would let me go, for indeed I made but one mistake in my Ave."

Vain was the attempt to make her lift her face from the black serge shoulder where she had hidden it. Sister Grethel coaxed and scolded, Sir Kasimir reproved, the housemother offered comfits, and Christina's soft voice was worst of all, for the child, probably taking her for Our Lady herself, began to gasp forth a general confession. "I will never do so again! Yes, it was a fib, but Mother Hildegard gave me a bit of marchpane not to tell——" Here the lay-sister took strong measures for closing the little mouth, and Christina drew back, recommending that the child should be left gradually to discover their terrestrial nature. Ebbo had looked on with extreme disgust, trying to hurry Friedel, who had delayed to trace some lines for his mother on her broidery pattern. In passing the step where Grethel sat with Thekla on her lap, the clank of their armour caused the uplifting of the little flaxen head, and two wide blue eyes looked over Grethel's shoulder, and met Friedel's sunny glance. He smiled; she laughed back again. He held out his arms, and, though his hands were gauntleted, she let him lift her up, and curiously smoothed and patted his cheek, as if he had been a strange animal.

"You have no wings," she said. "Are you St. George, or St. Michael?"

"Neither the one nor the other, pretty one. Only your poor cousin Friedel von Adlerstein, and here is Ebbo, my brother."

It was not in Ebbos' nature not to smile encouragement at the fair little face, with its wistful look. He drew off his glove to caress her silken hair, and for a few minutes she was played with by the two brothers like a newly-invented toy, receiving their attentions with pretty half-frightened graciousness, until Count Rudiger hastened in to summon them.

Her extreme delight, when towards evening the Junkern returned, was flattering even to Ebbo; and, when it was time for her to be taken home, she made strong resistance, clinging fast to Christina, with screams and struggles. To the lady's promise of coming to see her she replied, "Friedel and Ebbo, too," and, receiving no response to this request, she burst out, "Then I won't come! I am the Freiherrinn Thekla, the heiress of Adlerstein Wildschloss and Felsenbach. I won't be a nun. I'll be married! You shall be my husband," and she made a dart at the nearest youth, who happened to be Ebbo.

"Ay, ay, you shall have him. He will come for you, sweetest Fraulein," said the perplexed Grethel, "so only you will come home! Nobody will come for you if you are naughty."

"Will you come if I am good?" said the spoilt cloister pet, clinging tight to Ebbo.

"Yes," said her father, as she still resisted, "come back, my child, and one day shall you see Ebbo, and have him for a brother."

Thereat Ebbo shook off the little grasping fingers, almost as if they had belonged to a noxious insect.

CHAPTER IX

ONE SUMMER EVENING, when shooting at a bird on a pole was in full exercise in the tilt-yard, the sports were interrupted by a message from the Provost that a harbinger had brought tidings that the Imperial court was within a days' journey.

All was preparation. Fresh sand had to be strewn on the arena. New tapestry hangings were to deck the galleries, the houses and balconies to be brave with drapery, the fountain in the market-place was to play Rhine wine, all Ulm was astir to do honour to itself and to the Kaiser, and Ebbo stood amid all the bustle, subject to all that oppressive self-magnification so frequent in early youth, which made it seem to him as if the Kaiser and the King of the Romans were coming to Ulm with the mere purpose of destroying his independence, and as if the eyes of all Germany were watching for his humiliation.

"See! see!" suddenly exclaimed Friedel; "look! there is something among the tracery of the Dome Kirk Tower. Is it man or bird?"

"Bird, folly! Thou couldst see no bird less than an eagle from hence," said Ebbo. "No doubt they are about to hoist a banner."

"That is not their wont," returned Sir Kasimir.

"I see him," interrupted Ebbo. Nay," but he is a bold climber. We went up to that stage, close to the balcony, but there's no footing beyond but crockets and canopies. Shouldst thou deem it worse than the Red Eyrie, Friedel?"

"Yea, truly! The depth beneath is plainer! It is fearful! He is like a fly against the sky. Look! look! The saints protect him! He is on that narrowest topmost ledge—measuring; his heel is over the parapet—half his foot!"

"Holding on by the rotten scaffold pole! St. Barbara be his speed; but he is a brave man!" shouted Ebbo. "Oh! the pole has broken."

"Heaven forfend!" cried Wildschloss, with despair on his face unseen by the boys, for Friedel had hidden his eyes, and Ebbo was straining his with the intense gaze of horror. He had carried his glance downwards, following the 380 feet fall that must be the lot of the adventurer. Then looking up again he shouted, "I see him! I see him! Praise to St. Barbara! He is safe! He has caught by the upright stone-work."

"Where? where? Show me!" cried Wildschloss, grasping Ebbo's arm.

"There! clinging to that upright bit of tracery, stretching his foot out to yonder crocket."

"I cannot see. Mine eyes swim and dazzle," said Wildschloss. "Merciful heavens! is this another tempting of Providence? How is it with him now, Ebbo?"

"Swarming down another slender bit of the stone network. It must be easy now to one who could keep head and hand steady in such a shock."

"There!" added Friedel, after a breathless space, "he is on the lower parapet, whence begins the stair. Do you know him, sir? Who is he?"

"Either a Venetian mountebank," said Wildschloss, "or else there is only one man I know of either so foolhardy or so steady of head."

"Be he who he may," said Ebbo, "he is the bravest man that ever I beheld. Who is he, Sir Kasimir?"

"An eagle of higher flight than ours, no doubt," said Wildschloss. "But come; we shall reach the Dome Kirk by the time the climber has wound his way down, and we shall see what like he is."

Their coming was well timed, for a small door at the foot of the tower was just opening to give exit to a very tall knight, in one of those short Spanish cloaks the collar of which could be raised so as to conceal the face. He looked to the right and left, and had one hand raised to put up the collar when he recognised Sir Kasimir, and, holding out both hands, exclaimed, "Ha, Adlerstein! well met! I looked to see thee here. No unbonneting; I am not come yet. I am at Strasburg, with the Kaiser and the Archduke, and am not here till we ride in, in purple and in pall, by the time the good folk have hung out their arras, and donned their gold chains, and conned their speeches, and mounted their mules."

"Well that their speeches are not over the lykewake of his kingly kaiserly highness," gravely returned Sir Kasimir.

"Ha! Thou sawest? I came out here to avoid the gaping throng, who don't know what a hunter can do. I have been in worse case in the Tyrol. Snowdrifts are worse footing than stone vine leaves."

"Where abides your highness?" asked Wildschloss.

"I ride back again to the halting-place for the night, and meet my father in time to do my part in the pageant. I was sick of the addresses, and, moreover, the purse-proud Flemings have made such a stiff little fop of my poor boy that I am ashamed to look at him, or hear his French accent. So I rode off to get a view of this notable Dome in peace, ere it be bedizened in holiday garb; and one can't stir without all the Chapter waddling after one. Ha! Adlerstein, where didst get such a perfect pair of pages? I would I could match my hounds as well."

"They are no pages of mine, so please you," said the knight; "rather this is the head of my name. Let me present to your kingly highness the Freiherr von Adlerstein."

"Thou dost not thyself distinguish between them!" said Maximilian, as Friedmund stepped back, putting forward Eberhard. They would have doffed their caps and bent the knee, but were hastily checked by Maximilian. "No, no, Junkern, I shall owe you no thanks for bringing all the street on me!—that's enough—Reserve the rest for Kaiser Fritz." Then, familiarly taking Sir Kasimir's arm, he walked on saying, "I remember now. Thou wentest after an inheritance from the old Mouser of the Debateable Ford, and wert ousted by a couple of lusty boys sprung of a peasant wedlock."

"Nay, my lord, of a burgher lady, fair as she is wise and virtuous; who, in spite of all hindrances, has bred up these youths in all good and noble nurture."

"Is this so?" said the king, turning sharp round on the twins. "Are you minded to quit freebooting, and come a-crusading against the Turks with me?"

"Everywhere with such a leader!" enthusiastically exclaimed Ebbo.

"What? up there?" said Maximilian, smiling. "Thou hast the tread of a chamois-hunter."

"Friedel has been on the Red Eyrie," exclaimed Ebbo; then, thinking he had spoken foolishly, he coloured.

"Which is the Red Eyrie?" good-humouredly asked the king.

"It is the crag above our castle," said Friedel modestly.

"None other has been there," added Ebbo, perceiving his auditor's interest; "but he saw the eagle flying away with a poor widow's kid, and the sight must have given him wings, for we never could find the same path; but here is one of the feathers he brought down"

—taking off his cap so as to show a feather rather the worse for wear, and sheltered behind a fresher one.

"Nay," said Friedel, "thou shouldst say that I came to a ledge where I had like to have stayed all night, but that ye all came out with men and ropes."

"We know what such a case is!" said the king. "It has chanced to us to hang between heaven and earth; I've even had the Holy Sacrament held up for my last pious gaze by those who gave me up for lost on the mountain-side. Adlerstein? The peak above the Braunwasser? Some day shall ye show me this eyrie of yours, and we will see whether we can amaze our cousins the eagles. We see you at our father's court to-morrow?" he graciously added, and Ebbo gave a ready bow of acquiescence.

"There," said the king, as after their dismissal he walked on with Sir Kasimir, "never blame me for rashness and imprudence. Here has this height of the steeple proved the height of policy. It has made a loyal subject of a Mouser on the spot."

"Pray Heaven it may have won a heart, true though proud!" said Wildschloss; "but mousing was cured before by the wise training of the mother. Your highness will have taken out the sting of submission, and you will scarce find more faithful subjects."

"How old are the Junkern?"

"Some sixteen years, your highness."

"That is what living in the mountains does for a lad. Why could not these thrice-accursed Flemish towns let me breed up my boy to be good for something in the mountains, instead of getting duck-footed and muddy-witted in the fens.?"

In the meantime Ebbo and Friedel were returning home in that sort of passion of enthusiasm that ingenuous boyhood feels when first brought into contact with greatness or brilliant qualities.

Ebbo had heard so much of the perfections of the king of the Romans as to be prepared to hate him; but the boy, as we have seen, was of a generous, sensitive nature, peculiarly prone to enthusiastic impressions of veneration; and Maximilian's high-spirited manhood, personal fascination, and individual kindness had so entirely taken him by surprise, that he talked of him all the evening in a more fervid manner than did even Friedel, though both could scarcely rest for their anticipation of seeing him on the morrow in the full state of his entry.

Richly clad, and mounted on cream-coloured steeds, nearly as much alike as themselves, the twins were a pleasant sight for a proud mother's eyes, as they rode out to take their place in the procession that was to welcome the royal guests.

Arrayed, as her sons loved to see her, in black velvet, and with pearl-bordered cap, Christina sat by her aunt in the tapestried balcony, and between them stood or sat little Thekla von Adlerstein Wildschloss, whose father had entrusted her to their care, to see the procession pass by. A rich Eastern carpet, of gorgeous colouring, covered the upper balustrade, over which they leant, in somewhat close quarters with the scarlet-bodiced dames of the opposite house, but with ample space for sight up and down the rows of smiling expectants at each balcony, or window, equally gay with hangings, while the bells of all the churches clashed forth their gayest chimes, and fitful bursts of music were borne upon the breeze.

On they came—stout lanzknechts first, the city guard with steel helmets unadorned buff, suits, and bearing either harquebuses, halberts, or those handsome but terrible weapons, morning stars. Then followed guild after guild, each preceded by the banner bearing its homely emblem—the cauldron of the smiths, the hose of the clothiers, the helmet of the armourers, the basin of the barbers, the boot of the shoemakers; even the sausage of the cooks, and the shoe of the shoeblacks, were represented, as by men who gloried in the calling in which they did life's duty and task.

First in each of these bands marched the prentices, stout, broad, flat-faced lads, from twenty to fourteen years of age, with hair like tow hanging from under their blue caps, staves in their hands, and knives at their girdles. Behind them came the journeymen, in leathern jerkins and steel caps, and armed with halberts or cross-bows; men of all ages, from sixty to one or two and twenty, and many of the younger ones with foreign countenances and garb betokening that they were strangers spending part of their wandering years in studying the Ulm fashions of their craft. Each trade showed a large array of these juniors; but the masters who came behind were comparatively few, mostly elderly, long-gowned, gold-chained personages, with a weight of solid dignity on their brows.

Then came the ragged regiment of scholars, wild lads from every part of Germany and Switzerland, some wan and pinched with hardship and privation, others sturdy, selfish rogues, evidently well able to take care of themselves.

Contrasting with these ill-kempt pupils marched the grave professors and teachers, in square ecclesiastic caps and long gowns, whose colours marked their degrees and the Universities that had conferred them—some thin, some portly, some jocund, others dreamy; some observing all the humours around, others still intent on Aristotelian ethics; all men of high fame, with doctor at the beginning of their names, and "or" or "us" at the close of them. After them rode the magistracy, a burgomaster from each guild, and the Herr Provost himself—as great a potentate within his own walls as the Doge of Venice of or Genoa, or perhaps greater, because less jealously hampered. In this dignified group was Uncle Gottfried, by complacent nod and smile acknowledging his good wife and niece, who indeed had received many a previous glance and bow from friends passing beneath. But Master Sorel was no new spectacle in a civic procession, and the sight of him was only a pleasant fillip to the excitement of his ladies.

Here was jingling of spurs and trampling of horses; heraldic achievements showed upon the banners, round which rode the mail-clad retainers of country nobles who had mustered to meet their lords. Then with still more of clank and tramp, rode a bright-faced troop of lads, with feathered caps and gay mantles. Young Count Rudiger looked up with courteous salutation; and just behind him, with smiling lips and upraised faces, were the pair whose dark eyes, dark hair, and slender forms rendered them conspicuous among the fair Teutonic youth. Each cap was taken off and waved, and each pair of lustrous eyes glanced up pleasure and exultation at the sight of the lovely "Mutterlein."[1] Thekla was shrieking with delight at the sight of her father, tall and splendid on his mighty black charger, with a smile for his child, and for the lady a bow so low and deferential that it was evidently remarked by those at whose approach every lady in the balconies was rising, every head in the street was bared.

A tall, thin, shrivelled, but exceedingly stately old man on a gray horse was in the centre. Clad in a purple velvet mantle, and bowing as he went, he looked truly the Kaiser, to whom stately courtesy was second nature. On one side, in black and gold, with the jewel of the Golden Fleece on his breast, rode Maximilian, responding gracefully to the salutations of the people, but his keen eye roving in search of the subject of Sir Kasimir's salute, and lighting on Christina with such a rapid, amused glance of discovery that, in her confusion, she missed what excited Dame Johanna's rapturous admiration—the handsome boy on the Emperor's other side, a fair, plump lad, the young sovereign of the Low Countries, beautiful in

1 Little Mother.

feature and complexion, but lacking the fire and the loftiness that characterised his father's countenance. The train was closed by the reitern of the Emperor's guard—steel-clad mercenaries who were looked on with no friendly eyes by the few gazers in the street who had been left behind in the general rush to keep up with the attractive part of the show.

Pageants of elaborate mythological character impeded the Imperial progress at every stage, and it was two full hours ere the two youths returned, heartily weary of the lengthened ceremonial.

Ebbo had to dress for the banquet spread in the town-hall. Space was wanting for the concourse of guests, and Master Sorel had decided that the younger baron should not be included in the invitation. Friedel pardoned him more easily than did Ebbo, who not only resented any slight to his double, but in his fits of shy pride needed the aid of his readier and brighter other self. But it might not be, and Sir Kasimir and Master Gottfried alone accompanied him, hoping that he would not look as wild as a hawk, and would do nothing to diminish the favourable impression he had made on the King of the Romans.

Late, according to mediaeval hours, was the return, and Ebbo spoke in a tone of elation. "The Kaiser was most gracious, and the king knew me," he said, "and asked for thee, Friedel, saying one of us was nought without the other. But thou wilt go to-morrow, for we are to receive knighthood."

"Already!" exclaimed Friedel.

"Yea," said Ebbo. "The Romish king said somewhat about waiting to win our spurs; but the Kaiser said I was in a position to take rank as a knight, and I thanked him, so thou shouldst share the honour."

"The Kaiser," said Wildschloss, "is not the man to let a knight's fee slip between his fingers. The king would have kept off their grip, and reserved you for knighthood from his own sword under the banner of the empire; but there is no help for it now, and you must make your vassals send in their dues."

"My vassals?" said Ebbo; "what could they send?"

"The aid customary on the knighthood of the heir."

"But there is—there is nothing!" said Friedel. "They can scarce pay meal and poultry enough for our daily fare; and if we were to flay them alive, we should not get sixty groschen[1] from the whole."

---

[1] Small silver coin.

"True enough! Knighthood must wait till we win it," said Ebbo gloomily.

"Nay, it is accepted," said Wildschloss. "The Kaiser loves his iron chest too well to let you go back. You must be ready with your round sum to the chancellor, and your spur-money and your fee to the heralds, and largess to the crowds."

"Mother, the dowry," said Ebbo.

"At your service, my son," said Christina, anxious to chase the cloud from his brow.

But it was a deep haul, for the avaricious Friedrich IV. made exorbitant charges for the knighting his young nobles; and Ebbo soon saw that the improvements at home must suffer for the honours that would have been so much better won than bought.

"If your vassals cannot aid, yet may not your kinsman——" began Wildschloss.

"No, sir!" interrupted Ebbo. "Rather will my mother, brother, and I ride back this very night to unfettered liberty on our mountain, without obligation to any living man."

"Less hotly, Sir Baron," said Master Gottfried gravely. "You broke in on your noble godfather, and you had not heard me speak. You and your brother are the old man's only heirs, nor do ye incur any obligation that need fret you by forestalling what would be your just right. I will see my nephews as well equipped as any young baron of them."

The mother looked anxiously at Ebbo. He bent his head with rising colour, and said, "Thanks, kind Uncle. From *you* I have learnt to look on goodness as fatherly."

"Only," added Friedel, "if the barons' station renders knighthood fitting for him, surely I might remain his esquire."

"Never, Friedel!" cried his brother. "Without thee, nothing."

"Well said, Freiherr," said Master Sorel; "what becomes the one becomes the other. I would not have thee left out, my Friedel, since I cannot leave thee the mysteries of my craft."

"To-morrow!" said Friedel gravely. "Then must the vigil be kept tonight."

"The boys think these are the days of Roland and Karl the Great." said Wildschloss. "He would fain watch his arms in the moonlight in the Dome Kirk! Alas! no, my Friedel! Knighthood in these days smacks more of bezants[1] than of deeds of prowess."

Nurtured in mountain solitude, on romance transmitted through

____

[1] Gold coins.

the pure medium of his mother's mind, and his spirit untainted by contact with the world, Friedmund von Adlerstein looked on chivalry with the temper of a Percival or Galahad, and regarded it with a sacred awe. Eberhard, though treating it more as a matter of business, was like enough to his brother to enter into the force of the vows they were about to make; and if the young Barons of Adlerstein did not perform the night-watch over their armour, yet they kept a vigil that impressed their own minds as deeply, and in early morn they went to confession and mass ere the gay parts of the city were astir.

If the sense that he was the last veritable *free* lord of Adlerstein rushed over Ebbo, he was, on the other hand, overmastered by the kingliness of Friedrich and Maximilian, and was aware that this submission, while depriving him of little or no actual power, brought him into relations with the civilized world, and opened to him paths of true honour. So the ceremonies were gone through, his oath of allegiance was made, investiture was granted to him by the delivery of a sword, and both he and Friedel were dubbed knights. Then they shared another banquet, where, away from the Junkern and among elder men, Ebbo was happier than the day before.

The crass obtuseness of most of the nobility made it a relief to return to the usual habits of the Sorel household when the court had left Ulm. Friedmund, anxious to prove that his new honours were not to alter his home demeanour, was drawing on a block of wood from a tinted pen-and-ink sketch; Ebbo was deeply engaged with a newly-acquired copy of Virgil; and their mother was embroidering some draperies for the long-neglected castle chapel—all sitting, as Master Gottfried loved to have them, in his studio, whence he had a few moments before been called away, when, as the door slowly opened, a voice was heard that made both lads start and rise.

"Yea, truly, Herr Guildmaster, I would see these masterpieces. Ha! What have you here for masterpieces? Our two new knights?" And Maximilian entered in a simple riding-dress, attended by Master Gottfried, and by Sir Kasimir of Adlerstein Wildschloss.

Christina would fain have slipped out unperceived, but the king was already removing his cap from his fair curling locks, and bending his head as he said, "The Frau Freiherrinn von Adlerstein? Fair lady. I greet you well, and thank you in the Kaiser's name and mine for having bred up for us two true and loyal subjects."

"May they so prove themselves, my liege!" said Christina, bending low.

"And not only loyal-hearted," added Maximilian, smiling, "but ready-brained, which is less frequent among our youth. What is thy book, young knight? Virgilius Maro? Dost thou read the Latin?" he added, in that tongue.

"Not as well as we wish, your kingly highness," readily answered Ebbo, in Latin, "having learnt solely of our mother till we came hither."

"Never fear for that, my young blade," laughed the king. "Know'st not that the wiseacres thought me too dull for teaching till I was past ten years? And what is thy double about? Drawing on wood? How now! An able draughtsman, my young knight?"

"My nephew Sir Friedmund is good to the old man," said Gottfried, himself almost regretting the lad's avocation. "My eyes are failing me, and he is aiding me with the graving of this border. He has the knack that no teaching will impart to any of my present journeymen."

"Born, not made," quoth Maximilian. "Nay," as Friedel coloured deeper at the sense that Ebbo was ashamed of him, "no blushes, my boy; it is a rare gift. I can make a hundred knights any day, but the Almighty alone can make a genius. It was this very matter of graving that led me hither."

For Maximilian had a passion for composition, and chiefly for autobiography, and his head was full of that curious performance, _Der Weisse Konig_,[1] which occupied many of the leisure moments of his life, being dictated to his former writing-master, Marcus Sauerwein, and he continued eagerly to talk to Master Gottfried about the mystery of graving, and the various scenes in which he wished to depict himself.

"And what is this?" he asked; "what is the daintily carved group I see yonder?"

"Your highness means, 'The Dove in the Eagle's Nest,'" said Kasimir. "It is the work of my young kinsmen, and their appropriate device."

"As well chosen as carved," said Maximilian, examining it. "Well is it that a city dove should now and then find her way to the eyrie. Some of my nobles would cut my throat for the heresey, but I am safe here, eh, Sir Kasimir? Fare ye well, ye dove-trained eaglets.

[1] _The White King._

We will know one another better when we bear the cross against the infidel."

The brothers kissed his hand, and he descended the steps from the hall-door. Ere he had gone far, he turned round upon Sir Kasimir with a merry smile: "A very white and tender dove indeed, and one who might easily nestle in another eyrie, methinks."

"Deems your kingly highness that consent could be won?" asked Wildschloss.

"From the Kaiser? Pfui, man, thou knowst as well as I do the golden key to his consent. So thou wouldst risk thy luck again! Thou hast no male heir."

"And I would fain give my child a mother who would deal well with her. Nay, to say sooth, that gentle, innocent face has dwelt with me for many years. But for my pre-contract, I had striven long ago to win her, and had been a happier man, mayhap. And, now I have seen what she has made of her sons, I feel I could scarce find her match among our nobility."

"Nor elsewhere," said the king; "and I honour thee for not being so besotted in our German haughtiness as not to see that it is our free cities that make refined and discreet dames. I give you good-speed, Adlerstein; but, if I read aright the brow of one at least of these young fellows, thou wilt scarce have a willing or obedient stepson."

Ebbo trusted that his kinsman of Wildschloss was safe gone with the court, and his temper smoothed and his spirits rose in proportion while preparations for a return to Adlerstein were being completed—preparations by which the burgher lady might hope to render the castle far more habitable, not to say baronial, than it had ever been.

The lady herself was one afternoon assisting her aunt in some of the duties of her *wirthschaft*, when Master Gottfried entered the apartment with an air of such extreme complacency that both turned round amazed; the one exclaiming, "Surely funds have come in for finishing the spire!" the other, "Have they appointed thee Provost for next year, housefather?"

"Neither the one nor the other," was the reply. "But heard you not here the horse's feet? Here has the Lord of Adlerstein Wildschloss been with me in full state, to make formal proposals for the hand of our child, Christina."

"For Christina!" cried Hausfrau Johanna, with delight; "truly that is well. Truly our maiden has done honour to her breeding.

A second nobleman demanding her—and one who should be able richly to endow her!"

"And who will do so," said Master Gottfried. "For morning gift he promises the farms and lands of Grunau—rich both in forest and corn glebe. Likewise, her dower shall be upon Wildschloss— where the soil is of the richest pasture, and there are no less than three mills, whence the lord obtains large rights of multure. Moreover, the castle was added to and furnished on his marriage with the late baroness, and might serve a Kurfurst; and though the jewels of Freiherrinn Valeska must be inherited by her daughter, yet there are many of higher price which have descended from his own ancestresses, and which will all be hers."

"And what a wedding we will have!" exclaimed Johanna; "it shall be truly baronial. I will take my hood and go at once to neighbour Sophie Lemsburg, who was wife to the Markgraf's Under-Keller-Meister.[1] She will tell me point device the ceremonies befitting the espousals of a baron's widow."

Poor Christina had sat all this time with drooping head and clasped hands, a tear stealing down as the formal terms of the treaty sent her spirit back to the urgent, pleading, imperious voice that had said, "Now, little one, thou wilt not shut me out;" and as she glanced at the ring that had lain on that broad palm, she felt as if her sixteen cheerful years had been an injury to her husband in his nameless bloody grave. But protection was so needful in those rude ages, and second marriages so frequent, that reluctance was counted as weakness. She knew her uncle and aunt would never believe that aught but compulsion had bound her to the rude outlaw, and her habit of submission was so strong that, only when her aunt was actually rising to go and consult her gossip, she found breath to falter:

"Hold, dear aunt—my sons——"

"Nay, child, it is the best thing thou couldst do for them. Wonders hast thou wrought, yet are they too old to be without fatherly authority. I speak not of Friedel; the lad is gentle and pious, though spirited; but for the baron. The very eye and temper of my poor brother Hugh—thy father, Stine—are alive again in him. Yea, I love the lad better for it, while I fear. He minds me precisely of Hugh ere he was prenticed to the weapon-smith, and all became bitterness."

"Ah, truly," said Christina, raising her eyes: "all would become

1 Under-butler.

bitterness with my Ebbo were I to give a father's power to one whom he would not love."

"Then were he sullen and unruly, indeed!" said the old burgomaster with displeasure; "none have shown him more kindness, none could better aid him in court and empire. The lad has never had restraint enough. I blame thee not, child, but he needs it sorely, by thine own showing."

"Alas, uncle! mine be the blame, but it is over late. My boy will rule himself for the love of God and of his mother, but he will brook no hand over him—least of all now he is a knight and thinks himself a man. Uncle, I should be deprived of both my sons, for Friedel's very soul is bound up with his brother's. I pray thee enjoin this thing not on me," she implored.

Child!" exclaimed Master Gottfried, "thou thinkst not that such a contract as this can be declined for the sake of a wayward Junker! Nay, little as I heed such toys, it will doubtless please the lads that the baron will obtain of the Emperor letters of nobility for this house, which verily sprang of good Walloon family, and so their shield will have no blank. The Romish king promises to give thee rank with any baroness, and hath fully owned what a pearl thou art, mine own sweet dove! Nay, Sir Kasimir is coming to-morrow in the trust to make the first betrothal, with Graf von Kaulwitz as a witness, and I thought of asking the Provost on the other hand."

"Verily, dear father and mother," said Christina, who had rallied a little, "have patience with me. I may not lightly or suddenly betroth myself; I know not that I can do so at all, assuredly not unless my sons were heartily willing. Have I your leave to retire?"

"Granted, my child, for meditation will show thee that this is too fair a lot for any but thee."

"Let me entreat one favour more," implored Christina. "Speak of this to no one ere I have seen my sons."

She made her way to her own chamber, there to weep and flutter. Marriage was a matter of such high contract between families that parties themselves had usually no voice in the matter, and only the widowed had any chance of a personal choice; nor was this always accorded in the case of females, who remained at the disposal of their relatives. Obedience first to the father, then to the husband, was the first requisite; love might shift for itself; and the fair widow of Adlerstein, telling her beads in sheer perplexity, knew not whether her strong repugnance to this marriage and warm sympathy with her son Ebbo were not an act of rebellion. Yet each moment did her husband rise before her mind more vividly, with his rugged looks, his warm, tender heart, his dawnings of comprehension, his generous forbearance and reverential love—the love of her youth—to be equalled by no other. The accomplished courtier and polished man of the world might be his superior, but she loathed the superiority, since it was to her husband. Might not his one chosen dove keep heart-whole for him to the last? "My husband! my loving Eberhard! left with none but me to love thee, unknown to thine own sons! I cannot, I will not give my heart away from thee! Thy little bride shall be faithful to thee, whatever betide. When we meet beyond the grave I will have been thine only, nor have set any before thy sons. Heaven forgive me if I be undutiful to my uncle; but thou must be preferred before even him! Hark!" and she started as if at Eberhard's footstep; then smiled, recollecting that Ebbo had his father's tread. But her husband had been too much in awe of her to enter with that hasty, agitated step and exclamation, "Mother, mother, what insolence is this!"

"Hush, Ebbo! I prayed mine uncle to let me speak to thee."

"It is true, then," said Ebbo, dashing his cap on the ground; "I had soundly beaten that grinning prentice for telling Heinz."

"Is it in sooth as we heard?" asked Friedel. "Mother, we know what you would say," he added, throwing himself on his knees beside her, his arm round her waist.

She bent down to kiss him. "Thou knew'st it, Friedel, and now must thou aid me to remain thy father's true widow, and to keep Ebbo from being violent."

Ebbo checked his hasty march to put his hand on her chair and kiss her brow. "Motherling, I will restrain myself, so you will give me your word not to desert us."

"Nay, Ebbo," said Friedel, "the motherling is too true and loving for us to bind her."

"Children," she answered, "hear me patiently. I have been communing with myself, and deeply do I feel that none other can I love save him who is to you a mere name, but to me a living presence. Nor would I put any between you and me. Fear me not, Ebbo. But, my son, this is no matter for rage or ingratitude, Remember it is no small condescension in a noble to stoop to thy citizen mother."

"He knew what painted puppets noble ladies are," growled Ebbo.

"Moreover," continued Christina, "thine uncle is highly gratified, and cannot believe that I can refuse. He understands not my love

for thy father, and sees many advantages for us all. I doubt me
if he believes I have the power to resist his will, and for thee, he would
he would not count thine opposition valid. And the more angry
and vehement thou art, the more will he deem himself doing thee
a service by overruling thee."

"Come home, mother, and when we are back in free Adlerstein
it will be plain who is master."

"Such a flitting would scarce prove our wisdom," said Christina,
"to run away with thy mother like a lover in a ballad. Nay, let
me first deal gently with thine uncle, and speak myself with Sir
Kasimir. Then will we back to Adlerstein without leaving wounds
to requite kindness."

Ebbo was wrought on to promise not to attack the burgomaster
on the subject, but he was moody and silent, and Master Gottfried
let him alone, forbearing to provoke his fiery spirit.

But when Sir Kasimir's visit was imminent, and Christina had
refused to make the change in her dress by which a young widow
was considered to lay herself open to another courtship, Master
Gottfried called the twins apart.

"My young lords," he said, "I fear me ye are vexing your gentle
mother by needless strife at what must take place."

"Pardon me, good uncle," said Ebbo, "I utterly decline the
honour of Sir Kasimir's suit to my mother."

Master Gottfried smiled. "Sons are not wont to be the judges
in such cases, Sir Eberhard."

"Perhaps not," he answered; "but my mother's will is to the
nayward, nor shall she be coerced."

"It is merely because of you and your pride," said Master
Gottfried.

"I think not so," rejoined the calmer Friedel; "my mother's love
for my father is still afresh."

"Young knights," said Master Gottfried, "it would scarce become
me to say, nor you to hear, how much matter of fancy such love
must have been towards one whom she knew but for a few short
months, though her pure sweet dreams, through these long years,
have moulded him into a hero. Boys, I verily believe ye love her
truly. Would it be well for her still to mourn and cherish a dream
while yet in her fresh age, capable of new happiness, fuller than she
has ever enjoyed ?"

"Did I even think she had for this man a quarter of the love
she bears to my dead father," said Ebbo, "I would strive for en-

durance; but in good sooth we found her in tears, praying us to guard her from him. I may be a boy, but I am man enough to prevent her from being coerced."

"Was this so, Friedel?" asked Master Gottfried. "Ach, I thought ye all wiser. And spake she not of Sir Kasimir's offers?—Interest with the Romish king?—Yea, and a grant of nobility and arms to this house, so as to fill the blank in your scutcheon?"

"My father never asked if she were noble," said Ebbo. "Nor will I barter her for a cantle of a shield."

"There spake a manly spirit," said his uncle, delighted. "Her worth hath taught thee how little to prize these gew-gaws! Yet, if you look to mingling with your own proud kind, ye may fall among greater slights than ye can brook. It may matter less to you, Sir Baron, but Friedel here, ay, and your sons, will be ineligible to the choicest orders of knighthood, and the canonries and chapters that are honourable endowments."

Friedel looked as if he could bear it, and Eberhard said, "The order of the Dove of Adlerstein is enough for us."

The Baron of Adlerstein Wildschloss, unprepared for the opposition that awaited him, was riding down the street equipped point-device, and with a goodly train of followers, in brilliant suits. The suitor was ushered into the full family assembly, where Christina rose and came forward a few steps to meet him, curtseying as low as he bowed, as he said, "Lady, I have preferred my suit to you through your honour-worthy uncle, who is good enough to stand my friend."

"You are over good, sir. I feel the honour, but a second wedlock may not be mine."

"Now," murmered Ebbo to his brother, as the knight and lady seated themselves in full view, "now will the smooth-tongued fellow talk her out of her senses."

Wildschloss did not talk like a young wooer; but he spoke as a grave and honourable man, deeply penetrated with true esteem and affection. He said that at their first meeting he had been struck with her sweetness and discretion, and would soon after have endeavoured to release her from her durance, but that he was bound by the contract already made with the Trautbachs, who were dangerous neighbours to Wildschloss. He had delayed his distasteful marriage as long as possible, and it had caused him nothing but trouble and strife; his children would not live, and Thekla, the only survivor, was, as his sole heiress, a mark for the cupidity of her uncle, the Count of Trautbach, and his almost savage son Lassla; while the right to the Wildschloss barony would become so doubtful between her and Ebbo, as heir of the male line, that strife and blood-shed would be wellnigh inevitable. These causes made it almost imperative that he should re-marry, and his own strong preference and regard for little Thelka directed his wishes towards the Frei-herrinn von Adlerstein. He backed his suit with courtly com-pliments, as well as with representations of his child's need of a mother's training, and the twin's equal want of fatherly guidance, dilating on the benefits he could confer on them.

Christina felt his kindness, and had full trust in his intentions. "No" was a difficult syllable to her, but she had that within her which could not accept him; and she firmly told him that she was too much bound to both her Eberhards. But there was no daunting him, nor preventing her uncle and aunt from encouraging him. He professed that he would wait, and give her time to consider; and though she reiterated that consideration would not change her mind, Master Gottfried came forward to thank him, and express his confidence of bringing her to reason.

"While I, sir," said Ebbo, with flashing eyes, and low but resentful voice, "beg to decline the honour in the name of the elder house of Adlerstein."

He held himself upright as a dart, but was infinitely annoyed by the little mocking bow and smile that he received in return, as Sir Kasimir, with his long mantle, swept out of the apartment, attended by Master Gottfried.

"Burgomaster Sorel," said the boy, standing in the middle of the floor as his uncle returned, "let me hear whether I am a person of any consideration in this family or not."

"Nephew baron," quietly replied Master Gottfried, "it is not the use of us Germans to be dictated to by youths not yet arrived at years of discretion."

"Then, mother," said Ebbo, "we leave to-morrow morn."   And at her nod of assent the housefather looked deeply grieved, the housemother began to clamour about ingratitude. "Not so," answered Ebbo fiercely. "We quit the house as poor as we came, in homespun and with the old mare."

"Peace, Ebbo!" said his mother, rising; "peace, I entreat, house-mother! pardon, uncle, I pray thee. Oh, why will not all who love me let me follow that which I believe to be best?"

"Child," said her uncle, "I cannot see thee domineered over by a youth whose whole conduct shows his need of restraint."

"Nor am I," said Christina. "It is I who am utterly averse to this offer. My sons and I are one in that; and, uncle, if I pray of you to consent to let us return to our castle, it is that I would not see the visit that has made us so happy stained with strife and dissension! You cannot be angered with my son for his love for me!"

And when, by and by, Master Gottfried went out to call on Sir Kasimir, and explain how he had thought it best to yield to the hot-tempered lad, and let the family learn how to be thankful for the goods they had rejected, he found affairs in a state that made him doubly anxious that the young barons should be safe on their mountain without knowing of them. The Trautbach family had heard of Wildschloss's designs, and they had set abroad such injurious reports respecting the Lady of Adlerstein, that Sir Kasimir was in the act of inditing a cartel to be sent by Count Kaulwitz, to demand an explanation—not merely as the lady's suitor, but as the only Adlerstein of full age. Now, if Ebbo had heard of the rumour, he would certainly have given the lie direct, and taken the whole defence on himself; and it may be feared that, just as his cause might have been, Master Gottfried's faith did not stretch to believing that it would make his sixteen-year-old arm equal to the brutal might of Lassla of Trautbach. So he heartily thanked the Baron of Wildschloss, agreed with him that the young knights were not as yet equal to the maintenance of the cause, and went home again to watch carefully that no report reached either of his nephews. Nor did he breathe freely till he had seen the little party ride safe off in the early morning, in much more lordly guise than when they had entered the city.

As to Wildschloss and his nephew of Trautbach, in spite of their relationship they had a sharp combat on the borders of their own estates, in which both were severely wounded; but Sir Kasimir, with the misericorde[1] in his grasp, forced Lassla to retract whatever he had said in dispraise of the lady of Adlerstein. Wily old Gottfried took care that the tidings should be sent in a form that might at once move Christina with pity and gratitude towards her champion, and convince her sons that the adversary was too much hurt for them to attempt a fresh challenge.

---

[1] The dagger with which the duellist gave the death-blow

M

CHAPTER X

The reconciliation made Ebbo retract his hasty resolution of relinquishing all the benefits resulting from his connection with the Sorel family, and his mother's fortune made it possible to carry out many changes that rendered the castle and its inmates far more prosperous in appearance than had ever been the case before.

A chaplain had been secured. The youths had insisted on his being capable of assisting their studies, and a good man had been found who was fearfully learned, having studied at all possible universities, but then failing as a teacher, because he was so dreamy and absent as to be incapable of keeping the unruly students in order. Jobst Schon was his proper name, but he was translated into Jodocus Pulcher. The chapel was duly adorned, the hall and other chambers were fitted up with some degree of comfort; the castle court was cleansed, the cattle-sheds removed to the rear, and the serfs were presented with seed, and offered payment in coin if they would give their labour in fencing and clearing the cornfield and vineyard which the barons were bent on forming on the sunny slope of the ravine. The serfs had much rather their lord had turned out a freebooter than an improver. Why should they sow new seeds, when the old had sufficed their fathers? Work, beyond the regulated days when they scratched up the soil of his old enclosure, was abhorrent to them. As to his offered coin, they needed nothing it would buy, and had rather bask in the sun or sleep in the smoke. A vineyard had never been heard of on an Adlerstein mountain: it was clean contrary to his forefathers' habits; and all came of the bad drop of restless burgher blood, that could not let honest folk rest.

Ebbo stormed, not merely with words, but blows, became ashamed of his violence, tried to atone for it by gifts and kind words. Had not Koppel and a few younger men been more open to influence, his agricultural schemes could hardly have begun; but Friedel's persuasions were not without success, and every rood that was dug was achieved by his patience and perseverance.

386

Next came home the Graf von Schlangenwald. He had of late inhabited his castle in Styria, but in a quarrel with some of his neighbours he had lost his eldest son, and the pacification enforced by the King of the Romans had so infuriated him that he had deserted that part of the country and returned to Swabia more fierce and bitter than ever. Thenceforth began a petty border warfare such as had existed when Christina first knew Adlerstein, but had of late died out. The shepherd lad came home weeping with wrath. Three mounted Schlangenwaldern had driven off his four best sheep, and beaten himself with their halberds, though he was safe on Adlerstein ground. Then a light thrown by a Schlangenwald reiter consumed all Jobst's pile of wood. The swine did not come home, and were found with spears sticking in them; the great broad-horned bull that Ebbo had brought from the pastures of Ulm vanished from the Alp below the Gemsbock's Pass, and was known to be salted for winter use at Schlangenwald.

Still Christina tried to persuade her sons that this might be only the retainers' violence, and induced Ebbo to write a letter, complaining of the outrages, but not blaming the count, only begging that his followers might be better restrained. The letter was conveyed by a lay-brother—no other messenger being safe. Ebbo had protested from the first that it would be of no use, but he waited anxiously for the answer.

Thus it stood, when conveyed to him by a tenant of the Ruprecht cloister:

"Wot you, Eberhard, Freiherr von Adlerstein, that your house have injured me by thought, word, and deed. Your great-grandfather usurped my lands at the ford. Your grandfather stole my cattle and burnt my mills. Then, in the war, he slew my brother Johann and lamed for life my cousin Matthias. Your father slew eight of my retainers and spoiled my crops. You yourself claim my land at the ford, and secure the spoil which is justly mine. Therefore do I declare war and feud against you. Therefore to you and all yours, to your helpers and helpers' helpers, am I a foe. And thereby shall I have maintained my honour against you and yours.

"WOLFGANG, Graf von Schlangenwald.

HIEROM, Graf von Schlangenwald—
his cousin."

etc.   etc.   etc.

And a long list of names, all connected with Schlangenwald, followed; and a large seal, bearing the snake of Schlangenwald, was appended thereto.

"The old miscreant!" burst out Ebbo; "it is a feud brief."

"A feud brief!" exclaimed Friedel; "they are no longer according to the law."

"Law?—what cares he for law or mercy either? Is this the way men act by the League? Did we not swear to send no more feud letters, nor have recourse to fistright?"

"We must appeal to the Markgraf of Wurtemburg," said Friedel.

It was the only measure in their power, though Ebbo winced at it; but his oaths were recent, and his conscience would not allow him to transgress them by doing himself justice. Besides, neither party could take the castle of the other, and the only reprisals in his power would have been on the defenceless peasants of Schlangenwald. He must therefore lay the whole matter before the Markgraf, who was the head of the Swabian League, and bound to redress his wrongs. He made his arrangements without faltering, selecting the escort who were to accompany him, and insisting on leaving Friedel to guard his mother and the castle. He would not for the world have admitted the suggestion that the council and introduction of Adlerstein Wildschloss would have been exceedingly useful to him.

The blue banner came safe up the pass again, but Ebbo was gloomy and indignant. The Markgraf of Wurtemburg had been formally civil to the young Freiherr; but he had laughed at the feud letter as a mere old-fashioned habit of Schlangenwald's that it was better not to notice, and he evidently regarded the stealing of a bull or the misusing of a serf as far too petty a matter for his attention. He told Ebbo that, being a free baron of the empire, he must keep his bounds respected; he was free to take and hang any spoiler he could catch, but his bulls were his own affair: the League was not for such gear.

Ebbo returned home in a mood that rejoiced Heinz and Hatto with hopes of the old days, while it filled his mother with dreary dismay and apprehension.

"Schlangenwald shall suffer next time he transgresses," said Ebbo.

The "next time" was when the first winter cold was setting in. A party of reitern came to harry an outlying field, where Ulrich had raised a scanty crop of rye. Tidings reached the castle in such good time that the two brothers, with Heinz, the two Ulm grooms, Koppel, and a troop of serfs, fell on the marauders before they had effected much damage, and while some remained to trample out the fire, the rest pursued the enemy even to the village of Schlangenwald.

"Burn it, Herr Freiherr," cried Heinz, hot with victory. "Let them learn how to make havoc of our corn."

But a host of half-naked beings rushed out shrieking about sick children, bed-ridden grandmothers, and crippled fathers, and falling on their knees, with their hands stretched out to the young barons. Ebbo turned away his head with hot tears in his eyes; "Friedel, what can we do?"

"Not barbarous murder," said Friedel.

"But they brand us for cowards!"

"The cowardice were in striking here," and Friedel sprang to withhold Koppel, who had lighted a bundle of dried fern ready to thrust into the thatch.

"Peasants," said Ebbo, with the same impulse, "I spare you. You did not this wrong. But bear word to your lord, that if he will meet me with lance and sword, he will learn the valour of Adlerstein."

The serfs flung themselves before him in transports of gratitude, but he turned hastily away and strode up the mountain, his cheek glowing as he remembered, too late, that his defiance would be scoffed at, as a boy's vaunt.

Christina perceived that this was one of the most critical periods of Ebbo's life, baited as he was by the enemy of his race, and feeling all the disadvantages which heart and conscience gave him in dealing with a man who had neither, at a time when public opinion was always with the most masterful. The necessity of arming his retainers and having fighting-men as a guard were temptations to hereditary habits of violence; and that so proud and fiery a nature as his should never become involved in them was almost beyond hope. Even present danger seemed more around than ever before. The estate was almost in a state of siege, and Christina never saw her sons quit the castle without thinking of their father's fate. The snow, which she had so often hailed as a friend, was never more welcome than this winter; not merely as shutting the enemy out, and her sons in, but as cutting off all danger of a visit from her suitor, who would now come armed with his late sufferings in her behalf; and, moreover, with all the urgent need of a wise and respected head and protector for her sons. Yet the more evident the expediency became, the greater grew her distaste.

.   .   .   .

The snow melted, the torrent became a flood, then contracted itself, but was still a broad stream, when one spring afternoon Ebbo showed his brother some wains making for the ford, adding, "It cannot be rightly passable. They will come to loss. I shall get the men together to aid them."

"See," and Friedel pointed to the thicket to the westward of the meadow around the stream, where the beech trees were budding, but not yet forming a full mass of verdure, "is not the snake in the wood? Methinks I spy the glitter of his scales."

"By heavens, the villians are lying in wait for the travellers at our landing-place," cried Ebbo, and raising the bugle to his lips, he sent forth three notes well known as a call to arms. Their echoes came back from the rocks, followed instantly by lusty jodels,[1] and the brothers rushed into the hall to take down their light headpieces and corselets, answering in haste their mother's startled questions, by telling of the endangered travellers, and the Schlangenwald ambush. She looked white and trembled, but said no word to hinder them; only as she clasped Friedel's corselet, she entreated them to take fuller armour.

"We must speed the short way down the rock," said Ebbo, "and cannot be cumbered with heavy harness. Sweet motherling, fear not; but let a meal be spread for our rescued captives. Ho, Heinz, 'tis against the Schlangenwald rascals. Art too stiff to go down the rock path?"

"No; nor down the abyss, could I strike a good stroke against Schlangenwald at the bottom of it," qouth Heinz.

The convoy had by this time halted, evidently to try the ford. A horseman crossed, and found it practicable, for a waggon proceeded to make the attempt.

"Now is our time," said Ebbo, who was standing on the narrow ledge between the castle and the precipitous path leading to the meadow. "One waggon may get over, but the second or third will stick in the ruts that it leaves. Now we will drop from our crag, and if the Snake falls on them, why, then for a pounce of the Eagle."

The two young knights, so goodly in their bright steel, knelt for their mother's blessing, and then sprang like chamois down the ivy-twined steep, followed by their men, and were lost to sight among the bushes and rocks. Yet even while her frame quivered with fear, her heart swelled at the thought what a gulf there was between these days and those when she had hidden her face in despair, while Ermentrude watched the Debateable Ford.

[1] The loud musical cry made for signalling in mountain districts (the *j* is pronounced *y*).

She watched now in suspense, indeed, but with exultation instead of shame, as two waggons safely crossed; but the third stuck fast, and presently turned over in the stream, impelled sideways by the efforts of the struggling horses. Then, amid endeavours to disentangle the animals and soccour the driver, the travellers were attacked by a party of armed men, who dashed out of the beechwood, and fell on the main body of the waggons, which were waiting on the bit of bare shingly soil that lay between the new and old channels. A wild melee was all that Christina could see—weapons raised, horses starting, men rushing from the river, while the clang and the shout rose even to the castle.

Hark! Out rings the clear call, "The Eagle to the rescue!" There they speed over the meadow, the two slender forms with glancing helms! Oh, overrun not the followers, rush not into needless danger! There is Koppel almost up with them with his big axe—Heinz's broad shoulders near. Heaven strike with them! Some are flying. Some one has fallen! O heavens! on which side? Ah! it is into the Schlangenwald woods that the fugitives direct their flight. Three—four—the whole troop pursued! Go not too far! Run not into needless risk! Your work is done, and gallantly. Well done, young knights of Adlerstein! Which of you is it that stands pointing out safe standing-ground for the men that are raising the wagon? Which of you is it who stands in converse with a burgher form? Thanks and blessings! the lads are safe, and full knightly hath been their first emprise.

A quarter of an hour later, a step mounted the ascent, and Friedel's bright face laughed from his helmet, "There, mother, will you crown your knights? Could you see Ebbo bear down the chief squire? for the old Snake was not there himself. And whom do you think we rescued besides a whole band of Venetian traders to whom he had joined himself? Why, my uncle's friend, the architect, of whom he used to speak—Master Moritz Schleiermacher."

"Poor Master Moritz! Is he much hurt? Is Ebbo bringing him up hither?"

"No, mother, he is but giddied and stunned, and now must you send down store of sausage, sourkraut, meat, wine, and beer; for the wains cannot all cross till daylight, and we must keep ward all night lest the Schlangenwaldern should fall on them again. Plenty of good cheer, mother, to make a right merry watch."

"Take heed, Friedel mine; a merry watch is scarce a safe one."

"Even so, sweet motherling, and therefore must Ebbo and I share it. You must mete out your liquor wisely, you see, enough for the credit of Adlerstein, and enough to keep out the marsh fog, yet not enough to make us snore too soundly. I am going to take my lute; it would be using it ill not to let it enjoy such a chance as a midnight watch."

So away went the boy, and by and by Christina saw the red watch-fire as she gazed from her window. She would have been pleased to see how, marshalled by a merchant who had crossed the desert from Egypt to Palestine, the wagons were ranged in a circle, and the watches told off, while the food and drink were carefully portioned out.

Freiherr Ebbo, on his own ground, as champion and host, was far more at ease than in the city, and became very friendly with the merchants and architect as they sat round the fire, conversing, or at times challenging the mountain echoes by songs to the sound of Friedel's lute. When the stars grew bright, most lay down to sleep in the wagons, while the others watched, till Karl's wagon should be over the mountain, and the vigil was relieved.

No disturbance took place, and at sunrise a hasty meal was partaken of, and the work of crossing the river was set in hand.

"Pity," said Moritz, the architect, "that this ford were not spanned by a bridge, to the avoiding of danger and spoil."

"Who could build such a bridge?" asked Ebbo.

"Yourself, Herr Freiherr, in union with us burghers of Ulm. It were well worth your while to give land and stone, and ours to give labour and skill, provided we fixed a toll on the passage, which would be willingly paid to save peril and delay."

The brothers caught at the idea, and the merchants agreed that such a bridge would be an inestimable boon to all traffickers between Constance, Ulm, and Augsburg, and would attract many travellers who were scared away by the evil name of the Debateable Ford. Master Moritz looked at the stone of the mountain, pronounced it excellent material, and already sketched the span of the arches with a view to winter torrents. As to the site, the best was on the firm ground above the ford; but here only one side was Adlerstein, while on the other Ebbo claimed both banks, and it was probable that an equally sound foundation could be obtained, only with more cost and delay.

After this survey the travellers took leave of the barons, promising to write when their fellow-citizens should have been sounded as to the bridge; and Ebbo remained in high spirits, with such brilliant purposes that he had quite forgotten his gloomy forebodings. "Peace instead of war at home," he said; "with the revenue it will bring, I will build a mill, and set our lads to work, so that they may become less dull and doltish than their parents. Then we will follow the Emperor with a train that none need despise! No one will talk now of Adlerstein not being able to take care of himself!"

Letters came from Ulm, saying that the guilds of mercers and wine merchants were delighted with the project, and invited the Baron of Adlerstein to a council at the Rathhaus. Master Sorel begged the mother to come with her sons to be his guest; but, fearing the neighbourhood of Sir Kasimir, she remained at home, while her sons rode to the city. There Ebbo found that his late exploit and his future plan had made him a person of much greater consideration than on his last visit, and he demeaned himself with far more ease and affability in consequence. He had affairs on his hands too, and felt more than one year older.

The two guilds agreed to build the bridge, and share the toll with the baron in return for the ground and materials; but they preferred the plan that placed one pier on the Schlangenwald bank, and proposed to write to the count an offer to include him in the scheme, awarding him a share in the profits in proportion to his contribution. However vexed at the turn affairs had taken, Ebbo could offer no valid objection, and was obliged to affix his signature to the letter in company with the guildmasters.

It was despatched by the city pursuivants—

> The only men who safe might ride
> Their errands on the border side;

and a meeting was appointed in the Rathhaus for the day of their expected return. The higher burghers sat on their carved chairs in the grand old hall, the lesser magnates on benches, and Ebbo, in an elbowed seat far too spacious for his slender proportions, met a glance from Friedel that told him his merry brother was thinking of the frog and the ox. The pursuivants entered—hardy, shrewd-looking men, with the city arms decking them wherever there was room for them.

"Honour-worthy sirs," they said, "no letter did the Graf von Schlangenwald return."

"Sent he no message?" demanded Moritz Schleiermacher.

"Yea, worthy sir, but scarce befitting this reverend assembly."
On being pressed, however, it was repeated: "The Lord Count was

pleased to swear at what he termed the insolence of the city in sending him heralds, 'as if,' said he, 'the dogs,' your worships, 'were his equals.' Then having cursed your worships, he reviled the crooked writing of Herr Clerk Diedrichson, and called his chaplain to read it to him. Herr Priest could scarce read three lines for his foul language about the ford. 'Never,' said he, 'would he consent to raising a bridge—a mean trick,' so said he, 'for defrauding him of his rights to what the flood sent him.'"

"But," asked Ebbo, "took he no note of our explanation, that if he give not the upper bank, we will build lower, where both sides are my own?"

"He passed it not entirely over," replied the messenger.

"What said he—the very words?" demanded Ebbo, with the paling cheek and low voice that made his passion often seem like patience.

"He said—(the Herr Freiherr will pardon me for repeating the words)—he said, 'Tell the misproud mongrel of Adlerstein that he had best sit firm in his own saddle ere meddling with his betters, and if he touch one pebble of the Braunwasser, he will rue it. And before your city-folk take up with him or his, they had best learn whether he have any right at all in the case.'"

"His plan is plain," said Master Gottfried; "full proofs were given in, and his investiture by the Kaiser forms a title in itself."

"Even so did I explain, Herr Guildmaster," said the pursuivant; "but, pardon me, the count laughed me to scorn, and quoth he, 'Asked the Kaiser for proof of his father's death?'"

"Mere mischief-making, as before," said Master Gottfried, while his nephews started with amaze. "His father's death was proved by an eye-witness, whom you still have in your train, have you not, Herr Freiherr?"

"Yea," replied Ebbo, "he is at Adlerstein now, Heinrich Bauermann, called the Schneiderlein, from whom we have often heard how my father died, choked in his own blood, from a deep breast-wound, immediately after he had sent home his last greetings to my lady mother."

"Was the corpse restored?" asked the able Rathsherr Ulrich.

"No," said Ebbo. "Almost all our retainers had perished, and when a friar was sent to the hostel to bring home the remains, it appeared that the treacherous foe had borne them off—nay, my grandfather's head was sent to the Diet!"

The assembly agreed that the count could only mean to make the absence of direct evidence about a murder committed eighteen years ago tell in sowing distrust between the allies. The suggestion was not worth a thought, and it was plain that no site would be available except the Debateable Strand. To this, however, Ebbo's title was assailable, both on account of his minority, as well as his father's unproved death, and of the disputed claim to the ground. The Rathsherr, Master Gottfried, and others, therefore recommended deferring the work till the baron should be of age, when, on again tendering his allegiance, he might obtain a distinct recognition of his marches. But this policy did not consort with the quick spirit of Moritz Schleiermacher, nor with the convenience of the mercers and wine merchants, who were constant sufferers by the want of a bridge, and afraid of waiting four years in which a lad like the baron might return to the normal instincts of his class, or the Braunwasser might take back the land it had given; whilst Ebbo himself was urgent, with all the defiant fire of youth, to begin building at once in spite of all gainsayers.

"Strife and blood will it cost," said Master Sorel gravely.

"What can be had worth the having save at cost of strife and blood?" said Ebbo, with a glance of fire.

So the young knights mounted, and had ridden about half the way in silence, when Ebbo exclaimed, "Friedel"—and as his brother started, "what art musing on?"

"What thou art thinking of," said Friedel, turning on him an eye that had not only something of the brightness but of the penetration of a sunbeam.

"I do not think thereon at all," said Ebbo gloomily. "It is a figment of the old serpent to hinder us from snatching his prey from him."

"Nevertheless," said Friedel, "I cannot but remember that the Genoese merchant of old told us of a German noble sold by his foes to the Moors."

"Folly! That tale was too recent to concern my father."

"I did not think it did," said Friedel; "but mayhap that noble's family rest equally certain of his death."

"Pfui!" said Ebbo hotly; "hast not heard fifty times how he died even in speaking, and how Heinz crossed his hands on his breast? What wouldst have more?"

"Hardly even that," said Friedel, slightly smiling.

"Tush!" hastily returned his brother, "I meant only by way of proof. Would an honest old fellow like Heinz be a deceiver?"

"Not wittingly. Yet I would fain ride to that hostel and make inquiries!"

"The traitor host met his deserts, and was broken on the wheel for murdering a pedlar a year ago," said Ebbo. "I would I knew where my father was buried, for then would I bring his corpse honourably back; but as to his being a living man, I will not have it spoken of to trouble my mother. Her heart is at peace, believing him in his grave; but let her imagine him in Schlangenwald's dungeon, or some Moorish galley, if thou likest it better, and how will her mild spirit be rent!"

"It might be so," said Friedel thoughtfully. "It may be best to keep this secret from her till we have fuller certainty."

"Agreed then," said Ebbo, "unless the Wildschloss fellow should again molest us, when his answer is ready."

"Is this just towards my mother?" said Friedel.

"Just! What mean'st thou? Is it not our office and our dearest right to shield our mother from care? And is not her chief wish to be rid of the Wildschloss suit?"

Friedel, however, could not rest till he had followed Heinz to the stable, and speaking over the back of the old white mare, the only other survivor of the massacre, has asked him once more for the particulars, a tale he was never loth to tell: but when Friedel further demanded whether he was certain of having seen the death of his younger lord, he replied, as if hurt, "What! think you I would have quitted him while life was yet in him?"

"No, certainly, good Heinz; yet I would fain know by what tokens thou knewest his death."

"Ah! Sir Friedel; when you have seen a stricken field or two, you will not ask how I know death from life."

"Is a swoon so utterly unlike death?"

"I say not but that an inexperienced youth might be mistaken," said Heinz; "but for one who had learned the bloody trade, it were impossible."

Yet while Ebbo plunged more eagerly into plans for the bridge-building, Friedel drew more and more into his old world of musings; and many a summer afternoon was spent by him at the Ptarmigan's Mere, in deep communings with himself, as one revolving a purpose.

Christina could not but observe, with a strange sense of foreboding, that, while one son was more than ever in the lonely mountain heights, the other was far more at the base. Master Moritz Schleiermacher was a constant guest at the castle, and Ebbo was much taken up with his companionship. He was a strong, shrewd man, still young, but with much experience, and he knew how to adapt himself to intercourse with the proud nobility, preserving an independent bearing, while avoiding all that haughtiness could take umbrage at; and thus he was acquiring a greater influence over Ebbo than was perceived by any save the watchful mother, who began to fear lest her son was acquiring an infusion of worldly wisdom and eagerness for gain that would indeed be a severance between him and his brother.

CHAPTER XI

THE STONE was quarried high on the mountain, and a direct road was made for bringing it down to the waterside. The castle profited by the road in accessibility, but its impregnability was so far lessened. However, as Ebbo said, it was to be a friendly harbour, instead of a robber crag, and in case of need the communication could easily be destroyed. The blocks of stone were brought down, and wooden sheds were erected for the workmen in the meadow.

In August, however, came tidings that, after two amputations of a diseased limb, the Kaiser Freidrich III. had died—it was said from over-free use of melons in the fever consequent on the operation. His death was not likely to make much change in the government, which had of late been left to his son. At this time the King of the Romans (for the title of Kaiser was conferred only by coronation by the Pope, and this Maximilian never received) was at Innspruck collecting troops for the deliverance of Styria and Carinthia from a horde of invading Turks. The Markgraf of Wurtemburg sent an intimation to all the Swabian League that the new sovereign would be pleased if their homage were paid to him in his camp at the head of their armed retainers.

Here was the way of enterprise and honour open at last, and the

young Barons of Adlerstein eagerly prepared for it, equipping their
vassals and sending to Ulm to take three or four men-at-arms into
their pay, so as to make up twenty lances as the contingent of Adlerstein. It was decided that Christina should spend the time of
their absence at Ulm, whither her sons would escort her on their way
to the camp. The last busy day was over, and in the summer
evening Christina was sitting on the castle steps listening to Ebbo's
eager talk of his plans of interesting his hero, the King of the Romans,
in his bridge, and obtaining full recognition of his claim to the
Debateable Strand, where the busy workmen could be seen far below.

Presently Ebbo, as usual when left to himself, grew restless for
want of Friedel, and exclaiming, "The musing fit is on him!—he will
stay all night at the tarn if I fetch him not," he set off in quest of him,
passing through the hamlet to look for him in the chapel on his way.

Not finding Friedel there, he was, however, some way up towards
the tarn, when he met his brother wearing the beamy yet awestruck
look that he often brought from the mountain height, yet with a
steadfast expression of resolute purpose on his face.

"Ah, dreamer!" said Ebbo, "I knew where to seek thee! Ever in
the clouds!"

"Yes, I have been to the tarn," said Friedel, throwing his arm
round his brother's neck in their boyish fashion. "It has been very
dear to me, and I longed to see its grey depths once more."

"Once! Yea, manifold times shalt thou see them," said Ebbo.
"Schleiermacher tells me that these are no Janissaries, but a mere
miscreant horde, even by whom glory can scarcely be gained, and no
peril at all."

"I know not," said Friedel, "but it is to me as if I were taking my
leave of all these purple hollows and heaven-lighted peaks cleaving
the sky. All the more, Ebbo, since I have made up my mind to a
resolution, I am convinced that it is my duty to strive to ascertain my
father's fate. Hold, I say not that it is thine. Thou hast thy charge
here——"

"Looking for a dead man," growled Ebbo; "a proper quest!"

"Not so," returned Friedel. "At the camp it will surely be
possible to learn, through either Schlangenwald or his men, how it
went with my father. Men say that his surviving son, the Teutonic
knight, is of very different mould. He might bring something to
light. Were it proved to be as the Schneiderlein avers, then would
our conscience be at rest; but, if he were in Schlangenwald's
dungeon——"

"Folly! Impossible!"

"Yet men have pined eighteen years in dark vaults," said Friedel.

"If the serpent hath dared," cried Ebbo, "though it is mere folly to think of it, we would summon the League and have his castle about his ears! Not that I believe it."

"Scarce do I," said Friedel; "but there haunts me evermore the description of the kindly German chained between the decks of the Corsair's galley. Once and again have I dreamt thereof."

"Thou wilt learn," returned Ebbo, drawing him closer, "as I also trust to do—in what nameless hole the serpent hid his remains. Then shall they be duly coffined and blazoned. All the monks in the cloisters for twenty miles round shall sing requiems, and thou and I will walk bareheaded, with candles in our hands, by the bier, till we rest him in the Blessed Friedmund's chapel; and there Lucas Handlein shall carve his tomb, and thou shalt sit for the likeness."

"So may it end," said Friedel, "but either I will know him dead, or endeavour somewhat in his behalf. And that the need is real as well as the purpose blessed, I have become the more certain, for, Ebbo, as I rose to descend the hill, I saw on the cloud our patron's very form—I saw myself kneel before him and receive his blessing."

Ebbo burst out laughing. "Now know I that it is indeed as saith Schleiermacher," he said, "and that these phantoms of the Blessed Friedmund are but shadows cast by the sun on the vapours of the ravine. See, Friedel, I had gone to seek thee at the chapel, and meeting Father Norbert, I bent my knee, that I might take his farewell blessing. I had the substance, thou the shadow, thou dreamer!"

Friedel was as much mortified for the moment as his gentle nature could be. Then he resumed his sweet smile, saying, "Be it so! I have oft read that men are too prone to take visions and special providences to themselves, and now I have proved the truth of the saying."

"And," said Ebbo, "thou seest thy purpose is as baseless as thy vision?"

"No, Ebbo. It grieves me to differ from thee, but my resolve is older than the fancy, and may not be shaken because I was vain enough to believe that the Blessed Friedmund could stoop to bless me."

"Ha!" shouted Ebbo, glad to see an object on which to vent his secret annoyance. "Who goes there, skulking round the rocks? Here, rogue, what art after here?"

"No harm," sullenly replied a half-clad boy.

"Whence art thou? From Schlangenwald, to spy what more we can be robbed of? This comes of sparing the nest of thankless adders!"

"Nay," said Friedel, "mayhap it is because they are not thankless that the poor fellow is here."

"Sir," said the boy, coming nearer, "I will tell *you*—*you* I will tell —not him who threatens. Mother said you spared our huts, and the lady gave us bread when we came to the castle gate in winter, and she would not see the reiters lay waste your folk's doings down there without warning you"

"My good lad! What saidst thou?" cried Ebbo; but the boy seemed dumb before him, and Friedel repeated the question ere he answered: "All the lanzknechts and reiters are at the castle, and the Herr Graf has taken all my father's young sheep for them, a plague upon him! And our folk are warned to be at the muster rock to-morrow morn, each with a bundle of straw and a pine brand; and Black Berend heard the body squire say the Herr Graf had sworn not to go to the wars till every stick at the ford be burnt, every stone drowned, every workman hung."

Ebbo, in a transport of indignation and gratitude, thrust his hand into his pouch, and threw the boy a handful of groschen, while Friedel gave warm thanks, in utmost haste, ere both brothers sprang with headlong speed down the wild path, to take advantage of the timely intelligence.

The council of war was speedily assembled, consisting of the barons, their mother, Master Moritz Schleiermacher, Heinz, and Hatto. To bring up to the castle the workmen, their families, and the more valuable implements, was at once decided; and Christina asked whether there would be anything left worth defending, and whether the Schlangenwalden might not expend their fury on the scaffold, which could be newly supplied from the forest, the huts, which could be quickly restored, and the stones, which could hardly be damaged. The enemy must proceed to the camp in a day or two, and the building would be less assailable by their return; and, besides, it was scarcely lawful to enter on a private war when the Imperial banner was in the field.

"Craving your pardon, gracious lady," said the architect, "that blame rests with him who provokes the war. See, Lord Baron, there is time to send to Ulm, where the two guilds, our allies, will at once equip their trained bands and dispatch them. We meanwhile will hold the knaves in check, and, by the time our burghers come up, the snake brood will have had such a lesson as they will not soon forget. Said I well, Herr Freiherr?"

"Right bravely," said Ebbo. "It consorts not with our honour or rights, with my pledges to Ulm, or the fame of my house, to shut ourselves up and see the rogues work their will scathless. My own score of men, besides the stouter masons, carpenters, and serfs, will be fully enough to make the old serpent of the wood rue the day, even without the aid of the burghers. Not a word against it, dearest mother. None is so wise as thou in matters of peace, but honour is here concerned."

"My question is," persevered the mother, "whether honour be not better served by obeying the summons of the king against the infidel, with the men thou hast called together at his behest? Let the count do his worst; he gives thee legal ground for complaint to lay before the king and the League, and all may there be more firmly established."

"That were admirable counsel, lady," said Schleiermacher, "well suited to the honour-worthy Guildmaster Sorel, and to our justice-loving city; but, in matters of baronial rights and aggressions, king and League are wont to help those that help themselves, and those that are over-nice as to law and justice come by the worst."

"Not the worst in the long run," said Friedel.

"Thine unearthly code will not serve us here, Friedel mine," returned his brother. "Did I not defend the work I have begun, I should be branded as a weak fool. Nor will I see the foes of my house insult me without striking a fair stroke. Call in the serfs, Hatto, and arm them. Mother, order a good supper for them. Master Moritz, let us summon thy masons and carpenters, and see who is a good man with his hands among them."

Christina saw that remonstrance was vain. The days of peril and violence were coming back again; and all she could take comfort in was, that, if not wholly right, her son was far from wholly wrong, and that with a free heart she could pray for a blessing on him and on his arms.

CHAPTER XII

BY THE EARLY September sunrise the thicket beneath the pass was sheltering the twenty well-appointed reiters of Adlerstein, each standing, holding his horse by the bridle, ready to mount at the instant. In their rear were the serfs and artisans, some with axes, scythes, or ploughshares, a few with crossbows, and Jobst and his sons with the long blackened poles used for stirring their charcoal fires. In advance were Master Moritz and the two Barons, the former in a stout plain steel helmet, cuirass, and gauntlets, a sword, and those new-fashioned weapons, pistols; the latter in full knightly armour, exactly alike, from the gilt-spurred heel to the eagle-crested helm, and often moved restlessly forward to watch for the enemy, though taking care not to be betrayed by the glitter of their mail. So long did they wait that there was even a doubt whether it might not have been a false alarm; the boy was vituperated, and it was proposed to dispatch a spy to see whether anything were doing at Schlangenwald.

At length a rustling and rushing were heard; then a clank of armour. Ebbo vaulted into the saddle, and gave the word to mount; Schleier-macher, who always fought on foot, stepped up to him. "Keep back your men, Herr Freiherr. Let his design be manifest. We must not be said to have fallen on him on his way to the muster."

"It would be but as he served my father!" muttered Ebbo, forced, however, to restrain himself, as the tramp of horses shook the ground, and bright armour became visible on the further side of the stream.

For the first time the brothers beheld the foe of their line. He was seated on a clumsy black horse, and sheathed in full armour, and was apparently a large, heavy man, whose powerful proportions were becoming unwieldy as he advanced in life. As the armed troop, outnumbering the Adlersteiners by about a dozen, and followed by a rabble with straw and pine brands, came forth on the meadow, the count halted, and appeared to be giving orders.

"The ruffian! He is calling them on! Now——" began Ebbo.

"Nay, there is no sign yet that he is not peacefully on his journey to the camp," responded Moritz; and, chafing with impatient fury, the knight waited while Schlangenwald rode towards the old channel of the Braunwasser, and there, drawing his rein, and sitting like a statue in his stirrups, he could hear him shout: "The lazy dogs are not astir yet. We will give them a reveille. Forward with your brands!"

"Now!" and Ebbo's cream-coloured horse leapt forth, as the whole band flashed into the sunshine from the greenwood covert.

"Who troubles the workmen on my land?" shouted Ebbo.

"Who you may be I care not," replied the count, "but when I

find strangers unlicensed on my lands, I burn down their huts. On, fellows!"

"Back, fellows!" called Ebbo. "Whoso touches a stick on Adlerstein ground shall suffer."

"So!" said the count, "this is the burgher-bred, burgher-fed varlet, that calls himself of Adlerstein! Boy, thou had best be warned. Wert thou true-blooded, it were worth my while to maintain my rights against thee. Craven as thou art, not even with spirit to accept my feud, I would fain not have the trouble of sweeping thee from my path."

"Herr Graf, as true Freiherr and belted knight, I defy thee! I proclaim my right to this ground, and whoso damages those I place there must do battle with me."

"Thou wilt have it then," said the count, taking his heavy lance from his squire, closing his visor, and wheeling back his horse, so as to give space for his career.

Ebbo did the like, while Friedel on one side, and Hierom von Schlangenwald on the other, kept their men in array, awaiting the issue of the strife between their leaders—the fire of seventeen against the force of fifty-six.

They closed in full shock, with shivered lances and rearing, pawing horses, but without damage to either. Each drew his sword, and they were pressing together, when Heinz, seeing a Schlangenwalder aiming with his crossbow, rode at him furiously, and the melee became general; shots were fired, not only from crossbows, but from arquebuses, and in the throng Friedel lost sight of the main combat between his brother and the count.

Suddenly, however, there was a crash, as of falling men and horses, with a shout of victory strangely mingled with a cry of agony, and both sides became aware that their leaders had fallen. Each party rushed to its fallen head. Friedel beheld Ebbo under his struggling horse, and an enemy dashing at his throat, and, flying to the rescue, he rode down the assailant, striking him with his sword; and, with the instinct of driving the foe as far as possible from his brother, he struck with a sort of frenzy, shouting fiercely to his men, and leaping over the dry bed of the river, rushing onward with an intoxication of ardour that would have seemed foreign to his gentle nature, but for the impetuous desire to protect his brother. Their leader down, the enemy had no one to rally them, and, in spite of their superiority in number, gave way in confusion before the furious onset of Adlerstein. So soon, however, as Friedel perceived that he had forced the enemy far back from the scene of conflict, his anxiety for his brother returned, and, leaving the retainers to continue the pursuit, he turned his horse. There on the green meadow, lay on the one hand Ebbo's cream-coloured charger, with his master under him, on the other the large figure of the count; and several other prostrate forms likewise struggled on the sand and pebbles of the strand, or on the turf.

"Ay," said the architect, who had turned with Friedel, "'twas a gallant feat, Sir Friedel, and I trust there is no great harm done. Were it the mere dint of the count's sword, your brother will be little worse."

"Ebbo! Ebbo mine, look up!" cried Friedel, leaping from his horse, and unclasping his brother's helmet.

"Friedel!" groaned a half-suffocated voice. "Oh, take away the horse."

One or two of the artisans were at hand, and with their help the dying steed was disengaged from the rider, who could not restrain his moans, though Friedel held him in his arms, and endeavoured to move him as gently as possible. It was then seen that the deep gash from the count's sword in the chest was not the most serious injury, but that an arquebus ball had pierced his thigh, before burying itself in the body of his horse; and that the limb had been further crushed and wrenched by the animal's struggles. He was nearly unconscious, and gasped with anguish, but, after Moritz had bathed his face and moistened his lips, as he lay in his brother's arms, he looked up with clearer eyes, and said, "Have I slain him? It was the shot, not he, that sent me down. Lives he? See—thou, Friedel—thou. Make him yield."

Transferring Ebbo to the arms of Schleiermacher, Friedel obeyed, and stepped towards the fallen foe. The wrongs of Adlerstein were indeed avenged, for the blood was welling fast from a deep thrust above the collar-bone, and the failing, feeble hand was wandering uncertainly among the clasps of the gorget.

"Let me aid," said Friedel, kneeling down, and in his pity for the dying man omitting the summons to yield, he threw back the helmet, and beheld a grizzled head and stern, hard features, so embrowned by weather and inflamed by intemperance, that even approaching death failed to blanch them. A scowl of malignant hate was in the eyes, and there was a thrill of angry wonder as they fell on the lad's face. "Thou again,—thou whelp! I thought at least I had made an end of thee," he muttered, unheard by Friedel who, intent on the thought that had recurred to him with greater vividness than ever, was again filling Ebbo's helmet with water. He refreshed the dying man's face with it, held it to his lips, and said, "Herr Graf, variance and strife are ended now. For Heaven's sake, say where I may find my father!"

"So! Wouldst find him?" replied Schlangenwald, fixing his look on the eager countenance of the youth, while his hand, with a dying man's nervous agitation, was fumbling at his belt.

"I would bless you for ever, could I but free him."

"Know then," said the count, speaking very slowly, and still holding the young knight's gaze with a sort of intent fascination, "that thy villain father is a Turkish slave, unless he be—as I hope— where his mongrel son may find him."

Therewith came a flash, a report; Friedel leaped back, staggered, fell; Ebbo started to a sitting posture, with horrified eyes, and a loud shriek, calling on his brother; Moritz sprang to his feet, shouting, "Shame! treason!"

"I call you to witness that I had not yielded." said the count. "There's an end of the brood!" and with a grim smile he straightened his limbs, and closed his eyes as a dead man, ere the indignant artisans fell on him in savage vengeance.

All this had passed like a flash of lightning, and Friedel had almost at the instant of his fall flung himself towards his brother, and raising himself on one hand, with the other clasped Ebbo's, saying, "Fear not; it is nothing." and he was bending to take Ebbo's head again on his knee, when a gush of dark blood, from his left side, caused Moritz to exclaim, "Ah! Sir Friedel, the traitor did his work! That is no slight hurt."

"Where? How? The ruffian!" cried Ebbo, supporting himself on his elbow, so as to see his brother, who rather dreamily put his hand to his side, and, looking at the fresh blood that immediately dyed it, said, "I do not feel it. This is more numb dulness than pain."

"A bad sign that," said Moritz apart to one of the workman, with whom he held counsel how to carry back to the castle the two young knights, who remained on the bank, Ebbo partly extended on the ground, partly supported on the knee and arm of Friedel, who sat with his head drooping over him, their looks fixed on one another, as if conscious of nothing else on earth.

"Herr Freiherr," said Moritz presently, "have you breath to wind your bugle to call the men back from the pursuit?"

Ebbo essayed, but was too faint, and Friedel, rousing himself from the stupor, took the horn from him, and made the mountain echoes ring again, but at the expense of a great effusion of blood.

By this time, however, Heinz was riding back, and in a moment his exultation changed to rage and despair, when he saw the condition of his young lords. Master Schleiermacher proposed to lay them on some of the planks prepared for the building, and carry them up the new road.

"Methinks," said Friedel, "that I could ride if I were lifted on horseback, and thus would our mother be less shocked."

"Well thought," said Ebbo. "Go on, and cheer her. Show her thou canst keep the saddle, however it may be with me." he added, with a groan of anguish.

Ebbo was lifted on the shoulders of his bearers, and Friedel strove to rise, with the aid of Heinz, but sank back, unable to use his limbs; and Schleiermacher was the more concerned. "It goes so with the backbone," he said. "Sir Friedmund, you had best be carried."

"Nay, for my mother's sake! And I would fain be on my good steed's back once again!" he entreated. And when with much difficulty he had been lifted to the back of his cream-colour, who stood as gently and patiently as if he understood the exigency of the moment, he sat upright, and waved his hand as he passed the litter, while Ebbo, on his side, signed to him to speed on and prepare their mother. Long, however, before the castle was reached, dizzy confusion and leaden helplessness, when no longer stimulated by his brother's presence, so grew on him that it was with much ado that Heinz could keep him in his saddle; but, when he saw his mother in the castle gateway, he again collected his forces, bade Heinz withdraw his supporting arm, and, straightening himself, waved a greeting to her, as he called cheerily: "Victory, dear mother. Ebbo has overthrown the count, and you must not be grieved if it be at some cost of blood."

"Alas, my son!" was all Christina could say, for his effort at gaiety formed a ghastly contrast with the grey, livid hue that overspread his fair young face, his bloody armour, and damp disordered hair, and even his stiff unearthly smile.

"Nay, motherling," he added, as she came so near that he could put his arm round her neck, "sorrow not, for Ebbo will need thee much. And, mother, " as his face lighted up, "there is joy coming to you. Only I would that I could have brought him. Mother, he died not under the Schlangenwald swords."

"Who? Not Ebbo?" cried the bewildered mother.

"Your own Eberhard, our father," said Friedel, raising her face to him with his hand, and adding, as he met a startled look, "The cruel count owned it with his last breath. He is a Turkish slave, and surely Heaven will give him back to comfort you, even though we may not work his freedom! Oh, mother, I had so longed for it, but God be thanked that at least certainty was bought by my life." The last words were uttered almost unconsciously, and he had nearly fallen, as the excitement faded.

The mother had no time for grief. Alas! She might have full time for that by and by! The one wish of the twins was to be together, and presently both were laid on the great bed in the upper chamber, Ebbo in a swoon from the pain of the transport, and Friedel lying so as to meet the first look of recovery. And, after Ebbo's eyes had reopened, they watched one another in silence for a short space, till Ebbo said, "Is that the hue of death on thy face, brother?"

"I well believe so," said Friedel.

"Ever together," said Ebbo, holding his hand. "But alas! My mother! Would I had never sent thee to the traitor."

"Ah! So comes her comfort," said Friedel. "Heard not you? He owned that my father was among the Turks."

"And I," cried Ebbo. "I have withheld thee! Oh, Friedel, had I listened to thee, thou hadst not been in this fatal broil!"

"Nay, ever together," repeated Friedel. "Through Ulm merchants will my mother be able to ransom him. I know she will, so oft have I dreamt of his return. Then, mother, you will give him our duteous greetings;" and he smiled again.

Like one in a dream Christina returned his smile, because she saw he wished it, just as the moment before she had been trying to stanch his wound.

It was plain that the injuries, except Ebbo's sword-cut, were far beyond her skill, and she could only endeavour to check the bleeding till better aid could be obtained from Ulm. Thither Moritz Schleiermacher had already sent, and he assured her that he was far from despairing of the elder baron, but she derived little hope from his words, for gunshot wounds were then so ill understood as generally to prove fatal.

Moreover, there was an undefined impression that the two lives must end in the same hour, even as they had begun. Indeed, Ebbo was suffering so terribly, and was so much spent with pain and the loss of blood, that he seemed sinking much faster than Friedel, whose wound bled less freely, and who only seemed benumbed and torpid, except when he roused himself to speak, or was distressed by the writhing and moans which, however, for his sake, Ebbo restrained as much as he could.

To be together seemed an all-sufficient consolation, and, when the chaplain came sorrowfully to give them the last rites of the Church, Ebbo implored him to pray that he might not be left behind long.

The farewell greetings of the Church on earth breathed soft and sweet in their loftiness, and Friedel, though lying motionless, and with closed eyes, never failed in the murmured response, whether fully conscious or not, while his brother only attended by fits and starts, and was evidently often in too much pain to know what was passing.

Help was nearer than had been hoped. The summons dispatched the night before had been responded to by the vintners and mercers; the trained bands had set forth, and their captain, a cautious man, never rode into the way of blows without his surgeon at hand. And so it came to pass that, before the sun was low on that long and grievous day, Doctor Johannes Butteman was led into the upper chamber, where the mother looked up to him with a kind of hopeless gratitude on her face, which was nearly as white as those of her sons. The doctor soon saw that Friedel was past human aid; but, when he declared that there was fair hope for the other youth, Friedel, whose torpor had been dispelled by the examination, looked up with his beaming smile, saying, "There, motherling."

The doctor then declared that he could not deal with the baron's wound unless he were the sole occupant of the bed, and this sentence brought the first cloud of grief or dread to Friedel's brow, but only for a moment. He looked at his brother, who had again fainted at the first touch of his wounded limb, and said, "It is well. Tell the dear Ebbo that I cannot help it if I go to the praying, and leave him the fighting. Dear, dear Ebbo!" With much effort he signed the cross on his brother's brow, and kissed it long and fervently, whilst almost giving himself to Heinz and Moritz to be carried to his own bed in the turret chamber.

There, even as they laid him down, began what seemed to be the mortal agony, and, though he was scarcely sensible, his mother felt that her prime call was to him, while his brother was in other hands. Perhaps it was well for her. Surgical practice was rough, and wounds made by firearms were thought to have imbibed a poison that made treatment be supposed efficacious in proportion to the pain inflicted. When Ebbo was recalled by the torture to see no white reflection of his own face on the pillow beside him, a delirious frenzy seized him, and his struggles were frustrating the doctor's attempts, when a low, soft, sweet song stole through the open door.

"Friedel!" he murmered, and held his breath to listen. All through the declining day did the gentle sound continue; now of grand chants or hymns caught from the cathedral choir, now of songs of chivalry or saintly legend so often sung over the evening fire, the one flowing into the other in the wandering of the failing powers, but never failing in the tender sweetness that had distinguished Friedel through life. And, whenever that voice was heard, let them do to him what they would, Ebbo was still absorbed in intense listening so as not to lose a note, and lulled almost out of sense of suffering by that swan-like music. If his attendants made such noise as to break in on it, or if it ceased for a moment, the anguish returned, but was charmed away by the weakest, faintest resumption of the song.

The September sun had set, twilight was coming on, the doctor had worked his stern will, and Ebbo, quivering in every fibre, lay spent on his pillow, when his mother glided in, and took her seat near him, though where she hoped he would not notice her presence. But he raised his eyelids, and said, "He is not singing now."

"Singing indeed, but where we cannot hear him," she answered. "'Whiter than the snow, clearer than the ice-cave, more solemn than the choir. They will come at last.' That was what he said, even as he entered there." And the low dove-like tone and tender calm face continued upon Ebbo the spell that the chant had left. He dozed as though still lulled by its echo.

CHAPTER XIII

EBBO'S LIFE HUNG in the balance, and he had hardly consciousness
to realise either his brother's death or his own state, save as much as
was shown by the words, "Let him not be taken away, mother; let
him wait for me."

Friedmund did wait, in his coffin before the altar in the castle
chapel, covered with a pall of blue velvet, and great white cross,
mournfully sent by Hausfrau Johanna; his sword, shield, helmet,
and spurs laid on it, and wax tapers burning at the head and feet.
And, when Christina could leave the one son on his couch of suffering, it was to kneel beside the other son on his narrow bed of rest,
and recall, like a breath of solace, the heavenly loveliness and peace
that rested on his features when she had taken her last long look at
them.

Moritz Schleiermacher assisted at Sir Friedmund's first solemn
requiem, and then made a journey to Ulm, whence he returned to
find the baron's danger so much abated that he ventured on begging
for an interview with the lady, in which he explained his purpose
of repairing at once to the Imperial camp, taking with him a letter
from the guilds concerned in the bridge, and using his personal
influence with Maximilian to obtain not only pardon for the combat
but authoritative sanction to the erection. Dankwart of Schlangenwald, the Teutonic knight, and only heir of old Wolfgang, was
supposed to be with the emperor, and it might be possible to come
to terms with him, since his breeding in the Prussian commanderies
had kept him aloof from the feuds of his father and brother. This
mournful fight had to a certain extent equalised the injuries on either
side, since the man whom Friedel had cut down was Hierom, one
of the few remaining scions of Schlangenwald, and there was thus
no dishonour in trying to close the deadly feud, and coming to an
amicable arrangement about the Debateable Strand, the cause of
so much bloodshed. What was now wanted was Freiherr Eberhard's
signature to the letter to the emperor, and his authority for making
terms with the new count; and haste was needed, lest the Markgraf

410

of Wurtemburg should represent the affray in the light of an outrage against a member of the League.

Christina saw the necessity, and undertook if possible to obtain her son's signature, but, at the first mention of Master Moritz and the bridge, Ebbo turned away his head, groaned, and begged to hear no more of either. He thought of his bold declaration that the bridge must be built, even at the cost of blood! Little did he then guess whose blood! He hated the very name, he said, and hid his face with a shudder. He hoped the torrent would sweep away every fragment of the bridge.

"Nay, Ebbo mine, wherefore wish ill to a good work that our blessed one loved? Listen, and let me tell you my dream for making yonder strand a peaceful memorial of our peaceful boy."

"To honour Friedel?" and he gazed on her with something like interest in his eyes.

"Yes, Ebbo, and as he would best brook honour. Let us seek for ever to end the rival claims to yon piece of meadow by praying this knight of a religious order, the new count, to unite with us in building there—or as near as may be safe—a church of holy peace, and a cell for a priest, who may watch over the bridge, and offer the hold sacrifice for the departed of either house. There will we place our gentle Friedel to be the first to guard the peace of the ford, and there we will sleep ourselves when our time shall come, and so may the cruel feud of many generations be slaked for ever."

"In his blood!" sighed Ebbo. "Ah! would that it had been mine, mother. It is well, as well as anything can be again. So shall the spot where he fell be made sacred, and fenced from rude feet, and we shall see his fair effigy keeping his armed watch there."

And Christina was thankful to see his look of gratification, sad though it was. She sat down near his bed, and began to write a letter in their joint names to Graf Dankwart von Schlangenwald proposing that thus, after the even balance of the wrongs of the two houses, their mutual hostility might be laid to rest for ever by the consecration of the cause of their long contention. It was a stiff and formal letter, full of the set, pious formularies of the age, scarcely revealing the deep heart-feeling within; but it was to the purpose, and Ebbo, after hearing it read, heartily approved, and consented to sign both it and those that Schleiermacher had brought. Christina held the scroll, and placed the pen in the fingers that had lately so easily wielded the heavy sword, but now felt it a far greater effort to guide the slender quill.

Moritz Schleiermacher went his way in search of the King of the Romans, far off in Carinthia. A full reply could not be expected till the campaign was over, and all that was known for some time was through a messenger sent back to Ulm by Schleiermacher with the intelligence that Maximilian would examine into the matter after his return, and that Count Dankwart would reply when he should come to perform his father's obsequies after the army was dispersed. There was also a letter of kind though courtly condolence from Kasimir of Wildschloss, much grieving for gallant young Sir Friedmund, proffering all the advocacy he could give the cause of Adlerstein, and covertly proffering the protection that she and her remaining son might now be more disposed to accept. Christina suppressed this letter, knowing it would only pain and irritate Ebbo, and that she had her answer ready. Indeed, in her grief for one son, and her anxiety for the other, perhaps it was this letter that first made her fully realise the drift of those earnest words of Friedel's respecting his father.

Meantime the mother and son were alone together, with much of suffering and of sorrow, yet with a certain tender comfort in the being all in all to one another, with none to intermeddle with their mutual love and grief.

One October afternoon, as Ebbo lay on his bed, Hatto's aged step was on the stair. "Gracious lady," he said, "here is a huntsman bewildered in the hills, who has been asking for shelter from the storm that is drifting up."

"See to his entertainment, then, Hatto," said the lady.

"My lady—Sir Baron," added Hatto, "I had not come up but that this guest seems scarce gear for us below. He is none of the foresters of our tract. His hair is perfumed, his shirt is fine holland, his buff suit is of softest skin, his baldric has a jewelled clasp, and his arblast![1] It would do my lord baron's heart good only to cast eyes on the perfect make of that arblast! He has a lordly tread and a stately presence, and, though he has a free tongue, and made friends with us as he dried his garments, he asked after my lord like his equal."

"Oh, mother, must you play the chatelaine?" asked Ebbo. "Who can the fellow be? Why did none ever so come when they would have been more welcome?"

---

[1] Crossbow.

"Welcomed must he be," said Christina, rising, "and thy state shall be my excuse for not tarrying longer with him than may be needful."

Yet, though shrinking from a stranger's face, she was not without hope that the variety might wholesomely rouse her son from his depression, and in effect Ebbo, when left with Hatto, minutely questioned him on the appearance of the stranger, and watched, with much curiosity, for his mother's return.

"Ebbo mine," she said, entering, after a long interval, "the knight asks to see thee either after supper, or to-morrow morn."

"Then a knight he is?"

"Yea truly, a knight in every look and gesture, bearing his head like the leading stag of the herd, and yet right gracious."

"Gives he no name?" said Ebbo.

"He calls himself Ritter Theurdank, of the suite of the late Kaiser, but I should deem him wont rather to lead than to follow."

"Theurdank," repeated Eberhard, "I know no such name! So, motherling, are you going to sup? I shall not sleep till I have seen him!"

"Hold, dear son." She leant over him and spoke low. "See him thou must, but let me first station Heinz and Koppel at the door with halberts, not within earshot, but thou art so entirely defence-less."

She had the pleasure of seeing him laugh. "Less defenceless than when the kinsman of Wildschloss here visited us, mother? I see for whom thou takest him, but let it be so; a spiritual knight would scarce wreak his vengeance on a wounded man in his bed. I will not have him insulted with precautions. If he has freely risked himself in my hands, I will as freely risk myself in his. Moreover, I thought he had won thy heart."

"Reigned over it, rather," said Christina. "It is but the disguise that I suspect and mistrust. Bid me not leave thee alone with him, my son."

"Nay, dear mother," said Ebbo, "the matters on which he is like to speak will brook no presence save our own, and even that will be hard enough to bear. Prop me more upright! So! And comb out these locks somewhat smoother. Thanks, mother. Now can he see whether he will choose Eberhard of Adlerstein for friend or foe."

By the time supper was ended, the only light in the upper room came from the flickering flames of the fire of pine knots on the hearth.

It glanced on the pale features and dark sad eyes of the young baron, sad in spite of the eager look of scrutiny that he turned on the figure that entered at the door, and approached so quickly that the partial light only served to show the gloss of long fair hair, the glint of a jewelled belt, and the outline of a tall, well-knit, agile frame.

"Welcome, Herr Ritter," he said, "I am sorry we have been unable to give you a fitter reception."

"No host could be more fully excused than you," said the stranger, and Ebbo started at his voice. "I fear you have suffered much, and still have much to suffer."

"My sword wound is healing fast," said Ebbo; "it is the shot in my broken thigh that is so tedious and painful."

"And I dare be sworn the leeches made it worse. I have hated all leeches ever since they kept me three days a prisoner in a pothe-cary's shop stinking with drugs. Why, I have cured myself with one pitcher of water of a raging fever, in their very despite! How did they serve thee, my poor boy?"

"They poured hot oil into the wound to remove the venom of the lead," said Ebbo.

"Had it been my case the lead should have been in their own brains first, though that were scarce needed, the heavy-witted Hans Sausages. Why should there be more poison in lead than in steel? I have asked all my surgeons that question, nor ever had a reasonable answer. Greater havoc of warriors do they make than ever with the arquebus—ay, even when every lanzknecht bears one."

"Alack!" Ebbo could not help exclaiming, "where will be room for chivalry?"

"Talk not old-world nonsense," said Theurdank; "chivalry is in the heart, not in the weapon. A youth beforehand enough with the world to be building bridges should know that, when all our troops are provided with such an arm, then will their platoons in serried ranks be as a solid wall breathing fire, and as impregnable as the lines of English archers with long bows, or the phalanx of Macedon. And, when each man bears a pistol instead of the miseri-corde, his life will be far more his own."

Ebbo's face was in full light, and his visitor marked his contracted brow and trembling lip. "Ah!" he said, "thou hast had foul experience of these weapons."

"Not mine own hurt," said Ebbo; "that was but fair chance of war."

"I understand," said the knight; "it was the shot that severed the goodly bond that was so fair to see, Young man, none has grieved more truly than King Max."

"And well he may," said Ebbo. "He has not lost merely one of his best servants, but all the better half of another."

"There is still stuff enough left to make that *one* well worth having." said Theurdank, kindly grasping his hand, "though I would it were more substantial! How didst get old Wolfgang down, boy? He must have been a tough morsel for slight bones like these, even when better covered than now. Come, tell me all. I promised the Markgraf of Wurtemburg to look into the matter when I came to be guest at St. Ruprecht's cloister, and I have some small interest too with King Max."

His kindliness and sympathy were more effectual with Ebbo than the desire to represent his case favourably, for he was still too wretched to care for policy; but he answered Theurdank's questions readily, and explained how the idea of the bridge had originated in the vigil beside the broken wagons.

"I hope," said Theurdank, "the merchants made up thy share? These overthrown goods are a seignorial right of one or other of you lords of the bank."

"True, Herr Ritter; but we deemed it unknightly to snatch at what travellers lost by misfortune."

"Freiherr Eberhard, take my word for it, while thou thus holdest all the arquebuses yet to be cut out of the Black Forest will not mar thy chivalry. Where didst get these ways of thinking?"

"My brother was a very St. Sebastian! My mother—"

"Ah! her sweet wise face would have shown it, even had not poor Kasimir of Adlerstein raved of her. Ah! lad, thou hast crossed a case of true love there! Canst not brook even such a gallant stepfather?"

"I may not," said Ebbo, with spirit; "for with his last breath Schlangenwald owned that my own father died not at the hostel, but may now be alive as a Turkish slave."

"The devil!" burst out Theurdank. "Well! That might have been a pretty mess! A Turkish slave, saidst thou? What year chanced all this matter—thy grandfather's murder and all the rest?"

"The year before my birth," said Ebbo. "It was in the September of 1475."

"Ha!" muttered Theurdank, musing to himself; "that was the year the dotard Schenk got his overthrow at the fight of Rain on Sare from the Moslem. Some composition was made by them, and old

Wolfgang was not unlikely to have been the go-between. So! Say on, young knight," he added, "let us to the matter in hand. How rose the strife that kept back two troops from our—from the banner of the empire ?"

Ebbo proceeded with the narration, and concluded it just as the bell now belonging to the chapel began to toll for Compline,[1] and Theurdank prepared to obey its summons, first, however, asking if he should send any one to the patient. Ebbo thanked him, but said he needed no one till his mother should come after prayers.

At length, lamp in hand, she appeared with tears shining in her eyes, and bending over him said:

"He hath done honour to our blessed one, my Ebbo; he knelt by him, and crossed him with holy water, and when he led me from the chapel he told me any mother in Germany might envy me my two sons now. Thou must love him now, Ebbo."

"Love him as one loves one's loftiest model," said Ebbo; "value the old castle the more for sheltering him."

"Hath he made himself known to thee ?"

"Not openly, but there is only one that he can be."

Christina smiled; knowing as she did that Ebbo's admiration was apt to be enthusiastic, and might now be rendered the more fervent by fever and solitude, she was still at a loss to understand his dazzled, fascinated state.

When Heinz entered, bringing the castle key, which was always laid under the baron's pillow, Ebbo made a movement with his hand that surprised them both, as if to send it elsewhere—then muttered, "No, no, not till he reveals himself. Take care all due honour is shown to him! Good-night, Heinz."

"Gracious lady," said Heinz, when by a sign he had intimated to her his desire of speaking with her unobserved by the baron, "never fear; I know who the fellow is as well as you do. I shall be at the foot of the stairs, and woe to whoever tries to step up them past me."

"There is no reason to apprehend treason, Heinz, yet to be on our guard can do no harm."

"Nay, lady, I could look to the gear for the oubliette if you would speak the word."

"For Heaven's sake, no, Heinz. This man has come hither trusting to our honour, and you could not do your lord a greater

[1] The last service of the day.

wrong, nor one that he could less pardon, than by any attempt on our guest."

"Would that he had never eaten our bread!" muttered Heinz. "Vipers be they all, and who knows what may come next?"

"Watch, watch, Heinz; that is all," implored Christina, "and, above all, not a word to any one else."

And Christina dismissed the man-at-arms gruff and sullen, and herself retired ill at ease between fears of, and for, the unwelcome guest whose strange powers of fascination had rendered her, in his absence, doubly distrustful.

The snow fell all night without ceasing, and was still falling on the morrow, when the guest explained his desire of paying a short visit to the young baron, and then taking his departure. Christina would gladly have been quit of him, but she felt bound to remonstrate, for their mountain was absolutely impassable during a fall of snow, above all when accompanied by wind, since the drifts concealed fearful abysses, and the shifting masses ensured destruction to the unwary wayfarer; nay, natives themselves had perished between the hamlet and the castle.

"Not the hardiest cragsman, not my son himself," she said, "could venture on such a morning to guide you to—"

"Whither, gracious dame?" asked Theurdank, half smiling.

"Nay, sir, I would not utter what you would not make known."

"You know me, then?"

"Surely, sir, for our noble foe, whose generous trust in our honour must win my son's heart."

"So!" he said, with a peculiar smile, "Theurdank—Dankwart— I see! May I ask if your son likewise smelt out the Schlangenwald?"

"Verily, Sir Count, my Ebbo is not easily deceived. He said our guest could be but one man in all the empire."

Theurdank smiled again, saying, "Then, lady, you shudder not at a man whose kin and yours have shed so much of one another's blood?"

"Nay, ghostly knight. I regard you as no more stained therewith than are my sons by the deeds of their grand-father."

"If there were more like you, lady," returned Theurdank, "deadly feuds would soon be starved out. May I to your son? I have more to say to him, and I would fain hear his views of the storm."

N

Christina could not be quite at ease with Theurdank in her son's room, but she had no choice, and she knew that Heinz was watching on the turret stair, out of hearing indeed, but as ready to spring as a cat who sees her young ones in the hand of a child that she only half trusts.

Ebbo lay eagerly watching for his visitor, who greeted him with the same almost paternal kindness he had evinced the night before, but consulted him upon the way from the castle. Ebbo confirmed his mother's opinion that the path was impracticable so long as the snow fell, and the wind tossed it in wild drifts.

"Truly it is dismal work for a lusty hunter to lie here," said Theurdank, "but soon shalt thou take thy crags again in full vigour, I hope. How call'st thou the deep grey lonely pool under a steep frowning crag, sharpened well-nigh to a spear point, that I passed yester afternoon?"

"The Ptarmigan's Mere, the Red Eyrie," murmured Ebbo, scarcely able to utter the words as he thought of Friedel's delight in the pool, his exploit at the eyrie, and the gay bargain made in the streets of Ulm, that he should show the scaler of the Dome steeple the way to the eagle's nest.

"I remember," said his guest gravely, coming to his side. "Ah, boy! thy brother's flight has been higher yet. Weep freely; fear me not. Do I not know what it is, when those who were over-good for earth have found their eagle's wings, and left us here? Never owned I brother, but I trow ye two were one in no common sort."

"Such brothers as we saw at Ulm were little like us," returned Ebbo, from the bottom of his heart. "We were knit together so that all will begin with me as if it were the left hand remaining alone to do it! I am glad that my odd life may not even in shadow be renewed till after I have gone in quest of my father."

"Be not over hasty in that quest," said the guest, "or the infidels may chance to gain two Freiherren instead of one. Hast any designs?"

Ebbo explained that he thought of making his way to Genoa to consult the merchant Gian Battista dei Battiste, whose description of the captive German noble had so strongly impressed Friedel. Ebbo knew the difference between Turks and Moors, but Friedel's impulse guided him, and he further thought that at Genoa he should learn the way to deal with either variety of infidel. Theurdank thought this a prudent course, since the Genoese had dealings both at Tripoli and Constantinople; and, moreover, the transfer was not impossible since the two different hordes of Moslems trafficked among themselves when either had made an unusually successful razzia.[1]

"Dost know Italian?" said Theurdank. "There is something of Italy in thine eye."

"My mother's mother was Italian, my lord; but she died so early that her language has not descended to my mother or myself."

"Thou shouldst learn it. It will be pastime while thou art bed-fast, and serve thee well in dealing with the Moslem. Moreover, I may have work for thee in Welschland. Books? I will send thee books."

Such were the discourses of that morning: now on poetry and book-lore; now admiration of the carvings that decked the room; now talk on grand architectural designs, or improvements in fire-arms, or the discussion of hunting adventures. There seemed nothing in art, life, or learning in which the versatile mind of Theurdank was not at home, or that did not end in some strange personal reminiscence of his own. All was so kind, so gracious, and brilliant, that at first the interview was full of wondering delight to Ebbo, but latterly it became very fatiguing from the strain of attention, above all towards a guest who evidently knew that he was known, while not permitting such recognition to be avowed. Ebbo began to long for an interruption, but, though he could see by the lightened sky that the weather had cleared up, it would have been impossible to have suggested to any guest that the way might now probably be open, and more especially to such a guest as this. Considerate as his visitor had been the night before, the pleasure of talk seemed to have done away with the remembrance of his host's weakness, till Ebbo so flagged that at last he was scarcely alive to more than the continued sound of the voice; but his guest seemed too much immersed in his own plans, theories, and adventures, to mark the condition of his auditor.

Interruption came at last, however. There was a sudden knock at the door at noon, and with scant ceremony Heinz entered, followed by three other of the men-at-arms, fully equipped.

"Ha! what means this?" demanded Ebbo.

"Peace, Sir Baron," said Heinz, advancing so as to place his large person between Ebbo's bed and the strange hunter. "You know nothing of it. We are not going to lose you as well as your brother, and we mean to see how this knight likes to serve as a

[1] Plundering raid.

hostage instead of opening the gates as a traitor spy. On him, Koppel! it is thy right."

"Hands off! at your peril, villains!" exclaimed Ebbo, sitting up, and speaking in the steady resolute voice that had so early rendered him thoroughly their master, but much perplexed and dismayed, and entirely unassisted by Theurdank, who stood looking on with almost a smile, as if diverted by his predicament.

"By your leave, Herr Freiherr," said Heinz, putting his hand on his shoulder, "this is no concern of yours. While you cannot guard yourself or my lady, it is our part to do so. I tell you his minions are on their way to surprise the castle."

Even as Heinz spoke, Christina came panting into the room, and, hurrying to her son's side, said, "Sir Count, is this just, is this honourable, thus to return my son's welcome, in his helpless condition?"

"Mother, are you likewise distracted?" exclaimed Ebbo. "What is all this madness?"

"Alas, my son, it is no frenzy! There are armed men coming up the Eagle's Stairs on the one hand, and by the Gemsbock's Pass on the other!"

"But not a hair of your head shall they hurt, lady," said Heinz. "This fellow's limbs shall be thrown to them over the battlements. On, Koppel!"

"Off, Koppel!" thundered Ebbo. "Would you brand me with shame for ever? Were he all the Schlangenwalds in one, he should go as freely as he came; but he is no more Schlangenwald than I am."

"He has deceived you, my lord," said Heinz. "My lady's own letter to Schlangenwald was in his chamber. 'Tis a treacherous disguise."

"Fool that thou art!" said Ebbo. "I know this gentleman well. I knew him at Ulm. Those who meet him here mean me no ill. Open the gates and receive them honourably! Mother, mother, trust me; all is well. I know what I am saying."

The men looked one upon another. Christina wrung her hands, uncertain whether her son were not under some strange, fatal deception.

"My lord has his fancies," growled Koppel. "I'll not be balked of my right of vengeance for his scruples. Will he swear that this fellow is what he calls himself?"

"I swear," said Ebbo slowly, "that he is a true, loyal knight, well known to me."

"Swear it distinctly, Sir Baron," said Heinz. "We have all too deep a debt of vengeance to let off any one who comes here lurking in the interest of our foe. Swear that this is Theurdank, or we send his head to greet his friends."

Drops stood on Ebbo's brow, and his breath laboured as he felt his senses reeling, and his powers of defence for his guest failing him. Even should the stranger confess his name, the people of the castle might not believe him; and here he stood like one indifferent, evidently measuring how far his young host would go in his cause.

"I cannot swear that his real name is Theurdank," said Ebbo, rallying his forces, "but this I swear, that he is neither friend nor fosterer of Schlangenwald, that I know him, and I had rather die than the slightest indignity were offered him here," and with a great effort that terribly wrenched his wounded leg, he reached past Heinz, and grasped his guest's hand, pulling him as near as he could.

"Sir," he said, "if they try to lay hands on you, strike my death-blow!"

A bugle-horn was wound outside. The men stood daunted—Christina in extreme terror for her son, who lay gasping, breathless, but still clutching the stranger's hand, and with eyes of fire glaring on the mutinous warriors. Another bugle-blast! Heinz was almost in the act of grappling with the silent foe, and Koppel cried as he raised his halberd, "Now or never!" but paused.

"Never, so please you," said the strange guest. "What if your young lord could not forswear himself that my name is Theurdank! Are you foes to all the world save Theurdank?"

"No masking," said Heinz sternly. "Tell your true name as an honest man, and we will judge whether you be friend or foe."

"My name is a mouthful, as your master knows," said the guest slowly, looking with strangely amused eyes on the confused lanz-knechts, who were trying to devour their rage. "I was baptized Maximilianus; Archduke of Austria, by birth; by choice of the Germans, King of the Romans."

"The Kaiser!"

Christina dropped on her knee; the men-at-arms tumbled backwards; Ebbo pressed the hand he held to his lips, and fainted away. The bugle sounded for the third time.

CHAPTER XIV

SLOWLY AND PAINFULLY did Ebbo recover from his swoon, and presently dropped into a profound slumber, whence he awoke to find it still broad daylight, and his mother sitting by the side of his bed, all looking so much as it had done for the last six weeks that his first inquiry was if all that had happened had been but a strange dream. His mother would scarcely answer till she had satisfied herself that his eye was clear, his voice steady, his hand cool, and that, as she said, "That Kaiser had done him no harm."

"Ah, then it was true! Where is he? Gone?" cried Ebbo eagerly.

"No, in the hall below, busy with letters they have brought him. Lie still, my boy; he has done thee quite enough damage for one day."

"But, mother, what are you saying? Something disloyal, was it not?"

"Well, Ebbo, I was very angry that he should have half killed you when he could so easily have spoken one word. Heaven forgive me if I did wrong, but I could not help it."

"Did *he* forgive you, mother?" said Ebbo anxiously.

"He—oh, yes. To do him justice, he was greatly concerned; devised ways of restoring thee, and now has promised not to come near thee again without my leave," said the mother, quite as persuaded of her own rightful sway in her son's sick chamber as ever Kunigunde had been of her dominion over the castle.

"And is he displeased with me? Those cowardly, vindictive rascals, to fall on him, and set me at naught! Before him, too!" exclaimed Ebbo bitterly.

"Nay, Ebbo, he thought thy part most gallant. I heard him say so, not only to me, but below stairs—both wise and true. Thou did'st know him, then?"

"From the first glance of his princely eye—the first of his keen smiles. I had seen him disguised before. I thought you knew him too, mother; I never guessed that your mind was running on Schlangenwald."

"Would that I had; but, though I breathed no word openly, I
encouraged Heinz's precautions. My boy, I could not help it; my
heart would tremble for my only one, and I saw he could not be
what he seemed."

"And what doth he here? Who were the men who were advancing?"

"They were the followers he had left at St. Ruprecht's, and
likewise Master Schleiermacher and Sir Kasimir of Wildschloss."

"Ha!"

"What—he had not told thee?"

"No. He knew that I knew him, was at no pains to disguise
himself, yet evidently meant me to treat him as a private knight.
But what brought Wildschloss here?"

"It seems," said Christina, "that, on the return from Carinthia,
the Kaiser expressed his intention of slipping away from his army
in his own strange fashion, and himself inquiring into the matter
of the ford. So he took with him his own personal followers,
the new Graf von Schlangenwald, Herr Kasimir, and Master
Schleiermacher. The others he sent to Schlangenwald; he himself
lodged at St. Ruprecht's, appointing that Sir Kasimir should meet
him there this morning. From the convent he started on a chamois
hunt, and made his way hither; but, when the snow came on, and he
returned not, his followers became uneasy, and came in search of
him."

"Motherling, prithee let him know that I am at his service,"
said Ebbo.

And, after having fed and refreshed her patient, the gentle potentate of his chamber consented to intimate her consent to admit the
invader. But not till after delay enough to fret the impatient nerves
of illness did Maximilian appear, saying, in the cheery voice that
was one of his chief fascinations:

"Yea, truly, fair dame, I know thou wouldst sooner trust
Schlangenwald himself than me alone with thy charge. How goes
it, my true knight?"

"Well, right well, my liege," said Ebbo, "save for my shame and
grief."

"Thou art the last to be ashamed for that," said the good-natured
prince. "Have I never seen my faithful vassals more bent on their
own feuds than on my word?—I who reign over a set of kings, who
brook no will but their own."

"And may we ask your pardon," said Ebbo, "not only for ourselves, but for the men-at-arms?"

"What! the gruesome giant that was prepared with the axe, and the honest lad that wanted to do his duty by his father? I honour that lad, Freiherr; I would enroll him in my guard, but that probably he is better off here than with me. But what I came hither to say was this," and he spoke gravely: "thou art sincere in desiring reconciliation with the House of Schlangenwald?"

"With all my heart," said Ebbo, "do I loathe the miserable debt of blood for blood!"

"And," said Maximilian, "Graf Dankwart is of like mind. Bred from pagedom in his Prussian commandery, he has never been exposed to the irritations that have fed the spirit of strife, and he will be thankful to lay it aside. The question next is how to solemnise this conciliation, ere your retainers on one side or the other do something to set you by the ears together again, which, judging by this morning's work, is not improbable."

"Alas! no," said Ebbo, "while I am laid by."

"Had you both been in our camp, you should have sworn friendship in my chapel. Now must Dankwart come hither to thee, as I trow he had best do, while I am here to keep the peace. See, friend Ebbo, we will have him here to-morrow; thy chaplain shall deck the altar here, the Father Abbot shall say mass, and ye shall swear peace and brotherhood before me. And," he added, taking Ebbo's hand, "I shall know how to trust thine oaths as of one who sets the fear of God above that of his king."

This was truly the only chance of impressing on the wild vassals of the two houses an obligation that perhaps might override their ancient hatred; and the baron and his mother gladly submitted to the arrangement. Maximilian withdrew to give directions for summoning the persons required, and Christina was soon obliged to leave her son, while she provided for her influx of guests.

Ebbo was alone till nearly the end of the supper below stairs. He had been dozing, when a cautious tread came up the turret steps, and he started, and called out, "Who goes there? I am not asleep."

"It is your kinsman, Freiherr," said a well-known voice; "I come by your mother's leave."

"Welcome, Sir Cousin," said Ebbo, holding out his hand. "You come to find everything changed."

"I have knelt in the chapel," said Wildschloss.

"And he loved you better than I!" said Ebbo.

"Your jealousy of me was a providential thing, for which all may be thankful," said Wildschloss gravely; "yet it is no small thing to lose the hope of so many years! However, young baron, I have grave matter for your consideration. Know you the service on which I am to be sent? The Kaiser deems that the Armenians or some of the Christian nations on the skirts of the Ottoman empire might be made our allies, and attack the Turk in his rear. I am chosen as his envoy, and shall sail so soon as I can make my way to Venice. I only knew of the appointment since I came hither, he having been led thereto by letters brought him this day; and mayhap by the downfall of my hopes. He was peremptory, as his mood is, and seemed to think it no small favour," added Wildschloss, with some annoyance. "And meantime, what of my poor child? There she is in the cloister at Ulm, but an inheritance is a very millstone round the neck of an orphan maid. That insolent fellow, Lassla von Trautbach, hath already demanded to espouse the poor babe; he—a blood-stained, dicing, drunken rover, with whom I would not trust a dog that I loved! Yet my death would place her at the disposal of his father, who would give her at once to him. Nay, even his aunt, the abbess, will believe nothing against him, and hath even striven with me to have her betrothed at once. On the barest rumour of my death will they wed the poor little thing, and then woe to her, and woe to my vassals!"

"The King," suggested Ebbo. "Surely she might be made his ward."

"Young man," said Sir Kasimir, bending over him, and speaking in an undertone, "he may well have won your heart. As friend, when one is at his side, none can be so winning or so sincere as he; but with all his brilliant gifts, he says truly of himself that he is a mere reckless huntsman. To-day, while I am with him, he would give me half Austria, or fight single-handed in my cause or Thekla's. Next month, when I am out of sight, comes Trautbach, just when his head is full of keeping the French out of Italy, or reforming the Church, or beating the Turk, or parcelling the empire into circles, or, maybe, of a new touchhole for a cannon—nay, of a flower-garden, or of walking into a lion's den. He just says, 'Yea, well,' to be rid of the importunity, and all is over with my poor little maiden. Hare-brained and bewildered with schemes has he been as Romish King—how will it be with him as Kaiser? It is but of his wonted

madness that he is here at all, when his Austrian states must be all
astray for want of him. No, no; I would rather make a weather-
cock guardian to my daughter. You yourself are the only guard to
whom I can safely entrust her."

"My sword as knight and kinsman—" began Ebbo.

"No, no; 'tis no matter of errant knight or distressed damsel.
There is only one way in which you can save her, and that is as her
husband."

Ebbo started, as well he might, but Sir Kasimir laid his hand
on him with a gesture that bade him listen ere he spoke. "My
first wish for my child," he said, "was to see her brought up by that
peerless lady below stairs. The saints—in pity to one so like themselves—spared her the distress our union would have brought her.
Now, it would be vain to place my little Thekla in her care, for
Trautbach would easily feign my death, and claim his niece, nor
are you of age to be made her guardian as head of our house. But,
if this marriage rite were solemnised, then would her person and
lands alike be yours, and I could leave her with an easy heart."

"But," said the confused, surprised Ebbo, "what can I do?
They say I shall not walk for many weeks to come. And, even if I
could, I am so young—I have so blundered in my dealings with my
own mountaineers, and with this fatal bridge—how should I manage
such estates as yours? Some better—"

"Look you, Ebbo," said Wildschloss; "you have erred—you have
have been hasty; but tell me where to find another youth, whose
strongest purpose was as wise as your errors, or who cared for others'
good more than for his own violence and vainglory? Brief as your
time has been, one knows when one is on your bounds by the aspect
of your serfs, the soundness of their dwellings, the prosperity of
their crops and cattle; above all, by their face and tone if one asks
for their lord. You are the only youth I know to whom I could
entrust my child or my lands. The old Wildschloss castle is a male
fief, and would return to you, but there are domains since granted
that will cause intolerable trouble and strife, unless you and my poor
little heiress are united. As for age, you are—"

"Eighteen next Easter."

"Then there are scarce eleven years between you. You will find
the little one a blooming bride when your first deeds in arms have
been fought out."

"And, if my mother trains her up," said Ebbo thoughtfully, "she
will be all the better daughter to her. But, Sir Cousin, you know I

too must be going. So soon as I can brook the saddle, I must seek out and ransom my father."

"That is like to be a far shorter and safer journey than mine. The Genoese and Venetians understand traffic with the infidels for their captives, and only by your own fault could you get into danger. Even at the worst, should mishap befall you, you could so order matters as to leave your girl-widow in your mother's charge."

"Then," added Ebbo, "she would still have one left to love and cherish her. Sir Kasimir, it is well; though, if you knew me without my Friedel, you would repent of your bargain."

"Thanks from my heart," said Wildschloss, "but you need not be concerned. You have never been over-friendly with me even with Friedel at your side. But to business, my son. You will endure that title from me now? My time is short."

"What would you have me do? Shall I send the little one a betrothal ring, and ride to Ulm to wed and fetch her home in spring?"

"That may hardly serve. These kinsmen would have seized on her and the castle long ere that time. The only safety is the making wedlock as fast as it can be made with a child of such tender years. Mine is the only power that can make the abbess give her up, and therefore will I ride this moonlight night to Ulm, bring the little one back with me by the time the reconciliation be concluded, and then shall ye be wed by the Abbot of St. Ruprecht's, with the Kaiser for a witness, and thus will the knot be too strong for the Trautbachs to untie."

Ebbo looked disconcerted and gasped, as if this were over-quick work. "To-morrow!" he said. "Knows my mother?"

"I go to speak with her at once. The Kaiser's consent I have, as he says, 'If we have one vassal who has common sense and honesty, let us make the most of him.' Ah! my son, I shall return to see you his counsellor and friend."

Those days had no delicacies as to the lady's side taking the initiative; and, in effect, the wealth and power of Wildschloss so much exceeded those of the older branch that it would have been presumptuous on Eberhard's part to have made the proposal. It was more a treaty than an affair of hearts, and Sir Kasimir had not even gone through the form of inquiring if Ebbo were fancy-free. It was true, indeed, that he was still a boy, with no passion for any one but his mother; but had he even formed a dream of a lady love, it would scarcely have been deemed a rational objection. The days of romance were no days of romance in marriage.

CHAPTER XV

No ONE COULD bear to waken the young baron till the sun had risen high enough to fall on his face and unclose his eyes. Christina made her son ready for the day's solemnities, arraying him in a fine holland shirt with exquisite broidery of her own on the collar and sleeves, and carefully disposing his long, glossy, dark brown hair so as to fall on his shoulders as he lay propped up by cushions. She would have thrown his crimson mantle round him, but he repelled it indignantly. "Gay braveries for me, while my Friedel is not yet in his resting-place? Here—the black velvet cloak."

"Alas, Ebbo! it makes thee look more of a corpse than a bridegroom. Thou wilt scare thy poor little spouse. Ah! it was not thus I had fancied myself decking thee for thy wedding."

"Poor little one!" said Ebbo. "If, as your uncle says, mourning is the seed of joy, this bridal should prove a gladsome one! But let her prove a loving child to you, and honour my Friedel's memory, then shall I love her well. Do not fear, motherling; with the roots of hatred and jealousy taken out of the heart, even sorrow is such peace that it is almost joy."

It was over early for pain and sorrow to have taught that lesson, thought the mother, as with tender tears she gave place to the priest, who was to begin the solemnities of the day by shriving the young baron.

A temporary altar was erected between the windows, and hung with the silk and embroidery belonging to that in the chapel: a crucifix was placed on it, with the shrine of the stone of Nicaea, one or two other relics brought from St. Ruprecht's cloister, and a beautiful mother-of-pearl and gold pyx also from the abbey, containing the Host. These were arranged by the chaplain, Father Norbert, and three of his brethren from the abbey. And then the Father Abbot, a kindly, dignified old man, who had long been on friendly terms with the young baron, entered; and after a few kind though serious words to him, assumed a gorgeous cope stiff with gold embroidery, and, standing by the altar, awaited the arrival of the other assistants at the ceremony.

The slender, youthful-looking, pensive lady of the castle, in her wonted mourning dress, was courteously handed to her son's bedside by the Emperor. He was in his plain buff leathern hunting garb, unornamented, save by the rich clasp of his sword-belt and his gold chain, and his head was only covered by the long silken locks of fair hair that hung round his shoulders; but, now that his large, keen dark blue eyes were gravely restrained, and his eager face composed, his countenance was so majestic, his bearing so lofty, that not all his crowns could have better marked his dignity.

Behind him came a sunburnt, hardy man, wearing the white mantle and black fleur-de-lis-pointed cross of the Teutonic Order. A thrill passed through Ebbo's veins as he beheld the man who to him represented the murderer of his brother and both his grandfathers, the cruel oppressor of his father, and the perpetrator of many a more remote, but equally unforgotten, injury. And in like manner Sir Dankwart beheld the actual slayer of his father, and the heir of a long score of deadly retribution. No wonder then that, while the Emperor spoke a few words of salutation and inquiry, gracious though not familiar, the two foes scanned one another with a shiver of mutual repulsion, and a sense that they would fain have fought it out as in the good old times.

However, Ebbo only beheld a somewhat dull, heavy, honest-looking visage of about thirty years old, good-nature written in all its flat German features, and a sort of puzzled wonder in the wide, light eyes that stared fixedly at him, no doubt in amazement that the mighty, huge-limbed Wolfgang could have been actually slain by the delicately-framed youth. Schleiermacher was also present, and the chief followers on either hand had come into the lower part of the room—Hatto, Heinz, and Koppel, looking far from contented; some of the Emperor's suite; and a few attendants of Schlangenwald, like himself connected with the Teutonic Order.

The Emperor spoke: "We have brought you together, Herr Graff von Schlangenwald, and Herr Freiherr von Adlerstein, because ye have given us reason to believe you willing to lay aside the remembrance of the foul and deadly strifes of your forefathers, and to live as good Christians in friendship and brotherhood."

"Sir, it is true," said Schlangenwald; and "It is true," said Ebbo.

"That is well," replied Maximilian. "Nor can our reign better begin than by the closing of a breach that has cost the land some

of its bravest sons. Dankwart von Schlangenwald, art thou willing
to pardon the heir of Adlerstein for having slain thy father in free
and honourable combat, as well as, doubtless, for other deeds of
his ancestors, more than I know or can specify?"

"Yea, truly; I pardon him, my liege, as befits my vow."

"And thou, Eberhard von Adlerstein, dost thou put from thee
vengeance for thy twin brother's death, and all the other wrongs
that thine house has suffered?"

"I put revenge from me for ever."

"Ye agree, further, then, instead of striving as to your rights to
the piece of meadow called the Debateable Strand, and to the wrecks
of burthens there cast up by the stream, ye will unite with the citizens
of Ulm in building a bridge over the Braunwasser, where, your
mutual portions thereof being decided by the Swabian League, toll
may be taken from all vehicles and beasts passing thereover?"

"We agree," said both knights.

"And I, also, on behalf of the two guilds of Ulm," added Moritz
Schleiermacher.

"Likewise," continued the Emperor, "for avoidance of debate, and
to consecrate the spot that has caused so much contention, ye will
jointly erect a church, where may be buried both the relatives who
fell in the late unhappy skirmish, and where ye will endow a perpetual
mass for their souls, and those of others of your two races."

"Thereto I willingly agree," said the Teutonic knight.

But to Ebbo it was a shock that the pure, gentle Friedmund
should thus be classed with his treacherous assassin; and he had
almost declared that it would be sacrilege, when he received from
the Emperor a look of stern, surprised command, which reminded
him that concession must not be all on one side, and that he could
not do Friedel a greater wrong than to make him a cause of strife.
So, though they half choked him, he contrived to utter the words,
"I consent."

"And in token of amity I here tear up and burn all the feud
briefs of Adlerstein," said Schlangenwald, producing form his pouch
a collection of hostile literature, beginning from a crumpled strip
of yellow parchment, and ending with a coarse paper missive in
the clerkly hand of burgher-bred Hugh Sorel, and bearing the
crooked signatures of the last two Eberhards of Adlerstein—all with
great seals of the eagle shield appended to them. A similar collection—which, with one or two other family defiances, and the letters
of investiture recently obtained at Ulm, formed the whole archives

of Adlerstein—had been prepared within Ebbo's reach; and each of the two, taking up a dagger, made extensive gashes in these documents, and then—with no mercy to the future antiquaries, who would have gloated over them—the whole were hurled into the flames on the hearth, where the odour they emitted, if not grateful to the physical sense, should have been highly aggreeable to the moral.

"Then, holy Father Abbot," said Maximilian, "let us ratify this happy and Christian reconciliation by the blessed sacrifice of peace, over which these two faithful knights shall unite in swearing goodwill and brotherhood."

Such solemn reconciliations were frequent, but, alas! were too often a mockery. Here, however, both parties were men who felt the awe of the promise made before the Pardon-winner of all mankind. Ebbo's deep, repressed ardour and excitement were no small contrast to the sober, matter-of-fact demeanour of the Teutonic knight, who comported himself with the mechanical decorum of an ecclesiastic, but quite as one who meant to keep his word. Maximilian served the mass in his royal character as sub-deacon. He was fond of so doing, either from humility, or love of incongruity, or both. No one, however, communicated except the clergy and the parties concerned—Dankwart first, as being monk as well as knight, then Eberhard and his mother; and then followed, interposed into the rite, the oath of pardon, friendship, and brotherhood administered by the abbot, and followed by the solemn kiss of peace.

The service ended, it was part of the pledge of amity that the reconciled enemies should break their fast together, and a collation of white bread and wine was provided for the purpose. The Emperor tried to promote free and friendly talk between the two adversaries, but not with great success; for Dankwart, though honest and sincere, seemed extremely dull. He appeared to have few ideas beyond his Prussian commandery and its routine discipline, and to be lost in a castle where all was at his sole will and disposal, and he caught eagerly at all proposals made to him as if they were new lights. As, for instance, that some impartial arbitrator should be demanded from the Swabian League to define the boundary; and that next Rogationtide the two knights should ride or climb it in company, while meantime the serfs should be strictly charged not to trespass, and any transgressor should be immediately escorted to his own lord.

"But," quoth Sir Dankwart in a most serious tone, "I am told that a she-bear dwells in a den on yonder crag, between the pass you call the Gemsbock's and the Schlangenwald valley. They told me the right in it had never been decided, and I have not been up myself. To say truth, I have lived so long in the sand plains as to have lost my mountain legs, and I hesitated to see if a hunter could mount thither for fear of fresh offence; but, if she bide there till Rogation-tide, it will be ill for the lambs."

"Is that all?" cried Maximilian. "Then will I, a neutral, kill your bear for you, gentlemen, so that neither need transgress this new crag of debate. I'll go down and look at your bear-spears, friend Ebbo, and be ready so soon as Kasimir has done with his bridal."

At that moment, half a dozen horsemen were seen coming up from the ford, by the nearer path, and a fore-runner arrived with the tidings that the Baron of Adlerstein Wildschloss was close behind with the little Baroness Thekla.

Half the moonlight night had Sir Kasimir and his escort ridden; and, after a brief sleep at the nearest inn outside Ulm, he had entered in early morning, demanded admittance to the convent, claimed his daughter, and, placing her on a cushion before him on his saddle, had borne her away, telling her of freedom, of the kind lady, and the young knight who had dazzled her childish fancy.

Christina went down to receive her. There was no time to lose, for the huntsman Kaiser was bent on the slaughter of his bear before dark, and, if he were to be witness of the wedding, it must be immediate.

Thus nothing could be done to prepare the little maiden but to divest her of her mufflings, and comb out her flaxen hair, crowning it with a wreath which Christina had already woven form the myrtle of her own girlhood, scarcely waiting to answer the bewildered queries and entreaties save by caresses and admonitions to her to be very good.

Poor little thing! She was tired, frightened, and confused; and, when she had been brought upstairs, she answered the half smiling, half shy greeting of her bridegroom with a shudder of alarm, and the exclamation, "Where is the beautiful young knight? That's a lady going to take the veil lying under the pall."

"You look rather like a little nun yourself," said Ebbo, for she wore a little conventual dress, "but we must take each other for such as we are;" and, as she hid her face and clung to his mother, he added in a more cheerful, coaxing tone, "You once said you would be my wife."

"Ah, but then there were two of you, and you were all shining bright."

Before she could be answered, the impatient Emperor returned, and brought with him the abbot, who proceeded to find the place in his book, and to ask the bridegroom for the rings. Ebbo looked at Sir Kasimir, who owned that he should have brought them from Ulm, but that he had forgotten.

"Jewels are not plenty with us," said Ebbo, with a glow of amusement and confusion dawning on his cheek, such as reassured the little maid that she beheld one of the two beautiful knights. "Must we borrow?"

Christina looked at the ring she had first seen lying on her own Eberhards' palm, and she felt as if to let it be used would sever the renewed hope she scarcely yet durst entertain; and at the same moment Maximilian glanced at his own fingers, and muttered, "None but this! Unlucky!" For it was the very diamond which Mary of Burgundy had sent to assure him of her faith, and summon him to her aid after her father's death. Sir Kasimir had not retained the pledge of his own ill-omened wedlock; but, in the midst of the dilemma, the Emperor, producing his dagger, began to detach some of the massive gold links of the chain that supported his hunting-horn. "There," said he, "the little elf of a bride can get her finger into this lesser one; and you—verily this largest will fit, and the goldsmith can beat it out when needed. So on with you in St. Hubert's name, Father Abbot!"

Slender-boned and thin as was Ebbo's hand, it was a very tight fit, but the purpose was served. The service commenced; and fortunately, thanks to Thekla's conventual education, she was awed into silence and decorum by the sound of the Latin and the sight of an abbot. It was a strange marriage, if only in the contrast between the pale, expressive face and sad, dark eyes of the prostrate youth, and the frightened, bewildered little girl, standing upon a stool to reach up to him, with her blue eyes stretched with wonder, and her cheeks flushed and pouting with unshed tears, her rosy plump hand enclosed in the long white wasted one that was thus for ever united to it by the broken fragments of Kaiser Max's chain.

The rite over, two attestations of the marriage of Eberhard, Freiherr von Adlerstein, and Thekla, Freiherrin von Adlerstein Wildschloss and Felsenbach, were drawn up and signed by the abbot, the Emperor, Count Dankwart, and the father and mother of the two contracting parties; one to be commited to the care of the abbot, the other to be preserved by the House of Adlerstein.

Then the Emperor, as the concluding grace of the ceremonial, bent to kiss the bride; but, tired, terrified, and cross, Thekla, as if quite relieved to have some object for her resentment, returned his attempt with a vehement buffet, struck with all the force of her small arm, crying out, "Go away with you! I know I've never married *you*!"

"The better for my eyes!" said the good-natured Emperor, laughing heartily. "My lady Bearess is like to prove the more courteous bride! Fare thee well, Sir Bridegroom," he added, stooping over Ebbo, and kissing his brow; "Heaven give thee joy of this day's work, and of thy faithful little fury. I'll send her the bearskin as her meetest wedding-gift."

And the next that was heard from the Kaiser was the arrival of a parcel of Italian books for the Freiherr Eberhard, and for the little Freiherrin a large bundle, which proved to contain a softly-dressed bearskin, with the head on, the eyes being made of rubies, a gold muzzle and chain on the nose, and claws tipped with gold. The Emperor had made a point that it should be conveyed to the castle snow or no snow, for a yule gift.

CHAPTER XVI

THE CLEAR SUNSHINE of early summer was becoming low on the hillsides. Sparkling and dimpling, the clear amber-coloured stream of the Braunwasser rippled along its stony bed, winding in and out among the rocks so humbly that it seemed to be mocked by the wide span of the arch that crossed it in all the might of massive bulwarks, and dignified masonry of huge stones.

Some way above, a clearing of the wood below the mountain showed huts, and labourers apparently constructing a mill so as to take advantage of the leap of the water from the height above; and, on the left bank, an enclosure was traced out, within which were rising the walls of a small church, while the noise of the mallet and chisel echoed back from the mountain-side, and masons, white with stone-dust, swarmed around.

Across the bridge came a pilgrim, marked out as such by hat, wallet, and long staff, on which he leant heavily, stumbling along as if both halting and footsore, and bending as one bowed down by past toil and present fatigue. Pausing in the centre, he gazed round with a strange disconcerted air,—at the castle on the terraced hillside, looking down with bright eyes of glass glittering in the sunshine, and lighting up even that grim old pile; at the banner hanging so lazily that the tinctures and bearings were hidden in the folds; then at the crags, rosy purple in evening glow, rising in broad step above step to the Red Eyrie, bathed in sunset majesty of dark crimson; and above it the sweep of the descending eagle, discernible for a moment in the pearly light of the sky. The pilgrim's eye lighted up as he watched it; but then, looking down at bridge and church and trodden wheel-tracked path, he frowned with perplexity, and each painful step grew heavier and more uncertain.

Near the opposite side of the enclosure there waited a tall, rugged-looking, elderly man with two horses—one an aged mare, mane, tail, and all of the snowiest silvery white; the other a little shaggy dark mountain pony, with a pad-saddle. And close to the bank of the stream might be seen its owner, a little girl of seven years, whose tight round lace cap had slipped back, as well as her blue silk hood, and exposed a profusion of loose flaxen hair, and a plump, innocent face.

The pilgrim looked at her unperceived, and for a moment was about to address her; but then, with a strange air of repulsion, dragged himself on to the porch of the rising church, where, seated on a block of stone, he could look into the interior. All was unfinished, but the portion which had made the most progress was a chantry-chapel opposite to the porch, and containing what were evidently designed to be two monuments. One was merely blocked out, but it showed the outline of a warrior bearing a shield on which a coiled serpent was rudely sketched in red chalk. The other, in a much more forward state, was actually under the hands of the sculptor, and represented a slender youth, almost a boy, though in the full armour of a knight, his hands clasped on his breast over a lute, an eagle on his shield, an eagle-crest on his helmet, and, under the arcade supporting the alter-tomb, shields alternately of eagles and doves.

But the strangest thing was that this young knight seemed to be sitting for his own effigy. The very same face, under the very same helmet, only with the varied, warm hues of life instead of in cold white marble, was to be seen on the shoulders of a young man in a grey cloth dress, with a black scarf passing from shoulder to waist, crossed by a sword-belt. The hair was hidden by the helmet, whose raised visor showed keen, finely-cut features, and a pair of dark brown eyes of somewhat grave and sad expression.

"Have a care, Lucas," he presently said; "I fear me you are chiselling away too much. It must be a softer, more rounded face than mine has become; and, above all, let it not catch any saddened look. Keep that air of solemn waiting in glad hope, as though he saw the dawn through his closed eyelids, and were about to take up his song again!"

"Verily, Herr Freiherr, now the likeness is so far forward, the actual sight of you may lead me to mar it rather than mend."

"So is it well that this should be the last sitting. I am to set forth for Genoa in another week. If I cannot get letters from the Kaiser, I shall go in search of him, that he may see that my lameness is no more an impediment."

The pilgrim passed his hand over his face, as though to dissipate a bewildering dream; and just then the little girl flew rushing up from the stream, but came to a sudden standstill at sight of the stranger, who at length addressed her. "Little lady," he said, "is this the Debateable Ford?"

"No; now it is the Friendly Bridge," said the child.

The pilgrim started, as with a pang of recollection. "And what is yonder castle?" he further asked.

"Schloss Adlerstein," she said proudly.

"And you are the little lady of Adlerstein Wildschloss?"

"Yes," again she answered; and then, gathering courage—"You are a holy pilgrim! Come up to the castle for supper and rest." And then, springing past him, she flew up to the knight, crying, "Herr Freiherr, here is a holy pilgrim, weary and hungry. Let us take him home to the mother."

"Did he take thee for a wild elf?" said the young man, with an elder-brotherly endeavour to right the little cap that had slidden under the chin, and to push back the unmanageable wealth of hair under it, ere he rose; and he came forward and spoke with kind courtesy, as he observed the wanderer's worn air and feeble step. "Dost need a night's lodging, holy palmer? My mother will make thee welcome, if thou canst climb as high as the castle yonder."

The pilgrim made an obeisance, but instead of answering, demanded hastily, "See I yonder the bearing of Schlangenwald?"

"Even so. Schloss Schlangenwald is about a league farther on, and thou wilt find a kind reception there, if thither thou art bent."

"Is that Graf Wolfgang's tomb?" still eagerly pursued the pilgrim; and receiving a sign in the affirmative, "What was his end?"

"He fell in a skirmish."

"By whose hand?"

"By mine."

"Ha!" and the pilgrim surveyed him with undisguised astonishment; then, without another word, took up his staff and limped out of the building, but not on the road to Schlangenwald. It was nearly a quarter of an hour afterwards that he was overtaken by the young knight and the little lady on their horses, just where the new road to the castle parted from the old way by the Eagle's Ladder. The knight reined up as he saw the poor man's slow, painful steps, and said, "So thou art not bound for Schlangenwald?"

"I would to the village, so please you—to the shrine of the Blessed Friedmund."

"Nay, at this rate thou will not be there till midnight," said the young knight, springing off his horse; "thou canst never brook our sharp stones! See, Thekla, do thou ride on with Heinz to tell the mother I am bringing her a holy pilgrim to tend. And thou, good man, mount my old grey. Fear not; she is steady and surefooted, and hath of late been used to a lame rider. Ah! that is well. Thou hast been in the saddle before."

To go afoot for the sake of giving a lift to a holy wayfarer was one of the most esteemed acts of piety of the Middle Age, so that no one durst object to it, and the palmer did no more than utter a suppressed murmur of acknowledgment as he seated himself on horseback, the young knight walking by his rein. "But what is this?" he exclaimed, almost with dismay. "A road to the castle up here!"

"Yes, we find it a great convenience. Thou art surely from these parts?" added the knight.

"I was a man-at-arms in the service of the baron," was the answer, in an odd, muffled tone.

"What!—of my grandfather?" was the exclamation.

"No!" gruffly. "Of old Freiherr Eberhard. Not of any of the Wildschloss crew."

"But I am not a Wildschloss! I am grandson to Freiherr Eberhard! Oh, wast thou with him and my father when they were set upon in the hostel?" he cried, looking eagerly up to the pilgrim; but the man kept his broad-leaved hat slouched over his face, and only muttered, "The son of Christina!" the last word so low that Ebbo was not sure that he caught it, and the next moment the old warrior exclaimed exultingly, "And you have had vengeance on them! When—how —where?"

"Last harvest-tide—at the Debateable Strand," said Ebbo, never able to speak of the encounter without a weight at his heart, but drawn on by the earnestness of the old foe of Schlangenwald. "It was a meeting in full career—lances broken, sword-stroke on either hand. I was sore wounded, but my sword went through his collar-bone."

"Well struck! good stroke!" cried the pilgrim, in rapture. "And with that sword?"

"With this sword. Didst know it?" said Ebbo, drawing the weapon, and giving it to the old man, who held it for a few moments, weighed it affectionately, and with a long low sigh restored it, saying, "It is well. You and that blade have paid of the core. I should be content. Let me dismount. I know my way to the hermitage."

"Nay, what is this?" said Ebbo; "thou must have rest and food. The hermitage is empty, scarce habitable."

"But let me go, ere I bring evil on you all. I can pray up there, and save my soul, but I cannot see it all."

"See what?" said Ebbo, again trying to see his guest's face. "There may be changes, but an old faithful follower of my father's must ever be welcome."

"Not when his wife has taken a new lord," growled the stranger bitterly, "and he a Wildschloss! Young man, I could have pardoned aught else!"

"I know not who you may be who talk of pardoning my lady-mother," said Ebbo, "but new lord she has neither taken nor will take. She has refused every offer; and, now that Schlangenwald with his last breath confessed that he slew not my father, but sold him to the Turks, I have been only awaiting recovery from my wound to go in search of him."

"Who, then, is yonder child, who told me she was Wildschloss?"

"That child," said Ebbo, with half a smile and half a blush, "is my wife, the daughter of Wildschloss, who prayed me to espouse her thus early, that so my mother might bring her up."

By this time they had reached the castle court, now a well-kept, lordly-looking enclosure, where the pilgrim looked about him as one bewildered. He was so infirm that Ebbo carefully helped him up the stone stairs to the hall, where he already saw his mother prepared for the hospitable reception of the palmer. Leaving him at the entrance, Ebbo crossed the hall to say to her in a low voice, "This pilgrim is one of the old lanzknechts of my grandfather's time. One of the old sort—supremely discontented at change."

"And thou hast walked up, and wearied thyself!" exclaimed Christina, grieved to see her son's halting step.

"A rest will soon cure that," said Ebbo, seating himself as he spoke on a settle near the hall fire; but the next moment a strange wild low, shriek from his mother made him start up and spring to her side. She stood with hands clasped, and wondering eyes. The pilgrim—his hat on the ground, his white head and rugged face displayed was gazing as though devouring her with his eyes, murmuring, "Unchanged! unchanged!"

"What is this?" thundered the young baron. "What are you doing to the lady?"

"Hush! hush, Ebbo!" exclaimed Christina. "It is thy father! On thy knees! Thy father is come! It is our son, my own lord. Oh, embrace him! Kneel to him, Ebbo!" she wildly cried.

"Hold, mother," said Ebbo, keeping his arm round her, though she struggled against him, for he felt some doubts as he looked back at his walk with the stranger, and remembered Heinz's want of recognition. "Is it certain that this is indeed my father?"

"Oh, Ebbo," was the cry of poor Christina, almost beside herself, "how could I not be sure? I know him! I feel it! Oh, my lord, bear with him. It is his wont to be so loving! Ebbo, cannot you see it is himself?"

"The young fellow is right," said the stranger slowly. "I will answer all he may demand."

"Forgive me," said Ebbo, abashed, "forgive me"; and, as his mother broke from him, he fell upon his knee; but he only heard his father's cry, "Ah! Stine, Stine, thou alone art the same," and, looking up, saw her, with her face hidden in the white beard, quivering with a rapture such as he had never seen in her before. It seemed long to him ere she looked up again in her husband's face to sob on, "My son! Oh! my beautiful twins! Our son! Oh, see him, dear lord!" And the pilgrim turned to hear Ebbo's "Pardon, honoured father, and your blessing."

Almost bashfully the pilgrim laid his hand on the dark head, and murmured something; then said, "Up, then! The slayer of

Schlangenwald kneeling! Ah, Stine, I knew thy little head was wondrous wise, but I little thought thou wouldst breed him up to avenge us on old Wolfgang! So slender a lad too! Ha! Schneiderlein, old rogue, I knew thee," holding out his hand. "So thou didst get home safe?"

"Ay, my lord; though, if I left you alive, never more will I call a man dead," said Heinz.

"Worse luck for me—till now," said Sir Eberhard, whose tones, rather than his looks, carried perfect conviction of his identity. It was the old homely accent, and gruff good-humoured voice, but with something subdued and broken in the tone. His features had grown like his father's, but he looked much older than ever the hale old mountaineer had done, or than his real age; so worn and lined was his face, his skin tanned, his eyelids and temples puchered by burning sun, his hair and beard white as the mane of his old mare, the proud Adlerstein port entirely gone. He stooped even more without his staff than with it; and, when he yielded himself with a sigh of repose to his wife's tendance, she found that he had not merely the ordinary hurts of travelling, but that there were old festering scars on his ankles. "The gyves,"[1] he said, as she looked up at him with startled, pitying eyes. "Little deemed I that they would ever come under thy tender hands." As he almost timidly smoothed the braid of dark hair on her brow—"So they never burnt thee for a witch after all, little one? I thought my mother would never keep her hands off thee, and used to fancy I heard the crackling of the flame."

"She spared me for my children's sake," said Christina; "and truly Heaven has been very good to us, but never so much as now. My dear lord, will it weary thee too much to come to the castle chapel and give thanks?" she said timidly.

"With all my heart," he answered earnestly. "I would go even on my knees. We were not without masses even in Tunis; but, when Italian and Spaniard would be ransomed, and there was no mind of the German, I little thought I should ever sing Brother Lambert's psalm about turning our captivity as rivers in the south."

Ebbo was hovering round, supplying all that was needed for his father's comfort; but his parents were so completely absorbed in one another that he was scarcely noticed.

When the chapel bell rang, and the pair rose to offer their thanksgiving, Ebbo dutifully offered his support, but was absolutely

[1] Fetter, ankle-iron.

unseen, so fondly was Sir Eberhard leaning on his wife; and her bright exhulting smile and shake of the head gave a pang to the son who had hitherto been all in all to her.

The pair knelt side by side with hands locked together, while notes of praise rang from all voices; and meantime Ebbo, close to Friedmund's coffin, strove to share the joy, and to lift up a heart that *would* sink in the midst of self-reproach for undutifulness, and would dislike the thought of the rude untaught man, holding aloof from him, likely to view him with distrust and jealousy, and to undo all he had achieved, and further absorbing the mother, the mother who was to him all the world, and for whose sake he had given his best years to the child-wife, as yet nothing to him.

It was reversing the natural order of things that, after reigning from infancy, he should have to give up at eighteen to one of the last generation; and some such thought rankled in his mind when the whole household trooped joyfully out of the chapel to prepare a banquet for their old new lord, and their young old lord was left alone.

Alone with the coffin where the armour lay upon the white cross, Ebbo threw himself on his knees, and laid his head upon it, murmuring, "Ah, Friedel! Friedel! Would that we had changed places! Thou wouldst brook it better. At least thou didst never know what it is to be lonely."

"Herr Baron!" said a little voice.

His first movement was impatient. Thekla was apt to pursue him wherever he did not want her; but here he had least expected her, for she had a great fear of that coffin, and could hardly be brought to the chapel at prayer times, when she generally occupied herself with fancies that the empty helmet glared at her. But now Ebbo saw her standing as near as she durst, with a sweet wistfulness in her eyes, such as he had never seen there before.

"What is it, Thekla?" he said. "Art sent to call me?"

"No; only I saw that you stayed here all alone," she said, clasping her hands.

"Must I not be alone, child?" he said bitterly. "Here lies my brother. My mother has her husband again!"

"But you have me!" cried Thekla; and, as he looked up between amusement and melancholy, he met such a loving eager little face, that he could not help holding out his arms, and letting her cling to him. "Indeed," she said, "I'll never be afraid of that helmet again, if only you will not lay down your head there, and say you are alone."

"Never, Thekla! while you are my little wife," said he; and, child as she was, there was strange solace to his heart in the eyes that, once vacant and wondering, had now gained a look of love and intelligence.

"What are you going to do?" she said, shuddering a little, as he rose and laid his hand on Friedel's sword.

"To make thee gird on thine own knight's sword," said Ebbo, unbuckling that which he had so long worn. "Fridel," he added, "thou wouldst give me thine. Let me take up thy temper with it, thine open-hearted love and humility."

He guided Thekla's happy little fingers to the fastening of the belt, and then, laying his hand on hers, said gravely, "Thekla, never speak of what I said just now—not even to the mother. Remember it is thy husband's first secret."

And feeling no longer solitary when his hand was in the clasp of hers, he returned to the hall, where his father was installed in the baronial chair, in which Ebbo had been at home from babyhood. His mother's exclamation showed that her son had been wanting to her; and she looked fuller than ever of bliss when Ebbo gravely stood before his father, and presented him with the good old sword that he had sent to his unborn son.

"You are like to use it more than I—nay, you have used it to some purpose," said he. "Yet must I keep mine old comrade at least a little while. Wife, son, sword, should make one feel the same man again, but it is all too wonderful!"

All that evening, and long after, his hand from time to time sought the hilt of his sword, as if that touch above all proved to him that he was again a free noble in his own castle.

The story he told was thus. The swoon in which Heinz had left him had probably saved his life by checking the gush of blood, and he had known no more till he had found himself in a rough cart among the corpses. At Schlangenwald's castle he had been found still breathing, and had been flung into a dungeon, where he lay unattended, for how long he never knew, since all the early part of the time was lost in the clouds of fever. On coarse fare and scanty drink, in that dark vault, he had struggled by sheer obstinacy of vitality into recovery. In the very height of midsummer alone did the sun peep through the grating of his cell, and he had newly hailed this cheerful visitor when he was roughly summoned, placed on horseback with eyes and hands bound, and only allowed sight again to find himself among a herd of his fellow Germans in the

Turkish camp. They were the prisoners of the terrible Turkish raid of 1475, when Georg von Schenk and fourteen other noblemen of Austria and Styria were all taken in one unhappy fight, and dragged away into captivity, with hundreds of lower rank.

To Sir Eberhard the change had been greatly for the better. The Turk had treated him much better than the Christian; and walking in the open air, chained to a German comrade, was far pleasanter than pining in his lonely dungeon. At Adrianople, an offer had been made to each of the captives, if they would become Moslems, of entering the Ottoman service as Spahis;[1] but with one voice they had refused, and had then been drafted into different divisions. The fifteen nobles, who had been offered for ransom, were taken to Constantinople, to await its arrival, and they had promised Sir Eberhard to publish his fate on their return to their homes; and, though he knew the family resources to well to have many hopes, he was rather hurt to find that their promise had been unfulfilled.

"Alas! they had no opportunity," said Ebbo. "Gulden[2] were scarce, or were all in Kaiser Friedrich's great chest; the ransoms could not be raised, and all died in captivity. I heard about it when I was at Wurms last month."

"The boy at Wurms?" almost gasped Sir Eberhard, in amaze.

"I had to be there about matters concerning the Wildschloss lands and the bridge," said Ebbo; "and both Dankwart von Schlangenwald and I made special inquiries about that company in case you should have shared their fate. I hoped to have set forth at that time, but the Kaiser said I was still too lame, and refused me licence, or letters to the Sultan."

"You would not have found me," said his father, narrating how he with a large troop of captives had been driven down to the coast, where they were transferred to a Moorish slave-dealer, who shipped them off for Tunis. He had then been allotted to a corsair, and had thenceforth been chained to the bench of rowers, between the two decks, where, in stifling heat and stench, in storm or calm, healthy or diseased, the wretched oarsmen were compelled to play the part of machinery in propelling the vessel, in order to capture Christian ships—making exertions to which only the perpetual lash of the galley-master could have urged their exhausted frames; often not desisting for twenty or thirty hours, and rowing still while sustenance was put into their mouths by their drivers. Many a man drew his

---

[1] Horse soldiers.
[2] Florins.

last breath with his last stroke, and was at the first leisure moment hurled into the waves. It was the description that had so deeply moved Friedel long ago, and Christina wept over it, as she looked at the bowed form once so proud and free, and thought of the unhealed scars. But there, her husband added, he had been chained next to a holy friar of German blood, like himself a captive of the great Styrian raid; and, while some blasphemed in their misery, or wildly chid their patron saints, this good man strove to show that all was to work out good. "See"—and he took out a rosary of strung bladders of seaweed; "that is what he left me when he died, and what I meant to have been telling for ever up in the hermitage."

It was plain that Sir Eberhard had learnt more Christianity in the hold of his Moorish pirate ship than ever in the Holy Roman Empire, and he had vowed never to return to a life of violence, even though fancying a life of penance in a hermitage the only alternative.

Ebbo asked if the Genoese merchant, Ser Gian Battista dei Battiste, had indeed been one of his fellow-captives. "Ha!—what?" and on the repetition, "Truly I knew him, Merchant Gian as we used to call him; but you twang off his name as they speak it in his own stately city."

Christina smiled. "Ebbo learnt the Italian tongue this winter from our chaplain, who had studied at Bologna. He was told it would aid in his quest of you."

"Tell me not!" said the traveller, holding up his hands in deprecation; "the Junker is worse than a priest! And yet he killed old Wolfgang! But what of Gian?"

Ebbo briefly narrated the adventure, when it evidently appeared that his having led at least one foray gave his father for the first time a fellow-feeling for him, and a sense that he was one of the true old stock; but, when he heard of the release, he growled, "So! How would a lad have fared who so acted in my time? My poor old mother! She must have been changed indeed not to have scourged him till he had no strength to cry out."

"He was my prisoner!" said Ebbo, in his old defiant tone; "I had the right."

"Ah, well! the Junker has always been master here, and I never!" said the elder knight, looking round rather piteously; and Ebbo, with a sudden movement, exclaimed, "Nay, sir, you are the only lord and master, and I stand ready to be the first to obey you."

"You! A fine young book-learned scholar, already knighted, and with all these Wildschloss lands too!" said Sir Eberhard, gazing with a strange puzzled look at the delicate but spirited features of this strange, perplexing son. "Reach hither your hand, boy."

And as he compared the slender, shapely hand of such finely-textured skin with the breadth of his own horny giant's paw, he tossed it from him, shaking his head with a gesture as if he had no commands for such feminine-looking fingers to execute, and mortifying Ebbo not a little. "Ah!" said Christina apologetically, "it always grieved your mother that the boys would resemble me and mine. But, when daylight comes, Ebbo will show you that he has not lost the old German strength."

"No doubt—no doubt," said Sir Eberhard hastily, "since he has slain Schlangenwald; and, if the former state of things be at an end, the less he takes after the ancient stock the better. But I am an old man now, Stine, though thou look'st fair and fresh as ever, and I do not know what to make of these things. White napery on the table; glass drinking things—nay, were it not for thee and the Schneiderlein, I should not know I was at home."

He was led back to his narration, and it appeared that, after some years spent at the oar, certain bleedings from the lungs, the remains of his wound, had become so much more severe as to render him useless for naval purposes; and, as he escaped actually dying during a voyage, he was allowed to lie by on coming into port till he had in some degree recovered, and then had been set to labour at the fortifications, chained to another prisoner, and toiling between the burning sand and burning sun, but treated with less horrible severity than the necessities of the sea had occasioned on board ship, and experiencing the benefit of intercourse with the better class of captives, whom their miserable fate had thrown into the hands of the Moors.

It was a favourite alms-deed among the Provencals, Spaniards, and Italians to send money for the redemption of prisoners to the Moors, and there was a regular agency for ransoms through the Jews; but German captives were such an exception that no one thought of them, and many a time had the summons come for such and such a slave by name, or for five poor Sicilians, twenty Genoese, a dozen Marseillais, or the like, but still no word for the Swabian; till he had made up his mind that he should either leave his bones in the hot mud of the harbour, or be only set free by some gallant descent either of the brave King of Portugal, of or the Knights of Rhodes, of whom the captives were ever dreaming and whispering.

At length his own slave name was shouted; he was called up by the captain of his gang, and, while expecting some fresh punishment or, maybe, to find himself sold into some domestic form of slavery, he was set before a Jewish agent, who, after examining him on his name, country, and station, and comparing his answers with a paper of instructions, informed him that he was ransomed, caused his fetters to be struck off, and shipped him off at once for Genoa, with orders to the captain to consign him to the merchant Signor dei Battiste. By him Sir Eberhard had been received with the warmest hospitality, and treated as befitted his original station, but Battista disclaimed the merit of having ransomed him. He had but acted, he said, as the agent of an Austrian gentleman, from whom he had received orders to inquire after the Swabian baron who had been his fellow-captive, and, if he were still living, to pay his ransom, and bring him home.

"The name—the name?" eagerly asked Ebbo and his mother at once.

"The name? Gian was wont to make bad work of our honest German names, but I tried to learn this—being so beholden to him. I even caused it to be spelt over to me, but my letters long ago went from me. It seems to me that the man is a knight-errant, Stine— one Ritter Theur—Theur——"

"Theurdank!" cried Ebbo.

"Ay, Theurdank. What, you know him? There is nothing you and your mother don't know, I believe."

"Know him! Father, he is our greatest and noblest! He has been kind to me beyond description. He is the Kaiser! Now I see why he had that strange arch look which so vexed me when he forbade me on my allegiance to set forth till my lameness should be gone! Long ago had he asked me all about Gian Battista. To him he must have written."

"The Kaiser!" said Sir Eberhard. "Nay, the poor fellows I left in Turkey ever said he was too close of fist for them to have hope from him."

"Oh! that was old Kaiser Friedrich. This is our own gallant Maximilian—a knight as true and brave as ever was paladin," said Christina; "and most truly loving and prizing our Ebbo."

"And yet I wish—I wish," said Ebbo, "that he had let me win my father's liberty for myself."

"Yea, well," said his father, "there spoke the Adlerstein. We never were wont to be beholden to king or kaiser."

"Nay," said Ebbo, after a moment's recollection, colouring as he spoke; "it is true that I deserved it not. Nay, Sir Father, it is well. You owe your freedom in very truth to the son you have not known. It was he who treasured up the thought of the captive German described by the merchant, and even dreamt of it, while never doubting of your death; it was he who caught up Schlangenwald's first hint that you lived, while I, in my pride, passed it by as merely meant to perplex me; it was he who had formed an absolute purpose of obtaining some certainty; and at last, when my impetuosity had brought on the fatal battle, it was he who bought with his own life the avowal of your captivity. I had hoped to have fulfilled Friedel's trust, and to have redeemed my own backwardness; but it is not to be. While I was yet lying helpless on my bed, the Emperor has taken it out of my power. Mother, you receive him from Friedel's hands, after all."

"And well am I thankful that so it should be," said Christina. "Ah, Ebbo! sorely should I have pined with anxiety when thou wast gone. And thy father knows that thou hadst the full purpose."

"Yea, I know it," said the old man; "and, after all, small blame to him even if he had not. He never saw me, and light grieves the heart for what the eye hath not seen."

"But," added the wife, "since the Romish king freed you, dear lord, cared he not better for your journey than to let you come in this forlorn plight?"

This, it appeared, was far from being his deliverer's fault. Money had been supplied, and Sir Eberhard had travelled as far as Aosta with a party of Italian merchants; but no sooner had he parted with them than he was completely astray. His whole experience of life had been as a robber-baron or as a slave, and he knew not how to take care of himself as a peaceful traveller; he suffered fresh extortions at every stage, and after a few days was plundered by his guides, beaten, and left devoid of all means of continuing his journey to which he could hardly hope for a cheerful end. He did not expect to find his mother living—far less that his unowned wife could have survived the perils in which he had involved her; and he believed that his ancestral home would, if not a ruin, be held by his foes, or at best by the rival branch of the family, whose welcome of the outlawed heir would probably be to a dungeon, if not a halter. Yet the only magnet on earth for the lonely wanderer was his native mountain, where from some old peasant he might learn how his fair young bride had perished, and perhaps the sins of his youth might be expiated by continual prayer in the hermitage chapel where his sister lay buried, and whence he could see the crags for which his eye and heart had craved so long with the homesickness of a mountaineer.

And now, when his own Christina had welcomed him with all the overflow of her loving heart, unchanged save that hers had become a tenderer yet more dignified loveliness; when his gallant son, in all the bloom of young manhood, received him with dutiful submission; when the castle, in a state of defence, prosperity, and comfort, of which he had never dreamt, was again his own;—still the man was bewildered, and sometimes oppressed almost to distress. He had, as it were, fallen asleep in one age of the world and wakened in another, and it seemed as if he really wished to defer his wakening, or else that repose was an absolute novelty to him; for he sat dozing in his chair in the sun the whole of the next day, and scarcely spoke.

Ebbo, who felt it a necessity to come to an understanding of the terms on which they were to stand, tried to refer matters to him, and to explain the past, but he was met sometimes by a shake of the head, sometimes by a nod—not of assent, but of sleep; and his mother advised him not to harass the wearied traveller, but to leave him to himself for at least that day, and let him take his own time for exertion, letting things meantime go on as usual. Ebbo obeyed, but with a load at his heart, as he felt that all he was doing was but provisional, and that it would be his duty to resign all that he had planned, and partly executed, to this incompetent ignorant rule. He could certainly, when not serving the Emperor, go and act for himself at Thekla's dower castle of Felsenbach, and his mother might save things from going to utter ruin at Adlerstein; but no reflection or self-reproach could make it otherwise than a bitter pill to any Telemachus to have to resign to one so unlike Ulysses[1] in all but the length of his wanderings—one, also, who seemed only half to like, and not at all to comprehend, his Telemachus.

Meantime Ebbo attended to such matters as were sure to come each day before the Herr Freiherr. Now it was a question whether the stone for the mill should be quarried where it would undermine a bit of grass land, or farther on, where the road was rougher; now Berend's swine had got into Barthel's rye, and Barthel had severely hurt one of them—the Herr Freiherr's interference could alone prevent a hopeless quarrel; now a wagon with ironwork for the mill

---

[1] The Greek hero who wandered about for ten years after the siege of Troy, and at last returned home to his wife, Penelope, and his son, Telemachus.

claimed exemption from toll as being for the baron; and he must send down the toll, to obviate injustice towards Schlangenwald and Ulm.

Old Ulrich's grandson, who had run away for a lanzknecht, had sent a letter home (written by a comrade): the baron must read and answer it. Steinmark's son wanted to be a poor student: the Herr Freiherr must write him a letter of recommendation. Mother Grethel's ewe had fallen into a cleft; her son came to borrow a rope, and ask aid, and the baron must superintend the hoisting the poor beast up again. Hans had found the track of a wolf, and knew the hole where a litter of cubs abode: the Freiherr, his wolf-hound, and his spear were wanted for their destruction. Dietrich could not tell how to manage his new arquebus: the baron must teach him to take aim. Then there was a letter from Ulm to invite the baron to consult on the tax demanded by the Emperor for his Italian war, and how far it should concern the profits of the bridge; and another letter from the Markgraf of Wurtemburg, as chief of the Swabian League, requesting the Lord of Adlerstein to be on the look-out for a band of robbers, who were reported to be in neighbouring hills, after being hunted out of some of their other lurking places.

That very night, or rather nearly at the dawn of a summer morning, there was a yelling below the castle, and a flashing of torches, and tidings ran through it that a boor on the outskirts of the mountain had had his ricks fired and his cattle driven by the robbers, and his young daughters carried off. Old Sir Eberhard hobbled down to the hall in time to see weapons flashing as they were dealt out, to hear a clear decided voice giving orders, to listen to the tramp of horse, and watch more reitern pass out under the gateway than ever the castle counted in his father's time. Then he went back to his bed, and when he came down in the morning found all the women-kind of the castle roasting and boiling. And, at noon, little Thekla came rushing down from the watch-tower with news that all were coming home up the Eagle's Steps, and she was sure *her* baron had seen her, and waved to her. Soon after, *her* baron in his glitter-ing steel rode his cream-coloured charger (once Friedel's) into the castle court, followed by his exultant merry-men. They had over-taken the thieves in good time, made them captives, and recovered the spoil unhurt; and Heinz and Koppel made the castle ring with the deed of their young lord, who had forced the huge leader of the band to earth, and kept him down by main strength till they could come to bind him.

o

"By main strength?" slowly asked Sir Eberhard, who had been stirred into excitement.

"He was a loose-limbed, awkward fellow," said Ebbo, "less strong than he looked."

"Not only that, sir," said Heinz, looking from his old master to his young one; "but old iron is not a whit stronger than new steel, though the one looks full of might, and you would think the other but a toy."

"And what have you done with the rogues' heads?" asked the old knight. "I looked to see them on your spears. Or have you hung them?"

"Not so, sir," said Ebbo. "I sent the men off to Stuttgart with an escort. I dislike doing execution ourselves; it makes the men so lawless. Besides, this farmer was Schlangenwalder."

"And yet he came to you for redress?"

"Yes, for Sir Dankwart is at his commandery, and he and I agreed to look after each other's lands."

Sir Eberhard retired to his chair as if all had gone past his understanding, and thence he looked on while his son and wife hospitably regaled, and then dismissed, their auxiliaries in the rescue.

Afterwards Christina told her son that she thought his father was rested, and would be better able to attend to him, and Ebbo, with a painful swelling in his heart, approached him deferentially, with a request that he would say what was his pleasure with regard to the Emperor, to whom acknowledgments must in the first place be made for his release, and next would arise the whole question of homage and investiture.

"Look you here, fair son," said Sir Eberhard, rousing himself, "these things are all past me. I'll have none of them. You and your Kaiser understand one another, and your homage is paid. It boots not changing all for an old fellow that is but come home to die."

"Nay, father, it is in the order of things that you should be lord here."

"I never was lord here, and, what is more, I would not, and could not be. Son, I marked you yesterday. You are master as never was my poor father, with all the bawling and blows that used to rule the house, while these fellows mind you at a word, in a voice as quiet as your mother's. Besides, what should I do with all these mills and bridges of yours, and Diets, and Leagues, and councils enough to addle a man's brain? No, no; I could once slay a bear, or strike a fair stroke at a Schlangenwalder, but even they got the better of me, and I am good for nothing now but to save my soul. So, young sir, if you can give the old man a corner of the hearth while he lives, he will never interfere with you. And, maybe, if the castle were in jeopardy in your absence, with that new-fangled road up to it, he could tell the fellows how to hold it out."

"Sir—dear father," cried the ardent Ebbo, "this is not a fit state of things. I will spare you all the trouble and care; only make me not undutiful; take your own place. Mother, convince him!"

"No, my son," said Sir Eberhard; "your mother sees what is best for me. I only want to be left to her to rest a little while. As Heinz says, the rusty old iron must lie by while the new steel does the work. It is quiet that I need. It is joy enough for me to see what she has made you, and all around. Ah! Stine, my white dove, I knew thine was a wise head; but when I left thee, gentle little frightened, fluttering thing, how little could I have thought that, all alone, unaided, thou wouldst have kept that little head above water, and made thy son work out all these changes—thy doing— and so I know they are good and seemly."

"I did it not, dear husband; God did it for me. He gave the boys the loving, true tempers that worked out the rest! He shielded them and me in our days of peril."

"Yes, father," added Ebbo, "Providence guarded us; but above all, our chief blessing has been the mother who has made one of us a holy saint, and taught the other to seek after him! Father, I am glad you see how great has been the work of the Dove you brought to the Eagle's Nest."

CHAPTER XVII

THE YEAR 1531 has begun, and Schloss Adlerstein remains in its strength on the mountain-side, but with a look of cultivation on its environs such as would have amazed Kunigunde.

The old hall is still the chief place of assembly, and now that it has been wainscoted, with a screen of carved wood to shut off the draughty passages, and a stove of bright tiles to increase the warmth, it is far more cheerful. Moreover, a window has been opened showing the rich green meadow below, with the bridge over the Braunwasser, and the little church, with a spire of pierced lacework, and white cottages peeping out of the retreating forest.

That is the window which the Lady Baroness loves. See her there, the lovely old lady of seventy-five—yes, lovelier than ever, for her sweet brown eyes have the same pensive, clear beauty, enhanced by the snowy whiteness of her hair, of which a soft braid shows over the pure pale brow beneath the white band, and sweeping black veil, that she has worn by right for twenty years. But the slight form is active and brisk, and there are ready smiles and looks of interest for the pretty fair-haired maidens, three in number, who run in and out from their household avocations to appeal to the "dear grandmother," mischievously to tell of the direful yawns proceeding from brothers Ebbo and Gottfried over their studies with their tutor, or to gaze from the window and wonder if the father, with the two brothers, Friedel Max and Kasimir, will return from Ulm in time for the "mid-day eating."

Ah! there they are. Quick-eyed Vittoria has seen the cavalcade first, and dances off to tell Ermentrude and Stine time enough to prepare their last batch of fritters for the newcomers. The Lady Baroness lays down her distaff, and gazes with eyes of satisfied content at the small party of horsemen climbing up the footpath. Then, when they have wound out of sight round a rock, she moves out towards the hall-door with a light, quick step, for never yet has she resigned her great enjoyment, that of greeting her son on the steps of the porch—those steps where she once met such fearful news, but where that memory has been effaced by many a cheerful welcome.

There, then, she stands, amid the bright throng of grandchildren, while the baron and his sons spring from their horses and come up to her. The baron doffs his Spanish hat, bends the knee, kisses her hand, and receives her kiss on his brow, with the fervour of a life-devotion, before he turns to accept the salutation of his daughters, and then takes her hand, with pretty affectionate ceremony, to hand her back to her seat.

No sooner is the meal over than, with a formal entreaty for dismissal, the seven young folks, and all the dogs, move off together, to that favourite gathering-place round the stove, where all their merry tongues are let loose together.

To them, the Herr Vater and the Frau Grossmutter[1] seem nearly of the same age, and of the same generation; and verily the eighteen years between the mother and son have dwindled into a very small difference even in appearance, and a lesser one in feeling. She is a youthful, beautiful old lady; he a grave, spare, worn, elderly man, in his full strength, but with many a trace of care and thought, and far more of silver than of brown in his thin hair and pointed beard, and with a melancholy thoughtfulness in his clear brown eyes—all well corresponding with the gravity of the dress in which he has been meeting the burghers of Ulm: a black velvet suit—only relieved by his small white lace ruff, and the ribbon and jewel of the Golden Fleece, the only other approach to ornament that he wears being that ring long ago twisted off the Emperor Maximilian's chain. But now, as he has bowed off the chaplain to his study, and excused himself from aiding his two gentlemen-squires in consuming their krug[2] of beer, and hands his mother to her favourite nook in the sunny window, taking his seat by her side, his features assume an expression of repose and relaxation as if here indeed were his true home.

He has chosen his seat in full view of a picture that hangs on the wainscoted wall, near his mother—a picture whose pure ethereal tinting, of colour limpid as the rainbow, yet rich as the most glowing flower-beds, its soft lovely *pose*, and rounded outlines, prove it to be no produce even of one of the great German artists of the time, but to have been wrought, under an Italian sky, by such a hand as left us the marvellous smile of Mona Lisa. It represents two figures, one unmistakably himself when in the prime of life, his brow

---

[1] Grandmother.   [2] Tankard.

and cheeks unfurrowed, and his hair still thick, shining brown, but
with the same grave earnestness of the dark eye that came with the
early sense of responsibility, and with the first sorrow of his youth.
The other figure, one on which the painter loved to dwell, is of a
lady, so young that she might almost pass for his daughter, except
for the peculiar, tender sweetness that could only become the wife
and mother. Fair she is as snow, with scarce a deepening of the
rose on cheek, or even lip, fragile and transparent as a spiritual form,
and with a light in the blue eyes, and a grace in the soft fugitive
smile, that scarce seems to belong to earth.

"What, thou nestling here, my little Vittoria, away from all yonder
prattle?"

"Dear father, if I may, I love far best to hear you and the grandmother talk."

"Hear the child! She alone hath your face, mother, or Friedel's
eyes! Is it that thou wouldst be like thy noble Roman godmother,
the Marchesa di Pescara, that makes thee seek our grave company,
little one?"

"I always long to hear you talk of her, and of the Italian days,
dear father, and how you won this noble jewel of yours."

"Ah, child, that was before those times! It was the gift of good
Kaiser Max at his godson's christening, when he filled your sweet
mother with pretty spite by persuading her that it was a little golden
bear skin."

"Tell her how you had gained it, my son."

"By vapouring, child; and by the dull pride of my neighbours.
Heard'st thou never of the siege of Padua, when we had Bayard,
the best knight in Europe, and five hundred Frenchmen for our
allies? Our artillery had made a breach, and the Kaiser requested
the French knights to lead the storm, whereto they answered, Well
and good, but our German nobles must share the assault, and not
leave them to fight with no better backers the the hired lanzknechts.
All in reason, quoth I, and more shame for us not to have been foremost in our Kaiser's own cause; but what said the rest of our misproud chivalry? They would never condescend to climb a wall on
foot in company with lanzknechts! On horseback must their
worships fight, or not at all; and when to shame them I called myself
a mountaineer, more used to climb than to ride, and vowed that I
should esteem it an honour to follow such a knight as Bayard, were
it on all-fours, then cast they my burgher blood in my teeth. Never
saw I the Kaiser so enraged; he swore that all the common sense

in the empire was in the burgher blood, and that he would make me a knight of the noblest order in Europe to show how he esteemed it. And next morning he was gone! So ashamed was he of his own army that he rode off in the night, and sent orders to break up the siege. I could have torn my hair, for I had just lashed up a few of our nobles to a better sense of honour, and we would yet have redeemed our name! And after all, the Chapter of proud Flemings would never have admitted me had not the heralds hunted up that the Sorels were gentlemen of blood and coat armour long ago at Liege. I am glad my father lived to see that proved, mother. He could not honour thee more than he did, but he would have been sorely grieved had I been rejected. He often thought me a mechanical burgher, as it was."

"Not quite so, my son. He never failed to be proud of thy deeds, even when he did not understand them; but this, and the grandson's birth, were the crowning joys of his life."

"Yes, those were glad triumphant years, take them all in all, ere the Emperor sent me to act ambassador in Rome, and we left you the two elder little girls and the boy to take care of. My dear little Thekla! She had a foreboding that she might never see those children more, yet would she have pined her heart away more surely had I left her at home! I never was absent a week but I found her wasted with watching for me."

"It was those weary seven years of Italy that changed thee most, my son."

"Apart from you, mother, and knowing you now indeed to be widowed, and with on the one hand such contradictory commands from the Emperor as made me sorely ashamed of myself, of my nation, and of the man whom I loved and esteemed personally the most on earth, yet bound there by his express command, while I saw my tender wife's health wasting in the climate day by day! Yet still, while most she gasped for a breath of Swabian hills, she ever declared it would kill her outright to send her from me. And thus it went on till I laid her in the stately church of her own patroness. Then how it would have fared with me and the helpless little ones I know not, but for thy noble godmother, my Vittoria, the wise and ready helper of all in trouble, the only friend thy mother had made at Rome, and who had been able, from all her heights of learning and accomplishment, to value my Thekla's golden soul in its simplicity. Even then, when too late, came one of the Kaiser's kindest letters, recalling me—a letter whose every word I would have paid for with a drop of my own blood six weeks before! and which he had only failed to send because his head was running on the plan of that gorgeous tomb where he is not buried! Well, at least it brought us home to you again once more, mother, and, where you are, comfort never has been utterly absent from me. He could think, but could not act; and now we have a man who acts, but *will* not think. It may have been a good day for our German reputation among foreign princes when Charles V. put on the crown; but only two days in my life have been as mournful to me as that when I stood by Kaiser Max's death-bed at Wells, and knew that generous, loving, fitful spirit was passing away from the earth! Never owned I friend I loved so well as Kaiser Max! Nor has any Emperor done so much for this our dear land."

Travellers in Wurtemburg may perhaps turn aside from glorious old Ulm, and the memories of the battlefields around it, to the romantic country round the Swabian mountains, through which descend the tributaries of the Danube. Here they may think themselves fortunate if they come upon a green valley, with a bright mountain torrent dashing through it, fresh from the lofty mountain, with terraced sides that rise sheer above. An old bridge, a mill, and a neat German village lie clustered in the valley; a seignorial mansion peeps out of the forest glades; and a lovely church, of rather late Gothic, but beautifully designed, attracts the eye so soon as it can be persuaded to quit the romantic outline of the ruined baronial castle high upon one of the mountain ledges. Report declares that there are tombs in the church well worth inspection. You seek out an old venerable blue-coated peasant who has charge of the church.

"What is yonder castle?"

"It is the castle of Adlerstein."

"Are the family still extant?"

"Yea, yea; they built yonder house when the Schloss became ruinous. They have always been here."

The church is very beautiful in its details, the carved work of the east end and pulpit especially so, but nothing is so attractive as the altar tomb in the chantry chapel. It is a double one, holding not, as usual, the recumbent effigies of a husband and wife, but of two knights in armour.

"Who are these, good friend?"

"They are the good Barons Ebbo and Friedel."

Father and son they appear to be, killed at the same time in some fatal battle, for the white marble face of one is round with youth, no hair on lip or chin, and with a lovely peaceful solemnity, almost cheerfulness, in the expression. The other, a bearded man, has the glory of old age in his worn features, beautiful and restful, but it is as if one had gone to sleep in the light of dawn, the other in the last glow of sunset. Their armour and their crests are alike, but the young one bears the eagle shield alone, while the elder has the same bearing repeated upon an escutcheon of pretence.[1] They are surely father and son, a maiden knight and tried warrior, who fell together?

"No," the guide shakes his head; "they are twin brothers, the good Barons Ebbo and Friedel, who were born when their father had been taken captive by the Saracens while on a crusade. Baron Friedel was slain at the bridge foot, and his brother built the church in his memory. He first planted vines upon the mountains, and freed the peasants from the lords' dues on their flax. And it is true that the two brothers may still be seen hovering on the mountain-side in the mist at sunset, sometimes one, sometimes both."

You turn with a smile to the inscription, sure that those windows, those porches, that armour, never were of crusading date, and ready to refute the old peasant. You spell out the upright Gothic letters around the cornice of the tomb, and you read, in mediaeval Latin:

'Orate pro Anima Friedmundis Equitis Baronis Adlersteini.[2] A.D. mcccxciii.'

Then turn to the other side and read:

'Hic jacet Eberardus Eques Baro Adlersteini.[3]   A.D. mdxliii Demum.[4]

Yes, the guide is right. They are brothers, with well-nigh a lifetime between their deaths. Is that the meaning of that strange *Demum*?

Few of the other tombs are worth attention, each lapsing further into the bad taste of later ages; yet there is one still deserving ad-

---

[1] A shield with a coat of arms that includes a "bearing," *i.e.* a device, indicating a claim to estates, in this case those of his wife.
[2] "Pray for the soul of Friedmund, Knight, Baron of Adlerstein."
[3] "Here lies Eberhard, Knight, Baron of Adlerstein."
[4] At last.

miration, placed close to the head of that of the two barons. It
is the effigy of a lady, aged and serene, with a delicately-carved
face beneath her stiff headgear.   Surely this monument was erected
somewhat later, for the inscription is in German.   Stiff, contracted,
hard to read, but this is the rendering of it :

'𝕳ere lies 𝕮hristina 𝕾orel, wife of 𝕰berhard, xxth 𝕭aron von
𝕬dlerstein, and mother of the 𝕭arons 𝕰berhard and 𝕱riedmund.   𝕾he
fell asleep two days before her son, on the feast of 𝕾t. 𝕵ohn, mdxliii.
    '𝕳er children shall rise up and call her blessed.
'𝕰rected with full hearts by her grandson, 𝕭aron 𝕱riedmund
𝕸aximilianus, and his brothers and sisters.   𝕱arewell.'

The Gate of the Giant Scissors

CHAPTER I.

IN THE PEAR-TREE

JOYCE WAS CRYING, up in old Monsieur Greville's tallest pear-tree. She had gone down to the farthest corner of the garden, out of sight of the house, for she did not want any one to know that she was miserable enough to cry.

She was tired of the garden with the high stone wall around it, that made her feel like a prisoner; she was tired of French verbs and foreign faces; she was tired of France, and so homesick for her mother and Jack and Holland and the baby, that she couldn't help crying. No wonder, for she was only twelve years old, and she had never been out of the little Western village where she was born, until the day she started abroad with her Cousin Kate.

Now she sat perched up on a limb in a dismal bunch, her chin in her hands and her elbows on her knees. It was a grey afternoon in November; the air was frosty, although the laurel-bushes in the garden were all in bloom.

"I s'pect there is snow on the ground at home," thought Joyce, "and there's a big cheerful fire in the sitting-room grate.

"Holland and the baby are shelling corn, and Mary is popping it. Dear me! I can smell it just as plain! Jack will be coming in from the post-office pretty soon, and maybe he'll have one of my letters. Mother will read it out loud, and there they'll all be, thinking that I am having such a fine time; that it is such a grand thing for me to be abroad studying, and having dinner served at night in so many courses, and all that sort of thing. They don't know that I am sitting up here in this pear-tree, lonesome enough to die. Oh, if I could only go back home and see them for even five minutes," she sobbed, "but I can't I can't! There's a whole wide ocean between us!"

She shut her eyes, and leaned back against the tree as that desolate feeling of homesickness settled over her like a great miserable ache. Then she found that shutting her eyes, and thinking very hard about the little brown house at home, seemed to bring it into plain sight. It was like opening a book, and seeing picture after picture as she turned the pages.

There they were in the kitchen, washing dishes, she and Mary;

461

and Mary was standing on a soap-box to make her tall enough to handle the dishes easily. How her funny little braid of yellow hair bobbed up and down as she worked, and how her dear little freckled face beamed, as they told stories to each other to make the work seem easier.

Mary's stories all began the same way: "If I had a witch with a wand, this is what we would do." The witch with a wand had come to Joyce in the shape of Cousin Kate Ware, and that coming was one of the pictures that Joyce could see now, as she thought about it with her eyes closed.

There was Holland swinging on the gate, waiting for her to come home from school, and trying to tell her by excited gestures, long before she was within speaking distance, that some one was in the parlour. The baby had on his best plaid kilt and new tie, and the tired little mother was sitting talking in the parlour, an unusual thing for her. Joyce could see herself going up the path, swinging her sun-bonnet by the strings and taking hurried little bites of a big June apple in order to finish it before going into the house. Now she was sitting on the sofa beside Cousin Kate, feeling very awkward and shy with her little brown fingers clasped in this stranger's soft white hand. She had heard that Cousin Kate was a very rich old maid, who had spent years abroad, studying music and languages, and she had expected to see a stout, homely woman with bushy eyebrows, like Miss Teckla Schaum, who played the church organ, and taught German in the High School.

But Cousin Kate was altogether unlike Miss Teckla. She was tall and slender, she was young-looking and pretty, and there was a stylish air about her, from the waves of her soft golden brown hair to the bottom of her tailor-made gown, that was not often seen in this little Western village.

Joyce saw herself glancing admiringly at Cousin Kate, and then pulling down her dress as far as possible, painfully conscious that her shoes were untied, and white with dust. The next picture was several days later. She and Jack were playing mumble-peg outside under the window by the lilac-bushes, and the little mother was just inside the door, bending over a pile of photographs that Cousin Kate had dropped in her lap. Cousin Kate was saying, "This beautiful old French villa is where I expect to spend the winter, Aunt Emily. These are views of Tours, the town that lies across the river Loire from it, and these are some of the chateaux near by that I intend to visit. They say the purest French in the world

is spoken there. I have prevailed on one of the dearest old ladies
that ever lived to give me rooms with her. She and her husband
live all alone in this big country place, so I shall have to provide
against loneliness by taking my company with me. Will you let
me have Joyce for a year?"

Jack and she stopped playing in sheer astonishment, while Cousin
Kate went on to explain how many advantages she could give the
little girl to whom she had taken such a strong fancy.

Looking through the lilac-bushes, Joyce could see her mother
wipe her eyes and say, "It seems like pure providence, Kate, and I
can't stand in the child's way. She'll have to support herself soon,
and ought to be prepared for it; but she's the oldest of the five, you
know, and she has been like my right hand ever since her father
died. There'll not be a minute while she is gone, that I shall not
miss her and wish her back. She's the life and sunshine of the
whole home."

Then Joyce could see the little brown house turned all topsy-
turvey in the whirl of preparation that followed, and the next thing,
she was standing on the platform at the station, with her new steamer
trunk beside her. Half the town was there to bid her good-by. In
the excitement of finding herself a person of such importance she
forgot how much she was leaving behind her, until looking up, she
saw a tender, wistful smile on her mother's face, sadder than any
tears.

Luckily the locomotive whistled just then, and the novelty of
getting aboard a train for the first time, helped her to be brave at the
parting. She stood on the rear platform of the last car, waving her
handkerchief to the group at the station as long as it was in sight,
so that the last glimpse her mother should have of her, was with her
bright little face all ashine.

All these pictures passed so rapidly through Joyce's mind, that
she had retraced the experiences of the last three months in as
many minutes. Then, somehow, she felt better. The tears had
washed away the ache in her throat. She wiped her eyes and climbed
like a squirrel to the highest limb that could bear her weight.

This was not the first time that the old pear-tree had been shaken
by Joyce's grief, and it knew that her spells of homesickness always
ended in this way. There she sat, swinging her plump legs back
and forth, her long light hair blowing over the shoulders of her
blue jacket, and her saucy little mouth puckered into a soft whistle.
She could see over the high wall now. The sun was going down

behind the tall Lombardy poplars that lined the road, and in a distant field two peasants still at work reminded her of the picture of "The Angelus." They seemed like acquaintances on account of the resemblance, for there was a copy of the picture in her little bedroom at home.

All around her stretched quiet fields, sloping down to the ancient village of St. Symphorien and the river Loire. Just across the river, so near that she could hear the ringing of the cathedral bell, lay the famous old town of Tours. There was something in these country sights and sounds that soothed her with their homely cheerfulness. The crowing of a rooster and the barking of a dog fell on her ear like familiar music.

"It's a comfort to hear something speak English," she sighed, "even if it's nothing but a chicken. I do wish that Cousin Kate wouldn't be so particular about my using French all day long. The one little half-hour at bedtime when she allows me to speak English isn't a drop in the bucket. It's a mercy that I had studied French some before I came, or I would have a lonesome time. I wouldn't be able to ever talk at all."

It was getting cold up in the pear-tree. Joyce shivered and stepped down to the limb below, but paused in her descent to watch a peddler going down the road with a pack on his back.

"Oh, he is stopping at the gate with the big scissors!" she cried, so interested that she spoke aloud. "I must wait to see if it opens."

There was something mysterious about that gate across the road, Like Monsieur Gréville's, it was plain and solid, reaching as high as the wall. Only the lime-trees and the second story windows of the house could be seen above it. On the top it bore an iron medallion, on which was fastened a huge pair of scissors. There was a smaller pair on each gable of the house, also.

During the three months that Joyce had been in Monsieur Greville's home, she had watched every day to see it open; but if any one ever entered or left the place, it was certainly by some other way than this queer gate.

What lay beyond it, no one could tell. She had questioned Gabriel the coachman, and Berthe the maid, in vain. Madame Gréville said that she remembered having heard, when a child, that the man who built it was named *Ciseaux*, and that was why the symbol of this name was hung over the gate and on the gables. He had been regarded as half crazy by his neighbours. The place was still owned by a descendant of his, who had gone to Algiers, and left it in charge of two servants.

The peddler rang the bell of the gate several times, but failing to arouse any one, shouldered his pack and went off grumbling. Then Joyce climbed down and walked slowly up the gravelled path to the house. Cousin Kate had just come back from Tours in the pony cart, and was waiting in the door to see if Gabriel had all the bundles that she had brought out with her.

Joyce followed her admiringly into the house. She wished that she could grow up to look exactly like Cousin Kate, and wondered if she would ever wear such stylish silk-lined skirts, and catch them up in such an airy, graceful way when she ran up-stairs; and if she would ever have a Paris hat with long black feathers, and always wear a bunch of sweet violets on her coat.

She looked at herself in Cousin Kate's mirror as she passed it, and sighed. "Well, I am better-looking than when I left home," she thought. "That's one comfort. My face isn't freckled now, and my hair is more becoming this way than in tight little pigtails, the way I used to wear it."

Cousin Kate, coming up behind her, looked over her head and smiled at the attractive reflection of Joyce's rosy cheeks and straightforward grey eyes. Then she stopped suddenly and put her arms around her, saying, "What's the matter, dear? You have been crying."

"Nothing," answered Joyce, but there was a quaver in her voice, and she turned her head aside. Cousin Kate put her hand under the resolute little chin, and tilted it until she could look into the eyes that dropped under her gaze. "You have been crying," she said again, this time in English, "crying because you are homesick. I wonder if it would not be a good occupation for you to open all the bundles that I got this afternoon. There is a saucepan in one, and a big spoon in the other, and all sorts of good things in the others, so that we can make some molasses candy here in my room, over the open fire. While it cooks you can curl up in the big armchair and listen to a fairy tale in the firelight. Would you like that, little one?"

"Oh, yes!" cried Joyce, ecstatically. "That's what they are doing at home this minute, I am sure. We always make candy every afternoon in the winter time."

Presently the saucepan was sitting on the coals, and Joyce's little pug nose was rapturously sniffing the odour of bubbling molasses.

"I know what I'd like the story to be about," she said, as she stirred the delicious mixture with the new spoon. "Make up something about the big gate across the road, with the scissors on it."

Cousin Kate crossed the room, and sat down by the window, where she could look out and see the top of it.

"Let me think for a few minutes," she said. "I have been very much interested in that old gate myself."

She thought so long that the candy was done before she was ready to tell the story; but while it cooled in plates outside on the window-sill, she drew Joyce to a seat beside her in the chimney-corner. With her feet on the fender, and the child's head on her shoulder, she began this story, and the firelight dancing on the walls, showed a smile on Joyce's contented little face.

CHAPTER II

A NEW FAIRY TALE

ONCE UPON A time, on a far island of the sea, there lived a King with seven sons. The three eldest were tall and dark, with eyes like eagles, and hair like a crows' wing for blackness, and no princes in all the land were so strong and fearless as they. The three youngest sons were tall and fair, with eyes as blue as cornflowers, and locks like the summer sun for brightness, and no princes in all the land were so brave and beautiful as they.

But the middle son was little and lorn; he was neither dark nor fair; he was neither handsome nor strong. So when the King saw that he never won in the tournaments nor led in the boar hunts, nor sang to his lute among the ladies of the court, he drew his royal robes aroused him, and henceforth frowned on Ethelried.

To each of his other sons he gave a portion of his kingdom, armour and plumes, a prancing charger, and a trusty sword; but to Ethelried he gave nothing. When the poor Prince saw his brothers riding out into the world to win their fortunes, he fain would have followed. Throwing himself on his knees before the King, he cried, "Oh royal Sire, bestow upon me also a sword and a steed, that I may up and away to follow my brethren."

But the King laughed him to scorn. "Thou a sword!" he quoth. "Thou who hast never done a deed of valour in all thy life! In sooth thou shalt have one, but it shall be one befitting thy maiden size and courage, if so small a weapon can be found in all my kingdom!"

Now just at that moment it happened that the Court Tailor came into the room to measure the King for a new mantle of ermine. Forthwith the grinning jester began shrieking with mirth, and all the little bells upon his motley cap began shaking too.

"Why do you laugh?" demanded the King.

"Because I think the sword of Ethelried has now been found," responded the Jester, pointing to the Court Tailor and the scissors hanging from his waist.

"So be it," exclaimed the King, and he commanded that the scissors should be taken from the Court Tailor and fastened into the belt of Ethelried. "Wear these until thou hast proved thyself a prince and with their aid come into thy kingdom," he said with an oath, "Until that far day, let me never more set eyes upon thy face!"

So Ethelried left the palace and wandered away over mountain and moor with a heavy heart. No one knew that he was a prince; no fireside offered him welcome; no lips gave him a friendly greeting. The scissors hung useless and rusting by his side.

One night as he lay in a deep forest, too unhappy to sleep, he heard a noise near at hand in the bushes. By the light of the moon he saw that a ferocious wild beast had been caught in a hunter's snare, and was struggling to free itself from the heavy net. His first thought was to slay the animal, for he had had no meat for many days. Then he bethought himself that he had no weapon large enough.

While he stood gazing at the struggling beast, it turned to him with such a beseeching look in its wild eyes, that he was moved to pity.

"Thou shalt have thy liberty," he cried, "even though thou shouldst rend me in pieces the moment thou art free. Better dead than this craven life to which my father hath doomed me!"

So he set to work with the scissors to cut the great ropes of the net in twain. At first each strand seemed as hard as steel, and the blades of the scissors were so rusty and dull that he could scarcely move them. Great beads of sweat stood out on his brow as he bent himself to the task.

Presently, as he worked, the blades began to grow sharper and sharper, and brighter and brighter, and longer and longer. By the time that the last rope was cut the scissors were as sharp as a broadsword, and half as long as his body.

At last he raised the net to let the beast go free. Then he sank on his knees in astonishment. It had suddenly disappeared, and in its place stood a beautiful Fairy with filmy wings, which shone like rainbows in the moonlight.

"Prince Ethelried," she said in a voice that was like a crystal bell's for sweetness, "dost thou not know that thou art in the domain of a frightful Ogre? It was he who changed me into the form of a wild beast, and set the snare to capture me. But for thy fearlessness and faithful perseverence in the task which thou didst in pity undertake, I must have perished at dawn."

At this moment there was a distant rumbling as of thunder. "'Tis the Ogre!" cried the Fairy. "We must hasten." Seizing the scissors that lay on the ground where Ethelried had dropped them, she opened and shut them several times, exclaiming:

> "Scissors, grow a giant's height
> And save us from the Ogre's might!"

Immediately they grew to an enormous size, and, with blades extended, shot through the tangled thicket ahead of them, cutting down everything that stood in their way,—bushes, stumps, trees, vines; nothing could stand before the fierce onslaught of those mighty blades.

The Fairy darted down the path thus opened up, and Ethelried followed as fast as he could, for the horrible roaring was rapidly coming nearer. At last they reached a wide chasm that bounded the Ogre's domain. Once across that, they would be out of his power, but it seemed impossible to cross. Again the Fairy touched the scissors, saying:

> "Giant scissors, bridge the path,
> And save us from the Ogre's wrath."

Again the scissors grew longer and longer, until they lay across the chasm like a shining bridge. Ethelried hurried across after the Fairy, trembling and dizzy, for the Ogre was now almost upon them. As soon as they were safe on the other side, the Fairy blew upon the scissors, and, presto, they became shorter and shorter until they were only the length of an ordinary sword.

"Here," she said, giving them into his hands; "because thou wast persevering and fearless in setting me free, these shall win for thee thy heart's desire. But remember that thou canst not keep them sharp and shining, unless they are used at least once each day in some unselfish service."

Before he could thank her she had vanished, and he was left in the forest alone. He could see the Ogre standing powerless to hurt him, on the other side of the chasm, and gnashing his teeth, each one of which was as big as a millstone.

The sight was so terrible, that he turned on his heel, and fled away as fast as his feet could carry him. By the time he reached the edge of the forest, he was very tired and ready to faint from hunger. His heart's greatest desire being for food, he wondered if the scissors could obtain it for him as the Fairy had promised. He had spent his last coin and knew not where to go for another.

Just then he spied a tree, hanging full of great, yellow apples. By standing on tiptoe he could barely reach the lowest one with his scissors. He cut off an apple, and was about to take a bite, when an old Witch sprang out of a hollow tree across the road.

"So you are the thief who has been stealing my gold apples all this last fortnight!" she exclaimed. "Well, you shall never steal again, that I promise you. Ho, Frog-eye Fearsome, seize on him and drag him into your darkest dungeon!"

At that, a hideous-looking fellow, with eyes like a frog's, green hair, and horrid clammy webbed fingers, clutched him before he could turn to defend himself. He was thrust into the dungeon and left there all day.

At sunset, Frog-eye Fearsome opened the door to slide in a crust and a cup of water, saying in a croaking voice, "You shall be hanged in the morning, hanged by the neck until you are quite dead." Then he stopped to run his webbed fingers through his damp green hair, and grin at the poor captive Prince, as if he enjoyed his suffering. But the next morning no one came to take him to the gallows, and he sat all day in total darkness. At sunset Frog-eye Fearsome opened the door again to thrust in another crust and some water and say, "In the morning you shall be drowned; drowned in the Witch's mill-pond with a great stone tied to your heels."

Again the croaking creature stood and gloated over his victim, then left him to the silence of another long day in the dungeon. The third day he opened the door and hopped in, rubbing his webbed hands together with fiendish pleasure, saying, "You are to have no food and drink to-night, for the Witch has thought of a far more horrible punishment for you. In the morning I shall surely come again, and then—beware!"

Now as he stopped to grin once more at the poor Prince, a Fly darted in, and, blinded by the darkness of the dungeon, flew straight into a spider's web, above the head of Ethelried.

"Poor creature!" thought Ethelried. "Thou shalt not be left a prisoner in this dismal spot while I have the power to help thee." He lifted the scissors and with one stroke destroyed the web, and gave the Fly its freedom.

As soon as the dungeon had ceased to echo with the noise that Frog-eye Fearsome made in banging shut the heavy door, Ethelried heard a low buzzing near his ear. It was the Fly, which had alighted on his shoulder.

"Let an insect in its gratitude teach you this," buzzed the Fly. "Tomorrow, if you remain here, you must certainly meet your doom, for the Witch never keeps a prisoner past the third night. But escape is possible. Your prison door is of iron, but the shutter which bars the window is only of wood. Cut your way out at midnight, and I will have a friend in waiting to guide you to a place of safety. A faint glimmer of light on the opposite wall shows me the keyhole. I shall make my escape thereat and go to repay thy unselfish service to me. But know that the scissors move only when bidden in rhyme. Farewell."

The Prince spent all the following time until midnight, trying to think of a suitable verse to say to the scissors. The art of rhyming had been neglected in his early education, and it was not until the the first cock-crowing began that he succeeded in making this one:

"Giant scissors, serve me well,
And save me from the Witch's spell!"

As he uttered the words the scissors leaped out of his hand, and began to cut through the wooden shutters as easily as through a cheese. In a very short time the Prince had crawled through the opening. There he stood, outside the dungeon, but it was a dark night and he knew not which way to turn.

He could hear Frog-eye Fearsome snoring like a tempest up in the watch-tower, and the old Witch was talking in her sleep in seven languages. While he stood looking around him in bewilderment, a Firefly alighted on his arm. Flashing its little lantern in the Prince's face, it cried, "This way! My friend, the Fly, sent me to guide you to a place of safety. Follow me and trust entirely to my guidance."

The Prince flung his mantle over his shoulder, and followed on with all possible speed. They stopped first in the Witch's orchard, and the Firefly held its lantern up while the Prince filled his pockets with the fruit. The apples were gold with emerald leaves, and the cherries were rubies, and the grapes were great bunches of amethyst. When the Prince had filled his pockets he had enough wealth to provide for all his wants for at least a twelvemonth.

The Firefly led him on until they came to a town where was a fine inn. There he left him, and flew off to report the Prince's safety to the Fly and recieve the promised reward.

Here Ethelried stayed for many weeks, living like a king on the money that the fruit jewels brought him. All this time the scissors were becoming little and rusty, because he never once used them, as the Fairy bade him, in unselfish service for others. But one day he bethought himself of her command, and started out to seek some opportunity to help somebody.

Soon he came to a tiny hut where a sick man lay moaning, while his wife and children wept beside him. "What is to become of me?" cried the poor peasant. "My grain must fall and rot in the field from overripeness because I have not the strength to rise and harvest it; then indeed must we all starve."

Ethelried heard him, and that night, when the moon rose, he stole into the field to cut it down with the giant scissors. They were so rusty from long idleness that he could scarcely move them. He tried to think of some rhyme with which to command them; but it had been so long since he had done any thinking, except for his own selfish pleasure, that his brain refused to work.

However, he toiled on all night, slowly cutting down the grain stalk by stalk. Towards morning the scissors became brighter and sharper, until they finally began to open and shut of their own accord. The whole field was cut by sunrise. Now the peasant's wife had risen very early to go down to the spring and dip up some cool water for her husband to drink. She came upon Ethelried as he was cutting the last row of the grain, and fell on her knees to thank him. From that day the peasant and all his family were firm friends of Ethelried's, and would have gone through fire and water to serve him.

After that he had many adventures, and he was very busy, for he never again forgot what the Fairy had said, that only unselfish service each day could keep the scissors sharp and shining. When the shepherd lost a little lamb one day on the mountain, it was Ethelried who found it caught by the fleece in a tangle of cruel thorns. When he had cut it loose and carried it home, the shepherd also became his firm friend, and would have gone through fire and water to serve him.

The grandame whom he supplied with faggots, the merchant whom he rescued from the robbers, the King's councillor to whom he gave aid, all became his friends. Up and down the land, to beggar or lord, homeless wanderer or high-born dame, he gladly gave unselfish service all unsought, and such as he helped straightway became his friends.

Day by day the scissors grew sharper and sharper and ever more quick to spring forward at his bidding.

One day a herald dashed down the highway, shouting through his silver trumpet that a beautiful Princess had been carried away by the Ogre. She was the only child of the King of this country, and the knights and nobles of all other realms and all the royal potentates were prayed to come to her rescue. To him who could bring her back to her father's castle should be given the throne and kingdom, as well as the Princess herself.

So from far and near, indeed from almost every country under the sun, came knights and princes to fight the Ogre. One by one their brave heads were cut off and stuck on poles along the moat that surrounded the castle.

Still the beautiful Princess languished in her prison. Every night at sunset she was taken up to the roof for a glimpse of the sky, and told to bid good-bye to the sun, for the next morning would surely be her last. Then she would ring her lily-white hands and wave a sad farewell to her home, lying far to the westward. When the knights saw this they would rush down to the chasm and sound a challenge to the Ogre.

They were brave men, and they would not have feared to meet the fiercest wild beasts, but many shrunk back when the Ogre came rushing out. They dared not meet in single combat, this monster with the gnashing teeth, each one of which was as big as a millstone.

Among those who drew back were Ethelried's brothers (the three that were dark and the three that were fair). They would not acknowledge their fear. They said, "We are only waiting to lay some wily plan to capture the Ogre."

After several days Ethelried reached the place on foot. "See him," laughed one of the brothers that was dark to one that was fair. "He comes afoot; no prancing steed, no waving plumes, no trusty sword; little and lorn, he is not fit to be called a brother to princes."

But Ethelried heeded not their taunts. He dashed across the drawbridge, and, opening his scissors, cried:

"Giant scissors, rise in power!
Grant me my heart's desire this hour!"

The crowds on the other side held their breath as the Ogre rushed out, brandishing a club as big as a church steeple. Then Whack! Bang! The blows of the scissors, warding off the blows of the mighty club, could be heard for miles around.

At last Ethelried became so exhausted that he could scarcely raise his hand, and it was plain to be seen that the scissors could not do battle much longer. By this time a great many people, attracted by the terrific noise, had come running up to the moat. The news had spread far and wide that Ethelried was in danger; so every one whom he had ever served dropped whatever he was doing, and ran to the scene of the battle. The peasant was there, and the shepherd, and the lords and beggars and high-born dames, all those whom Ethelried had ever befriended.

As they saw that the poor Prince was about to be vanquished, they all began a great lamentation, and cried out bitterly.

"He saved my harvest," cried one. "He found my lamb," cried another. "He showed me a greater kindness still," shouted a third. And so they went on, each telling of some unselfish service that the Prince had rendered him. Their voices all joined at last into such a roar of gratitude that the scissors were given fresh strength on account of it. They grew longer and longer, and stronger and stronger, until with one great swoop they sprang forward and cut the ugly old Ogre's head from his shoulders.

Every cap was thrown up, and such cheering rent the air as has never been heard since. They did not know his name, they did not know that he was Prince Ethelried, but they knew by his valour that their was royal blood in his veins. So they all cried out long and loud: "*Long live the Prince! Prince Ciseaux!*"

Then the King stepped down from his throne and took off his crown to give to the conqueror, but Ethelried put it aside.

"Nay," he said. "The only kingdom that I crave is the kingdom of a loving heart and a happy fireside. Keep all but the Princess."

So the Ogre was killed, and the Prince came into his kingdom that was his heart's desire. He married the Princess, and there was feasting and merrymaking for seventy days and seventy nights, and they all lived happily ever after.

When the feasting was over, and the guests had all gone to their homes, the Prince pulled down the house of the Ogre and built a new one. On every gable he fastened a pair of shining scissors to remind himself that only through unselfish service to others comes the happiness that is highest and best.

Over the great entrance gate he hung the ones that had served him so valiantly, saying, "Only those who belong to the kingdom of loving hearts and happy homes can ever enter here."

One day the old King, with the brothers of Ethelried (the three that were dark and the three that were fair), came riding up to the portal. They thought to share in Ethelried's fame and splendour. But the scissors leaped from their place and snapped so angrily in their faces that they turned their horses and fled.

Then the scissors sprang back to their place again to guard the portal of Ethelried, and, to this day, only those who belong to the kingdom of loving hearts may enter the Gate of the Giant Scissors.

CHAPTER III

BEHIND THE GREAT GATE

THAT WAS THE tale of the giant scissors as it was told to Joyce in the pleasant fire-lighted room; but behind the great gates the true story went on in a far different way.

Back of the Ciseaux house was a dreary field, growing drearier and browner every moment as the twilight deepened; and across its rough furrows a tired boy was stumbling wearily homeward. He was not more than nine years old, but the careworn expression of his thin white face might have belonged to a little old man of ninety. He was driving two unruly goats towards the house. The chase they led him would have been a laughable sight, had he not looked so small and forlorn plodding along in his clumsy wooden shoes, and a peasant's blouse of blue cotton, several sizes too large for his thin little body.

The anxious look in his eyes changed to one of fear as he drew nearer the house. At the sound of a gruff voice bellowing at him from the end of the lane, he winced as if he had been struck.

"Ha, there, Jules! Thou lazy vagabond! Late again! Canst thou never learn that I am not to be kept waiting?"

"But, Brossard," quavered the boy in his shrill, anxious voice, "it was not my fault, indeed it was not. The goats were so stubborn to-night. They broke through the hedge, and I had to chase them over three fields."

"Have done with thy lying excuses," was the rough answer. "Thou shalt have no supper to-night. Maybe an empty stomach will teach thee when my commands fail. Hasten and drive the goats into the pen."

There was a scowl on Brossard's burly red face that made Jules's heart bump up in his throat. Brossard was only the caretaker of the Ciseaux place, but he had been there for twenty years,—so long that he felt himself the master. The real master was in Algiers nearly all the time. During his absence the great house was closed, excepting the kitchen and two rooms above it. Of these Brossard had one and Henri the other. Henri was the cook ; a slow, stupid old man, not to be jogged out of either his good-nature or his slow gait by anything that Brossard might say.

Henri cooked and washed and mended, and hoed in the garden. Brossard worked in the fields and shaved down the expenses of their living closer and closer. All that was thus saved fell to his share, or he might not have watched the expenses so carefully.

Much saving had made him miserly. Old Therese, the woman with the fish-cart, used to say that he was the stingiest man in all Tourraine. She ought to know, for she had sold him a fish every Friday during all those twenty years, and he had never once failed to quarrel about the price. Five years had gone by since the master's last visit. Brossard and Henri were not likely to forget that time, for they had been awakened in the dead of night by a loud knocking at the side gate. When they opened it the sight that greeted them made them rub their sleepy eyes to be sure that they saw aright.

There stood the master, old Martin Ciseaux. His hair and fiercely bristling moustache had turned entirely white since they had last seen him. In his arms he carried a child.

Brossard almost dropped his candle in his first surprise, and his wonder grew until he could hardly contain it, when the curly head raised itself from monsieur's shoulder, and the sleepy baby voice lisped something in a foreign tongue.

"By all the saints!" muttered Brossard, as he stood aside for his master to pass.

"It's my brother Jules's grandson," was the curt explanation that monsieur offered. "Jules is dead, and so is his son and all the family,—died in America. This is his son's son, Jules, the last of the name. If I choose to take him from a foreign poorhouse and give him shelter, it's nobody's business, Louis Brossard, but my own."

With that he strode on up the stairs to his room, the boy still in his arms. This sudden coming of a four-year-old child into their daily life made as little difference to Brossard and Henri as the presence of the four-months-old puppy. They spread a cot for him in Henri's room when the master went back to Algiers. They gave him something to eat three times a day when they stopped for their own meals, and then went on with their work as usual.

It made no difference to them that he sobbed in the dark for his mother to come and sing him to sleep,—the happy young mother who had petted and humoured him in her own fond American fashion. They could not understand his speech; more than that, they could not understand him. Why should he mope alone in the garden with that beseeching look of a lost dog in his big, mournful eyes? Why should he not play and be happy, like the neighbour's children or the kittens or any other young thing that had life and sunshine?

Brossard snapped his fingers at him sometimes at first, as he would have done to a playful animal; but when Jules drew back, frightened by his foreign speech and rough voice, he began to dislike the timid child. After awhile he never noticed him except to push him aside or to find fault.

It was from Henri that Jules picked up whatever French he learned, and it was from Henri also that he had received the one awkward caress, and the only one, that his desolate little heart had known in all the five loveless years that he had been with them.

A few months ago Brossard had put him out in the field to keep the goats from straying away from their pasture, two stubborn creatures, whose self-willed wanderings had brought many a scolding down on poor Jules's head. To-night he was unusually unfortunate, for added to the weary chase they had led him was this stern command that he should go to bed without his supper.

He was about to pass into the house, shivering and hungry, when Henri put his head out at the window. "Brossard," he called, "there isn't enough bread for supper ; there's just this dry end of a loaf. You should have bought as I told you, when the baker's cart stopped here this morning."

Brossard slowly measured the bit of hard, black bread with his eye, and, seeing that there was not half enough to satisfy the appetites of two hungry men, he grudgingly drew a franc from his pocket.

"Here, Jules," he called. "Go down to the bakery, and see to it that thou art back by the time that I have milked the goats, or thou shalt go to bed with a beating, as well as supperless. Stay!" he added, as Jules turned to go. "I have a mind to eat white bread tonight instead of black. It will cost an extra sou, so be careful to count the change. It is only once or so in a twelvemonth," he muttered to himself as an excuse for his extravagance.

It was half a mile to the village, bur down hill all the way, so that Jules reached the bakery in a very short time.

Several customers were ahead of him, however, and he awaited his turn nervously. When he left the shop an old lamplighter was going down the street with torch and ladder, leaving a double line of twinkling lights in his wake, as he disappeared down the wide "Paris road." Jules watched him a moment, and then ran rapidly on. For many centuries the old village of St. Symphorien had echoed with the clatter of wooden shoes on its ancient cobblestones ; but never had foot-falls in its narrow, crooked streets kept time to the beating of a lonelier little heart.

The officer of Customs, at his window beside the gate that shuts in the old town at night, nodded in a surly way as the boy hurried past. Once outside the gate, Jules walked more slowly, for the road began to wind up-hill. Now he was out again in the open country, where a faint light lying over the frosty fields showed that the moon was rising.

Here and there lamps shone from the windows of houses along the road ; across the field came the bark of a dog, welcoming his master ; two old peasant women passed him in a creaking cart on their glad way home.

At the top of the hill Jules stopped to take breath, leaning for a moment against the stone wall. He was faint from hunger, for he had been in the fields since early morning, with nothing for his midday lunch but a handful of boiled chestnuts. The smell of the fresh bread tantalized him beyond endurance. Oh, to be able to take a mouthful,—just one little mouthful of that brown, sweet crust! He put his face down close, and shut his eyes, drawing in the delicious odour with long, deep breaths. What bliss it would be to have that whole loaf for his own,—he, little Jules, who was to have no supper that night! He held it up in the moonlight, hungrily looking at it on every side. There was not a broken place to be found anywhere on its surface ; not one crack in all that hard, brown glaze of crust, from which he might pinch the tiniest crumb.

For a moment a mad impulse seized him to tear it in pieces, and eat every scrap, regardless of the reckoning with Brossard afterwards. But it was only for a moment. The memory of his last beating stayed his hand. Then, fearing to dally with temptation, lest it should master him, he thrust the bread under his arm, and ran every remaining step of the way home.

Brossard took the loaf from him, and pointed with it to the stairway,—a mute command for Jules to go to bed at once. Tingling with a sense of injustice, the little fellow wanted to shriek out in all his hunger and misery, defying this monster of a man ; but a struggling sparrow might as well have tried to turn on the hawk that held it. He clenched his hands to keep from snatching something from the table, set out so temptingly in the kitchen, but he dared not linger even to look at it. With a feeling of utter helplessness he passed it in silence, his face white and set.

Dragging his tired feet slowly up the stairs, he went over to the casement window, and swung it open ; then, kneeling down, he laid his head on the sill, in the moonlight. Was it his dream that came back to him then, or only a memory ; He could never be sure, for if it were a memory, it was certainly as strange as any dream, unlike anything he had ever known in his life with Henri and Brossard. Night after night he had comforted himself with the picture that it brought before him.

He could see a little white house in the middle of a big lawn. There were vines on the porches, and it must have been early in the evening, for the fireflies were beginning to twinkle over the lawn. And the grass had just been cut, for the air was sweet with the smell of it. A woman, standing on the steps under the vines, was calling "Jules, Jules, it is time to come in, little son!"

But Jules, in his white dress and shoulder-knots of blue ribbon, was toddling across the lawn after a firefly.

Then she began to call him another way. Jules had a vague idea that it was a part of some game that they sometimes played together. It sounded like a song, and the words were not like any that he had ever heard since he came to live with Henri and Brossard. He could not forget them, though, for had they not sung themselves through that beautiful dream every time he had it ?

> "Little Boy Blue, oh, where are you ?
> O, where are you-u-u-u ?"

He only laughed in the dream picture and ran on after the firefly. Then a man came running after him, and, catching him, tossed him up laughingly, and carried him to the house on his shoulder.

Somebody held a glass of cool, creamy milk for him to drink, and by and by he was in a little white night-gown in the woman's lap. His head was nestled against her shoulder, and he could feel her soft lips touching him on cheeks and eyelids and mouth, before she began to sing :

> "Oh, little Boy Blue, lay by your horn,
> And mother will sing of the cows and the corn,
> Till the stars and the angels come to keep
> Their watch, where my baby lies fast asleep."

Now all of a sudden Jules knew that there was another kind of hunger worse than the longing for bread. He wanted the soft touch of those lips again on his mouth and eyelids, the loving pressure of those restful arms, a thousand times more than he had wished for the loaf that he had just brought home. Two hot tears, that made his eyes ache in their slow gathering, splashed down on the window-sill.

Down below Henri opened the kitchen door and snapped his fingers to call the dog. Looking out, Jules saw him set a plate of bones on the step. For a moment he listened to the animal's contented crunching, and then crept across the room to his cot, with a little moan. "O-o-oh—o-oh!" he sobbed. "Even the dog has more than I have, and I'm *so* hungry!" He hid his head awhile in the old quilt ; then he raised it again, and, with the tears streaming down his thin little face, sobbed in a heart-broken whisper : "Mother! Mother! Do you know how hungry I am ?"

A clatter of knives and forks from the kitchen below was the only answer, and he dropped despairingly down again.

"She's so far away she can't even hear me!" he moaned. "Oh, if I could only be dead, too!"

He lay there, crying, till Henri had finished washing the supper dishes and had put them clumsily away. The rank odour of tobacco, stealing up the stairs, told him that Brossard had settled down to enjoy his evening pipe. Through the casement window that was still ajar came the faint notes of an accordeon from Monsieur Gréville's garden, across the way. Gabriel, the coachman, was walking up and down in the moonlight, playing a wheezy accompaniment to the only song he knew. Jules did not notice it at first, but after awhile, when he had cried himself quiet, the faint melody began to steal soothingly into his consciousness. His eyelids closed drowsily, and then the accordeon seemed to be singing something to him. He could not understand at first, but just as he was dropping off to sleep he heard it quite clearly :

"Till the stars and angels come to keep
  Their watch, where my baby lies fast asleep."

Late in the night Jules awoke with a start, and sat up, wondering what had aroused him. He knew that it must be after midnight, for the moon was nearly down. Henri was snoring. Suddenly such a strong feeling of hunger came over him, that he could think of nothing else. It was like a gnawing pain. As if he were being led by some power outside of his own will, he slipped to the door of the room. The little bare feet made no noise on the carpetless floor. No mouse could have stolen down the stairs more silently than timid little Jules. The latch of the kitchen door gave a loud click that made him draw back with a shiver of alarm ; but that was all. After waiting one breathless minute, his heart beating like a trip-hammer, he went on into the pantry.

The moon was so far down now, that only a white glimmer of light showed him the faint outline of things ; but his keen little nose guided him. There was half a cheese on the swinging shelf, with all the bread that had been left from supper. He broke off great pieces of each in eager haste. Then he found a crock of goat's milk Lifting it to his mouth, he drank with big, quick gulps until he had to stop for breath. Just as he was about to raise it to his lips again, some instinct of danger made him look up. There in the doorway stood Brossard, bigger and darker and more threatening than he had ever seemed before.

A frightened little gasp was all that the child had strength to give. He turned so sick and faint that his nerveless fingers could no longer hold the crock. It fell to the floor with a crash, and the milk spattered all over the pantry. Jules was too terrified to utter a sound. It was Brossard who made the out-cry. Jules could only shut his eyes and crouch down trembling, under the shelf. The next instant he was dragged out ,and Brossard's merciless strap fell again and again on the poor shrinking little body, that writhed under the cruel blows.

Once more Jules dragged himself up-stairs to his cot, this time bruised and sore, too exhausted for tears, too hopeless to think of possible to-morrows.

Poor little prince in the clutches of the ogre! If only fairy tales might be true! If only some gracious spirit of elfin lore might really come at such a time with its magic wand of healing! Then there would be no more little desolate hearts, no more grieved little faces with undried tears upon them in all the earth. Over every threshold where a child's wee feet had pattered in and found a home, it would hang its guardian Scissors of Avenging, so that only those who belong to the kingdom of loving hearts and gentle hands would ever dare to enter.

CHAPTER IV.

A LETTER AND A MEETING

NEARLY A WEEK later Joyce sat at her desk, hurrying to finish a letter before the postman's arrival.

"Dear Jack," it began.

"You and Mary will each get a letter this week. Hers is the fairy tale that Cousin Kate told me, about an old gate near here. I wrote it down as well as I could remember. I wish you could see that gate. It gets more interesting every day, and I'd give most anything to see what lies on the other side. Maybe I shall soon, for Marie has a way of finding out anything she wants to know. Marie is my new maid. Cousin Kate went to Paris last week, to be gone until nearly Christmas, so she got Marie to take care of me.

"It seems so odd to have somebody button my boots and brush my hair, and take me out to walk as if I were a big doll. I have to be very dignified and act as if I had always been used to such things. I believe Marie would be shocked to death if she knew that I had ever washed dishes, or pulled weeds out of the pavement, or romped with you in the barn.

"Yesterday when we were out walking I got so tired of acting as if I were a hundred years old, that I felt as if I should scream.

P

'Marie,' I said, 'I've a mind to throw my muff in the fence-corner and run and hang on that wagon that's going down-hill.' She had no idea that I was in earnest. She just smiled very politely and said, 'Oh, mademoiselle, impossible! How you Americans do love to jest.' But it was no joke. You can't imagine how stupid it is to be with nobody but grown people all the time. I'm fairly aching for a good old game of hi spy or prisoner's base with you. There is nothing at all to do, but to take poky walks.

"Yesterday afternoon we walked down to the river. There's a double row of trees along it on this side, and several benches where people can wait for the tramcars that pass down this street and then across the bridge into Tours. Marie found an old friend of hers sitting on one of the benches,—such a big fat woman, and oh, such a gossip! Marie said she was tired, so we sat there a long time. Her friend's name is Clotilde Robard. They talked about everybody in St. Symphorien.

"Then I gossiped, too. I asked Clotilde Robard if she knew why the gate with the big scissors was never opened any more. She told me that she used to be one of the maids there, before she married the spice-monger and was Madame Robard. Years before she went to live there, when the old Monsieur Ciseaux died, there was a dreadful quarrel about some money. The son that got the property told his brother and sister never to darken his doors again.

"They went off to America, and that big front gate has never opened since they passed out of it. Clotilde says that some people say that they put a curse on it, and something awful will happen to the first one who dares to go through. Isn't that interesting?

"The oldest son, Mr, Martin Ciseaux, kept up the place for a long time, just as his father had done, but he never married. All of a sudden he shut up the house, sent away all the servants but the two who take care of it, and went off to Algiers to live. Five years ago he came back to bring his little grand-nephew, but nobody has seen him since that time.

"Clotilde says that an orphan asylum would have been a far better home for Jules (that is the boy's name), for Brossard, the caretaker, is so mean to him. Doesn't that make you think of Prince Ethelried in the fairy tale? 'Little and lorn; no fireside welcomed him and no lips gave him a friendly greeting.'

"Marie says that she has often seen Jules down in the field, back of his Uncle's house, tending the goats. I hope that I may see him sometime.

"Oh, dear, the postman has come sooner than I expected. He is talking down in the hall now, and if I do not post this letter now it will miss the evening train and be too late for the next mail steamer. Tell mamma that I will answer all her questions about my lessons and clothes next week. Oceans of love to everybody in the dear little brown house."

Hastily scrawling her name, Joyce ran out into the hall with her letter. "Anything for me?" she asked, anxiously, leaning over the banister to drop the letter into Marie's hand. "One, mademoiselle," was the answer. "But it has not a foreign stamp."

"Oh, from Cousin Kate!" exclaimed Joyce, tearing it open as she went back to her room. At the door she stooped to pick up a piece of paper that had dropped from the envelope. It crackled stiffly as she unfolded it.

"Money!" she exclaimed in surprise. "A whole twenty franc note. What could Cousin Kate have sent it for?" The last page of the letter explained.

"I have just remembered that December is not very far off, and that whatever little Christmas gifts we send home should soon be started on their way. Enclosed you will find twenty francs for your Christmas shopping. It is not much, but we are too far away to send anything but the simplest little remembrances, things that will not be spoiled in the mail, and on which little or no duty need be paid. You might buy one article each day, so that there will be some purpose in your walks into Tours.

"I am sorry that I can not be with you on Thanksgiving Day. We will have to drop it from our calendar this year; not the thanksgiving itself, but the turkey and mince pie part. Suppose you take a few francs to give yourself some little treat to mark the day. I hope my dear little girl will not be homesick all by herself. I never should have left just at this time if it had not been very necessary."

Joyce smoothed out the bank-note and looked at it with sparkling eyes. Twenty whole francs! The same as four dollars! All the money that she had ever had in her whole life put together would not have amounted to that much. Dimes were scarce in the little brown house, and even pennies seldom found their way into the children's hands when five pairs of little feet were always needing shoes, and five healthy appetites must be satisfied daily.

All the time that Joyce was pinning her treasure securely in her pocket and putting on her hat and jacket, all the time that she was walking demurely down the road with Marie, she was planning different ways in which to spend her fortune.

"Mademoiselle is very quiet," ventured Marie, remembering that one of her duties was to keep up an improving conversation with her little mistress.

"Yes," answered Joyce, half impatiently; "I've got something so lovely to think about, that I'd like to go back and sit down in the garden and just think and think until dark, without being interrupted by anybody."

This was Marie's opportunity. "Then mademoiselle might not object to stopping in the garden of the villa which we are now approaching," she said. "My friend, Clotilde Robard, is house-keeper there, and I have a very important message to deliver to her."

Joyce had no objection. "But, Marie," she said, as she paused at the gate, "I think I'll not go in. It is so lovely and warm out here in the sun that I'll just sit here on the steps and wait for you."

Five minutes went by and then ten. By that time Joyce had decided how to spend every centime in the whole twenty francs, and Marie had not returned. Another five minutes went by. It was dull, sitting there facing the lonely highway, down which no one ever seemed to pass. Joyce stood up, looked all around, and then slowly sauntered down the road a short distance.

Here and there in the crevices of the wall blossomed a few hardy wild flowers, which Joyce began to gather as she walked. "I'll go around this bend in the road and see what's there," she said to herself. "By that time Marie will surely be done with her messages."

No one was in sight in any direction, and feeling that no one could be in hearing distance, either, in such a deserted place, she began to sing. It was an old Mother Goose rhyme that she hummed over and over, in a low voice at first, but louder as she walked on.

Around the bend in the road there was nothing to be seen but a lonely field where two goats were grazing. On one side of it was a stone wall, on two others a tall hedge, but the side next her sloped down to the road, unfenced.

Joyce, with her hands filled with the yellow wild flowers, stood looking around her, singing the old rhyme, the song that she had taught the baby to sing before he could talk plainly :

"Little Boy Blue, come blow your horn,
The sheep's in the meadow, the cow's in the corn.
Little Boy Blue, oh, where are you?
Oh, where are you-u-u-u?"

The gay little voice that had been rising higher and higher, sweet as any bird's, stopped suddenly in mid-air; for, as if in answer to her call, there was a rustling just ahead of her, and a boy who had been lying on his back, looking at the sky, slowly raised himself out of the grass.

For an instant Joyce was startled; then seeing by his wooden shoes and old blue cotton blouse that he was only a little peasant watching the goats, she smiled at him with a pleasant good morning.

He did not answer, but came towards her with a dazed expression on his face, as if he were groping his way through some strange dream. "It is time to go in!" he exclaimed, as if repeating some lesson learned long ago, and half forgotten.

Joyce stared at him in open-mouthed astonishment. The little fellow had spoken in English. "Oh, you must be Jules," she cried. "Aren't you? I've been wanting to find you for ever so long."

The boy seemed frightened, and did not answer, only looked at her with big, troubled eyes. Thinking that she had made a mistake, that she had not heard aright, Joyce spoke in French. He answered her timidly. She had not been mistaken; he was Jules; he had been asleep, he told her, and when he heard her singing, he thought it was his mother calling him as she used to do, and had started up expecting to see her at last. Where was she? Did mademoiselle know her? Surely she must if she knew the song.

It was on the tip of Joyce's tongue to tell him that everybody knew that song; that it was as familiar to the children at home as the chirping of crickets on the hearth or the sight of dandelions in the spring-time. But some instinct warned her not to say it. She was glad afterwards, when she found that it was sacred to him, woven in as it was with his one beautiful memory of a home. It was all he had, and the few words that Joyce's singing had startled from him were all that he remembered of his mother's speech.

If Joyce had happened upon him in any other way, it is doubtful if their acquaintance would have grown very rapidly. He was afraid of strangers; but coming as she did with the familiar song that was like an old friend, he felt that he must have known her some-time,—that other time when there was always a sweet voice calling, and fireflies twinkled across a dusky lawn.

Joyce was not in a hurry for Marie to come now. She had a hundred questions to ask, and made the most of her time by talking very fast. "Marie will be frightened," she told Jules, "if she does not find me at the gate, and will think that the gypsies have stolen me. Then she will begin to hunt up and down the road, and I don't know what she would say if she came and found me talking to a strange child out in the fields, so I must hurry back. I am glad that I found you. I have been wishing so long for somebody to play with, and you seem like an old friend because you were born in America. I'm going to ask madame to ask Brossard to let you come over sometime."

Jules watched her as she hurried away, running lightly down the road, her fair hair flying over her shoulders and her short blue skirt fluttering. Once she looked back to wave her hand. Long after she was out of sight he still stood looking after her, as one might gaze longingly after some visitant from another world. Nothing like her had ever dropped into his life before, and he wondered if he should ever see her again.

CHAPTER V

A THANKSGIVING BARBECUE

This doesn't seem a bit like Thanksgiving Day, Marie," said Joyce, plaintively, as she sat up in bed to take the early breakfast that her maid brought in,—a cup of chocolate and a roll.

"In our country the very minute you wake up you can *feel* that it is a holiday. Outdoors it's nearly always cold and grey, with everything covered with snow. Inside you can smell turkey and pies and all sorts of good spicy things. Here it is so warm that the windows are open and flowers blooming in the garden, and there isn't a thing to make it seem different from any other old day."

Here her grumbling was interrupted by a knock at the door, and Madame Gréville's maid, Berthé, came in with a message.

"Madame and monsieur intend spending the day in Tours, and since Mademoiselle Ware has written that Mademoiselle Joyce is to have no lessons on this American holiday, they will be pleased to have her accompany them in the carriage. She can spend the morning with them there or return immediately with Gabriel."

"Of course I want to go," cried Joyce. "I love to drive. But I'd rather come back here to lunch and have it by myself in the garden. Berthé, ask madame if I can't have it served in the little kiosk at the end of the arbor."

As soon as she had received a most gracious permission, Joyce began to make a little plan. It troubled her conscience somewhat, for she felt that she ought to mention it to madame, but she was almost certain that madame would object, and she had set her heart on carrying it out.

"I won't speak about it now," she said to herself, "because I am not *sure* that I am going to do it. Mamma would think it was all right, but foreigners are so queer about some things."

Uncertain as Joyce may have been about her future actions, as they drove towards town, no sooner had madame and monsieur stepped from the carriage, on the Rue Nationale, than she was perfectly sure.

"Stop at the baker's, Gabriel," she ordered as they turned homeward, then at the big grocery on the corner. "Cousin Kate told me to treat myself to something nice," she said apologetically to her conscience, as she gave up the twenty francs to the clerk to be changed.

If Gabriel wondered what was in the little parcels which she brought back to the carriage, he made no sign. He only touched his hat respectfully, as she gave the next order: "Stop where the road turns by the cemetery, Gabriel; at the house with the steps going up to an iron-barred gate. I'll be back in two or three minutes," she said, when she had reached it, and climbed from the carriage.

To his surprise, instead of entering the gate, she hurried on past it, around the bend in the road. In a little while she came running back, her shoes covered with damp earth, as if she had been walking in a freshly ploughed field.

If Gabriel's eyes could have followed her around that bend in the road, he would have seen a sight past his understanding: Mademoiselle Joyce running at the top of her speed to meet a little goatherd in wooden shoes and blue cotton blouse,—a common little peasant goatherd.

"It's Thanksgiving Day, Jules," she announced, gasping, as she sank down on the ground beside him. "We're the only Americans here, and everybody has gone off; and Cousin Kate said to celebrate in some way. I'm going to have a dinner in the garden I've bought a rabbit, and we'll dig a hole, and make a fire, and barbecue it the way Jack and I used to do at home. And we'll roast eggs in the ashes, and have a fine time. I've got a lemon tart and a little iced fruit-cake, too."

All this was poured out in such breathless haste, and in such a confusion of tongues, first a sentence of English and then a word of

French, that it is no wonder that Jules grew bewildered in trying to follow her. She had to begin again at the beginning, and speak very slowly, in order to make him understand that it was a feast day of some kind, and that he, Jules, was invited to some sort of a strange, wonderful entertainment in Monsieur Gréville's garden. "But Brossard is away from home," said Jules, "and there is no one to watch the goats, and keep them from straying down the road. Still it would be just the same if he were home," he added, sadly. "He would not let me go, I am sure. I have never been out of sight of that roof since I first came here, except on errands to the village, when I had to run all the way back." He pointed to the peaked gables, adorned by the scissors of his crazy old ancestor.

"Brossard isn't your father," cried Joyce, indignantly, "nor your uncle, nor your cousin, nor anything else that has a right to shut you up that way. Isn't there a field with a fence all around it, that you could drive the goats into for a few hours?"

Jules shook his head.

"Well, I can't have my Thanksgiving spoiled for just a couple of old goats," exclaimed Joyce. "You'll have to bring them along, and we'll shut them up in the carriage-house. You come over in about an hour, and I'll be at the side gate waiting for you."

Joyce had always been a general in her small way. She made her plans and issued her orders both at home and at school, and the children accepted her leadership as a matter of course. Even if Jules had not been willing and anxious to go, it is doubtful if he could have mustered courage to oppose the arrangements that she made in such a masterful way; but Jules had not the slightest wish to object to anything whatsoever that Joyce might propose.

It is safe to say that the old garden had never before even dreamed of such a celebration as the one that took place that afternoon behind its moss-coated walls. The time-stained statue of Eve, which stood on one side of the fountain, looked across at the weather-beaten figure of Adam, on the other side, in stony-eyed surprise. The little marble satyr in the middle of the fountain, which had been grinning ever since its endless shower-bath began, seemed to grin wider than ever, as it watched the children's strange sport.

Jules dug the little trench according to Joyce's directions, and laid the iron grating which she had borrowed from the cook across it, and built the fire underneath. "We ought to have something especially patriotic and Thanksgivingey," said Joyce, standing on one foot to consider. "Oh, now I know," she cried, after a moment's thought. "Cousin Kate has a lovely big silk flag in the top of her trunk. I'll run and get that, and then I'll recite the 'Landing of the Pilgrims' to you while the rabbit cooks."

Presently a savoury odour began to steal along the winding paths of the garden, between the laurel-bushes,—a smell of barbecued meat sputtering over the fire. Above the door of the little kiosk, with many a soft swish of silken stirrings, hung the beautiful old flag. Then a clear little voice floated up through the pine-trees:

> "My country, 'tis of thee,
> Sweet land of liberty,
> Of thee I sing!"

All the time that Joyce sang, she was moving around the table, setting out the plates and rattling cups and saucers. She could not keep a little quaver out of her voice, for, as she went on, all the scenes of all the times that she had sung that song before came crowding up in her memory. There were the Thanksgiving days in the church at home, and the Washington's birthdays at school, and two Decoration days, when, as a granddaughter of a veteran, she had helped scatter flowers over the soldiers' graves.

Somehow it made her feel so hopelessly far away from all that made life dear to be singing of that "sweet land of liberty" in a foreign country, with only poor little alien Jules for company.

Maybe that is why the boy's first lesson in patriotism was given so earnestly by his homesick little teacher. Something that could not be put into words stirred within him, as, looking up at the soft silken flutterings of the old flag, he listened for the first time to the story of the Pilgrim Fathers.

The rabbit cooked slowly, so slowly that there was time for Jules to learn how to play mumble-peg while they waited. At last it was done, and Joyce proudly plumped it into the platter that had been waiting for it. Marie had already brought out a bountiful lunch, cold meats and salad and a dainty pudding. By the time that Joyce had added her contribution to the feast, there was scarcely an inch of the table left uncovered. Jules did not know the names of half the dishes.

Not many miles away from that old garden, scattered up and down the Loire throughout all the region of fair Tourraine, rise the turrets of many an old château. Great banquet halls, where kings and queens once feasted, still stand as silent witnesses of a gay bygone court life ; but never in any château or palace among them all was feast more thoroughly enjoyed than this impromptu dinner in the garden, where a little goatherd was the only guest.

It was an enchanted spot to Jules, made so by the magic of Joyce's wonderful gift of story-telling. For the first time in his life that he could remember, he heard of Santa Claus and Christmas trees, of Bluebeard and Aladdin's lamp, and all the dear old fairy tales that were so entrancing he almost forgot to eat.

Then they played that he was the prince, Prince Ethelried, and that the goats in the carriage-house were his royal steeds, and that Joyce was a queen whom he had come to visit.

But it came to an end, as all beautiful things must do. The bells in the village rang four, and Prince Ethelried started up as Cinderella must have done when the pumpkin coach disappeared. He was no longer a king's son; he was only Jules, the little goatherd, who must hurry back to the field before the coming of Brossard.

Joyce went with him to the carriage-house. Together they swung open the great door. Then an exclamation of dismay fell from Joyce's lips. All over the floor were scattered scraps of leather and cloth and hair, the kind used in upholstering. The goats had whiled away the hours of their imprisonment by chewing up the cushions of the pony cart.

Jules turned pale with fright. Knowing so little of the world, he judged all grown people by his knowledge of Henri and Brossard. "Oh, what will they do to us?" he gasped.

"Nothing at all," answered Joyce, bravely, although her heart beat twice as fast as usual as monsieur's accusing face rose up before her.

"It was all my fault," said Jules, ready to cry. "What must I do?" Joyce saw his distress, and with quick womanly tact recognized her duty as hostess. It would never do to let this, his first Thanksgiving Day be clouded by a single unhappy remembrance. She would pretend that it was a part of their last game; so she waved her hand, and said, in a theatrical voice, "You forget, Prince Ethelried, that in the castle of Irmingarde she rules supreme. If it is the pleasure of your royal steeds to feed upon cushions they shall not be denied, even though they choose my own coach pillows, of gold-cloth and velour."

"But what if Gabriel should tell Brossard?" questioned Jules, his teeth almost chattering at the mere thought.

"Oh, never mind, Jules," she answered, laughingly. "Don't worry about a little thing like that. I'll make it all right with madame as soon as she gets home."

Jules, with utmost faith in Joyce's power to do anything that she might undertake, drew a long breath of relief. Half a dozen times between the gate and the lane that led into the Ciseaux field, he turned around to wave his old cap in answer to the hopeful flutter of her little white handkerchief ; but when he was out of sight she went back to the carriage-house and looked at the wreck of the cushions with a sinking heart. After that second look, she was not so sure of making it all right with madame.

Going slowly up to her room, she curled up in the window-seat to wait for the sound of the carriage wheels. The blue parrots on the wallpaper sat in their blue hoops in straight rows from floor to ceiling, and hung all their dismal heads. It seemed to Joyce as if there were thousands of them, and that each one was more unhappy than any of the others. The blue roses on the bed-curtains, that had been in such gay blosson a few hours before, looked ugly and unnatural now.

Over the mantel hung a picture that had been a pleasure to Joyce ever since she had taken up her abode in this quaint blue room. It was called "A Message from Noel," and showed an angel flying down with gifts to fill a pair of little wooden shoes that some child had put out on a window-sill below. When madame had explained that the little French children put out their shoes for Saint Noël to fill, instead of hanging stockings for Santa Claus, Joyce had been so charmed with the picture that she declared that she intended to follow the French custom herself, this year.

Now, even the picture looked different, since she had lost her joyful anticipations of Christmas. "It is all No-el to me now," she sobbed. "No tree, no Santa Claus, and now, since the money must go to pay for the goats' mischief, no presents for anybody in the dear little brown house at home,—not even mamma and the baby!"

A big salty tear trickled down the side of Joyce's nose and splashed on her hand; then another one. It was such a gloomy ending for her happy Thanksgiving Day. One consoling thought came to her in time to stop the deluge that threatened. "Any way, Jules has had a good time for once in his life." The thought cheered her so much that, when Marie came in to light the lamps, Joyce was walking up and down the room with her hands behind her back, singing.

As soon as she was dressed for dinner she went down-stairs, but found no one in the drawing-room. A small fire burned cozily on the hearth, for the November nights were growing chilly. Joyce picked up a book and tried to read, but found herself looking towards the door fully as often as at the page before her. Presently she set her teeth together and swallowed hard, for there was a rustling in the hall. The portiere was pushed aside and madame swept into the room in a dinner-gown of dark red velvet.

To Joyce's waiting eyes she seemed more imposing, more elegant, and more unapproachable than she had ever been before. At madame's entrance Joyce rose as usual, but when the red velvet train had swept on to a seat beside the fire, she still remained standing. Her lips seemed glued together after those first words of greeting.

"Be seated, mademoiselle," said the lady, with a graceful motion of her hand towards a chair. "How have you enjoyed your holiday?"

Joyce gave a final swallow of the choking lump in her throat, and began her humble confession that she had framed up-stairs among the rows of dismal blue wall-paper parrots. She started with Clotilde Robard's story of Jules, told of her accidental meeting with him, of all that she knew of his hard life with Brossard, and of her longing for some one to play with. Then she acknowledged that she had planned the barbecue secretly, fearing that madame would not allow her to invite the little goatherd. At the conclusion, she opened the handkerchief which she had been holding tightly clenched in her hand, and poured its contents in the red velvet lap.

"There's all that is left of my Christmas money," she said, sadly "seventeen francs and two sous. If it isn't enough to pay for the cushions, I'll write to Cousin Kate, and maybe she will lend me the rest."

Madame gathered up the handful of coin, and slowly rose. "It is only a step to the carriage-house," she said, "If you will kindly ring for Berthé to bring a lamp we will look to see how much damage has been done."

It was an unusual procession that filed down the garden walk a few minutes later. First came Berthé, in her black dress and white cap, holding a lamp high above her head, and screwing her forehead into a mass of wrinkles as she peered out into the surrounding darkness. After her came madame, holding up her dress and step- ping daintily along in her high-heeled little slippers. Joyce brought up the rear, stumbling along in the darkness of madame's large shadow, so absorbed in her troubles that she did not see the amused expression on the face of the grinning satyr in the fountain.

Eve, looking across at Adam, seemed to wink one of her stony eyes, as much as to say, "Humph! Somebody else has been getting into trouble. There's more kinds of forbidden fruit than one; pony-cart cushions, for instance."

Berthé opened the door, and madame stepped inside the carriage-house. With her skirts held high in both hands, she moved around among the wreck of the cushions, turning over a bit with the toe of her slipper now and then.

Madame wore velvet dinner-gowns, it is true, and her house was elegant in its fine old furnishings bought generations ago; but only her dressmaker and herself knew how many times those gowns had been ripped and cleaned and remodelled. It was only constant housewifely skill that kept the antique furniture repaired and the ancient brocade hangings from falling into holes. None but a French woman, trained in petty economies, could have guessed how little money and how much thought was spent in keeping her table up to it high standard of excellence.

Now as she looked and estimated, counting the fingers of one hand with the thumb of the other, a wish stirred in her kind old heart that she need not take the child's money; but new cushions must be bought, and she must be just to herself before she could be generous to others. So she went on with her estimating and counting, and then called Gabriel to consult him.

"Much of the same hair can be used again," she said, finally, "and the cushions were partly worn, so that it would not be right for you to have to bear the whole expense of new ones. I shall keep six-teen,—no, I shall keep only fifteen francs of your money, mademoiselle. I am sorry to take any of it, since you have been so frank with me; but you must see that it would not be justice for me to have to suffer in consequence of your fault. In France, children do nothing without the permission of their elders, and it would be well for you to adopt the same rule, my dear madamoi-selle."

Here she dropped two francs and two sous into Joyce's hand. It was more than she had dared to hope for. Now there would be at least a little picture-book apiece for the children at home.

This time Joyce saw the grin on the satyr's face when they passed the fountain. She was smiling herself when they entered the house, where monsieur was waiting to escort them politely in to dinner.

CHAPTER VI

JOYCE PLAYS GHOST

MONSIEUR CISEAUX was coming home to live. Gabriel brought the news when he came back from market. He had met Henri on the road and heard it from him. Monsieur was coming home. That was all they knew; as to the day or the hour, no one could guess. That was the way with monsieur, Henri said. He was so peculiar one never knew what to expect.

Although the work of opening the great house was begun immediately, and a thorough cleaning was in process from garret to cellar, Brossard did not believe that his master would really be at home before the end of the week. He made his own plans accordingly, although he hurried Henri relentlessly with the cleaning.

As soon as Joyce heard the news she made an excuse to slip away, and ran down to the field to Jules. She found him paler than usual, and there was a swollen look about his eyes that made her think that maybe he had been crying.

"What's the matter?" she asked. "Aren't you glad that your uncle is coming home?"

Jules gave a cautious glance over his shoulder towards the house, and then looked up at Joyce. Heretofore, some inward monitor of pride had closed his lips about himself whenever he had been with her, but, since the Thanksgiving Day that had made them such firm friends, he had wished every hour that he could tell her of his troubles. He felt that she was the only person in the world who took any interest in him. Although she was only three years older than himself, she had that motherly little way with her that eldest daughters are apt to aquire when there is a whole brood of little brothers and sisters constantly claiming attention.

So when Joyce asked again, "What's the matter, Jules?" with so much anxious sympathy in her face and voice, the child found himself blurting out the truth.

"Brossard beat me again last night," he exclaimed. Then, in response to her indignant exclamation, he poured out the whole story of his ill-treatment. "See here!" he cried, in conclusion, unbuttoning his blouse and baring his thin little shoulders. Great

494

red welts lay across them, and one arm was blue with a big mottled bruise.

Joyce shivered and closed her eyes an instant to shut out the sight that brought the quick tears of sympathy.

"Oh, you poor little thing!" she cried. "I'm going to tell madame."

"No, don't!" begged Jules. "If Brossard ever found out that I had told anybody, I believe that he would half kill me. He punishes me for the least thing. I had no breakfast this morning because I dropped an old plate and broke it."

"Do you mean to say," cried Joyce, "that you have been out here in the field since sunrise without a bite to eat?"

Jules nodded.

"Then I'm going straight home to get you something." Before he could answer she was darting over the fields like a little flying squirrel.

"Oh, what if it were Jack!" she kept repeating as she ran. "Dear old Jack, beaten and starved, without anybody to love him or say a kind word to him." The mere thought of such misfortune brought a sob.

In a very few minutes Jules saw her coming across the fields again, more slowly this time, for both hands were full, and without their aid she had no way to steady the big hat that flapped forward into her eyes at every step. Jules eyed the food ravenously. He had not known how weak and hungry he was until then.

"It will not be like this when your uncle comes home," said Joyce, as she watched the big mouthfuls disappear down the grateful little throat. Jules shrugged his shoulders, answering tremulously "Oh, yes, it will be lots worse. Brossard says that my Uncle Martin has a terrible temper, and that he turned his poor sister and my grandfather out of the house one stormy night. Brossard says he shall tell him how troublesome I am, and likely he will turn me out, too. Or, if he doesn't do that, they will both whip me every day."

Joyce stamped her foot. "I don't believe it," she cried, indignantly. "Brossard is only trying to scare you. Your uncle is an old man now, so old that he must be sorry for the way he acted when he was young. Why, of course he must be," she repeated, "or he never would have brought you here when you were a left homeless baby, More than that, I believe he will be angry when he finds how you have been treated. Maybe he will send Brossard away when you tell him."

"I would not dare to tell him," said Jules, shrinking back at the bare suggestion.

"Then *I* dare," cried Joyce with flashing eyes. "I am not afraid of Brossard or Henri or your uncle, or any man that I ever knew. What's more, I intend to march over here just as soon as your uncle comes home, and tell him right before Brossard how you have been treated."

Jules gasped in admiration of such reckless courage. "Seems to me Brossard himself would be afraid of you if you looked at him that way." Then his voice sank to a whisper. "Brossard is afraid of one thing, I've heard him tell Henri so, and that is *ghosts*. They talk about them every night when the wind blows hard and makes queer noises in the chimney. Sometimes they are afraid to put out their candles for fear some evil spirit might be in the room."

"I'm glad he is afraid of something, the mean old thing!" exclaimed Joyce. For a few moments nothing more was said, but Jules felt comforted now that he had unburdened his long pent up little heart. He reached out for several blades of grass and began idly twisting them around his finger.

Joyce sat with her hands clasped over her knees, and a wicked little gleam in her eyes that boded mischief. Presently she giggled as if some amusing thought had occurred to her, and when Jules looked up inquiringly she began noiselessly clapping her hands together.

"I've thought of the best thing," she said. "I'll fix old Brossard now. Jack and I have played ghost many a time, and have even scared each other while we were doing it, because we were so frightful-looking. We put long sheets all over us and went about with pumpkin jack-o'-lanterns on our heads. Oh, we looked awful, all in white, with fire shining out of those hideous eyes and mouths. If I knew when Brossard was likely to whip you again, I'd suddenly appear on the scene and shriek out like a banshee and make him stop. Wouldn't it be lovely?" she cried, more carried away with the idea the longer she thought of it. "Why, it would be like acting our fairy story. You are the Prince, and I will be the giant scissors and rescue you from the Ogre. Now let me see if I can think of a rhyme for you to say whenever you need me."

Joyce put her hands over her ears and began to mumble something that had no meaning whatever for Jules: "Ghost—post—roast—toast,—no that will never do; need—speed—deed,—no! Help—

yelp (I wish I could make him yelp),—friend—spend—lend,—thats it. I shall try that."

There was a long silence, during which Joyce whispered to herself with closed eyes. "Now I've got it," she announced, triumphantly, "and it's every bit as good as Cousin Kate's:

"Giant scissors, fearless friend,
      Hasten, pray, thy aid to lend."

"If you could just say that loud enough for me to hear, I'd come rushing in to save you."

Jules repeated the rhyme several times, until he was sure that he could remember it, and then Joyce stood up to go.

"Good-by, fearless friend," said Jules. "I wish I were brave like you." Joyce smiled in a superior sort of way, much flattered by the new title. Going home across the field she held her head a trifle higher than usual, and carried on an imaginary conversation with Brossard, in which she made him quail before her scathing rebukes.

Joyce did not take her usual walk that afternoon. She spent the time behind locked doors busy with paste, scissors, and a big muff-box, the best foundation she could find for a jack-o'-lantern. First she covered the box with white paper and cut a hideous face in one side,—great staring eyes, and a frightful grinning mouth. With a bit of wire she fastened a candle inside and shut down the lid.

"Looks too much like a box yet," she said, after a critical examination. "It needs some hair and a beard. Wonder what I can make it of." She glanced all around the room for a suggestion, and then closed her eyes to think. Finally she went over to her bed, and, turning the covers back from one corner, began ripping a seam in the mattress. When the opening was wide enough she put in her thumb and finger and pulled out a handful of the curled hair. "I can easily put it back when I have used it, and sew up the hole in the mattress," she said to her conscience. "My! This is exactly what I needed."

The hair was mixed, white and black, coarse and curly as a negro's wool.

She covered the top of the pasteboard head with it, and was so pleased that she added long beard and fierce moustache to the already hideous mouth. When that was all done she took it into a dark closet and lighted the candle. The monster's head glared at her from the depth of the closet, and she skipped back and forth in front of it, wringing her hands in delight.

"Oh, if Jack could only see it! If he could only see it!" she kept exclaiming. "It is better than any pumpkin head we ever made, and scary enough to throw old Brossard into a fit. I can hardly wait until it is dark enough to go over."

Meanwhile the short winter day drew on towards the close. Jules, out in the field with the goats, walked back and forth, back and forth, trying to keep warm. Brossard, who had gone five miles down the Paris road to bargain about some grain, sat comfortably in a little tobacco shop, with a pipe in his mouth and a glass and bottle on the table at his elbow. Henri was at home, still scrubbing and cleaning. The front of the great house was in order, with even the fires laid on all the hearths ready for lighting. Now he was scrubbing the back stairs. His brush bumped noisily against the steps, and the sound of its scouring was nearly drowned by the jerky tune which the old fellow sung through his nose while he worked.

A carriage drove slowly down the road and stopped at the gate with the scissors; then, in obedience to some command from within, the vehicle drove on to the smaller gate beyond. An old man with white hair and bristling moustache slowly alighted. The master had come home. He put out his hand as if to ring the bell, then on second thought drew a key from his pocket and fitted it in the lock. The gate swung back and he passed inside. The old house looked grey and forbidding in the dull light of the late afternoon. He frowned up at it, and it frowned down at him, standing there as cold and grim as itself. That was his only welcome.

The doors and windows were all shut, so that he only caught a faint sound of the bump, thump of the scrubbing-brush as it accompanied Henri's high-pitched tune down the back stairs.

Without giving any warning of his arrival, he motioned the man beside the coachman to follow with his trunk, and silently led the way upstairs. When the trunk had been unstrapped and the man had departed, monsieur gave one slow glance round the room. It was in perfect readiness for him. He set a match to the kindling laid in the grate, and then closed the door into the hall. The master had come home again, more silent, more mysterious in his movements than before.

Henri finished his scrubbing and his song, and, going down into the kitchen, began preparations for supper. A long time after,

Jules came up from the field, put the goats in their place, and crept in behind the kitchen stove.

Then it was that Joyce, from her watch-tower of her window, saw Brossard driving home in the market-cart. "Maybe I'll have a chance to scare him while he is putting the horse up and feeding it." she thought. It was in the dim gloaming when she could easily slip along by the hedges without attracting attention. Bareheaded, and in breathless haste to reach the barn before Brossard, she ran down the road, keeping close to the hedge, along which the wind raced also, blowing the dead leaves almost as high as her head.

Slipping through a hole in the hedge, just as Brossard drove in at the gate, she ran into the barn and crouched down behind the door. There she wrapped herself in the sheet that she had brought with her for the purpose, and proceeded to strike a match to light the lantern. The first one flickered and went out. The second did the same. Brossard was calling angrily for Jules now, and she struck another match in nervous haste, this time touching the wick with it before the wind could interfere. Then she drew her dress over the lantern to hide the light.

"Wouldn't Jack enjoy this," she thought, with a daring little giggle that almost betrayed her hiding-place.

"I tell thee it is thy fault," cried Brossard's angry voice, drawing nearer the barn.

"But I tried," began Jules's, timidly.

His trembling excuse was interrupted by Brossard, who had siezed him by the arm. They were now on the threshold of the barn, which was as dark as a pocket inside.

Joyce, peeping through the crack of the door, saw the man's arm raised in the dim twilight outside. "Oh, he is really going to beat him," she thought, turning faint at the prospect. Then her indignation overcame every other feeling as she heard a heavy halter-strap whiz through the air and fall with a sickening blow across Jules's shoulders. She had planned a scene something like this while she worked away at the lantern that afternoon. Now she felt as if she were acting a part in some private theatrical performance. Jules's cry gave her the cue, and the courage to appear.

As the second blow fell across Jules's smarting shoulders, a low blood-curdling wail came from the dark depths of the barn. Joyce had not practised that dismal moan of a banshee to no purpose in her ghost dances at home with Jack. It rose and fell and quivered and rose again in cadences of horror. There was something awful, something inhuman, in that fiendish, long-drawn shriek.

Brossard's arm fell to his side paralysed with fear, as that same hoarse voice cried, solemnly: "Brossard, beware! Beware!" But worse than that voice of sepulchral warning was the white-sheeted figure, coming towards him with a wavering, ghostly motion, fire shooting from the demon-like eyes, and flaming from the hideous mouth.

Brossard sank on his knees in a shivering heap, and began crossing himself. His hair was upright with horror, and his tongue stiff. Jules knew who it was that danced around them in such giddy circles, first darting towards them with threatening gestures, and then gliding back to utter one of those awful, sickening wails. He knew that under that fiery head and wrapped in that spectral dress was his "fearless friend," who according to promise, had hastened her aid to lend; nevertheless, he was afraid of her himself. He had never imagined that anything could look so terrifying.

The wail reached Henri's ears and aroused his curiosity. Cautiously opening the kitchen door, he thrust out his head, and then nearly fell backwards in his haste to draw it in again and slam the door. One glimpse of the ghost in the barnyard was quite enough for Henri.

Altogether the performance probably did not last longer than a minute, but each of the sixty seconds seemed endless to Brossard. With a final die-away moan Joyce glided towards the gate, delighted beyond measure with her success; but her delight did not last long. Just as she turned the corner of the house, someone standing in the shadow of it clutched her. A strong arm was thrown around her, and a firm hand snatched the lantern, and tore the sheet away from her face.

It was Joyce's turn to be terrified. "Let me go!" she shrieked, in English. With one desperate wrench she broke away, and by the light of the grinning jack-o'-lantern saw who was her captor. She was face to face with Monsieur Ciseaux.

"What does this mean?" he asked, severely. "Why do you come masquerading here to frighten my servants in this manner?"

For an instant Joyce stood speechless. Her boasted courage had forsaken her. It was only for an instant, however, for the rhyme that she had made seemed to sound in her ears as distinctly as if Jules were calling to her:

"Giant scissors, fearless friend,
Hasten, pray, thy aid to lend."

"I will be a fearless friend," she thought. Looking defiantly up into the angry face she demanded: "Then why do you keep such servants? I came because they needed to be frightened, and I'm glad you caught me, for I told Jules that I should tell you about them as soon as you got home. Brossard has starved and beaten him like a dog ever since he has been here. I just hope that you will look at the stripes and bruises on his poor little back. He begged me not to tell, for Brossard said you would likely drive him away, as you did your brother and sister. But even if you do, the neighbours say that an orphan asylum would be a far better home for Jules than this has been. I hope you'll excuse me, monsieur, I truly do, but I'm an American, and I can't stand by and keep still when I see anybody being abused, even if I am a girl, and it isn't polite for me to talk so to older people."

Joyce fired out the words as if they had been bullets, and so rapidly that monsieur could scarcely follow her meaning. Then, having relieved her mind, and fearing that maybe she had been rude in speaking so forcibly to such an old gentleman, she very humbly begged his pardon. Before he could recover from her rapid change in manner and her torrent of words, she reached out her hand, saying, in the meekest of little voices, "And will you please give me back those things, monsieur? The sheet is Madame Greville's, and I've got to stuff that hair back in the mattress to-night."

Monsieur gave them to her, still too astonished for words. He had never before heard any child speak in such a way. This one seemed more like a wild, uncanny little sprite than like any of the little girls he had known heretofore. Before he could recover from his bewilderment, Joyce had gone. "Good-night, monsieur," she called, as the gate clanged behind her.

CHAPTER VII

OLD "NUMBER THIRTY-ONE"

NO SOONER HAD the gate closed upon the subdued little ghost, shorn now of its terrors, than the old man strode forward to the place where Brossard crouched in the straw, still crossing himself. This sudden appearance of his master at such a time only added to

Brossard's fright. As for Jules, his knees shook until he could scarcely stand.

Henri, his curiosity lending him courage, cautiously opened the kitchen door to peer out again. Emboldened by the silence, he flung the door wide open, sending a broad stream of lamplight across the little group in the barnyard. Without a word of greeting monsieur laid hold of the trembling Jules and drew him nearer to the door. Throwing open the child's blouse, he examined the thin little shoulders, which shrank away as if to dodge some expected blow.

"Go to my room," was all the old man said to him. Then he turned fiercely towards Brossard. His angry tones reached Jules even after he had mounted the stairs and closed the door. The child crept close to the cheerful fire, and, crouching down on the rug, waited in a shiver of nervousness for his uncle's step on the stair.

Meanwhile, Joyce, hurrying home all a-tingle with the excitement of her adventure, wondered anxiously what would be the result of it. Under cover of the dusk she slipped into the house unobserved. There was barely time to dress for dinner. When she made her appearance monsieur complimented her unusually red cheeks.

"Doubtless mademoiselle has had a fine promenade," he said.

"No," answered Joyce, with a blush that made them redder still, and that caused madame to look at her so keenly that she felt those sharp eyes must be reading her inmost thoughts. It disturbed her so that she upset the salt, spilled a glass of water, and started to eat her soup with a fork. She glanced in an embarrassed way from madame to monsieur, and gave a nervous little laugh.

"The little mademoiselle has been in mischief again," remarked monsieur, with a smile. "What is it this time?"

The smile was so encouraging that Joyce's determination not to tell melted away, and she began a laughable account of the afternoon's adventure. At first both the old people looked shocked. Monsieur shrugged his shoulders and pulled his grey beard thoughtfully. Madame threw up her hands at the end of each sentence like horrified little exclamation points. But when Joyce had told the entire story neither of them had a word of blame, because their sympathies were so throughly aroused for Jules.

"I shall ask Monsieur Ciseaux to allow the child to visit here sometimes," said madame, her kind old heart full of pity for the motherless little fellow; "and I shall also explain that it was only your desire to save Jules from ill treatment that caused you to do such an unusual thing. Otherwise he might think you too bold and too—well, peculiar, to be a fit playmate for his little nephew."

"Oh, was it really so improper and horrid of me, madame?" asked Joyce, anxiously.

Madame hesitated. "The circumstances were some excuse," she finally admitted. "But I certainly should not want a little daughter of mine to be out after dark by herself on such a wild errand. In this country a little girl would not think it possible to do such a thing."

Joyce's face was very sober as she rose to leave the room. "I do wish that I could be proper like little French girls," she said, with a sigh.

Madame drew her towards her, kissing her on both cheeks. It was such an unusual thing for madame to do that Joyce could scarcely help showing some surprise. Feeling that the caress was an assurance that she was not in disgrace, as she had feared, she ran upstairs, so light-hearted that she sang on the way.

As the door closed behind her, monsieur reached for his pipe, saying, as he did so, "She has a heart of gold, the little mademoiselle."

"Yes," assented madame; "but she is a strange little body, so untamed and original. I am glad that her cousin returns soon, for the responsibility is too great for my old shoulders. One never knows what she will do next."

Perhaps it was for this reason that madame took Joyce with her when she went to Tours next day. She felt safer when the child was in her sight.

"It is so much nicer going around with you than Marie," said Joyce, giving Madame an affectionate little pat, as they stood before the entrance of a great square building, awaiting admission. "You take me to places that I have never seen before. What place is this?" She stooped to read the inscription on the door-plate:

"LITTLE SISTERS OF THE POOR."

Before her question could be answered, the door was opened by a wrinkled old woman, in a nodding white cap, who led them into a reception-room at the end of the hall.

"Ask for Sister Denisa," said madame, "and give her my name."

The old woman shuffled out of the room, and madame, taking a small memorandum book from her pocket, began to study it. Joyce sat looking about her with sharp, curious glances. She wondered if these little sisters of the poor were barefoot beggar girls, who went about the streets with ragged shawls over their heads, and with baskets in their hands. In her lively imagination she pictured row after row of such unfortunate children, marching out in the morning, empty-handed, and creeping back at night with the results of the day's begging. She did not like to ask about them, however, and, in a few minutes, her curiosity was satisfied without the use of questions.

Sister Denisa entered the room. She was a beautiful woman, in the plain black habit and white head-dress of a sister of charity. "Oh, they're nuns!" exclaimed Joyce, in a disappointed whisper. She had been hoping to see the beggar girls. "Oh, they're nuns!" She had often passed the convent in St. Sumphorien, and caught glimpses of the nuns, through the high barred gate. She had wondered how it must feel to be shut away from the world; to see only the patient white faces of the other sisters, and to walk with meekly folded hands and downcast eyes always in the same old paths. She had been hoping to see the beggar girls. She had often passed the convent in St. Symphorien, and caught glimpses of the nuns, through the high barred gate. She had wondered how it must feel to be shut away from the world; to see only the patient white faces of the other sisters, and to walk with meekly folded hands and downcast eyes always in the same old paths.

But Sister Denisa was different from the nuns that she had seen before. Some inward joy seemed to shine through her beautiful face and make it radiant. She laughed often and there was a happy twinkle in her clear, grey eyes. When she came into the room, she seemed to bring the outdoors with her, there was such sunshine and fresh air in the cheeriness of her greeting.

Madame had come to visit an old pensioner of hers who was in the home. After a short conversation, Sister Denisa rose to lead the way to her. "Would the little mademoiselle like to go through the house while madame is engaged?" asked the nun.

"Oh, yes, thank you," answered Joyce, who had found by this time that this home was not for little beggar girls, but for old men and women. Joyce had known very few old people in her short life, except her Grandmother Ware; and this grandmother was one of those dear, sunny old souls, whom everybody loves to claim, whether they are in the family or not. Some of Joyce's happiest days had been spent in her grandmother's country home, and the host of happy memories that she had stored up during those visits served to sweeten all her after life.

Old age, to Joyce, was associated with the most beautiful things that she had ever known: the warmest hospitality, the tenderest love, the cheeriest home-life. Strangers were in the old place now, and Grandmother Ware was no longer living, but, for her sake, Joyce held sacred every wrinkled face set round with snow-white hair, just as she looked tenderly on all old-fashioned flowers, because she had seen them first in her grandmother's garden.

Sister Denisa led the way into a large, sunny room and Joyce looked around eagerly. It was crowded with old men. Some were sitting idly on the benches around the walls, or dozing in chairs near the stove. Some smoked, some gathered around the tables where games of checkers and chess were going on; some gazed listlessly out of the windows. It was good to see how dull faces brightened, as Sister Denisa passed by with a smile for this group, a cheery word for the next. She stopped to brush the hair back from the forehead of an old paralytic, and pushed another man gently aside, when he blocked the way, with such a sweet-voiced "Pardon, little father," that it was like a caress. One white-haired old fellow, in his second childhood, reached out and caught at her dress, as she passed by.

Crossing a porch where were more old men sitting sadly alone, or walking sociably up and down in the sunshine, Sister Denisa passed along a court and held the door open for Joyce to enter another large room.

"Here is the rest of our family," she said. "A large one, is it not? Two hundred poor old people that nobody wants, and nobody cares what becomes of."

Joyce looked around the room and saw on every hand old age that had nothing beautiful, nothing attractive. "Were they beggars when they were little?" she asked.

"No, indeed," answered the nun. "That is the saddest part of it to me. Nearly all these poor creatures you see here once had happy homes of their own. That pitiful old body over by the stove, shaking with palsy, was once a gay, rich countess; the invalid whom madame visits was a marquise. It would break your heart, mademoiselle, to hear the stories of some of these people, especially those who have been cast aside by ungrateful children, to whom their support has become a burden. Several of these women have prosperous grandchildren, to whom we have appealed in vain. There is no cruelty that hurts me like such cruelty to old age."

Just then another nun came into the room, said something to Sister Denisa in a low voice, and glided out like a silent shadow, her rosary swaying back and forth with every movement of her clinging black skirts. "I am needed upstairs." said Sister Denisa, turning to Joyce. "Will you come up and see the sleeping-rooms.?"

They went up the freshly scrubbed steps to a great dormitory, where, against the bare walls, stood long rows of narrow cots. They were all empty, except one at the farthest end, where an old woman lay with her handkerchief across her eyes.

"Poor old Number Thirty-one!" said Sister Denisa. "She seems to feel her unhappy position more than anyone in the house. The most of them are thankful for mere bodily comfort,—satisfied with food and shelter and warmth; but she is continually pining for her old home surroundings. Will you not come and speak to her in English? She married a countryman of yours, and lived over thirty years in America. She speaks of that time as the happiest in her life. I am sure that you can give her a great deal of pleasure."

"Is she ill?" said Joyce, timidly drawing back as the nun started across the room.

"No, I think not," was the answer. "She says she can't bear to to be herded in one room with all those poor creatures, like a flock of sheep, with nothing to do but wait for death. She has always been accustomed to having a room of her own, so that her greatest trial is in having no privacy. She must eat, sleep, and live with a hundred other old women always around her. She comes up here to bed whenever she can find the slightest ache for an excuse, just to be by herself. I wish that we could give her a little spot that she could call her own, and shut the door on, and feel alone. But it cannot be," she added, with a sigh. "It taxes our strength to the utmost to give them all even a bare home."

By this time they had reached the cot, over the head of which hung a card, bearing the number "Thirty-one."

"Here is a little friend to see you, grandmother," said Sister Denisa, placing a chair by the bedside, and stooping to smooth back the locks of silvery hair that had strayed out from under the coarse white night-cap. Then she passed quickly on to her other duties, leaving Joyce to begin the conversation as best she could. The old woman looked at her sharply with piercing dark eyes, which must have been beautiful in their youth. The intense gaze embarrassed Joyce, and to break the silence she hurriedly stammered out the first thing that came into her mind.

"Are you ill, to-day?"

The simple question had a startling effect on the old woman. She raised herself on one elbow, and reached out for Joyce's hand, drawing her eagerly nearer. "Ah," she cried, "you speak the language that my husband taught me to love, and the tongue my little children lisped; but they are all dead now, and I've come back to my native land to find no home but the one that charity provides."

Her words ended in a wail, and she sank back on her pillow. "And this is my birthday," she went on. "Seventy-three years old, and a pauper, cast out to the care of strangers."

The tears ran down her wrinkled cheeks, and her mouth trembled pitifully. Joyce was distressed; she looked around for Sister Denisa, but saw that they were alone, they two, in the great bare dormitory, with its long rows of narrow white cots. The child felt utterly helpless to speak a word of comfort, although she was so sorry for the poor old lonely creature that she began to cry softly to herself. She leaned over, and taking one of the thin, blue-veined hands in hers, patted it tenderly with her plump little fingers.

"I ought not to complain," said the trembling voice, still broken by sobs. "We have food and shelter and sunshine and the sisters. Ah, that little Sister Denisa, she is indeed a smile of God to us all. But at seventy-three one wants more than a cup of coffee and a clean handkerchief. One wants something besides a bed and being just Number Thirty-one among two hundred other paupers."

"I am *so* sorry!" exclaimed Joyce, with such heartfelt earnestness that the sobbing woman felt the warmth of her sympathy, and looked up with a brighter face.

"Talk to me," she exclaimed. "It has been so long since I have heard your language."

While she obeyed Joyce kept thinking of her Grandmother Ware. She could see her outdoors among her flowers, the dahlias and touch-me-nots, the four-o'clocks and the cinnamon roses, taking such pride and pleasure in her sweet posy beds. She could see her beside the little table on the shady porch, making tea for some old neighbour who had dropped in to spend the afternoon with her. Or she was asleep in her armchair by the western window, her Bible in her lap and a smile on her sweet, kindly face. How dreary and empty the days must seem to poor old Number Thirty-one, with none of these things to brighten them.

Joyce could scarcely keep the tears out of her voice while she talked. Later, when Sister Denisa came back, Joyce was softly humming a lullaby, and Number Thirty-one, with a smile on her pitiful old face, was sleeping like a little child.

"You will come again, dear mademoiselle," said Sister Denisa, as she kissed the child goodbye at the door. "You have brought a blessing, may you carry one away as well!"

Joyce looked inquiringly at madame. "You may come whenever you like," was the answer. "Marie can bring you whenever you are are in town."

Joyce was so quiet on the way home that madame feared the day had been too fatiguing for her. "No," said Joyce, soberly. "I was only thinking about poor old Number Thirty-one. I am sorrier for her than I was for Jules. I used to think that there was nothing so sad as being a little child without any father or mother, and having to live in an asylum. I've often thought how lovely it would be go around and find a beautiful home for every little orphan in the world. But I believe now, that it is worse to be old that way. Old people can't play together, and they haven't anything to look forward to, and it makes them so miserable to remember all the things they have had and lost. If I had enough money to adopt anybody, I would adopt some poor old grandfather or grandmother and make them happy all the rest of their days."

CHAPTER VIII

CHRISTMAS PLANS AND AN ACCIDENT

THAT NIGHT, WHEN Marie came in to light the lamps and brush Joyce's hair before dinner, she had some news to tell.

"Brossard has been sent away from the Ciseaux place," she said. A new man is coming to-morrow, and my friend, Clotilde Robard, has already taken the position of housekeeper. She says that a very different life has begun for little Monsieur Jules, and that in his fine new clothes one could never recognise the little goatherd. He looks now like what he is, a gentleman's son. He has the room next to monsieur's, all freshly furnished, and after New Year a tutor is coming from Paris."

"But they say that it is pitiful to see how greatly the child fears his uncle. He does not understand the old man's cold, forbidding manner, and it provokes monsieur to have the little one tremble and grow pale whenever he speaks. Clotilde says that Madame Gréville told monsieur that the boy needed games and young companions to make him more like other children, and he promised her that Monsieur Jules should come over here tomorrow afternoon to play with you."

"Oh, good!" cried Joyce. "We'll have another barbecue if the day is fine. I am so glad that we do not have to be bothered any more by those tiresome old goats."

By the time the next afternoon arrived, however, Joyce was far too much interested in something else to think of a barbecue. Cousin Kate had come back from Paris with a trunk full of pretty things, and a plan for the coming Christmas. At first she thought of taking only madame into her confidence, and preparing a small Christmas tree for Joyce; but afterwards she concluded that it would give the child more pleasure if she were allowed to take part in the preparations. It would keep her from being homesick by giving her something else to think about.

Then madame proposed inviting a few of the little peasant children who had never seen a Christmas tree. The more they discussed the plan the larger it grew, like a rolling snowball. By lunch-time madame had a list of thirty children, who were to be bidden to the Noel fete, and Cousin Kate had decided to order a tree tall enough to touch the ceiling.

When Jules came over, awkward and shy with the consciousness of his new clothes, he found Joyce sitting in the midst of yards of gaily coloured tarletan. It was heaped up around her in bright masses of purple and orange and scarlet and green, and she was making it into candy-bags for the tree.

In a few minutes Jules had forgotten all about himself, and was as busy as she, pinning the little stocking-shaped patterns in place, and carefully cutting out those fascinating bags.

"You would be lots of help," said Joyce, "if you could come over every day, for there's all the ornaments to unpack, and the corn to shell, and pop, and string. It will take most of my time to dress the dolls, and there's such a short time to do everything in."

"You never saw any pop-corn, did you, Jules?" asked Cousin Kate. "When I was here last time, I couldn't find it anywhere in France; but the other day a friend told me of a grocer in Paris, who imports it for his American customers every winter. So I went there. Joyce, suppose you get the popper and show Jules what the corn is like."

Madame was interested also, as she watched the little brown kernels shaken back and forth in their wire cage over the glowing coals. When they began popping open, the little seeds suddenly turning into big white blossoms, she sent Rosalie running to bring monsieur to see the novel sight.

"We can eat and work at the same time," said Joyce, as she filled a dish with the corn. and called Jules back to the table, where he had been cutting tarletan. "There's no time to lose. See what a funny grain this is!" she cried, picking up one that lay on the top of the dish. "It looks like Therese, the fishwoman, in her white cap."

"And here is a goat's head," said Jules, picking up another grain. "And this one looks like a fat pigeon."

He had forgotten his shyness entirely now, and was laughing and talking as easily as Jack could have done.

"Jules," said Joyce, suddenly, looking around to see that the older people were too busy with their own conversation to notice hers. "Jules, why don't you talk to your Uncle Martin the way you do to me? He would like you lots better if you would. Robard says that you get pale and frightened every time he speaks to you, and it provokes him for you to be so timid."

Jules dropped his eyes. "I cannot help it," he exclaimed. "He looks so grim and cross that my voice just won't come out of my throat when I open my mouth."

Joyce studied him critically, with her head tipped a little to one side. "Well, I must say," she exclaimed, finally, "that, for a boy born in America, you have the least dare about you of anybody I ever saw. Your Uncle Martin isn't any grimmer or crosser than a man I knew at home. There's Judge Ward, so big and solemn and dignified that everybody is half way afraid of him. Even grown people have always been particular about what they said to him.

"Last summer his little nephew, Charley Ward, came to visit him. Charley's just a little thing, still in dresses, and he calls his uncle, Bill. Think of anybody daring to call Judge Ward, *Bill*! No matter what the judge was doing, or how glum he looked, if Charley took a notion, he would go up and stand in front of him, and say, 'Laugh, Bill, laugh!' If the judge happened to be reading, he'd have to put down his book, and no matter whether he felt funny or not, or whether there was anything to laugh at or not, he would have to throw his head back and just roar. Charley liked to see his fat sides shake, and his white teeth shine. I've heard people say that the judge likes Charley better than anybody else in the world, because he's the only person who acts as if he wasn't afraid of him."

Jules sat still a minute, considering, and then asked, anxiously, "But what do you suppose would happen if I should say 'Laugh, Martin, laugh,' to my uncle?"

Joyce shrugged her shoulders impatiently. "Mercy, Jules, I did not mean that you should act like a three-year-old baby. I meant that you ought to talk up to your uncle some. Now this is the way you are." She picked up a kernel of the unpopped corn, and held it out for him to see. "You shut yourself up in a little hard ball like this, so that your uncle can't get acquainted with you. How can he know what is inside of your head if you always shut up like a clam whenever he comes near you? This is the way you ought to be." She shot one of the great white grains towards him with a deft flip of her thumb and finger. "Be free and open with him."

Jules put the tender morsel in his mouth and ate it thoughtfully. "I'll try," he promised, "if you really think that it would please him, and I can think of anything to say. You don't know how I dread going to the table when everything is always so still that we can hear the clock tick."

"Well, you take my advice," said Joyce. "Talk about anything. Tell him about our Thanksgiving feast and the Christmas tree, and ask him if you can't come over every day to help. I wouldn't let anybody think that I was a coward."

Joyce's little lecture had a good effect, and monsieur saw the wisdom of Madame Greville's advice when Jules came to the table that night. He had brought a handful of the wonderful corn to show his uncle, and in the conversation that it brought about he unconsciously showed something else,—something of his sensitive inner self that aroused his uncle's interest.

Every afternoon of the week that followed found Jules hurrying over to Madame Greville's to help with the Christmas preparations. He strung yards of corn, and measured out the nuts and candy for each of the gay bags. Twice he went in the carriage to Tours with Cousin Kate and Joyce, to help buy presents for the thirty little guests. He was jostled by the holiday shoppers in crowded aisles. He stood enraptured in front of wonderful show windows, and he had the joy of choosing fifteen things from piles of bright tin trumpets, drums, jumping-jacks, and picture-books. Joyce chose the presents for the girls.

THE GATE OF THE GIANT SCISSORS

The tree was bought and set up in a large unused room back of the library, and as soon as each article was in readiness it was carried in and laid on a table beside it. Jules used to steal in sometimes and look at the tapers, the beautiful glass balls, the gilt stars, and glittering tinsel, and wonder how the stately cedar would look in all that array of loveliness. Everything belonging to it seemed sacred, even the unused scraps of bright tarletan and the bits of broken candles. He would not let Marie sweep them up to be burned, but gathered them carefully into a box and carried them home. There were several things that he had rescued from her broom,—one of those beautiful red balls, cracked on one side it is true, but gleaming like a mammoth red cherry on the other. There were scraps of tinsel and odds and ends of ornaments that had been broken or damaged by careless handling. These he hid away in a chest in his room, as carefully as a miser would have hoarded a bag of gold.

Clotilde Robard, the housekeeper, wondered why she found his candle burned so low several mornings. She would have wondered still more if she had gone into his room a while before daybreak. He had awakened early, and, sitting up in bed with the quilts wrapped around him, spread the scraps of tarletan on his knees. He was piecing together with his awkward little fingers enough to make several tiny bags.

Henri missed his spade one morning, and hunted for it until he was out of patience. It was nowhere to be seen. Half an hour later, coming back to the house, he found it hanging in its usual place, where he had looked for it a dozen times at least. Jules had taken it down to the woods to dig up a little cedar tree, so little that it was not over a foot high when it was planted in a box.

Clotilde had to be taken into the secret, for he could not hide it from her. "It is for my Uncle Martin," he said, timidly. "Do you think he will like it?"

The motherly housekeeper looked at the poor little tree, decked out in its scraps of cast-off finery, and felt a sob rising in her throat, but she held up her hands with many admiring exclamations that made Jules glow with pride.

"I have no beautiful white strings of popcorn to hang over it like wreaths of snow," he said, "so I am going down the lane for some mistletoe that grows in one of the highest trees. The berries are like lovely white wax beads."

"You are a good little lad," said the housekeeper, kindly, as she gave his head an affectionate pat. "I shall have to make something to hang on that tree myself; some gingerbread figures, maybe. I used to know how to cut out men and horses and pigs,—nearly all the animals. I must try it again some day soon."

A happy smile spread all over Jules's face as he thanked her. The words, "You are a good little lad," sent a warm glow of pleasure through him, and rang like music in his ears all the way down the lane. How bright the world looked this frosty December morning! What cheeriness there was in the ring of Henri's axe as he chopped away at the stove-wood! What friendliness in the baker's whistle, as he rattled by in his big cart! Jules found himself whistling, too, for sheer gladness, and all because of no more kindness than might have been thrown to a dog; a pat on the head and the words, "You are a good little lad."

Sometime after, it may have been two hours or more, Madame Greville was startled by a wild, continuous ringing of the bell at her front gate. Somebody was sending peal after peal echoing through the garden, with quick, impatient jerks of the bell-wire. She hurried out herself to answer the summons.

Berthe had already shot back the bolt and showed Clotilde leaning against the stone post, holding her fat sides and completely exhausted by her short run from the Ciseaux house.

"Will madame send Gabriel for the doctor?" she cried, gasping for breath at every word. "The little Monsieur Jules has fallen from a tree and is badly hurt. We do not know how much, for he is still unconscious and his uncle is away from home. Henri found him lying under a tree with a big bunch of mistletoe in his arms. He carried him up-stairs while I ran over to ask you to send Gabriel quickly on a horse for the doctor."

"Gabriel shall go immediately," said Madame Greville, "and I shall follow you as soon as I have given the order."

Clotilde started back in as great haste as her weight would allow, puffing and blowing and wiping her eyes on her apron at every step. Madame overtook her before she had gone many rods. Always calm and self-possessed in every emergency, madame took command now; sent the weeping Clotilde to look for old linen, Henri to the village for Monsieur Ciseaux, and then turned her attention to Jules.

"To think," said Clotilde, coming into the room, "that the last thing the poor little lamb did was to show me his Christmas tree that he was making ready for his uncle!" She pointed to the corner where it stood, decked by awkward boyish hands in its pitiful collection of scraps.

"Poor little fellow!" said madame, with tears in her own eyes. "He has done the best he could. Put it in the closet, Clotilde. Jules would not want it to be seen before Christmas."

Madame stayed until the doctor had made his visit; then the report that she carried home was that Jules had regained consciousness, and that, as far as could be discovered, hjs only injury was a broken leg.

Joyce took refuge in the pear-tree. It was not alone because Jules was hurt that she wanted to cry, but because they must have the Noel fete without him. She knew how bitterly he would be disappointed.

CHAPTER IX

A GREAT DISCOVERY

"ONLY TWO more nights till Christmas eve, two more nights, two more nights," sang Joyce to Jules in a sort of chant. She was sitting beside his bed with a box in her lap, full of little dolls, which she was dressing. Every day since his accident she had been allowed to make him two visits,—one in the morning, and one in the afternoon. They helped wonderfully in shortening the long, tedious days for Jules. True, Madame Greville came often with broths and jellies, Cousin Kate made flying visits to leave rare hothouse grapes and big bunches of violets; Clotilde hung over him with motherly tenderness, and his uncle looked into the room many times a day to see that he wanted nothing.

Jule's famished little heart drank in all this unusual kindness and attention as greedily as the parched earth drinks in the rain. Still, he would have passed many a long, restless hour, had it not been for Joyce's visits.

She brought over a photograph of the house at home, with the family seated in a group on the front porch. Jules held it close while she introduced each one of them. By the time he had heard all about Holland's getting lost the day the circus came to town, and Jack's taking the prize in a skating contest, and Mary's setting her apron on fire, and the baby's sweet little ways when he said his prayers, or played peek-a-boo, he felt very well acquainted with the entire Ware family. Afterward, when Joyce had gone, he felt his loneliness more than ever. He lay there, trying to imagine how it must feel to have a mother and sisters and brothers all as fond of each other as Joyce's were, and to live in the midst of such good times as always went on in the little brown house.

Monsieur Ciseaux, sitting by his fire with the door open between the two rooms, listened to Joyce's merry chatter with almost as much interest as Jules. He would have been ashamed to admit how eagerly he listened for her step on the stairs every day, or what longings wakened in his lonely old heart, when he sat by his love-less fireside after she had gone home, and there was no more sound of children's voices in the next room.

There had been good times in the old Ciseaux house also, once, and two little brothers and a sister had played in that very room; but they had grown up long ago, and the ogre of selfishness and misunderstanding had stolen in and killed all their happiness. Ah, well, there was much that the world would never know about that misunderstanding. There was much to forgive and forget on both sides.

Joyce had a different story for each visit. To-day she had just finished telling Jules the fairy tale of which he never tired, the tale of the giant scissors.

"I never look at those scissors over the gate without thinking of you," said Jules, "and the night you played that I was the Prince, and you came to rescue me."

"I wish I could play scissors again, and rescue somebody else that I know," answered Joyce. "I'd take poor old Number Thirty-one away from the home of the Little Sisters of the Poor."

"What's Number Thirty-one?" asked Jules. "You never told me about that."

"Didn't I?" asked Joyce, in surprise. "She is a lonely old woman that the sisters take care of. I have talked about her so often, and written home so much, that I thought I had told everybody. I can hardly keep from crying whenever I think of her. Marie and I stop every day we go into town and take her flowers. I have been there four times since my first visit with madame. Sometimes she tells me things that happened when she was a little girl here in France, but she talks to me oftenest in English about the time when she lived in America. I can hardly imagine that she was ever as young as I am, and that she romped with her brothers as I did with Jack."

"Tell some of the things that she told you," urged Jules; so Joyce began repeating all that she knew about Number Thirty-one.

It was a pathetic little tale that brought tears to Jules's eyes, and a dull pain to the heart of the old man who listened in the next room. "I wish I were rich," exclaimed Joyce, impulsively, as she finished. "I wish I had a beautiful big home, and I would adopt her for my grandmother. She should have a great lovely room, where the sun shines in all day long, and it should be furnished in rose colour like the one that she had when she was a girl. I'd dress her grey satin and soft white lace. She has the prettiest silvery hair, and beautiful dark eyes. She would make a lovely grandmother. And I would have a maid to wait on her, and there'd be mignonette always growing in boxes on the window-sill. Every time I came back from town, I'd bring her a present just for a nice little surprise; and I'd read to her, and sing to her, and make her feel that she belonged to somebody, so that she'd be happy all the rest of her days.

"Yesterday while I was there she was holding a little cut glass vinaigrette. It had a big D engraved on the silver top. She said that it was the only thing that she had left except her wedding ring, and that it was to be Sister Denisa's when she was gone. The D stands for both their names. Hers is Desire. She said the vinaigrette was too precious to part with as long as she lives, because her oldest brother gave it to her on her twelfth birthday, when she was exactly as old as I am. Isn't Desire a pretty name?"

"Mademoiselle," called Monsieur Ciseaux from the next room, "mademoiselle, will you come—will you tell me—what name was that? Desire, did you say?"

There was something so strange in the way he called that name Desire, almost like a cry, that Joyce sprang up, startled, and ran into the next room. She had never ventured inside before.

"Tell me again what you were telling Jules," said the old man. "Seventy-three years, did you say? And how long has she been back in France?"

Joyce began to answer his rapid questions, but stopped with a frightened cry as her glance fell on a large portrait hanging over the mantel. "There she is!" she cried, excitedly dancing up and down as she pointed to the portrait. "There she is! That's Number Thirty-one, her very own self."

"You are mistaken!" cried the old man, attempting to rise from his chair, but trembling so that he could scarcely pull himself up on his feet. "That is a picture of my mother, and Desire is dead; long dead."

"But it is *exactly* like Number Thirty-one,—I mean Madame Desire," persisted Joyce.

Monsieur looked at her wildly from under his shaggy brows, and then, turning away, began to pace up and down the room. "I had a sister once," he began. "She would have been seventy-three this month, and her name was Desire."

Joyce stood motionless in the middle of the room, wondering what was coming next. Suddenly turning with a violence that made her start, he cried, "No, I never can forgive! She has been dead to me nearly a lifetime. Why did you tell me this, child? Out of my sight! What is it to me if she is homeless and alone? Go! Go!"

He waved his hands so wildly in motioning her away, that Joyce ran out of the room and banged the door behind her.

"What do you suppose is the matter with him?" asked Jules, in a frightened whisper, as they listened to his heavy tread, back and forth, back and forth, in the next room.

Joyce shook her head. "I don't know for sure," she answered, hesitatingly, "but I believe that he is going crazy."

Jules's eyes opened so wide that Joyce wished she had not frightened him. "Oh, you know that I didn't mean it," she said reassuringly. The heavy tread stopped, and the children looked at each other.

"What can he be doing now?" Jules asked, anxiously.

Joyce tiptoed across the room, and peeped through the keyhole. "He is sitting down now, by the table, with his head on his arms. He looks as if he might be crying about something."

"I wish he didn't feel bad," said Jules, with a swift rush of pity. "He has been so good to me ever since he sent Brossard away. Sometimes I think that he must feel as much alone in the world as I do, because all his family are dead, too. Before I broke my leg I was making him a little Christmas tree, so that he need not feel left out when we had the big one. I was getting mistletoe for it when I fell. I can't finish it now, but there's five pieces of candle on it, and I'll get Clotilde to light them while the fete is going on, so that I'll not miss the big tree so much. Oh, nobody knows how much I want to go to that fete! Sometimes it seems more than I can bear to have to stay away."

"Where is your tree?" asked Joyce. "May I see it?"

Jules pointed to the closet. "It's in there," he said, proudly. "I trimmed it with pieces that Marie swept up to burn. Oh, shut the door! Quick!" he cried, excitedly, as a step was heard in the hall. "I don't want anybody to see it before the time comes."

The step was Henri's. He had come to say that Marie was waiting to take mademoiselle home. Joyce was glad of the interruption. She could not say anything in praise of the poor little tree, and she knew that Jules expected her to. She felt relieved that Henri's presence made it impossible for her to express any opinion.

She bade Jules good-by gaily, but went home with such a sober little face that Cousin Kate began to question her about her visit. Madame, sitting by the window with her embroidery-frame, heard the account also. Several times she looked significantly across at Cousin Kate, over the child's head.

"Joyce," said Cousin Kate, "you have had so little outdoor excercise since Jules's accident that it would be a good thing for you to run around in the garden awhile before dark."

Joyce had not seen madame's glances, but she felt vaguely that Cousin Kate was making an excuse to get rid of her. She was disappointed, for she thought that her account of monsieur's queer actions and Jules's little tree would have made a greater impression on her audience. She went out obediently, walking up and down the paths with her hands in her jacket pockets, and her red tam-o'-shanter pulled down over her eyes. The big white cat followed her, ran on ahead, and then stopped, arching its back as if waiting for her to stroke it. Taking no notice of it, Joyce turned aside to the pear-tree and climbed up among the highest branches.

The cat rubbed against the tree, mewing and purring by turns, then sprang up in the tree after her. She took the warm, furry creature in her arms and began talking to it.

"Oh, Solomon," she said, "what do you suppose is the matter over there? My poor old lady must be monsieur's sister, or she couldn't have looked exactly like that picture, and he would not have acted so queerly. What do you suppose it is that he can never forgive? Why did he call me in there and then drive me out in such a crazy way, and tramp around the room, and put his head down on his arms as if he were crying?"

Solomon purred louder and closed his eyes.

"Oh, you dear, comfortable old thing," exclaimed Joyce, giving the cat a shake. "Wake up and take some interest in what I am saying. I wish you were as smart as Puss in Boots; then maybe you could find out what is the matter. How I wish fairy tales could be true! I'd say 'Giant scissors, right the wrong and open the gate that's been shut so long.' There! Did you hear that, Solomon Greville? I said a rhyme right off without waiting to make it up. Then the scissors would leap down and cut the mis-understanding or trouble or whatever it is, and the gate would fly open, and there the brother and sister would meet each other. All the unhappy years would be forgotten, and they'd take each other by the hand, just as they did when they were little children, Martin and Desire, and go into the old home together,—on Christmas Day, in the morning."

Joyce was half singing her words now, as she rocked the cat back and forth in her arms. "And then the scissors would bring Jules a magnificent big tree, and he'd never be afraid of his uncle any more. Oh, they'd all have such a happy time on Christmas Day, in the morning!"

Joyce had fully expected to be homesick all during the holidays; but now she was so absorbed in other people's troubles, and her day-dreams to make everybody happy, that she forgot all about herself. She fairly bubbled over with the peace and good-will of the approaching Christmas-tide, and rocked the cat back and forth in the pear-tree to the tune of a happy old-time carol.

A star or two twinkled out through the gloaming, and, looking up beyond them through the infinite stretches of space, Joyce thought of a verse that she and Jack had once learned together, one rainy Sunday at her Grandmother Ware's, sitting on a little stool at the old lady's feet:

"Behold thou hast made the heaven and the earth by thy great power and outstreched arm, and *there is nothing too hard for thee.*" Her heart gave a bound at the thought. Why should she be sitting there longing for fairy tales to be true, when the great Hand that had set the stars to swinging could bring anything to pass; could even open that long-closed gate and bring the brother and sister together again, and send happiness to little Jules?

Joyce lifted her eyes again and looked up, out past the stars. "Oh, if you please, God," she whispered, "for the little Christ-child's sake."

When Joyce went back to the house, Cousin Kate sat in the drawing-room alone. Madame had gone over to see Jules, and did not return until long after dark. Berthe had been in three times to ask monsieur if dinner should be served, before they heard her ring at the gate.   When she finally came, there was such an air of mystery about her that Joyce was puzzled.   All that next morning, too, the day before Christmas, it seemed to Joyce as if something unusual were afloat.   Everybody in the house was acting strangely.

Madame and Cousin Kate did not come home to lunch.   She had been told that she must not go to see Jules until afternoon, and the doors of the room where the Christmas tree was kept had all been carefully locked.   She thought that the morning never would pass.   It was nearly three o'clock when she started over to see Jules.   To her great surprise, as she ran lightly up the stairs to his room, she saw her Cousin Kate hurrying across the upper hall, with a pile of rose-coloured silk curtains in her arms.

Jules tried to raise himself up in bed as Joyce entered, forgetting all about his broken leg in his eagerness to tell the news.   "Oh, what do you think!" he cried.   "They said that I might be the one to tell you.   She *is* Uncle Martin's sister, the old woman you told about yesterday, and he is going to bring her home to-morrow."

Joyce sank into a chair with a little gasp at the suddenness of his news.   She had not expected this beautiful ending of her day-dreams to be brought about so soon, although she had hoped that it would be sometime.

"How did it all happen?" she cried, with a beaming face.   "Tell me about it!   Quick!"

"Yesterday afternoon madame came over soon after you left. She gave me my wine jelly, and then went into Uncle Martin's room, and talked and talked for the longest time.   After she had gone he did not eat any dinner, and I think that he must have sat up all night, for I heard him walking around every time that I waked up. Very early this morning, madame came back again, and M. Greville was with her.   They drove with Uncle Martin to the little Sisters of the Poor.   I don't know what happened out there, only that Aunt Desire is to be brought home to-morrow.

"Your Cousin Kate was with them when they came back, and they had brought all sorts of things with them from Tours.   She is in there now, making Aunt Desire's room look like it did when she was a girl."

"Oh, isn't it lovely!" exclaimed Joyce.   "It is better than all the fairy tales I have ever read or heard,—almost too good to be true!" Just then Cousin Kate called her, and she ran across the hall. Standing in the doorway, she looked all around the freshly furnished room, that glowed with the same soft, warm pink that colours the heart of a shell.

"How beautiful!" cried Joyce, glancing from the rose on the dressing-table to the soft curtains of the windows, which all opened towards the morning sun. "What a change it will be from that big bare dormitory with its rows of narrow little cots." She tiptoed around the room, admiring everything, and smiling over the happiness in store for poor old Number Thirty-one, when she should find herself in the midst of such loveliness.

Joyce's cup of pleasure was so full, that it brimmed over when they turned to leave the room. Cousin Kate slipped an arm around her, and kissed her softly on the forehead.

"You dear little fairy tale lover," she said. "Do you know that it is because of you that this desert has blossomed? If you had never made all those visits to the Little Sisters of the Poor, and had never won old Madame Desire's love and confidence by your sympathy, if you had never told Jules the story of the giant scissors, and wished so loud that you could fly to her rescue, old monsieur would never have known that his sister is living. Even then, I doubt if he would have taken this step, and brought her back home to live, if your stories of your mother and the children had not brought his own childhood back to him. He said that he used to sit there hour after hour, and hear you talk of your life at home, until some of its warmth and love crept into his own frozen old heart, and thawed out its selfishness and pride."

Joyce lifted her radiant face, and looked towards the half opened window, as she caught the sound of chimes. Across the Loire came the deep-toned voice of a cathedral bell, ringing for vespers.

"Listen!" she cried. "Peace on earth,—good-will—oh, Cousin Kate! It really does seem to say it! My Christmas has begun the day before."

CHAPTER X

CHRISTMAS

LONG BEFORE THE Christmas dawn was bright enough to bring the blue parrots into plain view on the walls of Joyce's room, she had climbed out of bed to look for her "messages from Noel." The night before, following the old French custom, she had set her little slippers just outside the threshold. Now, candle in hand, she softly slipped to the door and peeped out into the hall. Her first eager glance showed that they were full.

Climbing back into her warm bed, she put the candle on the table beside it, and began emptying the slippers. They were filled with bonbons and all sorts of little trifles, such as she and Jules had admired in the gay shop windows. On the top of one Madame had laid a slender silver pencil, and monsieur a pretty purse. In the other was a pair of little wooden shoes, fashioned like the ones that Jules had worn when she first knew him. They were only half as long as her thumb, and wrapped in a paper on which was written that Jules himself had whittled them out for her, with Henri's help and instructions.

"What little darlings!" exclaimed Jouce. "I hope he will think as much of the scrapbook that I made for him as I do of these. I know that he will be pleased with the big microscope that Cousin Kate bought for him."

She spread all the things out on the table, and gave the slippers a final shake. A red morocco case, no larger than half a dollar, fell out of the toe of one of them. Inside the case was a tiny buttonhole watch, with its wee hands pointing to six o'clock. It was the smallest watch that Joyce had ever seen, Cousin Kate's gift. Joyce could hardly keep back a little squeal of delight. She wanted to wake up everybody on the place and show it. Then she wished that she could be back in the brown house, showing it to her mother and the children. For a moment, as she thought of them, sharing the pleasure of their Christmas stockings without her, a great wave of homesickness swept over her, and she lay back on the pillow with that miserable, far-away feeling that, of all things, makes one most desolate.

Then she heard the rapid "tick, tick, tick, tick," of the little watch, and was comforted. She had not realised before that time could go so fast. Now thirty seconds were gone; then sixty. At this rate it could not be such a very long time before they would be packing their trunks to start home; so Joyce concluded not to make herself unhappy by longing for the family, but to get as much pleasure as possible out of this strange Christmas abroad.

That little watch seemed to make the morning fly. She looked at it at least twenty times an hour. She had shown it to everyone in the house, and was wishing that she could take it over to Jules for him to see, when Monsieur Ciseaux's carriage stopped at the gate.

He was on his way to the Little Sisters of the Poor, and had come to ask Joyce to drive with him to bring his sister home.

He handed her into the carriage as if she had been a duchess, and then seemed to forget that she was beside him; for nothing was said all the way. As the horses spun along the road in the keen morning air, the old man was busy with his memories, his head dropped forward on his breast. The child watched him, entering into this little drama as sympathetically as if she herself were the forlorn old woman, and this silent, white-haired man at her side were Jack.

Sister Denisa came running out to meet them, her face shining and her eyes glistening with tears. "It is for joy that I weep." she exclaimed, "that poor madame should have come to her own again. See the change that has already been made in her by the blessed news."

Joyce looked down the corridor as monsieur hurried forward to meet the old lady coming towards them, and to offer his arm. Hope had straightened the bowed figure; joy had put lustre into her dark eyes and strength into her weak frame. She walked with such proud stateliness that the other inmates of the home looked up at her in surprise as she passed. She was no more like the tearful, broken-spirited woman who had lived among them so long, than her threadbare dress was like the elegant mantle which monsieur had brought to fold around her.

Joyce had brought a handful of roses to Sister Denisa, who caught them up with a cry of pleasure, and held them against her face as if they carried with them some sweetness of another world.

Madame came up then, and taking the nun in her arms, tried to thank her for all that she had done, but she could find no words for a gratitude so deep, and turned away, sobbing.

They said good-bye to Sister Denisa,—brave Little Sister of the Poor, whose only joy was the pleasure of unselfish service; who had no time to even stand at the gate and be a glad witness of other people's Christmas happiness, but must hurry back to her morning task of dealing out coffee and clean handkerchiefs to two hundred old paupers. No, there were only a hundred and ninety-nine now. Down the streets, across the Loire, into the old village and out again, along the wide Paris road, one of them was going home.

The carriage turned and went for a little space between brown fields and closely clipped hedgerows, and then madame saw the windows of her old home flashing back the morning sunlight over the high stone wall. Again the carriage turned, into the lane this time, and now the sunlight was caught up by the scissors over the gate, and thrown dazzlingly down into their faces.

Monsieur smiled as he looked at Joyce, a tender, gentle smile that one would have supposed never could have been seen on those harsh lips. She was almost standing up in the carriage, in her excitement.

"Oh, it has come true!" she cried ,clasping her hands together. "The gates are really opening at last.!"

Yes, the Ogre, whatever may have been its name, no longer lived. Its spell was broken, for now the giant scissors no longer barred the way. Slowly the great gate swung open, and the carriage passed through. Joyce sprang out and ran on ahead to open the door. Hand in hand, just as when they were little children, Martin and Desire, this white-haired brother and sister went back to the old home together; and it was Christmas Day, in the morning.

At five o'clock that evening the sound of Gabriel's accordian went echoing up and down the garden, and thirty little children were marching to its music along the paths, between the rows of blooming laurel. Joyce understood, now, why the room where the Christmas tree stood had been kept so carefully locked. For two days that room had been empty and the tree had been standing in Monsieur Ciseaux's parlour. Cousin Kate and madame and Bertha and Marie and Gabriel had all been over there, busily at work, and neither she nor Jules had suspected what was going on downstairs.

Now she marched with the others, out of the garden and across the road, keeping time to the music of the wheezy old accordeon that Gabriel played so proudly. Surely every soul, in all that long procession filing through the gate of the giant scissors, belonged to the kingdom of loving hearts and gentle hands; for they were all children who had passed through, or else mothers who carried in their arms the little ones who, but for these faithful arms, must have missed this Noel fete.

Jules had been carried downstairs and laid on a couch in the corner of the room where he could see the tree to its best advantage. Beside him sat his great-aunt, Desire, dressd in a satin gown of silvery grey that had been her mother's, and looking as if she had just stepped out from the frame of the portrait upstairs. She held Jules's hand in hers, as if with it she grasped the other Jules, the little brother of the olden days for whom this child had been named. And she told him stories of his grandfather and his father. Then

Jules found that this Aunt Desire had known his mother; had once sat on the vine-covered porch while he ran after fireflies on the lawn in his little white dress; had heard the song the voice still sang to him in his dreams:

"Till the stars and the angels come to keep
Their watch where my baby lies fast asleep."

When she told him this, with her hand stroking his and folding it tight with many tender little claspings, he felt that he had found a part of his old home, too, as well as Aunt Desire.

One by one the tapers began to glow on the great tree, and when it was all ablaze the doors were opened for the children to flock in. They stood about the room, bewildered at first, for not one of them had ever seen such a sight before; a tree that glittered and sparkled and shone, that bore stars and rainbows and snow wreaths and gay toys. At first they only drew deep, wondering breaths, and looked at each other with shining eyes. It was all so beautiful and so strange.

Joyce flew here and there, helping to distribute the gifts, feeling her heart grow warmer and warmer as she watched the happy children. "My little daughter never had anything like that in all her life," said one grateful mother as Joyce laid a doll in the child's outstretched arms. "She'll never forget this to her dying day, nor will any of us, dear mademoiselle! We knew not what it was to have so beautiful a Noel!"

When the last toy had been stripped from the branches, it was Cousin Kate's turn to be surprised. At a signal from madame, the children began circling around the tree, singing a song that the sisters at the village school had taught them for the occasion. It was a happy little song about the green pine-tree, king of all trees and monarch of the woods, because of the crown he yearly wears at Noel. At the close every child came up to madame and Cousin Kate and Joyce, to say "Thank you, madame," and "Good night," in the politest way possible.

Gabriel's accordian led them out again, and the music, growing fainter and fainter, died away in the distance; but in every heart that heard it had been born a memory whose music could never be lost,—the memory of one happy Christmas.

Joyce drew a long breath when it was all over, and, with her arm around Madame Desire's shoulder, smiled down at Jules.

"How beautifully it has all ended!" she exclaimed. "I am sorry that we have come to the place to say 'and they all lived happily ever after,' for that means that it is time to shut the book."

"Dear heart," murmered Madame Desire, drawing the child closer to her, "it means that a far sweeter story is just beginning, and it is you who have opened the book for me."

Joyce flushed with pleasure, saying, "I thought this Christmas would be so lonely; but it has been the happiest of my life."

"And mine, too," said Monsieur Ciseaux from the other side of Jules's couch. He took the little fellow's hand in his. "They told me about the tree that you prepared for me. I have been up to look at it, and now I have come to thank you." To the surprise of everyone in the room, monsieur bent over and kissed the flushed little face on the pillow. Jules reached up, and, putting his arms around his uncle's neck, laid his cheek a moment against the face of his stern old kinsman. Not a word was said, but in that silent caress every barrier of coldness and reserve was forever broken down between them. So the little Prince came into his kingdom,— the kingdom of love and real home happiness.

It is summer now, and far away in the little brown house across the seas Joyce thinks of her happy winter in France and the friends that she found through the gate of the giant scissors. And still those scissors hang over the gate, and may be seen to this day, by anyone who takes the trouble to walk up the hill from the little village that lies just across the river Loire, from the old town of Tours.

How Fauntleroy Occurred

CHAPTER I

HIS ENTRANCE INTO THE WORLD

IT HAS ALWAYS been rather interesting to me to remember that he first presented himself in an impenetrable disguise. It was a disguise sufficiently artful to have disarmed the most wary. I, who am not at all a far-sighted person, was completely taken in by him. I saw nothing to warrant in the slightest degree any suspicion that he had descended to earth with practical intentions; that he furtively cherished plans of making himself into the small hero of a book, the picturesque subject of illustrations, the inspiration of a fashion in costume, the very *jeune premiere* in a play over which people in two continents would laugh and cry.

Perhaps in periods before he introduced himself to his family that morning of April 5, 1876, in a certain house in Paris, he may have known all this and laid out his little plans with adroitness and deliberation; but when I first examined him carefully as he lay on my arm looking extremely harmless and extremely fast asleep in his extremely long night-gown, he did not bear at all the aspect of a crafty and designing person; he only looked warm and comfortable and quite resigned to his situation.

He had been clever enough to disguise himself as a baby, a quite new baby in violet powder and a bald head and a florid complexion. He had even put on small, indefinite features and entirely dispensed with teeth, besides professing inability to speak, a fastidious simplicity of taste in the matter of which limited him to the most innocuous milk diet. But beneath this disguise there he lurked, the small individual who, seven years later—apparently quite artlessly and unconsciously—presented his smiling, ingenuous little face to the big world and was smiled back upon by it—Little Lord Fauntleroy. He was a quite unromantic little person. Only a prejudiced maternal parent could have picked him out from among seventy-five other babies of the same age; but somehow we always felt that he had a tiny character of his own, and somehow it was always an amusing little character, and one's natural tendency was to view him in rather a jocular light.

In the first place he had always been thought of as a little girl. It was the old story of "your sister, Betsy Trotwood," and when he presented himself with an unflinching firmness in the unexpected character of a little boy serious remonstrance was addressed to him.

"This habit you have contracted of being a little boy," his mamma said to him, "is most inconvenient. Your name was to be Vivien, 'Vivien, is early English and picturesque and full of colour; Vivian, which is a boy's name, I don't think so much of. It sounds like a dandy, and reminds me of Vivian Grey; but after the way you have behaved it is about all I can do for you, because I am too tired of thinking of names to be equal to inventing anything else."

If it had not been for his disguise and his determination not to be betrayed into the weakness of speech it is quite possible he might have responded:

"If you will trust the matter to me I will manage to reconcile you to the name, and make you feel there is some consolation for the fact that I preferred to be myself, instead of Vivien. Just give me time."

We were, of course, obliged to give him time, and he wasted none if it. One of the favourite jokes was that he was endeavouring to ingratiate himself with us, and by a strict attention to business to merit future patronage. We felt it very clever of him to elect to do this quietly, to occupy the position he had chosen for himself with such unobtrusiveness that no one could possibly object to him. This might really have been the deepest craft. To have proved one's self an individual to whom no one can object on any pretext is really an enormous step in the direction of gaining a foothold. It is quite possible that he realized that the step he had taken had been somewhat premature; that to introduce himself to a family absorbed in study and foreign travel, and a elder brother, aged eighteen months, had not been entirely discreet, and that a general decorum of manner would be required to obliterate the impression that he had been somewhat inconsiderate.

His elder brother had decided to become a stately beauty, and after some indeterminate months had set up as premonitory symptoms large brown eyes, a deepening golden tinge of hair, and a distinguished and gracefully exclusive demeanour.. His opinion of the newcomer was that he was an interloper. I think his private impression was that he was vulgar, also that he was fatuous and unnecessary. He used to stand by his nurse's knee when she held the intruder, and regard her with haughty reflection from under his eyelids. She had hitherto been his sole property, and her defection seemed to him to denote inferior taste and instability of

character. On one occasion, after standing by her in disapproving
silence for some time while he alternately looked at her and then at
the white bundle on her knee, he waved his hand toward the grate,
remarking with more dignity of demeanour than clearness of enun-
ciation:

"F'ow him in 'er fire!"

We were sure that the new member of the family appreciated
the difficulty of his position. We wondered if he had understood
when he had heard us refer to him as the "Little Calamity." After
a few day's acquaintance with him we were afraid he had, and felt
a delicacy in using the term, which we had at first thought rather
a good joke.

Dear Little Calamity, how often we have spoken of that misnomer
since! From his first hour his actions seemed regulated by the
peaceful resolve never to be in the way, and never to make anyone
uncomfortable.

The unvarying serenity with which he devoted himself to absorbing as much nourishment as his small system would hold, and then
sleeping sweetly for hours and most artistically assimilating it, was
quite touching.

"Look at him," his mamma would say. "He is trying to insinuate
himself. He intends to prove that he is really an addition, and that
no family should be without him. But no family can have him,"
she burst forth in a very short time, "no family but ours. Nobody
is rich enough to buy him. He has made his own price, and it is
five hundred thousand million dollars!" When he had selected her
as a parent he had probably observed that she was a susceptible
person—peculiarly susceptible to the special variety of charms he
had to offer. He had analyzed her weakness and his strength, and
had known she was a fitting victim for his seductive arts.

The unflinchingness with which he applied himself to the fine
art of infant fascination was really worth reflecting upon. At thirty
there are numerous methods by which a person may prove that
he is worthy of affection and admiration, at three months his
charms and virtues are limited to a good digestion, a tendency to
somnolence and an unobtrusive temper. The new arrival did not
obtrude upon us any ostentatiously novel attractions. He merely
applied himself to giving his family the most superior specimens
of the meritorious qualities his tender age was entitled to. He
never complained of feeling unwell; he was generally asleep, and

a much longer period than is submitted to usually by persons of his months. And when he did so he invariably wore the air of being engaged in sweet-tempered though profound reflection.

He had not seemed to regret being born in Paris, but he seemed agreeably impressed by America when he was taken there at the age of six weeks. Feeling himself restored to a land of Republican freedom he began to feel at liberty to unfold his hitherto concealed resources. He began by giving less time to sleep and more to agreeable, though inarticulate, conversation. He began to sit up and look around him with soft, shadowy and peculiarly thoughtful eyes. The expression—the dear little dreamy, reflective expression —of his eyes was his most valuable possession. It was a capital. It attracted the attention of his immediate relatives, and ensnared them into discussing his character and wondering what he was thinking of. His eyes were brown, and having heard their colour remarked on in a complimentary manner, he, with great artistic presence of mind, stealthily applied himself to developing upon his hitherto bald head golden hair with a curl in it.

It was his mamma who first discovered this. She was lying upon a grassy slope playing with him and holding him up in the sunlight at arm's length; she saw in the brightness a sort of faint little nimbus of gold crowning him.

"Oh, the Lammie day!" she cried out. ("Lammie day" is not in the dictionary; it was a mere maternal inspiration.) "See what he is doing now! He is putting out a lovely little golden fuzz all over his head—and there is a tiny curl at the ends—like little duck tails! He has asked somebody, or something, perhaps a fairy, what kind of hair I like with brown eyes, and he is doing it on purpose." It seemed not improbable that on inquiring into her character before selecting her he had grounded himself thoroughly in the matter of her tastes, and had found that an insistent desire for a certain beauty in the extremely young was one of her weaknesses also.

From his earliest hours he considered her. He had not anticipated walking alone at nine months old, but in their intimate moments he discovered she had really set her heart upon his doing so.

"Your brother walked alone so beautifully when he was nine months old," she would remark, "and if you wait until you are ten months old I shall feel that you have dishonoured your family and brought my reddish hair with sorrow to the grave."

This being the case, he applied himself to making determined, if slow, little pilgrimages upon the carpet on his hands and knees.

When he was awake he would lie upon his back without revolt for His reward was that the first time he essayed this he was saluted with cries of adulation and joy, notwithstanding the fact that his attempt was rather wobbly in character, and its effect was marred by his losing his balance and rolling over in a somewhat ignominious manner.

"He is creeping!" his mamma said. "He has begun to creep! He is going to walk as soon as Lionel did!" and everything available in the form of an audience was gathered together in the room to exult with acclamations over the enrapturing spectacle of a small thing dragging its brief white frock and soft, plump body, accompanied and illuminated by a hopeful smile, over a nursery carpet.

"He is so original!" his unprejudiced parent exclaimed, with fine discrimination. "He's creeping, of course, and babies have crept before, but he gives it a kind of air, as if he had invented it, and yet was quite modest."

Her discrimination with regard to his elder brother had been quite as fine. There were even persons who regarded her as being prejudiced by undue affection. It has never been actually proved that the aspirant for pedestrian honours had privately procured a calendar and secreted it for daily reference as to the passage of time, but if this were not the case, it was really by a rather singular coincidence that the day before his ninth month was completed he arrested his creeping over the carpet, and dragging himself up by a chair to a standing position, covered himself with glory by staggering, flushed, uncertain, but triumphant, at least six steps across the floor unaided and alone.

He was snatched up and kissed until he was breathless. He was ruffled and tumbled with delightful little shakes and ecstatic little hugs. He bore it all with the modest composure of a conqueror who did not deign trivial airs and graces. His cheeks were warm and pink; he made no remark whatever, but there was in his eyes a soft, coy little smile which only a person of his Machiavelian depth of character could have accomplished. By that time, by adroit machinations and an unbounded knowledge of human weakness, he had assured his position in the respectable family of which he had chosen to become a member. It would have been impossible to oust him, or to work upon the feelings of his relatives in any such manner as would have induced them to listen for a moment to any animadversions upon his conduct. His eyelashes, his indefinite features, his totter, his smile were considered to become matters of the most thrilling national importance.   On the magnificent occasion when he first decided to follow his mamma upstairs, and consequently applied himself to the rather prolonged and serious athletic task of creeping up step by step on his dusty little hands and soft knees, and electrifying her by confronting her when she turned and saw him, with a sweetly smiling and ardent little upturned face, on that occasion it seemed really that it could only be by the most remarkable oversight that there were not columns of editorials on the subject in the London *Times*.

"They write about the passing of Bills in Parliament," his parent remarked, "and about wars and royal marriages, why don't they touch on things of really vital importance?"   It was at this period of existance that his papa was frequently distracted in moments of deep absorption in scientific subjects by being implored to leave his essay upon astigmatism and fix his attention upon his offspring.

"Don't waste him!" he was besought.   "He could not possibly keep up this degree of fascination always.   He might grow out of it, and then just think how you would feel when you reflected that you had read medical books when you might have been watching him pretending to be looking at pictures.   He ought to be economized every moment!"

But the most charming feature of his character was that his knowledge of the possession of glittering accomplishments, which were innumerable, never betrayed him into forgetting his attitude toward the entire world was one of the most perfect good fellowship.   When he was spoken to he smiled, when he kissed, even by unprepossessingly familiar persons, he always comported himself with graceful self-control and dignity.   The trying fact, which I am sure was more apparent to no one than to himself, that there were individuals whose idea of entertaining him was to make blatant idiots of themselves, was never resented by him openly.   When they uttered strange sounds and poked his soft cheeks, or tumbled him about in an unseemly manner, it was his habit to gaze at them with deep but not disdainful curiosity and interest, as if he were trying to be just toward them and explain to himself their point of view.

"It really must be rather fatiguing to him not to be able to express himself," was his mamma's opinion.   "He has evidently so many opinions in reserve."

He was so softly plump, he was so sweet-tempered, he was so pretty! One forget all about his early English sister Vivien.   It was as if she had never been contemplated for a moment.   The word "calamity" was artfully avoided in conversation. One felt unworthy and rather blushed if one caught sight of it in literature. When he invented a special little habit of cuddling up to his mamma in a warm, small heap, and in his sleep making for her a heavenly downy necklace of both his arms, with his diminutive palms locked together to hold her prisoner through the night, she began to feel it quite possible that his enslaving effect upon her might be such as to enfeeble an intellect never of the most robust. But she knew him by this time well enough to realize that it would be useless to rebel, and that she might as well succumb.

She succumbed more and more as the days went by. But she also observed that everybody else succumbed. While making the most of his mental charms and graces he gave a great deal of attention to his physical attractions. It was believed that he concentrated his attention upon his hair. He encouraged it to develop from the golden fuzz into a golden silk, from the tiny duck tails to shining rings, from rings to a waving aureole, from the aureole to an entrancing mop of yellow, which tumbled over his forehead and gave his up-looking eyes a prettiness of expression.

And how like him it was to make a point of never objecting to have this wayward, though lovely growth brushed. What a *supplice* he might have made of the ceremony for his family if he had resented it and rebelled. But, on the contrary, it was believed that he siezed upon the opportunity offered by it to gild the refined gold of his amiability of disposition as it were. Speaking as a person with some knowledge of the habits of the extremely young, I should say that there may be numbers of maternal parents who will scarcely believe that one of the most enchanting hours of the day was a certain time in the morning when he leaned against his mamma's knee and gave himself up to engaging conversation while his tangles were being taken out. He made not the slightest objection to being curled and brushed and burnished up and made magnificent. His soft, plump body rested confidingly against the supporting knee, and while the function proceeded he devoted himself to agreeable remark and analytical observation.

There was an expression of countenance it was his habit to wear at such times which was really a matter of the finest art. It combined philosophic patience, genial leniency, and a sweet determination to make the very best of a thing which was really beautiful to behold. It was at these times that a series of nursery romances, known as "The Hair-Curling Series," was invented and related.

They were notable chiefly for good, strong dramatic colouring, and their point was the illustration of the useful moral that little boys with a great deal of beautiful curly hair are naturally rewarded—if they are always good when it is brushed—by delightful adventures, such as being played with by fairies and made friends with by interesting wild animals, whose ravenous propensities are softened to the most affectionate mildness by the sight of such high-mindedness in tender youth.   There was one story, known as "The Good Wolf," which lasted for months and was a never-ending source of delight, as it rejoiced in features which could be varied to adapt themselves to any circumstance or change of taste in playthings. It was the laudable habit of the good wolf to give presents to little boys who were deserving, besides taking them delightful rides in a little sleigh, and one could vary the gifts and excursions to an unlimited extent.   Another, known as "The Mournful Story of Benny," was a fearful warning, but ended happily, and as it was not of a personal nature was not disapproved of, and was listened to with respectful and sympathising interest, though "The Good Wolf" was preferred.

A delightfully intelligent little expression, and an occasional dear little gurgling laugh when the best points were made, convinced me that the point of view of the listener had a appreciation of the humour between the lines quite as clear in a four-year-old way as that of the relater of the incidents.   He revelled in the good wolf, and was concerned by the misfortunes of Benny, who had brought tragedy upon himself by being so lost to all sense of virtue as to cut off his curls; but he knew they were highly-coloured figures, and part of a subtle and delightful joke.

But long before this he had learned to talk, and it was then that we were introduced to the treasures of his mind.

What was the queer little charm which made everyone like him so much, which made everyone smile when he looked at them, which made everyone listen when he spoke, which made arms quite involuntarily close around his small body when he came within reach?

The person who made the closest study of his character devoted five or six years to it before she was quite sure what this charm consisted in.   Then she decided that it was formed of a combination of fortunate characteristics, which might have lost all their value of fascination but for their being illumined by the warmth and brightness of a purely kind little heart full of friendliness to the whole world.

He was pretty, but many little boys were pretty; he was quaint and amusing, but so are many scores. The difference between this one tiny individuality and others was that he seemed to have been born without sense of the existence of any barrier between his own innocent heart and any other.

I think it had never occurred to him that anyone could possibly be unfriendly or unloving to him. He was a perfectly human little thing, not a young cherub, but a rational baby, who made his frocks exceedingly dirty, and rejoiced sweetly in the making of mud pies. But, somehow, his radiant smile of belief in one's sympathy, even with his mud pies, minimized the trouble of contending with the earthly features of him.

His opinion evidently was that the world was made of people who loved him and smiled if they saw him, of things one could play with, and stories one could listen to, and of friends and relations who were always ready to join in the play and tell the stories. He went peacefully to the curl-brushing ordeal, perhaps, because of this confiding sureness that any hand that dealt with him would touch him tenderly. He never doubted it.

One morning, before he was three years old, he trotted into the dining-room with a beautifully preoccupied expression, evidently on business thoughts intent. The breakfast was over, but his mamma was still sitting at the table reading.

She heard the tiny pattering of feet coming down the hall before he entered. She had thought him with his nurse, but he appeared to be returning from some unusual expedition to the front door, which, as it was a warm, early summer morning, stood open.

She was always curious about his mental processes, and so when he trotted to the table with his absorbed air, and stood upon his tiptoes making serious efforts to gain possession of a long loaf of French bread, she regarded him with interest. He was so little and the roll of bread was so long, and his intentions to do something practical with it were so evident. Somehow one of his allurenemts was that he was always funny, and he was so, purely because his small point of view was always so innocently serious.

"What does mamma's baby want?" she asked.

He looked at her with an air of sweet good faith, and secured the bread, tucking it in all its dignity of proportion under the very shortest possible arm.

"Lady," he said, "lady, f'ont door—want b'ead."

And he trotted off with a simple security in the sense of doing the right and only admissible thing, which it was reposeful to behold.

His mamma left her book hurriedly and trotted after him. Such a quaint baby figure he was with the long French roll under his arm! And he headed straight for the front door.

Standing upon the top step was an exceedingly dilapidated and disreputable little negro girl with an exceedingly dirty and broken basket on her arm. This basket was intended to contain such scraps of food as she might beg for. She was grinning a little, and at the same time looking a little anxious as the baby came toddling to her, the sun on his short curls, the loaf under his short arm.

He dropped the loaf into her basket with sweet friendliness.

"B'ead, lady," he said.

And as she scurried away he turned to smile at his approaching mamma with the confidence of a two-year-old angel.

"Lady, b'ead," he remarked succinctly, and the situation was explained.

The dirty little coloured girl was a human thing in petticoats, consequently she was a lady. His tender mind saw no other conclusion to be arrived at. She had expressed a desire for bread. On his mamma's breakfast-table there was a beautiful long loaf. Of course it must be given to her. The question of demand and supply was so easily settled, so he trotted after the bread. The mere circumstances of short legs and short arms did not deter a spirit like his.

And it was this simple and unquestioning point of view which made him adorable.

CHAPTER II

IN WHITE FROCK AND SASH

IN THE DRAWING-ROOM, in full war paint of white frock and big sash, he was the spirit of innocent and friendly hospitality, in the nursery he was a brilliant entertainment, below stairs he was the admiration and delight of the domestics. The sweet temper which prompted him to endeavour to sustain agreeable conversation with the guest who admired him led him, also, to enter into friendly converse with the casual market-man at the back door, and to entertain with lively anecdote and sparkling repartee the extremely stout coloured cook in the kitchen. He endeavoured to assist her in the performance of her more arduous culinary duties, and by his sympathy and interest sustained her in many trying moments. When he was visiting her department chuckles and giggles might be heard issuing from the kitchen when the door opened. Those who heard them always knew that they were excited by the moral or social observations or affectionate advice and solace of the young but distinguished guest.

"Me an' Carrie made that pudding," he would kindly explain at dinner. "It's a very good pudding. Carrie's such a nice cook. She lets me help her."

And his dimples would express such felicity, and his eyes beam from under his tumbling love locks with such pleasure at his confidence in the inevitable rapture of his parents at the announcement of his active usefulness, that no one possessed sufficient strength of mind to correct the grammatical structure of the remarks.

There is a picture—not one of Mr. Birch's—which I think will always remain with me. It is ten years since I saw it, but I see it still. It is the quaint one of a good-looking, stout, coloured woman climbing slowly up a back staircase with a sturdy little fellow on her back, his legs astride her spacious waist, his arms clasped round her neck, his lovely mop of yellow hair tumbling over her shoulder, upon which his cheek affectionately and comfortably rests.

It does not come within the province of cooks to toil up stairs with little boys on their backs, especially when the little boys have stout little legs of their own, and are old enough to wear Jersey suits and warlike scarfs of red; but in this case the carrying upstairs was an agreeable ceremony, partly jocular and wholly affectionate, engaged in by two confidants, and the bearer enjoyed it as much as did her luxurious burden.

"We're friends, you know," he used to say. "Carrie's my friend and Dan's my friend. Carrie's such a kind cook and Dan's such a nice waiter."

That was the whole situation in a nutshell. They were his friends, and they formed together a mutual admiration society.

His conversation with them we knew was enriched by gems of valuable and entertaining information. Among his charms was his desire to acquire information, and the amiable readiness with which he imparted it to his acquaintances. We gathered that while assisting in the making of pudding he was lavish in the bestowal of useful knowledge. Intimate association and converse with him had revealed to his mamma that there was no historical, geographical or scientific fact which might not be impressed upon him in story form, and fill him with rapture.   Monsoons and typhoons, and the crossing of the Great Desert on camels he found absorbing; the adventures of Romulus and Remus and their good wolf, and the founding of Rome held him spellbound.   He found the vestal virgins and their task of keeping up the sacred fires in the temple sufficiently interesting to be made into a species of dramatic entertainment during his third year. It was his habit to creep out of his crib very early in the morning, and entertain himself agreeably in the nursery until other people got up.   One morning his mamma, lying in her room, which opened into the nursery, heard a suspicious sound of unlawful poking at the fire.

"Vivvie," she said, "is that you?"

The poking ceased, but there was no reply.   Silence reigned for a few moments, and then the sound was heard again.

"Vivain," said his anxious parent, "you are not allowed to touch the fire."

Small, soft feet came pattering hurriedly into the room; round the footboard of the bed a ruffled head and seriously expostulatory little countenance appeared.

"Don't you know," he said with an air of lenient remonstrance, "don't you *know* I's a westal wirgin?"

It would be impossible to explain him without relating anecdotes. Is there not an illustration of the politeness of his demeanour and the grace of his infant manners in the reply renowned in his history, made at the age of four, when his mamma was endeavouring to explain some interesting point in connection with the structure of his small, plump body?   It was his habit to ask so many searching questions that it was necessary for his immediate relatives to endeavour to render their minds compact masses of valuable facts. But on this occasion his inquires had led him into such unknown depths as were beyond him for the moment—only for the moment of course.   He listened to the statement made, his usual engaging expression of delighted interest gradually becoming tinged with polite doubtfulness.   When the effort at explanation was at an end he laid his hand upon his mamma's knee with apologetic but firm gentleness.

"Well, you see," he said, "of course you know I *believe* you, dearest" (the most considerate stress was laid upon the "believe"), "but *ascuse* me," with infinite delicacy, "*ascuse* me, I do *not* think it is true."

The tender premonitory assurance that his confidence was unimpaired, even though he was staggered by the statement made, was so affectionately characteristic of him, and the apologetic grace of the "ascuse me, dearest," was all his own.

There might be little boys who were oblivious of, and indifferent to the attractions of simoons who saw no charm in the interior arrangements of camels, and were indifferent to the strata of the earth, but in his enterprising mind such subjects wakened the liveliest interest, and a little habit he had of suddenly startling his family by revealing to them the wealth of his store of knowledge by making casual remarks was at once instructive and enlivening.

"A camel has ever so many stomachs," he might sweetly announce while sitting in his high chair and devoting himself to his breakfast, the statement appearing to evolve itself from dreamy reflection. "It fills them with water. Then it goes across the desert and carries things. Then it isn't thirsty."

He was extremely pleased with the camel, and was most exhaustive in his explanations of him. It was not unlikely that Carrie and Dan might have passed a strict examination on the subject of incidents connected with the crossing of the Great Desert. He also found his bones interesting, and was most searching in his inquiries as to the circulation of his blood. But he had been charmed with his bones from his first extremely early acquaintance with them, as witness an incident of his third year which is among the most cherished by his family of their recollections of him.

He sat upon his mamma's knee before the nursery fire, a small round, delightful thing, asking questions. He had opened up the subject of his bones by discovering that his short, plump arm seemed built upon something solid, which he felt at once necessary to investigate.

"It is a little bone," his mamma said, "and there is one in your other arm, and one in each of your legs. Do you know," giving him a caressing little shake, "if I could see under all the fat on your little body I should find a tiny, weenty skeleton?"

He looked up enraptured. His dimples had a power of expressing delight never equalled by any other baby's dimples. His eyes and his very curls themselves seemed to have something to do with it.

"If you did," he said, "if you did *would you give it to me to play with?*"

He was a very fortunate small person in the fact that nature had been extremely good to him in the matter of combining his mental sweetness and quaintness with the great charm of physical picturesqueness. All his little attitudes and movements were picturesque. When he stood before one to listen he fell unconsciously into some quaint attitude, when he talked he became ingenuously dramatic, when he sat down to converse he mentally made a droll or delightful and graceful little picture of himself. His childish body was as expressive as his glowing little face. Any memory of him is always accompanied by a distinct recollection of the expression of his face and some queer or pretty position which seemed to be part of his mental attitude. When he wore frocks his habit of standing with his hands clasped behind his back in the region of a big sash, and his trick of sitting down with a hand upon each of the plump knees, a brevity of skirt disclosed, were things to be remembered; when he was inserted into Jersey suits and velvet doublet and knickerbockers his manly little fashion of standing hands upon hips, and sitting in delicious, all unconsciously aesthetic poses were positively features of his character. What no dancing-master could have taught him his graceful, childish body fell into with entire naturalness, merely because he was a picturesque, small person in both body and mind.

Could one ever forget him as he appeared one day at the seaside when coming up from the beach with his brief trousers rolled up to his stalwart little thighs? He stood upon the piazza, spade and bucket in hand, looking with deep, sympathetic interest at a male visitor who was on the point of leaving the house. This visitor was a man who had recently lost his wife suddenly. He was a near relative of a guest in the house, and the young friend of all the world had possibly heard his bereavement discussed. But at six years old it is not the custom of small boys to concern themselves about such events. It seems that this one did, however, though the caller was not one of his intimates. He stood apart for a few moments looking at him with a tenderly reflective countenance. His mamma seeing his absorption privately wondered what he was thinking of. But presently he transferred both spade and bucket to one hand, and came forward holding out the other. I do think not anything could have been quainter and more sweet than the kind little face which uplifted itself to the parting guest.

"Mr. Wenham," he said, "I'm *very* sorry for you, Mr. Wenham, about your wife being dead. I'm very sorry for you. I know how you must miss her."

Even the sympathy of six years old does not go for nothing. There was a slight moisture in Mr. Wenham's eyes as he shook the small, sandy hand, and his voice was not quite steady as he answered, "Thank you, Vivvie, thank you."

It was when he was spending the summer at this place that he made the acquaintance of the young lady whose pony he regarded as a model of equine strength and beauty. It was the tiniest possible pony, whose duty it was to draw a small phaeton containing a small girl and her governess. But I was told it was a fine sight to behold the blooming little gentleman caller standing before this stately equipage, his hands on his hips, his head upon one side, regarding the steed with quite the experienced air of an aged jockey.

"That's a fine horse," he said. "You see it's got plenty of muscle. What I like is a horse with plenty of muscle."

And when we drove away from the cottage at the end of the summer, I myself perhaps a shade saddened, as one often is by the thought that the days of sunshine and roses are over, he put his small hand in mine and looked up at me wistfully.

"We liked that little house, didn't we, dearest?" he said. "We will always like it, won't we?"

"Do you know my friend Mrs. Wilkins?" he inquired one day when he was still small enough to wear white frocks, and not old enough to extend his explorations further than the part of the quiet street opposite the house he lived in.

"And who is your friend Mrs. Wilkins?" his mamma inquired.

"She is a very nice lady that saw me through her window when I was playing on the pavement, and we talked to each other, and she asked me to come into her house. She's such a kind lady, and she paints beautiful cups and saucers. She's my friend. And her cook is a nice lady too. She lives in the basement and she talks to me through the window. She likes little boys. I have two friends in that house."

"My friend Mrs. Wilkins" became one of his cherished intimates. His visits to her were frequent and prolonged.

"I've just been to see my friend Mrs. Wilkins," he would say, or, "My friend Mrs. Wilkins' husband is very kind to me. We go to his store, and he gives me oranges."

It is not improbable that he also painted china during his calls upon his friend Mrs. Wilkins. It is certain that if he did not otherwise assist his attitude was that of an enthusiastic admirer of the art. That his conversation with the lady embraced many subjects we have evidence in an anecdote frequently related with great glee by those to whom the incident was reported. I myself was not present during the ingenuous summing up of the charm of social life, but I have always mentally seen him taking his part in the scene in one of his celebrated conversational attitudes, in which he usually sat holding his plump knee in a manner which somehow seemed to express deep, speculative thought.

"Are you in society, Mrs. Wilkins?" he inquired ingenuously.

"What *is* being in society, Vivvie?" Mrs. Wilkins replied probably with the intention of drawing forth his views.

"It's—well—there are a great many carriages, you know, and a great many ladies come to see you. And they say 'How *are* you, Mrs. Burnett? So glad to find you at home.' Gabble, gabble, gabble, gabble. '*Good* morning!' And they go away. That's it."

I am not quite sure that I repeat the exact phrasing, but the idea is intact, and the point which inspired the hearers with such keen joy was that he had absolutely no intention of making an unfriendly criticism. He was merely painting an impressionist's picture. On his own part he was fond of society. It delighted him to be allowed to come into the drawing-room on the days when his mamma was "at home." This function impressed him as an agreeable festivity. As he listened to the "gabble, gabble, gabble," he beamed with friendly interest. He admired the ladies, and regarded them as beautiful and amiable. It was his pleasure to follow the departing ones into the hall and render them gallant assistance with their wraps.

"I like ladies, dearest," he would say. "They are so pretty."

At what age he became strongly imbued with the staunchest Republican principles it would be difficult to say. He was an unflinching Republican.

"My dearest Mamma," he wrote me in one of the splendid epistolary efforts of his earliest years,—

"I am sorry that I have not had time to write to you before. I have been so occupied with the presidential election. The boys in my school knock me down and jump on me because they want me to go Democrat. But I am still a strong Republican. I send you a great many hugs and kisses.

"Yout obedient and humble son and servant,

"VIVIAN."

He was given to inventing picturesque terminations to his letters, and he seemed particularly pleased with the idea of being my humble or obedient son and servant. The picture the letter brought to my mind of a flushed and tumbled but staunch little Republican engaged in a sort of kindergarten political tussle with equally flushed and tumbled little Democrats wore an extremely American aspect. Figuratively speaking, he plunged into the thick of the electioneering fray. He engaged in political argument upon all available occasions. Fortunately for his peace of mind, Carrie and Dan favoured the Republican party. Dan took him to see Republican torchlight processions, and held him upon his shoulders while he waved his small hat, his hair flying about his glowing face while he shouted himself hoarse. No unworthy party cry of " 'Rah for Hancock!" went unanswered by the clarion response. At the sound of such a cry in the street the nursery windows flew open with a bang, and two ecstatic Republicans (himself and brother) almost precipitated themselves into space shouting " 'Rah for Garfield!" Without such precautions he felt his party would be lost. I think he was six when he discovered that he was a supporter of the movement in favour of female suffrage. It was rather a surprise to us when this revealed itself, but his reasons were such of a serious and definite nature that they were arguments not to be refuted.

When he gave them he was leaning against a window-ledge in a room in a seaside home, his hands in his red sash, his countenance charming with animation.

"I believe they ought to be allowed to vote if they like it," he said, " 'cause what should we do if there were no ladies? Nobody would have any mothers or any wives."

"That is true," his maternal audience encouraged him by saying. "The situation would be serious."

"And nobody could grow up," he proceeded. "When anyone's a baby, you know, he hasn't any teeth, and he can't eat bread and things. And if there were no ladies to take care of him when he was very first born he'd die. I think people ought to let them vote if they want to."

This really seemed so to go to the root of things that the question appeared disposed of.

One laughed, and laughed at him. All his prettiness was quaint, and so innocent that its unconsciousness made one smile. Only sometimes—quite often—while one was smiling one was queerly touched and stirred.

What a picture of a beautiful, brave little spirit, aflame with young young fervour, he was the day I went into a room and found him reading for the first time in his brief life the story of the American Revolution.

He sat in a large chair, one short leg tucked under him, a big book on his knee, his love locks tumbling over his ecstasied child face. He looked up glowing when I entered. His cheeks were red, his eyes were beautiful.

"Dearest," he said, "dearest, listen. *Here's* a brave man, here's a brave man! This is what he says, 'Give me liberty or give me death!' " It was somehow so movingly incongruous. This "pretty page with dimpled chin," stirred so valiantly by his "liberty or death." I kissed his golden thatch, laughing and patting it; but a little lump was in my throat.

Where did he learn—faithful and tender heart—to be such a lover as he was? Surely no woman ever had such a lover before! What taught him to pay such adorable, childish court, and to bring the first fruits of every delight to lay upon one shrine? In the small garden where he played—a toddling thing accumulating stains of grass and earth in truly human fashion on his brief white frock— the spring scattered sparsely a few blue violets. How he applied himself to searching for them, to gather them with pretty laborious- ness until he had collected a small, warm handful, somewhat dilapidated before it was large enough to be brought upstairs in the form of a princely floral gift.

It is nearly fourteen years since they were first laid at my feet— these darling little grubby handfuls of exhausted violets—but I can hear yet the sound of the small feet climbing the staircase stoutly but carefully, the exultant voice shouting at intervals all the way up from the first flight, "Sweet dearest! Sweet de-ar-est! I got somefin' for you! Please let me in."

So many beautiful names had been tried by turns by himself and brother, but they found "sweetest" and "sweet dearest" the most satisfactory. Finally they decided upon "dearest" as combining and implying the sentiment they were inspired by.

There was in a certain sacred workroom at the top of the house a receptacle known as the "treasure drawer." It was always full of wonderful things, rich gifts brought carefully and with lavish generosity from the grass in the back yard, from dust heaps, from the street, from anywhere; bits of glass or pebble, gorgeous advertis- ing cards, queerly-shaped twigs or bits of wood, pictures out of papers, small, queer toys, possessing some charm which might make them valuable to an appreciative maternal relative. And just before they were presented I always heard the small feet on the stairs, the knock on the door, and the delightful, confiding voice outside,—

"Please may I come in? I've brought a treasure for you, dearest."

We always spoke of them as "treasures." They seemed so beautiful and valuable to the donor that love brought them at once as a gift to love, and the recipient saw them with his eyes.

The very first bud which appeared on the old-fashioned rose-bushes at the back of the house was watched for and discovered when it was a tiny, hard, green thing.

"There's a bud," he would say, "and I'm watching till it is a rose, so that I can give it to you."

There is nothing so loving as a child who is loved. What valuable assistance he rendered in the matter of toilette. How charmed he was with any pretty new thing. How delighted to be allowed to put on slippers or take them off, stand by the dressing-table and hand pins, and give the benefit of his admiring advice. And how adorable it was to come home late from a party and find the pin-cushion adorned with a love-letter scrawled boldly in lead pencil and secured by a long pin. In conjunction with his brother—who was the troubadour of love from his infancy, and who has a story of his own—he invented the most delightful surprises for those late returns. Sometimes pieces of candy wrapped in paper awaited the arrival, sometimes *billets doux*, sometimes singular rhymes courageously entitled, "A Valentine." The following was the fine flower of all:—

MY MAMA

"O my swetest little mama,
Sweteness that can ne'er be told
Dwells all decked in glory behind thy bosom folds.
In love and tender sweteness
Thy heart has no compare
And as through the path of sorrow
Thy heart goes wandering on
Thow always lend a helping hand
To all who are alone.

"ESEX ESEX."

"What does 'Essex' mean, darling?" I asked.

"I don't know what it means," he said sweetly, "and I didn't spell it right at first. But you know when anyone writes poetry they nearly always put another name at the end, and I thought Essex would do." He was so desirous of making it complete!

CHAPTER III

IN BOYHOOD AND NOW

As a travelling companion what a success he was! How he made friends in the train, at railway stations, on steamers. How, if one lost sight of him for a moment, he invariably reappeared full of delight with the information that he had "found a friend."

As I was struggling in the usual manner up the crowded gangway of an ocean steamer on one occasion his flushed and radiant countenance appeared over the rail where he had climbed.

"Dearest, dearest," he said, "I've found a friend. He's a French gentleman and can't speak English."

He found him on the tug, and they had apparently sworn eternal amity between the wharf and the steamer, though how this had been accomplished I was never quite able to determine, as he had only just begun to attack valiantly a verb or so of the first conjugation. But with the assistance of "donnor," "aller," "aimer," and a smile like his nothing was impossible.

His circle of acquaintances during an ocean voyage was choice and large. And one languid passenger lying in her steamer chair with cushions behind her and fur robes over her was never passed without the affectionate, inquiring smiles of a protector, and at intervals through all the day he presented himself to "look after" her.

"Are you all right, dearest?" he would say. "Do you want your feet tucked in? Did the desk-steward bring you your lunch? Are your cushions comfortable?" And these matters being attended to he would kiss her gaily and run off to explore engines, or gather valuable information about walking beams.

On several occasions he and his brother made some rather long railway journeys alone. It was quite safe to send them. If they had not been able to take care of themselves half the world would have taken care of them. Conductors conversed with them, passengers were interested in them, and they arrived at the end of their travels laden with tribute. After one such journey taken together between Washington and Boston with what joy they performed their toilettes through an entire summer, with the assistance of a large box of wonderful soaps and perfumes sent to them by acquaintance made *en voyage*.

"He was Lionel's friend," Vivian explained. "I think he said he was a drummer. He was so nice to us. My friend that I made was a professor in a college, I believe, and he gave me this to remember him by."

"This" was a pretty nugget of gold, and was accompanied by a card, on which the donor had written the most affectionately kind things of the pleasure he had had in his brief acquaintance with his young travelling companion, whose *bonne mine* he should not soon forget.

One could always be quite sure that he would give no trouble during a journey, that he would always be ready to perform any service, that no railroad nor ocean boat official could withstand him when he presented himself with a smiling request.

It is easy to call to mind, at any moment, some memory of him, his face flushed, his hair damp on his forehead, his eyes courageous, as he struggled with something too big for him he had felt it his duty to take charge of, as he swayed with the crowd down the gangway of some steamer at Southampton or some *paquebot* at Calais.

"It is too heavy for you, darling," one would say. "You look so hot. Let me carry it."

"Oh, no," would be his valiant answer. "I'm all right, dearest. It's rather a warm day, but a boy doesn't mind being warm."

Even foreign languages did not appal him.

"I'm only a little boy, you know," he would say, cheerfully. "It doesn't matter if it does sound funny, just so that they understand me. I like to talk to them."

So he conversed with Annunciata in the kitchen and Luigi in the dining-room, as it had been his habit to converse with Carrie and Dan years before, for by this time his love-locks had been cropped and had changed to brown; but he still remained the same charming and engaging little person.

"Boys are sometimes a great trouble," commented Luigi, in referring to him and his brother, "but these—they are little *signorini*."

Fauntleroy had "occurred" nearly four years before the time when he exhausted all the resources of the Paris Exposition; but it was still Fauntleroy, though a taller one in schoolboy suit and Eton collar, and shorn of his *boucles blonde*, who marched off at nine o'clock every morning for two weeks, and spent the day exploring the treasures of the Exhibition. Sometimes he was quite alone, sometimes he had appointments with some "friends" he had made in the passage from New York to Havre—three interesting men whose connection with the electrical exhibit inspired him with admiration and delight. My impression is that they did not speak French, and that it enraptured him to place his vocabulary at their disposal.

"They are so kind to me, dearest," he said, just as he had said it at three years old when he visited his "friend Mrs. Wilkins."

"It must be an entertaining spectacle," I often thought, "to see him walk into the restaurant quite unattended, order his little *dejeuner a la fourchette*, dispose of it in dignified solitude at a small table, and present the *garçon* with a *pourboire* as if he were forty. I should like to be a spectator from afar. No doubt the waiters know him and make jocular remarks among themselves."

But it was when he was only seven that Fauntleroy really occurred. He had been so amusing and interesting that summer, and I had reflected upon him so much. Every few days I heard some delightful anecdote about him, or saw him do something incomparably quaint. What led me most into speculation was the effect he invariably produced upon people, touching little fascinations he exercised.

"Do you know I never saw a child like him?" said a clever man of the world who had spent an hour talking to him.

And curiously enough it was exactly the idea expressed by an old coloured aunty years before.

"Dat chile," she said, "he suttanly ain't like no other chile. 'Tain't jest dat he's smart—though cose he's smart, smart as they make 'em. It's sump'n else. An' he's the frien'liest little human I ever seed—he suttanly is!"

I had been ill that year and the year before it; and of that illness I have many memories which are beautiful and touching things. One is of many disturbed and weary nights when the door of my room opened quietly and a little figure entered; such an adorable little figure, in a white night-gown, and with bright hair tumbled by sleep falling about a serious small face.

"I've come to take care of you, dearest," he would say with his indescribable protecting and comforting air. "I'll sit by you and make you go to sleep."

And somehow there seemed to emanate from his childish softness a sort of soothing which could not have been put into words.

It was his special province to put me to sleep when I was restless. He assumed it as a sacred duty, and had the utmost confidence in his power to do it.

"I'll put you to sleep," he would say. "I will just sit by you and hold your hand and make you quiet."

How long had he sat by me on that one night which I shall always remember? I do not know. But he had been so quiet and had sat holding my hand so long that I could not find it in my heart to let him know that the charm had not worked and that I was not really asleep. I pretended that I was, lying very still and breathing with soft regularity.

He stayed quite a long time after I knew he thought I was quiet for the night, he was so determined to be quite sure that nothing would disturb me. At last he began with the most cautious softness to take his hand away. When he had been a baby I had sometimes laid him down to sleep with just such cautious movement. How gradually and softly the small fingers released themselves one by one, how slowly, with what infinite precaution of slowness the warm, kind little palm was detached from mine. Then there was a mysterious, careful movement, and I knew he was leaving his chair. I dared not open my eyes for fear he would see me and be heart-broken because I was awake. What was he doing? There were no footsteps, and yet he was moving a little—a very little it seemed. And the movement was so slow and interrupted by such pauses that the length of time it lasted added to my curiousness. What idea had he been inspired by? Whatsoever he was doing he was putting his entire soul into, and he should not be crushed by the thought that it was all in vain. When I could hear that he had reached the door I opened an eye very cautiously. The opening of the door was as clever and quiet as the mysterious movement. It was opened only a little, there was more careful movement, and then it was drawn to. But though I had been looking directly at the slip of light I had not seen him. Somehow he had passed through without coming within my line of vision.

I lay mystified. The incomprehensibleness of it gave me something to think about. His room was near my own, and I knew that he went to it and got into bed. I knew, also, that he would be asleep as soon as his curly head touched the pillow.

He had been asleep perhaps an hour when his brother came in.

He had been spending the evening at the house of a friend. He was usually a tender and thoughtful thing himself, but this night the excitement of festivity had intoxicated him and made him forgetful. He came up the staircase and ran into the bedroom with a childish rush.

Exactly what happened I could only guess at. I had reason to suppose that my young protector and medical attendant was wakened with some extra sense of flurry taking place. He evidently sat up in bed in reproachful despair.

"What have I done?" said his brother. "What is the matter?"

I heard tears in the plaintive little voice that answered—actual tears.

"Oh!" he said. "I know you've wakened her! I know you have! It was so hard to get her to sleep. And at last I did, and then I was so afraid of wakening her that I went down on the floor and crawled out of the room on my hands and knees. And I think it took an hour."

"Darling," I murmured in the drowsiest possible tone when he crept into the room to look at me, "I've had a lovely sleep, and I'm going to sleep again. You made me so quiet." But with the most serious difficulty I restrained myself from clutching him in my arms with a force which would have betrayed to him all my adoring duplicity.

It was things such as these I remembered when he was so deliciously amusing, and I heard stories of him every day.

Sometimes when swinging in my hammock on the piazza I caught sight of him flying on his small bicycle down the tree-shaded avenue, a delightful, animated picture, his strong, graceful child body beautifully defined in his trim, close-fitting Jersey suit, his red scarf and fez brilliant touches of colour, his waving, flying hair brightened to gold as he darted through the sunshine and into the shade. I used to say to myself:

"He is so good to look at! He is so pretty; that is why everyone likes him so." And then when I heard him say some quaint thing which was an actual delight through its droll ingenuousness, I said: "It is because he is so amusing!"

So I studied him day after day, often trying to imagine the effect his fearless candour and unsophisticated point of view would have upon certain persons who did not know his type.

I was convalescing from my long illness and had plenty of time to amuse myself with such speculations. He was such a patriotic young American; he was so engaged in an impending presidential election at the time; his remarks were so well worth hearing. I began, among other fancies about him, to imagine his making them with that frankly glowing face to conservative English people. He had English blood in his veins, and things more unheard of had occurred than that through a combination of circumstances he might be surrounded by things very new to him.

"When a person is a duke," he had said to me once, "what makes him one? What has he done?" His opinion evidently was, that dukedoms were a species of reward for superhuman sweetness of character and brilliant intellectual capacity. I began to imagine the interest that would be awakened in his mind by the contemplation of ducal personages.

It amused me to analyze the subject of what his point of view would be likely to be. I knew it would be productive of immense entertainment to his acquaintances. I was sure that the duke would be subjected to sweet but searching cross-questioning, and that much lively interest would be felt in the subject of coronets. He would regard them as a species of eccentric hat. What questions he would ask, what enthusiasm he would display when he was impressed by things beautiful or stately and interesting! Would he seem "a cheeky little beggar" to less republican minds than his own? I asked myself this curiously. But no, I was sure he would not. He would be so simple; he would expect such splendour of mind and of noble friendliness that the hupothetical duke would like him as Dan and Carrie did, and he would end by saying "My friend, the Duke of Blankshire," as affectionately as he had said "My friend, the milkman."

It was only a thread of fancy for a while, but one day I had an idea.

"I will write a story about him," I said. "I will put him in a world quite new to him and see what he will do. How shall I bring a small American boy into close relationship with an English nobleman—irascible, conservative, disagreeable? He must live with him talk to him, show him his small, unconscious republican mind. He will be more effective if I make him a child who has lived in the simplest possible way. Eureka! Son of younger son, separated from ill-tempered noble father because he has married a poor young American beauty. Young father dead, elder brothers dead, boy comes into title! How it would amaze him and bewilder him!

Yes, there it is, and Vivian shall be he—just Vivian with his curls and his eyes, and his friendly, kind, little soul. Little Lord Something-or-other. What a pretty title—Little Lord—, Little Lord—, what?"

And a day later it was Little Lord Fauntleroy. A story like that is easily written. In part it was being lived before my eyes.

"I can wash myself quite well, thank you," he would say, scrubbing vigorously one day. "I can do it quite well, dearest, if some one will just 'zamine the corners."

He had always spoken very clearly, but there were a few words his pronunciation of which endeared them inexpressibly to me. On the evening of the day before "Fauntleroy" spent his first morning with "Lord Dorincourt" he brought into my room a parlour baseball game to show me.

It was a lovely thing to see his delight over it, and to note the care with which he tried to make all technical points clear to an interested but unintelligent parent. What vigorous little attitudes he threw himself into when he endeavoured to show me how the ball was thrown in the real game!

"I'm afraid that I am a very stupid little mammy," I said. "What does the first base do? And what is the pitcher for? I'm very dull, you see."

"Oh, no!" he said. "No, you're not, dearest! It's me, you know. I'm afraid that I'm not a very good 'splainer. And besides, you are a lady, you know, and ladies don't play base-ball."

Almost every day I recorded something he had said or suggested.

And how delightful it was to read the manuscript to him and his brother. He used to sit in a large arm-chair holding his knee or with his hands in his pockets.

"Do you know," he said to me once, "I like that boy? There's one thing about him, he never forgets about dearest."

When the first appearance of the false claimant occurred he turned quite pale; so did his brother.

"Oh, dearest!" they gasped, "why did you do that? Oh, don't do it!"

"What will he do?" the occupant of the arm-chair asked. "Won't he, dearest, be the Earl's boy any more?"

"'That other boy,' said Fauntleroy tremulously, to Lord Dorincourt, the next day, 'he will have to—to be your boy now—as I was—won't he?'"

" 'No,' answered the Earl, and he said it so fiercely that Cedric quite jumped.

" 'Shall I be your boy even if I'm not going to be an earl?' he said. 'Shall I be your boy just as I was before?' "

But it was a real little heart that had beaten at the thought.

He has been considered such an ideal little person—Cedric Errol, Lord Fauntleroy—and he was so real after all. Perhaps it is worth while explaining that he was only a simple, natural thing—a child, whose great charm was that he was the innocent friend of the whole world.

I have reason to believe that an impression exists that the passage of years has produced no effect whatever on the great original, that he has still waving, golden hair, and wears black velvet doublets and broad collars of lace. This is an error. He is sixteen. He plays football and tennis and battles sternly with Greek. He is anxious not to "flunk" in geometry, and his hair is exceedingly short and brown. He has a fine sense of humour, and his relatives consider it rather a good joke to present him to intimates, as he appears before them, looking particularly cheerful and robust, in the words first heard by Mr. Wenham:

"This is—'Little Lord Fauntleroy.' "